"Like most of Irving's work, *Last Night in Twisted River* is long, complicated, funny and sad. It can be relentlessly grim and laugh-out-loud funny, often on the same page. But it's also riveting. . . . It ranks as one of the year's most imaginative and complex reads."
—*Calgary Herald*

"One of our most accomplished writers . . . Irving has laid bare his own self-torture in his work. . . . Readers familiar with Irving's oeuvre will not only appreciate this latest attempt to unearth that which is most fundamental to the human experience, but will also celebrate the fact that the author of masterful works such as *The Cider House Rules* and *A Prayer for Owen Meany* seems to be back—older, yes, but definitely wiser, a mellow vintage that is all the better for its time spent in the cellar, waiting to be uncorked."
—*The Globe and Mail*

"With his new novel, *Last Night in Twisted River*, John Irving once again performs the most death-defying of literary feats: He negotiates the delicate line between familiarity and novelty in such impressive style as to create a work that is at once comfortable, vintage Irving yet wholly new and unique. He manages to create an utterly immersive world while continuing his exploration of his lifelong concerns. . . . This is among Irving's most rewarding and satisfying novels. . . . It is realistically rooted in the richest story of all: the blood, guts, joys, dreams and sorrows of real human lives, as captured by one of our greatest writers."
—*National Post*

"The John Irving novel of John Irving novels, a writer's deep rumination on why one writes, and written in the only form that the writer . . . feels can accommodate such extensive creative self-surgery: as a good old-fashioned—although hardly traditional—epic of a novel . . . Irving's new novel is some extraordinary feat of surgical inspirational deconstruction. The most compelling story here isn't the story of Danny's fraught, tragedy-laden life, but how that life—or creatively tailored elements taken from it—is assembled, shuffled and ultimately reassembled into the book we're reading."

—*Toronto Star*

PRAISE FROM THE UNITED STATES

"Sheer reading pleasure . . . rich in detail, yet never less than a page-turner . . . *Last Night in Twisted River* is a novel of excellence. . . . It's not difficult to make the case that John Irving is the greatest American novelist of his generation . . . [and] of all the great American novelists of his generation, he has been the timeless one who has unerringly delivered. . . . Irving is a master."

—*Financial Times*

"Full-throated, hot-blooded and clear-eyed; not since *A Widow for One Year* has he sculpted a story with such poise; not since *Garp* has he so trenchantly assessed the writer's craft. Majestic yet intimate, shot with whimsy, dread and molten pathos . . . [*Last Night in Twisted River*] isn't a comeback so much as a coming-of-age."

—*Los Angeles Times*

"An epic that winds its way through love and hate, hope and despair . . . *Last Night in Twisted River* forms a sort of literary triptych with *Garp* and *A Widow for One Year*, in that each takes on the imaginative power of fiction."

—*St. Louis Post-Dispatch*

"A satisfying tale of loss and redemption . . . an impressive feat of sustained narrative craftsmanship . . . *Last Night in Twisted River* is a marvel."

—*San Francisco Chronicle*

"Mesmerizing . . . I found myself enjoying the book to no end. . . . Irving offers writing lessons and cooking lessons, but also life lessons, one of which is to pick up a long novel and read to your heart's content if you want to see how the chaos we all live in takes on some superior momentum and graceful awareness of just how dangerous and glorious and luxurious and tasty life can be."

—*The Dallas Morning News*

"John Irving crafts another gem. . . . Irving's story is engrossing, and he gives us a satisfying assortment of fully realized characters."

—*Houston Chronicle*

"Epic and cinematic . . . a book with the Dickensian scope that Irving is known for." —*Minneapolis Star Tribune*

"Deeply felt and often moving . . . keenly observed and affecting . . . an entertaining . . . commentary on the fiction-making process itself." —*The New York Times*

"Irving's skill as a storyteller is impressive." —*The New Yorker*

"If you're a fan of ambitious, chaotic, plot- and character-driven storytelling, you'll love this book. . . . Irving . . . has created another sprawling, sentimental, emotional tale, the kind that readers crave."

—*Entertainment Weekly*

"Thrilling . . . a vigorous burst of storytelling." —*Playboy*

"A big, juicy novel to satisfy readers of . . . *The World According to Garp*." —*Chicago Tribune*

"A luxuriously written book that can distract a reader for many a chilly evening . . . Irving is a master plotter. . . . With tons of warmth and intrigue, *Last Night in Twisted River* is an Irving success and a novel lover's book for a long winter." —*The Plain Dealer*

"Tightly plotted . . . suspenseful . . . evocative." —*The Seattle Times*

"*Last Night in Twisted River* is about the forces that shape a writer's life. . . . Much of the novel's charm lies in how Irving infuses it with his passion for craft and storytelling." —*The Boston Globe*

"A wonderful, long read to carry us away . . . just as satisfying as *The Cider House Rules, A Prayer for Owen Meany,* or *The World According to Garp*. . . . It's the long, winding plot that lures us in. And the confident voice of a master storyteller." —*The Providence Journal*

"If you like sprawling family stories with sexual complications, memorable characters and reflections on writing, then *Last Night in Twisted River* is for you." —*USA Today*

"A novel that feels a lot like life writ large, filled with the kind of unplanned accidents and haphazard moments, sudden threats and humorous asides that we can all recognize." —*The Philadelphia Inquirer*

"Full to bursting with story, character, and emotion . . . at once a moving portrait of a father-and-son relationship, [an] homage to a quintessentially American fortitude forged by treacherous work and scant wages, and a tribute to the bonds of friendship . . . Irving is a natural-born storyteller with a unique and compelling authorial voice." —*Booklist* (starred review)

PRAISE FROM THE UNITED KINGDOM

"Irving's fluency is astonishing. He renders incidental detail riveting and extraneous explanations . . . absorbing. . . . Every place and time he takes us to is so full of intriguing stories, musings and events that . . . the reader longs to take up residence, put down roots and try her best to hang around for a while. . . . This is Irving's twelfth novel and, as ever, the surface shines like midwinter ice in his beloved New Hampshire." —*New Statesman*

"Critics tend to reach for Dickens—an acknowledged inspiration, along with Melville, Hawthorne and Hardy—when trying to define the Irving touch. Anyone attuned to recent fiction of his own northern states might also put him on a blessed middle-ground between John Updike and Stephen King. . . . Irving's novels steer a zigzagging course through those forests of imagination where history, myth and yarn merge." —*The Independent*

"The stunts Irving pulls . . . are nothing less than show-stopping. . . . Spreading like the canopy of a tree, the historical and geographical breadth of this story is a growing surprise. You think you are in a backwoods melodrama then suddenly the fall of the twin towers is being described." —*The Guardian*

"John Irving writes long, busy books on serious themes. . . . His faith in a populous, eventful plot and his belief in the moral importance of literature make him an amiable companion for the long haul."

—*Daily Express*

"The most poetic and powerful of Irving's work to date . . . Though the book is too subtle and gentle to trumpet itself as Irving's Great American Novel, the story of Dominic and Daniel, as they leave their past behind . . . is none the less the story of the United States itself. . . . That history—the fall of Saigon, 9/11—plays out on TV sets in the background to major events in the novel's own twisted tale is merely Irving, at his most masterly, making metaphorical mischief. . . . Irving is also, perhaps, the only modern American writer able to seamlessly merge the small detail with the significant event, while writing books that balance literary authority with mass-market appeal. . . . For all its loss, sadness, change and uncertainty, *Twisted River* is, then, like all Irving's best works, the sound of hope echoing gently against the madness of modern life."

—*The Independent on Sunday*

"Intricately crafted . . . Through his most overtly autobiographical character, Irving mounts a passionate defense of the art of fiction. . . . Irving draws back the curtain to reveal something of the novelist's process. . . . Once again, he demonstrates his instinctive ear for language, for the subtle distinctions in voice and idiom that give his full-bodied characters their individual resonances. . . . *Last Night in Twisted River* is a big, old-fashioned novel in the best sense; Irving has created in painstaking, loving detail a whole and complete world, a record of momentous social changes, but, above all a testament to the enduring power of love and fiction."

—*The Observer*

LAST NIGHT IN
TWISTED RIVER

VINTAGE CANADA

JOHN IRVING

LAST
NIGHT
IN
TWISTED
RIVER

A NOVEL

VINTAGE CANADA EDITION, 2010

Published in Canada by Vintage Canada, a division of Random House of Canada Limited, Toronto, in 2010, and simultaneously in the United States of America by Ballantine Books, a division of Random House Inc., New York. Originally published in hardcover in Canada by Alfred A. Knopf Canada, a division of Random House of Canada Limited, in 2009, and simultaneously in the United States of America by Random House, a division of Random House Inc. Distributed by Random House of Canada Limited.

Vintage Canada with colophon is a registered trademark.

www.randomhouse.ca

Grateful acknowledgement is made to the following for permission to reprint previously published material:

HAL LEONARD CORPORATION: Excerpt from "After the Gold Rush," words and music by Neil Young, copyright © 1970 by Broken Arrow Music Corporation. Copyright renewed. All rights reserved. Reprinted by permission of Hal Leonard Corporation.

RAM'S HORN MUSIC: Excerpt from "Tangled Up in Blue" by Bob Dylan, copyright © 1974 by Ram's Horn Music. All rights reserved. International copyright secured. Reprinted by permission.

Library and Archives Canada Cataloguing in Publication

Irving, John
Last night in Twisted River : a novel / John Irving.

Includes bibliographical references.

ISBN 978-0-307-39837-6

I. Title.

PS3559.R8L37 2010   813'.54   C2009-906715-3

Book design by Barbara M. Bachman

Printed and bound in the United States of America

2 4 6 8 9 7 5 3 1

For Everett—my pioneer, my hero

I had a job in the great north woods
Working as a cook for a spell
But I never did like it all that much
And one day the ax just fell.

—*Bob Dylan,* "Tangled Up in Blue"

CONTENTS

I.

COOS COUNTY, NEW HAMPSHIRE, 1954

II.

BOSTON, 1967

III.

WINDHAM COUNTY, VERMONT, 1983

IV.

TORONTO, 2000

V.

COOS COUNTY, NEW.HAMPSHIRE, 2001

VI.

POINTE AU BARIL STATION, ONTARIO, 2005

COOS COUNTY,
NEW HAMPSHIRE, 1954

—

CHAPTER 1

UNDER THE LOGS

THE YOUNG CANADIAN, WHO COULD NOT HAVE BEEN MORE than fifteen, had hesitated too long. For a frozen moment, his feet had stopped moving on the floating logs in the basin above the river bend; he'd slipped entirely underwater before anyone could grab his outstretched hand. One of the loggers had reached for the youth's long hair—the older man's fingers groped around in the frigid water, which was thick, almost soupy, with sloughed-off slabs of bark. Then two logs collided hard on the would-be rescuer's arm, breaking his wrist. The carpet of moving logs had completely closed over the young Canadian, who never surfaced; not even a hand or one of his boots broke out of the brown water.

Out on a logjam, once the key log was pried loose, the river drivers had to move quickly and continually; if they paused for even a second or two, they would be pitched into the torrent. In a river drive, death among moving logs could occur from a crushing injury, before you had a chance to drown—but drowning was more common.

From the riverbank, where the cook and his twelve-year-old son could hear the cursing of the logger whose wrist had been broken, it was immediately apparent that someone was in more serious trouble than the would-be rescuer, who'd freed his injured arm and had managed to regain his footing on the flowing logs. His fellow river drivers ignored him; they moved with small, rapid steps toward shore, calling out the lost boy's name. The loggers ceaselessly prodded with their pike poles, directing the floating logs ahead of them. The rivermen were, for the most part, picking the safest way ashore, but to the cook's hopeful son it seemed that they might have been trying to create a gap of sufficient width for the young Canadian to emerge. In truth, there were now only intermittent gaps between the logs. The boy who'd told them his name was "Angel Pope, from Toronto," was that quickly gone.

"Is it *Angel*?" the twelve-year-old asked his father. This boy, with his dark-brown eyes and intensely serious expression, could have been mistaken for Angel's younger brother, but there was no mistaking the family resemblance that the twelve-year-old bore to his ever-watchful father. The cook had an aura of controlled apprehension about him, as if he routinely anticipated the most unforeseen disasters, and there was something about his son's seriousness that reflected this; in fact, the boy looked so much like his father that several of the woodsmen had expressed their surprise that the son didn't also walk with his dad's pronounced limp.

The cook knew too well that indeed it was the young Canadian who had fallen under the logs. It was the cook who'd warned the loggers that Angel was too green for the river drivers' work; the youth should not have been trying to free a logjam. But probably the boy had been eager to please, and maybe the rivermen hadn't noticed him at first.

In the cook's opinion, Angel Pope had also been too green (and too clumsy) to be working in the vicinity of the main blade in a sawmill. That was strictly the sawyer's territory—a highly skilled position in the mills. The planer operator was a relatively skilled position, too, though not particularly dangerous.

The more dangerous and less skilled positions included working on the log deck, where logs were rolled into the mill and onto the saw carriage, or unloading logs from the trucks. Before the advent of mechanical loaders, the logs were unloaded by releasing trip bunks on the sides of the trucks—this allowed an entire load to roll off a truck at once. But the trip bunks sometimes failed to release; the men were occasionally caught under a cascade of logs while they were trying to free a bunk.

As far as the cook was concerned, Angel shouldn't have been in *any* position that put the boy in close proximity to moving logs. But the lumberjacks had been as fond of the young Canadian as the cook and his son had been, and Angel had said he was bored working in the kitchen. The youth had wanted more physical labor, and he liked the outdoors.

The repeated *thunk-thunk* of the pike poles, poking the logs, was briefly interrupted by the shouts of the rivermen who had spotted Angel's pike pole—more than fifty yards from where the boy had vanished. The fifteen-foot pole was floating free of the log drive, out where the river currents had carried it away from the logs.

The cook could see that the river driver with the broken wrist had come ashore, carrying his pike pole in his good hand. First by the familiarity of his cursing, and only secondarily by the logger's matted hair and tangled beard, did the cook realize that the injured man was Ketchum—no neophyte to the treachery of a log drive.

It was April—not long after the last snowmelt and the start of mud season—but the ice had only recently broken up in the river basin, the first logs falling through the ice upstream of the basin, on the Dummer ponds. The river was ice-cold and swollen, and many of the lumberjacks had heavy beards and long hair, which would afford them some scant protection from the blackflies in mid-May.

Ketchum lay on his back on the riverbank like a beached bear. The moving mass of logs flowed past him. It appeared as if the log drive were a life raft, and the loggers who were still out on the river seemed like castaways at sea—except that the sea, from one moment to the next, turned from greenish brown to bluish black. The water in Twisted River was richly dyed with tannins.

"*Shit,* Angel!" Ketchum shouted from his back. "I said, 'Move your feet, Angel. You have to keep moving your *feet!*' Oh, shit."

The vast expanse of logs had been no life raft for Angel, who'd surely drowned or been crushed to death in the basin above the river bend, although the lumberjacks (Ketchum among them) would follow the log drive at least to where Twisted River poured into the Pontook

Reservoir at Dead Woman Dam. The Pontook Dam on the Androscoggin River had created the reservoir; once the logs were let loose in the Androscoggin, they would next encounter the sorting gaps outside Milan. In Berlin, the Androscoggin dropped two hundred feet in three miles; two paper mills appeared to divide the river at the sorting gaps in Berlin. It was not inconceivable to imagine that young Angel Pope, from Toronto, was on his way there.

COME NIGHTFALL, THE COOK and his son were still attempting to salvage leftovers, for tomorrow's meals, from the scores of untouched dinners in the small settlement's dining lodge—the cookhouse in the so-called town of Twisted River, which was barely larger and only a little less transient than a logging camp. Not long ago, the only dining lodge on a river drive hadn't been a lodge at all. There once was a traveling kitchen that had been permanently built onto a truck body, and an adjacent truck on which a modular dining hall could be taken down and reassembled—this was when the trucks used to perpetually move camp to another site on Twisted River, wherever the loggers were working next.

In those days, except on the weekends, the rivermen rarely went back to the town of Twisted River to eat or sleep. The camp cook had often cooked in a tent. Everything had to be completely portable; even the sleeping shelters were built onto truck bodies.

Now nobody knew what would become of the less-than-thriving town of Twisted River, which was situated partway between the river basin and the Dummer ponds. The sawmill workers and their families lived there, and the logging company maintained bunkhouses for the more transient woodsmen, who included not only the French Canadian itinerants but most of the river drivers and the other loggers. The company also maintained a better equipped kitchen, an *actual* dining lodge—the aforementioned cookhouse—for the cook and his son. But for how much longer? Not even the owner of the logging company knew.

The lumber industry was in transition; it would one day be possible for every worker in the logging business to work from home. The logging camps (and even the slightly less marginal settlements like Twisted River) were dying. The wanigans themselves were disappearing; those curious shelters for sleeping and eating and storing equipment had not only been mounted on trucks, on wheels, or on crawler tracks, but they were often attached to rafts or boats.

The Indian dishwasher—she worked for the cook—had long ago told the cook's young son that *wanigan* was from an Abenaki word, leading the boy to wonder if the dishwasher herself was from the Abenaki tribe. Perhaps she just happened to know the origin of the word, or she'd merely claimed to know it. (The cook's son went to school with an Indian boy who'd told him that *wanigan* was of Algonquian origin.)

While it lasted, the work during a river drive was from dawn till dark. It was the protocol in a logging operation to feed the men four times a day. In the past, when the wanigans couldn't get close to a river site, the two midday meals had been trekked to the drivers. The first and last meal were served in the base camp—nowadays, in the dining lodge. But out of their affection for Angel, tonight many of the loggers had missed their last meal in the cookhouse. They'd spent the evening following the log drive, until the darkness had driven them away—not only the darkness, but also the men's growing awareness that none of them knew if Dead Woman Dam was open. From the basin below the town of Twisted River, the logs—probably with Angel among them—might already have flowed into the Pontook Reservoir, but not if Dead Woman Dam was closed. And if the Pontook Dam *and* Dead Woman were open, the body of the young Canadian would be headed pell-mell down the Androscoggin. No one knew better than Ketchum that there would likely be no finding Angel there.

The cook could tell when the river drivers had stopped searching—from the kitchen's screen door, he could hear them leaning their pike poles against the cookhouse. A few of the tired searchers found their way to the dining lodge after dark; the cook didn't have the heart to turn them away. The hired help had all gone home—everyone but the Indian dishwasher, who stayed late most nights. The cook, whose difficult name was Dominic Baciagalupo—or "Cookie," as the lumberjacks routinely called him—made the men a late supper, which his twelve-year-old son served.

"Where's Ketchum?" the boy asked his dad.

"He's probably getting his arm fixed," the cook replied.

"I'll bet he's hungry," the twelve-year-old said, "but Ketchum is wicked tough."

"He's impressively tough for a drinking man," Dominic agreed, but he was thinking that maybe Ketchum wasn't tough enough for *this*. Losing Angel Pope might be hardest on Ketchum, the cook thought, because the veteran logger had taken the young Canadian under his wing. He'd looked after the boy, or he had tried to.

Ketchum had the blackest hair and beard—the charred-black color of charcoal, blacker than a black bear's fur. He'd been married young—and more than once. He was estranged from his children, who had grown up and gone their own ways. Ketchum lived year-round in one of the bunkhouses, or in any of several run-down hostel-ries, if not in a wanigan of his own devising—namely, in the back of his pickup truck, where he had come close to freezing to death on those winter nights when he'd passed out, dead drunk. Yet Ketchum had kept Angel away from alcohol, and he'd kept not a few of the older women at the so-called dance hall away from the young Cana-dian, too.

"You're too young, Angel," the cook had heard Ketchum tell the youth. "Besides, you can catch things from those ladies."

Ketchum would know, the cook had thought. Dominic knew that Ketchum had done more damage to himself than breaking his wrist in a river drive.

THE STEADY HISS and intermittent flickering of the pilot lights on the gas stove in the cookhouse kitchen—an old Garland with two ovens and eight burners, and a flame-blackened broiler above—seemed perfectly in keeping with the lamentations of the loggers over their late supper. They had been charmed by the lost boy, whom they'd adopted as they would a stray pet. The cook had been charmed, too. Perhaps he saw in the unusually cheerful teenager some future incarna-tion of his twelve-year-old son—for Angel had a welcoming expres-sion and a sincere curiosity, and he exhibited none of the withdrawn sullenness that appeared to afflict the few young men his age in a rough and rudimentary place like Twisted River.

This was all the more remarkable because the youth had told them that he'd recently run away from home.

"You're Italian, aren't you?" Dominic Baciagalupo had asked the boy.

"I'm not from Italy, I don't speak Italian—you're not much of an Italian if you come from Toronto," Angel had answered.

The cook had held his tongue. Dominic knew a little about *Boston* Italians; some of them seemed to have issues regarding how Italian they were. And the cook knew that Angel, in the old country, might have been an Angelo. (When Dominic had been a little boy, his mother had called him Angelù—in her Sicilian accent, this sounded like an-geh-LOO.)

But after the accident, nothing with Angel Pope's written name could be found; among the boy's few belongings, not a single book or letter identified him. If he'd had any identification, it had gone into the river basin with him—probably in the pocket of his dungarees— and if they never located the body, there would be no way to inform Angel's family, or whoever the boy had run away from.

Legally or not, and with or without proper papers, Angel Pope had made his way across the Canadian border to New Hampshire. Not the way it was usually done, either—Angel hadn't come from Quebec. He'd made a point of arriving from Ontario—he was not a French Canadian. The cook hadn't once heard Angel speak a word of French *or* Italian, and the French Canadians at the camp had wanted nothing to do with the runaway boy—apparently, they didn't like English Canadians. Angel, for his part, kept his distance from the French; he didn't appear to like the Québécois any better than they liked him.

Dominic had respected the boy's privacy; now the cook wished he knew more about Angel Pope, and where he'd come from. Angel had been a good-natured and fair-minded companion for the cook's twelve-year-old son, Daniel—or Danny, as the loggers and the saw- mill men called the boy.

Almost every male of working age in Twisted River knew the cook and his son—some women, too. Dominic had needed to know a num- ber of women—mainly, to help him look after his son—for the cook had lost his wife, Danny's young mother, a long-seeming decade ago.

Dominic Baciagalupo believed that Angel Pope had had some experience with kitchen work, which the boy had done awkwardly but uncomplainingly, and with an economy of movement that must have been born of familiarity—despite his professed boredom with cooking-related chores, and his penchant for cutting himself on the cutting board.

Moreover, the young Canadian was a reader; he'd borrowed many books that had belonged to Dominic's late wife, and he often read aloud to Daniel. It was Ketchum's opinion that Angel had read Robert Louis Stevenson to young Dan "to excess"—not only *Kidnapped* and *Treasure Island* but his unfinished deathbed novel, *St. Ives*, which Ketchum said should have died with the author. At the time of the accident on the river, Angel had been reading *The Wrecker* to Danny. (Ketchum had not yet weighed in with his opinion of *that* novel.)

Well, whatever Angel Pope's background had been, he'd had some schooling, clearly—more than most of the French Canadian woodsmen the cook had known. (More than most of the sawmill workers and the *local* woodsmen, too.)

"Why did Angel have to die?" Danny asked his dad. The twelve-year-old was helping his father wipe down the dining tables after the late-arriving loggers had gone off to bed, or perhaps to drink. And although she often kept herself busy in the cookhouse quite late into the night, at least well past Danny's bedtime, the Indian dishwasher had finished with her chores; by now, she'd driven her truck back to town.

"Angel didn't have to die, Daniel—it was an *avoidable* accident." The cook's vocabulary often made reference to *avoidable* accidents, and his twelve-year-old son was overfamiliar with his father's grim and fatalistic thoughts on human fallibility—the recklessness of youth, in particular. "He was too green to be out on a river drive," the cook said, as if that were all there was to it.

Danny Baciagalupo knew his dad's opinion of *all* the things Angel, or any boy that age, was too green to do. The cook also would have wanted to keep Angel far away from a peavey. (The peavey's most important feature was the hinged hook that made it possible to roll a heavy log by hand.)

According to Ketchum, the "old days" had been more perilous. Ketchum claimed that working with the horses, pulling the scoots out of the winter woods, was risky work. In the winter, the lumberjacks tramped up into the mountains. They'd cut down the trees and (not that long ago) used horses to pull the timber out, one log at a time. The scoots, or wheelless drays, were dragged like sleds on the frozen snow, which not even the horses' hooves could penetrate because the sled ruts on the horse-haul roads were iced down every night. Then the snowmelt and mud season came, and—"back then," as Ketchum would say—all the work in the woods was halted.

But even this was changing. Since the new logging machinery could work in muddy conditions and haul much longer distances to improved roads, which could be used in all seasons, mud season itself was becoming less of an issue—and horses were giving way to crawler tractors.

The bulldozers made it possible to build a road right to a logging site, where the wood could be hauled out by truck. The trucks moved the wood to a more central drop point on a river, or on a pond or lake; in fact, highway transport would very soon supplant the need for river drives. Gone were the days when a snubbing winch had been used to ease the horses down the steeper slopes. "The teams could slide on their haunches," Ketchum had told young Dan. (Ketchum rated oxen highly, for their steady footing in deep snow, but oxen had never been widely used.)

Gone, too, was railroad logging in the woods; it came to an end in the Pemigewasset Valley in '48—the same year one of Ketchum's cousins had been killed by a Shay locomotive at the Livermore Falls paper mill. The Shay weighed fifty tons and had been used to pull the last of the rails from the woods. The former railroad beds made for firm haul roads for the trucks in the 1950s, although Ketchum could still remember a murder on the Beebe River Railroad—back when he'd been the teamster for a bobsled loaded with prime virgin spruce behind a four-horse rig. Ketchum had been the teamster on one of the early Lombard steam engines, too—the one steered by a horse. The horse had turned the front sled runners, and the teamster sat at the front of the log hauler; later models replaced the horse and teamster with a helmsman at a steering wheel. Ketchum had been a helmsman, too, Danny Baciagalupo knew—clearly, Ketchum had done everything.

The old Lombard log-hauler roads around Twisted River were

truck roads now, although there were derelict Lombards abandoned in the area. (There is one still standing upright in Twisted River, and another one, tipped on its side, in the logging camp in West Dummer— or Paris, as the settlement was usually called, after the Paris Manufacturing Company of Paris, Maine.)

Phillips Brook ran to Paris and the Ammonoosuc—and into the Connecticut River. The rivermen drove hardwood sawlogs along Phillips Brook to Paris, and some pulpwood, too. The sawmill in Paris was strictly a hardwoods operation—the manufacturing company in Maine made toboggans—and the logging camp in Paris, with its steam-powered sawmill, had converted the former horse hovel to a machine shop. The mill manager's house was also there, together with a seventy-five-man bunkhouse and a mess hall, and some rudimentary family housing—not to mention an optimistically planted apple orchard and a schoolhouse. That there was no schoolhouse in the town of Twisted River, nor had anyone been optimistic enough about the settlement's staying power to plant any apple trees, gave rise to the opinion (held chiefly in Paris) that the logging camp was a more civilized community, and less temporary, than Twisted River.

At the height of land between the two outposts, no fortune-teller would have been foolish enough to predict success or longevity for either settlement. Danny Baciagalupo had heard Ketchum declare certain doom for the logging camp in Paris *and* for Twisted River, but Ketchum "suffered no progress gladly"—as the cook had cautioned his son. Dominic Baciagalupo was not a storyteller; the cook routinely cast doubt on some of Ketchum's stories. "Daniel, don't be in too big a hurry to buy into the Ketchum version," Dominic would say.

Had Ketchum's aunt, an accountant, truly been killed by a toppled stack of edging in the lathe mill in Milan? "I'm not sure there is, or ever was, a lathe mill in Milan, Daniel," the cook had warned his son. And according to Ketchum, one thunderstorm had killed four people in the sawmill at the outlet dam to Dummer Pond—the bigger and uppermost of the Dummer ponds. Allegedly, lightning had struck the log carriage. "The dogger and the setter, not to mention the sawyer holding the band-saw levers *and* the takeaway man, were killed by a single bolt," Ketchum had told Danny. Witnesses had watched the entire mill burn to the ground.

"I'm surprised that another of Ketchum's relatives wasn't among the victims, Daniel," was all that Dominic would say.

Indeed, another of Ketchum's cousins had fallen into the slasher in a pulpwood slasher mill; an uncle had been brained by a flying four-foot log at a cut-up mill, where they'd been cutting long spruce logs into pulpwood length. And there'd once been a floating steam donkey on Dummer Pond; it was used to bunch logs for the sawmill entrance at the outlet dam, but the engine had exploded. A man's ear was found frozen in the spring snow on the island in the pond, where all the trees had been singed by the explosion. Later, Ketchum said, an ice fisherman used the ear for bait in the Pontook Reservoir.

"More relatives of yours, I assume?" the cook had asked.

"Not that I'm aware of," Ketchum had replied.

Ketchum claimed to have known the "legendary asshole" who'd constructed a horse hovel upstream of the bunkhouse and mess hall at Camp Five. When all the men in the logging camp got sick, they strung up the purported legend in a network of bridles in the horse hovel above the manure pit—"until the asshole fainted from the fumes."

"You can see why Ketchum misses the old days, Daniel," the cook had said to his son.

Dominic Baciagalupo knew some stories—most of them not for telling. And what stories the cook could tell his son didn't capture young Dan's imagination the way Ketchum's stories did. There was the one about the bean hole outside the cook's tent on the Chickwolnepy, near Success Pond. In the aforementioned old days, on a river drive, Dominic had dug a bean hole, four feet across, and started the beans cooking in the ground at bedtime, covering the hole with hot ashes and earth. At 5 A.M., when it would be piping hot, he planned to dig the covered pot out of the ground for breakfast. But a French Canadian had wandered out of the sleeping wanigan (probably to take a pee) when it was still dark; he was barefoot when he fell into the bean hole, burning both his feet.

"That's it? That's the whole story?" Danny had asked his dad.

"Well, it's kind of a *cooking* story, I guess," Ketchum had said, to be kind. Ketchum would tease Dominic on the subject that spaghetti was replacing baked beans and pea soup on the upper Androscoggin.

"We never used to have so many *Italian* cooks around," Ketchum would say, winking at Danny.

"You're telling me you'd rather have baked beans and pea soup than pasta?" the cook asked his old friend.

"Your dad is a *touchy* little fella, isn't he?" Ketchum would say to Danny, winking again. "Constipated Christ!" Ketchum had more than once declared to Dominic. "Are you ever *touchy*!"

NOW IT WAS THAT mud-season, swollen-river time of year again. There'd been a strong surge of water coming through one of the sluice gates—what Ketchum called a "driving head," probably from the sluice gate at the east end of Little Dummer Pond—and a green kid from Toronto, whom they barely knew, had been swept away.

For only a while longer would the loggers increase the volume of water in Twisted River. They did this by building sluice dams on the tributary streams flowing into the main driving river; the water above these dams was released in the spring, adding torrents of water volume to a log drive. The pulpwood was piled in these streams (and on the riverbanks) during the winter and then sluiced into Twisted River on the water released from the dams. If this was soon after the snowmelt, the water ran fast, and the riverbanks were gouged by the moving logs.

In the cook's opinion, there were not enough bends in Twisted River to account for the river's name. The river ran straight down out of the mountains; there were only two bends in it. But to the loggers, particularly those old-timers who'd named the river, these two bends were bad enough to cause some treacherous logjams every spring— especially upstream of the basin, nearer the Dummer ponds. At both bends in the river, the trapped logs usually needed to be pried loose by hand; at the bend upriver, where the current was strongest, no one as green as Angel would have been permitted out on a logjam.

But Angel had perished in the basin, where the river was comparatively calm. The logs themselves made the water in the river basin choppy, but the currents were fairly moderate. And at both bends, the more massive jams were broken up with dynamite, which Dominic Baciagalupo deplored. The blasting wreaked havoc with the pots and pans and dangling utensils in the cookhouse kitchen; in the dining hall, the sugar bowls and the ketchup bottles slid off the tables. "If your dad is not a storyteller, Danny, he is definitely not a dynamite man," was how Ketchum had put it to the boy.

From the basin below the town of Twisted River, the water ran downstream to the Androscoggin. In addition to the Connecticut, the big log-driving rivers in northern New Hampshire were the Ammonoosuc and the Androscoggin: Those rivers were documented killers.

But some rivermen had drowned, or been crushed to death, in the relatively short stretch of rapids between Little Dummer Pond and the town of Twisted River—and in the river basin, too. Angel Pope wasn't the first; nor would the young Canadian be the last.

And in the compromised settlements of Twisted River and Paris, a fair share of sawmill workers had been maimed, or had even lost their lives—no small number of them, unfortunately, because of the fights they got into with the loggers in certain bars. There weren't enough women—that was usually what started the fights—although Ketchum had maintained that there weren't enough bars. There were no bars in Paris, anyway, and only married women lived in the logging camp there.

In Ketchum's opinion, that combination put the men from Paris on the haul road to Twisted River almost every night. "They never should have built a bridge over Phillips Brook," Ketchum also maintained.

"You see, Daniel," the cook said to his son. "Ketchum has once again demonstrated that progress will eventually kill us all."

"Catholic thinking will kill us first, Danny," Ketchum would say. "Italians are Catholics, and your dad is Italian—and so are you, of course, although neither you nor your dad is very Italian, or very Catholic in your thinking, either. I am mainly speaking of the French Canadians when I refer to Catholic thinking. French Canadians, for example, have so many children that they sometimes number them instead of name them."

"Dear God," Dominic Baciagalupo said, shaking his head.

"Is that true?" young Dan asked Ketchum.

"What kind of name is Vingt Dumas?" Ketchum asked the boy.

"Roland and Joanne Dumas do not have twenty children!" the cook cried.

"Not together, maybe," Ketchum replied. "So what was little Vingt? A slip of the tongue?"

Dominic was shaking his head again. "What?" Ketchum asked him.

"I promised Daniel's mother that the boy would get a proper education," the cook said.

"Well, I'm just making an effort to *enhance* Danny's education," Ketchum reasoned.

"*Enhance*," Dominic repeated, still shaking his head. "Your vocabulary, Ketchum," the cook began, but he stopped himself; he said nothing further.

Neither a storyteller nor a dynamite man, Danny Baciagalupo thought of his father. The boy loved his dad dearly, but there was also a habit the cook had, and his son had noticed it—Dominic often didn't finish his thoughts. (Not out loud, anyway.)

NOT COUNTING THE Indian dishwasher—and a few of the sawmill workers' wives, who helped the cook in the kitchen—there were rarely any women eating in the cookhouse, except on the weekends, when some of the men ate with their families. That alcohol was not permitted was the cook's rule. Dinner (or "supper," as the older rivermen used to eating in the wanigans called it) was served as soon as it was dark, and the majority of loggers and sawmill men were sober when they ate their evening meal, which they consumed quickly and with no intelligible conversation—even on weekends, or when the loggers weren't engaged in the river drives.

As the men had usually come to eat directly from some manner of work, their clothes were soiled and they smelled of pitch and spruce gum and wet bark and sawdust, but their hands and faces were clean and freshly scented by the pine-tar soap that the cavernous washroom of the cookhouse made readily available—at the cook's request. (Washing your hands before eating was another of Dominic's rules.) Furthermore, the washroom towels were always clean; the clean towels were part of the reason that the Indian dishwasher generally stayed late. While the kitchen help was washing the last of the supper dishes, the dishwasher herself was loading the towels into the washing machines in the cookhouse's laundry room. She never went home until the washing cycles had ended and she'd put all the towels in the dryers.

The dishwasher was called Injun Jane, but not to her face. Danny Baciagalupo liked her, and she appeared to dote on the boy. She was more than a decade older than his dad (she was even older than Ketchum), and she had lost a son—possibly he'd drowned in the Pemigewasset, if Danny hadn't misheard the story. Or maybe Jane and her dead son were from the Pemigewasset Wilderness—they may have come from that part of the state, northwest of the mills in Conway—and the doomed son had drowned elsewhere. There was a bigger, uncontained wilderness north of Milan, where the spruce mill was; there were more logging camps up there, and lots of places where a young logger might drown. (Jane had told Danny that Pemigewasset meant "Alley of the Crooked Pines," which conjured to the impressionable boy a likely place to drown.)

All young Dan could really remember was that it had been a wilderness river-driving accident—and from the fond way the dishwasher looked at the cook's son, perhaps her lost boy had been about twelve when he drowned. Danny didn't know, and he didn't ask; everything he knew about Injun Jane was something he'd silently observed or had imperfectly overheard.

"Listen only to those conversations that are directed to you, Daniel," his father had warned him. The cook meant that Danny shouldn't eavesdrop on the disjointed or incoherent remarks the men made to one another when they were eating.

Most nights, after their evening meal—but never as flagrantly as in the wanigan days, and not usually when there was an early-morning river drive—the loggers and the sawmill men drank. The few who had actual homes in Twisted River drank at home. The transients— meaning most of the woodsmen and all the Canadian itinerants— drank in their bunkhouses, which were crudely equipped in that dank area of town immediately above the river basin. These hostelries were within walking distance of the dismal bars and the seedy, misnamed dance hall, where there was no actual dancing—only music and the usual too-few women to meet.

The loggers and sawmill workers with families preferred the smaller but contentiously more "civilized" settlement in Paris.

Ketchum refused to call the logging camp "Paris," referring instead to what he said was the real name of the place—West Dummer. "No community, not even a logging camp, should be named for a manufacturing company," Ketchum declared. It further offended Ketchum that a logging operation in New Hampshire was named after a company in *Maine*—one that manufactured toboggans, of all things.

"Dear God!" the cook cried. "Soon all the wood on Twisted River will be pulpwood—for paper! What about toboggans is worse than *paper*?"

"*Books* are made from paper!" Ketchum declared. "What role do toboggans play in your son's *education*?"

There was a scarcity of children in Twisted River, and they went to school in Paris—as Danny Baciagalupo did, when he went to school at all. For the betterment of young Dan's *education*, the cook not infrequently kept his son home from school—so that the boy could read a book or two, a practice not necessarily encouraged by the Paris (or, as Ketchum would have it, the West Dummer) school. "Perish the thought that the children in a logging camp should learn to *read*!" Ketchum railed. As a child, he had not learned to read; he was forever angry about it.

THERE WERE—THERE still *are*—good markets for both sawlogs and pulpwood over the Canadian border. The north country of New Hampshire continues to feed wood in huge quantities to paper mills in New Hampshire and Maine, and to a furniture mill in Vermont. But of the logging camps, as they used to be, mere tumbledown evidence remains.

In a town like Twisted River, only the weather wouldn't change. From the sluice dam at the bottom of Little Dummer Pond to the basin below Twisted River, a persistent fog or mist lay suspended above the violent water until midmorning—in all seasons, except when the river was frozen. From the sawmills, the keen whine of the blades was both as familiar and expected as the songs of birds, though neither the sounds of sawing nor the birdsongs were as reliable as the fact that there was never any spring weather in that part of New Hampshire—except for the regrettable period of time from early

April till the middle of May, which was distinguished by frozen, slowly thawing mud.

Yet the cook had stayed, and there were few in Twisted River who knew why. There were fewer who knew why he'd come in the first place, and from where or when. But his limp had a history, of which everyone was aware. In a sawmill or logging-camp kind of town, a limp like Dominic Baciagalupo's was not uncommon. When logs of any size were set in motion, an ankle could get crushed. Even when he wasn't walking, it was obvious that the boot on the cook's maimed foot was two sizes bigger than the one he wore on his good foot—and when he was either sitting down or standing still, his bigger boot pointed the wrong way. To those knowledgeable souls in the settlement of Twisted River, such an injury could have come from any number of logging accidents.

Dominic had been pretending to be a teenager; in his own estimation, he was not as green as Angel Pope, but he was "green enough," as the cook would tell his son. He'd had an after-school job on the loading platforms at one of the big mills in Berlin, where a friend of Dominic's absent father was a foreman. Until World War II, the supposed friend of Dominic's dad was a fixture there, but the cook remembered so-called Uncle Umberto as an alcoholic who repeatedly bad-mouthed Dominic's mom. (Even after the accident, Dominic Baciagalupo was never contacted by his absconding father, and "Uncle" Umberto not once proved himself as a family friend.)

There was a load of hardwood sawlogs on the log deck—mostly maple and birch. Young Dominic was using a peavey, rolling the logs into the mill, when a bunch of logs rolled all at once and he couldn't get out of their way. He was only twelve in 1936; he handled a peavey with a rakish confidence. Dominic had been the same age as his son was now; the cook would never have allowed his beloved Daniel on a log deck, not even if the boy had been *ambidextrous* with a peavey. And in Dominic's case, when he had been knocked down by the logs, the hinged hook of his own peavey was driven into his left thigh, like a fishhook without the barb, and his left ankle was crunched sideways—it was shattered and mangled under the weight of the wood. From the peavey wound, he was in no danger of bleeding to death, but one could always die of blood poisoning in those days. From the ankle injury, he might have died of gangrene later—or, more likely, had the left foot amputated, if not the entire leg.

There were no X-rays in Coos County in 1936. The medical authorities in Berlin were disinclined to undertake any fancy reassembly of a crushed ankle; in such cases, little or no surgery was recommended. It was a wait-and-see category of accident: Either the blood vessels were mashed flat and there would be a subsequent loss of circulation—then the doctors would have to cut the foot off—or the broken and displaced bits of the ankle would fuse together and heal every which way, and Dominic Baciagalupo would walk with a limp and be in pain for the rest of his life. (That would turn out to be the case.)

There was also the scar where the peavey had hooked him, which resembled the bite wound of a small, peculiar animal—one with a curved, solitary tooth and a mouth that wasn't big enough to enclose the twelve-year-old's thigh. And even before he took a step, the angle of Dominic's left foot indicated a sharp left turn; the toes were aimed in a sideways direction. People often noticed the deformed shape of the ankle and the misdirected foot before they saw the limp.

One thing was certain: Young Dominic wouldn't be a logger. You need your balance for that kind of work. And the mills were where he'd been injured—not to mention that his runaway father's drunken "friend" was a foreman there. The mills were not in Dominic Baciagalupo's future, either.

"Hey, Baciagalupo!" Uncle Umberto had often hailed him. "You may have a Neapolitan name, but you hang around like a Sicilian."

"I *am* Sicilian," Dominic would dutifully say; his mother seemed inordinately proud of it, the boy thought.

"Yeah, well, your *name* is *napolitano*," Umberto told him.

"After my dad, I suppose," young Dominic ventured to guess.

"Your dad was no Baciagalupo," Uncle Umberto informed him. "Ask *Nunzi* where your name came from—she gave it to you."

The twelve-year-old didn't like it when Umberto, who clearly disliked Dominic's mother, called her "Nunzi"—an affectionate family nickname, shortened from Annunziata—which Umberto didn't say affectionately at all. (In a play, or in a film, the audience would have had no trouble recognizing Umberto as a minor character; yet the best actor to play Umberto would be one who always believed he was cast in a major role.)

"And you're not really my uncle, I suppose?" Dominic inquired of Umberto.

"Ask your mama," Umberto said. "If she wanted to keep you *siciliano,* she shoulda given you *her* name."

His mother's maiden name was Saetta—she was very proud of the sigh-AY-tah, as she pronounced the Sicilian name, and of all the Saettas Dominic had heard her speak of when she chose to talk about her heritage.

Annunziata was reluctant to speak of Dominic's heritage at all. What little the boy had gleaned—bits of information, or misinformation—had been gathered slowly and insufficiently, like the partial evidence, the incomplete clues, in the increasingly popular board game of young Dan's childhood, one the cook and Ketchum played with the boy, and sometimes Jane joined them. (Was it Colonel Mustard in the kitchen with the candlestick, or had the murder been committed by Miss Scarlet in the ballroom with the revolver?)

All young Dominic knew was that his father, a Neapolitan, had abandoned the pregnant Annunziata Saetta in Boston; he was rumored to have taken a boat back to Naples. To the question "Where is he now?" (which the boy had asked his mother, many times), Annunziata would shrug and sigh, and looking either to Heaven or in the direction of the exhaust vent above her kitchen stove, she would say mysteriously to her son: *"Vicino di Napoli."* "In the vicinity of Naples," young Dominic had guessed. With the help of an atlas, and because the boy had heard his mother murmur the names of two hill towns (and provinces) in the vicinity of Naples in her sleep—Benevento and Avellino—Dominic had concluded that his dad had fled to that region of Italy.

As for Umberto, he was clearly not an uncle—and definitely a "legendary asshole," as Ketchum would have said.

"What kind of name is Umberto?" Dominic had asked the foreman.

"From da king!" Umberto had answered indignantly.

"I mean it's a Neapolitan name, right?" the boy had asked.

"What are you questioning me for? You da twelve-year-old, pretending to be sixteen!" Umberto cried.

"You told me to say I was sixteen," Dominic reminded the foreman.

"Look, you gotta job, Baciagalupo," Umberto had said.

Then the logs rolled, and Dominic became a cook. His mother, a Sicilian-born Italian-American transported by an unwanted pregnancy from Boston's North End to Berlin, New Hampshire, could cook. She'd left the city and had moved to the north country when Gennaro Capodilupo had slipped away to the docks off Atlantic Avenue and Commercial Street, leaving her with child as he sailed (figuratively, if not literally) "back to Naples."

Asshole (if not Uncle) Umberto was right: Dominic's dad was no Baciagalupo. The absconding father was a Capodilupo—cah-poh-dee-LEW-poh, as Annunziata told her son, meant "Head of the Wolf." What was the unwed mother to do? "For the lies he told, your father should have been a *Bocca*dalupo!" she said to Dominic. This meant "*Mouth* of the Wolf," the boy would learn—a fitting name for Asshole Umberto, young Dominic often thought. "But *you*, Angelù—you are my *kiss* of the wolf!" his mom said.

In an effort to legitimize him, and because his mother had a high-handed love of words, she would not name Dominic a head of (or a mouth of) the wolf; for Annunziata Saetta, only a kiss of the wolf would do. It should have been spelled "Baciacalupo," but Nunzi always pronounced the second "c" in Baciacalupo like a "g." Over time, and due to a clerical error in kindergarten, the misspelled name had stuck. He'd become Dominic Baciagalupo before he became a cook. His mother also called him Dom, for short—Dominic being derived from *doménica*, which means "Sunday." Not that Annunziata was a tireless adherent of what Ketchum called "Catholic thinking." What was both Catholic *and* Italian in the Saetta family had driven the young, unmarried woman north to New Hampshire; in Berlin, other Italians (presumably, also Catholics) would look after her.

Had they expected she would put her child up for adoption, and come back to the North End? Nunzi knew that this was done, but she wouldn't consider giving up her baby, and—notwithstanding the sizable nostalgia she expressed for the Italian North End—she was never tempted to go back to Boston, either. In her unplanned condition, she had been sent away; understandably, she resented it.

While Annunziata remained a loyal Sicilian in her own kitchen, the proverbial ties that bind were irreparably frayed. Her Boston family—and, by association, the Italian community in the North End, and whatever represented "Catholic thinking" there—had disowned her. In turn, she disowned them. Nunzi never went to Mass herself, nor did she make Dominic go. "It's enough if we go to confession, when we want to," she would tell young Dom—her little kiss of the wolf.

She wouldn't teach the boy Italian, either—some essential cooking lingo excepted—nor was Dominic inclined to learn the language of "the old country," which to the boy meant the North End of Boston, not Italy. It was both a language and a place that had rejected his mother. Italian would never be Dominic Baciagalupo's language; he said, adamantly, that Boston was nowhere he ever wanted to go.

Everything in Annunziata Saetta's new life was defined by a sense of starting over. The youngest of three sisters, she could read and speak English as well as she could cook *siciliano*. Nunzi taught children how to read in a Berlin elementary school—and after the accident, she took Dominic out of school and taught him some fundamental cooking skills. She also insisted that the boy read books—not just cookbooks but everything she read, which were mostly novels. Her son had been crippled while violating the generally overlooked child-labor laws; Annunziata had taken him out of circulation, her version of homeschooling being both culinary and literary.

Neither area of education was available to Ketchum, who had left school when he was younger than twelve. At nineteen, in 1936, Ketchum could neither read nor write, but when he wasn't working as a logger, he was loading lumber onto the railroad flatcars from the open platforms at the end of the biggest Berlin mill. The deck crew tapered the load at the top, so that the flatcars could safely pass through the tunnels or under the bridges. "That was the extent of my education, before your mom taught me to read," Ketchum enjoyed telling Danny Baciagalupo; the cook would commence to shake his head again, although the story of Dominic's late wife teaching Ketchum to read was apparently incontestable.

At least the saga of Ketchum belatedly learning to read seemed *not* in the tall-tale category of Ketchum's other stories—the one about the low-roofed bunkhouse at Camp One, for example. According to Ketchum, "some Injun" had been assigned the task of shoveling snow off the roof, but the Indian had neglected the job. When the roof collapsed under the weight of the snow, all but one logger escaped the bunkhouse alive—not the Indian, who was suffocated by what Ketchum called "the concentrated odor of wet socks." (Of course the cook and his son were well aware of Ketchum's nearly constant complaint—namely, that the stink of wet socks was the bane of bunkhouse life.)

"I don't remember an Indian at Camp One," was all Dominic had said to his old friend.

"You're too young to remember Camp One, Cookie," Ketchum had said.

Danny Baciagalupo had often observed that his father bristled at the mere mention of the seven-year age difference between himself and Ketchum, whereas Ketchum was inclined to overemphasize the discrepancy in their ages. Those seven years would have seemed insurmountable to them had the two young men met in the Berlin of their youth—when Ketchum had been a rawboned but strapping nineteen, already sporting a full if ragged beard, and Annunziata's little Dom was not yet a teenager.

He'd been a strong, wiry twelve-year-old—not big, but compact and sinewy—and the cook had retained the appearance of a lean-muscled young logger, although he was now thirty and looked older, especially to his young son. It was his dad's seriousness that made him look older, the boy thought. You could not say "the past" or "the future" in the cook's presence without making him frown. As for the present, even the twelve-year-old Daniel Baciagalupo understood that the times were changing.

Danny knew that his father's life had been changed forever because of an ankle injury; a different accident, to the boy's young mother, had altered the course of his own childhood and changed his dad's life forever *again*. In a twelve-year-old's world, change couldn't be good. *Any* change made Danny anxious—the way missing school made him anxious.

On the river drives, in the not-so-old days, when Danny and his dad were working and sleeping in the wanigans, the boy didn't go to school. That he didn't like school—but that he always, and far too easily, made up the work he missed—also made Danny anxious. The boys in his grade were all older than he was, because they skipped school as often as they could and they *never* made up the work they missed; they'd all been held back and had repeated a grade or two.

When the cook saw that his son was anxious, he invariably said: "Stand your ground, Daniel—just don't get killed. I promise you, one day we'll leave here."

But this made Danny Baciagalupo anxious, too. Even the wanigans had felt like home to him. And in Twisted River, the twelve-year-old had his own bedroom above the cookhouse—where his father also had a bedroom, and where they shared a bathroom. These were the only second-story rooms in the cookhouse, and they were spacious and comfortable. Each room had a skylight and big windows with a view of the mountains, and—below the cookhouse, at the foothills of the mountains—a partial view of the river basin.

Logging trails circumscribed the hills and mountains; there were big patches of meadow and second growth, where the woodcutters had harvested the hardwoods and the coniferous forest. From his bedroom, it seemed to young Daniel Baciagalupo that the bare rock and second growth could never replace the maples and birch, or the softwoods—the spruce and fir, the red and white pine, and the hemlock and tamarack. The twelve-year-old thought that the meadows were running wild with waist-high grass and weeds. Yet, in truth, the forests in the region were being managed for sustainable yields of timber; those woods are still producing—"in the twenty-first fucking century," as Ketchum would one day say.

And as Ketchum regularly suggested, some things would never change. "Tamarack will always love swamps, yellow birch will forever be highly prized for furniture, and gray birch will never be good for fuck-all except firewood." As for the fact that the river drives in Coos County would soon be limited to four-foot pulpwood, Ketchum was morosely disinclined to utter any prophecies. (All the veteran logger would say was that the smaller pulpwood tended to stray out of the current and required cleanup crews.)

What *would* change the logging business, and what might put an end to the cook's job, was the restless spirit of modernity; the changing times could kill a mere "settlement" like Twisted River. But Danny Baciagalupo was just wondering, obsessively: What work would there be in Twisted River after the woodcutters moved on? Would the *cook* then move on? Danny worried. (Could Ketchum *ever* move on?)

As for the river, it just kept moving, as rivers do—as rivers do. Under the logs, the body of the young Canadian moved with the river, which jostled him to and fro—to and fro. If, at this moment in time, Twisted River also appeared restless, even impatient, maybe the river itself wanted the boy's body to move on, too—move on, too.

CHAPTER 2

DO-SI-DO

N A STORAGE CLOSET OFF THE PANTRY IN THE COOKHOUSE kitchen, the cook kept a couple of folding cots—from the wanigan days, when he'd slept in any number of portable kitchens. Dominic had salvaged a couple of sleeping bags, too. It was not out of nostalgia for the wanigans that the cook had kept the old cots and mildewed sleeping bags. Sometimes Ketchum slept in the cookhouse kitchen; occasionally, if Danny was awake, the boy would tirelessly endeavor to get his dad's permission to sleep in the kitchen, too. If Ketchum hadn't had too much to drink, Danny hoped to hear another of the logger's stories—or the same story, wildly revised.

THE FIRST NIGHT after Angel Pope had disappeared under the logs, it snowed a little. It was still cold at night in April, but Dominic had turned the two gas ovens on in the kitchen. The ovens were set at 350 and 425 degrees, and the cook had premixed the dry ingredients for the scones, the corn muffins, and the banana bread before going to bed. His French toast (from the banana bread) was popular, and he would make pancakes from scratch in the morning. Because of the raw eggs, Dominic didn't like to keep the pancake batter in the fridge more than two days. Also last-minute, almost every morning, he made buttermilk biscuits, which he baked quickly in the 425-degree oven.

It was usually Danny's job to be sure that the potatoes were peeled and cubed and soaking overnight in salted water. His dad would fry the potatoes on the griddle in the morning, when he fried the bacon. The griddle on the old Garland was above the broiler, which was eye-level to the cook. Even with a long-handled spatula, and standing on tiptoe or on a low stool—neither method of elevating himself was the easiest thing for a cook with a crooked foot—Dominic would frequently burn his forearm when he reached to the back of the griddle. (Sometimes Injun Jane would spell the cook at the griddle, because she was taller and her reach was longer.)

It would be dark when Dominic got up to fry the bacon and do his baking, and dark when Danny woke in the upstairs of the cookhouse to the smell of bacon and coffee, and *still* dark when the kitchen help and the Indian dishwasher arrived from town—the headlights of their vehicles heralding their arrival almost simultaneously with the engine sounds. Most mornings, the Garland's broiler was flaming hot—for melting the cheese on top of the omelets. Among young Dan's before-school jobs were cutting up the peppers and tomatoes for the omelets, and warming the big saucepan of maple syrup on one of the back burners of the eight-burner stove.

The outside door to the cookhouse kitchen didn't open or close properly; it was so loose-fitting that it rattled in the wind. The inside screen door opened into the kitchen, which could be added to the list of things that made Danny Baciagalupo anxious. For any number of practical reasons, you wanted the door to open to the outside. There was enough traffic in the busy kitchen to not want a door getting in the way—and once, long ago, a bear had come into the cookhouse kitchen. It had been a balmy night—the troublesome outside door to the cookhouse was propped open—and the bear had just butted the screen door with its head and walked inside.

Danny had been too young to remember the bear, although he'd asked his father to tell him the story many times. The boy's mother had long before put him to bed upstairs; she was having a late-night snack with Danny's dad when the bear joined them. The cook and his wife were sharing a mushroom omelet and drinking white wine. When he used to drink, Dominic Baciagalupo had explained to his son, he had often felt compelled to fix late-night snacks for himself and his wife. (Not anymore.)

Danny's mother screamed when she saw the bear. That made the bear stand up on its hind legs and squint at her, but Dominic had had quite a lot of wine; at first, he didn't know it was a bear. He must have thought it was a hairy, drunken logger, coming to assault his beautiful wife.

On the stove was an eight-inch cast-iron skillet, in which the cook had recently sautéed the mushrooms for the omelet. Dominic picked up the skillet, which was still warm in his hand, and hit the bear in the face—mostly on its nose but also on the broad, flat bridge of its nose between the bear's small, squinty eyes. The bear dropped to all fours and fled through the kitchen door, leaving the torn screen and the broken wooden slats hanging from the frame.

Whenever the cook told this story, he always said: "Well, the door had to be fixed, of course, but it still opens the wrong way." In telling the story to his son, Dominic Baciagalupo usually added: "I would never hit a bear with a cast-iron skillet—I thought it was a *man!*"

"But what would you do with a bear?" Danny asked his dad.

"Try to reason with it, I guess," the cook replied. "In that sort of situation, you can't reason with a man."

As for what "that sort of situation" was, Dan could only guess. Had his father imagined he was protecting his pretty wife from a dangerous man?

As for the eight-inch cast-iron skillet, it had acquired a special place for itself in the cookhouse. It no longer made its home in the kitchen with the other pots and pans. The skillet was hung at shoulder height on a hook in the upstairs of the cookhouse, where the bedrooms were—it resided just inside Dominic's bedroom door. That skillet had proved its worth; it had become the cook's weapon of choice, should he ever hear someone's footsteps on the stairs or the sound of an intruder (animal or human) sneaking around in the kitchen.

Dominic didn't own a gun; he didn't want one. For a New Hampshire boy, he had missed out on all the deer hunting—not only because of the ankle injury but because he hadn't grown up with a dad.

As for the loggers and the sawmill men, the deer hunters among them brought the cook their deer; he butchered the deer for them, and kept enough meat for himself so that he could occasionally serve venison in the cookhouse. It wasn't that Dominic disapproved of hunting; he just didn't like venison, or guns. He also suffered from a recurrent dream; he'd told Daniel about it. The cook repeatedly dreamed that he was murdered in his sleep—shot to death in his own bed—and whenever he woke from that dream, the sound of the shot was still ringing in his ears.

So Dominic Baciagalupo slept with a skillet in his bedroom. There were cast-iron skillets of all sizes in the cookhouse kitchen, but the eight-inch size was preferable for self-defense. Even young Dan could manage to swing it with some force. As for the ten-and-a-half-inch skillet, or the eleven-and-a-quarter-inch one, they may have been more accommodating to cook in, but they were too heavy to be reliable weapons; not even Ketchum could swing those bigger skillets quickly enough to take out a lecherous logger, or a bear.

THE NIGHT AFTER Angel Pope had gone under the logs, Danny Baciagalupo lay in bed in the upstairs of the cookhouse. The boy's bedroom was above the inside-opening screen door to the kitchen, and the loose-fitting outer door, which he could hear rattling in the wind. He could hear the river, too. In the cookhouse, you could always hear Twisted River—except when the river ran under the ice. But Danny must have fallen asleep as quickly as his father, because the twelve-year-old didn't hear the truck. The light from the truck's headlights had not shone into the cookhouse. Whoever was driving the truck must have been able to navigate the road from town in near-total darkness, because there wasn't much moonlight that night—or else the driver was drunk and had forgotten to turn on the truck's headlights.

Danny thought he heard the door to the truck's cab close. The mud, which was soft in the daytime, could get crunchy underfoot at night—it was still cold enough at night for the mud to freeze, and now there was a dusting of new snow. Perhaps he hadn't heard a truck door close, Dan was thinking; that *clunk* might have been a sound in whatever dream the boy had been having. Outside the cookhouse, the footsteps on the frozen mud made a shuffling sound—ponderous and wary. Maybe it's a bear, Danny thought.

The cook kept a cooler outside the kitchen. The cooler was sealed tight, but it contained the ground lamb, for the lamb hash, and the bacon—and whatever other perishables wouldn't fit in the fridge. What if the bear had smelled the meat in the cooler? Danny was thinking.

"Dad?" the boy spoke out, but his father was probably fast asleep down the hall.

Like everyone else, the bear seemed to be having trouble with the outer door to the cookhouse kitchen; it batted at the door with one paw. Young Dan heard grunting, too.

"Dad!" Danny shouted; he heard his father swipe the cast-iron skillet off the hook on the bedroom wall. Like his dad, the boy had gone to bed in his long johns and a pair of socks. The floor in the upstairs hall felt cold to Danny, even with his socks on. He and his dad padded downstairs to the kitchen, which was dimly lit by the pilot lights flickering from the old Garland. The cook had a two-handed grip on the black skillet. When the outer door opened, the bear—if it was a bear—pushed against the screen door with its chest. It came inside in an upright position, albeit unsteadily. Its teeth were a long, white blur.

"I'm not a bear, Cookie," Ketchum said.

The flash of white, which Danny had imagined was the bear's bared teeth, was the new cast on Ketchum's right forearm; the cast went from the middle of the big man's palm to where his arm bent at the elbow. "Sorry I startled you fellas," Ketchum added.

"Close the outer door, will you? I'm trying to keep it warm in here," the cook said. Danny saw his father put the skillet on the bottom step of the stairs. Ketchum struggled to secure the outer door with his left hand. "You're drunk," Dominic told him.

"I've got one arm, Cookie, and I'm right-handed," Ketchum said.

"You're still drunk, Ketchum," Dominic Baciagalupo told his old friend.

"I guess you remember what that's like," Ketchum said.

Dan helped Ketchum close the outer door. "I'll bet you're real hungry," he said to Ketchum. The big man, swaying slightly, ruffled the boy's hair.

"I don't need to eat," Ketchum said.

"It might help to sober you up," the cook said. Dominic opened the fridge. He told Ketchum: "I've got some meat loaf, which isn't bad cold. You can have it with applesauce."

"I don't need to eat," the big man said again. "I need you to come with me, Cookie."

"Where are we going?" Dominic asked, but even young Dan knew when his father was pretending not to know something he clearly knew.

"You know where," Ketchum told the cook. "I just have trouble remembering the exact spot."

"That's because you drink too much, Ketchum—that's why you can't remember," Dominic said.

When Ketchum lowered his head, he swayed more; for a moment, Danny thought that the logger might fall down. And by the way both men had lowered their voices, the boy understood that they were negotiating; they were also being careful not to say too much, because Ketchum didn't know what the twelve-year-old knew about his mother's death, and Dominic Baciagalupo didn't want his son to hear whatever odd or unwelcome detail Ketchum might remember.

"Just try the meat loaf, Ketchum," the cook said softly.

"It's pretty good with applesauce," Danny said. The riverman lowered himself onto a stool; he rested his new white cast on the countertop. Everything about Ketchum was hardened and sharp-edged, like a whittled-down stick—and, as Danny had observed, "wicked tough"—which made the sterile, fragile-looking cast as unsuited to the man as a prosthetic limb. (If Ketchum had lost an arm, he would have made do with the stump—he might have used it as a club.)

But now that Ketchum was sitting down, Danny thought the river driver looked safe enough to touch. The boy had never felt a cast before. Even drunk, Ketchum somehow knew what Dan was thinking. "Go on—you can touch it," the logger said, extending his cast in the boy's direction. There was dried blood, or pitch, on what Danny could see of Ketchum's crooked fingers; they protruded from the cast, unmoving. With a broken wrist, it hurt to move your fingers for the first few days. The boy gently touched Ketchum's cast.

The cook gave Ketchum a generous serving of meat loaf and applesauce. "There's milk or orange juice," Dominic said, "or I could make you some coffee."

"What a disheartening choice," Ketchum said, winking at Danny.

"Disheartening," the cook repeated, shaking his head. "I'll make some coffee."

Danny wished that the two men would just talk about everything; the boy knew much of their history, but not enough about his mother. Of her death, *no* detail could be odd or unwelcome—Danny wanted to hear every word of it. But the cook was a careful man, or he had become one; even Ketchum, who had driven his own children away from him, was especially cautious and protective with Danny, much as the veteran logger had behaved around Angel.

"I wouldn't go there with you when you've been drinking, anyway," the cook was saying.

"I took you there when you'd been drinking," Ketchum said; so he wouldn't say more, he took a mouthful of meat loaf and applesauce.

"Except when it's under a logjam, a body doesn't move downstream as fast as a log," Dominic Baciagalupo said, as if he were speaking to the coffeepot—not to Ketchum, whose back was turned to him. "Not unless the body is caught on a log."

Danny had heard this explanation, in another context. It had taken a few days—three, to be exact—for his mother's body to make the journey from the river basin to the narrows, where it had bumped up against the dam. First a drowned body sinks, the cook had explained to his son; then it rises.

"They're keeping the dams closed through the weekend," Ketchum said. (He meant not only Dead Woman Dam but the Pontook Dam, on the Androscoggin.) Ketchum ate steadily but not fast, the fork held unfamiliarly, and a little clumsily, in his left hand.

"It's good with applesauce, isn't it?" the boy asked him. Ketchum nodded in agreement, chewing vigorously.

They could smell the coffee brewing, and the cook said—more to himself than to his son, or Ketchum—"I might as well start the bacon, while I'm at it." Ketchum just went on eating. "I suppose the logs are already at the first dam," Dominic added, as if he were still speaking to no one but himself. "I mean *our* logs."

"I know which logs you mean, and which dam," Ketchum told

him. "Yes, the logs are already at the dam—they were there while you were making supper."

"So you saw that moron doctor there?" the cook asked. "Not that you need a genius to put a cast on a broken wrist, but you must be a man who loves to take chances." Dominic went out of the cookhouse to get the bacon from the cooler. It was black outside, and the sound of the river rushed into the warm kitchen.

"You used to take chances, Cookie!" Ketchum called out to his old friend; he looked cautiously at Danny. "Your dad used to be happier, too—when he drank."

"I used to be happier—period," the cook said; the way he dropped the slab of bacon on the cutting board made Danny look at his father, but Ketchum never turned his attention away from the meat loaf and applesauce.

"Given that bodies move downstream slower than logs," Ketchum said with deliberate slowness, his speech slightly slurred, "what would you guess as to Angel's estimated time of arrival at that spot I'm having trouble remembering, exactly?"

Danny was counting to himself, but it was clear to the boy, and to Ketchum, that the cook had already been estimating the young Canadian's journey. "Saturday night or Sunday morning," Dominic Baciagalupo said. He had to raise his voice above the hissing bacon. "I'm not going there with you at night, Ketchum."

Danny quickly looked at Ketchum, anticipating the big man's response; it was, after all, the story that most interested the boy, and the one closest to his heart. "I went there with *you* at night, Cookie."

"The odds are better you'll be sober Sunday morning," the cook told Ketchum. "Nine o'clock, Sunday morning—Daniel and I will meet you there." (They meant Dead Woman Dam, though young Dan knew that neither man would say it.)

"We can all go in my truck," Ketchum said.

"I'll drive Daniel with me, in case you're not quite sober," Dominic replied.

Ketchum pushed his clean plate away; he rested his shaggy head on the countertop and stared at his cast. "You'll meet me at the mill-pond, you mean?" Ketchum asked.

"I don't call it that," the cook said. "The dam was there before the mill. How can they call it a pond, when it's where the river *narrows*?"

"You know mill people," Ketchum said with contempt.

"The dam was there before the mill," Dominic repeated, still not naming the dam.

"One day the water will breach that dam, and they won't bother to build another one," Ketchum said; his eyes were closing.

"One day they won't be driving logs on Twisted River," the cook said. "They won't need a dam where the river runs into the reservoir, though I believe they'll keep the Pontook Dam on the Androscoggin."

"One day *soon*, Cookie," Ketchum corrected him. His eyes were closed—his head, his chest, and both his arms were sprawled on the countertop. The cook quietly removed the clean plate, but Ketchum wasn't asleep; he spoke more slowly than before. "There's a sort of spillway off to one side of the dam. The water makes a pool—it's almost like an open well—but there's a kind of containment boom, just a rope with floats, to keep the logs out."

"It sounds like you remember it as *exactly* as I do," Dominic told him.

That was where they'd found his mother, Danny knew. Her body floated lower in the water than the logs; she must have drifted under the containment boom and into the spillway. Ketchum had found her all alone in the pool, or the well—not a log around her.

"I can't quite see how to *get* there," Ketchum said, with some frustration. With his eyes still closed, he was slowly curling the fingers of his right hand, his fingertips reaching for but not quite touching the palm of his cast; both the cook and his son knew that the logger was testing his tolerance of the pain.

"Well, I can show you, Ketchum," Dominic said gently. "You have to walk out on the dam, or across the logs—remember?"

The cook had carried one of the folding cots into the kitchen. He nodded to his son, who helped him set up the cot—where it wouldn't be in the way of the ovens, or the inside-opening screen door. "I want to sleep in the kitchen, too," Danny told his dad.

"If you make a little distance between yourself and the conversation, you might actually go back to sleep," Dominic said to his son.

"I want to hear the conversation," Danny said.

"The conversation is almost over," the cook whispered in the boy's ear, kissing him.

"Don't count on it, Cookie," Ketchum said, with his eyes still closed.

"I've got the baking to do, Ketchum—and I might as well start the potatoes."

"I've heard you talk and cook at the same time," Ketchum told him; he hadn't opened his eyes.

The cook gave his son a stern look, pointing to the stairs. "It's cold upstairs," Danny complained; the boy paused on the bottom step, where the skillet was.

"On your way, please put the skillet back where it belongs, Daniel."

The boy went grudgingly upstairs, pausing on every step; he listened to his father work with the mixing bowls. Young Dan didn't need to see in order to know what his dad was doing—the cook always made the banana bread first. As Danny hung the eight-inch cast-iron skillet on the hook in his father's bedroom, he counted sixteen eggs cracked into the stainless-steel bowl; then came the mashed bananas and the chopped walnuts. (Sometimes, his dad topped the bread with warm apples.) The cook made the scones next, adding the eggs and the butter to the dry ingredients—the fruit, if he had any, he added last. From the upstairs hall, Danny could hear his father greasing the muffin tins, which he then sprinkled with flour—before he put the corn-muffin mixture into the tins. There was oatmeal in the banana bread—and sweet bran flour, which the boy could soon smell from his bedroom.

It was warmer under the covers, from where Danny heard the oven doors open and the baking pans and muffin tins slide in; then he heard the oven doors close. The unusual sound, which made the boy open his eyes and sit up in bed, was his father struggling to lift Ketchum—holding the big man under both arms while he dragged him to the folding cot. Danny hadn't known that his dad was strong enough to lift Ketchum; the twelve-year-old crept quietly down the stairs and watched his father settle Ketchum on the cot, where the cook covered the logger with one of the unzipped sleeping bags, as if the opened bag were a blanket.

Dominic Baciagalupo was putting the potatoes on the griddle when Ketchum spoke to him. "There was no way I could let you see her, Cookie—it wouldn't have been right."

"I understand," the cook said.

On the stairs, Danny closed his eyes again, seeing the story, which he knew by heart—Ketchum, taking small steps on the logs, drunk, while he reached into the pool created by the spillway. "Don't come out here, Cookie!" Ketchum had called ashore. "Don't you try walking on the logs—or on the dam, either!"

Dominic had watched Ketchum carry his dead wife along the edge of the containment boom. "Get away from me, Cookie!" Ketchum had called, as he came across the logs. "You can't see her anymore—she's not the same as she was!"

The cook, who was also drunk, had taken the blanket from the back of Ketchum's truck. But Ketchum would not come ashore with the body; even drunk, he had kept walking on the logs with small, rapid steps. "Spread the blanket in the back of the truck, Cookie—then walk away!" When Ketchum came ashore, Dominic was standing at a triangular point—equidistant from the riverbank and Ketchum's truck. "Just stand your ground, Cookie—till I cover her," Ketchum had said.

Danny wondered if that was the source of his father's frequent admonition: "Stand your ground, Daniel—just don't get killed." Maybe it had come from Ketchum, who had gently placed the cook's dead wife in the back of his truck, covering her with the blanket. Dominic had kept his distance.

"Didn't you want to see her?" Danny had asked his dad, too many times.

"I trust Ketchum," his father had answered. "If anything ever happens to me, Daniel, you trust him, too."

Danny realized that he must have crept back upstairs to his bedroom, and fallen asleep, when he smelled the lamb hash in addition to all the baking; he'd not been aware of his dad opening the difficult outer door to the cookhouse kitchen and getting the ground lamb from the cooler. The boy lay in his bed with his eyes still closed, savoring all the smells. He wanted to ask Ketchum if his mom had been faceup in the water when he'd first spotted her, or if he'd found her in the spillway facedown.

Danny got dressed and went downstairs to the kitchen; only then did he realize that his father had found the time to come upstairs and get dressed, probably after Ketchum had passed out on the cot. Dan watched his dad working at the stove; when the cook was concentrating on three or four tasks that were all in close proximity to one another, his limp was almost undetectable. At such moments, Danny could imagine his father at the age of twelve—before the ankle accident. At twelve, Danny Baciagalupo was a lonely kid; he had no friends. He often wished that he could have known his dad when they were both twelve-year-olds.

WHEN YOU'RE TWELVE, four years seems like a long time. Annunziata Saetta knew that it wouldn't take her little Dom's ankle four years to heal; Nunzi's beloved Kiss of the Wolf was off the crutches in four *months,* and he was reading as well as any fifteen-year-old by the time he was only thirteen. The homeschooling worked. In the first place, Annunziata was an elementary-school teacher; she knew how much of the school day was wasted on discipline, recess, and snacks. The boy did his homework, and double-checked it, during what amounted to Nunzi's school day; Dominic had time for lots of extra reading, and he kept a journal of the recipes he was learning, too.

The boy's cooking skills were more slowly acquired, and—after the accident—Annunziata made her own child-labor laws. She would not permit young Dominic to go off to work at a breakfast place in Berlin until the boy really knew his way around a kitchen, and he had to wait until he'd turned sixteen; in those four years, Dom became an extremely well-read sixteen-year-old, and an accomplished cook, who was less experienced at shaving than he was at walking with a limp.

It was 1940 when Dominic Baciagalupo met Danny's mom. She was a twenty-three-year-old teaching in the same elementary school as Annunziata Saetta; in fact, the cook's mother introduced her sixteen-year-old son to the new teacher.

Nunzi had no choice in the matter. Her cousin Maria, another Saetta, had married a Calogero—a common Sicilian surname. "After some Greek saint who died there—the name has something to do with children in general, I think, or maybe orphans in particular,"

Nunzi had explained to Dominic. She pronounced the name cah-LOH-ger-roh. It was used as a first name, too, his mother explained—"frequently for bastards."

At sixteen, Dominic was sensitive to the subject of illegitimacy—not that Annunziata wasn't. Her cousin had sent her pregnant daughter away to the wilds of New Hampshire, bemoaning the fact that the daughter was the first woman in the Calogero family to have graduated from college. "It was only a teachers' college, and a lot of good it did her—she still got knocked up!" the poor girl's mother told Nunzi, who repeated this insensitivity to Dom. The boy understood without further detail that the pregnant twenty-three-year-old was being sent to them because Annunziata and *her* bastard were considered in the same boat. Her name was Rosina, but—given Nunzi's fondness for abbreviations—the banished girl was already a Rosie before she made the trip from Boston to Berlin.

As was often the way "back then"—not only in the North End, and by no means limited to Italian *or* Catholic families—the Saettas and the Calogeros were sending one family scandal to live with another. Thus Annunziata was given a reason to resent her Boston relatives *twice*. "Let this be a lesson to you, Dom," the teenager's mother told him. "We are not going to judge poor Rosie for her unfortunate condition—we are going to *love* her, like nothing was the matter."

While Annunziata should be commended for her spirit of forgiveness—especially in 1940, when unwed mothers could generally be counted among America's most unforgiven souls—it was both reckless and unnecessary to tell her sixteen-year-old son that he was going to *love* his second cousin "like nothing was the matter."

"Why is she my *second* cousin?" the boy asked his mom.

"Maybe that's not what she is—maybe she's called your cousin *once-removed*, or something," Nunzi said. When Dominic looked confused, his mother said: "Whatever she's called, she's not really your cousin—not a first cousin, anyway."

This information (or misinformation) posed an unknown danger to a crippled sixteen-year-old boy. His accident, his rehabilitation, his homeschooling, not to mention his reinvention as a cook—all these—had deprived him of friends his own age. And "little" Dom had a full-time job; he already saw himself as a young man. Now Nunzi had told him that the twenty-three-year-old Rosie Calogero was "not really" his cousin.

As for Rosie, when she arrived, she was not yet "showing"; that she soon would be posed another problem.

Rosie had a B.S. in education from the teachers' college; at that time, frankly, she was overqualified to teach at a Berlin elementary school. But when the young woman started to *look* pregnant, she would need to temporarily quit her job. "Or else we'll have to come up with a husband for you, either real or imaginary," Annunziata told her. Rosie was certainly pretty enough to find a husband, a *real* one— Dominic thought she was absolutely beautiful—but the poor girl wasn't about to sally forth on the requisite social adventures necessary for meeting available young men, not when she was expecting!

FOR FOUR YEARS, the boy had cooked with his mother. In some ways, because he wrote every recipe down—not to mention each variation of the recipes he would make, occasionally, without her—he was surpassing her, even as he learned. As it happened, on that life-changing night, Dominic was making dinner for the two women and himself. He was on his way to becoming famous at the breakfast place in Berlin, and he got home from work well before Rosie and his mom came home from school; except on weekends, when Nunzi liked to cook, Dominic was becoming the principal cook in their small household. Stirring his marinara sauce, he said: "Well, *I* could marry Rosie, or I could *pretend* to be her husband—until she finds someone more suitable. I mean, who needs to know?"

To Annunziata, it seemed like such a sweet and innocent offer; she laughed and gave her son a hug. But young Dom couldn't imagine anyone "more suitable" for Rosie than himself—he had been faking the *pretend* part. He would have married Rosie for real; the difference in their ages, or that they were vaguely related, was no stumbling block for him.

As for Rosie, it didn't matter that the sixteen-year-old's proposal, which was both sweet and *not*-so-innocent, was unrealistic—and probably illegal, even in northern New Hampshire. What affected the poor girl, who was still in the first trimester of her pregnancy, was that the lout who'd knocked her up had *not* offered to marry her—not even under what had amounted to considerable duress.

Given the predilections of the male members of both the Saetta and Calogero families, this "duress" took the form of multiple threats of castration ending with death by drowning. Whether it was Naples or Palermo the lout sailed back to was not made clear, but no marriage proposal was ever forthcoming. Dominic's spontaneous and heartfelt offer was the first time *anyone* had proposed to Rosie; overcome, she burst into tears at the kitchen table before Dominic could poach the shrimp in his marinara sauce. Sobbing, the distraught young woman went to bed without her dinner.

In the night, Annunziata awoke to the confusing sounds of Rosie's miscarriage—"confusing" because, at that moment, Nunzi didn't know if the loss of the baby was a blessing or a curse. Dominic Baciagalupo lay in his bed, listening to his second or once-removed cousin crying. The toilet kept flushing, the bathtub was filling—there must have been blood—and, over it all, came the sympathetic crooning of his mother's most consoling voice. "Rosie, maybe it's better this way. Now you don't need to quit your job—not even temporarily! Now we don't have to come up with a husband for you—not a real one *or* the imaginary kind! Listen to me, Rosie—it wasn't a baby, not yet."

But Dominic lay wondering, What have I done? Even an *imaginary* marriage to Rosie gave the boy a nearly constant erection. (Well, he was sixteen years old—no wonder!) When he heard that Rosie had stopped crying, young Dom held his breath. "Did Dominic hear me—did I wake him up, do you think?" the boy heard the girl ask his mother.

"Well, he sleeps like the dead," Nunzi said, "but you did make quite a ruckus—understandably, of course."

"He must have heard me!" the girl cried. "I have to talk to him!" she said. Dominic could hear her step out of the tub. There was the vigorous rubbing of a towel, and the sound of her bare feet on the bathroom floor.

"*I* can explain to Dom in the morning," his mother was saying, but his not-really-a-cousin's bare feet were already padding down the hall to the spare room.

"No! I have something to tell him!" Rosie called. Dominic could hear a drawer open; a coat hanger fell in her closet. Then the girl was in his room—she just opened his door, without knocking, and lay down on the bed beside him. He could feel her wet hair touch his face.

"I heard you," he told her.

"I'm going to be fine," Rosie began. "I'll have a baby, some other day."

"Does it hurt?" he asked her. He kept his face turned away from her on the pillow, because he had brushed his teeth too long ago—he was afraid his breath was bad.

"I didn't think I wanted the baby until I lost it," Rosie was saying. He couldn't think of what to say, but she went on. "What you said to me, Dominic, was the nicest thing anyone ever said to me—I'll never forget it."

"I would marry you, you know—I wasn't just saying it," the boy said.

She hugged him and kissed his ear. She was on top of the covers, and he was under them, but he could still feel her body pressing against his back. "I'll never have a nicer offer—I know it," his not-really-a-cousin said.

"Maybe we could get married when I'm a little older," Dominic suggested.

"Maybe we *will*!" the girl cried, hugging him again.

Did she mean it, the sixteen-year-old wondered, or was she just being nice?

From the bathroom, where Annunziata was draining and scrubbing the tub, their voices were audible but indistinct. What surprised Nunzi was that Dominic was talking; the boy rarely spoke. His voice was still changing—it was getting lower. But from the moment Annunziata had heard Rosie say, "Maybe we *will*!"—well, Dominic began to talk and talk, and the girl's interjections grew fainter but lengthier. What they said was indecipherable, but they were whispering as breathlessly as lovers.

As she went on compulsively cleaning the bathtub, Annunziata no longer wondered if the miscarriage had been a blessing or a curse; the miscarriage was no longer the point. It was Rosie Calogero herself—was *she* a blessing or a curse? What had Nunzi been thinking? She'd opened her house to a pretty, intelligent (and clearly *emotional*) young woman—one who'd been rejected by her lover and banished from

home by her family—without realizing what an irresistible temptation the twenty-three-year-old would be for a lonely boy coming of
age.

Annunziata got off her knees in the bathroom and went down the
hall to the kitchen, noting that the door to her son's bedroom was partially open and the whispering went on and on. In the kitchen, Nunzi
took a pinch of salt and threw it over her shoulder. She resisted the
impulse to intrude on the two of them, but—first stepping back into
the hall—she raised her voice.

"My goodness, Rosie, you must forgive me," Annunziata announced. "I never even asked you if you wanted to *go back to Boston*!"
Nunzi had tried to make this not appear to be *her* idea; she'd attempted a neutral or indifferent tone, as if she were speaking strictly
out of consideration for what Rosie herself wanted to do. But the
murmuring from Dominic's bedroom was broken by a sudden, shared
intake of breath.

Rosie felt the boy gasp against her chest the second she was aware
of her own gasp. It was as if they had rehearsed the answer, so perfectly in unison was their response. "No!" Annunziata heard her son
and Rosie cry; they were a chorus.

Definitely not a blessing, Nunzi was thinking, when she heard
Rosie say, "I want to stay here, with you and Dominic. I want to teach
at the school. I don't *ever* want to go back to Boston!" (I can't blame
her for *that,* Annunziata realized; she knew the feeling.)

"I want Rosie to stay!" Nunzi heard her son call out.

Well, of *course* you do! Annunziata thought. But what would the
repercussions of the difference in their ages be? And what would happen if and when the country went to war, and all the young men went?
(But *not* her beloved Kiss of the Wolf—not with a limp like that,
Nunzi knew.)

ROSIE CALOGERO KEPT her job and did it well. The young cook also
kept his job and did it well—well enough that the breakfast place
started serving lunch, too. In a short time, Dominic Baciagalupo became a much better cook than his mom. And whatever the young
cook made for lunch, he brought the best of it home for dinner; he fed
his mother and his not-really-a-cousin very well. On occasion,

mother and son would still cook together, but on most culinary matters, Annunziata yielded to Dominic.

He made meat loaf with Worcestershire sauce and provolone, and served it warm with his multipurpose marinara sauce—or cold, with applesauce. He did breaded chicken cutlets *alla parmigiana;* in Boston, his mother had told him, she'd made *veal* Parmesan, but in Berlin he couldn't get good veal. (He substituted pork for veal—it was almost as good.) Dominic made eggplant Parmesan, too—the sizable contingent of French Canadians in Berlin knew what *aubergine* was. And Dom did a leg of lamb with lemon and garlic and olive oil; the olive oil came from a shop Nunzi knew in Boston, and Dominic used it to rub roast chicken or baste turkey, both of which he stuffed with cornbread and sausage and sage. He did steaks under the broiler, or he grilled the steaks, which he served with white beans or roasted potatoes. But he didn't much care for potatoes, and he loathed rice. He served most of his main dishes with pasta, which he did very simply—with olive oil and garlic, and sometimes with peas or asparagus. He cooked carrots in olive oil with black Sicilian olives, and more garlic. And although he detested baked beans, Dominic would serve them; there were lumbermen and mill workers, mostly old-timers who'd lost their teeth, who ate little else. ("The baked beans and pea soup crowd," Nunzi called them disparagingly.)

Occasionally, Annunziata could get fennel, which she and Dom cooked in a sweet tomato sauce with sardines; the sardines came in cans from another shop Nunzi knew in Boston, and mother and son mashed them to a paste in garlic and olive oil, and served them with pasta topped with bread crumbs, and browned in the oven. Dominic made his own pizza dough. He served meatless pizzas every Friday night—in lieu of fish, which neither the young cook nor his mom trusted was fresh enough in the north country. Shrimp, frozen in chunks of ice the size of cinder blocks, arrived unthawed in trains from the coast; hence Dominic trusted the shrimp. And the pizzas made more use of his beloved marinara sauce. The ricotta, Romano, Parmesan, and provolone cheese all came from Boston—as did the black Sicilian olives. The cook, who was still learning his craft, chopped a lot of parsley and put it on everything—even on the ubiquitous pea soup. (Parsley was "pure chlorophyll," his mother had told him; it offset garlic and freshened your breath.)

Dominic kept his desserts simple, and—to Nunzi's vexation—there was nothing remotely Sicilian about them: apple pie, and blueberry cobbler or johnnycake. In Coos County, you could always get apples and blueberries, and Dominic was good with dough.

His breakfasts were even more basic—eggs and bacon, pancakes and French toast, corn muffins and blueberry muffins and scones. In those days, he would make banana bread only when the bananas had turned brown; it was wasteful to use good bananas, his mother had told him.

There was a turkey farm in the Androscoggin Valley, roughly between Berlin and Milan, and the cook made turkey hash with peppers and onions—and a minimal amount of potatoes. "Corned beef isn't fit for hash—it must be Irish!" Annunziata had lectured to him.

That alcoholic asshole Uncle Umberto, who would drink himself to death before the war was over, never ate a meal cooked by his not-really-a-nephew. The veteran lumberman could scarcely tolerate being a foreman to the ever-increasing numbers of female mill workers, and the women refused to tolerate Umberto at all, which only served to exacerbate the troubled foreman's drinking. (Minor character or not, Umberto would haunt Dominic's memory, where the not-really-an-uncle played a major role. How had Dominic's father been Umberto's friend? And did Umberto dislike Nunzi because she wouldn't sleep with him? Given his mother's banishment from Boston, and her situation in Berlin, Dominic would often torture himself with the thought that Umberto had wrongly imagined Nunzi might be rather easily seduced.) And one winter month, some years ahead of Asshole Umberto's demise, Annunziata Saetta caught the same flu all the schoolchildren had; Nunzi died before the United States had officially entered the war.

What were Rosie Calogero and young Dom to do? They were twenty-four and seventeen, respectively; they couldn't very well live together in the same house, not after Dominic's mother died. Nor could they tolerate living apart—hence the not-quite-cousins had a quandary on their hands. Not even Nunzi could tell them what to do, not anymore; the young woman and noticeably younger man only did what they thought poor Annunziata would have wanted, and maybe she would have.

Young Dom simply lied about his age. He and his (not-really-a) cousin Rosie Calogero were married in mud season, 1941—just before the first big log drives of that year on the Androscoggin, north of Berlin. They were a successful, if not prosperous, young cook and a successful, though not prosperous, schoolteacher. At least their work wasn't transient, and what need did they have to be prosperous? They were both (in their different ways) young and in love, and they wanted only one child—just one—and, in March 1942, they would have him.

Young Dan was born in Berlin—"just before mud season," as his father always put it (mud season being more definitive than the calendar)—and almost immediately upon his birth, the boy's hardworking parents moved away from the mill town. To the cook's sensibilities, the stench of the paper mill was a constant insult. It seemed plausible to believe that one day the war would be over, and when it was, Berlin would grow bigger—beyond all recognition, except for the smell. But in 1942, the town was already too big and too fetid—and too full of mixed memories—for Dominic Baciagalupo. And Rosie's prior experience in the North End had made her wary of moving back to Boston, although both the Saetta and Calogero families entreated the young cousins to come "home."

Children know when they are not loved unconditionally. Dominic was aware that his mother had felt she was spurned. And while Rosie never appeared to resent the circumstances that had compelled her to marry a mere *boy*, she truly resented how her family had banished her to Berlin in the first place.

The entreaties by the Saetta and Calogero families fell on deaf ears. Who were they to say all was forgiven? Apparently, it was okay with them that the cousins were married, and that they had a child; but what Dominic and Rosie remembered was how it had *not* been okay for either a Saetta or a Calogero to be pregnant and *un*married.

"Let them find someone else to forgive," was how Rosie put it. Dominic, knowing how Nunzi had felt, agreed. Boston was a bridge that had been burned behind them; more to the point, the young couple felt confident that *they* hadn't burned it.

Surely moral condemnation wasn't new to New England, not in

1942; and while most people might have chosen Boston over Twisted River, the decisions made by many young married couples are circumstantial. To the newly formed Baciagalupo family, Twisted River may have seemed remote and raw-looking, but there was no paper mill. The sawmill and logging-camp settlement had never kept a cook through a single mud season, and there was no school—not in a town largely inhabited by itinerants. There was, however, the potential for a school in the smaller but more permanent-seeming settlement on Phillips Brook—namely, Paris (formerly, West Dummer), which was only a few miles on the log-hauler road from the visibly scruffier settlement in Twisted River, where the logging company had heretofore refused to invest in a permanent cookhouse. According to the company, the portable, makeshift kitchen and the dining wanigans would have to do. That this made Twisted River look more like a logging camp than an actual town failed to discourage Dominic and Rosie Baciagalupo, to whom Twisted River beckoned as an opportunity— albeit a rough one.

In the summer of '42—leaving themselves enough time to order textbooks and other supplies, in preparation for the new Paris school—the cook and the schoolteacher, together with their infant son, followed the Androscoggin north to Milan, and then traveled north-northwest on the haul road from the Pontook Reservoir. Where Twisted River poured into the Pontook was simply called "the narrows"; there wasn't even a sawmill, and the rudimentary Dead Woman Dam was as yet unnamed. (As Ketchum would say: "Things were a lot less fancy then.")

The couple with their child arrived at the basin below Twisted River before nightfall and the mosquitoes. To those few who remembered the young family's arrival, the man with the limp and his pretty but older-looking wife with her new baby must have appeared hopeful—although they carried only a few clothes with them. Their books and the rest of their clothes, together with the cook's kitchenware, had come ahead of them—all of it on an empty logging truck, covered with a tarp.

The kitchen and dining wanigans needed more than a good cleaning: A full-scale restoration was what the wanigans wanted—and what the cook would insist on having, if he was going to stay. And if the logging company expected the cook to remain past the next mud season, they would have to build a permanent cookhouse—with bedrooms above the cookhouse, where the cook and his family intended to live.

Rosie was more modest in her demands: A one-room school would be sufficient for Paris, née West Dummer, where there had never been a school before; there were only a few families with school-age children on Phillips Brook in 1942, and fewer still in Twisted River. There would soon be more—after the war, when the men came home—but Rosie Baciagalupo, née Calogero, wouldn't get to see the men return from war, nor would she ever educate their children.

The young schoolteacher died in the late winter of 1944—shortly after her son, Dan, had turned two. The boy had no memory of his mother, whom he knew only by the photographs his father had kept— and by the passages she'd underlined in her many books, which his dad had saved, too. (As in the case of Dominic Baciagalupo's mother, Rosie had liked to read novels.)

To judge Dominic by his apparent pessimism—there was an air of aloofness about his conduct, or a noticeable detachment in his demeanor, and even something melancholic in his bearing—you might conclude that he had never recovered from the tragic death of his twenty-seven-year-old wife. Yet, in addition to his beloved son, Dominic Baciagalupo had got one thing that he'd wanted: The cookhouse had been built to his specifications.

Apparently, there was a Paris Manufacturing Company connection; some bigwig's wife, passing through Berlin, had raved about Dominic's cooking. The word had gotten around: The food was way better than standard logging-camp fare. It wouldn't have been right for Dominic to just pack up and leave, but the cook and his son had stayed for ten years.

Of course there was an old logger or two—chief among them, Ketchum—who knew the miserable reason. The cook, who was a widower at twenty, blamed himself for his wife's death—and he wasn't the only man who made living in Twisted River resemble a mercilessly extended act of penance. (One had only to think of Ketchum.)

IN 1954, DOMINIC BACIAGALUPO was only thirty—young to have a twelve-year-old son—but Dominic had the look of a man long resigned to his fate. He was so unflinchingly calm that he radiated a

kind of acceptance that could easily be mistaken for pessimism. There
was nothing pessimistic about the good care he took of his boy,
Daniel, and it was only for the sake of his son that the cook ever complained about the harshness or the limitations of life in Twisted
River—the town still didn't have a school, for example.

As for the school the Paris Manufacturing Company had built on
Phillips Brook, there'd been no discernible improvements on the quality of education Rosie Baciagalupo had provided. Granted, the one-
room schoolhouse had been rebuilt since the forties, but the school's
thuggish culture was dominated by the older boys who'd been held
back a grade or two. There was no controlling them—the long-
suffering schoolteacher was no Rosie Baciagalupo. The Paris school's
thugs were inclined to bully the cook's son—not only because Danny
lived in Twisted River and his dad limped. They also teased the boy
for the proper way in which he invariably spoke. Young Dan's enunciation was exact; his diction never descended to the dropped conso-
nants and broad vowels of the Paris kids, and they abused him for it.
("The West Dummer kids," Ketchum unfailingly called them.)

"Stand your ground, Daniel—just don't get killed," his father predictably told him. "I promise you, one day we'll leave here."

But whatever its faults, and his family's sad story, the Paris Manufacturing Company School on Phillips Brook was the only school the
boy had attended; even the thought of leaving that school made
Danny Baciagalupo anxious.

"ANGEL WAS TOO GREEN to be felling trees in the forest, or working
on the log brows," Ketchum said from the folding cot in the kitchen.
Both the cook and his son knew that Ketchum talked in his sleep, especially when he'd been drinking.

A log brow, which was made of log cribwork and built into a bank
on the side of a haul road, had to be slightly higher than the bed of the
logging truck, which was pulled up beside it. Logs brought in from
the woods could be stored behind the cribwork until they were ready
to be loaded. Alternatively, log skids formed a ramp up to the truck
bed; then a horse, or a tractor-powered jammer (a hoist), was used to
load the logs. Ketchum wouldn't have wanted Angel Pope to have
anything to do with loading or unloading logs.

Danny Baciagalupo had begun his kitchen chores when Ketchum spoke again in his drunken stupor. "He should have been sticking lumber, Cookie." The cook nodded at the stove, though he knew perfectly well that Ketchum was still asleep, without once looking at the veteran riverman.

Stacking boards—or "sticking lumber," as it was called—was usually a beginning-laborer position at a sawmill. Even the cook wouldn't have considered Angel too green for that. The lumber was stacked by alternating layers of boards with "stickers"; these were narrow slats of wood laid perpendicular to the boards to separate them, to allow the air to circulate for drying. Dominic Baciagalupo might have allowed Danny to do that.

"Progressively increasing mechanization," Ketchum mumbled. If the big man had so much as attempted to roll over on the folding cot, he would have fallen off or collapsed the cot. But Ketchum lay unmoving on his back, with his cast held across his chest—as if he were about to be buried at sea. The unzipped sleeping bag covered him like a flag; his left hand touched the floor.

"Oh, boy—here we go again," the cook said, smiling at his son. *Progressively increasing mechanization* was a sore point with Ketchum. By 1954, rubber-tired skidders were already appearing in the woods. The larger trees were generally being yarded by tractors; the smaller horse-logging crews were being paid what was called a "piece rate" (by the cord or thousand board feet) to cut and haul timber to an assigned roadside location. As rubber-tired logging equipment became more common, an old horse-logger like Ketchum knew that the trees were being harvested at a faster rate. Ketchum was not a faster-rate man.

Danny opened the tricky outer door of the cookhouse kitchen and went outside to pee. (Although his father disapproved of peeing outdoors, Ketchum had taught young Dan to enjoy it.) It was still dark, and the mist from the rushing river was cold and wet on the boy's face.

"Fuck the donkey-engine men!" Ketchum shouted in his sleep. "Fuck the asshole truck drivers, too!"

"You're quite right about that," the cook said to his sleeping friend. The twelve-year-old came back inside, closing the kitchen's outer door. Ketchum was sitting up on the cot; perhaps his own shouting had woken him. He was frightening to behold. The unnatural blackness of his hair and beard gave him the appearance of someone who'd been burned in a terrible fire—and now the livid scar on his forehead seemed especially ashen in the whitish light from the fluorescent lamps. Ketchum was assessing his surroundings in an unfocused but wary way.

"Don't forget to fuck Constable Carl, too," the cook said to him.

"Absolutely," Ketchum readily agreed. "That fucking cowboy."

Constable Carl had given Ketchum the scar. The constable routinely broke up fights at the dance hall and in the hostelry bars. He'd broken up one of Ketchum's fights by cracking the logger's head with the long barrel of his Colt .45—"the kind of show-off weapon only an asshole would have in New Hampshire," in Ketchum's opinion. (Hence Constable Carl was a "cowboy.")

Yet, in Danny Baciagalupo's opinion, getting smacked on your forehead with a Colt .45 was preferable to Constable Carl shooting you in the foot, or in the knee—a method of breaking up fights that the cowboy generally favored with the Canadian itinerants. This usually meant that the French Canadians couldn't work in the woods; they had to go back to Quebec, which was okay with Constable Carl.

"Was I saying something?" Ketchum asked the cook and his son.

"You were positively eloquent on the subject of the donkey-engine men and the truck drivers," Dominic told his friend.

"Fuck them," Ketchum automatically replied. "I'm going north— anywhere but here," he announced. Ketchum was still sitting on the cot, where he regarded his cast as if it were a newly acquired but utterly useless limb; he stared at it with hatred.

"Yeah, sure," Dominic said.

Danny was working on the countertop, cutting up the peppers and tomatoes for the omelets; the boy knew that Ketchum talked about "going north" all the time. Both the Millsfield and the Second College Grant regions of New Hampshire, which is now officially known as the Great North Woods, and the Aziscohos Mountain area southeast of Wilsons Mills, Maine, were the logging territories that beckoned to Ketchum. But the veteran river driver and horse-logger knew that the aforementioned "progressively increasing mechanization" would go north, too; in fact, it was already there.

"You should leave here, Cookie—you know you should," Ketchum said, as the first of the headlights from the kitchen help shone into the cookhouse.

"Yeah, sure," the cook said again. Like Dominic Baciagalupo, Ketchum talked about leaving, but he stayed.

The engine sound of the Indian dishwasher's truck stood out among the other vehicles. "Constipated Christ!" said Ketchum, as he finally stood up. "Does Jane ever shift out of first gear?"

The cook, who had not once looked at Ketchum while he was working at the stove, looked at him now. "I didn't hire her for her driving, Ketchum."

"Yeah, sure," was all Ketchum said, as Injun Jane opened the outer door; the Indian dishwasher and the rest of the kitchen help came inside. (Danny briefly wondered why Jane was the only one who seemed to have no trouble dealing with that tricky door.)

Ketchum had folded up the cot and the sleeping bag; he was putting them away when Jane spoke. "Uh-oh—there's a logger in the kitchen," she said. "That's never a good sign."

"You and your signs," Ketchum said, without looking at her. "Is your husband dead yet, or do we have to postpone the celebration?"

"I haven't married him yet, and I have no plans to," Jane replied, as always. The Indian dishwasher lived with Constable Carl—a bone of contention with Ketchum and the cook. Dominic didn't like the cowboy any better than Ketchum did—nor had Jane been with the constable long, and (speaking of signs) she gave some vague indication that she might leave him. He beat her. The cook and Ketchum had more than once remarked on Jane's black eyes and split lips, and even Danny had noticed the thumb-size and fingerprint-shaped bruises on her upper arms, where the constable had evidently grabbed her and shaken her.

"I can take a beating," was what Jane usually said to Ketchum or the cook, though it clearly pleased her that they were concerned for her safety. "But Carl should watch out," she only occasionally added. "One day, I just might beat him back."

Jane was a big woman, and she greeted the twelve-year-old (as she always did) by hugging him against one of her massive hips. The boy came up to her breasts, which were monumental; not even the baggy sweatshirt that she wore in the early-morning cold could conceal them. Injun Jane had a ton of coal-black hair, too—although this was unfailingly arranged in one thick braid, which hung to her rump. Even in sweatpants, or baggy dungarees—her kitchen clothes of choice—Jane couldn't hide her rump.

On top of her head, with a hole cut out of it for the braid, was a 1951 Cleveland Indians baseball cap—a gift from Ketchum. One summer, sick of the blackflies and the mosquitoes, Ketchum had tried driving a truck; it was a long-distance lumber hauler, and he'd actually acquired the baseball cap in far-off Cleveland. (Danny could only imagine that this must have happened before Ketchum had decided that all truck drivers were assholes.)

"Well, Jane, you're an Injun—this is the cap for you," Ketchum had told her. The logo on the cap was the red face of Chief Wahoo, a toothy Indian with a crazed grin, his head, and part of his feather, encircled with the letter *C*. The wishbone-shaped *C* was red; the cap was blue. As for who Chief Wahoo was, neither Ketchum nor Injun Jane knew.

The twelve-year-old had heard the story frequently; it was one of Jane's favorites. One of the more memorable times Danny saw her take the Cleveland Indians cap off was when she told the boy how Ketchum had given the cap to her. "Ketchum was actually kind of good-looking, when he was younger," Jane never failed to tell the boy. "Though he was never as good-looking as your dad—or as good-looking as *you're* going to be," the Indian dishwasher always added. Her grinning-Indian baseball cap was water-marked and stained with cooking oil. Jane liked to put the Chief Wahoo cap on the twelve-year-old's head, where it rested low on his forehead, just above the boy's eyes; he could feel his hair sticking out of the hole in the back of the cap.

Danny had never seen Injun Jane's hair unbraided, although she'd been his babysitter many times, especially when he was younger—too young, at the time, to accompany his dad on the river drives, which meant that the boy was too young to get a decent night's sleep in the kitchen wanigan. Jane had regularly put young Dan to bed in his room above the cookhouse kitchen. (Danny had assumed that she must have slept in his dad's bedroom on those nights when his father was away.)

The next morning, when Jane made the boy breakfast, there was no evidence that her long black braid had ever been undone—though it was hard to imagine that sleeping with a braid of hair that long and thick could be very comfortable. For all Danny knew, Jane might have slept in the Cleveland Indians baseball cap, too. The crazily grinning Chief Wahoo was a demonic, ever-watchful presence.

"I'll leave you ladies to your chores," Ketchum was saying. "Lord knows, I wouldn't want to be in the way."

"Lord knows," one of the kitchen helpers said. She was one of the sawmill workers' wives—most of the kitchen helpers were. They were all married and fat; only Injun Jane was fatter, and she *wasn't* married to Constable Carl.

The constable was fat, too. The cowboy was as big as Ketchum—although Ketchum wasn't fat—and Carl was *mean*. Danny had the impression that everyone despised the cowboy, but Constable Carl always ran for office unopposed; quite possibly, no one else in Twisted River had the slightest desire to be constable. The job chiefly entailed breaking up fights, and finding ways to send the French Canadian itinerants back to Quebec. Constable Carl's way—namely, shooting them in the feet or in their knees—was mean, but it worked. Yet who *wanted* to split open people's heads with a gun barrel, or shoot people in the feet and knees? Danny wondered. And why would Injun Jane, whom the boy adored, want to live with a cowboy like that?

"Living here can be compromising, Daniel," the boy's father often said.

"Women have to lose their looks before they'll live with Constable Carl," Ketchum had tried to explain to young Dan. "But when the women lose too much of their looks, Carl finds someone else."

All the kitchen help, certainly each and every one of those sawmill workers' wives, had lost their looks—in Danny Baciagalupo's estimation. If Injun Jane was fatter than all of them, she still had a pretty face and amazing hair; and she had such sensational breasts that the cook's son couldn't bear to think about them, which meant (of course) that he couldn't keep his thoughts from drifting to Jane's breasts at unexpected times.

"Is it their *breasts* that men like about women?" Danny had asked his father.

"Ask Ketchum," the cook had replied, but Danny thought that Ketchum was too old to take an interest in breasts—Ketchum seemed too old to even *notice* breasts anymore. Granted, Ketchum had lived hard; he'd been roughed up and looked older than he was. Ketchum was only thirty-seven—he just looked a lot older (except for how black his hair and beard were).

And Jane—how old was she? Danny wondered. Injun Jane was twelve years older than Danny's dad—she was forty-two—but she looked older, too. She'd been roughed up as well, and not only by Constable Carl. To the twelve-year-old, everyone seemed old—or older than they were. Even the boys in Danny's grade at school were older.

"I'll bet you had a great night's sleep," Jane was saying to the cook. She smiled at Danny. When she reached behind herself to tie the apron strings around her thick waist, her breasts were *gigantic*! the boy was thinking. "Did you get any sleep, Danny?" the Indian dishwasher asked him.

"Sure, I got enough," the boy answered. He wished his dad and the sawmill workers' wives weren't there, because he wanted to ask Jane about his mother.

His dad could talk to him about Ketchum retrieving her battered body from the spillway; maybe that was because Ketchum had prevented the cook from seeing what the river and the logs had done to her. But Danny's father could never talk about the accident itself—at least not to his son, and not with anything approximating specific details. Ketchum could barely bring himself to say more. "We were all drunk, Danny," Ketchum always began. "Your dad was drunk, I was drunk—your mom was a little drunk, too."

"I was the drunkest," Dominic would assert, without fail. There was such blame attached to his drunkenness that the cook had stopped drinking, though not immediately.

"Maybe I was drunker than you, Cookie," Ketchum sometimes said. "After all, I let her go out on the ice."

"That was my fault," the cook usually insisted. "I was so drunk that you had to carry me, Ketchum."

"Don't think I don't remember," Ketchum would say. But neither man could (or would) say exactly what had *happened*. Danny doubted that the details had eluded them; it was more a matter of the details being unutterable, or that it was unthinkable for either man to divulge such details to a child.

Injun Jane, who had not been drinking—she never drank—told the twelve-year-old the story. As many times as the boy had asked her, she'd told him the same story every time; that's how he knew it was probably true.

JANE HAD BEEN DANNY's babysitter that night; Danny would have been two. On a Saturday night, there was dancing in the dance hall—there was both *actual* dancing and square dancing then. Dominic Baciagalupo didn't dance; with a limp like his, he couldn't. But his somewhat older wife—Ketchum called her "Cousin Rosie"—loved to dance, and the cook loved to watch her dance, too. Rosie was pretty and small, both thin and delicate—in a way that most of the women her age in Twisted River and Paris, New Hampshire, were not. ("Your mom didn't have the body of someone pushing thirty—not someone from around here, anyway," as Injun Jane put it, whenever she told the story to young Dan.)

Apparently, Ketchum was either too old or already too banged-up for the war. Although Constable Carl had fairly recently split open Ketchum's forehead, Ketchum had already had a host of other injuries and maimings—enough to make him ineligible for military service, but not of sufficient severity to stop him from dancing. "Your mother taught Ketchum to read *and* dance," the cook had told his son—in a curiously neutral-sounding way, as if Dominic either had no opinion or didn't know which of these acquired skills was the more remarkable or important for Ketchum to have learned. In fact, Ketchum was Rosie Baciagalupo's *only* dance partner; he looked after her as if she were his daughter, and (out on the dance floor) the cook's wife was so small beside Ketchum that she almost could have passed for his child.

Except for the "noteworthy coincidence," as Danny had heard Injun Jane say, that the boy's mom and Ketchum were both twenty-seven years old.

"Ketchum and your dad liked to drink together," Jane told young Dan. "I don't know what it is that men like about drinking *together*, but Ketchum and your dad liked it a little too much."

Perhaps the drinking had allowed them to say things to each other, Danny thought. Since Dominic Baciagalupo had become a teetotaler—though Ketchum *still* drank like a riverman in his early twenties—maybe the men had more guarded conversations; even the twelve-year-old knew there was a lot they left unsaid.

According to Ketchum, "Injuns" couldn't or shouldn't drink at all—he took it as simple common sense that Injun Jane didn't drink. Yet she lived with Constable Carl, who was a mean drunk. After the dance hall and the hostelry bars had closed, the constable drank himself into a belligerent temper. It was often late when Jane drove herself home—when she'd finished with washing the towels and had put them in the dryers in the laundry room, and could only then drive home from the cookhouse. Late or not, Constable Carl was occasionally awake and warlike when Jane was ready to go to bed. After all, she got up early and the cowboy didn't.

"I'll draw you a picture," Injun Jane would say to young Dan, sometimes apropos of nothing. "Your father couldn't drink as much as Ketchum, but he would try to keep up. Your mother was more sensible, but she drank too much, too."

"My dad can't drink as much as Ketchum because he's *smaller*?" Danny always asked Jane.

"Weight has something to do with it, yes," the dishwasher generally replied. "It wasn't the first night that Ketchum carried your dad back to the cookhouse from the dance hall. Your mom was still dancing around them, doing her pretty little do-si-dos." (Did young Dan ever detect a degree of envy or sarcasm in the way Injun Jane referred to Cousin Rosie's *pretty little do-si-dos?*)

Danny knew that a do-si-do was a square-dance figure; he'd asked Ketchum to show him, but Ketchum had shaken his head and burst into tears. Jane had demonstrated a do-si-do for Danny; with her arms folded on her enormous bosom, she passed by his right shoulder, circling him back-to-back.

The boy tried to imagine his mother do-si-doing Ketchum as the big man carried his dad. "Was Ketchum dancing, too?" Danny asked.

"I suppose so," Jane replied. "I wasn't with them until later. I was with *you*, remember?"

At the frozen river basin, Rosie Baciagalupo stopped do-si-doing

Ketchum and called across the ice to the mountainside. When Twisted River was frozen, there was more of an echo; the ice brought your voice back to you quicker and truer than if it had traveled over the open water.

"I wonder why that is," Danny usually said to Jane.

"I heard them from the cookhouse," Injun Jane went on, never offering any speculation on the echo. "Your mom called, 'I love you!' Your dad, over Ketchum's shoulder, called back, 'I love you, too!' Ketchum just yelled, 'Shit!' and other such things; then he yelled, 'Assholes!' Pretty soon all three of them were yelling, 'Assholes!' I thought the yelling would wake you up, although nothing woke you up at night—not even when you were two."

"My mom went out on the ice first?" Danny always asked.

"Do-si-dos on the ice were hard to do," Jane answered. "Ketchum went out on the ice to do-si-do with her; he was still carrying your dad. It was black ice. There was snow in the woods, but not on the river basin. The basin was windblown, and there'd been no new snow for almost a week." Jane usually added: "Most years, the ice didn't break up in the river basin this way."

The drunken cook couldn't stand, but he wanted to slide around on the ice, too; he made Ketchum put him down. Then Dominic fell down—he just sat down on the seat of his pants, and Ketchum pushed him like a human sled. Danny's mom do-si-doed the two of them. If they hadn't been yelling, "Assholes!" so loudly, one of them might have heard the logs.

In those days, the horse-loggers dumped as many logs as they could on the river ice between Little Dummer Pond and the basin in Twisted River—and on the tributary streams upriver, too. Sometimes, the weight of the logs broke through the ice on Dummer Pond first; it was the bigger of the Dummer ponds, held back by a sluice dam that didn't always hold. One way or another, the ice upstream of the town of Twisted River always broke up first, and in the late winter of 1944, the logs shot down the rapids from Little Dummer Pond, the ice breaking ahead of the logs—both the broken slabs of ice and all the logs coming into the river basin in an unimpeded torrent.

In the late winter or early spring, this invariably happened; it just usually happened in the daytime, because the daytime weather was warmer. In 1944, the avalanche of logs came into the river basin at night. Ketchum was pushing Dominic across the ice on the seat of his pants; the cook's pretty, "somewhat older" wife was dancing around them.

Was the phrase "somewhat older" a part of Injun Jane's account of that night? (Danny Baciagalupo wouldn't remember, although he knew for a fact that Jane never failed to interject—at the moment the logs rushed into the river basin—the aforementioned "noteworthy co-incidence" that Ketchum and Cousin Rosie were the same age.)

Injun Jane had opened the door from the cookhouse kitchen; she was going to tell them to stop yelling, "Assholes!" or they would wake up little Danny. Jane was high enough above the river basin to hear the rushing water and the logs. All winter long, the sound of the river was muffled under the ice and snow. Not that Saturday night. Jane closed the kitchen door and ran down the hill.

No one was yelling, "Assholes!" now. The first of the logs skidded onto the ice in the river basin; the logs were wet, and they seemed to pick up speed when they hit the ice. Some of the logs were driven deep into the basin, under the ice; when they rose, the bigger logs broke through the ice from underwater. "Like torpedoes," Injun Jane always said.

By the time Jane reached the river basin, the sheer weight of the logs was breaking up the ice; when the ice first broke, some of the slabs were as big as cars. Ketchum had left the cook in a sitting position when he first saw Rosie disappear. One second, she was do-si-doing; in the next second, she had slipped out of sight behind a slab of ice the size of a wall. Then the logs completely covered where she'd been. Ketchum picked his way back across the chunks of ice and bobbing logs to where the cook had fallen on one side. Dominic Baciagalupo was drifting downstream on a pulpit-size slab of ice.

"She's gone, Cookie—*gone!*" Ketchum was calling. The cook sat up, surprised to see a log rise out of the basin and come crashing down beside him.

"Rosie?" Dominic asked. If he had yelled, "I love you, too," there would have been no discernible echo now—not with the noisy music the logs and broken ice were making. Ketchum put the cook over his shoulder and tiptoed from log to log ashore; sometimes he stepped on an ice floe instead of a log, and his sinking leg would get wet above his knee.

"Assholes!" Injun Jane was yelling from the riverbank—to both of them, or all three of them. "Assholes! Assholes!" she cried and cried.

The cook was wet and cold and shivering, and his teeth were chattering, but Ketchum and Jane could understand him well enough. "She can't be gone, Ketchum—she can't just *disappear* like that!"

"But she was gone that fast, Danny," the dishwasher told the boy. "Faster than the moon can slide behind a cloud—your mom was gone like that. And when we got back to the cookhouse, you were wide awake and screaming—it was worse than any nightmare I ever saw you have. I took it as a sign that you somehow knew your mom was gone. I couldn't get you to stop crying—you *or* your father. Ketchum had got hold of a cleaver. He just stood in the kitchen with his left hand on a cutting board, holding the cleaver in his right hand. 'Don't,' I told him, but he kept staring at his left hand on the cutting board— imagining it gone, I guess. I left him in order to look after you and your dad. When I came back to the kitchen, Ketchum was gone. I looked everywhere for his left hand; I was sure I was going to find his hand somewhere. I didn't want you or your father finding it."

"But he didn't cut his hand off?" Danny always interrupted her.

"Well, no—he didn't," Jane told the boy, with some impatience. "You've noticed that Ketchum still has a left hand, haven't you?"

Sometimes, especially when Ketchum was drunk, Danny had seen the way the logger looked at his left hand; it was the way he'd stared at his cast last night. If Injun Jane had seen Ketchum staring at his cast, she might have taken this as a sign that Ketchum *still* thought about cutting off his hand. (But why the *left* one? Danny Baciagalupo would wonder. Ketchum was right-handed. If you hated yourself, if you were *really* taking yourself to task or holding yourself accountable, wouldn't you want to cut off your *good* hand?)

THEY WERE BUSTLING about the kitchen—all the fat women, and the lean cook with his leaner son. You didn't pass behind someone without saying, "Behind you!" or putting your hand on the person's back. When the sawmill workers' wives passed behind Danny, they often patted the boy on his bum. One or two of them would pat the cook on his bum, too, but not if Injun Jane was watching. Danny had noticed how Jane often placed herself between his father and the kitchen helpers—especially in the narrow gauntlet between the stove and the countertop, which got narrower whenever the oven doors needed to be opened. There were other tight quarters in the cook-house kitchen, challenging the cooks and the servers, but that passage between the stove and the countertop was the tightest.

Ketchum had gone outside to pee—a seemingly unbreakable habit from the wanigan days—while Injun Jane went into the dining room to set the tables. In those "good old days" in the portable logging camps, Ketchum liked to wake up the rivermen and the other loggers by pissing on the metal siding of the sleeping wanigans. "There's a wanigan in the river!" he was fond of hollering. "Oh, sweet Jesus—it's floating away!" A cacophony of swearing followed, from inside the portables.

Ketchum also liked to beat on the metal siding of the sleeping wanigans with one of the river drivers' pike poles. "Don't let the bear in!" he would holler. "Oh, Lord—it's got one of the women! Oh, Lord—dear God, *no!*"

Danny was ladling the warm maple syrup from the big saucepan on the back burner into the pitchers. One of the sawmill workers' wives was breathing down the back of the boy's neck. "Behind you, cutie!" the woman said hoarsely. His dad was dipping the banana bread in the egg mixture; one of the kitchen helpers was putting the banana-bread French toast on the griddle, while another kept turning the lamb hash with a spatula.

Before he went outside for an apparently never-ending piss, Ketchum had spoken to the twelve-year-old. "Nine o'clock, Sunday morning—don't let your dad forget, Danny."

"We'll be there," the boy had said.

"What plans are you making with Ketchum?" Injun Jane whispered in the twelve-year-old's ear. Big as she was, the boy hadn't noticed her behind him; he first mistook her for the sawmill worker's wife who'd been breathing down his neck, but Jane had returned from the dining room.

"Dad and I are meeting Ketchum at Dead Woman Dam on Sunday morning," Danny told her.

Jane shook her head, her long braid, longer than a horse's tail, swishing above her big rump. "So Ketchum talked him into it," she said disapprovingly; the boy couldn't see her eyes above the pulled-down visor of her Cleveland Indians cap. As always, Chief Wahoo was grinning insanely at the twelve-year-old.

The near-perfect choreography in the kitchen would have been imperceptible to a stranger, but Danny and the Indian dishwasher were used to it. They saw that everything was always the same, right down to the cook holding the hot tray of scones with the oven mitts while the sawmill workers' wives deftly got out of his way—one of them knocking the corn muffins out of the muffin tins into a big china bowl as she did so. No one bumped into anyone, big as they all were—save Danny and his dad, who were (in the present company) noticeably small.

In the cramped aisle between the countertop and the stove, where there was a pan or a pot on six of the eight burners, the cook and the Indian dishwasher passed back-to-back. This wasn't new—it happened all the time—but Danny caught a nuance in their dance, and he overheard (as he previously hadn't) the brief but distinct dialogue between them. As they passed, back-to-back, Jane deliberately bumped Dominic—she just touched her big rump to the middle of his back, because the top of the cook's head came up only to Jane's shoulders.

"Do-si-do your partner," the dishwasher said.

Despite his limp, the cook caught his balance; not one scone slid off the hot tray. "Do-si-do," Dominic Baciagalupo softly said. Injun Jane had already passed behind him. No one but Danny had noticed the contact, though if Ketchum had been there—drunk or sober—Ketchum surely would have noticed. (But Ketchum, of course, was outside—presumably, still pissing.)

CHAPTER 3

A WORLD OF ACCIDENTS

ANGEL POPE HAD GONE UNDER THE LOGS ON THURSDAY. After breakfast on Friday, Injun Jane drove Danny in her truck to the Paris Manufacturing Company School, on Phillips Brook, and then drove back to the cookhouse in Twisted River.

The river-driving crew would be prodding logs on a site just upstream of Dead Woman Dam. The cook and his kitchen helpers would prepare four midday meals; they would backpack two meals to the rivermen, and drive two meals to the loggers loading the trucks along the haul road between the town of Twisted River and the Pontook Reservoir.

Fridays were hard enough without the woe of losing Angel. Everyone was in too much of a hurry for the weekend to start, although weekends in Twisted River (in the cook's opinion) amounted to little more than drinking too much and the usual sexual missteps—"not to mention the subsequent embarrassment or shame," as Danny Baciagalupo had heard his dad say (repeatedly). And from Dominic's point of view, the Friday-night meal in the cookhouse was the week's most demanding. For the practicing Catholics among the French Canadians, the cook made his renowned meatless pizzas, but for the "*non-mackerel-snappers*"—as Ketchum was fond of describing himself, and most of the loggers and sawmill workers—a meatless pizza on a Friday night wouldn't suffice.

When Injun Jane dropped Danny at the Paris school, she punched him lightly on his upper arm; it was where the older boys at school would hit him, if he was lucky. Naturally, the older boys hit him harder than Jane did—whether they hit him on the upper arm or somewhere else. "Keep your chin down, your shoulders relaxed, your elbows in, and your hands up around your face," Jane told him. "You want to look like you're going to throw a punch—then you kick the bastard in the balls."

"I know," the twelve-year-old told her. He had never thrown a punch at anyone—nor had he ever kicked someone in the balls. Jane's instructions to the boy bewildered him; he thought that her directions must have been based on some advice Constable Carl had given her, but Jane only had to worry about the *constable* hitting her. Young Dan believed that nobody else would have dared to confront her—maybe not even Ketchum.

While Jane would kiss Danny good-bye at the cookhouse, or virtually anywhere in Twisted River, she never kissed him when she dropped him at the Paris Manufacturing Company School—or when she picked him up in the vicinity of Phillips Brook, where those West Dummer kids might be hanging out. If the older boys saw Injun Jane kiss Danny, they would give him more trouble than usual. On this particular Friday, the twelve-year-old just sat beside Jane in the truck, not moving. Young Dan might have momentarily forgotten where they were—in which case, he was expecting her to kiss him—or else he'd thought of a question to ask Jane about his mother.

"What is it, Danny?" the dishwasher said.

"Do you do-si-do my dad?" the boy asked her.

Jane smiled at him, but it was a more measured smile than he was used to seeing on her pretty face; that she didn't answer made him anxious. "Don't tell me to ask Ketchum," the boy blurted out. This made Injun Jane laugh; her smile was more natural, and more immediately forthcoming. (As always, Chief Wahoo was madly grinning.)

"I was going to say that you should ask your father," the dishwasher said. "Don't be anxious," she added, punching his upper arm again—

this time a little harder. "Danny?" Jane said, as the twelve-year-old was climbing out of the truck cab. "*Don't* ask Ketchum."

IT WAS A WORLD of accidents, the cook was thinking. In the kitchen, he was cooking up a storm. The lamb hash, which he'd served for breakfast, would be good for a midday meal, too; he'd also made a chickpea soup (for the Catholics) and a venison stew with carrots and pearl onions. Yes, there was the infernal pot of baked beans, and the omnipresent pea soup with parsley. But there was little else that was standard logging-camp fare.

One of the sawmill workers' wives was cooking some Italian sweet sausage on the griddle. The cook kept telling her to break up the sausage meat as she cooked it—whereupon another of the sawmill workers' wives started singing. "Try beatin' your meat with a spatula!" she sang to the unlikely but overfamiliar tune of "Vaya con Dios"; the other women joined in.

The lead singer among the sawmill workers' wives was the woman the cook had put in charge of proofing the yeast for the pizza dough—he was keeping an eye on her. Dominic wanted to mix the pizza dough and start it rising before they drove off on the haul road to deliver the midday meals. (On a Friday night, there would be a bunch of pissed-off French Canadians if there weren't enough meatless pizzas for the mackerel-snappers.)

The cook was making cornbread, too. He wanted to start the stuffing for the roast chickens he was also serving in the cookhouse Friday night; he would mix the sausage with the cornbread and some celery and sage, adding the eggs and butter when he got back to his kitchen from the river site and wherever they were loading the trucks. In a large saucepan, in which Danny had warmed the maple syrup, Dominic was boiling the butternut squash; he would mash it up and mix it with maple syrup, and add the butter when he returned to town. On Friday night, together with the stuffed roast chickens, he would serve scalloped potatoes with the whipped squash. This was arguably Ketchum's favorite meal; most Fridays, Ketchum ate some of the meatless pizza, too.

Dominic was feeling sorry for Ketchum. The cook didn't know if

Ketchum truly believed they would find Angel in the spillway of the upper dam Sunday morning, or if Ketchum hoped they would never find the boy's body. All the cook had determined was that he didn't want young Daniel to see Angel's body. Dominic Baciagalupo wasn't sure if *he* wanted to see Angel's body—or ever find the boy, either.

The pot of water—in which the cook had poured a couple of ounces of vinegar, for the poached eggs—was coming to a boil again. For breakfast, he'd served the lamb hash with poached eggs, but when he served the hash as a midday meal, he would just have lots of ketchup handy; poached eggs didn't travel well. When the water and vinegar came to a boil, Dominic poured it over the cutting boards to sterilize them.

One of the sawmill workers' wives had made about fifty bacon, lettuce, and tomato sandwiches with the leftover breakfast bacon. She was eating one of the sandwiches while she eyed the cook—some mischief was on her mind, Dominic could tell. Her name was Dot; she was far too large to be a Dot, and she'd had so many children that she seemed to be a woman who had abandoned every other capacity she'd ever conceivably possessed, except her appetite, which the cook didn't like to think about at all. (She had too *many* appetites, Dominic imagined.)

The sawmill worker's wife with the spatula—the one who needed to be reminded to break up the sausage on the griddle—appeared to be in on the mischief, because she had her eye on the cook, too. Since the woman eating the BLT had her mouth full, the one with the spatula spoke first. Her name was May; she was bigger than Dot and had been married twice. May's children with her second husband were the same age as her grandchildren—that is, the children of her children from her first marriage—and this unnatural phenomenon had completely unhinged May *and* her second husband, to the degree that they couldn't recover sufficiently to console each other concerning the sheer strangeness of their lives.

What Dominic found unnatural was May's ceaseless need to lament the fact that she had children the age of her grandchildren. Why was it such a big deal? the cook had wondered.

"Just *look* at her," Ketchum had said, meaning May. "For her, *everything* is a big fucking deal."

Maybe so, the cook considered, as May pointed the spatula at him. Wiggling her hips in a seductive manner, she said in a purring voice: "Oh, Cookie, I would leave my miserable life behind—if only you would marry me, and cook for me, too!"

Dominic was using the long-handled dish scrubber on the cutting boards, which were soaking in boiling water; the vinegar in the hot water made his eyes tear. "You're married already, May," he said. "If you married me, and we had children, you'd have kids *younger* than your grandchildren. I dare not guess how *that* would make you feel."

May looked genuinely stricken by the idea; maybe he shouldn't have raised the dreaded subject, the cook was thinking. But Dot, who was still eating the BLT, spasmodically laughed with her mouth full— whereupon she commenced to choke. The kitchen helpers, May among them, stood waiting for the cook to do something.

Dominic Baciagalupo was no stranger to choking. He'd seen a lot of loggers and mill workers choke—he knew what to do. Years ago, he'd saved one of the dance-hall women; she was drunk, and she was choking on her own vomit, but the cook had known how to handle her. It was a famous story—Ketchum had even *titled* it, "How Cookie Saved Six-Pack Pam." The woman was as tall and rawboned as Ketchum, and Dominic had needed Ketchum's help to knock her to her knees, and then wrestle her to all fours, where the cook could apply a makeshift Heimlich maneuver. (Six-Pack Pam was so named because this was Ketchum's estimate of the woman's nightly quota, before she started on the bourbon.)

Dr. Heimlich was born in 1920, but his now-famous maneuver hadn't been introduced in Coos County in 1954. Dominic Baciagalupo had been cooking for big eaters for fourteen years. Countless people had choked in front of him; three of them had died. The cook had observed that pounding someone on the back didn't always work. Ketchum's original maneuver, which entailed holding the chokers upside down and vigorously shaking them, had been known to fail, too.

But once Ketchum had been forced to improvise, and Dominic had witnessed the astonishingly successful result. A drunken logger had been too pugnacious and too big for Ketchum to shake upside down. Ketchum kept dropping the man, who was not only choking to death—he was trying to kill Ketchum, too.

Ketchum repeatedly punched the madman in the upper abdomen—all uppercuts. Upon the fourth or fifth uppercut, the choker expectorated a large, unchewed piece of lamb, which he had inadvertently inhaled.

Over the years, the cook had modified Ketchum's improvisational method to suit his own smaller size and less violent nature. Dominic would slip under the flailing arms of the choker and get behind him or her. He would hold the victim around the upper abdomen and apply sudden, upward pressure with his locked hands—just under the rib cage. This had worked every time.

In the kitchen, when Dot began to flail her arms, Dominic quickly ducked behind her. "Oh, my God, Cookie—*save* her!" May cried; the children-grandchildren crisis was momentarily off her mind, if not entirely forgotten.

With his nose in the warm, sweaty area at the back of Dot's neck, the cook could barely join his hands together as he reached around her. Dot's breasts were too big and low; Dominic needed to lift them out of the way to locate where Dot's rib cage ended and her upper abdomen began. But when he held her breasts, albeit briefly, Dot covered his hands with her own and forcefully shoved her butt into his stomach. She was laughing hysterically, not choking at all; crazy May and the rest of the kitchen helpers were laughing with her. "Oh, Cookie—how did you know that's how I like it?" Dot moaned.

"I always thought that Cookie was a do-it-from-behind kind of guy," May said matter-of-factly.

"Oh, you little *dog!*" Dot cried, grinding against the cook. "I just love how you always say, 'Behind you!' "

Dominic finally freed his hands from her breasts; he lightly pushed himself away from her.

"I guess we're not *big* enough for him, Dot," May said sorrowfully. Something mean had entered her voice; the cook could hear it. I'm going to pay for the children-grandchildren remark, Dominic was thinking. "Or maybe we're just not *Injun* enough," May said.

The cook didn't so much as look at her; the other kitchen helpers, even Dot, had turned away. May was defiantly patting the lamb hash flat against the griddle with the spatula. Dominic reached around her and turned the griddle off. He touched his fingers to the small of her back as he passed behind her. "Let's pack up, ladies," he said, almost the same way he usually said it. "You and May can pack the meals to the rivermen," the cook told Dot. "The rest of us will drive till we find the loggers on the haul road." He didn't speak to May, *or* look at her.

"So Dot and I do all the walkin'?" May asked him.

"You should walk more than you do," Dominic said, still not looking at her. "Walking's good for you."

"Well, I made the damn BLTs—I guess I can carry them," Dot said.

"Take the lamb hash with you, too," the cook told her.

Someone asked if there were any "ultra-Catholic" French Canadians among the river drivers; maybe Dot and May should pack some of the chickpea soup to the river site, too.

"I'm not carryin' *soup* on my back," May said.

"The mackerel-snappers can pick the bacon out of the BLTs," Dot suggested.

"I don't think there are any mackerel-snappers among these rivermen," Dominic said. "We'll take the chickpea soup and the venison stew to the loggers on the haul road. If there are any angry Catholics among the river drivers, tell them to blame me."

"Oh, I'll tell them to blame you, all right," May told him. She kept staring at him, but he wouldn't once look at her. When they were going their separate ways, May said: "I'm too big for you to ignore me, Cookie."

"Just be glad I'm ignoring you, May," he told her.

THE COOK HAD NOT expected to see Ketchum among the loggers loading the trucks on the haul road; even injured, Ketchum was a better river driver than any of the men on the river site. "That moron doctor told me not to get the cast wet," Ketchum explained.

"Why would you get the cast wet?" Dominic asked him. "I've never seen you fall in."

"Maybe I saw enough of the river yesterday, Cookie."

"There's venison stew," one of the kitchen helpers was telling the loggers.

There'd been an accident with one of the horses, and another accident with the tractor-powered jammer. Ketchum said that one of the

French Canadians had lost a finger unloading logs from a log brow, too.

"Well, it's Friday," Dominic said, as if he expected accidents among fools on a Friday. "There's chickpea soup for those of you who *care* that it's Friday," the cook announced.

Ketchum noted his old friend's impatience. "What's the matter, Cookie? What happened?" Ketchum asked him.

"Dot and May were just fooling around," the cook explained. He told Ketchum what had happened—what May had said about Injun Jane, too.

"Don't tell me—tell *Jane*," Ketchum told him. "Jane will tear May a new asshole, if you tell her."

"I know, Ketchum—that's why I'm *not* telling her."

"If Jane had seen Dot holding your hands on her tits, she would have already torn Dot a new asshole, Cookie."

Dominic Baciagalupo knew that, too. The world was a precarious place; the cook didn't want to know the statistics regarding how many new assholes were being torn every minute. In his time, Ketchum had torn many; he would think nothing of tearing a few more.

"There's roast chicken tonight, with stuffing and scalloped potatoes," Dominic told Ketchum.

Ketchum looked pained to hear it. "I have a date," the big man said. "Just my luck to miss stuffed chicken."

"A *date*?" the cook said with disgust. He never thought of Ketchum's relationships—mainly, with the dance-hall women—as *dates*. And lately Ketchum had been seeing Six-Pack Pam. God only knew how much they could drink *together*! Dominic Baciagalupo thought. Having saved her, the cook had a soft spot for Six-Pack, but he sensed that she didn't like him much; maybe she resented being saved.

"Are you still seeing Pam?" Dominic asked his hard-drinking friend.

But Ketchum didn't want to talk about it. "You should be concerned that May knows about you and Jane, Cookie. Don't you think you should be a little worried?"

Dominic turned his attention to where the kitchen helpers were, and what they were doing; they had set up a folding table by the side of the haul road. There were propane burners in the wanigan; the burners kept the soup and the stew hot. There were big bowls and spoons on the folding table; the loggers went into the wanigan, each with a bowl and a spoon in hand. The women served them in the wanigan.

"You don't look worried enough, Cookie," Ketchum told him. "If May knows about Jane, Dot knows. If Dot knows, every woman in your kitchen knows. Even *I* know, but I don't give a shit about it."

"I know. I appreciate it," Dominic said.

"My point is, how long before Constable Carl knows? Speaking of assholes," Ketchum said. He rested his heavy cast on the cook's shoulder. "Look at me, Cookie." With his good hand, Ketchum pointed to his forehead—at the long, livid scar. "My head's harder than yours, Cookie. You don't want the cowboy to know about you and Jane— believe me."

Who's your date? Dominic Baciagalupo almost asked his old friend, just to change the subject. But the cook didn't really want to know who Ketchum was screwing—especially if it *wasn't* Six-Pack Pam.

Most nights, increasingly, when Jane went home, it was so late that Constable Carl had already passed out; the cowboy wouldn't wake up until after she'd left for work in the morning. There was only the occasional trouble—mostly when Jane went home too early. But even a dumb drunk like the constable would eventually figure it out. Or one of the kitchen helpers would say something to her husband; the sawmill workers were not necessarily as fond of the cook and Injun Jane as the rivermen and the other loggers were.

"I get your point," the cook said to Ketchum.

"Shit, Cookie," Ketchum said. "Does *Danny* know about you and Jane?"

"I was going to tell him," Dominic answered.

"*Going to*," Ketchum said derisively. "Is that like saying you were *going to* wear a condom, or is that like wearing one?"

"I get your point," the cook said again.

"Nine o'clock, Sunday morning," Ketchum told him. Dominic could only guess that it was a date of two nights' duration that Ketchum was having—more like a *spree* or a *bender*, maybe.

—

IN TWISTED RIVER, if there were nights the cook could have concealed from his son, they would have been Saturday nights, when the whoring around and drinking to excess were endemic to a community staking an improbable claim to permanence in such close proximity to a violent river—not to mention the people, who made a plainly perilous living and looked upon their Saturday nights as an indulgence they deserved.

Dominic Baciagalupo, who was both a teetotaler and a widower *not* in the habit of whoring around, was nonetheless sympathetic to the various self-destructions-in-progress he would witness on an average Saturday night. Maybe the cook revealed more disapproval for Ketchum's behavior than he would ever show toward Twisted River's other louts and miscreants. Because Ketchum was no fool, perhaps the cook had less patience for Ketchum's foolishness, but to a smart twelve-year-old—and Danny was both observant and smart—there appeared to be more than impatience motivating his father's everlasting disappointment in Ketchum. And if Injun Jane didn't defend Ketchum from the cook's condemnation, young Dan did.

That Saturday night, when Angel had possibly arrived at Dead Woman Dam—where, because people float lower than logs, the boy's battered body might already have passed under the containment boom, in which case the young Canadian would be eddying in either a clockwise or counterclockwise direction to the right or left of the main dam and the sluice spillway—Danny Baciagalupo was helping his dad wipe down the tables after supper had been served in the cookhouse. The kitchen help had gone home, leaving Injun Jane to scour the last of the pots and pans while she waited for the washing cycles to end, so she could put all the towels and other linens in the dryers.

Whole families came to the cookhouse for Saturday-night supper; some of the men were already drunk and fighting with their wives, and a few of the women (in turn) lashed out at their children. One of the sawmill men had puked in the washroom, and two drunken loggers had shown up late for supper—naturally, they'd insisted on being fed. The spaghetti and meatballs, which the cook made every Saturday night—for the kids—was congealed and growing cold and was so beneath Dominic Baciagalupo's standards that he fixed the men some fresh penne with a little ricotta and the perpetual parsley.

"This is fuckin' delicious!" one of the drunks had declared.

"What's it called, Cookie?" the other hammered logger asked.

"Prezzémolo," Dominic said importantly, the sheer exoticness of the word washing over the drunken loggers like another round of beer. The cook had made them repeat the word until they could say it correctly—*prets–ZAY-mo-loh.*

Jane was disgusted; she knew it was nothing more exotic than the Italian word for *parsley.* "For two drunks who were *born* late!" Jane complained.

"You would let Ketchum go hungry, if it was Ketchum," Danny said to his father. "You're wicked harsh on Ketchum."

But the two drunks had been given a special supper and sent on their contented way. Danny and his dad and Jane were at the tail end of their Saturday-night chores when the wind from the suddenly kicked-open door to the dining room heralded another late arrival at the cookhouse.

From the kitchen, Jane couldn't see the visitor. She shouted in the direction of the rushing wind at the dining-room door. "You're too late! Supper is *over!*"

"I ain't hungry," said Six-Pack Pam.

Indeed, there was nothing hunger-driven in Pam's appearance; what little flesh she had hung loosely from her big bones, and her lean, feral-looking face, tight-lipped and drawn, suggested more of a mostly-beer diet than a penchant for overeating. Yet she was tall and broad-shouldered enough to wear Ketchum's wool-flannel shirt without looking lost in it, and her lank blond hair, which was streaked with gray, appeared to be clean but uncared for—like the rest of her. She held a flashlight as big as a billy club. (Twisted River was not a well-lit town.) Not even the sleeves of Ketchum's shirt were too long for her.

"So I guess you've killed him and claimed his clothes for your own," the cook said, watching her warily.

"I ain't chokin', either, Cookie," Pam told him.

"Not *this* time, Six-Pack!" Jane called from the kitchen. Danny guessed that the ladies must have known each other well enough for Jane to have recognized Pam's voice.

"It's kinda late for the hired help to still be here, ain't it?" Pam asked the cook.

Dominic recognized Six-Pack's special drunkenness with an envy and nostalgia that surprised him—the big woman could hold her beer and bourbon, better than Ketchum. Jane had come out of the kitchen with a pasta pot under her arm; the open end of the pot was leveled at Pam like the mouth of a cannon.

Young Dan, in a presexual state of one-third arousal and two-thirds premonition, remembered Ketchum's remark about women losing their looks, and how the various degrees of lost looks registered with Constable Carl. To the twelve-year-old, Jane *hadn't* lost her looks—not quite yet. Her face was still pretty, her long braid was striking, and more radiant to imagine was all that coal-black hair when she undid the braid. There were her stupendous breasts to contemplate, too.

Yet seeing Six-Pack Pam unhinged Danny in a different but similar way: She was as handsome (in the category of strong-looking) as a man, and what was womanly about her came with a rawness—how she had insouciantly thrown on Ketchum's shirt, without a bra, so that her loose breasts swelled the shirt—and now her eyes darted from Jane to Danny, and then fixed upon the cook with the venturesome but nervous daring of a young girl.

"I need your help with Ketchum, Cookie," Pam said. Dominic was fearful that Ketchum had had a heart attack, or worse; he hoped that Six-Pack would spare young Daniel the gruesome details.

"*I* can help you with Ketchum," Injun Jane told Pam. "I suppose he's passed out somewhere—if so, I can carry him easier than Cookie can."

"He's passed out naked on the toilet, and I ain't got but one toilet," Pam said to Dominic, not looking at Jane.

"I hope he was just reading," the cook replied.

Ketchum appeared to be making his dogged way through Dominic Baciagalupo's books, which were really Dominic's mother's books and Rosie's beloved novels. For someone who'd left school when he was

younger than Danny, Ketchum read the books he borrowed with a de-
termination bordering on lunacy. He returned the books to the cook
with words circled on almost every page—not underlined passages, or
even complete sentences, but just isolated words. (Danny wondered if
his mom had taught Ketchum to read that way.)

Once young Dan had made a list of the words Ketchum had circled in his mother's copy of Hawthorne's *The Scarlet Letter*. Collec-
tively, the words made no sense at all.

symbolize

whipping-post

sex

malefactresses

pang

bosom

embroidered

writhing

ignominious

matronly

tremulous

punishment

salvation

plaintive

wailings

possessed

misbegotten

sinless

innermost

retribution

paramour

besmirches

hideous

And these were only the words Ketchum had circled in the first
four chapters!

"What do you suppose he's thinking?" Danny had asked his dad.

The cook had held his tongue, though it was hard to resist

the temptation to reply. Surely "sex" and "bosom" were much on Ketchum's mind; as for "malefactresses," Ketchum had known some. (Six-Pack Pam among them!) Regarding the "paramour," Dominic Baciagalupo was more of an authority than he wanted to be—the hell with what Ketchum made of the word! And considering "whipping-post" and "writhing"—not to mention "wailings," "misbegotten," "besmirches," and "hideous"—the cook had no desire to investigate Ketchum's prurient interest in those words.

The "matronly," the "sinless," the "innermost," and above all "symbolize," were mild surprises; nor would Dominic have imagined that Ketchum gave much thought to what was "embroidered" or "ignominious" or "tremulous" or "plaintive." The cook believed that "retribution" (especially the "punishment" part) was as much up his old friend's alley as the "possessed" factor, because Ketchum surely was possessed—to the degree that the "salvation" ingredient seemed highly unlikely. (And did Ketchum regularly feel a "pang"—a pang for whom or what? Dominic wondered.)

"Maybe they're just words," young Dan had reasoned.

"What do you mean, Daniel?"

Was Ketchum trying to improve his vocabulary? For an uneducated man, he was very well spoken—and he kept borrowing books!

"It's a list of kind of *fancy* words, most of them," Danny had speculated.

Yes, the cook concurred—"sex" and "bosom," and perhaps "pang," excluded.

"All I know is, I was readin' out loud to him, and then he took the fuckin' book and went into the bathroom and passed out," Six-Pack was saying. "He's got himself wedged in a corner, but he's still on the toilet," she added.

Dominic didn't want to know about the reading out loud. His impression of Ketchum's dance-hall women did not include an element of literary interest or curiosity; it was the cook's opinion that Ketchum rarely spoke to these women, or listened to them. But Dominic had once asked Ketchum (insincerely) what he did for "foreplay."

To the cook's considerable surprise, Ketchum had answered: "I ask them to read out loud to me. It gets me in the mood."

Or in the mood to take the book to the bathroom and pass out with it, Dominic now thought dryly. Nor did the cook imagine that the literacy level among Ketchum's dance-hall women was especially high. How did Ketchum know which women could read at all? And what was the book that had put him *out* of the mood with Six-Pack Pam? (Quite possibly, Ketchum simply had needed to go to the bathroom.)

Injun Jane had gone into the kitchen and now returned with a flashlight. "So you can find your way back," she said to Dominic, handing him the light. "I'll stay with Danny, and get him ready for bed."

"Can I go with you?" the boy asked his dad. "I could help you with Ketchum."

"My place ain't very suitable for kids, Danny," Pam told him.

That concept begged a response, but all the cook said was: "You stay with Jane, Daniel. I'll be right back," he added, more to Jane than to his son, but the Indian dishwasher had already gone back inside the kitchen.

FROM THE UPSTAIRS OF THE COOKHOUSE, where the bedrooms were, there was a partial view of the river basin and a better view of the town above the basin. However, the town was so dark at night that one had little sense of the activities in the various saloons and hostelries from the distant cookhouse—nor could Danny and Injun Jane hear the music from the dance hall, where no one was dancing.

For a while, the boy and the Indian dishwasher had watched the two flashlights making their way to town. The cook's bobbing light was easily identified by his limp—and by his shorter steps, for Dominic needed to take twice as many steps to keep up with the longer strides of Six-Pack Pam. (It was their conversation Jane might have wished she could hear; it was Ketchum naked on the toilet Danny definitely wanted to see.) But soon the flashlights were lost in the fog shrouding the river basin, and in the dimmer lights of the town.

"He'll be back soon," the twelve-year-old said, because he must have sensed that Jane hoped so. She made no response, other than to turn down the bed in his father's room—she also turned the night-table light on.

Danny followed her into the upstairs hall, watching her touch the eight-inch cast-iron skillet as she left the bedroom. Shoulder-high to his dad, the skillet was breast-high to Injun Jane; it was level with Danny's eyes as he passed by it, touching it, too.

"Thinking about whacking a bear?" Jane asked the boy.

"I guess *you* were thinking about it," he told her.

"Go brush your teeth, and all that other stuff," she said.

The boy went into the bathroom he shared with his father. When he'd put on his pajamas and was ready for bed, Jane came into Danny's bedroom and sat on his bed beside him.

"I've never seen you undo your braid," the boy said. "I wonder what you look like with your hair down."

"You're too young to see me with my hair down," Jane told him. "I wouldn't want it on my conscience that I frightened you to death." The boy could see the playfulness in her eyes, under the visor of her Cleveland Indians cap.

There was a shout from the area of the town, and either a corresponding shout or an echo from the nearby river basin, but no words were distinguishable in the shouting, and any interconnected disputes or follow-up shouts were whipped away by the wind.

"It's dangerous in town on a Saturday night, isn't it?" Danny asked Injun Jane.

"I know this little fella with a limp—maybe you know who I mean—and he's always saying how it's 'a world of accidents.' Maybe that sounds familiar to you," Jane said. Her big hand had sneaked under the covers and found young Dan's armpit, where she knew he was the most ticklish.

"I know who you mean!" the twelve-year-old cried. "No tickling!"

"Well, the accidents are just more numerous on a Saturday night," Jane continued, not tickling him but keeping her hand in his armpit. "However, nobody's going to mess with your dad—not when Six-Pack is with him."

"There's the coming-home-alone part," the boy pointed out.

"Don't worry about your father, Danny," Jane told him; she let go of his armpit and straightened up on the bed.

"Could you take Six-Pack?" Danny asked her. It was one of Daniel Baciagalupo's favorite questions; he was always asking Injun Jane if she could "take" someone, the equivalent of Ketchum tearing an actual or alleged combatant a new asshole. Could Jane *take* Henri Thibeault, or No-Fingers La Fleur, or the Beaudette brothers, or the Beebe twins—or Scotty Fernald, Earl Dinsmore, Charlie Clough, and Frank Bemis?

Injun Jane generally answered: "I suppose so." (When Danny had asked her if she could take Ketchum, she'd said: "If he were drunk enough, maybe.")

But when the imaginary opponent was Six-Pack Pam, Jane hesitated. Danny had not known her to hesitate a whole lot. "Six-Pack is a lost soul," Jane finally said.

"But could you take her?" young Dan insisted.

Jane leaned over the boy as she got up from the bed; squeezing his shoulders with her strong hands, she kissed him on his forehead. "I suppose so," said Injun Jane.

"Why wasn't Six-Pack wearing a bra?" Danny asked her.

"She looked like she got dressed in a hurry," Jane told him; she blew him another kiss from the doorway of his bedroom, closing the door only halfway behind her. The light from the hall was Danny's night-light—for as long as he could remember.

He heard the wind shake the loose-fitting outer door to the kitchen; there was a rattling sound as the wind tugged at that bothersome door. The twelve-year-old knew it wasn't his dad coming home, or another night visitor.

"Just the wind!" Injun Jane called to him, from down the hall. Ever since the bear story, she knew the boy had been apprehensive about intruders.

Jane always left her shoes or boots downstairs, and came upstairs in her socks. If she had gone downstairs, Danny would have heard the stairs creak under her weight, but Jane must have stayed upstairs, as silent in her socks as a nocturnal animal. Later, young Dan heard water running in the bathroom; he wondered if his father had come home, but the boy was too sleepy to get up and go see. Danny lay listening to the wind and the omnipresent turmoil of the river. When someone kissed him on his forehead again, the twelve-year-old was too deeply asleep to know if it was his dad or Injun Jane—or else he was dreaming about being kissed, and it was Six-Pack Pam who was kissing him.

—

STRIDING THROUGH TOWN—with the cook limping after her like a loyal but damaged dog—Pam was too formidable and purposeful a figure to inspire anyone to dream of kissing her, or of being kissed by her. Certainly, the cook was dreaming of no such thing—not consciously.

"Slow down, Six-Pack," Dominic said, but either the wind carried his words beyond her hearing or Pam willfully lengthened her stride.

The wind tunneled furrows in the three-story tower of sawdust outside the sawmill, and the dust blew into their eyes. It was very flammable, what Ketchum called a "potential inferno"—at this time of year, especially. The winter-long pile wouldn't be trucked out of town until the haul roads hardened up at the end of mud season; only then would they truck it away, and sell it to the farmers in the Androscoggin Valley. (Of course, there was more inside the mill.) A fire in the sawdust would ignite the whole town; not even the cookhouse on the hill nearest the river bend would be spared, because the hill and the cookhouse bore the brunt of the wind off the river. The bigger, more brightly burning embers would be blown uphill from the town to the cookhouse.

Yet the building the cook had insisted upon was the most substantial in the settlement of Twisted River. The hostelries and saloons—even the sawmill itself, and the so-called dance hall—were mere kindling for the sawdust fire Ketchum imagined in his doomsayer dreams of ever-impending calamities.

Possibly, Ketchum was even dreaming now—on the toilet. Or so Dominic Baciagalupo considered, as he struggled to keep pace with Six-Pack Pam. They passed the bar near the hostelry favored by the French Canadian itinerants. In the muddy lane alongside the dance hall was a 1912 Lombard steam log hauler; it had been parked there so long that the dance hall had been torn down and rebuilt around it. (They'd used gasoline-powered log haulers to pull the loaded sleds of logs through the woods since the 1930s.)

If the town burned, Dominic was thinking, maybe the old Lombard forwarder would be the only surviving remains. To the cook's surprise, when he regarded the Lombard now, he saw the Beaudette brothers asleep or dead in the front seat over the sled runners. Perhaps they'd been evicted from the dance hall and had passed out (or been deposited) there.

Dominic slowed as he limped by the slumped-over brothers, but Pam had seen them, too, and she wasn't stopping. "They won't freeze—it ain't even snowin'," Six-Pack said.

Outside the next saloon, four or five men had gathered to watch a desultory fight. Earl Dinsmore and one of the Beebe twins had been brawling so long that they'd exhausted their best punches, or maybe the men were too inebriated to be fighting in the first place. They seemed beyond hurting each other—at least, intentionally. The other Beebe twin, out of either boredom or sheer embarrassment for his brother, suddenly started fighting with Charlie Clough. In passing, Six-Pack Pam knocked Charlie down; then she leveled Earl Dinsmore with a forearm to his ear, leaving the Beebe twins to aimlessly regard each other, the recognition slowly dawning on them that there was no one to fight—not unless they dared to take on Pam.

"It's Cookie with Six-Pack," No-Fingers La Fleur observed.

"I'm surprised you can tell us apart," Pam told him, shoving him out of her way.

They reached the flat-roofed row houses—the newer hostelries, where the truckers and donkey-engine men stayed. As Ketchum said, any contractor who would construct a flat-roofed, two-story building in northern New Hampshire was enough of a moron to not know how many assholes a human being had. Just then, the dance-hall door blew (or was shoved) open and the miserable music reached them—Perry Como singing "Don't Let the Stars Get in Your Eyes."

There was an outside flight of stairs to the nearest hostelry, and Pam turned, catching Dominic by his shirtsleeve and pulling him after her.

"Watch the next-to-last step, Cookie," she told him, tugging him up the stairs.

Stairs had never worked well with his limp—especially not at the pace Six-Pack led him. The next-to-last step from the top was missing. The cook stumbled forward, catching his balance against Pam's broad back. She simply turned again and lifted him under both arms—hoisting him to the topmost step, where the bridge of his nose collided with her collarbone. There was a womanly smell at her throat, if not exactly perfume, but the cook was confused by whatever odors of maleness clung to Ketchum's wool-flannel shirt.

The music from the dance hall was louder at the top of the stairs—Patti Page singing "(How Much Is) That Doggie in the Window?" No wonder no one dances anymore, Dominic Baciagalupo was thinking, just as Six-Pack lowered her shoulder and forced open the door. "Shit, I *hate* this song," she was saying, dragging the cook inside. "Ketchum!" she shouted, but there was no answer. Thankfully, the awful music stopped when Pam closed the door.

The cook couldn't comprehend where the kitchen, which they had entered, ended and the bedroom began; scattered pots and pans and bottles gave way to strewn undergarments and the giant, unmade bed, the only light on which was cast by a greenish aquarium. Who knew that Six-Pack Pam was a fish person, or that she liked pets of any species? (If fish were what was in the aquarium—Dominic couldn't see anything swimming around in the algae. Maybe Six-Pack was an *algae* person.)

They navigated the bedroom; it was hard, even without a limp, to get around the enormous bed. And while it was easy for Dominic to imagine the extreme situation and awkward location of Ketchum's collapse, and why this might have made it necessary for Pam to hastily dress herself without a bra, they passed *three* bras en route to the bathroom—any one of which, even in a hurry, surely would have been opportune.

Six-Pack now scratched her breast under Ketchum's wool-flannel shirt. Dominic wasn't immediately worried that she was fondling herself suggestively, or otherwise flirting with him; it was as unplanned a gesture as her knocking Charlie Clough to the muddy ground, or the spontaneous forearm to the ear that had dropped Earl Dinsmore. The cook knew that if Six-Pack were to *suggest* anything, she would be far less ambiguous about it than to merely touch her breast in passing. Besides, Ketchum's wool-flannel shirt must have been itchy against her bare skin.

They found Ketchum on the toilet, more or less as Pam must have discovered him—with the paperback he'd been reading pinned by his cast, and held open on one of his bare thighs, and with both knees splayed wide apart. The water in the toilet was laced with bright bloodred streaks—as if Ketchum had been slowly bleeding to death.

"He's gotta be bleedin' *internally!*" Six-Pack exclaimed, but the cook realized that Ketchum had dropped a pen with red ink into the toilet; he must have been using the pen to circle certain words. "I already flushed, before leavin' him," Pam was saying, as Dominic rolled up his sleeve and (reaching between Ketchum's knees) picked the pen out of the toilet bowl—flushing again. Dominic washed his hands and the pen in the sink, drying them with a towel.

It was only then that he noticed Ketchum's erection. One of the cook's most fervent hopes—namely, to never see Ketchum with an erection—may have caused him to first overlook the obvious. Naturally, Six-Pack hadn't overlooked it. "Well, I wonder what he thinks he's goin' to do with *that!*" she was saying, as she lifted Ketchum under his heavy arms. She was able to prop him more upright on the toilet seat, rescuing him from his wedged position. "If you take hold of his ankles, Cookie, I can handle the rest."

The book, which nearly followed the pen's path into the toilet, slid off Ketchum's thigh to the floor. Dostoyevsky's *The Idiot* was a surprise to Dominic Baciagalupo, who could more easily understand Ketchum passing out with the novel on (or off) a toilet than he could imagine Six-Pack reading out loud to Ketchum from the gigantic greenly-lit bed. Dominic instinctively uttered aloud the book's title, which was misunderstood by Pam.

"You're tellin' *me* he's an idiot!" she said.

"How were you liking the book?" the cook asked her, as they lugged Ketchum out of the bathroom; they managed to hit Ketchum's head on the doorknob as they passed the open door. Ketchum's cast was dragging on the floor.

"It's about fuckin' Russians," Six-Pack said dismissively. "I wasn't payin' much attention to the story—I was just readin' it to *him*."

The passing blow to his head hadn't awakened Ketchum, although it seemed to serve as an invitation for him to speak. "As for those kind of *dives*, where you could get into a shitload of trouble just *looking* at some super-sensitive asshole, there was never anything in downtown Berlin to equal Hell's Half Acre in Bangor—not in my experience,"

Ketchum said, his erection as upstanding and worthy of attention as a weather vane.

"What do you know about Maine?" Pam asked him, as if Ketchum were conscious and could understand her.

"I didn't kill Pinette—they could never pin it on me!" Ketchum declared. "That wasn't my stamping hammer."

They'd found Lucky Pinette, murdered in his bed, in the old Boom House on the Androscoggin—about two miles north of Milan. He'd had his head bashed in with a stamping hammer, and there were those rivermen who claimed that Lucky had had a dispute with Ketchum at the sorting gaps on the river earlier in the afternoon. Ketchum, typically, was discovered to be spending the night at the Umbagog House in Errol—with a dim-witted woman who worked in the kitchen there. Neither the stamping hammer that had repeatedly hit Pinette (indenting his forehead with the letter *H*) nor Ketchum's hammer was ever found.

"So who killed Lucky?" Six-Pack asked Ketchum, as she and Dominic dropped him onto the bed, where the river driver's undying erection trembled at them like a flagpole in a gale-force wind.

"I'll bet Bergeron did it," Ketchum answered her. "He had a stamping hammer just like mine."

"And Bergeron wasn't bangin' some *re*tard from Errol!" Pam replied.

With his eyes still closed, Ketchum merely smiled. The cook resisted the urge to go back into the bathroom and see what words Ketchum had circled in *The Idiot*—anything to get away from his old friend's towering erection.

"Are you awake, or what?" Dominic asked Ketchum, who appeared to have passed completely out again—or else he was imagining himself as one of the passengers in a third-class compartment on the Warsaw–St. Petersburg train, because Ketchum had only recently borrowed *The Idiot*, and the cook found it unlikely that Six-Pack had read very far into the first chapter before the passing-out-on-the-toilet episode had interrupted what Ketchum called his chosen *foreplay*.

"Well, I guess I'll go home," Dominic said, as Ketchum's finally drooping erection seemed to signify the end of the evening's entertainment. Perhaps not to Pam—facing the cook, she began to unbutton her borrowed shirt.

Here comes *suggestive,* Dominic Baciagalupo was thinking. There was no room between the foot of the bed and the bedroom wall, where Six-Pack blocked his way; he would have had to walk on the bed, stepping over Ketchum, to get around her.

"Come on, Cookie," Pam said. "Show me what you got." She tossed the wool-flannel shirt on the bed, where it covered Ketchum's face but not his fallen erection.

"She was *semi*-retarded," Ketchum mumbled from under the shirt, "and she wasn't from Errol—she came from Dixville Notch." He must have meant the kitchen worker in the Umbagog House, the woman he'd been banging the night Lucky Pinette was hammered to death in the old Boom House on the Androscoggin. (It could have been just a coincidence that neither Ketchum's stamping hammer nor the murder weapon was ever found.)

Six-Pack fiercely took hold of the cook's shoulders and snapped his face between her breasts—no ambiguity now. It was half a Heimlich maneuver that he made on her, ducking under her arms to get behind her—his hands locking on her lower rib cage, under her pretty breasts. With his nose jammed painfully between Pam's shoulder blades, Dominic said: "I can't do this, Six-Pack—Ketchum's my friend."

She easily broke his grip; her long, hard elbow smacked him in the mouth, splitting his lower lip. Then she headlocked him, half smothering him between her armpit and the soft side of her breast. "You ain't no friend of his if you let him find Angel! He's tearin' himself up over that damn kid, Cookie," Pam told him. "If you let him so much as *see* that boy's body, or what's left of it, you ain't no friend of Ketchum's!"

They were rolling around on the bed beside Ketchum's covered face and his naked, unmoving body. The cook couldn't breathe. He reached around Six-Pack's shoulder and punched her in the ear, but she lay on him unflinchingly, with her weight on his chest; she had his head and neck, and his right arm, locked up tight. All the cook could do was hit her again with his awkward left hook—his fist struck her cheekbone, her nose, her temple, and her ear again.

"Christ, you can't fight worth shit, Cookie," Six-Pack said with contempt. She rolled off him, letting him go. Dominic Baciagalupo would remember lying there, his chest heaving alongside his snoring friend. The ghastly green light from the aquarium washed over the gasping cook; in the tank's murky water, the unseen fish might have been mocking him. Pam had picked up a bra and was putting it on, with her back to him. "The least you can do is take Danny with you, *earlier* than when you're goin' to meet Ketchum. You two find Angel's body—*before* Ketchum gets there. Just don't let Ketchum *see* that boy!" she shouted.

Ketchum pulled the shirt off his face and stared unseeing at the ceiling; the cook sat up beside him. Pam had put the bra on and was angrily struggling into a T-shirt. Dominic would also remember this: Six-Pack's unbelted dungarees, low on her broad but bony hips, and the unzipped fly, through which he caught a glimpse of her blond pubic hair. She'd dressed herself in a hurry, to be sure—and she was hurrying now. "Get out, Cookie," she told him. He looked once at Ketchum, who had closed his eyes and covered his face with his cast. "Did Ketchum let you see your wife when he found her?" Pam asked the cook.

Dominic Baciagalupo would try to forget this part—how he got up from the bed, but Six-Pack wouldn't let him step around her. "Answer me," she said to him.

"No, Ketchum didn't let me see her."

"Well, Ketchum was bein' your *friend*," she said, letting the cook limp past her to the door in the kitchen area. "Watch that step, second from the top," she reminded him.

"You ought to ask Ketchum to fix that step for you," Dominic said.

"Ketchum *removed* the step—so he could hear someone comin' up the stairs, or sneakin' down," Six-Pack informed the cook.

There was no doubt Ketchum had to take certain precautions, Dominic was thinking, as he let himself out the door. The missing step awaited him—he stepped over it carefully. The depressing music from the dance hall hit him on the stairs. Teresa Brewer was singing "Till I Waltz Again with You" when the wind blew open the door the cook thought he had closed.

"Shit!" he heard Pam say.

Either the wind or the dance-hall music momentarily revived

Ketchum—enough for the riverman to make a final comment before
Six-Pack slammed the door. "Not so fucking lucky now—are you,
Lucky?" Ketchum asked the windy night.

Poor Pinette, Dominic Baciagalupo was thinking. Lucky Pinette
may already have been past hearing the question—that is, the first
time Ketchum had asked it, *if* he'd really asked it. (Certainly, Lucky
was long past hearing anything now.)

The cook skirted the shabby hostelry bars with their broken, interrupted lettering.

NO MINO S! the neon blinked at him.

TH RD BEER FR E! another sign blinked.

After he passed the neon announcements, Dominic would realize
he'd forgotten his flashlight. He was pretty sure that Six-Pack wouldn't
be friendly if he went back for it. The cook tasted the blood from his
split lip before he put his hand to his mouth and looked at the blood on
his fingers. But the available light in Twisted River was dim and growing dimmer. The dance-hall door blew (or was slammed) closed, cutting
off Teresa Brewer as suddenly as if Six-Pack had taken the singer's slen-
der throat in her hands. When the dance-hall door blew (or was kicked)
open again, Tony Bennett was crooning "Rags to Riches." Dominic
didn't for a moment doubt that the town's eternal violence was partly
spawned by irredeemable music.

Out in front of the saloon where the Beebe twins had been fighting, there was no evidence of a brawl; Charlie Clough and Earl Dinsmore had managed to pick themselves up from the muddy ground.
The Beaudette brothers, either murdered or passed out, had roused
themselves (or been removed) from the old Lombard forwarder forever occupying the lane alongside the dance hall, which it would almost certainly outlive.

Dominic Baciagalupo wove his way forward in the darkness, where
his limp could easily have been mistaken for the tentative progress of
a drunk. At the bar near the hostelry most frequented by the French
Canadian itinerants, a familiar figure lurched toward Dominic out of
the dark, but before the cook could be certain it was Constable Carl, a
flashlight blinded him. "Halt! That means 'Stop!' *Arrête,* if you're
fuckin' French," the cowboy said.

"Good evening, Constable," Dominic said, squinting into the

light. Both the flashlight and the windblown sawdust were causing him problems.

"You're out kinda late, Cookie—and you're *bleedin',*" the constable said.

"I was checking up on a friend," the cook replied.

"Whoever hit you wasn't your friend," the cowboy said, stepping closer.

"I forgot my flashlight—I just bumped into something, Carl."

"Like a knee . . . or an elbow, maybe," Constable Carl speculated; his flashlight was almost touching Dominic's bloody lower lip. The boilermakers on the constable's rank breath were as evident as the sawdust stinging the cook's face.

As luck would have it, someone had upped the volume on the music from the dance hall, where the virtual revolving door was flung open again—Doris Day singing "Secret Love"—while Injun Jane's two lovers stood face-to-face, the drunken cowboy patiently examining the sober cook's lip injury. Just then, the favorite hostelry of the French Canadian itinerants rudely disgorged one of the night's luckless souls. Young Lucien Charest, yipping like a coyote pup, was hurled out naked and landed on all fours in the muddy road. The constable swung his flashlight toward the frightened Frenchman.

It was deathly quiet then, as the dance-hall door slammed shut on Doris Day—as abruptly as the indiscriminate door had released "Secret Love" into the night—and both Dominic Baciagalupo and Lucien Charest clearly heard the knuckle-cracking sound of Constable Carl cocking his absurd Colt .45.

"Jesus, Carl, *don't . . .*" Dominic was saying, as the constable took aim at the young Frenchman.

"Get your naked French ass back indoors where you belong!" the constable shouted. "Before I blow your balls off, and your pecker with 'em!"

On all fours, Lucien Charest peed straight down at the ground— the puddle of piss quickly spreading to his muddy knees. The Frenchman turned and, still on all fours, scampered like a dog toward the hostelry, where the mischief-makers who'd thrown the young man outside now greeted him at the hostelry door as if his naked life depended on it. (It probably did.) Cries of "Lucien!" were followed by

French-speaking gibberish too fast and hysterical for either the cook or the constable to comprehend. When Charest was safely back inside the hostelry, Constable Carl turned off his flashlight. The ridiculous Colt .45 was still cocked; the cook was disconcerted that the cowboy slowly uncocked the weapon while it was pointed at the knee of Dominic Baciagalupo's good leg.

"You want me to walk you home, little Cookie?" Carl asked.

"I'm okay," Dominic answered. They could both make out the lights of the cookhouse, uphill from the river-basin end of town.

"I see you got my darlin' Jane workin' late again tonight," the constable said. Before the cook had time to consider a careful reply, Carl added: "Isn't that boy of yours gettin' old enough to put himself to bed?"

"Daniel's old enough," Dominic answered. "I just don't like leaving him alone at night, and he's wicked fond of Jane."

"That makes two of us," Constable Carl said, spitting.

That makes *three* of us! Dominic Baciagalupo was thinking, but the cook said nothing. He was also remembering how Pam had pressed his face between her breasts, and how close she had come to suffocating him. He felt ashamed, and disloyal to Jane, because Six-Pack had also aroused him—in a peculiarly life-threatening way.

"Good night, Constable," the cook said. He had started uphill before the cowboy shone his flashlight on him, briefly illuminating the way ahead.

"Good night, Cookie," Carl said. When the flashlight went out, the cook could feel that the constable was still watching him. "You get around pretty good for a *cripple*!" the cowboy called up the dark hill. Dominic Baciagalupo would remember that, too.

Just a snatch of the song from the dance hall reached him, but Dominic was now too far from town to hear the words clearly. It was only because he'd heard the song so many times that he knew what it was—Eddie Fisher singing "Oh My Papa"—and long after the cook could no longer hear the stupid song, he was irritated to find himself singing it.

CHAPTER 4

THE EIGHT-INCH CAST-IRON SKILLET

THE COOK COULDN'T ENTIRELY DISPEL THE FEELING THAT the constable had followed him home. For a while, Dominic Baciagalupo stood at the window in the darkened dining hall, on the lookout for a flashlight coming up the hill from town. But if the cowboy were intent on investigating the goings-on at the cookhouse, not even he would have been dumb enough to use his flashlight.

Dominic left the porch light on by the kitchen door, so that Jane could see the way to her truck; he put his muddy boots beside Jane's at the foot of the stairs. The cook considered that, perhaps, he had lingered downstairs for another reason. How would he explain his lip injury to Jane, and should he tell her about his meeting with the constable? Shouldn't Jane know that Dominic had encountered the cowboy, and that both Constable Carl's behavior and his disposition were as unpredictable and unreadable as ever?

The cook couldn't even say for certain if the constable somehow *knew* that Jane was Dominic's "paramour," as Ketchum might have put it—in reference to the toilet-reader's list of words from another illicit love story.

Dominic Baciagalupo went quietly upstairs in his socks—though the stairs creaked in a most specific way because of his limp, and he could not manage to creep past his open bedroom door without Jane sitting up in bed and seeing him. (He sneaked enough of a look at her to know she'd let her hair down.) Dominic had wanted to clean up his wounded lower lip before he saw her, but Jane must have sensed he was hiding something from her; she sailed her Cleveland Indians cap into the hall, nearly hitting him. Chief Wahoo landed upside down but still grinning—the chief appearing to stare crazily down the hall, in the direction of the bathroom and young Dan's bedroom.

In the bathroom mirror, the cook saw that his lower lip probably needed to be stitched; the wound would heal eventually, without stitches, but his lip would heal faster and there would be less of a scar if he had a couple of stitches. For now, after he'd painfully brushed his teeth, he poured some hydrogen peroxide on his lower lip and patted it dry with a clean towel—noting the blood on the towel. It was just bad luck that tomorrow was Sunday; he would rather let Ketchum or Jane stitch up his lip than try to find that moron doctor on a Sunday, in that place Dominic wouldn't even think of by its ill-fated name.

The cook came out of the bathroom and continued down the hall to Daniel's room. Dominic Baciagalupo kissed his sleeping son good night, leaving an unnoticed spot of blood on the boy's forehead. When the cook came out into the hall, there was Chief Wahoo grinning upside down at him—as if to remind him that he better watch his words carefully with Injun Jane.

"Who hit you?" she asked him, as he was getting undressed in the bedroom.

"Ketchum was wild and unruly—you know how he can be when he's passed out and talking at the same time."

"If Ketchum had hit you, Cookie, you wouldn't be standing here."

"It was just an *accident*," the cook insisted, relying on a favorite word. "Ketchum didn't mean to hurt me—he just caught me with his cast, by accident."

"If he'd hit you with his cast, you would be dead," Jane told him. She was sitting up in bed, with her hair all around her; it hung down below her waist, and she had folded her arms over her breasts, which were hidden by both her hair and her arms.

Whenever she took her hair down, and later went home that way, she could get in real trouble with Constable Carl—if he hadn't already passed out. It was a night when Jane should stay late and leave early in the morning, if she went home at all, Dominic was thinking.

"I saw Carl tonight," the cook told her.

"It wasn't Carl who hit you, either," Jane said, as he got into bed beside her. "And it doesn't look as if he shot you," she added.

"I can't tell if he knows about us, Jane."

"I can't tell, either," she told him.

"Did Ketchum kill Lucky Pinette?" the cook asked.

"Nobody knows, Cookie. We haven't known doodley-squat about that for *ages*! Why did Six-Pack hit you?" Jane asked him.

"Because I wouldn't fool around with her—that's why."

"If you had screwed Six-Pack, I would have hit you so hard you wouldn't ever have *found* your lower lip," Jane told him.

He smiled, which the lip didn't like. When he winced at the pain, Jane said, "Poor baby—no kissing for you tonight."

The cook lay down next to her. "There are other things besides kissing," he said to her.

She pushed him to his back and lay on top of him, the sheer weight of her pressing him into the bed and taking his breath away. If the cook had closed his eyes, he would have seen himself in Six-Pack's suffocating headlock again, so he kept his eyes wide open. When Injun Jane straddled his hips and firmly seated herself in his lap, Dominic felt a sudden intake of air fill his lungs. With an urgency possibly prompted by Six-Pack having assaulted him, Jane mounted the cook; she wasted no time in slipping him inside her.

"I'll show you *other things*," the Indian dishwasher said, rocking herself back and forth; her breasts fell on his chest, her mouth brushed his face, carefully *not* touching his lower lip, while her long hair cascaded forward, forming a tent around the two of them.

The cook could breathe, but he couldn't move. Jane's weight was too great for him to budge her. Besides, Dominic Baciagalupo wouldn't have wanted to change a single element of the way she was rocking back and forth on top of him—or her gathering momentum. (Not even if Injun Jane had been as light as Dominic's late wife, Rosie, and the cook himself were as big as Ketchum.) It was a little like riding a train, Dominic imagined—except all he could do was hold tightly to the train that was, in reality, riding *him*.

IT DIDN'T MATTER NOW that Danny was certain he'd heard water running in the bathroom, or that the kiss on his forehead—either his father's kiss or a second good-night kiss from Jane—had been real. It didn't matter, either, that the boy had incorporated the kiss into a dream he was having about Six-Pack Pam, who'd been ardently kissing him—not necessarily on his forehead. Nor did it matter that the twelve-year-old knew the odd creak his dad's limp made on the stairs, because he'd heard the limp a while ago and there was a different, unfamiliar creaking now. (On stairs, his father always put his good foot forward; the lame foot followed, more lightly, after it.)

What mattered now was the new and never-ending creaking, and where the anxious, wide-awake boy thought the creaking came from. It wasn't only the wind that was shaking the whole upstairs of the cookhouse; Danny had heard and felt the wind in every season. The frightened boy quietly got out of bed, and—holding his breath— tiptoed to his partially open bedroom door and into the upstairs hall.

There was Chief Wahoo with his lunatic, upside-down grin. But what had happened to *Jane*? young Dan wondered. If her hat had ended up in the hall, where was her *head*? Had the intruder (for surely there was a predator on the loose) decapitated Jane—either with one swipe of its claws or (in the case of a *human* predator) with a bush hook?

As he made his cautious way down the hall, Danny half expected to see Jane's severed head in the bathtub; as he passed the open bathroom door, without spotting her head, the twelve-year-old could only imagine that the intruder was a bear, not a man, and that the bear had *eaten* Jane and was now attacking his dad. For there was no denying where the violent creaks and moans were coming from—his father's bedroom—and that was definitely moaning (or worse, *whimpering*) that the boy could hear as he came closer. When he passed the Cleveland Indians cap, the recognition that Chief Wahoo had landed upside down only heightened the twelve-year-old's fears.

What Danny Baciagalupo would see (more accurately, what he

thought he saw), upon entering his dad's bedroom, was everything the twelve-year-old had feared, and worse—that is, both bigger and *hairier* than what the boy had ever imagined a bear could be. Only his father's knees and feet were visible beneath the bear; more frightening still, his dad's lower legs weren't moving. Maybe the boy had arrived too late to save him! Only the bear was moving—the rounded, hump-backed beast (its head not discernible) was rocking the entire bed, its glossy-black hair both longer and more luxuriant than Danny had ever imagined a black bear's hair would be.

The bear was *consuming* his father, or so it appeared to the twelve-year-old. With no weapon at hand, one might have expected the boy to throw himself on the animal attacking his dad in such a savage or frenzied manner—if only to be hurled into a bedroom wall, or raked to death by the beast's claws. But family histories—chiefly, perhaps, the stories we are told as children—invade our most basic instincts and inform our deepest memories, especially in an emergency. Young Dan reached for the eight-inch cast-iron skillet as if it were *his* weapon of choice, not his father's. That skillet was a legend, and Danny knew exactly where it was.

Holding the handle in both hands, the boy stepped up to the bed and took aim at where he thought the bear's head ought to be. He'd already started his two-handed swing—as Ketchum had once shown him, with an ax, being sure to get his hips behind the swinging motion—when he noticed the bare soles of two clearly human feet. The feet were in a prayerful position, just beside his dad's bare knees, and Danny thought that the feet looked a lot like *Jane's*. The Indian dishwasher was on her feet all day, and—for such a heavy woman—it was only natural that her feet often hurt her. She liked nothing better, she'd told young Dan, than a foot rub, which Danny had more than once given her.

"Jane?" Danny asked—in a small, doubting voice—but nothing slowed the forward momentum of the cast-iron skillet.

Jane must have heard the boy utter her name, because she raised her head and turned to face him. That was why the skillet caught her full-force on her right temple. The ringing sound, a dull but deep *gong*, was followed by a stinging sensation young Dan first felt in his hands; a reverberant tingle passed through both wrists and up his forearms. For the rest of his life, or as long as his memory endured, it would be small consolation to Danny Baciagalupo that he didn't see the expression on Jane's pretty face when the skillet struck her. (Her hair was so long that it simply covered everything.)

Jane's massive body shuddered. She was *too* massive, and her hair was too sleekly beautiful, for her ever to have been a black bear—not in this life or the next, where she most assuredly was going. Jane rolled off the cook and crashed to the floor.

There was no mistaking her for a bear now. Her hair had fanned out—flung wide as wings, to both sides of her inert, colossal torso. Her big, beautiful breasts had slumped into the hollows of her armpits; her motionless arms reached over her head, as if (even in death) Jane sought to hold aloft a heavy, descending universe. But as astonishing as her nakedness must have been to an innocent twelve-year-old, Danny Baciagalupo would best remember the faraway gaze in Jane's wide-open eyes. Something more than the final, split-second recognition of her fate lingered in Injun Jane's dead eyes. What had she suddenly seen in the immeasurable distance? Danny would wonder. Whatever Jane had glimpsed of the unforeseeable future had clearly terrified her—not just *her* fate but *all* their fates, maybe.

"Jane," Danny said again; this time it wasn't a question, though the boy's heart was racing and he must have had many questions on his mind. Nor did Danny more than glance at his dad. Was it his father's nakedness that made the boy so quickly look away? (Perhaps it was what Ketchum had called the *little-fella* aspect of the cook; the latter aspect was greatly enhanced by how near Dominic now was to the dead dishwasher.) "Jane!" Danny cried, as if the boy needed a third utterance of the Indian's name to finally register what he had done to her.

The cook quickly covered her private parts with a pillow. He knelt in the vast expanse of her far-flung hair, putting his ear to her quiet heart. Young Dan held the skillet in both hands, as if the reverberation still stung his palms; possibly, the ongoing tingle in his forearms would last forever. Though he was only twelve, Danny Baciagalupo surely knew that the rest of his life had just begun. "I thought she was a bear," the boy told his dad.

Dominic could not have looked more shocked if, at that moment, the dead dishwasher had turned herself into a bear; yet the cook could see for himself that it was his beloved Daniel who needed some consoling. Trembling, the boy stood clutching the murder weapon as if he believed a *real* bear would be the next thing to assail them.

"It's understandable that you thought Jane was a bear," his father said, hugging him. The cook took the skillet from his shaking son, hugging him again. "It's not your fault, Daniel. It was an accident. It's *nobody's* fault."

"How can it be *nobody's* fault?" the twelve-year-old asked.

"It's *my* fault, then," his dad told him. "It will never be your fault, Daniel. It's all mine. *And* it was an accident."

Of course the cook was thinking about Constable Carl; in the constable's world, there was no such thing as a no-fault accident. In the cowboy's mind, if you could call it that, good intentions didn't count. You can't save yourself, but you can save your son, Dominic Baciagalupo was thinking. (And for how many years might the cook manage to save them both?)

For so long, Danny had wanted to see Jane undo her braid and let down her hair—not to mention how he had dreamed of seeing her enormous breasts. Now he couldn't look at her. "I loved Jane!" the boy blurted out.

"Of course you did, Daniel—I know you did."

"Were you *do-si-doing* her?" the twelve-year-old asked.

"Yes," his father answered. "I loved Jane, too. Just not like I loved your mom," he added. Why was it necessary for him to say that? the cook asked himself guiltily. Dominic had truly loved Jane; he must have been yielding to the fact that there was no time to grieve for her.

"What happened to your lip?" the boy asked his dad.

"Six-Pack smacked me with her elbow," the cook answered.

"Were you *do-si-doing* Six-Pack, too?" his son asked him.

"No, Daniel. Jane was my girlfriend—just Jane."

"What about Constable Carl?" young Dan asked.

"We have a lot to do, Daniel," was all his dad would tell him. And they didn't have a lot of time, the cook knew. Before long, it would be light outside; they had to get started.

IN THE CONFUSION and sheer clumsiness that followed, and in their frantic haste, the cook and his son would find a multitude of reasons to relive the night of their departure from Twisted River—though they would remember the details of their forced exit differently. For young Dan, the monumental task of dressing the dead woman—not to mention bringing her body down the cookhouse stairs, and toting her to her truck—had been herculean. Nor did the boy at first understand why it was so important to his father that Jane be *correctly* dressed— that is, exactly as she would have dressed herself. Nothing missing, nothing awry. The straps to her stupendous bra could not be twisted; the waistband of her mammoth boxer shorts could not be rolled under; her socks could not be worn inside out.

But she's *dead*! What does it matter? Danny was thinking. The boy wasn't considering the scrutiny that Injun Jane's body might soon come under—what the examining physician would conclude was the cause of death, for example. (A blow to the head, obviously, but what was the instrument—and where was it?) The approximate time of death would need to be factored in, too. Clearly it mattered to the cook that, at the time of her death, Jane would appear to have been fully clothed.

As for Dominic, he would forever be grateful to Ketchum—for it was Ketchum who'd acquired a dolly for the cookhouse, on one of his drunken binges in Maine. The dolly was useful in unloading the dry goods from the trucks, or the cases of olive oil and maple syrup—even egg cartons, and anything heavy.

The cook and his son had strapped Jane onto the dolly; thus they were able to bring her down the cookhouse stairs in a semi-upright position, and wheel her standing (almost straight) to her truck. However, the dolly had been no help getting Injun Jane into the cab, which the cook would later recall as the "herculean" part of the task—or one herculean part, among several.

As for the instrument of death, Dominic Baciagalupo would pack the eight-inch cast-iron skillet among his most cherished kitchen items—namely, his favorite cookbooks, because the cook knew he had no time, and scant room, to pack his kitchenware. The other pots and pans would stay behind; the rest of the cookbooks, and all the novels, Dominic would leave for Ketchum.

Danny scarcely had time to gather some photos of his mom, but not the books he'd kept her pictures pressed flat in. As for clothing, the cook packed only the bare necessities of his own and young Dan's clothes—and Dominic would pack more clothes for himself than he did for his son, because Daniel would soon outgrow what he was wearing.

The cook's car was a 1952 Pontiac station wagon—the so-called semiwoodie Chieftain Deluxe. They'd made the last real "woodie" in 1949; the semiwoodie had fake wooden panels outside, offset against the maroon exterior, and real wood inside. The interior had maroon leather upholstery, too. Because of Dominic's lame left foot, the Pontiac Chieftain Deluxe came with automatic transmission—in all likelihood making it the only vehicle with automatic transmission in the settlement of Twisted River—which made it possible for Danny to drive the car, too. The twelve-year-old's legs weren't long enough to depress a clutch pedal all the way to the floor, but Danny had driven the semiwoodie station wagon on the haul roads. Constable Carl didn't cruise the haul roads. There were many boys Danny's age, and even younger, driving cars and trucks on the back roads around Phillips Brook and Twisted River—unlicensed preteens with pretty good driving skills. (The boys who were a little taller than Danny could depress the clutch pedals all the way to the floor.)

Considering the contingencies of their escape from Twisted River, it was a good thing that Danny could drive the Chieftain, because the cook would not have wanted to be seen *walking* through town, back to the cookhouse, after he drove Jane (in her truck) to Constable Carl's. By that early hour of the morning, in the predawn light, Dominic Baciagalupo's limp would have made him recognizable to anyone who might have been up and about—and for the cook and his son to have been seen walking *together* at that ungodly hour would have been most unusual and suspicious.

Of course, Dominic's maroon semiwoodie was the only car of its kind in town. The '52 Pontiac Chieftain might not pass unnoticed, although it would pass more quickly through the settlement than the cook with his limp, and the station wagon would never be parked within sight of where Dominic would leave Jane's truck—at Constable Carl's.

"Are you crazy?" Danny would ask his father, as they were preparing to leave the cookhouse—for the last time. "Why are we bringing the body to the constable?"

"So the drunken cowboy will wake up in the morning and think *he* did it," the cook told his son.

"What if Constable Carl is awake when we get there?" the boy asked.

"That's why we have a back-up plan, Daniel," his dad said.

A misty, almost imperceptible rain was falling. The long maroon hood of the Chieftain Deluxe glistened. The cook wet his thumb on the hood; he reached inside the open driver's-side window and rubbed the spot of dried blood off his son's forehead. Remembering his good-night kiss, Dominic Baciagalupo knew whose blood it was; he hoped it hadn't been the last kiss he would give Daniel, and that no more blood (not *anyone's* blood) would touch his boy tonight.

"I just follow you, right?" young Dan asked his dad.

"That's right," the cook said, the back-up plan foremost in his mind as he climbed into the cab of Jane's truck, where Jane was slumped against the passenger-side door. Jane wasn't bleeding, but Dominic was glad that he couldn't see the bruise on her right temple. Jane's hair had fallen forward, covering her face; the contusion (it was swollen to the size of a baseball) was pressed against the passenger-side window.

They drove, a caravan of two, to the flat-roofed, two-story hostelry where Six-Pack was renting what passed for a second-floor apartment. In the rearview mirror of Jane's truck, the cook had only a partial view of his son's small face behind the wheel of the '52 Pontiac. The Chieftain's exterior visor resembled that of a baseball cap pulled low over the windshield-eyes of the eight-cylinder station wagon with its shark-toothed grille and aggressive hood ornament.

"Shit!" Dominic said aloud. He had suddenly thought of Jane's Cleveland Indians cap. Where was it? Had they left Chief Wahoo upside down in the upstairs hall of the cookhouse? But they were already at Six-Pack's place; not a soul had been on the streets, and the dance-hall door had not once opened. They couldn't go back to the cookhouse now.

Danny parked the Pontiac at the foot of the outside stairs to Pam's apartment. The boy had squeezed into the cab of Jane's truck, between poor dead Jane and his father, before Dominic noticed Injun Jane's missing baseball cap—young Dan was wearing it.

"We need to leave Chief Wahoo with her, don't we?" the twelve-year-old asked.

"Good boy," his dad said, his heart welling with pride and fear. Regarding the back-up plan, there was so much for a twelve-year-old to remember.

The cook needed his son's help in getting Injun Jane from the cab of the truck to Constable Carl's kitchen door, which Jane had said was always left unlocked. It would be all right if they dragged her feet through the mud, because the constable would expect Jane's boots to be muddy; they just couldn't allow another part of her to touch the ground. Naturally, the dolly would have left wheel tracks in the mud—and what would Dominic have done with the dolly? Leave it in Jane's truck, or at Constable Carl's door?

They drove to that forlorn part of town near the sawmill and the hostelry favored by the French Canadian itinerants. (Constable Carl liked living near his principal victims.) "What would you guess Ketchum weighs?" Danny asked, after his dad had parked Jane's truck in her usual spot. They were standing on the running board of the truck; young Dan held Jane upright in the passenger seat while his father managed to guide her stiffening legs out the open door. But once her feet were on the running board, what then?

"Ketchum weighs about two-twenty, maybe two-thirty," the cook said.

"And Six-Pack?" young Dan asked.

Dominic Baciagalupo would feel the stiffness in his neck from Six-Pack's headlock for about a week. "Pam probably weighs about one-seventy-five—one-eighty, tops," his dad answered.

"And what do *you* weigh?" Danny asked.

The cook could see where this line of questioning was going. He let Injun Jane's feet slide all the way to the mud; he stood on the wet ground beside her, holding her around her hips while Daniel (still standing on the running board) hugged her under her arms. We will both end up in the mud with Jane on top of us! Dominic was thinking, but he said, as casually as possible, "Oh, I don't know what I weigh—about one-fifty, I guess." (He weighed all of 145 with his winter clothes on, he knew perfectly well—he had never weighed as much as 150 pounds.)

"And *Jane?*" young Dan grunted, stepping down to the ground from the truck's running board. The body of the Indian dishwasher pitched forward into his and his father's waiting arms. Though Jane's knees buckled, they did not touch the mud; the cook and his son staggered to hold her, but they didn't fall.

Injun Jane weighed at least 300 pounds—maybe 315 or 320—although Dominic Baciagalupo would profess not to know. The cook could scarcely get his breath as he dragged his dead paramour to her bad boyfriend's kitchen door, but he managed to sound almost unconcerned as he answered his son in a whisper: "Jane? Oh, she weighs about the same as Ketchum—maybe a little more."

To their mutual surprise, the cook and his son saw that Constable Carl's kitchen door was not only unlocked—it was open. (The wind, maybe—or else the cowboy had come home so drunk that he'd left the door open in a blind, unthinking stupor.) The misty rain had wet what they could see of the kitchen floor. While the kitchen was dimly lit, at least one light was on, but they couldn't see beyond the kitchen; they could not know more.

When Jane's splayed feet were touching the kitchen floor, Dominic felt confident that he could slide her the rest of the way inside by himself; it would help him that her boots were muddy and the floor was wet. "Good-bye, Daniel," the cook whispered to his son. In lieu of a kiss, the twelve-year-old took Jane's baseball cap off his head and put it on his father's.

When the cook could no longer hear Danny's retreating steps on the muddy street, he steered Jane's great weight forward into the kitchen. He could only hope that the boy would remember his instructions. "If you hear a gunshot, go to Ketchum. If you wait for me in the Pontiac for more than twenty minutes—even if there is *no* shot—go to Ketchum."

Dominic had told the twelve-year-old that if anything *ever* happened to his dad—not just tonight—go to Ketchum, and tell Ketchum everything. "Watch out for the next-to-last step at the top of Pam's stairs," the cook had also told his son.

"Won't Six-Pack be there?" the boy had asked.

"Just tell her you need to talk to Ketchum. She'll let you in," his father had said. (He could only *hope* that Pam would let Daniel in.)

Dominic Baciagalupo slid Injun Jane's body past the wet area on the kitchen floor before he let her come to rest against a cabinet. Holding her under her arms, he allowed her immense weight to sag onto the countertop; then, with excruciating slowness, he stretched her body out upon the floor. While he was bending over her, the Cleveland Indians cap fell off the cook's head and landed upside down beside Jane; Chief Wahoo was grinning insanely while Dominic waited for the cocking-sound of the Colt .45, which the cook was certain he would hear. Just as Danny would be sure to hear the discharging of the gun—it was more than loud. At that hour, everyone in town would hear a gunshot—maybe even Ketchum, still sleeping off his bender. (On occasion, even from the distance of the cookhouse, Dominic had heard that Colt .45 discharge.)

But nothing happened. The cook let his breathing return to normal, choosing not to look around. If Constable Carl was there, Dominic didn't want to see him. The cook would rather let the cowboy shoot him in the back as he was leaving; he left carefully, using the outward-turned toe of his bad foot to smear his muddy footprints as he left.

Outside, a wooden plank was stretched across the gutter from the road. Dominic used the plank to wipe flat the drag marks where the toes and heels of Jane's boots had carved deep ruts—marking the tortured path from her truck to the constable's kitchen door. The cook returned the plank to its proper place, wiping the mud from his hands on the wet fender of Jane's truck, which the increasingly steady rain would wash clean. (The rain would take care of his and young Dan's footprints, too.)

No one saw the cook limp past the silent dance hall; the Beaudette brothers, or their ghosts, had not reoccupied the old Lombard log hauler, which stood as the lone sentinel in the muddy lane alongside the hall. Dominic Baciagalupo was wondering what Constable Carl might make of Injun Jane's body when he stumbled over it in the bleary-eyed morning. What had he hit her with? the cowboy might speculate, having hit her more than once before. But where is the weapon, the blunt instrument? the constable would be sure to ask himself. Maybe I'm *not* the one who hit her, the cowboy might later conclude—once his head cleared, or most certainly when he learned that the cook and his son had left town.

Please, God, give me *time,* the cook was thinking, as he saw his boy's small face behind the water-streaked windshield of the Chieftain Deluxe. Young Dan was waiting in the passenger seat, as if he'd never lost faith that his father would safely return from Constable Carl's and be their driver.

By *time,* that dogged companion, Dominic Baciagalupo meant more than the time needed for this most immediate getaway. He meant the necessary time to be a good father to his precious child, the time to watch his boy become a man; the cook prayed he would have *that* much time, though he had no idea how he might arrange such an unlikely luxury.

He got into the driver's seat of the station wagon without receiving the .45-caliber bullet he'd been expecting. Young Dan began to cry. "I kept listening for the gunshot," the twelve-year-old said.

"One day, Daniel, you may hear it," his dad told him, hugging him before he started the Pontiac.

"Aren't we going to tell Ketchum?" Danny asked.

All the cook could say might one day be in danger of sounding like a mantra, but Dominic would say it nonetheless: "We haven't time."

Like a long, slowly moving hearse, the maroon semiwoodie took the haul road out of the settlement. As they drove south-southeast, sometimes within sight of Twisted River, the dawn was fast approaching. There would be the dam to deal with, when they reached the Pontook Reservoir; then, wherever they went next, they would be on Route 16, which ran north and south along the Androscoggin.

Exactly how *much* time remained to them, in their more immediate future, would be determined by what they found at Dead Woman Dam—and how long they would need to linger there. (Not too long, Dominic would hope as he drove.)

"Are we *ever* going to tell Ketchum?" young Dan asked his dad.

"Sure we are," his father answered, though the cook had no idea how he might get the necessary message to Ketchum—one that would be safe yet somehow manage to be clear.

For now, the wind had dropped and the rain was letting up. Ahead of them, the haul road was slick with tire-rutted mud, but the sun was rising; it shone in the driver's-side window, giving Dominic Baciagalupo a bright (albeit unrealistic) view of the future.

Only hours ago, the cook had been worried about finding Angel's body—specifically, how the sight of the dead Canadian youth might affect his beloved Daniel. Since then, the twelve-year-old had killed his favorite babysitter, and both father and son had wrestled with her body—bringing Injun Jane the not-inconsiderable distance from the upstairs of the cookhouse to her near-final resting place at Constable Carl's.

Whatever the cook and his dear boy would find at Dead Woman Dam, Dominic was optimistically thinking, how bad could it really be? (Under stress, as he was, the cook had uncharacteristically thought of the place by its ill-gotten name.)

AS THE CHIEFTAIN CAME CLOSER to the Pontook Reservoir, the boy and his dad could see the seagulls. Although the Pontook was more than one hundred miles from the ocean, there were always seagulls around the Androscoggin—it was such big water.

"There's a kid in my class named Halsted," Danny was saying worriedly.

"I think I know his father," the cook said.

"His dad kicked him in the face with his caulk boots on—the kid has holes in his forehead," young Dan reported.

"That would definitely be the Halsted I know," Dominic replied.

"Ketchum says someone should stick a sawdust blower up Halsted's ass, and see if the fat bastard can be inflated—Ketchum means the dad," Danny explained.

"Ketchum recommends the sawdust blower for no small number of assholes," the cook said.

"I'll bet you we're going to miss Ketchum wicked," the boy said obsessively.

"I'll bet you we do," his father agreed. "Wicked*ly.*"

"Ketchum says you can't ever dry out hemlock." Danny talked on and on. The twelve-year-old was clearly nervous about where they were going—not just Dead Woman Dam, but where they might go after that.

"Hemlock beams are good for bridges," Dominic countered.

"Hook your whiffletree as close to the load as possible," young Dan recited, from memory—for no apparent reason. "Success Pond has the biggest fucking beaver pond there is," Danny continued.

"Are you going to quote Ketchum the whole way?" his dad asked him.

"The whole way *where*?" the twelve-year-old asked anxiously.

"I don't know yet, Daniel."

"Hardwoods don't float very well," the boy replied, apropos of nothing.

Yes, but softwoods float pretty *high*, Dominic Baciagalupo was thinking. Those had been softwoods in the river drive, when Angel went under the logs. And with the wind last night, some of the topmost logs might have been blown outside the containment boom; those logs would be eddying in the overflow spillway to either side of the sluice dam. The stray logs, mostly spruce and pine, would make it hard to get Angel out of the circling water. Both the high-water shoreline and the more slowly moving water in the millpond had been formed by the dam; with any luck, they might find Angel's body there, in the shallows.

"Who would kick his own kid in the face with a caulk boot?" the distraught boy asked his dad.

"No one we'll ever see again," Dominic told his son. The sawmill at Dead Woman Dam looked abandoned, but that was just because it was Sunday.

"Tell me once more why they call it Dead Woman Dam," Danny said to his father.

"You know perfectly well why they call it that, Daniel."

"I know why you don't like to call it that," the boy quickly rejoined. "*Mom* was the dead woman—that's why, right?"

The cook parked the '52 Pontiac next to the loading dock at the mill. Dominic wouldn't answer his son, but the twelve-year-old knew the whole history—"perfectly well," as his dad had said. Both Jane and Ketchum had told the boy the story. Dead Woman Dam was named for his mother, but Danny never ceased wanting his father to talk about it—more than his father ever would.

"Why does Ketchum have a white finger? What does the chainsaw have to do with it?" young Dan started up; he simply couldn't stop talking.

"Ketchum has more than one white finger, and you *know* what the chainsaw has to do with it," his father said. "The vibration, remember?"

"Oh, right," the boy said.

"Daniel, please relax. Let's just try to get through this, and move on."

"Move on *where*?" the twelve-year-old shouted.

"Daniel, please—I'm as upset as you are," his father said. "Let's look for Angel. Let's just see what we find, okay?"

"We can't do anything about Jane, can we?" Danny asked.

"No, we can't," his dad said.

"What will Ketchum think of us?" the boy asked.

Dominic wished he knew. "That's enough about Ketchum," was all the cook could say. Ketchum will know what to do, his old friend was hoping.

But how would they manage to tell Ketchum what had happened? They couldn't wait at Dead Woman Dam until nine o'clock in the morning. If it took half that long to find Angel, they couldn't even wait until they found him!

It all depended on when Constable Carl woke up and discovered Jane's body. At first, the cowboy would surely think he was the culprit. And the cookhouse never served breakfast on a Sunday morning; an early supper was the only meal served on Sundays. It would be midafternoon before the kitchen helpers arrived at the cookhouse; when they learned that the cook and his son were gone, they wouldn't necessarily tell the constable. (Not right away.) The cowboy would have no immediate reason to go looking for Ketchum, either.

Dominic was beginning to think that it might be all right to wait for Ketchum at Dead Woman Dam until nine o'clock in the morning. From what the cook knew about Constable Carl, it would be just like him to *bury* Jane's body and forget about her—that is, until the cowboy heard that the cook and his son were gone. Most people in Twisted River would conclude that Injun Jane had left town with them! Only the constable would know where Jane was, and, under the circumstances (the guilty-looking, premature burial), the cowboy wouldn't be likely to dig up Jane's body just to prove what he knew.

Or was this wishful thinking on Dominic Baciagalupo's part? Constable Carl wouldn't hesitate to bury Injun Jane, *if* he believed he killed her. What *would* be wishful thinking on the cook's part was to imagine that the cowboy might feel contrite about killing Jane—enough to blow his brains out, one could only hope. (*That* would be wishful thinking—to dream of a *penitent* Constable Carl, as if the cowboy could even conceive of contrition!)

To the right of the flashboards and the sluice spillway, outside the containment boom, the water was eddying against the dam in a clockwise direction, a few windblown logs (some stray red pine and tamarack among the spruce) circling in the open water. Young Dan and his dad couldn't spot a body there. Where the main water passed through the sluice spillway, the containment boom bulged with tangled logs, but nothing stood out from the wet-bark, dark-water tones.

The cook and his son carefully crossed the dam to the open water on the left side of the boom; here the water and some stray logs were eddying in a counterclockwise direction. A deerskin glove was twirling in the water, but they both knew Angel hadn't been wearing gloves. The water was deep and black, with floating slabs of bark; to Dominic's disappointment *and* relief, they didn't see a body there, either.

"Maybe Angel *got out*," Danny said, but his dad knew better; no one that young slipped under moving logs and *got out*.

It was already past seven in the morning, but they had to keep looking; even the family Angel had run away from would want to know about their boy. It would take longer to search the broader reaches of the millpond—at some distance from the dam—although the footing would be safer there. The closer they were to the dam and the containment boom, the more the cook and his son worried about each other. (They weren't wearing caulk boots, they weren't Ketchum—they weren't even rivermen of the greenest kind. They simply weren't loggers.)

It would be half past eight before they found Angel's body. The long-haired boy, in his red, white, and green plaid shirt, was floating facedown in the shallows, close to shore—not one log was anywhere around him. Danny didn't even get his feet wet bringing the body ashore. The twelve-year-old used a fallen branch to hook Angel's Royal Stewart shirt; young Dan called to his dad while he towed the Canadian youth to within his grasp. Together they got Angel to higher ground on the riverbank; lifting and dragging the body was light work compared to toting Injun Jane.

They unlaced the young logger's caulk boots and converted one of the boots to a pail, to bring fresh water ashore. They used the water to wipe the mud and pieces of bark from Angel's face and hands, which were a pale pearl color tinged with blue. Danny did his best to run his fingers like a comb through the dead youth's hair.

The twelve-year-old was the first to find a leech. As long and thick as Ketchum's oddly bent index finger, it was what the locals called a northern bloodsucker—it was attached to Angel's throat. The cook knew it wouldn't be the only leech on Angel. Dominic Baciagalupo also knew how Ketchum hated leeches. The way things were working out, Dominic might not be able to spare his old friend the sight of Angel's body, but—with Daniel's help—they might spare Ketchum the bloodsuckers.

By nine o'clock, they had moved Angel to the loading dock at the sawmill, where the platform was at least dry and partly sunny—and in view of the parking lot. They had stripped the body and removed almost twenty leeches; they'd wiped Angel clean with his wet plaid shirt, and had managed to re-dress the dead boy in an anonymous combination of the cook's and his son's unrecognizable clothes. A T-shirt that had always been too big for Danny fit Angel fine; an old pair of Dominic's dungarees completed the picture. For Ketchum's sake, if Ketchum ever showed up, at least the clothes were clean and dry. There was nothing they could do about the pearl-gray, bluish tint to Angel's skin; it was unreasonable to hope that the weak April sun would return the natural color to the dead youth, but somehow Angel *looked* warm.

"Are we waiting for Ketchum?" Danny asked his dad.

"For just a little while longer," the cook replied. His dad was the anxious one now, young Dan realized. (The thing about time, Dominic knew, was that it was relentless.)

The cook was wringing out Angel's soaking-wet and dirty clothes when he felt the wallet in the left-front pocket of the Canadian's dungarees—just a cheap, imitation-leather wallet with a photo of a pretty, heavy-looking woman under a plastic window, which was now fogged by its immersion in the cold water. Dominic rubbed the plastic on his shirtsleeve; when he could see the woman more clearly, her resemblance to Angel was apparent. Surely, she was the dead boy's mother—a woman a little older than the cook but younger than Injun Jane.

There wasn't much money in the wallet—just some small bills, only American dollars (Dominic had expected to find some Canadian dollars, too), and what appeared to be a business card from a restaurant with an Italian name. This confirmed the cook's earliest impression that Angel was no stranger to working in a kitchen, though it might not have been the boy's foremost career choice.

However, something else was *not* as Dominic Baciagalupo had expected: The restaurant wasn't in Toronto, or anywhere else in Ontario; it was an Italian restaurant in Boston, Massachusetts, and the name of the restaurant was an even bigger surprise. It was a phrase that the illegitimate son of Annunziata Saetta knew well, because he'd heard his mother utter it with a bitterness born of rejection. *"Vicino di Napoli,"* Nunzi had said—in reference to where Dominic's absconding father had gone—and the boy had thought of those hill towns and provinces "in the vicinity of Naples," where his dad had come from (and, allegedly, gone back to). The names of those towns and provinces that Annunziata had said in her sleep—Benevento and Avellino—came to Dominic's mind.

But was it possible that his deadbeat dad had run no farther than an Italian restaurant on Hanover Street—what Nunzi had called "the main drag" of the North End of Boston? Because, according to the business card in Angel's wallet, the restaurant was called Vicino di Napoli—clearly a Neapolitan place—and it was on Hanover Street, near Cross Street. The street names themselves were as familiar to Dominic's childhood as Nunzi's oft-repeated recommendations for parsley (*prezzémolo*), or her frequent mention of Mother Anna's and the Europeo—two other restaurants on Hanover Street.

Nothing struck the cook as too coincidental to be believed—not on a day when twelve-year-old Daniel Baciagalupo had killed his father's lover with the same skillet the cook had put to such legendary use. (Who would believe he'd once saved his now-dead wife from a *bear*?) Even so, Dominic was unprepared for the last item he discovered in Angel Pope's wallet. As near as the cook could tell, this was a summer pass to Boston's streetcar and subway system—a transit pass, Dominic had heard his mother call it. The pass declared that the bearer was under the age of sixteen in the summer of 1953—and there was Angel's date of birth, to prove it. The boy had been born on February 16, 1939, which meant that Angel had only recently turned fifteen. The youth would have had to have run away from home when he was only *fourteen*—if he had really run away. (And of course there was no way of knowing if Boston was still the dead boy's "home," although the transit pass and the business card from Vicino di Napoli strongly suggested that this was so.)

What would most convincingly catch Dominic Baciagalupo's attention was Angel's real name—it wasn't exactly Angel Pope.

ANGELÙ DEL POPOLO

"Who?" Danny asked, when his father read the name on the streetcar and subway pass out loud.

The cook knew that Del Popolo meant "Of the People," and that Pope was a common Americanization of the Sicilian name; while Del Popolo was probably but not necessarily Sicilian, the an-geh-LOO was *definitely* Sicilian, which the cook knew, too. Had the boy worked in a Neapolitan restaurant? (At fourteen, a part-time job was permitted.) But what had made him run away? From the photograph, it appeared he had still loved his mom.

But all the cook said to his son was: "It seems that Angel wasn't who he said he was, Daniel." Dominic let Danny look over the transit pass—it and the business card from Vicino di Napoli in the North End were all they had to go on, if they were going to try to find Angelù Del Popolo's family.

Naturally, there was a more pressing problem. Where the hell was Ketchum? Dominic Baciagalupo was wondering. How long could they afford to wait? What if Constable Carl hadn't been all that drunk? What if the cowboy had found Injun Jane's body, but he'd known in an instant that he hadn't laid a hand on her—at least not last night?

It was hard to imagine what written message the cook could leave for Ketchum on Angel's body, because what if Ketchum didn't find Angel first? Wouldn't the message have to be in code?

> Surprise! Angel isn't Canadian!
> And, by the way, Jane was in an accident!
> Nobody did it—not even Carl!

Well, just how could the cook leave a note like that?

"Are we still waiting for Ketchum?" young Dan asked his dad.

It was with notably less conviction that his father replied: "For just a little while longer, Daniel."

THE SONG ON THE RADIO in Ketchum's badly lived-in truck reached them on the loading dock of the sawmill before the truck itself appeared on the haul road—maybe it was Jo Stafford singing "Make Love to Me," but Ketchum turned off the radio before the cook could be sure about the song. (Ketchum was on his way to becoming chainsaw-deaf. The radio in his truck was always overloud, the windows—now that it was what passed for spring—usually open.) Dominic was relieved to see that Six-Pack hadn't come along for the ride; that would have seriously complicated matters.

Ketchum parked his rattling heap a discreet distance from the Pontiac; he sat in the cab with his white cast resting on the steering wheel, his eyes looking past them on the platform to where Angel was reclining in the uncertain sunlight.

"You found him, I see," Ketchum said; he looked away, toward the dam, as if he were counting the logs in the containment boom.

As always, both predictable and unaccountable things were transported in the back of Ketchum's pickup truck; a homemade shelter covered the bed of the pickup, turning the entire truck into a wanigan. Ketchum carried his chainsaws around, together with an assortment of axes and other tools—and, under a canvas tarp, an inexplicable half-cord of firewood, in case the suddenly urgent need to build a bonfire possessed him.

"Daniel and I can put Angel in the back of your pickup, where you don't have to see him," Dominic said.

"Why can't Angel ride with you in the Chieftain?" Ketchum asked.

"Because we're not going back to Twisted River," the cook told his old friend.

Ketchum sighed, his eyes coming slowly to rest on Angel. The river driver got out of his truck and walked with an unexplained limp to the loading dock. (Dominic wondered if Ketchum was limping to mock him.) Ketchum picked up the dead youth's body as if it were a sleeping baby; the logger carried the fifteen-year-old to the cab of his truck, where Danny had run ahead to open the door.

"I guess I might as well see him now as wait till I have to unload him back in town," Ketchum told them. "I suppose these are your clothes on him?" he asked young Dan.

"Mine and my dad's," the twelve-year-old said.

The cook limped over to the truck, carrying Angel's wet and dirty clothes; he put them on the floor of the cab, by the dead boy's feet. "Angel's clothes could stand some washing and drying," he told Ketchum.

"I'll have Jane wash and dry his clothes," Ketchum told them. "Jane and I can clean Angel up a little, too—then we'll dress him in his own clothes."

"Jane is dead, Ketchum," the cook told him. (*It was an accident*, he was about to add, but his beloved Daniel was quicker.)

"I killed her with the skillet—the one Dad hit the bear with," Danny blurted out. "I thought Jane was a bear," the boy told Ketchum.

The cook confirmed the story by immediately looking away from his old friend. Ketchum put his good arm around Danny's shoulders and pulled the boy against him. Young Dan buried his face in the stomach of Ketchum's wool-flannel shirt—the same green and blue Black Watch plaid that Six-Pack Pam had been wearing. To the twelve-year-old, the commingled smells of Ketchum and Six-Pack inhabited the shirt as confidently as their two strong bodies.

Raising his cast, Ketchum pointed to the Pontiac. "Christ, Cookie, you haven't got poor Jane in the Chieftain, have you?"

"We took her to Constable Carl's," Danny said.

"I don't know if Carl had passed out in another room, or if he wasn't home, but I left Jane on his kitchen floor," the cook explained. "With any luck, the cowboy will find her body and think *he* did it."

"Of *course* he'll think he did it!" Ketchum thundered. "I'll bet he buried her an hour ago, or he's digging the damn hole as we speak. But when Carl hears that you and Danny have left town, he'll begin to think he *didn't* do it! He'll think *you* did it, Cookie—if you and Danny don't get your asses back to Twisted River!"

"Bluff it out, you mean?" Dominic asked.

"What's to bluff?" Ketchum asked. "For the rest of his rotten life, the cowboy will be trying to remember exactly how and why he killed Jane—or he'll be looking for you, Cookie."

"You're assuming he won't remember last night," the cook said. "That's a pretty big assumption, isn't it?"

"Six-Pack told me you paid us a visit last night," Ketchum told his old friend. "Well, do you think I remember you being there?"

"Probably not," Dominic answered. "But what you're suggesting is that I gamble *everything*." It was both unconscious and uncontrollable that, when the cook said *everything*, he looked straight at young Daniel.

"You go back to the cookhouse, I help you unpack the Chieftain, you and Danny are completely settled in by the time the kitchen helpers show up this afternoon. Then, around suppertime," Ketchum continued, "you send Dot or May—or one of those worthless fucking sawmill workers' wives—to Constable Carl's. You have her say, 'Where's Jane? Cookie's going crazy without his dishwasher!' *That's* bluffing it out! You win that bluff hands down," Ketchum told him. "The cowboy will be shitting his pants. He'll be shitting them for years—just waiting for some dog to dig up the Injun's body!"

"I don't know, Ketchum," the cook said. "It's a huge bluff. I can't take a chance like that—not with Daniel."

"You're taking a bigger chance if you leave," his old friend told him. "Shit, if the cowboy blows your head off, I'll take good care of Danny."

Young Dan's eyes kept moving from his father to Ketchum, and back to his father again. "I think we should go back to the cookhouse," the twelve-year-old told his dad.

But the cook knew how change—*any* change—made his son anxious. Of course Daniel Baciagalupo would vote to stay and bluff it out; *leaving* represented a more unknown fear.

"Look at it this way, Cookie," Ketchum was saying, his white cast leveled at his friend—as heavy as the cowboy's Colt .45—"if I'm wrong and Carl shoots you, he won't dare lay so much as a finger on Danny. But if I'm right, and the cowboy comes after you, he could kill you both—because you'd both be fugitives."

"Well, that's what we are—we're fugitives," Dominic said. "I'm not a gambler, Ketchum—not anymore."

"You're gambling now, Cookie," Ketchum told him. "Either way, it's a gamble, isn't it?"

"Give Ketchum a hug, Daniel—we should be going," his dad said. Danny Baciagalupo would remember that hug, and how he thought it strange that his father and Ketchum didn't hug each other—they were such old friends, and such good ones.

"Big changes are coming, Cookie," Ketchum tried to tell his friend. "They won't be moving logs over water much longer. Those dams on the Dummer ponds will be gone—this dam here won't last, either," he said, with a wave of his cast indicating the containment boom but choosing to leave Dead Woman Dam unnamed.

"Dummer Pond and Little Dummer *and* Twisted River will just flow into the Pontook. I suspect the old boom piers on the Androscoggin will last, but they won't be using them anymore. And the first time there's a fire in West Dummer or Twisted River, do you think anyone will bother to rebuild those sorry settlements? Who wouldn't rather move to Milan or Errol—or even Berlin, if you were old and feeble enough?" Ketchum added. "All you have to do is stay and *outlast* this miserable place, Cookie—you and Danny." But the cook and his son were making their way to the Chieftain. "If you run now, you'll be running forever!" Ketchum called after them. He limped around his truck from the passenger's to the driver's side.

"Why are you limping?" the cook called to him.

"Shit," Ketchum said. "There's a step missing on Six-Pack's stairs—I fucking forgot about it."

"Take care of yourself, Ketchum," his old friend told him.

"You, too, Cookie," Ketchum said. "I won't ask you about your lip, but I'm familiar with that injury."

"By the way, Angel wasn't Canadian," Dominic Baciagalupo told Ketchum.

"His real name was Angelù Del Popolo," young Dan explained, "and he came from Boston, not Toronto."

"I suppose that's where you're going?" Ketchum asked them. "Boston?"

"Angel must have had a family—there's got to be someone who needs to know what happened to him," the cook said.

Ketchum nodded. Through the windshield of his truck, the insufficient sunlight was playing tricks with the way Angelù Del Popolo sat up (almost straight) and faced alertly forward. Angel not only looked alive, but he seemed to be just starting the journey of his young life—not ending it.

"Suppose I tell Carl that you and Danny are delivering the bad news to Angel's family? You didn't leave the cookhouse looking like you were leaving it for good, did you?" Ketchum asked.

"We took nothing anybody would notice," Dominic said. "It would appear that we were coming back."

"Suppose I tell the cowboy that I was surprised Injun Jane wasn't with you?" Ketchum asked. "I could say that, if I were Jane, I would have gone to Canada, too." Danny saw how his dad considered this, before Ketchum said, "I think I *won't* say you've gone to Boston. Maybe it's better to say, 'If I were Jane, I would have gone to *Toronto*.' Suppose I say that?"

"Just don't say too much, whatever you say," the cook told him.

"I believe I'll still think of him as 'Angel,' if that's okay," Ketchum said, as he climbed into his truck; he glanced only briefly at the dead boy, quickly looking away.

"I'll *always* think of him as 'Angel'!" young Dan called.

To what extent a twelve-year-old is aware, or not, of the start of an adventure—or whether this misadventure had begun long before Danny Baciagalupo mistook Injun Jane for a bear—neither Ketchum nor the cook could say, though Danny seemed very "aware." Ketchum must have known that he might be seeing them for the last time, and he wanted to cast this phase of the gamble the cook was taking in a more positive light. "Danny!" Ketchum called. "I just want you to know that, on occasion, I more than once mistook Jane for a bear myself."

But Ketchum was not one for casting a positive light for long. "I don't suppose Jane was wearing the Chief Wahoo hat—when it happened," the logger said to Danny.

"No, she wasn't," the twelve-year-old told him.

"Damn it, Jane—oh, shit, Jane!" Ketchum cried. "Some fella in Cleveland told me it was a lucky hat," the river driver explained to the boy. "This fella said Chief Wahoo was some kind of spirit; he was supposed to look after Injuns."

"Maybe he's looking after Jane now," Danny said.

"Don't get religious on me, Danny—just remember the Injun as she was. Jane truly loved you," Ketchum told the twelve-year-old. "Just honor her memory—that's all you can do."

"I am missing you already, Ketchum!" the boy suddenly cried out.

"Oh, shit, Danny—you best get going, if you're going," the riverman said.

Then Ketchum started his truck and drove off on the haul road, toward Twisted River, leaving the cook and his son to their lengthier and less certain journey—to their next life, no less.

II.

BOSTON, 1967

—

NOM DE PLUME

I T WAS ALMOST EXACTLY AN UNLUCKY THIRTEEN YEARS SINCE Constable Carl had tripped over the body of the Indian dishwasher in his kitchen, and not even Ketchum could say for certain if the cowboy was suspicious of the cook and his son, who had disappeared that same night. To hear it from the most insightful gossips in that area of Coos County—that is to say, all along the upper Androscoggin— Injun Jane had disappeared with them.

According to Ketchum, it bothered Carl that people *thought* Jane had run off with the cook—more than the constable seemed troubled by the likelihood that he had murdered his companion with an unknown blunt instrument. (The murder weapon was never found.) And Carl must have *believed* he'd killed Jane; surely, he'd disposed of her body. Absolutely no one had seen her. (Her body hadn't turned up, either.)

Yet Ketchum continued to get insinuating inquiries from the cowboy, whenever their paths crossed. "Have you *still* not heard a word from Cookie?" Carl would never fail to ask Ketchum. "I thought you two were friends."

"Cookie never had a whole lot to *say*," Ketchum would point out repeatedly. "I'm not surprised I haven't heard from him."

"And what about the boy?" the cowboy occasionally asked.

"What *about* him? Danny's just a kid," Ketchum faithfully answered. "Kids don't write much, do they?"

But Daniel Baciagalupo wrote a lot—not only to Ketchum. From their earliest correspondence, the boy had told Ketchum that he wanted to become a writer.

"In that case, it would be best not to expose yourself to too much Catholic thinking," Ketchum had replied; his handwriting struck young Dan as curiously feminine. Danny had asked his dad if his mom had taught *her* handwriting to Ketchum—this in addition to the dancing, not to mention teaching the logger how to read.

All Dominic had said was: "I don't think so."

The puzzle of Ketchum's pretty penmanship remained unsolved, nor did Dominic appear to give his old friend's handwriting much thought—not to the degree young Dan did. For thirteen years, Danny Baciagalupo, the would-be writer, had corresponded with Ketchum more than his father had. The letters that passed between Ketchum and the cook were generally terse and to the point. Was Constable Carl looking for them? Dominic always wanted to know.

"You better assume so," was essentially all that Ketchum had conveyed to the cook, though lately Ketchum had had more to say. He'd sent Danny and Dominic the exact same letter; a further novelty was that the letter was *typed.* "Something's up," Ketchum had begun. "We should talk."

This was easier said than done—Ketchum had no phone. He was in the habit of calling both Dominic and young Dan collect from a public phone booth; these calls often ended abruptly, when Ketchum announced he was freezing his balls off. Granted, it was cold in northern New Hampshire—and in Maine, where Ketchum appeared to be spending more and more of his time—but, over the years, Ketchum's collect calls were almost invariably made in the cold-weather months. (Perhaps by choice—maybe Ketchum liked to keep things brief.)

Ketchum's very first *typed* letter to young Dan and his dad went on to say that the cowboy had let slip "an ominous insinuation." This was nothing new—Constable Carl *was* ominous, and he was forever *insinuating,* both Dominic and Danny already knew—but this time there'd been specific mention of Canada. In Carl's opinion, the Vietnam War was the reason relations between the United States and

Canada had soured. "I'm not gettin' shit in the area of cooperation from the Canadian authorities," was all the cowboy had said to Ketchum, who took this to mean that Carl was still making inquiries across the border. For thirteen years, the cop had believed that the cook and his son went to Toronto. If the cowboy *was* looking for them, he wasn't making inquiries in Boston—not yet. But now Ketchum had written that something was up.

KETCHUM'S LONG-AGO ADVICE TO DANNY—namely, if the boy wanted to be a writer, he shouldn't expose himself to too much *Catholic thinking*—may have been a misunderstanding on Ketchum's part. The Michelangelo School—Danny's new school in the North End—was a middle school, and a public one. The kids called the school the Mickey because the teachers were Irish, but there were no nuns among them. Ketchum must have assumed that the Michelangelo was a Catholic school. ("Don't let them brainwash you," he had written to Danny—the *them* word, though probably connected to *Catholic thinking*, was forever unclear.)

But young Dan was not struck (or even remotely influenced) by what was Catholic about the Mickey; what he had noticed about the North End, from the start, was what was *Italian* about it. The Michelangelo School Center had been a frequent site of the mass meetings where Italian immigrants gathered for Americanization. The overcrowded, cold-water tenement buildings, where so many of Danny's schoolmates at the Mickey lived, had originally been built for the Irish immigrants, who'd come to the North End before the Italians. But the Irish had moved—to Dorchester and Roxbury, or they were "Southies" now. Not all that long ago, there'd been a small number of Portuguese fishermen—maybe there still was a family or two, in the vicinity of Fleet Street—but in 1954, when Danny Baciagalupo and his dad arrived, the North End was virtually *all* Italian.

The cook and his son were not treated as strangers—not for long. Too many relatives wanted to take them in. There were countless Calogeros, ceaseless Saettas; cousins, and not-really-cousins, called the Baciagalupos "family." But Dominic and young Dan were unused to large families—not to mention extended ones. Hadn't being stand-offish helped them to survive in Coos County? The Italians didn't understand "standoffish"; either they gave you *un abbràccio* ("an embrace") or you were in for a fight.

The elders still gathered on street corners and in the parks, where one heard not only the dialects of Naples and Sicily, but of Abruzzi and Calabria as well. In the warm weather, both the young and the old lived outdoors, in the narrow streets. Many of these immigrants had come to America at the turn of the century—not only from Naples and Palermo, but also from innumerable southern Italian villages. The street life they had left behind had been re-created in the North End of Boston—in the open-air fruit and vegetable stands, the small bakeries and pastry shops, the meat markets, the pushcarts with fresh fish every Friday on Cross and Salem streets, the barbershops and shoeshine shops, the summertime feasts and festivals, and those curious religious societies whose street-level windows were painted with figures of patron saints. At least the saints were "curious" to Dominic and Daniel Baciagalupo, who (in thirteen years) had failed to find exactly what was Catholic *or* Italian within themselves.

Well, to be fair, perhaps Danny hadn't entirely "failed" with the Italian part—he was still *trying* to lose that northern New Hampshire coldness. Dominic, it seemed, would never lose it; he could cook Italian, but *being* one was another matter.

Despite Ketchum's likely misunderstanding that the Michelangelo was a Catholic school, it had long seemed unfair to Danny that his dad blamed Ketchum for giving young Dan the idea of going "away" to a boarding school. All Ketchum had said, in one of his earlier letters to Danny—in that positively *girlish* handwriting—was that the smartest "fella" he ever knew had attended a private school in the vicinity of the New Hampshire seacoast. Ketchum meant Exeter, not a long drive north of Boston—and in those days you could take the train, what Ketchum called "the good old Boston and Maine." From Boston's North Station, the Boston & Maine ran to northern New Hampshire, too. "Hell, I'm sure you can walk from the North End to North Station," Ketchum wrote to young Dan. "Even a fella with a limp could walk that far, I imagine." (The *fella* word was increasingly common in Ketchum's vocabulary—maybe from Six-Pack, though Jane had also used the word. Both Danny and his dad said it, too.)

The cook had not taken kindly to what he called Ketchum's "interference" in Daniel's secondary-school education, though young Dan had argued with his father on that point; illogically, Dominic *didn't* blame the boy's seventh- and eighth-grade English teacher at the Mickey, Mr. Leary, who'd had far more to do with Danny eventually going to Exeter than Ketchum had ever had.

For that matter, the cook should have blamed himself—for when Dominic learned that Exeter (in those days) was an all-boys' school, he was suddenly persuaded to allow his beloved Daniel to leave home in the fall of 1957, when the boy was only fifteen. Dominic would be heartbroken by how much he missed his son, but the cook could sleep at night, secure in the knowledge (or, as Ketchum would say, "the illusion") that his boy was safe from girls. Dominic let Daniel go to Exeter because he wanted to keep his son away from girls "for as long as possible," as he wrote to Ketchum.

"Well, that's *your* problem, Cookie," his old friend wrote back.

Indeed, it was. It hadn't been such an apparent problem when they'd first come to the North End—when young Dan was only twelve, and he appeared to take no notice of girls—but the cook saw how the girls already noticed his son. Among those cousins and not-really-cousins in the Saetta and Calogero clans, there would soon be some *kissing* cousins among them, the cook could easily imagine—not to mention all the other girls the boy would meet, for the North End was a *neighborhood*, where you met people like crazy. The cook and his twelve-year-old had never lived in a neighborhood before.

On that April Sunday in '54, father and son had had some difficulty *finding* the North End, and—even back then—it was easier to walk in the North End than it was to drive. (Both driving and parking the Pontiac Chieftain in that neighborhood had been a task—certainly not equal to transporting Injun Jane's body from the cookhouse to Constable Carl's kitchen, but a task nonetheless.) When they wove their way, on foot, to Hanover Street—passing once within view of the gold dome of the Sumner Tunnel Authority, which appeared to shine down on them like a new sun on a different planet—they saw two other restaurants (the Europeo and Mother Anna's) near Cross Street before they spotted Vicino di Napoli.

It was late afternoon—it had been a long drive from northern New Hampshire—but it was a warm, sunny day compared to the cold-morning light at Dead Woman Dam, where they'd left Angel's bluish body with Ketchum.

Here, the sidewalks teemed with families; people were actually talking—some of them *shouting*—to one another. (There—at Dead Woman Dam *and* in Twisted River, on the morning they left—they'd seen only the slain Indian dishwasher, the drowned boy, and Ketchum.) Here, from the moment they'd parked the Pontiac and started walking, Danny had been too excited to speak; he'd never seen such a place, except in the movies. (There were no movies to see in Twisted River; occasionally, Injun Jane had taken young Dan to Berlin to see one. The cook had said he would never go back to Berlin, "except in handcuffs.")

That April Sunday on Hanover Street, when they stopped walking outside Vicino di Napoli, Danny glanced at his father, who looked as if he'd been *dragged* to the North End in handcuffs—or else the cook felt doomed to be darkening the restaurant's door. Was a curse attached to the bearer of sad tidings? Dominic was wondering. What becomes of the man who brings bad news? One day, does something worse happen to him?

Young Dan could sense his dad's hesitation, but before either father or son could open the door, an old man opened it from inside the restaurant. "Come een-a, come een-a!" he said to them; he took Danny by the wrist, pulling him into the welcoming smell of the place. Dominic mutely followed them. At first glance, the cook could tell that the old man was not his despised father; the elderly gentleman looked nothing like Dominic, and he was too old to have been Gennaro Capodilupo.

He was, as he very much appeared to be, both the maître d' and owner of Vicino di Napoli, and he had no memory of having met Annunziata Saetta, though he'd known Nunzi (without knowing it) and he knew plenty of Saettas—nor did the old man realize, on this particular Sunday, that it was Dominic's father, Gennaro Capodilupo, whom he'd *fired;* Gennaro, that pig, had been an overly flirtatious busboy at Vicino di Napoli. (The restaurant was where Nunzi and Dominic's philandering dad had met!) But the aged owner and maître d' had *heard* of Annunziata Saetta; he'd heard of Rosina or "Rosie" Calogero, too. Scandals are the talk of neighborhoods, as young Dan and his dad would soon learn.

As for Vicino di Napoli, the dining room was not big, and the tables were small; there were red-and-white-checkered tablecloths, and two young women and a kid (about Angel's age) were arranging the place settings. There was a stainless-steel serving counter, beyond which Dominic could see a brick-lined pizza oven and an open kitchen, where two cooks were at work. Dominic was relieved that neither of the cooks was old enough to be his father.

"We're not quite ready to serve, but you can sit down—have-a something to drink, maybe," the old man said, smiling at Danny.

Dominic reached into an inside pocket of his jacket, where he felt Angelù Del Popolo's wallet—it was still damp. But he had barely taken the wallet out when the maître d' backed away from him. "Are you a *cop*?" the old man asked. The *cop* word got the attention of the two cooks Dominic had spotted in the kitchen; they came cautiously out from behind the serving counter. The kid and the two women setting the tables stopped working and stared at Dominic, too.

"Cops don't usually work with their children," one of the cooks said to the old man. This cook was covered with flour—not just his apron but his hands and bare forearms were a dusty white. (The pizza chef, probably, Dominic thought.)

"I'm not a cop, I'm a cook," Dominic told them. The two younger men and the old one laughed with relief; the two women and the kid went back to work. "But I have something to show you," Dominic said. The cook was fishing around in Angel's wallet. He couldn't make up his mind what to show them first—the Boston transit pass with Angelù Del Popolo's name and date of birth, or the photograph of the pretty but plump woman. He chose the streetcar and subway pass with the dead boy's actual name, but before Dominic could decide which of the men to show the pass to, the old man saw the photo in the open wallet and grabbed the wallet out of Dominic's hands.

"Carmella!" the maître d' cried.

"There was a *boy*," Dominic began, as the two cooks hovered over the picture under plastic in the wallet. "Maybe she's his mother."

Dominic got no further. The pizza chef hid his face in his hands, completely whitening both cheeks. "An-geh-LOO!" he wailed.

"No! No! No!" the old man sang, grabbing Dominic by both shoulders and shaking him.

The other cook (clearly the principal or first chef) held his heart, as if he'd been stabbed.

The pizza chef, as white-faced as a clown, lightly touched young Dan's hand with his flour-covered fingers. "What has happened to Angelù?" he asked the boy in such a gentle way that Dominic knew the man must have a child Daniel's age, or that he'd had one. Both cooks were about ten years older than Dominic.

"Angel drowned," Danny told them all.

"It was an accident," his father spoke up.

"Angelù was-a no fisherman!" the maître d' lamented.

"It was a logging accident," Dominic explained. "There was a river drive, and the boy slipped under the logs."

The young women and the kid about Angel's age had bolted—Danny hadn't seen them leave. (It would turn out that they had fled no farther than the kitchen.)

"Angelù used to work here, after school," the old man was saying, to Danny. "His mama, Carmella—she works here now."

The other cook had stepped closer, holding out his hand to Dominic. "Antonio Molinari," the principal chef said, somberly shaking Dominic's hand.

"Dominic Baciagalupo," the cook replied. "I was the cook in the logging camp. This is my son, Daniel."

"Giusé Polcari," the old man said to young Dan with downcast eyes. "Nobody calls me Giuseppe. I also like just plain Joe." Pointing to the pizza chef, old Polcari said: "This is my son Paul."

"You can call me Dan or Danny," the boy told them. "Only my dad calls me Daniel."

Tony Molinari had gone to the door of the restaurant; he was watching the passersby on Hanover Street. "Here she comes!" he said. "I see Carmella!" The two cooks fled into their kitchen, leaving the bewildered Baciagalupos with old Polcari.

"You gotta tell her—I no can-a do it," Giusé (or just plain Joe) was saying. "I introduce you," the maître d' said, pushing Dominic closer to the restaurant's door; Danny was holding his dad's hand. "Her husband drowned, too—they were a true-love story!" old Polcari was telling them. "But he was a fisherman—they drown a *lot*."

"Does Carmella have other children?" Dominic asked. Now the

three of them could see her—a full-figured woman with a beautiful face and jet-black hair. She was not yet forty; maybe she was Ketchum's age or a little older. Big breasts, big hips, big smile—only the smile was bigger than Injun Jane's, young Dan would notice.

"Angelù was her one and only," Giusé answered Dominic. Danny let go of his dad's hand, because old Polcari was trying to give him something. It was Angel's wallet, which felt wet and cold—the transit pass stuck out of it crookedly. Danny opened the wallet and put the pass back in place, just as Carmella Del Popolo walked in the door.

"Hey, Joe—am I late?" she asked the old man cheerfully.

"Not you, Carmella—you-a always on time!"

Maybe this was one of those moments that made Daniel Baciagalupo become a writer—his first and inevitably awkward attempt at *foreshadowing*. The boy suddenly saw into his father's future, if not so clearly into his own. Yes, Carmella was a little older and certainly plumper than the woman in the photo Angel had carried in his wallet, but in no one's estimation had she lost her looks. At twelve, Danny may have been too young to notice girls—or the girls themselves were too young to get his attention—but the boy already had an interest in *women*. (In Injun Jane, surely—in Six-Pack Pam, definitely.)

Carmella Del Popolo forcefully reminded young Dan of Jane. Her olive-brown skin was not unlike Jane's reddish-brown coloring; her slightly flattened nose and broad cheekbones were the same, as were her dark-brown eyes—like Jane's, Carmella's eyes were almost as black as her hair. And wouldn't Carmella soon have a *sadness* like Jane's inside her? Jane had lost a son, too, and Carmella—like Dominic Baciagalupo—had already lost an adored spouse.

It was not that Danny could see, at that moment, the slightest indication that his dad was attracted to Carmella, or she to him; it was rather that the boy knew one thing for certain. Angel's mother was the next woman his father would be attached to—for as long as the North End kept them safe from Constable Carl.

"You gotta sit down, Carmella," old Polcari was saying, as he retreated toward the kitchen, where the others were hiding. "This is that cook and his son, from up-a north—*you* know, Angelù's buddies."

The woman, who was already radiant, brightened even more. "You are *Dominic*?" she cried, pressing the cook's temples with her palms.

By the time she turned to Danny, which she did quickly, Giusé Polcari had disappeared with the other cowards. "And you must be *Danny!*" Carmella said with delight. She hugged him, hard—not as hard as Jane had hugged him, at times, but hard enough to make young Dan think of Jane again.

Dominic only now realized why there'd been so little money in Angel's wallet, and why they'd found next to nothing among the dead boy's few things. Angel had been sending his earnings to his mother. The boy had begged rides to the post office with Injun Jane; he'd told Jane that the postage to Canada was complicated, but he'd been buying money orders for his mom. He'd clearly been faithful about writing her, too, for she knew how the cook and his son had befriended her boy. All at once, she asked about Ketchum.

"Is Mr. Ketchum with you?" Carmella said to Danny, the boy's face held warmly in her hands. (Maybe this moment of speechlessness helped to make Daniel Baciagalupo become a writer. All those moments when you know you should speak, but you can't think of what to say—as a writer, you can never give enough attention to those moments.) But it was then that Carmella seemed to notice there was no one else in the dining room, and no one visible in the kitchen; the poor woman took this to mean that they intended to surprise her. Maybe her Angelù had made an unannounced visit to see her? Were the others hiding her dearest one in the kitchen, all of them managing to keep deathly quiet? "An-geh-LOO!" Carmella called. "Are you and Mr. Ketchum here, too? An-geh-LOO?"

Years later, when he'd grown accustomed to being a writer, Daniel Baciagalupo would think it was only natural, what happened then, back in the kitchen. They were not cowards; they were just people who loved Carmella Del Popolo, and they couldn't bear to see her hurt. But, at the time, young Dan had been shocked. It was Paul Polcari, the pizza chef, who started it. "An-geh-LOO!" he wailed.

"No! No! No!" his elderly father sang.

"Angelù, Angelù," Tony Molinari called, more softly.

The young women and the kid about Angel's age were crooning the dead boy's name, too. This chorus from the kitchen was not what Carmella had hoped to hear; they made such a dismal howl that the poor woman looked to Dominic for some explanation, seeing only the sorrow and panic in his face. Danny couldn't look at Angel's mom—it would have been like looking at Injun Jane a half-second before the skillet struck her.

A chair had been pulled out from the table nearest them—old Polcari's departing gesture, even before he had bid Carmella to sit down—and Carmella not so much sat in the chair as she collapsed into it, the olive-brown color abandoning her face. She had suddenly seen her son's wallet in young Dan's small hands, but when she'd reached and felt how wet and cold it was, she reeled backward and half fell into the chair. The cook was quick to hold her there, kneeling beside her with his arm around her shoulders, and Danny instinctively knelt at her feet.

She wore a silky black skirt and a pretty white blouse—the blouse would soon be spotted with her tears—and when she looked into Danny's dark eyes, she must have seen her son as he'd once looked to her, because she pulled the boy's head into her lap and held him there as if *he* were her lost Angelù.

"Not Angelù!" she cried.

One of the chefs in the kitchen now rhythmically beat on a pasta pot with a wooden spoon; like an echo, he called out, "Not Angelù!"

"I'm so sorry," young Dan heard his dad say.

"He drowned," the boy said, from Carmella's lap; he felt her hold his head more tightly there, and once again the immediate future appeared to him. For as long as he lived with his dad and Carmella Del Popolo, Danny Baciagalupo would be her surrogate Angelù. ("You can't blame the boy for wanting to go away to school," Ketchum would one day write his old friend. "Blame me, if you want to, Cookie, but don't blame Danny.")

"Not *drowned*!" Carmella screamed over the clamor from the kitchen. Danny couldn't hear what his father was whispering in the grieving woman's ear, but he could feel her body shaking with sobs, and he managed to slightly turn his head in her lap—enough to see the mourners come out of the kitchen. No pots and pans, or wooden spoons—they brought just themselves, their faces streaked with tears. (The face of Paul, the pizza chef, was streaked with flour, too.) But Daniel Baciagalupo already had an imagination; he didn't need to hear what his dad was saying in Carmella's ear. The *accident* word was surely part of it—it was a world of accidents, both the boy and his dad already knew.

"These are good people," old Polcari was saying; this sounded like a prayer. It was later that Danny realized Joe Polcari had not been praying; he'd been speaking to Carmella about the cook and his son "from up-a north." Indeed, the boy and his father were the ones who walked Carmella home. (She had needed to slump against them, at times close to swooning, but she was easy to support—she had to be more than a hundred pounds lighter than Jane, and Carmella was *alive*.)

But even before they left Vicino di Napoli that afternoon—when Danny's head was still held fast in the distraught mother's lap—Daniel Baciagalupo recognized another trick that writers know. It was something he already knew how to do, though he would not apply it to his method of writing for a few more years. All writers must know how to distance themselves, to *detach* themselves from this and that emotional moment, and Danny could do this—even at twelve. With his face secure in Carmella's warm grip, the boy simply *removed* himself from this tableau; from the vantage of the pizza oven, perhaps, or at least as far removed from the mourners as if he were standing, unseen, on the kitchen side of the serving counter, Danny saw how the staff of Vicino di Napoli had gathered around the seated Carmella and his kneeling dad.

Old Polcari stood behind Carmella, with one hand on the nape of her neck and the other hand on his heart. His son Paul, the pizza chef, stood in his aura of flour with his head bowed, but he had symmetrically positioned himself at Carmella's hip—perfectly opposite to the hip where Dominic knelt beside her. The two young women—waitresses, still learning their craft from Carmella—knelt on the floor directly behind young Dan, who, from the distance of the kitchen, could see himself on his knees with his head held in Carmella's lap. The other cook—the first or principal chef, Tony Molinari—stood slightly apart from the rest of them with his arm around the narrow shoulders of the kid about Angel's age. (He was the busboy, Danny would soon learn; being a busboy would be Danny's first job at Vicino di Napoli.)

But at this exact and sorrowful moment, Daniel Baciagalupo took in the whole tableau from afar. He would begin writing in the first-person voice, as many young writers do, and the tortured first sentence of one of his early novels would refer (in part) to this virtual Pietà on that April Sunday in Vicino di Napoli. In the novice writer's own words: "I became a member of a family I was unrelated to—long before I knew nearly enough about my own family, or the dilemma my father had faced in my early childhood."

"LOSE THE BACIAGALUPO," Ketchum had written to them both. "In case Carl comes looking for you—better change your last name, just to be safe." But Danny had refused. Daniel Baciagalupo was proud of his name—he even took some rebellious pride in what his father had told him of his name's history. All the years those West Dummer kids had called him a Guinea and a Wop made young Dan feel that he'd *earned* his name; now, in the North End (in an Italian neighborhood), why would he want to lose the Baciagalupo? Besides, the cowboy—*if* he came looking—would be trying to find a *Dominic* Baciagalupo, not a Daniel.

Dominic didn't feel the same way about his surname. To him, Baciagalupo had always been a made-up name. After all, Nunzi had named him—he'd been *her* Kiss of the Wolf, when in reality it would have made more sense for him to have been a Saetta, which he half was, or for his mother to have called him a Capodilupo, if only to shame his irresponsible father. ("That-a no-good fuck Gennaro," as old Joe Polcari would one day refer to the flirtatious, fired busboy who'd disappeared—only God knew where.)

And Dominic had lots of last names he could have chosen. Everyone in Annunziata's enormous family wanted him to become a Saetta, whereas Rosie's innumerable nieces and nephews—not to mention his late wife's more immediate family—wanted him to be a Calogero. Dominic didn't fall into that trap; he saw in an instant how insulted the Saettas would be if he changed his name to Calogero, and vice versa. Dominic's nickname at Vicino di Napoli, where he was almost immediately apprenticed to the first chef, Tony Molinari, and the pizza chef, Paul Polcari, would be Gambacorta—"Short Leg," an affectionate reference to his limp—which was soon shortened to Gamba (just plain "Leg"). But Dominic decided that, outside his life in the restaurant, neither Gambacorta nor Gamba was a suitable surname—not for a cook.

"What about Bonvino?" old Giusé Polcari would suggest. (The name meant "Good Wine," but Dominic didn't drink.)

Buonopane ("Good Bread") would be Tony Molinari's recommendation, whereas Paul Polcari, the pizza chef, was in favor of Capobianco ("White Head")—because Paul was usually white all over, due to the flour. But these names were too comical for a man with Dominic's sober disposition.

Their first night in the North End, Danny could have predicted what his dad would choose for a new last name. When father and son walked the widow Del Popolo to her brick tenement building on Charter Street—Carmella lived in a three-room walk-up near the old bathhouse and the Copps Hill Burying Ground; the only hot water was what she heated on her gas stove—young Dan could see far enough into his father's future to envision that Dominic Baciagalupo would (so to speak) quickly slip into the drowned fisherman's shoes. Although her late husband's shoes didn't actually fit Dominic, Carmella would one day be happy to discover that Dominic could wear the unfortunate fisherman's clothes—both men were slightly built, as was Danny, who would soon be wearing Angel's left-behind clothes. Naturally enough, father and son needed some city attire; people dressed differently in Boston than they did in Coos County. It would come as no surprise to Danny Baciagalupo, who *wouldn't* (at first) take Ketchum's advice and change his last name, that his dad became Dominic Del Popolo (after all, he was a cook "of the people")—if not on that first night in the North End.

In Carmella's kitchen was a bathtub bigger than the kitchen table, which already had the requisite three chairs. Two large pasta pots were full of water—forever hot, but not boiling, on the gas stove. Carmella did next to no cooking in her kitchen; she kept the water hot for her baths. For a woman who lived in a cold-water tenement, she was very clean and smelled wonderful; with Angel's help, she had managed to pay the gas bill. In the North End in those days, there weren't enough full-time jobs for young men of Angel's age. For young men who were strong enough, there were more full-time jobs to be found in the north country, in Maine and New Hampshire, but the work there could be dangerous—as poor Angel had discovered.

Danny and his dad sat at the small kitchen table with Carmella while she cried. The boy and his father told the sobbing mother stories about her drowned son; naturally, some of the stories led them to talk about Ketchum. When Carmella had temporarily cried herself out, the three of them, now hungry, went back to Vicino di Napoli, which served only pizza or quick pasta dishes on Sunday nights. (At that time, the Sunday midday meal was the main one for most Italians.) And the restaurant closed early on Sundays; the chefs prepared a dinner for the staff after the evening's customers had gone home. Most other nights, the restaurant was open for business fairly late, and the cooks fed themselves and the staff in the midafternoon, before dinner.

The aged owner and maître d' had been expecting the three of them to return; four of the small tables had been pushed together, and the place settings were already prepared for them. They ate and drank as at a wake, pausing only to cry—everyone but young Dan cried—and to toast the dead boy they'd all loved, though neither Danny nor his dad would touch a drop of wine. There were the oft-repeated "Hail Marys," many in unison, but there was no open coffin to view—no nightlong prayer vigil, either. Dominic had assured the mourners that Ketchum knew Angel was Italian; the river driver would have arranged "something Catholic" with the French Canadians. (Danny had given his dad a look, because they both knew that the woodsman would have done no such thing; Ketchum would have kept everything Catholic, *and* the French Canadians, as far away from Angel as possible.)

It was quite late when Tony Molinari asked Dominic where he and Danny were spending the night; surely they didn't want to drive all the way back to northern New Hampshire. As he'd told Ketchum, Dominic wasn't a gambler—not anymore—but he trusted the company he was in and (to his own and Danny's surprise) told them the truth. "We can't ever go back—we're on the run," Dominic said. It was Danny's turn to cry; the two young waitresses and Carmella were quick to comfort the boy.

"Say-a no more, Dominic—we don't-a need to know why, or who you're running from!" old Polcari cried. "You're-a safe with us."

"I'm not surprised, Dominic. Anyone can see you've been in a fight," Paul, the pizza chef, said, patting the cook's shoulder with a sympathetic, flour-covered hand. "That's one ugly-looking lip you've got—it's still bleeding, you know."

"Maybe you need stitches," Carmella said to the cook, with heart-felt concern. But Dominic dismissed her suggestion by shaking his head; he said nothing, but all of them could see the gratitude in the cook's shy smile. (Danny had given his dad another look, but the boy didn't doubt his father's reasoning for not explaining the circumstances of his lip injury; that father and son were on the run had nothing to do with the questionable character and aberrant behavior of Six-Pack Pam.)

"You can stay with me," Tony Molinari said to Dominic.

"They'll stay with *me*," Carmella told Molinari. "I have a spare room." Her offer was incontestable, because she meant Angel's room; even mentioning the room made Carmella commence to cry again. When Danny and his dad walked her back to the cold-water apartment on Charter Street, she told them to take the bigger bed—in her room. She would sleep in the single bed in her departed Angelù's room.

They would hear her crying herself to sleep—that is, she was trying to. When the crying had gone on for a long time, young Dan whispered to his father: "Maybe you should go to her."

"It wouldn't be appropriate, Daniel. It's her boy she misses—I think *you* should go to her."

Danny Baciagalupo went to Angel's room, where Carmella held out her arms to the boy, and he got into the narrow bed beside her. "An-geh-LOO," she whispered in his ear, until she finally fell asleep. Danny didn't dare get out of the bed, for fear he would wake her. He lay in her warm arms, smelling her good, clean smell, until he fell asleep, too. It had been a long, violent day for the twelve-year-old—counting the dramatic events of the previous night, of course—and young Dan must have been tired.

Wouldn't even the way he fell asleep somehow contribute to Danny becoming a writer? On the night of the same day he had killed the three-hundred-plus-pound Indian dishwasher, who happened to be his father's lover, Daniel Baciagalupo would find himself in the warm embrace of the widow Del Popolo, the voluptuous woman who would soon replace Injun Jane in his father's next life—his dad's sad but (for the time being) ongoing story. One day, the writer would recognize the near simultaneity of connected but dissimilar momentous events—these are what move a story forward—but at the moment Danny lost consciousness in Carmella's sweet-smelling arms, the exhausted boy had merely been thinking: How *coincidental* is this? (He was too young to know that, in any novel with a reasonable amount of forethought, there were no coincidences.)

Perhaps the photographs of his dead mother were sufficient to make young Dan become a writer; he had managed to take only some of them from the cookhouse in Twisted River, and he would miss the books he'd kept her photos pressed flat in—particularly, those novels that contained passages Rosie had underlined. The passages themselves were a way for the boy to better imagine his mother, together with the photos. Trying to remember those left-behind pictures was a way of imagining her, too.

Only a few of the photographs he brought to Boston were in color, and his dad had told Danny that the black-and-white photos were somehow "truer" to what Dominic called "the lethal blue of her eyes." (Why "lethal"? the would-be writer wondered. And how could those black-and-white pictures be "truer" to his mother's blue eyes than the standard color-by-Kodak photographs?)

Rosie's hair had been dark brown, almost black, but she was surprisingly fair-skinned, with sharply angular, fragile-looking features, which served to make her seem even more petite than she was. When young Dan would meet all the Calogeros—among them, his mother's younger sisters—he saw that two of these aunts were small and pretty, like his mom in the photographs, and the youngest of them (Filomena) also had blue eyes. But Danny would notice that, as much as he was drawn to stare at Filomena—she must have been about the same age as the boy's mother when Rosie had died (in her mid- to late twenties, in Danny's estimation)—his father was quick to say that Filomena's eyes were not the same blue as his mom's. (Not *lethal* enough, maybe, the boy could only guess.) Young Dan would notice, too, that his dad rarely spoke to Filomena; Dominic seemed almost rude to her, in that he purposely wouldn't look at her or ever comment on what she was wearing.

Was it *as a writer* that Daniel Baciagalupo began to notice such defining details? Had the boy already discerned what could be called a pattern-in-progress in his father's attraction, in turn, to Injun Jane and to Carmella Del Popolo—both of them big, dark-eyed women, as *opposite* to Rosie Calogero as the twelve-year-old could imagine? For if Rosie had truly been the love of his dad's life, might not Dominic *purposely* be denying himself contact with any woman remotely like her?

In fact, Ketchum would one day accuse the cook of maintaining an unnatural fidelity to Rosie by choosing to be with women who were grossly unlike her. Danny must have written Ketchum about Carmella, and the boy probably said she was big, because the cook had been careful—in his letters to his old friend—to make no mention of his new girlfriend's size, or the color of her eyes. Dominic would tell Ketchum next to nothing about Angel's mother and his developing relationship with her. Dominic wouldn't even respond to Ketchum's accusatory letter, but the cook was angry that the logger had criticized his apparent taste in women. At the time, Ketchum was still with Six-Pack Pam—speaking of women *opposite* to Cousin Rosie!

To remember Pam, Dominic needed only to look in a mirror, where the scar on his lower lip would remain very noticeable long after the night Six-Pack attacked him. It would be a surprise to Dominic Del Popolo, né Baciagalupo, that Ketchum and Six-Pack would last as a couple for very long. But they would be together for a few years longer than Dominic had been with Injun Jane—even a *little* longer than the cook would manage to stay with Carmella Del Popolo, Angel's large but lovely mom.

THE FIRST MORNING father and son would wake up in Boston, it was to the tantalizing sounds of Carmella having a bath in her small kitchen. Respecting the woman's privacy, Dominic and young Dan lay in their beds while Carmella performed her seductive-sounding ablutions; unbeknownst to them, she'd put a third and fourth pasta pot of water on the stove, and these would soon be coming to a near boil. "There's plenty of hot water!" she called to them. "Who wants the next bath?"

Because the cook had already been thinking about how he might fit, albeit snugly, in the same big bathtub with Carmella Del Popolo, Dominic somewhat insensitively suggested that he and Daniel could share a bath—he meant the same bathwater—an idea that the twelve-year-old found repellent. "No, Dad!" the boy called, from the narrow bed in Angel's room.

They could hear Carmella as the heavy woman rose dripping from the bathtub. "I know boys Danny's age—they need some *privacy*!" she said.

Yes, young Dan thought—not fully understanding that he would soon need *more* privacy from his dad and Carmella. After all, Danny was almost a teenager. While they wouldn't live together for long in the cold-water flat on Charter Street with the big bathtub in the small kitchen and an absurdly small water closet (with just a curtain, instead of a door)—the so-called WC contained only a toilet and a diminutive sink with a mirror above it—the apartment they would move into wasn't much larger, or half private enough for a *teenage* Daniel Baciagalupo, though it did have hot water. It would be another walk-up on what would one day be called Wesley Place—an alley that ran alongside the Caffè Vittoria—and in addition to having two bedrooms, there was a full-size bathroom with both a tub and a shower (and an actual door), and the kitchen was large enough for a table with six chairs.

Still, the bedrooms were next to each other; in the North End, there was nothing they could afford that was at all comparable to the spaciousness of the second floor of the cookhouse in Twisted River. And Danny was already too old to overhear his father and Carmella trying to keep their lovemaking quiet—certainly after the boy, with his excitable imagination, had heard and seen his dad and Injun Jane *doing it*.

The cook and Carmella, with young Dan increasingly aware of himself as the *surrogate* Angel, had an acceptable living arrangement, but it was not one that would last. It would soon be time for the teenager to create a little distance between himself and his dad—and, as he grew older, Danny was made more uncomfortable by another problem.

If he had once suffered from a presexual state of arousal, first inspired by Jane and then by Six-Pack Pam, the teenager could find no relief from his deepening desire for Carmella Del Popolo—his dad's "Injun replacement," as Ketchum called her. Danny's attraction to Carmella was a more troubling problem than the privacy issues.

"You need to get away," Ketchum would write to young Dan, although the boy truly liked his life in the North End. In fact, he *loved* it, especially in comparison to the life he'd had in Twisted River—at the Paris Manufacturing Company School, in particular.

The Michelangelo School thought little of the education Danny Baciagalupo had received among those Phillips Brook bums—those West Dummer dolts, as Ketchum called them. The authorities at the Mickey made Danny repeat a grade; he was a year older than most of his classmates. By seventh grade, when the would-be writer first mentioned Ketchum's Exeter idea to his English teacher, Mr. Leary, the Irishman already considered Danny Baciagalupo to be among his very best students. By the time the boy was taking eighth-grade English, Danny was far and away Mr. Leary's teacher's pet.

Several of Mr. Leary's former pupils had gone on to attend Boston Latin. A few had attended Roxbury Latin—in the old Irishman's opinion, a somewhat snooty Anglo school. Two boys Mr. Leary had taught had gone to Milton, and one to Andover, but no one from Mr. Leary's English classes had ever gone to Exeter; it was farther afield from Boston than those other good schools, and Mr. Leary knew it was a *very* good school. Might it have been a feather in Mr. Leary's cap if Daniel Baciagalupo were accepted at Exeter?

Mr. Leary felt bedeviled by most of the other seventh- and eighth-grade boys at the Mickey. It was notable that Danny didn't join in the teasing his teacher took, because teasing—and other, harsher forms of harassment—reminded the boy of his Paris school experience.

Mr. Leary was red-faced from drink; he had a potato-shaped nose, the veritable image of the alleged staple of his countrymen's diet. Wild white tufts of hair, like fur, stuck out above his ears, but Mr. Leary was otherwise bald—with a pronounced dent in the top of his head. He looked like a partially defeathered owl. "As a child," Mr. Leary told all his students, "I was hit on the head by an unabridged dictionary, which doubtless gave me my abundant love of words."

Both the seventh- and eighth-grade boys called him "O," for Mr. Leary had dropped the *O'* from his name. These badly behaved boys wrote no end of *O*'s on the blackboard when Mr. Leary was out of the classroom. They called to him, "O!"—but only when his back was turned.

Why this tormented the former Mr. O'Leary so, Danny didn't understand, nor did Daniel Baciagalupo think it was any big deal for his teacher to have dropped the *O'* from his name. (Just look at Angel Pope, and everything *he* had dropped. Did the Italian kids think that only the Irish occasionally tried to make less of their ethnicity?)

But Mr. Leary's foremost reason for finding Daniel Baciagalupo such an excellent student was that the boy loved to write, and he wrote and wrote. In the seventh and eighth grade at the Mickey, Mr. Leary had never seen anything quite like it. The boy seemed *possessed*—or at least *obsessed*.

True, it would not infrequently disturb Mr. Leary to read what young Dan would write about, but his stories—many of them far-fetched, most of them violent, and all of them with an undue amount of sexual content, totally inappropriate for a teenager—were invariably well-written and clear. The kid simply had a gift for storytelling; Mr. Leary just wanted to help him master the grammar, and all the rest of the *mechanics* of writing. At Exeter, Mr. Leary had heard, they were sticklers for grammar. They made a nuts-and-bolts business out of writing there—you had to write every day, about something.

When Mr. Leary wrote to the admissions people at Exeter, he made no mention of the subject matter of young Dan's creative writing. Exeter was not much interested in so-called creative writing, anyway; the essay, Mr. Leary assumed, was all-important there. And the Michelangelo School, where Daniel Baciagalupo was such an exceptional student, was in a neighborhood of Italo-Americans. (Mr. Leary was careful not to use the *immigrant* word, though this was very much his meaning.) These people were prone to laziness and exaggeration, Mr. Leary wanted Exeter to know. The Baciagalupo boy was "unlike the rest."

To listen to most of these Italians, Mr. Leary suggested, you would get the impression that they had *all* lived with rats (and other appalling conditions) in the steerage class of the ships that brought them to America—all of them orphans, or otherwise landing on the docks alone, and with no more than a few miserable lira to their names. And while many of the teenage girls were beautiful, they would all become hopelessly fat as women; this was because of the pasta and their unrestrained appetites. The latter, Mr. Leary suspected, were not limited to overeating. Truth be told, these Italians were not as industrious as those hardworking *earlier* immigrants—the Irish—and while Mr. Leary didn't exactly *say* these things to the admissions people at Exeter, he imparted no small amount of his prejudices while singing in praise of Daniel Baciagalupo's talents and character, not to mention citing the "difficulties" the boy had faced and overcome "at home."

There was a single parent—"a rather uncommunicative cook," as Mr. Leary described him. This cook lived with a woman Mr. Leary would describe as "a widow who has suffered multiple tragedies"—to wit, if ever there were a worthy candidate for the enviable position of a full-scholarship student at Exeter, Daniel Baciagalupo was his name! Cleverly, Mr. Leary was not only aware of his prejudices; he wanted to be sure that Exeter was aware of his prejudices, too. He intended to make the North End of Boston sound like a place Danny needed to be *rescued* from. Mr. Leary wanted someone from Exeter to come see the Michelangelo School—even if this meant seeing how disrespected Mr. Leary was there. For surely if a scholarship person met Daniel Baciagalupo in the company of those badly behaved boys at the Mickey—and, just as important, saw the would-be writer in the context of that noisy neighborhood restaurant where both the boy's father and the tragic widow worked—well, it would simply be obvious how Danny Baciagalupo stood out. The boy *did* stand out, but young Dan would have stood out anywhere—not only in the North End—though Mr. Leary didn't say this. As it would turn out, he said enough.

His letter had its desired effect. "Get a load of this guy!" (meaning Mr. Leary with his abundant prejudices) the first person in the admissions office at Exeter must have said. The letter was passed on to another reader, and to another; a lot of people at Exeter probably read that letter, among them the very "scholarship person" Mr. Leary had in mind all along.

And that person doubtless said, "I have to see this"—meaning not only the Mickey, and Mr. Leary, but also the underprivileged circumstances of Daniel Baciagalupo's Italo-American life.

There was much more that Mr. Leary *didn't* say. What need was there for Exeter to know about the boy's outrageous imagination? What had happened to the father in that one story? He'd been lamed (forever crippled) by a *bear*—the bear had eaten one of the father's feet—but the maimed man had somehow managed to beat back the bear with a frying pan! This same maimed man lost his wife in a square-dancing accident. There'd been a square dance outdoors, on a dock; the dock had collapsed, and all the dancers were drowned. The man who'd lost his foot to the bear had been spared because he couldn't dance! (He was just watching from afar, if Mr. Leary remembered the story correctly—it was all preposterous stuff, but well-written, very well-written.)

There was even a friend of this same fictional family who'd been brain-damaged by a corrupt cop. The victim was an unlikely lumberjack—"unlikely," in Mr. Leary's opinion, because the lumberjack was described as a great reader. Even more improbable, he'd been so badly beaten by the cop that he'd forgotten how to read! And the *women* in Daniel Baciagalupo's stories—Lord have mercy, thought Mr. Leary.

There was a native woman from a local Indian tribe—the story about the maimed man was set in the boondocks of northern New Hampshire and featured a dance hall where there was no dancing. (Come on, Mr. Leary had thought when he'd read the story—what would be the point of *that*?) But the story had been well-written, as always, and the Indian woman weighed three or four hundred pounds, and her hair hung below her waist; this caused a retarded boy (the child of the father who'd been attacked by the bear) to mistake the Indian for *another* bear! The unfortunate retard actually thought that the *same* bear had returned to eat the rest of his dad, when in truth the Indian woman was having sex with the cripple—in what Mr. Leary could only imagine must have been the *superior* position.

But when the teacher had said this to Danny ("I gather the Indian woman was in the—ah, well—*superior* position"), the Baciagalupo boy looked uncomprehending. The young writer had not understood.

"No, she was just on top," Danny had answered Mr. Leary. The teacher had smiled adoringly. In Mr. Leary's eyes, Daniel Baciagalupo was a genius-in-progress; the wonder boy could do no wrong.

Yet what had happened to the overweight Indian woman was horrendous. The retarded boy had *killed* her; he'd hit her with the exact same frying pan his father had used as a weapon against the bear! Young Baciagalupo's powers of description were perhaps at their best when he rendered the reposeful posture of the naked, dead Indian woman. The thoughtful father had quickly covered her exposed crotch with a pillow—perhaps to spare his damaged son any further misunderstanding. But the retarded boy had already seen more than his limited intelligence could stand. For years, he would be haunted by the sight of the slain woman's huge breasts—how they had lifelessly slumped into the hollows of her armpits. How did the kid keep coming up with *details* like those? Mr. Leary would wonder. (Mr. Leary would be haunted by the naked, dead Indian woman, too.)

But why say anything to Exeter about those questionable elements of the boy's imagination, which had even upset Mr. Leary? Those extreme details were mere indulgences the more mature writer would one day outgrow. For example, the woman who wore a man's wool-flannel shirt, without a bra; she had *raped* the retarded boy, after she'd consumed an entire six-pack of beer! Why did Exeter need to know about her? (Mr. Leary wished he could forget her.) Or the woman in one of the cold-water tenement buildings on Charter Street, near the bathhouse and the Copps Hill Burying Ground—as Mr. Leary remembered her, she had pretty big breasts, too. This was another Baciagalupo story, and the woman on Charter Street was referred to as the stepmother of the retarded boy—the same boy from that earlier story, but he was no longer *called* retarded. (In the new story, the boy was described as "just plain damaged.")

The father with the eaten foot had confusing dreams—both of the bear *and* of the slain Indian woman. Given the voluptuousness of the damaged boy's stepmother, Mr. Leary suspected the father of having a preternatural attraction to overweight women; naturally, it was entirely possible that the young *writer* found big women alluring. (Mr. Leary was beginning to feel the unwelcome allure of such women himself.)

And the stepmother was Italian, thus inviting Mr. Leary's prejudices to come into play; he looked for signs of laziness and exaggeration in the woman, finding (to his enormous satisfaction) a perfect example of the aforementioned "unrestrained appetites" Mr. Leary had long held Italian women accountable for. The woman overbathed herself.

She was so eccentrically devoted to her baths that an oversize bathtub was the centerpiece of the cold-water flat's undersize kitchen, where four pasta pots were constantly simmering—her bathwater was heated on the gas stove. The placement of the bathtub created quite a privacy problem for the indulgent woman's damaged stepson, who had bored a hole in his bedroom door, which opened into the kitchen.

What further damage was done to the boy by spying on his naked stepmother—well, Mr. Leary could only imagine! And, to talk about young Baciagalupo's inventiveness with *details,* when the voluptuary shaved her armpits, she left a small, spade-shaped patch of hair (in one armpit) purposely unshaven, "like an elf's meticulously trimmed goatee," young Dan had written.

"In *which* armpit?" Mr. Leary had asked the beginning writer.

"The left one," Danny answered, without a moment's hesitation.

"Why the left one, and not the right?" the English teacher asked.

The Baciagalupo boy looked thoughtful, as if he were trying to remember a rather complicated sequence of events. "She's right-handed," Danny answered. "She's not as skillful with the razor when she's shaving with her left hand. She shaves her right armpit with her left hand," he explained to his teacher.

"Those are good details, too," Mr. Leary told him. "I think you should put those details in the story."

"Okay, I will," young Dan said; he liked Mr. Leary, and did his best to protect his English teacher from the torments of the other boys.

The other boys didn't bother Danny. Sure, there were bullies at the Mickey, but they weren't as tough as those Paris Manufacturing Company thugs. If some bully in the North End gave Danny Baciagalupo any trouble, young Dan just told his older cousins. The bully would get the shit kicked out of him by a Calogero or a Saetta; the older cousins could have kicked the shit out of those West Dummer dolts, too.

Danny didn't show his writing to anyone but Mr. Leary. Of course the boy wrote rather long letters to Ketchum, but those letters weren't fiction; no one in his right mind would make up a story and try to pass it off on Ketchum. Besides, it was for pouring out his heart that young Dan needed Ketchum. Many of the letters to Ketchum began, "You know how much I love my dad, I really do, but . . ." and so on.

Like father, like son: The cook had kept things from his son, and Danny (in grades seven and eight, especially) was of an age to keep things back. He would be thirteen when he began grade seven and first met Mr. Leary; the Baciagalupo boy would be fifteen when he graduated from eighth grade. He was both fourteen *and* fifteen when he showed his English teacher the stories he made up with ever-increasing compulsion.

Despite Mr. Leary's misgivings about the subject matter—meaning the sexual content, chiefly—the wise old owl of an Irishman never said an unpraiseworthy word to his favorite pupil. The Baciagalupo boy was going to be a writer; in Mr. Leary's mind, there was no doubt about it.

The English teacher kept his fingers crossed about Exeter; if the boy was accepted, Mr. Leary hoped the school would be so rigorous that it might save young Baciagalupo from the more unsavory aspects of his imagination. At Exeter, maybe the *mechanics* of writing would be so thoroughly demanding and time-consuming that Danny would become a more *intellectual* writer. (Meaning what, exactly? Not quite such a *creative* one?)

Mr. Leary himself was not entirely sure what he meant by the mystifying thought that becoming a more intellectual writer might make Danny a less creative one—if that *was* what Mr. Leary thought—but the teacher's intentions were good. Mr. Leary wanted all the best for the Baciagalupo boy, and while he would never criticize a word young Dan had written, the old English teacher ventured out on a limb in making a bold suggestion. (Well, it wasn't *that* bold a suggestion; it merely seemed bold to Mr. Leary.) This happened to be in that almost-mud-season time of Danny's eighth-grade year—in March 1957, when Danny had just turned fifteen, and the boy and his teacher were waiting to hear from Exeter. That Mr. Leary made the afore-mentioned "bold suggestion" would (years later) prompt Daniel Baci-agalupo to write his own version of Ketchum's periodic claim.

"All the shit seems to happen in mud season!" Ketchum regularly complained, in seeming refutation of the fact that the cook and his beloved cousin Rosie were married in mud season, and young Dan had been born just before it. (Of course, there was no actual mud sea-son in Boston.)

"Danny?" Mr. Leary asked tentatively—almost as if he weren't sure of the boy's name. "Down the road, as a writer, you might want to consider a nom de plume."

"A *what*?" the fifteen-year-old asked.

"A pen name. Some writers choose their own names, instead of publishing under their given names. It's called a *nom de plume* in French," the boy's teacher explained. Mr. Leary felt his heart rise to his throat, because young Baciagalupo suddenly looked as if he'd been slapped.

"You mean lose the Baciagalupo," Danny said.

"It's just that there are easier names to say, and remember," Mr. Leary told his favorite pupil. "I thought that, since your father changed his name—and the widow Del Popolo hasn't become a Baci-agalupo, has she?—well, I merely imagined that you might not be so terribly *attached* to the Baciagalupo name yourself."

"I'm *very* attached to it," young Dan said.

"Yes, I can see that—then by all means you must hang on to that name!" Mr. Leary said with genuine enthusiasm. (He felt awful; he'd not meant to insult the boy.)

"I think Daniel Baciagalupo is a good name for a writer," the de-termined fifteen-year-old told his teacher. "If I write good books, won't readers go to the trouble of remembering my name?"

"Of course they will, Danny!" Mr. Leary cried. "I'm sorry about the nom-de-plume business—it was truly insensitive of me."

"That's okay—I know you're just trying to help me," the boy told him.

"We should be hearing some word from Exeter any day now," Mr. Leary said anxiously; he was desperate to change the subject from the pen-name faux pas.

"I hope so," Danny Baciagalupo said seriously. A more thoughtful expression had returned to young Dan's face; he'd stopped scowling.

Mr. Leary, who was agitated that he'd overstepped his bounds, knew that the boy went to work at Vicino di Napoli almost every afternoon after school; the well-meaning English teacher let Danny go on his way.

As he often did after school, Mr. Leary did some errands in the neighborhood. He still lived in the area of Northeastern University, where he'd gone to graduate school and met his wife; he took the subway to the Haymarket station every morning, and he took it home again, but he did his shopping (what little there was of it) in the North End. He'd taught at the Michelangelo for so long, virtually everyone in the neighborhood knew him; he'd taught either them or their children. Simply because they teased him—after all, he *was* Irish—didn't mean that they didn't *like* Mr. Leary, whose eccentricities amused them.

The afternoon of his ill-conceived "bold suggestion," Mr. Leary paused in the garden at St. Leonard Church, once again fretting at the absence of an *'s*—obviously, to the old English teacher, the church should have been named St. Leonard's. Mr. Leary did his confessing at St. Stephen's, which had a proper *'s*. He simply liked St. Stephen's better; it was more like a Catholic church anywhere. St. Leonard was somehow more *Italian*—even that familiar prayer in the garden of the church was translated into Italian. *"Ora sono qui. Preghiamo insieme. Dio ti aiuta."* ("Now I'm here. Let's pray together. God will help you.")

Mr. Leary prayed that God would help Daniel Baciagalupo get a full scholarship to Exeter. And there was another thing he'd never liked about St. Leonard, Mr. Leary thought, as he was leaving the garden. He hadn't gone inside the church; there was a plaster saint inside, San Peregrine, with his right leg bandaged. Mr. Leary found the statue vulgar.

And there was something else he preferred about St. Stephen's, the old Irishman was musing—how the church was across from the Prado, where the old men gathered to play checkers in the good weather. Mr. Leary occasionally stopped to play checkers with them. A few of those old guys were really good, but the ones who hadn't learned English irritated Mr. Leary; not learning English was either not American enough or too Italian to suit him.

A former pupil (a fireman now) called to the old teacher outside the fire station on the corner of Hanover and Charter streets, and Mr. Leary stopped to chat with the robust fellow. In no particular order, Mr. Leary then refilled a prescription at Barone's Pharmacy; in the same location, he paused at Tosti's, the record store, where he occasionally bought a new album. The one Italian "indulgence" that Mr. Leary loved was opera—well, to be fair, he also loved the way they served the espresso at the Caffè Vittoria, *and* the Sicilian meat loaf Danny Baciagalupo's dad made at Vicino di Napoli.

Mr. Leary made a small purchase at the Modern, a pastry shop on Hanover. He bought some cannoli to take home for his breakfast— the pastry cylinders were filled with sweetened ricotta cheese, nuts, and candied fruits. Mr. Leary had to confess to loving *those* Italian indulgences, too.

He didn't like to look up Hanover Street in the direction of Scollay Square, though he walked in that direction to take the subway home from the Haymarket station every school day. South of the Haymarket was the Casino Theatre, and in the near vicinity of the Scollay Square subway station was the Old Howard. At both establishments, Mr. Leary tried to see the new striptease shows on the nights they opened—before the censors saw the shows and inevitably "trimmed" them. His regular attendance at these striptease joints made Mr. Leary feel ashamed, although his wife had died long ago. His wife probably wouldn't have cared that he went to see the strippers—or she would have minded this indulgence less than if he'd remarried, which he hadn't. Yet Mr. Leary had seen a few of these strippers perform so many times, in a way he occasionally felt that he *was* married to them. He had memorized the mole (if it was a mole) on Peaches, the so-called Queen of Shake. Lois Dufee—whose name, Mr. Leary believed, was incorrectly spelled—was six feet four and had peroxide-blond hair. Sally Rand danced with balloons, and there was another dancer who used feathers. Precisely what he saw these and other strippers *do* was the usual subject of what he confessed at St. Stephen's—that and the repeated acknowledgment that he didn't miss his wife, not anymore. He'd once missed her, but—like his wife herself—the missing-her part had left him.

It was a relatively new habit of Mr. Leary's—since he had written to Exeter—that, before he finally left the North End every school day afternoon, he would stop back at the Michelangelo and see if there was anything in his mailbox. He was thinking to himself that he had a new confession to make at St. Stephen's—for it weighed on him like a sin that he'd proposed a nom de plume to the Baciagalupo boy— when he sorted through the mail, which had arrived late in the day. Yet what a good name for a writer Daniel *Leary* would have been! the old Irishman was thinking. Then he saw the pearl-gray envelope with the crimson lettering, and what very classy lettering it was!

Phillips Exeter Academy

Do you finally believe? Mr. Leary thought to himself. No prayer in a churchyard was ever wasted—even in that ultra-Italian garden at St. Leonard. "God will help you—*Dio ti aiuta,*" the crafty old Irishman said aloud, in English *and* Italian (just to be on the safe side, before he opened the envelope and read the letter from the scholarship person at Exeter).

Mr. Carlisle was coming to Boston. He wanted to visit the Michelangelo School and meet Mr. Leary. Mr. Carlisle very much looked forward to meeting Daniel Baciagalupo—and the boy's father, the cook, and the boy's stepmother, too. Mr. Leary realized that he may have overstepped his bounds, once more, by referring to the widow Del Popolo as Danny's "stepmother"; to the English teacher's knowledge, the cook and the curvy waitress weren't married.

Naturally, Mr. Leary had overstepped himself in a few other areas as well. While young Dan had told his English teacher that his dad was reluctant to let the boy leave home and go away to school—and Carmella Del Popolo had actually cried at the very idea—Mr. Leary had already submitted his favorite student's transcripts to the venerable academy. He'd even persuaded a couple of other teachers at the Mickey to write recommendations for young Baciagalupo. Mr. Leary had virtually applied for admission on behalf of Daniel Baciagalupo—

all without telling the boy's father what he was up to! Now, in Mr. Carlisle's letter, there were references to the family's need to submit financial statements—something the rather remote cook might be opposed to, it occurred to Mr. Leary, who was hoping he had not overstepped his bounds (again) to the degree that he'd utterly failed with the pen-name plan. The nom de plume had been an embarrassing mistake.

Oh, my, Mr. Leary was thinking—time to pray more! But he courageously took the Exeter letter in hand, together with his little parcel of pastries from the Modern, and he once more sallied forth on Hanover Street—this time not to the garden in the churchyard at St. Leonard but to Vicino di Napoli, where he knew he would find the Baciagalupo boy together with the "rather remote" cook, as Mr. Leary thought of Danny's dad, and that overweight woman the widow Del Popolo.

The voluptuous waitress had once come to a teacher's conference with Mr. Leary; her late son, Angelù, had been an open and friendly presence in Mr. Leary's seventh-grade English class. Angelù had never been among those badly behaved boys who tormented Mr. Leary for dropping the *O'* from his given name. The Del Popolo boy had been quite a good reader, too—though he was easily distracted, as Mr. Leary had told his mother. Then Angelù had dropped out of school, and gone to work in that godforsaken north country, where the lad had drowned like his father before him. (Quite a convincing argument for staying in school, if Mr. Leary had ever heard one!)

But ever since that teacher's conference with the widow Del Popolo, Mr. Leary had suffered the occasional dreams about her; probably every man who'd met that woman suffered those dreams, the old English teacher imagined. Nevertheless, her name had more than once come up in his confessions at St. Stephen's. (If Carmella Del Popolo had ever been a stripper at either the Casino Theatre or the Old Howard, they would have packed the place every night!)

With the Exeter letter returned to its envelope, and in his haste to beat a path to the little Italian restaurant, which had become (Mr. Leary knew) one of the most popular eating places in the North End, the owlish Irishman failed to notice the giant white *O'* that one of those badly behaved boys at the Mickey had rubbed with chalk onto the back of the teacher's navy-blue trench coat. Mr. Leary had not worn the trench coat on his earlier errands in the neighborhood, but now he donned the coat, unseeing; thus he went on his eager but anxious way, marked from behind with a chalk-white *O'* as identifiable (from a block away) as a bull's-eye.

WHEN IT WAS MUD SEASON in Coos County in 1967, Daniel Baciagalupo, the writer, was living in Iowa City, Iowa; they had a real spring in Iowa, no mud seasons there. But Danny, who was twenty-five with a two-year-old son—his wife had just left him—was very much in a mud-season frame of mind. He was also writing, at this moment, and trying to remember precisely what they had been talking about in Vicino di Napoli when Mr. Leary, with the letter from Exeter in his jacket, knocked fervently on the door, which was locked. (The staff was finishing its midafternoon meal.)

"It's the Irishman! Let him een-a!" cried old Polcari.

One of the young waitresses opened the door for Mr. Leary—Danny's cousin Elena Calogero. She was in her late teens or early twenties, as was the other young waitress assisting Carmella, Teresa DiMattia. Carmella's maiden name had been DiMattia. As the widow Del Popolo was fond of saying, she was a "twice-displaced Neapolitan"—the first time because she'd come as a child with her family to the North End from Sicily (her grandparents had long before moved from the vicinity of Naples), and the second time because she'd married a Sicilian.

By her own strange logic, Carmella had gone on *displacing* herself, the writer Daniel Baciagalupo thought, because *Angelù* was Sicilian (for "Angelo") and Carmella had attached herself to Dominic. But in the chapter Danny was writing, which he'd titled "Going Away to School," he was adrift and had lost his focus.

Too much of the crucial moment in the chapter—when the father is fighting back tears at the same time he is giving his son permission to go off to boarding school—was in the point of view of the boy's well-meaning but meddlesome English teacher.

"Hi, Mike!" Tony Molinari had said that afternoon in the restaurant. (Or had Paul Polcari, the pizza chef, greeted Mr. Leary first? Old Joe Polcari, who used to play checkers with Mr. Leary in the Prado, always addressed the English teacher as Michael—as my dad did, Danny Baciagalupo remembered.)

It was a bad night for Danny to try to write—perhaps this scene, especially. The wife (of three years) who'd just left him had always said she wouldn't stay, but he hadn't believed her—he hadn't *wanted* to believe her, as Ketchum had pointed out. Young Dan had met Katie Callahan when he was still an undergraduate at the University of New Hampshire; he'd been a junior when Katie was a senior, but they'd both been models in the life-drawing classes.

When she told him she was leaving, Katie said: "I still believe in you, as a writer, but the only stuff we ever had in common doesn't travel very far."

"What stuff is that?" he'd asked her.

"We're completely at ease being naked in front of strangers and total fuckheads," she'd told him. Maybe that's part of what being a writer entails, Danny Baciagalupo found himself thinking on that rainy spring night in Iowa City. He wrote mostly at night, when little Joe was sleeping. Absolutely everyone, but not Katie, called the two-year-old Joe. (Like the maître d' he was named after, the boy was never a Joseph; old Polcari had liked Giusé, or just plain Joe.)

As for being naked in front of strangers and total fuckheads, Katie meant this more literally—in her own case. His senior year in Durham, when Katie had been pregnant with Joe, she'd still modeled for the life-drawing classes and had slept with one of the art students. Now, in Iowa City—when Danny was about to graduate from the Writers' Workshop at the University of Iowa, with an M.F.A. in creative writing—Katie was still modeling for life-drawing classes, but this time she was sleeping with one of the faculty.

Yet that wasn't why she was moving on, she'd told her husband. She had proposed marrying Danny, and having a baby, before his graduation from college. "You don't want to go to Vietnam, do you?" she'd asked him.

Actually, Danny had thought (at the time) that he *did* want to go—not because he didn't oppose the war politically, though he would never be as political as Katie. (Ketchum called her a "fucking anarchist.") It was *as a writer* that Daniel Baciagalupo thought he should go to Vietnam; he believed he should see a war and know what one was like. Both his dad *and* Ketchum had told him his thinking was full of shit on that subject.

"I didn't let you go away from me, to goddamn Exeter, to let you die in a dumb war!" Dominic had cried.

Ketchum had threatened to come find Danny and cut a few fingers off his right hand. "Or your whole fucking hand!" Ketchum had thundered—freezing his balls off in a phone booth somewhere.

Both men had promised young Dan's mother that they would never let her boy go to war. Ketchum said he would use his Browning knife on Danny's right hand, or on just the fingers; the knife had a foot-long blade, and Ketchum kept it very sharp. "Or I'll put a deer slug in my twelve-gauge and shoot you point-blank in one of your knees!"

Daniel Baciagalupo would accept Katie Callahan's suggestion instead. "Go on, knock me up," Katie had said. "I'll marry you and have your kid. Just don't expect me to stay around for long—I'm not anybody's wife, and I'm not mother material, but I know how to have a baby. It's for a good cause—keeping one more body out of this fucking war. And you say you want to be a *writer*! Well, you have to live to do that, don't you? Fuckhead!"

It was never the case that she deceived him; he'd known from the first what she was like. They met when they were undressing together for a life-drawing class. "What's your name?" she'd asked him. "And what do you want to be when you grow up?"

"I'm going to be a writer," Danny said, even before he told her his name.

"If you think you are capable of living without writing, do not write," Katie Callahan said.

"What did you say?" he asked her.

"*Rilke* said that, fuckhead. If you want to be a fucking writer, you ought to read him," she said.

Now she was leaving him because she'd met (in her words) "another stupid boy who thinks he should go to Vietnam—just to fucking see it!" Katie was going to get this other boy to knock her up. Then, one day, she would move on again—"until this fucking war is over."

She would eventually run out of time; mathematically speaking, there were a limited number of would-be soldiers she could save from the war in this fashion. They called young dads like Danny Baciagalupo "Kennedy fathers"; in March 1963, President Kennedy had issued an executive order expanding paternity deferment. It would exist only for a little while—that having a child was a workable deferment from the draft—but it had served for Daniel Baciagalupo, the writer. He'd gone from 2-S (the student deferment) to 3-A—fathers maintaining a bona fide relationship with a child were deferred. Having a kid could get you out of the war; eventually, the fuckers would close that door, too, but Danny had walked right through it. Whether it would work or not for this other "stupid boy" she had met—well, at the time, not even Katie could say. She was leaving, anyway, whether or not she made a baby for the new would-be soldier, and regardless of how many more babies she would or wouldn't get to make for such a noble cause.

"Let me see if I have this right," were among Danny's last words to his departing wife, who'd never really been a wife, and who had no further interest in being a mother.

"If I stay any longer, fuckhead, the two-year-old is going to remember me," Katie had said. (She'd actually called her own child "the two-year-old.")

"His name's Joe," Danny had reminded her. That was when he'd said: "Let me see if I have this right. You're not just an anti-war activist and a sexual anarchist, you're also this radical chick who specializes in serial baby making for draft dodgers—have I got that right?"

"Put it in writing, fuckhead," Katie had suggested; and these were her last words to her husband: "Maybe it'll sound better in writing."

Both Ketchum and his dad had warned him. "I think letting me cut a few fingers off your right hand would be easier, and less painful in the long run," Ketchum had said. "How about just your fucking trigger finger? They won't draft you, I'll bet, if you can't squeeze a trigger."

Dominic had taken a dislike to Katie Callahan on the mere evidence of the first photograph Daniel showed him.

"She looks way too thin," the cook commented, scowling at the photo. "Does she ever eat anything?" (He should talk! Danny had thought; both Danny and his dad were thin, and they ate a lot.) "Are her eyes really *that* blue?" his father asked.

"Actually, her eyes are even *bluer*," Danny told his dad.

What is it about these preternaturally small women? Dominic found himself thinking, remembering his not-really-a-cousin Rosie. Had his beloved Daniel succumbed to one of those little-girl women whose petite appearance was deceiving? Even that first photograph of Katie conveyed to the cook the kind of childlike woman some men feel compelled to protect. But Katie didn't need protection; she didn't want it, either.

The first time they met, the cook couldn't look at her—it was the same way he had treated (*still* treated) Danny's aunt Filomena. "I should never have shown you your mother's photographs," Dominic said, when Danny told him he was marrying Katie.

I suppose I should have married some nice *fat* person! Daniel Baciagalupo found himself thinking, instead of working ahead on the chapter he was writing.

But the war in Vietnam would drag on, and on; Nixon would win the '68 election by promising voters an end to the war, but the war would continue until 1975. On April 23, 1970, issuing his own executive order, President Nixon put an end to the 3-A paternity deferment for new fathers—if the child was conceived on or after that date. In the last five years of the war, another 23,763 U.S. soldiers would be killed, and Daniel Baciagalupo would finally come to realize that he should have thanked Katie Callahan for saving his life.

"So what if she *was* a serial baby maker for draft dodgers," Ketchum would write to Danny. "She saved your ass, sure as shit. And I wasn't kidding—I would have chopped off your right hand to spare you getting your balls blown off, if she hadn't saved you. A finger or two, anyway."

But that April night in '67, when he kept trying to write in the rain in Iowa City, Daniel Baciagalupo preferred to think that it was his two-year-old, little Joe, who'd saved him.

Probably no one could have saved Katie. Many years later, Daniel Baciagalupo would read *Prime Green: Remembering the Sixties*, a memoir by the fiction writer Robert Stone. "Life had given Americans so much by the mid-sixties that we were all a little drunk on possibility," Stone would write. "Things were speeding out of control before we could define them. Those of us who cared most deeply about the changes, those who gave their lives to them, were, I think, the most deceived."

Well, that certainly rang true for Katie Callahan, Danny would think, when he read that passage. But that book by Robert Stone wouldn't be written in time to save Katie. So she wasn't looking for protection, and she couldn't be saved, but—in addition to her looks, which were both wanton and seemingly underage—no small part of her appeal, and what made her most desirable to Danny, was that Katie was a renegade. (She also had the edginess of a sexual deserter; you never knew what she would do next, because Katie didn't know, either.)

"SIT DOWN, MICHAEL, SIT DOWN—*eat* something!" old Polcari had kept urging Mr. Leary, but the agitated Irishman was too worked up to eat. He had a beer, and then a glass or two of red wine. Poor Mr. Leary couldn't look at Carmella Del Popolo, Danny knew, without imagining that spade-shaped elf's goatee she'd possibly left unshaven in her left armpit. And when Dominic limped off to the kitchen to bring Mr. Leary a slice of the English teacher's favorite Sicilian meat loaf, Danny Baciagalupo, the writer-in-progress, saw the old owl looking at his dad's limp with new and startled eyes. Maybe a *bear* did that to the cook's foot! Mr. Leary might have been thinking; maybe there really had been a three- or four-hundred-pound Indian woman whose hair had hung below her waist!

There was one other thing Mr. Leary had lied about to Exeter— the part about these immigrants being prone to *exaggeration*. Hadn't Mr. Leary said that the Baciagalupo boy was "unlike the rest"? In the area of *writerly* exaggeration, Daniel Baciagalupo was a born exaggerator! And Danny was still at it on that rainy night in Iowa City, though he was sorely distracted; he was still a little bit in love with Katie Callahan, too. (Danny was only beginning to understand what his father had meant by the color he'd called *lethal* blue.)

How did that Johnny Cash song go? He'd first heard it six or seven years ago, Danny was guessing.

> *Oh, I never got over those blue eyes,*
> *I see them everywhere.*

More distractions, the writer thought; it was as if he were determined to physically remove himself (to *detach* himself) from that night in Vicino di Napoli with dear Mr. Leary.

It had taken Mr. Leary a third or fourth glass of red wine, and most of the meat loaf, before he was brave enough to take the pearl-gray envelope out of his inside jacket pocket. From across the table, Danny spotted the crimson lettering; the fifteen-year-old knew what Exeter's school colors were.

"And it's all *boys*, Dominic," the writer could still hear Mr. Leary saying. The old English teacher had indicated, with a nod of his head, the attractive Calogero girl (Danny's older cousin Elena) and her overripe friend Teresa DiMattia. Those girls were all over Danny whenever the after-school busboy was trying to change into his black busboy pants back in the kitchen.

"Give Danny some privacy, girls," Tony Molinari would tell them, but they wouldn't let up with their ceaseless *vamping*. In addition to dear Mr. Leary, maybe Danny had those girls to thank for his dad's decision to let him go to Exeter.

The hard parts to write about were the tears in his father's eyes when he said, "Well, Daniel, if it's a good school, like Michael says, and if you really want to go there—well, I guess Carmella and I can come visit you there on occasion, and you can come home to Boston on the occasional weekends." His dad's voice had broken on the *occasion* and *occasional* words, Daniel Baciagalupo would remember on that rainy night when he absolutely could not write—but he kept trying to—in Iowa City.

Danny remembered, too, how he'd gone off to the back of the kitchen at Vicino di Napoli, so that his father wouldn't see him start to cry—by then Carmella was crying, too, but she was always crying—and Danny took a little extra time in the kitchen to wet a dishcloth. Unobserved by Mr. Leary, who was overly fond of red wine, Danny wiped clean the back of his teacher's trenchcoat. The chalk-white *O'* had been easy to erase, easier to erase than the *rest* of that evening.

Danny would never forget lying in his bedroom later that night, in the Wesley Place apartment, hearing his dad cry and cry—with Carmella crying, too, as she tried to comfort him.

Finally, young Dan had knocked on the wall between their bedrooms. "I love you! And I'll come home a lot—every weekend I can!"

"I love *you*!" his dad had blubbered back.

"I love you, too!" Carmella had called.

Well, he couldn't write *that* scene—he could never get it right, Daniel Baciagalupo was thinking.

The chapter titled "Going Away to School" was part of the twenty-five-year-old writer's second novel. He had finished his first novel at the end of his first year in the Iowa Writers' Workshop, and he'd spent much of his second and final year revising it. He had been lucky enough, in his senior year at the University of New Hampshire, to have one of the writers-in-residence in the English department introduce him to a literary agent. And his first novel was bought by the first publisher the book was sent to. It would be several years before Daniel Baciagalupo would realize how fortunate he'd been. Possibly, no other student graduating from the Writers' Workshop that year already had a novel accepted for publication. It had made Danny the envy of some other students. But he hadn't made many friends among those students; he was one of the few who was married and had a child, so he'd not been a regular at the parties.

Danny had written to Ketchum about the book. He hoped that the logger would be among the first to read it. The novel wouldn't be published until December of '67, or maybe not until the New Year, and though it had a northern New Hampshire setting, Daniel Baciagalupo assured Ketchum and his dad that they weren't in it. "It's not about either of you, or about me—I'm not ready for that," he'd told them.

"No Angel, no *Jane*?" Ketchum had asked; he'd sounded surprised, or perhaps disappointed.

"It's not autobiographical," Danny had told them, and it wasn't.

Maybe Mr. Leary would have called the novel "rather remote," had that dear man been alive to read it, but Mr. Leary had passed away. Thinking of that Exeter-letter afternoon in Vicino di Napoli, as Daniel Baciagalupo was, he remembered that old Giusé Polcari had died, too. The restaurant itself had moved twice—first to Fleet Street, then to North Square (where it was now)—and Tony Molinari and

Paul Polcari took turns at being the maître d', thus giving themselves a break from the kitchen. Dominic (with his limp) was not maître-d' material, though he subbed as the first or principal chef, and Danny's dad also took turns at the pizza-chef position—whenever Paul Polcari was the maître d'. Carmella, as before, was the most sought-after waitress in the place; there were always a couple of younger women under her supervision.

In those summers he was home from Exeter and UNH—that is, until he married Katie—Danny had worked as a waiter at Vicino di Napoli, and he would sub as the pizza chef when Paul needed a night off, or when his dad did. If he hadn't become a writer, Daniel Baciagalupo could have been a cook. That rainy night in Iowa, when the second novel wasn't going so well, and the first novel wasn't yet published, Danny was in a low enough mood to imagine that he might end up being a cook after all. (If the writing didn't work out, at least he could cook.)

As for the upcoming academic year, Danny already had a job—teaching creative writing, and some other English courses, at a small liberal arts college in Vermont. He had never heard of the college before he'd applied for the job, but with a first novel being published by Random House and an M.F.A. from a prestigious writing program like Iowa's—well, Danny was going to be a college teacher. The young writer was happy about returning to New England. He'd missed his dad, and Carmella—and, who knows, he might actually get to see more of Ketchum. Danny hadn't seen Ketchum but once since that terrible April Sunday when the boy and his dad had fled from Twisted River.

Ketchum had shown up in Durham when Danny was starting his freshman year at the University of New Hampshire. The veteran logger was in his mid-forties by then, and he'd come to Danny's dorm with a gruff announcement: "Your dad tells me you never learned how to drive on a real road."

"Ketchum, we didn't have a car in Boston—we sold the Chieftain the same week we arrived—and you don't have any time to take driving lessons at a place like Exeter," Danny explained.

"Constipated Christ!" Ketchum said. "A college kid who can't get a driver's license is no one I want to be associated with!"

Ketchum then taught Danny how to drive his old truck; those were hard lessons for a young man whose driving experience, heretofore, had been with automatic transmission on the haul roads around Twisted River. For the week or more that Ketchum was in Durham, he lived in his truck—"just like the wanigan days," the woodsman said. The parking authorities at UNH twice gave Ketchum parking tickets when the logger was sleeping in the back of his truck. Ketchum gave the tickets to Danny. "You can pay these," Ketchum told the young man. "The driving lessons are free." It upset Danny that he hadn't seen the woodsman but once in seven years. Now it had been six more years.

How can you *not see* someone as important to you as that? Daniel Baciagalupo was thinking in the Iowa spring rain. More perplexing, his father had not seen Ketchum once in thirteen years. What was the matter with them? But half of Danny's mind was still unfocused—lost in the run-amuck chapter he was blundering about in.

THE YOUNG WRITER had jumped ahead to his family's first meeting with Mr. Carlisle, the scholarship person at Exeter—once again in Vicino di Napoli. Maybe Danny also had Carmella to thank for getting him into the academy, because Mr. Carlisle had never laid eyes on anyone quite like Carmella—not in Exeter, New Hampshire, surely—and the smitten man must have thought, If the Baciagalupo kid doesn't get into Exeter, I might never see this woman again!

Mr. Carlisle would be crushed that Carmella wasn't with Danny when the boy first visited the prep school. Dominic didn't make the trip, either. How could they? In Boston, March 17 wasn't only St. Patrick's Day. (The young Irish puking green beer in the streets was an annual embarrassment to Mr. Leary.) It was also Evacuation Day, a big deal in the North End, because in 1774 or 1775—Danny could never remember the correct year; actually, it was 1776—the artillery was set up in the Copps Hill Burying Ground to escort the British ships out of Boston Harbor. You got a day off from school on Evacuation Day, and on Bunker Hill Day, if you lived in Boston.

That year, 1957, Evacuation Day had come on a Sunday. Monday was the school holiday, and Mr. Leary had taken Danny on the train to Exeter. (The Evacuation Day holiday was an impossible day for

Dominic and Carmella to be away from the restaurant.) The writer's unfocused mind had once more jumped ahead to that train ride to Exeter with Mr. Leary—and what would be their first look at the venerable academy. Mr. Carlisle had been a most welcoming host, but it must have killed him not to see Carmella.

And despite his promise to come home a lot—every weekend he could—Danny wouldn't do that. He rarely came home to Boston on his Exeter weekends—maybe twice a term, tops, and then he would meet his Exeter friends on a Saturday night in Scollay Square, usually to see the strippers at the Old Howard. You had to fake your age, but that was easy; they let the kids in most nights. You just had to be respectful to the ladies. On one of those nights at the Old Howard, Danny ran into his former English teacher. That was a sad night. For Mr. Leary, who loved Latin, it was an *errare humanum est* night—a "to err is human" night, for both the revered teacher and his prize student. Talk about jumping ahead! He would have to write about that unhappy night (or some version of it) one day, Daniel Baciagalupo supposed.

His first novel was dedicated to Mr. Leary. Because of the Irishman's love of Latin, Danny had written:

MICHAEL LEARY,

IN MEMORIAM

It was from Mr. Leary that he'd first heard the phrase *in medias res.* Mr. Leary had praised young Dan's writing by saying that, "as a reader," he liked how Danny often began a narrative in the middle of the story rather than at the chronological beginning.

"What's that called—is there a name for it?" the boy had innocently asked.

Mr. Leary had answered: "I call it *in medias res,* which in Latin means 'in the middle of things.' "

Well, that was kind of where he was at this moment in his life, Daniel Baciagalupo was thinking. He had a two-year-old son, whom he'd inexplicably not named after his father; he'd lost his wife, and had not yet met another woman. He was struggling to begin a second novel while the first one was not yet published, and he was about to go back to New England to his first noncooking, not-in-a-kitchen job. If that wasn't *in medias res,* Daniel Baciagalupo thought, what was?

And, continuing in Latin, when Danny had first gone to Exeter, he'd gone with Mr. Leary, who was with the boy *in loco parentis*—that is, "in the place of a parent."

Maybe that was why the first novel was dedicated to Mr. Leary. "Not to your dad?" Ketchum would ask Danny. (Carmella would ask the young writer the same question.)

"Maybe the next one," he would tell them both. His father never said anything about the dedication to Mr. Leary.

Danny got up from his desk to watch the rain streaking his windows in Iowa City. He then went and watched Joe sleeping. The way the chapter was going, the writer thought that he might as well go to bed, but he generally stayed up late. Like his dad, Daniel Baciagalupo didn't drink anymore; Katie had cured him of that habit, which was not a story he wanted to think about on a night when his writing wasn't working. He found himself wishing that Ketchum would call. (Hadn't Ketchum said they should talk?)

Whenever Ketchum called from those faraway phone booths, time seemed to stop; whenever he heard from Ketchum, Daniel Baciagalupo, who was twenty-five, usually felt that he was twelve and leaving Twisted River all over again.

One day, the writer would acknowledge this: It was *not* a coincidence when the logger called on that rainy April night. As usual, Ketchum called collect, and Danny accepted the call. "Fucking mud season," Ketchum said. "How the hell are you?"

"So you're a *typist* now," Danny said. "I'm going to miss your pretty handwriting."

"It was never my handwriting," Ketchum told him. "It was Pam's. Six-Pack wrote all my letters."

"Why?" Danny asked him.

"I can't write!" Ketchum admitted. "I can't read, either—Six-Pack read all your letters aloud to me, yours and your dad's."

This was a devastating moment for Daniel Baciagalupo; as the young writer would think of it later, it was right up there with his wife leaving him, but it would have more serious consequences. Danny thought of how he'd poured out his heart to Ketchum, of everything he'd written to the man—not to mention what Ketchum had to have told Pam, because it was obviously Six-Pack, not Ketchum, who'd replied. This meant that Six-Pack knew *everything*!

"I thought my mom taught you to read," Danny said.

"Not really," Ketchum replied. "I'm sorry, Danny."

"So now Pam is *typing*?" Danny asked. (This was truly hard to imagine; there'd not been a single typo in the typed letters both Danny and his dad had received from Ketchum.)

"There's a lady I met in the library—she turned out to be a school-teacher, Danny. She typed the letters for me."

"Where's Six-Pack?" Danny asked.

"Well, that's kind of the problem," Ketchum told him. "Six-Pack moved on. You know how that is," he added. Ketchum knew all about Katie moving on—there was no more to say about it.

"Six-Pack left you?" Danny asked.

"That's not the problem," Ketchum answered. "I'm not surprised she left me—I'm surprised she stayed so long. But I'm surprised that she's moved in with the cowboy," Ketchum added. "*That's* the problem."

Both Danny and his dad knew that Carl wasn't a constable any-more. (They also knew there was no more town of Twisted River; it had burned to the ground, and it had been a ghost town before it burned.) Carl was now a deputy sheriff of Coos County.

"Are you saying Six-Pack will tell the cowboy what she knows?" Danny asked Ketchum.

"Not immediately," Ketchum answered. "She has no reason to do me any dirt—or to do you and your dad any harm, as far as I know. We parted on good enough terms. It's what'll happen to her when Carl beats her up, because he will. Or when he throws her out, because he won't keep her for long. You haven't seen Six-Pack in a while, Danny—she's losing her looks something wicked."

Daniel Baciagalupo was counting to himself. He knew that Ketchum and Six-Pack were the same age, and that they both were the exact same age as Carl. When he got to fifty, Danny wrote the number down—that was how old they were. He could imagine that Six-Pack Pam's looks were going, and that the cowboy would one day kick her out. Carl would definitely beat her, even though the deputy sheriff had stopped drinking.

"Explain what you mean," Danny said to Ketchum.

"It'll be when Carl does something bad to Pam—that'll be when she'll tell him. Don't you see, Danny?" Ketchum asked him. "It's the only way she can hurt him. All these years, he's been wondering about you and your dad—all these years, he's been thinking he killed Jane. He just can't *remember* it! I think it's honestly driven him crazy—that he can't remember killing her, but he believes he did."

If he was a better man, it might be a relief to the cowboy to learn he *didn't* kill Injun Jane. And if Six-Pack had led a gentler life, maybe she *wouldn't* be tempted to use her knowledge of the situation as a weapon. (At worst, Pam might blurt out the truth to Carl—either accidentally, or while he was beating her up.) But Ketchum wasn't counting on the cowboy to discover some essential goodness within himself, and the river driver knew the life Six-Pack had led. (He'd led that life, too; there was nothing gentle about it.) And the cowboy *had* driven himself crazy—not because he believed he'd killed Jane; he didn't even feel guilty about that, much less crazy. Ketchum was right: What made Carl crazy was that he couldn't remember killing her; Ketchum knew the cowboy would have enjoyed remembering that.

That he couldn't remember was why the sheriff had eventually stopped drinking. Years ago, when Ketchum had first told Danny and his dad about "the new teetotaler in Coos County," both the cook and his son had laughed about it—they'd positively *howled*.

"Cookie's got to get out of Boston—that's for starters," Ketchum said now. "He ought to lose the Del Popolo, too. I'm going to tell him, but you've got to tell him, too, Danny. Your dad doesn't always listen to me."

"Ketchum, are you saying it's *inevitable* that Pam will tell Carl everything?"

"As inevitable as the fact that one day, Danny, the cowboy is going to beat her up."

"Jesus!" Danny suddenly cried. "What were you and Mom doing when she was supposed to be teaching you to read?"

"Talk to your dad, Danny—it's not my business to tell you."

"Were you sleeping with her?" Danny asked him.

"Talk to your dad, *please*," Ketchum said. Danny couldn't remember Ketchum ever saying the *please* word before.

"Does my dad know you slept with her?" Danny asked him.

"Constipated Christ!" Ketchum shouted into the phone. "Why do you think your dad busted half my head open with the damn skillet?"

"What did you just say?" Danny asked him.

"I'm drunk," Ketchum told him. "Don't listen to what I say."

"I thought Carl cracked your head open with his Colt forty-five," Danny said.

"Hell, if the cowboy had cracked my head open, I would have killed him!" Ketchum thundered. As soon as the logger said this, Danny knew it was true; Ketchum would never have tolerated having his head cracked open, unless Dominic had done it.

"I saw lights on in the cookhouse," Ketchum began, suddenly sounding weary. "Your mom and dad were up late talking, and—in those days—*drinking*. I walked in the screen door to the kitchen. I didn't know it was the night your mom told your dad about her and me."

"I get it," Danny said.

"Not all of it, you don't. Talk to your dad," Ketchum repeated.

"Did Jane know?" Danny asked.

"Shit, the Injun knew everything," Ketchum told him.

"Ketchum?" Danny asked. "Does my dad know that you didn't learn to read?"

"I'm trying to learn now," Ketchum said defensively. "I think that schoolteacher lady is going to teach me. She said she would."

"Does Dad know you can't read?" the young man asked his father's old friend.

"I suppose one of us will have to tell him," Ketchum said. "Cookie is probably of the opinion that Rosie must have taught me *something*."

"So that was why you called—what you meant by 'Something's up' in your letter—is that it?" Danny asked him.

"I can't believe you believed that bullshit about the fucking bear," Ketchum said. The bear story had found its way, in a more *remote* form, into Daniel Baciagalupo's first novel. But of course it hadn't *really* been a bear that walked into the kitchen—it had just been Ketchum. And if the bear story hadn't been planted in young Dan's heart and mind, maybe he wouldn't have reached for the eight-inch cast-iron skillet—maybe he wouldn't have imagined that the sound of his father and Jane making love was the sound of a mauling-in-progress. Then maybe he wouldn't have killed Jane.

"So there wasn't a bear," Danny said.

"Hell, there's probably three thousand bears at any given time in northern New Hampshire—I've seen a bunch of bears. I've shot some," Ketchum added. "But if a bear had walked into the cookhouse kitchen through that screen door, your father's best way to save himself, and Rosie, would be if the two of them had exited the kitchen through the dining room—not running, either, or ever turning their backs on the bear, but just maintaining eye contact and backing up real slowly. *No,* you dummy, it wasn't a bear—it was *me!* Anybody knows better than to hit a bear in the face with a fucking frying pan!"

"I wish I had never written about it," was all Danny could say.

"There's one more thing," Ketchum told him. "It's another kind of *writing* problem."

"Jesus!" Danny said again. "How much have you been drinking?"

"You're sounding more and more like your father," Ketchum told him. "I just mean that you're publishing a book, aren't you? And have you thought about what it might mean if that book were to become a bestseller? If suddenly you were to become a *popular* writer, with your name and picture in the newspapers and magazines—you might even get to be on television!"

"It's a first novel," Danny said dismissively. "It will have only a small first printing, and not much publicity. It's a *literary* novel, or I hope it is. It's highly unlikely it'll be a bestseller!"

"Think about it," Ketchum said. "Anything's *possible,* isn't it? Don't writers, even young ones, get lucky like other people—or unlucky, as the case may be?"

This time, Danny saw it coming—sooner than he'd seen it in Mr. Leary's classroom at the Mickey when the old English teacher made his "bold suggestion" about the boy possibly losing the Baciagalupo. The pen-name proposition—it was coming again. Ketchum had first proposed a version of it to both Danny and his dad; now Ketchum was asking Dominic to lose the Del Popolo.

"Danny?" Ketchum asked. "Are you still there? What's the name for it—when a writer chooses a name that's not his or her given name? That George Eliot did it, didn't she?"

"It's called a pen name," Danny told him. "Just how the fuck did you meet the schoolteacher lady in the *library* when you can't even *read*?"

"Well, I can read some of the authors' names and the titles," Ketchum said indignantly. "I can borrow books and find someone to read them to me!"

"Oh," Danny said. He guessed that was what Ketchum had done with his mother—this in lieu of learning to read. What had Ketchum called the reading-aloud part to Dominic? *Foreplay*, wasn't it? (Actually, that had been Dominic's word for it. Danny's dad had told his son this funny story!)

"A pen name," Ketchum repeated thoughtfully. "I believe there's another phrase for it, something French-sounding."

"A nom de plume," Danny told him.

"That's it!" Ketchum cried. "A nom de plume. Well, that's what you need—just to be on the safe side."

"I don't suppose you have any suggestions," Daniel Baciagalupo said.

"You're the writer—that's your job," Ketchum told him. "*Ketchum* kind of goes with Daniel, doesn't it? And it's a fine old Coos County kind of name."

"I'll think about it," Danny told him.

"I'm sure you can come up with something better," Ketchum said.

"Tell me one thing," Danny said. "If my mom hadn't died that night in the river, which one of you would she have left? You or my dad? I can't talk to my dad about *that*, Ketchum."

"Shit!" Ketchum cried. "I heard you call that wife of yours 'a free spirit.' Katie was a lawless soul, a political radical, a fucking anarchist, and a coldhearted woman—you should have known better, Danny. But *Rosie* was a free spirit! She wouldn't have left *either* of us—not ever! Your *mom* was a free spirit, Danny—like you young people today have never seen! Shit!" Ketchum cried again. "Sometimes you ask the dumbest questions—you make me think you're still a college kid who can't properly drive a car, or that you're still a twelve-year-old, one your dad and Jane and I could *still* fool about the world, if we wanted to. Talk to your *dad*, Danny—talk to him."

There was a click, followed by a dial tone, because Ketchum had disconnected the call, leaving the young writer alone with his thoughts.

CHAPTER 6

IN MEDIAS RES

N THEIR WALK-UP APARTMENT ON WESLEY PLACE, FOR REASONS that defied logic, the telephone was on Carmella's side of the bed. In those years Danny was away at boarding school and then at college, if the phone ever rang, young Dan was the reason the cook wanted to answer it—hoping it *was* Daniel, and not some terrible news about him. (More often, when the phone rang, it was Ketchum.)

Carmella had told Danny that he should call home more than he did. "You're the only reason we have a phone, your dad is always telling me!" The boy was pretty good, after that, about calling more frequently.

"Shouldn't the phone be on my side of the bed?" Dominic had asked Carmella. "I mean, you don't want to have to talk to Ketchum, and if it's Daniel—or worse, if there's any bad news about Daniel—"

Carmella wouldn't let him finish. "If there's bad news about Danny, I want to know it first—so I can tell you about it, and put my arm around your shoulders, the way you told me and held me," she said to him.

"That's crazy, Carmella," the cook said.

But that was the way it had worked out; the phone stayed on Carmella's side of the bed. Whenever Ketchum called collect, Carmella always accepted the call, and she usually said, "Hello, Mr.

Ketchum. When am I going to get to meet you? I would very much like to meet you one day." (Ketchum wasn't very talkative—not to her, anyway. She would soon pass the phone to Dominic—"Gamba," she fondly called him.)

But that spring of '67, when the news came about Danny's miserable marriage—that awful wife of his; the dear boy had deserved better—and there'd been more collect calls than usual from up north (most of them about that menacing cop), Ketchum had scared Carmella. Dominic would later think that Ketchum probably meant to. When she'd said the usual to the old woodsman—Carmella was about to hand the phone across the bed to Dominic—Ketchum said, "I don't know that you want to meet me, *ever,* because it might not be under the best of circumstances."

That had given Carmella quite a chill; she'd been upset enough with the way things were that spring, and now Mr. Ketchum had frightened her. And Carmella wished that Danny was as relieved as *she* was that Katie had left him. It was one thing to leave the man you were with—Carmella could understand that—but it was a sin for a mother to walk away from her own child. Carmella was relieved that Katie had left, because Carmella believed that Katie wouldn't have been any kind of mother if she'd *stayed.* Of course, Carmella and Dominic had never liked Katie Callahan; they'd both seen their share of customers like her in Vicino di Napoli. "You can smell the money on her," Carmella had said to the cook.

"It's not exactly on her, it's *under* her," the cook had commented. He meant that the money in Katie's family was a safety net for the wild girl; she could behave in any fashion she wanted because the family money was there to catch her if she fell. Dominic felt certain, as Ketchum did, that Katie Callahan's so-called free spirit was a fraud. Danny had misunderstood his dad; the boy thought that the cook didn't like Katie strictly because the young woman looked like Rosie, Danny's unfaithful mother. But Katie's looks had little to do with what Dominic *and* Ketchum didn't like about her; it was how she was *not* like Rosie Calogero that had bothered them, from the beginning.

Katie was nothing but a renegade young woman with a money cushion under her; "a mere sexual outlaw," Ketchum had called her. Whereas Rosie had loved both a boy and a man. She'd been trapped because she had genuinely loved the two of them—hence they'd been trapped, too. By comparison, the Callahan whore had just been fucking around; worse, with her high-minded politics, Katie thought she was above such mundanities as marriage and motherhood.

Carmella knew it pained Dominic that Danny believed his mother had been the same sort of lawless creature Katie was. Though Dominic had gone to great lengths to explain the threesome with Rosie and Ketchum to Carmella, she had to confess that she didn't understand it much better than Danny did. Carmella could understand the reason for it happening, but not for it continuing the way it had. Danny didn't get that part of it, either. Carmella also had been mad at her dear Gamba for not telling the boy about his mother sooner. Danny had long been old enough to know the story, and it would have been better if his dad had told him before the cat got let out of the bag in that conversation Danny had had with Mr. Ketchum.

Carmella had been the one who'd answered the phone on that early morning Danny called to talk about it. "Secondo!" she said, when she heard his voice on the phone. That had been Danny's nickname all the years he'd worked at Vicino di Napoli.

"Secondo Angelo," old Polcari had first named him—literally, "Second Angel."

All of them had been careful to call him Angelo, never Angelù, and around Carmella they would shorten the nickname to just plain Secondo—though Carmella herself was so fond of Danny that she often spoke of him as her *secondo figlio* (her "second son").

In restaurant language, *secondo* also means "second course," so it was the name that had stuck.

But now Carmella's Secondo Angelo was in no mood to speak to her. "I need to talk to my dad, Carmella," he said.

(Ketchum had warned the cook that Danny would be calling. "I'm sorry, Cookie," that call from Ketchum had begun. "I fucked up.")

On the April morning Danny called, Carmella knew that the young man would be angry at his dad for not telling him all those things. Of course she heard mostly Dominic's side of the conversation, but she could nevertheless tell how the phone call was going—badly.

"I'm sorry—I was going to tell you," the cook started.

Carmella could hear Danny's response to that, because he shouted into the phone at his father. "What were you waiting for?"

"Maybe for something like this to happen to you, so you might understand how difficult it can be with women," Dominic said. There in the bed, Carmella punched him. The "this" referred to Katie leaving, of course—as if that relationship, which was wrongheaded from the start, was at all comparable to what had gone on with Rosie and Ketchum. And why had they lied to the boy about the *bear* for so long? Carmella couldn't understand it; she certainly didn't expect Danny to.

She lay there listening to the cook tell his son about that night in the cookhouse kitchen, when Rosie had confessed to sleeping with Ketchum—and then Ketchum had walked through the screen door, when all of them were drunk, and Dominic had hit his old friend with the skillet. Luckily, Ketchum had been in enough fights; he never entirely believed that there was anyone alive who *wouldn't* take a swing at him. The big man's reactions were ingrained. He must have deflected the skillet with a forearm, slightly turning the weapon in Dominic's hand, so that only the cast-iron edge of the frying pan hit him—and it hit him in the dead center of his forehead, not in the temple, where even a partially blocked blow from such a heavy implement might have killed him.

There'd been no doctor in Twisted River, and there wasn't even a sawmill and a so-called millpond at what would become Dead Woman Dam, where there would later be an absolute *moron* of a doctor. Rosie had stitched up Ketchum's forehead on one of the dining-room tables; she'd used the ultra-thin stainless-steel wire the cook kept on hand for trussing up his chickens and turkeys. The cook had sterilized the wire by boiling it first, and Ketchum had bellowed like a bull moose throughout the process. Dominic had limped around and around the table while Rosie talked to the two of them. She was so angry that she was rough with the stitches.

"I wish I was stitching the *two* of you up," she said, looking at Dominic, before telling them both how it was going to be. "If there is *ever* another act of violence between the two of you, I will leave you *both*—is that clear enough?" she'd asked them. "If you promise never to hurt each other—in fact, you must always look after each other, like good brothers—then I will never leave either of you, not until the day I die," she told them. "So you can each have half of me, or you can both have none of me—in the latter case, I take Danny with me. Is everything understood?" They could tell she was totally serious about it.

"I suppose your mother was too proud to go back to Boston when she had the miscarriage—and she thought I was too young to be left alone when my mother died," Carmella heard Dominic telling Danny. "Rosie must have thought she had to take care of me, and of course she knew that I loved her. I don't doubt that she loved me, too, but I was still just a nice boy to her, and when she met Ketchum—well, he was her age. Ketchum was a man. We had no choice but to put up with it, Daniel—both Ketchum and I adored her, and in her own way I believe she loved the two of us."

"What did Jane think of it?" Danny asked his dad, because Ketchum had said that the Injun knew everything.

"Well, exactly what you would expect Jane to think of it," his father told him. "She said all three of us were assholes. Jane thought we were all taking a terrible chance—the Indian said it was a big gamble that any of it would work out. I thought so, too, but your mother wasn't giving us another option—and Ketchum was always a bigger gambler than I was."

"You should have told me earlier," his son said.

"I know I should have, Daniel—I'm sorry," Carmella heard the cook say.

Later, Dominic would tell Carmella what Danny had said to him then. "I don't care that much about the bear—it was a good story," Danny said to his dad. "But there's another thing you're wrong about. You told me you suspected that Ketchum killed Lucky Pinette. You and Jane, and half those West Dummer kids—that's what you all told me."

"I think Ketchum *may* have killed him, Daniel."

"I think you're wrong. Lucky Pinette was murdered in his bed—in the old Boom House on the Androscoggin. He'd had his head bashed in with a stamping hammer when they found him—isn't that the story?" Daniel Baciagalupo, the writer, asked his father.

"That's it, exactly," his dad answered. "Lucky Pinette's forehead was indented with the letter *H*."

"Cold-blooded murder—right, Dad?"

"It sure looked like it, Daniel."

"Then it wasn't Ketchum," Danny told him. "If Ketchum found it so easy to murder Lucky Pinette in bed, why doesn't he just kill Carl? There're any number of ways Ketchum could kill the cowboy—*if* Ketchum were a murderer."

Dominic knew that Daniel was right. ("Maybe the boy really *is* a writer!" the cook would say when he told Carmella the story.) Because if Ketchum were a murderer, the cowboy would already be dead. Ketchum had promised Rosie he would look after Dominic—they had both promised to look after each other—and, under the circumstances, what better way to look after Dominic was there? Just kill the cowboy—in bed, or wherever the woodsman could catch Carl napping.

"Don't you get it, Dad?" Danny had asked. "If Pam tells Carl everything, and the cowboy can't find you or me, why wouldn't he go after Ketchum? He'd know that Ketchum always knew everything—Six-Pack will tell him!"

But both father and son knew the answer to that. If the cowboy came after Ketchum, then Ketchum *would* kill him—both Ketchum and Carl knew that. Like most men who beat women, the cowboy was a coward; Carl probably wouldn't dare go after Ketchum, not even with a rifle with a scope. The cowboy knew that the logger would be hard to kill—not like the cook.

"Dad?" Danny asked. "When are you getting the hell out of Boston?" By the guilty, frightened way Dominic turned in bed to look at her, Carmella must have known what the new topic of conversation was. They had discussed Dominic leaving Boston, but the cook either couldn't or wouldn't tell Carmella when he was going.

When Dominic first told Carmella everything, he made one point particularly clear: If Carl ever came after him, and the cook had to go on the run again, Carmella couldn't come with him. She'd lost her husband and her only child. She had been spared just one thing—she'd not seen them die. If Carmella went on the run with Dominic, the cowboy might not kill her, too, but she would watch the cook get killed. "I won't allow it," Dominic had told her. "If that asshole comes after me, I go alone."

"Why can't you and Danny just tell the police?" Carmella had asked him. "What happened to Jane was an *accident*! Can't you make the police understand that Carl is crazy, and that he's dangerous?"

It was hard to explain to someone who wasn't from Coos County. In the first place, the cowboy *was* the police—or what passed for the police up there. In the second place, it wasn't a crime to be crazy and dangerous—not anywhere, but especially not in northern New Hampshire. Nor was it much of a crime that Carl had buried or otherwise disposed of Jane's body without telling anyone. The point was, the cowboy didn't kill her—Danny did. And the cook had been old enough to know better than to have run away the first time, when if he'd stayed and simply told the truth, to *someone*—well, maybe then it might have worked out. (Or Dominic could have just gone back to Twisted River with Daniel. The cook could have bluffed it out, as Ketchum had wanted him to—as young Dan also had wanted.)

Of course, it was too late to change any of that now. It was early enough in their relationship when the cook had told Carmella all this; she'd accepted the terms. Now that she loved him more than a little, she regretted what she'd agreed to. Not going with him, if Dominic had to go, would be very hard for her. Naturally, Dominic knew he would miss Carmella—more than he'd missed Injun Jane. Maybe not as much as both he and Ketchum still missed Rosie, but the cook knew that Carmella was special. Yet the more he loved Carmella, the more dead set Dominic was against her going with him.

As Carmella lay in bed, she thought about the places she could no longer go in the North End, first because she'd gone there with the fisherman, and then—more painfully—because she associated specific areas of the neighborhood with those special things she'd done with Angelù. Now where would she no longer be able to go when Dominic (her dear Gamba) had left her? the widow Del Popolo wondered.

After Angelù drowned, Carmella took no more walks on Parmenter Street—specifically, not in the vicinity of what had been Cushman's. The elementary school, where Angelù had gone to the early grades, had been torn down. (In '55, or maybe in '56—Carmella couldn't remember.) In its place, there would one day be a library, but Carmella wouldn't ever walk by that library.

Because she'd always been a waitress at Vicino di Napoli—it had been her first job and became her only one—she was free most mornings. When the little kids at Cushman's took their school trips in the neighborhood, Carmella had always volunteered to be one of the parents who went along—just to help the teachers out. Therefore, she no longer went anywhere near the Old North Church, where she and Angelù's class of schoolchildren had been shown the steeple that was restored in 1912 by the descendants of Paul Revere. It was an Episcopal church—one Carmella wouldn't have attended, because she was Catholic—but it was famous (foremost, for its role in Paul Revere's ride). Enshrined, under glass, were the bricks from the cell where the Pilgrim fathers had been imprisoned in England.

On two counts could Carmella not walk past the Mariners House on North Square, and this was awkward for her because it was so close to Vicino di Napoli. But it was the landmark of the Boston Port and Seamen's Society, "dedicated to the service of seafarers." The schoolchildren in Angelù's class had visited the Mariners House, but Carmella had skipped that school trip—after all, she'd lost a fisherman at sea.

It was just plain silly how more innocent connections to the fisherman and Angelù haunted her, but they did. She loved the Caffè Vittoria but avoided that room with the pictures of Rocky Marciano, because both the fisherman and Angelù had admired the heavyweight champion. And she'd eaten with her husband and son at the Grotta Azzurra on Hanover Street, where Enrico Caruso used to eat, too. Now there was no more going there.

The fisherman had told her that no sailor had ever been mugged on Hanover Street, or ever would be; it was a safe walk for even the drunken-most sailors, all the way from the waterfront to the Old Howard and back. In addition to the striptease places, there were cheap bars frequented by the sailors, and the arcades around Scollay Square. (Of course this would all change; Scollay Square itself would go.) But the world Carmella had lived in with her drowned husband and drowned son was both sacred and haunted to her—the whole length of Hanover Street!

Even the scavenging seagulls over the Haymarket reminded her of the Saturday people-watching she had done there, with Angelù holding her hand. Now she looked with caution at that restaurant on Fleet Street where Stella's used to be; she occasionally ate there with Dominic, on the nights Vicino di Napoli was closed. They ate at the Europeo, too—Dominic usually had the fried calamari, but never New York–style. ("Hold the red sauce—I like it just with lemon," the cook would say.) Would she no longer be able to eat in these places after her Gamba was gone? Carmella wondered.

She would certainly have to move into a smaller apartment. Would it be so hot in the apartment in the summer that she would become like one of those old ladies in the tenement building on Charter Street? They took their chairs out of their apartments so they could sit on the sidewalk, where it was cooler. Those cold-water tenements had been bedecked with streamers for the saints' feasts in the summer. Carmella suddenly recalled Angelù as a little boy sitting on the fisherman's shoulders; Hanover Street had been closed for a procession. It was the Feast of San Rocco, Carmella was remembering. Nowadays, she didn't like to watch the processions.

IN 1919, GIUSÉ POLCARI had been a young man. He remembered the Molasses Explosion, which killed twenty-one people in the North End—including the father of some kid Joe Polcari had known. "He was-a boiled to death in a tidal wave of hot molasses!" old Joe had said to Danny. Though the war was over, those who'd heard the explosion thought the Germans were coming—that Boston Harbor was being bombed, or something. "I saw a whole piano floating in the molasses!" old Polcari told young Dan.

In the kitchen of Vicino di Napoli was a black-and-white photograph of Nicola Sacco and Bartolomeo Vanzetti; the two anarchist immigrants were handcuffed together. Sacco and Vanzetti were sent to the electric chair for the murder of a paymaster and a guard at a shoe company in South Braintree. Old Polcari—in his final, addle-brained days—couldn't remember all the details, but he remembered the protest marches. "Sacco and Vanzetti were framed! A stool pigeon in the Charlestown Street jail fingered them, and the State of Massachusetts gave-a the stool pigeon a free ride back to Italy," old Joe had said to Danny. There'd been a procession for Sacco and Vanzetti that started on Hanover Street in the North End and went all the way to

Tremont Street, where the mounted police had broken up the crowd; there were thousands of protesters, Joe Polcari among them.

"If you or your son ever have a problem, Gamba, you tell me," Giusé Polcari said to Dominic. "I know-a some guys—they feex-a your problem for you."

Old Polcari meant the Camorra, the Neapolitan version of the Mafia—not that Dominic could truly understand the distinction. When he'd behaved wildly as a kid, Nunzi had called him her *camorrista*. But it was Dominic's impression that the Mafia was more or less in control of the North End, where both the Mafia and the Camorra were called the Black Hand.

When Dominic told Paul Polcari that the cowboy might be coming after him, Paul said, "If my dad were alive, he'd call his Camorra buddies, but I don't know about those guys."

"I don't know about the Mafia, either," Tony Molinari told Dominic. "If they do something for you, then you owe them."

"I don't want to involve you in my troubles," Dominic said to them. "I'm not asking the Mafia to help me, or the Camorra."

"The crazy cop won't come after Carmella, will he?" Paul Polcari asked the cook.

"I don't know—Carmella bears watching," Dominic answered.

"We'll watch her, all right," Molinari said. "If the cowboy comes here, to the restaurant—well, we've got knives, cleavers—"

"Wine bottles," Paul Polcari suggested.

"Don't even think about it," Dominic told them. "If Carl comes here looking for me, he'll be armed—he wouldn't go anywhere without that Colt forty-five on him."

"I know what my dad would say," Paul Polcari said. "He'd say, 'A Colt forty-five is-a *nothing*—not if you've ever tried to get-a cozy with one of those women who work as *stitchers* in the shirt factory. Even naked, they got-a needles on 'em!' " (Joe Polcari meant the Leopold Morse factory in the old Prince Macaroni building; his son Paul said Giusé must have banged some tough broad who worked there, or he'd tried to.)

The three cooks laughed; they made an effort to forget about the deputy sheriff up in Coos County. What else could they do but try to forget about him?

Old Polcari had had a hundred jokes like that one about the shirt-stitchers. "Do you remember the one about the woman who worked the night shift at the Boston Sausage and Provision Company?" Dominic asked Paul and Tony.

Both chefs roared. "Yeah, she worked in the skinless-meat department," Paul Polcari said.

"She had this sneaky little knife, for cutting the skin off the frankfurters!" Molinari remembered.

"She could peel-a your penis like it was a *grape!*" the three cooks shouted, almost in unison. Then Carmella came into the restaurant, and they stopped laughing.

"More dirty jokes?" she asked them. They were just firing up the pizza oven and waiting for the dough to rise; it was late morning, but the marinara sauce was already simmering. Carmella saw how worried they suddenly seemed, and they wouldn't look in her eyes. "You were talking about Carl, weren't you?" she asked them; they were like boys who'd been caught beating off. "Maybe you should do what Ketchum says—maybe, Gamba, you should listen to your old friend," she said to Dominic. Two months had passed since Ketchum's warning, but the cook still couldn't or wouldn't tell Carmella when he was leaving.

Now none of them could look at their beloved Gambacorta, the cook who limped. "Maybe you should go, if you're going," Carmella said to Dominic. "It's almost summer," she suddenly announced. "Do cops get summer vacations?" she asked them.

It was June—very nearly the last day of school, they all knew. That was a tough time of year for Carmella. All at once, there was nowhere she could go in the North End. The freed-from-school children were everywhere; they reminded Carmella of her Angelù *primù,* her first Angel.

The deputy sheriff had been with Six-Pack for these slowly passing two months. Yes, it was still a relatively new relationship, but—as Ketchum had pointed out—two months was a long time for Carl to go without whacking a woman. The cook couldn't remember a time when one *week* went by and the cowboy didn't hit Injun Jane.

THERE WERE THINGS Carmella had never told her dear Gamba about his beloved Daniel. How the boy had managed to get laid before he even went off to Exeter, for example. Carmella had caught Danny doing it with one of her nieces—one of those DiMattia girls, Teresa's younger sister Josie. Carmella had gone out to work in the restaurant, but she'd forgotten something and had to go back to the Wesley Place apartment. (Now she couldn't even remember what it was she'd forgotten.) It was Danny's day off from his busboy job. He already knew he had a full scholarship to Exeter—maybe he was celebrating. Of course Carmella knew that Josie DiMattia was older than Danny; probably Josie had started it. And all along Dominic had suspected that *Teresa* DiMattia—or her friend Elena Calogero, *definitely* a kissing cousin—would sexually initiate Danny.

Why was Gamba so worried about that? Carmella wondered. If the boy had had *more* sex—she meant in those years when he was a student at Exeter—maybe he wouldn't have become so infatuated with that Callahan girl when he went to college! And if he'd fucked a few *more* of his kissing cousins—Calogeros *and* Saettas, or for that matter every female in the DiMattia family—possibly he would have knocked up someone a whole lot nicer than Katie!

But because Dominic had obsessed about Elena Calogero and Teresa DiMattia, when Carmella came into the apartment and saw Danny fucking someone on her bed, she first assumed it *was* Teresa who was initiating the frightened-looking fifteen-year-old. Naturally, young Dan was frightened because Carmella had caught them at it!

"Teresa, you whore!" Carmella cried. (She actually called the girl a *troia*—from that notorious Trojan woman—but the word meant "whore," of course.)

"I'm Josie, Teresa's sister," the girl said indignantly. She must have been miffed that her aunt didn't recognize her.

"Well, yes, you are," Carmella replied. "And what are you doing using *our* bed, Danny? You've got your own bed, you *disgraziato*—"

"Jeez, yours is bigger," Josie told her aunt.

"And I hope you're using a condom!" Carmella cried.

Dominic used condoms; he didn't mind, and Carmella preferred it. Maybe the boy had found his father's condoms. When it came to condoms, it was a dumb world, Carmella knew. At Barone's Pharmacy, they kept the condoms hidden, completely out of sight. If kids asked for them, the pharmacist would give them shit about it. Yet any responsible parent who had a kid that age would tell the kid to use a condom. Where exactly were the kids supposed to get them?

"Was it one of your dad's condoms?" Carmella asked Danny, while the boy lay covered by a sheet; he looked mortified that she'd discovered him. The DiMattia girl, on the other hand, hadn't even bothered to cover her breasts. She just sat sullenly naked, staring at her aunt with defiance. "Are you going to confess this, Josie?" Carmella asked the girl. "How are you going to confess this?"

"I brought the condoms—Teresa gave them to me," Josie said, ignoring the larger question of confession.

Now Carmella was really angry. Just what did that *troia* Teresa think she was doing, giving her kid sister condoms! "How many did she give you?" Carmella asked. But before the girl could answer, Carmella asked Danny: "Don't you have any homework to do?" Then Carmella seemed to realize that she was guilty of a certain hypocrisy in her hasty judgment of Teresa. (Shouldn't Teresa be *thanked* for giving her kid sister condoms? Yet had the condoms *enabled* Josie to seduce Secondo?)

"Jeez, do you want me to count them or something?" Josie asked her aunt, about the condoms. Poor Danny just looked like he wanted to die, Carmella would always remember.

"Well, you kids be careful—I have to go to work," Carmella told them. "Josie!" Carmella had cried, as she walked out of the apartment, just before she'd slammed the door. "You wash my sheets, you make my bed—or I'll tell your mother!"

Carmella wondered if they had fucked all afternoon and evening, and if they'd had enough condoms. (She was so upset about it, she forgot that she'd gone back to the apartment because she'd forgotten something.)

Her dear Gamba had wanted his son to be safe from girls—and how the cook had cried when Danny went away to Exeter! Yet Carmella could never tell him that sending the boy to boarding school hadn't really worked. (Not in the way Dominic had hoped.) Dominic had also been overly impressed by the list of the colleges and universities many Exeter graduates attended; the cook couldn't understand why Danny hadn't been a good enough student at the academy to get into one of those Ivy League schools. The University of New Hampshire had been a disappointment to Dominic, as were his son's grades at Exeter. But the academy was a very hard school for someone coming from the Mickey, and Danny had demonstrated little aptitude for math and the sciences.

Mainly, the boy's grades weren't great because he *wrote* all the time. Mr. Leary had been right: So-called creative writing wasn't valued at Exeter, but the *mechanics* of good writing was. And there were individual English teachers there who'd played the Mr. Leary role for Danny—they read the fiction that young Baciagalupo showed them. (They hadn't once suggested a nom de plume, either.)

The other thing Danny did at Exeter was all that insane running. He ran cross-country in the fall, and ran on the track teams both winter and spring. He hated the required athletics at the school, but he liked running. He was a distance runner, primarily; it just went with his body, with his slightness. He was never very competitive; he liked to run as hard and as fast as he could, but he didn't care about beating anybody. He had never been able to run before going to Exeter, and you could run year-round there.

There'd been nowhere to run in the North End—not if you liked running any distance. And in the Great North Woods, there was nowhere safe to run; you would trip over something, trying to run in those woods, and if you ran on one of the haul roads, a logging truck would mow you down or force you off the road. The logging companies owned those roads, and the asshole truck drivers—as Ketchum called them—drove as if *they* owned them. (Of course there was also the deer hunting, both bow season and the firearm season. If you tried running in the woods or on a haul road during deer season, some asshole hunter might shoot you or run you through with a hunting arrow.)

When Danny wrote Ketchum about his running at Exeter, Ketchum wrote the boy back as follows: "Hell, Danny, it's a good thing you didn't do all that running around Twisted River. Most places I'm familiar with in Coos County, if I see a fella running, I assume he's done some dirt and is running away. It would be a safe bet to shoot most fellas you see running around here."

Danny loved the indoor track at Exeter. The Thompson Cage had a sloped wooden track above a dirt one. It was a good place to think about the stories he was imagining; he could think very clearly when he ran, Danny discovered, especially when he started to get tired.

When he left Exeter with B grades in English and history, and C grades in just about everything else, Mr. Carlisle told Dominic and Carmella that perhaps the boy would be a "late bloomer." But, as a writer, to publish a first novel less than a year after he left the Iowa Workshop was a fairly *early*-bloomer thing to do; of course Mr. Carlisle had been speaking strictly academically. And Danny's grades at UNH were excellent; compared to Exeter, the University of New Hampshire had been easy. The hard part about Durham was meeting Katie Callahan, and everything that had happened with her—both in Durham and in Iowa City. Neither Carmella nor her dear Gamba could talk about that young woman without feeling sick, almost poisoned.

"And here you were, Gamba, worried about a few hot Italian girls in the North End!" Carmella had once exploded at him. "What you should have seen coming was that University of New Hampshire iceberg!"

"A cold cunt," Ketchum had called Katie.

"It was all the *writing*, too," Dominic had replied to Carmella. "All that damn *imagining* all the time—it couldn't have been good for Daniel."

"You're crazy, Gamba," Carmella told him. "Danny didn't make up Katie. And would you really have wanted him to go to Vietnam instead?"

"Ketchum wouldn't have let that happen," Dominic told her. "Ketchum wasn't kidding, Carmella. Daniel would have become a writer with some missing fingers on his writing hand."

Maybe she *didn't* want to meet Mr. Ketchum after all, Carmella found herself thinking.

THE WRITER DANIEL BACIAGALUPO received his M.F.A. degree from the Iowa Writers' Workshop in June 1967. Together with his two-year-old son, Joe, the writer left for Vermont almost immediately upon his graduation. Despite his troubles with Katie, Danny had liked Iowa City and the Writers' Workshop, but Iowa was hot in the summer, and he wanted to take his time about finding a place to live in

Putney, Vermont, where Windham College was. It would also be necessary to set up a proper day-care situation for little Joe, and to hire a regular babysitter for the boy—though perhaps one or two of Danny's students at the college would be willing to help out.

He told only one of his teachers (and no one else) at Iowa about the nom-de-plume idea—the writer Kurt Vonnegut, who was a kind man and a good teacher. Vonnegut also knew about Danny's difficulties with Katie. Danny didn't tell Mr. Vonnegut the reason he was considering a pen name, just that he was unhappy about it.

"It doesn't matter what your name is," Vonnegut told him. He also told the young writer that *Family Life in Coos County,* Danny's first book, was one of the best novels he'd ever read. "*That's* what matters—not what name you use," Mr. Vonnegut said.

The one criticism the author of *Slaughterhouse-Five* would make of the young writer was what he called a punctuation problem. Mr. Vonnegut didn't like all the semicolons. "People will probably figure out that you went to college—you don't have to try to prove it to them," he told Danny.

But the semicolons came from those old-fashioned nineteenth-century novels that had made Daniel Baciagalupo want to be a writer in the first place. He'd seen the titles and the authors' names on the novels his mother had left behind—the books his father had bequeathed to Ketchum in Twisted River. Danny would be at Exeter before he actually read those books, but he'd paid special attention to those authors there—Nathaniel Hawthorne and Herman Melville, for example. They wrote long, complicated sentences; Hawthorne and Melville had *liked* semicolons. Plus they were New England writers, those two—they were Danny's favorites. And the English novelist Thomas Hardy naturally appealed to Daniel Baciagalupo, who—even at twenty-five—had seen his share of what looked like fate to him.

He'd been somewhat alone among his fellow workshop students at Iowa, in that he loved these older writers far better than most contemporary ones. But Danny did like Kurt Vonnegut's writing, and he liked the man, too. Danny was lucky with the teachers he had for his writing, beginning with Michael Leary.

"You'll find someone," Vonnegut said to Danny, when they said good-bye in Iowa City. (His teacher probably meant that Danny would meet the right woman, eventually.) "And," Kurt Vonnegut added, "maybe capitalism will be kind to you."

That last thought was the one Danny drove back East with. "Maybe capitalism will be kind to us," he said several times to little Joe, en route to Vermont.

"You better find a place with a spare room for your dad," Ketchum had told him, when they'd last talked. "Although Vermont isn't far enough away from New Hampshire—not in my opinion. Couldn't you get a teaching job out West somewhere?"

"For Christ's sake," Danny had said. "Southern Vermont is about the same driving distance from Coos County as Boston is, isn't it? And we were far enough away in Boston for thirteen years!"

"Vermont's too close—I just know it is," Ketchum told him, "but right now it's a lot safer for your father than staying in Boston."

"I keep telling him," Danny said.

"I keep telling him, too, but he's not listening worth shit," the woodsman said.

"It's because of Carmella," Danny told Ketchum. "He's very attached to her. He should take her with him—I know she'd go, if he asked her—but he won't. I think Carmella is the best thing that ever happened to him."

"Don't say that, Danny," Ketchum told him. "You didn't get to know your mother."

Danny kept quiet about that with Ketchum. He didn't want the old logger to hang up on him.

"Well, it looks to me like I'll just have to haul Cookie's ass out of Boston—one way or another," Ketchum said, after there was silence for a while.

"How are you going to do that?" Danny asked him.

"I'll put him in a cage, if I have to. You just find a house in Vermont that's big enough, Danny. I'll bring your dad to it."

"Ketchum—you didn't kill Lucky Pinette, did you?"

"Of course I didn't!" Ketchum shouted into the phone. "Lucky wasn't worth murdering."

"I sometimes think that *Carl* is worth murdering," the writer Daniel Baciagalupo ventured; he just floated that idea out there.

"I find that I keep thinking about it," Ketchum admitted.

"I wouldn't want you to get caught," Danny told him.

"That's not the problem I'm having with it," the woodsman said. "I don't imagine that Carl would care if *he* got caught—I mean for killing your dad."

"What's the problem, then?" Danny asked.

"I would like him to try to kill me first," Ketchum answered. "Then I *wouldn't* have a problem with it."

It was just as the writer Daniel Baciagalupo had imagined; the conundrum was that although the cowboy was exceedingly stupid, he was smart enough to stay alive. And he'd stopped drinking—that meant Carl wouldn't completely lose control of himself. That might have been why he hadn't beaten up Six-Pack in two whole months, or at least he hadn't beaten her enough for her to leave him and tell him what she knew.

Six-Pack still drank. Ketchum knew she could easily *and* completely lose control of herself—that was also a problem.

"I worry about something," Danny told Ketchum. "*You* haven't stopped drinking. Aren't you afraid you'll pass out dead drunk, and that's when Carl will come after you?"

"You haven't met my dog, Danny—he's a fine animal."

"I didn't know you had a dog," Danny said.

"Hell, when Six-Pack left me, I needed someone to talk to."

"What about that lady you met in the library—the schoolteacher who's teaching you how to read?" Danny asked the logger.

"She *is* teaching me, but it's not a very conversational experience," Ketchum said.

"You're actually learning to read?" Danny asked.

"Yes, I am—it's just slower going than counting coon shit," Ketchum told him. "But I'm aiming to be ready to read that book of yours, when it's published." There was a pause on the phone before Ketchum asked: "How's it going with the nom de plume? Have you come up with one?"

"My pen name is Danny Angel," the writer Daniel Baciagalupo told Ketchum stiffly.

"Not *Daniel*? Your dad is real fond of the Daniel. I like the Angel part," Ketchum said.

"Dad can still call me Daniel," Danny said. "Danny Angel is the best I can do, Ketchum."

"How's that little Joe doing?" Ketchum asked; he could tell that the young writer was touchy about the nom-de-plume subject.

ON THE TRIP BACK EAST, Danny mostly drove at night, when little Joe was sleeping. He would find a motel with a pool and play with Joe most of the day. Danny took a nap in the motel when his two-year-old did; then he drove all night again. The writer Danny Angel had lots of time to think as he drove. He could think the whole night through. But even with his imagination, Danny couldn't quite see a woodsman like Ketchum coming to Boston. Not even Danny Angel, né Daniel Baciagalupo, could have imagined how the fearsome logger would conduct himself there.

THAT WINDHAM COLLEGE would turn out to be a funny sort of place wouldn't matter much to Danny Angel, whose first novel, *Family Life in Coos County,* would be published to fairly good reviews with modest hardcover sales. The young author would sell the paperback rights, and he sold the movie rights, too, though no film was ever made from the book—and the two novels that followed the first would receive more mixed reviews, and sell fewer copies. (Novels two and three wouldn't even be published in paperback, and there was no interest in the movie rights for either book.) But all of that wouldn't matter much to Danny, who was consumed by the task of keeping his father from harm—all the while trying to be a good dad to Joe. Danny just kept writing and writing. He would need to keep teaching to support himself and his young son—all the while saying to little Joe, "Maybe capitalism will be kind to us *one day.*"

It hadn't been too tough to find a house to rent in Putney, one big enough to include his father—and Carmella, if she ever came to Vermont. It was a former farmhouse on a dirt road, which Danny liked because a brook ran alongside it; the road also crossed the brook in a couple of places. The running water was a reminder to Daniel Baciagalupo of where he'd come from. As for the farmhouse, it was a few miles from the village of Putney, which was little more than a general store and a grocery—called the Putney Food Co-op—and a convenience store with a gas station that was diagonally across from the old paper mill, on the road to the college. When Danny first saw the paper mill, he knew that his dad wouldn't like living in Putney. (The cook came from Berlin; he hated paper mills.)

Windham College was an architectural eyesore on an otherwise beautiful piece of land. The faculty were a mix of moderately distinguished and not-so-distinguished professors; Windham had no academic virtues to speak of, but some of its faculty were actually good teachers who could have been working at better colleges and universities, but they wanted to live in Vermont. Many of the male students might not have been attending college at all if there hadn't been a war in Vietnam; four years of college was the most widely available deferment from military service that young males of draft age had. Windham was that kind of place—not long for this world, but it would last as long as the war dragged on—and as the source of Danny's first not-in-a-restaurant job, it wasn't bad.

Danny wouldn't have many students who were genuinely interested in writing, and the few he had weren't talented or hardworking enough to suit him. At Windham, you were lucky if half the students in your classroom were interested in *reading*. But as a first novelist who'd been saved from the Vietnam War, which Daniel Baciagalupo knew was his case, he was a lenient teacher. Danny wanted everyone—his male students, especially—to stay in school.

If, as some cynics said, Windham's sole justification for existence was that it managed to prevent a few young men from going to Vietnam, that was okay with Danny Angel; he'd grown up enough politically to hate the war, and he was more of a writer than a teacher. Danny didn't really care how academically responsible (or not) Windham College was. The teaching was just a job to him—one that gave him enough time to write, and to be a good father.

Danny let Ketchum know as soon as he and Joe had moved into the old farmhouse on Hickory Ridge Road. Danny didn't care who was reading the logger's letters to him now; the young writer assumed it was the library lady, the schoolteacher whose work-in-progress was teaching Ketchum how to read.

"There's plenty of room for Dad," Danny wrote to the woodsman;

the writer included his new phone number and directions to the Putney house, from both Coos County and Boston. (It was nearly the end of June 1967.) "Maybe you'll show up for the Fourth of July," Danny wrote to Ketchum. "If so, I trust you to bring the fireworks."

Ketchum was a big fireworks fan. There'd once been a fish he couldn't catch. "I swear, it's the biggest damn trout in Phillips Brook," he'd declared, "and the smartest." He'd blown up the fish, and no small number of nearby brook trout, with dynamite.

"Don't bring any *dynamite*," Danny had added, as a postscript. "Just the fireworks."

IT WASN'T PRINCIPALLY "fireworks" that Ketchum brought to Boston, the first leg of his trip. The North Station was in that part of the West End that bordered on the North End. Ketchum got off the train, carrying a shotgun over one shoulder and a canvas duffel bag in the other hand; the duffel bag looked heavy, but not the way Ketchum was toting it. The gun was in a leather carrying case, but it was clear to everyone who saw the woodsman what the weapon was—it had to be either a rifle or a shotgun. The way the carrying case was tapered, you could tell that Ketchum was holding the barrel of the weapon with the butt-end over his shoulder.

The kid who was then the busboy at Vicino di Napoli had just put his grandmother on a train. He saw Ketchum and ran ahead of him, back to the restaurant. The busboy said it appeared that Ketchum was "taking the long way around"—meaning that the logger must have looked at a map, and he'd chosen the most obvious route, which was not necessarily the fastest. Ketchum must have come along Causeway Street to Prince Street, and then intersected with Hanover—a kind of roundabout way to get to North Square, where the restaurant was, but the busboy alerted them all that the big man with a gun was coming.

"*Which* big man?" Dominic asked the busboy.

"I just know he's got a gun—he's carrying it over his shoulder!" the busboy said. Everyone who worked at Vicino di Napoli had been forewarned that the cowboy might be coming. "And he's definitely from up north—he's fucking scary-looking!"

Dominic knew that Carl would have the Colt .45 concealed. It was big for a handgun, but no one carried a revolver over his shoulder. "It sounds like you mean a rifle or a shotgun," the cook said to the busboy.

"Jesus and Mary!" Tony Molinari said.

"He's got a scar on his forehead like someone split his face with a cleaver!" the busboy cried.

"Is it Mr. Ketchum?" Carmella asked Dominic.

"It must be," the cook told her. "It can't be the cowboy. Carl is big and fat, but he's not especially 'scary-looking,' and there's not much of the north country about him. He just looks like a cop—either in or out of uniform."

The busboy was still babbling. "He's wearing a flannel shirt with the sleeves cut off, and he's got a *huge* hunting knife on his belt—it hangs almost to his knee!"

"That would be the Browning," Dominic said. "It's definitely Ketchum. In the summer, he just cuts the sleeves off his old flannel shirts—the ones that have torn sleeves, anyway."

"What's the gun for?" Carmella asked her dear Gamba.

"Maybe he's going to shoot me before Carl gets a chance to," Dominic said, but Carmella didn't see the humor in it—none of them did. They went to the door and windows to look for Ketchum. It was that time of the afternoon they had to themselves; they were supposed to be eating their big meal of the day, before they started the dinner service.

"I'm setting a place for Mr. Ketchum," Carmella said, and she started to do so. The two younger waitresses were checking themselves out in a mirror. Paul Polcari held a pizza paddle in both hands; it was the size of a giant tennis racquet.

"Put the paddle down, Paul," Molinari told him. "You look ridiculous."

"There's a lot of stuff in the duffel bag he's carrying—ammunition, maybe," the busboy said.

"*Dynamite*, possibly," the cook said.

"The way the man looks, someone might arrest him before he gets here!" the busboy told them all.

"Why did he come? Why didn't he call first?" Carmella asked her Gamba.

The cook shook his head; they would all just have to wait and see what Ketchum wanted.

"He's coming to take you, Gamba, isn't he?" Carmella asked the cook.

"Probably," Dominic answered.

Even so, Carmella smoothed the little white apron over her black skirt; she unlocked the door and waited there. Someone should greet Mr. Ketchum, she was thinking.

What will I do in Vermont? the cook thought to himself. Who cares about eating Italian there?

Ketchum would waste little time with them. "I know who you are," he told Carmella pleasantly. "Your boy showed me your picture, and you haven't changed much." She *had* changed in the thirteen-plus years since that wallet photo had been taken—she was at least twenty pounds heavier, they all knew—but Carmella appreciated the compliment. "Are you all here?" Ketchum asked them. "Or is someone in the kitchen?"

"We're all here, Ketchum," the cook told his old friend.

"Well, I can see *you* are, Cookie," Ketchum said. "And from your disapproving expression, you don't look too happy to see me."

Ketchum didn't wait for a response. He just walked into the back of the kitchen until they couldn't see him. "Can you see me?" he called to them.

They hollered, "No!"—all but the cook.

"Well, I can still see you—this is perfect," Ketchum told them. When he came out of the kitchen, he had the shotgun out of its carrying case; to a one, the cook included, they recoiled from it. The gun had a foreign smell—the gun oil, maybe, and the oil-stained leather case—but there was another smell, something *truly* foreign (even to cooks, even in a restaurant's dining room and kitchen). Maybe the smell was death, because guns are designed to do just one thing—kill.

"This here is an Ithaca twenty-gauge—a single shot, no safety. It's as sweet and simple as a shotgun comes," Ketchum told them. "Even a child can shoot it." He broke open the shotgun, allowing the barrel to fall almost to a forty-five-degree angle. "There's no safety because you have to cock it with your thumb before it'll fire—there's no half-cock, either," the woodsman was saying. They watched, fascinated—all but Dominic.

Everything Ketchum said about the gun made no sense to them, but Ketchum kept patiently repeating himself. He showed them how to load it, and how to take out the empty shell—he showed them again and again, until even the busboy and the young waitresses could have done it. It broke the cook's heart to see the rapt attention Carmella gave to the old logger; even Carmella could have loaded and fired the damn shotgun by the time Ketchum had finished.

They didn't really comprehend the gravity of the demonstration until Ketchum got to the part about the two kinds of ammunition. "This here is buckshot. You keep the Ithaca loaded at all times with buckshot." Ketchum held up a big hand in front of Paul Polcari's flour-whitened face. "From back there, where I was standing in the kitchen, the buckshot would make a pattern about this size on a target standing here." They were getting the idea.

"You just have to see how it goes. If Carl is believing your story—and you all have to tell the cowboy the *same* story—maybe he'll leave without incident. No shots need to be fired," Ketchum was saying.

"What story is that?" the cook asked his old friend.

"Well, it's about how you walked out on this lady," Ketchum said, indicating Carmella. "Not that even a fool would, mind you—but that's what you did, and everyone here hates you for it. They would like to kill you themselves, if they could find you. Do any of you have trouble remembering that story?" Ketchum asked them. They shook their heads—even the cook, but for a different reason.

"Just so there's one of you back in the kitchen," Ketchum continued. "I don't care if the cowboy knows you're back there—just so he can't quite see you. You can be banging pots and pans around all you want to. If Carl asks to see you, and he will, just tell him you're busy cooking."

"Which one of us should be back in the kitchen with the gun?" Paul Polcari asked the woodsman.

"It doesn't matter which one of you is back there—just so you all know how to work the Ithaca," Ketchum answered.

"You know Carl will come here, I suppose?" Dominic asked him.

"It's inevitable, Cookie. He'll want to talk to Carmella most of all, but he'll come here to talk to everyone. If he doesn't believe your story, and there's any trouble—that's when one of you shoots him," Ketchum said to them all.

"How will we know there's going to be trouble?" Tony Molinari asked. "How will we know if he believes our story?"

"Well, you won't see the Colt forty-five," Ketchum answered. "Believe me, he'll have it on him, but you won't know there's going to be trouble until you see the weapon. When Carl lets you see the Colt, he intends to use it."

"Then we shoot him?" Paul Polcari asked.

"Whoever's in the kitchen should call out to him first," Ketchum told them. "You just say something like, 'Hey, cowboy!'—just so he looks at you."

"It would seem to me," Molinari said, "that we'd have a better chance just to shoot him—I mean before he's looking in the direction of the shooter."

"No, not really," Ketchum told him patiently. "If the cowboy is looking in your direction, assuming you take aim at his throat, you'll hit him in the face and chest—both—and you'll probably blind him."

The cook looked at Carmella, because he thought she might faint. The busboy appeared to be feeling sick. "When the cowboy is blind, you don't have to be in as big a hurry—when you take the empty shell out and put the deer slug in. The buckshot blinds him, but the deer slug is the kill-shot," Ketchum explained to them. "First you blind him, then you kill him."

The busboy dashed for the kitchen; they could hear him barfing in the overlarge sink the dishwasher used to scour pots and pans. "Maybe *he's* not the one to be back in the kitchen," Ketchum said softly to the others. "Hell, we used to jacklight deer in Coos County just like this. Shine the light on them, till the deer stared right at you. First the buckshot, then the deer slug." But here the woodsman paused before continuing. "Well, with a deer—if you're close enough—the buckshot will suffice. With the cowboy, we don't want to take any unnecessary chances."

"I don't think we can kill anybody, Mr. Ketchum," Carmella said. "We simply don't know how to do that."

"I just *showed* you how!" Ketchum told her. "That little Ithaca is the simplest gun I own. I won it in an arm-wrestling match in Milan—you remember, don't you, Cookie?"

"I remember," the cook told his old friend. It had turned into something more serious than an arm-wrestling match, as Dominic remembered it, but Ketchum had walked away with the single-shot Ithaca—there was no disputing that.

"Hell, just work on your *story*," Ketchum told them. "If the story is good enough, maybe you won't have to shoot the bastard."

"Did you come all this way just to bring us the gun?" the cook asked his old friend.

"I brought the Ithaca for *them*, Cookie—it's for your friends, not for you. I came to help you *pack*. We've got a little traveling to do."

Dominic reached back for Carmella's hand—he knew she was standing behind him—but Carmella was quicker. She wrapped her arms around her Gamba's waist and burrowed her face into the back of his neck. "I love you, but I want you to go with Mr. Ketchum," she told the cook.

"I know," Dominic told her; he knew better than to resist her, or Ketchum.

"What else is in the duffel bag?" the busboy asked the logger; the kid had come out of the kitchen and was looking a little better.

"Fireworks—for the Fourth of July," Ketchum said. "Danny asked me to bring them," he told Dominic.

Carmella went with them to the walk-up on Wesley Place. The cook didn't pack many things, but he took the eight-inch cast-iron skillet off the hook in their bedroom; Carmella supposed that the skillet was mostly symbolic. She walked with them to the car-rental place. They would drive the rental car to Vermont, and Ketchum would bring the car back to Boston; then he would take the train back to New Hampshire from North Station. Ketchum hadn't wanted his truck to be missing for a few days; he didn't want the deputy sheriff to know he was away. Besides, he needed a new truck, Ketchum told them; with all the driving he and Dominic had to do, Ketchum's truck might not have made it.

For thirteen years, Carmella had been hoping to meet Mr. Ketchum. Now she'd met him, *and* his violence. She could see in an instant what her Angelù had admired about the man, and—when Ketchum had been younger—Carmella could easily imagine how Rosie Calogero (or any woman her age) might have fallen in love with him. But now she hated Ketchum for coming to the North End and taking her Gamba away; she would even miss the cook's limp, she told herself.

Then Mr. Ketchum said something to her, and it completely won her over. "If, one day, you ever want to see the place where your boy perished, I would be honored to show you," Ketchum said to her. Carmella had to fight back tears. She had *so wanted* to see the river basin where the accident happened, but not the logs; she knew the logs would be too much for her. Just the riverbank, where the cook and young Dan had stood and seen it happen—and maybe the exact spot in the water—yes, she might one day want to see that.

"Thank you, Mr. Ketchum," Carmella said to him. She watched them get into the car. Ketchum, of course, was the driver.

"If you ever want to see me—" Carmella started to say to Dominic.

"I know," the cook said to her, but he wouldn't look at her.

COMPARED TO THE DAY HER GAMBA LEFT, the day Carl came to Vicino di Napoli was almost easy for Carmella. It had again been at the time of their midafternoon meal, and it was nearly the end of that summer—sometime in August '67, when they'd all started to imagine (or hope) that the cowboy wasn't ever coming.

Carmella saw the cop first. It was just as Gamba had told her: When Carl was out of uniform, he still looked like he was wearing one. Of course Ketchum had remarked on the jowls, and the way the cowboy's neck was bunched in folds. ("Maybe all cops have bad haircuts," Ketchum had said to her.)

"Someone go back in the kitchen," Carmella said, standing up from the table; the door was locked, and she went to unlock it. It was Paul Polcari who went back in the kitchen. The second the cowboy came inside, Carmella found herself wishing it had been Molinari back there.

"You would be the Del Popolo woman?" the deputy sheriff asked her. He showed them all his badge while saying, "Massachusetts is out of my jurisdiction—actually, everythin' outside Coos County is out of my jurisdiction—but I'm lookin' for a fella I think you all know. He's got some answerin' to do—name of Dominic, a little guy with a limp."

Carmella started to cry; she cried easily, but in this case she had to force herself.

"That prick," Molinari said. "If I knew where he was, I'd kill him."

"Me, too!" Paul Polcari cried from the kitchen.

"Can you come out of there?" the deputy called to Paul. "I like to see everyone."

"I'm busy cooking!" Paul screamed; pots and pans were banging.

The cowboy sighed. They all remembered how the cook and Ketchum had described Carl; they'd said the cop never stopped smiling, but it was the most insincere smile in the world. "Look," the cowboy said to them, "I don't know what the cook's done to you, but he's got some explainin' to do to me—"

"He walked out on her!" Molinari said, pointing to Carmella.

"He stole her *jewels*!" the busboy cried.

The kid is an idiot! the others thought. (Even the cop might be smart enough to know that Carmella wasn't the sort of woman who had *jewels*.)

"I didn't figure Cookie for a jewel thief," Carl said. "Are you people bein' honest with me? You really don't know where he is?"

"No!" one of the young waitresses cried out, as if her companion waitress had stabbed her.

"That prick," Molinari repeated.

"What about *you*?" the cowboy called into the kitchen. Paul seemed to have lost his voice. When the pots and pans commenced to banging again, the others took this as a signal to move a little bit away from the cop. Ketchum had told them not to scatter like a bunch of chickens, but to get some necessary separation between the cowboy and themselves—just to give the shooter a decent shot at the bastard.

"If I knew where he was, I would *cook* him!" Paul Polcari shouted. He held the Ithaca in his heavily floured hands, which were shaking. He sighted down the barrel till he found the cowboy's throat—what he could manage to see of it, under Carl's multiple chins.

"Can you come out of there, where I can see you?" the cop called to Paul, squinting into the kitchen. "*Wops*," the cowboy muttered. That was when Tony Molinari got a glimpse of the Colt. Carl had put his hand inside his jacket, and Molinari saw the big holster that was awkwardly at an angle under the deputy's armpit, the fat man's fingers just grazing the grip of the long-barreled handgun. The handle of the Colt .45 was inlaid with what looked like bone; it was probably deer antler.

For Christ's sake, Paul! Molinari was thinking. The cowboy's already *looking* at you—just shoot him! To her surprise, Carmella was thinking the same thing—just shoot him! She had all she could do not to cover both ears with her hands.

Paul Polcari just wasn't the one for the job. The pizza chef was a sweet, gentle man; now he found that his throat felt as if a cup of flour had clogged it. He was *trying* to say, "Hey, cowboy!" The words wouldn't come. And the cowboy kept squinting into the kitchen; Paul Polcari knew that he didn't have to say anything. He could just pull the trigger and Carl would be blinded. But Paul couldn't—more to the point, he *didn't*—do it.

"Well, shit," the deputy sheriff said. He was moving sideways, toward the restaurant door. Molinari was worried, because the cowboy was out of sight from Paul's spot in the back of the kitchen; then Carl reached inside his jacket again, and they all froze. (Here comes the Colt! Molinari was thinking.) But now they saw it was just a small card that the cowboy had pulled out of his pocket; he handed it to Carmella. "Call me if that little cripple calls you," Carl said to her; he was still smiling.

From the sound of the pots and pans falling in the kitchen, Molinari imagined that Paul Polcari had passed out back there.

"It should have been you in the kitchen, Tony," Carmella told Molinari later, "but I can't blame poor Paul."

Paul Polcari would blame himself, however; he would never shut up about it. It took Tony Molinari almost an hour to clean the Ithaca of all the flour, too. But the cowboy wouldn't come back. Maybe just having the gun in the kitchen had helped. As for the story Ketchum had told them to stick to, Carl must have believed it.

When their ordeal was over, Carmella cried and cried; they'd all assumed she was crying from the terrible tension of the moment. But her Gamba leaving had hurt her more; Carmella was crying because she knew that her Gamba's ordeal was *not* over. Contrary to what she had said to Ketchum, she would have fired the Ithaca herself if she'd been back in the kitchen. One look at the cowboy—and, as Ketchum had forewarned her, the way he'd looked at her—had convinced Carmella that she could have pulled the trigger. But that chance wouldn't come to her, or to any of them, again.

IN TRUTH, Carmella Del Popolo would miss Dominic more than she ever did the fisherman, and she would miss Secondo, too. She knew about that hole the boy had bored in his bedroom door in the cold-water Charter Street apartment. Maybe she bathed more modestly after she knew about the hole, but Carmella had let young Dan see her nonetheless. With the fisherman dead, and Angelù gone, there'd been no one to look at her for too long. When Dominic and Danny came into her life, Carmella didn't really mind that the twelve-year-old watched her in the bathtub in the kitchen; she only worried what an influence the sight of her might have on the boy later on. (Carmella didn't mean on Danny's *writing*.)

Of all the people who were surprised, puzzled, disappointed, or in-different regarding what the writer Daniel Baciagalupo would choose for a nom de plume, Carmella Del Popolo was without a doubt the most pleased. For when *Family Life in Coos County,* by Danny Angel, was published, Carmella was sure that Secondo had always known he was her surrogate son—just as surely as everyone in Vicino di Napoli knew (Carmella, most of all) that absolutely no one could replace her cherished but departed Angelù.

WINDHAM COUNTY,
VERMONT, 1983

—

CHAPTER 7

BENEVENTO AND AVELLINO

THE BUILDING WAS OLD AND MUCH ABUSED BY ITS PROXIMITY to the Connecticut River. A few of the apartments had been abused, too, but not exclusively by the river; back in the sixties, a couple of Windham College kids had made a mess of one of them. Once cheap, the apartments were slightly more expensive now. The Connecticut had been cleaned up, and the town of Brattleboro was much improved by it. The cook's second-floor apartment was in the back of the old Main Street building, overlooking the river. Most mornings, Dominic would go downstairs to his empty restaurant and the deserted kitchen to make himself some espresso; the kitchen was also in the back, with a good view of the river.

On the ground floor, there had always been a storefront or some kind of restaurant on the Main Street side of the weather-beaten apartment building, which was across the street from an army-navy clothing store and the local movie theater, known as the Latchis.

If you walked down the hill on Main Street, past the Latchis, you would come to Canal Street and the market where the cook did most of his shopping. From there, heading out of town, you could find your way to the hospital and a shopping mall—and, out by Interstate 91, a bunch of gas stations and the usual fast-food places.

If you walked north on Main Street, up the hill, you came to The

Book Cellar—quite a good bookstore, where the now-famous author Danny Angel had done a reading or two, and his share of book signings. The cook had met a couple of his Vermont lady friends in The Book Cellar, where they all knew Dominic Del Popolo, né Baciagalupo, as *Mr.* Angel—the celebrated novelist's father, and the owner-chef of the best Italian restaurant around.

After Daniel chose that nom de plume, Dominic had had to re-name himself, too.

"Shit, I suppose you should both be Angels—maybe that much is clear," Ketchum had said. "Like father, like son—and all that goes with that." But Ketchum had insisted that the cook lose the Dominic, too.

"How about *Tony*?" Danny had suggested to his dad. It was the Fourth of July, 1967, and Ketchum had nearly burned down the Putney farmhouse with his fireworks display; little Joe continued to scream for five minutes after the last cherry bomb went off.

The name Tony still sounded Italian but was nicely *anonymous,* Danny was thinking, while Dominic liked the name because of his fondness for Tony Molinari; only a few nights away from Boston, the cook already knew how much he was going to miss Molinari. Tony Angel, previously Dominic Del Popolo, previously Baciagalupo, would miss Paul Polcari, too—nor would the cook think any less of Paul when he heard about what happened in August of that same summer.

Tony Angel would blame Ketchum for the mishap of the cowboy getting out of Vicino di Napoli alive—not Paul Polcari. Poor Paul could never have squeezed the trigger. It was Ketchum's fault, in the cook's opinion, because Ketchum had told them all that it didn't matter which one of them was back in the kitchen with the shotgun. Come on! For someone who knew guns as well as Ketchum did, he should have known that *of course* it mattered who was taking aim and would (or would not) pull the trigger! Tony Angel would never blame sweet, gentle Paul.

"You blame Ketchum too much, for everything," Danny would tell his dad more than once, but that was just the way it was.

If Molinari had been back in the kitchen, Dominic Del Popolo would have changed his name back to Dominic Baciagalupo—and he would have gone back to Boston, to Carmella. The cook would never have had to become Tony Angel. And the writer Danny Angel, whose fourth novel was his first bestseller—now in 1983, his fifth novel had already been translated into more than thirty foreign languages—would have gone back to calling himself, as he dearly wanted to, Daniel Baciagalupo.

"Damn it, Ketchum!" the cook had said to his old friend. "If Carmella had been back in the kitchen with your blessed Ithaca, she would have shot Carl *twice* while he was still squinting at her. If the idiot *busboy* had been back there, I swear he would have pulled that trigger!"

"I'm sorry, Cookie. They were your friends—I didn't know them. You should have told me there was a nonshooter—a fucking *pacifist!*—among them."

"Stop blaming each other," Danny would tell them repeatedly.

After all, it had been sixteen years—or it would be, this coming August—since Paul Polcari failed to pull the trigger of Ketchum's single-shot 20-gauge. It had all worked out, hadn't it? the cook was thinking, as he sipped his espresso and watched the Connecticut River run by his kitchen window.

They had once run logs down the Connecticut. In the dining room of the restaurant, which looked out upon Main Street and the marquee with the name of whatever movie was currently playing at the Latchis Theatre, the cook had framed a big black-and-white photograph of a logjam in Brattleboro. The photo had been taken years ago, of course; they weren't moving logs over water in Vermont or New Hampshire anymore.

River driving had lasted longer in Maine, which was why Ketchum had worked so much in Maine in the sixties and seventies. But the last river drive in Maine was in 1976—from Moosehead Lake, down the Kennebec River. Naturally, Ketchum had been in the thick of it. He'd called the cook collect from some bar in Bath, Maine, not far from the mouth of the Kennebec.

"I'm trying to distract myself from some asshole shipyard worker, who is sorely tempting me to cause him a little bodily harm," Ketchum began.

"Just remember you're an out-of-stater, Ketchum. The local authorities will take the side of the shipyard worker."

"Christ, Cookie—do you know what it costs to move logs over water? I mean getting them from where you cut them to the mill— about fifteen fucking cents a cord! That's all a river drive will cost you."

The cook had heard this argument too many times. *I could hang up,* Tony Angel thought, but he stayed on the phone—perhaps out of pity for the shipyard worker.

"It'll cost you six or seven dollars a cord to get logs to the mill over *land*!" Ketchum shouted. "Most roads in northern New England aren't worth shit to begin with, and now there'll be nothing but ass-hole truck drivers on them! You may think it's already a world of acci-dents, Cookie, but imagine an overloaded logging truck tipping over and crushing a carload of skiers!"

Ketchum had been right; there'd been some terrible accidents in-volving logging trucks. In northern New England, it used to be that you could drive all over the place—according to Ketchum, only a moose or a drunken driver could kill you. Now the trucks were on the big roads and the little ones; the asshole truck drivers were every-where.

"This asshole country!" Ketchum had bellowed into the phone. "It'll always find a way to make something that was cheap expensive, and to take a bunch of jobs away from fellas in the process!"

There was an abrupt end to their conversation. In that bar in Bath, the sounds of an argument rose indistinctly; a violent scuffle ensued. No doubt somebody in the bar had objected to Ketchum defaming the entire country—in all likelihood, the aforementioned asshole shipyard worker. ("Some asshole *patriot,*" Ketchum later called the fella.)

THE COOK LIKED LISTENING to the radio when he started his pizza dough in the morning. Nunzi had taught him to always let a pizza dough rise twice; perhaps this was a silly habit, but he'd stuck to it. Paul Polcari, a superb pizza chef, had told Tony Angel that two rises were better than one, but that the second rise wasn't absolutely neces-sary. In the cookhouse kitchen in Twisted River, the cook's pizza dough had lacked one ingredient he now believed was essential.

Long ago, he'd said to those fat sawmill workers' wives—Dot and

May, those bad old broads—that he thought his crust could stand to be sweeter. Dot (the one who'd tricked him into feeling her up) said, "You're crazy, Cookie—you make the best pizza crust I've ever eaten."

"Maybe it needs honey," the then Dominic Baciagalupo had told her. But it turned out that he was out of honey; he'd tried adding a little maple syrup instead. That was a bad idea—you could taste the maple. Then he'd forgotten about the honey idea until May reminded him. She'd bumped him, on purpose, with her big hip while handing him the honey jar.

The cook had never forgiven May for her remark about Injun Jane—when she'd said that Dot and herself weren't "Injun enough" to satisfy him.

"Here, Cookie," May had said. "It's honey for your pizza dough."

"I changed my mind about it," he told her, but the only reason he hadn't tried putting honey in his dough was that he didn't want to give May the satisfaction.

It was in the kitchen at Vicino di Napoli where Paul Polcari first showed Tony Angel his pizza-dough recipe. In addition to the flour and water, and the yeast, Nunzi had always added a little olive oil to the dough—not more than a tablespoon or two, per pizza. Paul had shown the cook how to add an amount of honey about equal to the oil. The oil made the dough silky—you could bake the crust when it was thin, without its becoming too dry and brittle. The honey—as the cook himself had nearly discovered, back in Twisted River—made the crust a little sweet, but you never tasted the honey part.

Tony Angel rarely started a pizza dough without remembering how he'd *almost* invented the honey part of his recipe. The cook hadn't thought of big Dot and even bigger May in years. He was fifty-nine that morning he thought of them in his Brattleboro kitchen. How old would those old bitches be? Tony Angel wondered; surely they'd be in their sixties. He remembered that May had a slew of grandchildren—some of them the same age as her children with her second husband.

Then the radio distracted Tony from his thoughts; he missed what he imagined as the *Dominic* in himself, and the radio reminded him of all he missed. It had been better back in Boston—both the radio station they'd listened to in Vicino di Napoli *and* the music. The music

had been awful in the fifties, the cook thought, and then it got so un-
believably good in the sixties and seventies; now it was borderline
awful again. He liked George Strait—"Amarillo by Morning" and
"You Look So Good in Love"—but this very day they'd played two
Michael Jackson songs in a row ("Billie Jean" and "Beat It"). Tony
Angel detested Michael Jackson. The cook believed it was beneath
Paul McCartney to have done "The Girl Is Mine" with Jackson; they
had played that song, too, earlier in the morning. Now it was Duran
Duran on the radio—"Hungry Like the Wolf."

The music really had been better in Boston, in the sixties. Even old
Joe Polcari had sung along with Bob Dylan. Paul Polcari would bang
on the pasta pot to "(I Can't Get No) Satisfaction," and in addition to
The Rolling Stones and all the Dylan, there were Simon and Gar-
funkel and The Beatles. Tony imagined he could still hear how
Carmella sang "The Sound of Silence"; they had danced together in
the kitchen at Vicino di Napoli to "Eight Days a Week" and "Ticket
to Ride" and "We Can Work It Out." And don't forget there'd been
"Penny Lane" and "Strawberry Fields Forever." The Beatles had
changed everything.

The cook shut off the radio in his Brattleboro kitchen. He tried to
sing "All You Need Is Love" to himself instead of listening to the
radio, but neither Dominic Del Popolo, né Baciagalupo, *nor* Tony
Angel had ever been able to sing, and it wasn't long before that Beatles' song began to resemble a song by The Doors ("Light My Fire"),
which gave the cook a most unwelcome memory of his former
daughter-in-law, Katie. She'd been a big fan of The Doors and The
Grateful Dead and Jefferson Airplane. The cook kind of liked The
Doors and The Dead, but Katie had done a Grace Slick imperson-
ation that made it impossible for Tony Angel to like Jefferson Airplane—"Somebody to Love" and "White Rabbit," especially.

He remembered that time, just before Daniel and his wife and the
baby had left for Iowa, when Daniel brought Joe to Boston to stay
with the cook and Carmella. Daniel and Katie were going to a Beatles concert at Shea Stadium in New York; someone in Katie's la-di-da
family had gotten her the tickets. It was August; over fifty thousand
people had attended that concert. Carmella loved taking care of little

Joe—he'd been a March baby, like his father, so the boy had been only five months old at the time—but both Katie and Daniel were drunk when they came to the North End to pick up their baby.

They must have been smashed when they left New York, and they'd driven drunk the whole way to Boston. Dominic would not let them take Joe. "You're not driving back to New Hampshire with the baby—not in your condition," the cook told his son.

That was when Katie did her sluttish swaying and singing—*vamping* her way through "Somebody to Love" and "White Rabbit." Neither Carmella nor the cook could bear to look at Grace Slick after Katie's lewd, provocative performance.

"Come on, Dad," Danny said to his father. "We're fine to drive. Let little Joe come with us—we can't all sleep in this apartment."

"You'll just have to, Daniel," his father told him. "Joe can sleep in our room, with Carmella and me, and you and Katie will just have to find a way to fit in the single bed in your room—neither one of you is a large person," the cook reminded the young couple.

Danny was angry, but he held his temper. It was Katie who behaved badly. She went into the bathroom and peed with the door open—they could all hear her. Daniel gave his dad a look that said, Well, what did you expect? Carmella went into her bedroom and closed the door. (Little Joe was already asleep in there.) When Katie came out of the bathroom, she was naked.

Katie spoke to Danny as if her father-in-law weren't there. "Come on. If we have to do it in a single bed, let's get started."

Of course the cook knew that his son and Katie didn't *really* have noisy sex then and there, but that's what Katie wanted Danny's dad and Carmella to believe; she carried on like she was having an orgasm every minute. Both Danny and his wife were so drunk that they slept right through little Joe's nightmare later that night.

The cook and his son didn't speak to each other when Daniel left with his wife and child the next day; Carmella didn't look at Katie. But shortly before the would-be writer Daniel Baciagalupo took his family to Iowa, the cook had called his son.

"If you keep drinking the way you are, you won't write anything worth reading. The next day, you won't even remember what you wrote the day before," the young writer's father told him. "I stopped drinking because I couldn't handle it, Daniel. Well, maybe it's genetic—maybe you can't handle drinking, either."

Tony Angel didn't know what had happened to his son in Iowa City, but something had made Daniel stop drinking. Tony didn't really *want* to know what had happened to his beloved boy in Iowa, because the cook was certain that Katie had had something to do with it.

WHEN HE FINISHED WITH THE PIZZA DOUGH—the dough was having its first rise in the big bowls the cook covered with damp dish towels—Tony Angel limped up Main Street to The Book Cellar. He was fond of the young woman who ran the bookstore; she was always nice to him, and she often ate in his restaurant. Tony would buy her a bottle of wine on occasion. He cracked the same joke whenever he came into The Book Cellar.

"Have you got any women to introduce to me today?" Tony always asked her. "Someone about my age—or a little younger, maybe."

The cook really liked Brattleboro, and having his own restaurant. He had hated Vermont those first few years—better said, it was Putney he'd hated. Putney had an alternative style about it. ("Putney is an *alternative* to a town," the cook now liked to say to people.)

Tony had missed the North End—"something wicked," as Ketchum would say—and Putney was full of self-advertising hippies and other dropouts. There was even a commune a few miles out of town; the name of it had the word *clover* in it, but Tony couldn't remember what the rest of it was. He believed it was a women-only commune, which led the cook to suspect they were all lesbians.

And the butcher in the Putney Food Co-op kept cutting herself, or himself; cutting yourself wasn't what a butcher was supposed to do, and Tony thought the butcher's sex was "indeterminable."

"For God's sake, Dad, the butcher is clearly a woman," Danny told his father, with exasperation.

"You *say* she is, but have you taken all her clothes off—just to be sure?" his dad asked him.

Yet Tony Angel had opened his own pizza place in Putney, and despite the cook's constant complaints about Windham College—it didn't look like a "real" college to him (never mind that he'd not been to college), and all the college kids were "assholes"—the pizza place did very well, largely because of the Windham students.

"Constipated Christ, don't call it *Angel's* Pizza—or anything with the *Angel* name in it," Ketchum had told the cook. In retrospect, Ketchum had grown increasingly uncomfortable with Danny and his father choosing the name Angel—in case Carl ever remembered that the death of the *original* Angel had been coincident with the cook and his son leaving town in the first place. As for little Joe's name, Danny had chosen it, though he'd wanted to name his son after his dad— Dominic, Jr. (Katie hadn't liked either the Dominic or the Junior.) But Danny had refused to give little Joe the writer's nom de plume. Joe had remained a Baciagalupo; the boy didn't become an Angel. Both Danny and the cook remembered that Carl hadn't been able to *pro- nounce* Baciagalupo; they told Ketchum it was unlikely the cowboy could spell it, either—not even to save his own fat ass. So what if Joe was still a Baciagalupo? Ketchum just had to live with it. And now Ketchum kept complaining about the *Angel* name!

The cook often dreamed of that asshole Gennaro Capodilupo, his runaway father. Tony Angel could still hear the names of those two hill towns, which were also provinces, in the vicinity of Naples—those words his mother, Nunzi, had murmured in her sleep: Benevento and Avellino. Tony believed that his father really had gone back to the vicinity of Naples, where he'd come from. But the truth was, the cook didn't care. When someone abandons you, why should you care?

"And don't get cute and call the pizza place Vicinity of Naples," Ketchum had told the cook. "I know the cowboy doesn't speak Italian, but any fool might one day figure out that Vicino di Napoli, or how- ever the fuck you say it, *means* 'in the Vicinity of Naples.' "

So the cook had called his Putney pizza place Benevento; it was al- ways the first of the two towns or provinces Annunziata had uttered in her sleep, and no one but Tony Angel had heard his mother say it. The goddamn cowboy couldn't possibly come up with any connec- tions to Benevento.

"Shit, it sure sounds Italian—I'll give you that, Cookie," Ketchum had said.

The Putney pizza place had been right on Route 5, just before the fork in the center of town, where Route 5 continued north, past the paper mill and a tourist trap called Basketville. Windham College was a little farther north, up Route 5. The left-hand fork, where the Putney General Store was—and the Putney Food Co-op, with the self-lacerating butcher of "indeterminable" sex—went off in the direction of Westminster West. Out that way was the Putney School—a prep school Danny disdained, because he thought it wasn't up to *Exeter's* standards—and, on Hickory Ridge Road, where the writer Danny Angel still lived, there was an independent elementary school called the Grammar School, which had been very much up to *Danny's* standards.

He'd sent Joe there, and the boy had done well enough to get into Northfield Mount Hermon—a prep school Danny *did* approve of. NMH, as the school was called, was about half an hour south of Brattleboro, in Massachusetts—and an hour's drive from Danny's property in Putney. Joe, who was a senior in the spring of 1983, saw quite a lot of his dad and his grandfather.

In his Brattleboro apartment, the cook had a guest bedroom that was always ready for his grandson. Tony had torn out the kitchen in that apartment, but he'd kept the plumbing intact; he had built quite a spacious bathroom, which overlooked the Connecticut. The bathtub was big and reminded the cook of the one Carmella had had in her kitchen in that cold-water Charter Street apartment. Tony still didn't know for certain that Daniel had spied on Carmella in that bathtub, but he'd read all five of his son's novels, and in one of them there's a luscious-looking Italian woman who luxuriates in taking long baths. The woman's stepson is of an age where he's just beginning to masturbate, and the boy beats off while watching his stepmother bathe. (The clever kid bores a hole in the bathroom wall; his bedroom is conveniently next to the bathroom.)

While there were these little details of a recognizable kind in Danny Angel's novels, the cook more often noticed things that he was sure his son must have made up. If Carmella had put in an identifiable bathtub appearance, the character of the stepmother in that novel was definitely *not* based on Carmella; nor could the cook find any but the most superficial elements of himself in Daniel's novels, or much of Ketchum. (A minor character's broken wrist is mentioned in passing in one novel, and there's a different character's penchant for saying,

"Constipated Christ!" in another.) Both Ketchum and Tony Angel had talked about the absence of *anyone* in the novels who revealed to them their quintessential and beloved Daniel.

"Where is that boy hiding himself?" Ketchum had asked the cook, because even in Danny Angel's fourth (and most famous) novel, which was titled *The Kennedy Fathers*, the main character—who escapes the war in Vietnam with the same paternity deferment that kept Danny out of the war—bears little *essential* resemblance to the Daniel that Ketchum and the cook knew and loved.

There was a character based on Katie in *The Kennedy Fathers*—Caitlin, Danny Angel named her—a little sprite of a thing with a disproportionately oversize capacity for serial infidelities. She saves a truly hard-to-believe number of Kennedy fathers from the Vietnam War. The Caitlin character races through numerous husbands with the same casual frankness both the cook and Ketchum associated with the way Katie probably gave blow jobs—yet Caitlin *wasn't* Katie.

"She's way too nice," Tony Angel told his old friend.

"I'll say she is!" Ketchum agreed. "You even end up *liking* her!"

All her husbands end up liking Caitlin, too—or they can't get over her, if that amounts to the same thing. And all those babies who are born and get abandoned by their mother—well, we never find out what *they* think of their mother. The novel concludes when President Nixon puts an end to the 3-A deferment, while the war will drag on for five more years, and the Caitlin character just kind of disappears; she is a lost soul in the last chapter of *The Kennedy Fathers*. There's something that doesn't bode well about how she phones all her husbands and asks to speak to her kids, who have no memory of her. That's the last we hear about Caitlin—it's a sympathetic moment.

Ketchum and the cook knew very well that Katie had not once called Daniel and asked to speak to Joe; it seemed that she simply hadn't cared enough about them to even inquire how they were doing, though Ketchum always said that Danny might hear from Katie if he ever became famous.

When *The Kennedy Fathers* was published, and Danny *did* become famous, he still didn't hear from Katie. He did, however, hear from a few other Kennedy fathers. Most of the letters about the novel were favorable. Danny believed there was some shared guilt among such fathers, who'd all felt, at one time in their lives, that they probably *should* have gone to Vietnam, or (like Danny) they'd actually *wanted* to go. Now, of course, they all knew they were lucky that they hadn't gone to the war.

The novel was praised for seeing yet another dimension of how the war in Vietnam did permanent damage to America, and how the country would long be divided by that war. The young fathers in the novel might (or might not) turn out to be *good* fathers, and it was too soon to say if those children—those "tickets out of Vietnam," as Danny called them—would be damaged. Most reviewers thought that Caitlin was the novel's most memorable character, and the real hero of the story. She sacrifices herself to save these young men's lives, even though she leaves them—and quite possibly her own children—feeling haunted.

But the novel really pissed off Ketchum and the cook. They had hoped to read a hatchet job on Katie. But Danny didn't do that; instead, he'd turned his awful ex-wife into a fucking *hero*!

One letter Danny received from a Kennedy father was worth saving, and he would show it to his son—this was several years after *The Kennedy Fathers* was first published, in the spring of Joe's junior year at Northfield Mount Hermon, when the boy had been driving for only a year and had just turned seventeen. At young Joe's suggestion, Danny also showed the letter to his dad and Ketchum. While Danny and Joe had talked about the letter—both about what it meant, and what it didn't say—Ketchum and the cook were careful in their responses to Danny. The older men knew that Danny's feelings for Katie were a little different from theirs.

The letter was from a self-described "single parent" living in Portland, Oregon—a man named Jeff Reese. The letter began: "Like you, I am a Kennedy father—one of the stupid boys Katie Callahan saved. I'm not sure how many of us there are. I know of at least one other— I mean, in addition to you and me—and I am writing him, too. I regret to inform you both that Katie couldn't save herself—just a few of us stupid boys. I can't tell you more, but I know it was an accidental overdose." He didn't say of what. Perhaps Jeff Reese assumed that Danny would have known what substance Katie was abusing, but they'd not done any serious drugs together, only the occasional marijuana. In their case, the drinking and a little pot had been more than enough. (There wasn't a word about *The Kennedy Fathers,* though one would guess that Jeff Reese had somewhat belatedly read it. Maybe he'd read just enough of the book to see for himself that the Caitlin character wasn't really Katie. And if Katie had read *The Kennedy Fathers,* or any of Danny Angel's other novels, Jeff Reese didn't say; at least Katie must have known that Daniel Baciagalupo had become Danny Angel, for how else would Jeff Reese have made the connection?)

Danny had driven down to Northfield Mount Hermon for an impromptu visit with Joe at his son's school. The old James Gym was empty—it wasn't wrestling season—and they sat together on the sloped wooden track, reading and rereading the letter about Joe's mother. Maybe the boy had thought he would one day hear from his mom; Danny had never expected to hear from Katie, but the writer in him had thought she might try to make contact with her son.

At seventeen, Joe Baciagalupo often looked like he needed a shave, and he had the more defined facial features of a young man in his early twenties; yet there was something expectant and open in his expression that reminded his father of a more childlike Joe, or of the "little" Joe the boy had been. This might have made Danny say to him, "I'm sorry that you didn't have a mother, or that I didn't find someone who could have done a good job in that role for you."

"But it's not just a *role,* is it?" Joe asked his dad; he was still holding the letter about his mother dying from an overdose, and Danny would later think that the way the seventeen-year-old looked at the letter, it was as if it were foreign currency—a curiosity, exotic-looking, but of no particular use at the moment. "I mean, I had *you*—you've always been there," Joe continued. "And your dad—well, you know, he's like a second dad to me. And then there's Ketchum."

"Yes," was all the writer could say; when he talked to young Joe, Danny sometimes didn't know if he was talking to a child or a man. Was it part of the same anxiousness Danny had felt as a twelve-year-old that he suspected Joe kept things from him, or was it what Ketchum and the cook had kept from Danny that made him wonder about how forthcoming (or not) Joe was?

"I just want to be sure you're okay," Danny said to Joe, but the seventeen-year-old—child or man, or both—surely knew that by the *okay* word his father was implying much more than *okay*. The writer meant *thriving;* Danny also meant *safe,* as if regular father-son conversations could possibly ensure Joe's safety. (The child's or the man's.) Yet, as Danny would one day consider, maybe this was a writer's peculiar burden—namely, that the anxiety he felt as a father was conflated with the analysis he brought to bear on the characters in his fiction.

The day he showed Joe the letter about Katie, it struck Danny Angel that the news of Katie's death had an offstage, unreal quality; the distant report, from a stranger, had the effect of turning Katie into a minor fictional character. And if Danny had kept up the drinking with her, he would have turned out the same way—either an accident or a suicide, the finale disappointingly offstage. His dad had been right about the drinking; maybe not being able to handle it *was,* as his father had suggested, "genetic."

"AT LEAST HE HASN'T WRITTEN about Rosie—not yet," Ketchum wrote to his old friend.

Tony Angel had liked Ketchum's letters better before the old logger, who was now sixty-six, had learned to read. That lady he'd met in the library—"the schoolteacher" was all Ketchum ever called her—well, she'd done the job, but Ketchum was even crankier now that he could read and write, and the cook was convinced that Ketchum no longer listened as attentively. When you don't read, you *have* to listen; maybe those books the woodsman had heard were the books he'd understood best. Now Ketchum complained about almost everything he read. It also might have been that Tony Angel missed Six-Pack's handwriting. (In Ketchum's opinion, by the way, the cook had gotten crankier, too.)

Danny definitely missed Six-Pack Pam's influence on Ketchum; possibly his dependence on Pam had made Ketchum less lonely than he seemed to Danny now, and Danny had long ago accepted Six-Pack's role as a go-between in Ketchum's correspondence with the young writer and his dad.

Danny was forty-one in 1983. When men turn forty, most of them no longer feel young, but Joe—at eighteen—knew he had a relatively young dad. Even the girls Joe's age (and younger) at Northfield Mount Hermon had told the boy that his famous father was *very* good-looking. Maybe Danny was good-looking, but he wasn't nearly as good-looking as Joe.

The young man was almost eight inches taller than his dad and grandfather. Katie, the boy's mother, had been a noticeably small woman, but the men in the Callahan family were uniformly tall—not heavy but very tall. Their height went with their "patrician airs," the cook had declared.

He and Carmella had hated the wedding; they'd felt snubbed the whole time. It had been a lavish affair, at an expensive private club in Manhattan—Katie was already a couple of months pregnant—and for all the money the party cost, the food had been inedible. The Callahans weren't food people; they were the kind of ice-cube suckers who had too many cocktails and filled themselves with endless hors d'oeuvres. They looked like they had so much money that they didn't need to eat—that was what Tony Angel told Ketchum, who was still driving logs on the Kennebec at the time. He'd told Danny he had too much to do in Maine and couldn't come to the wedding. But the real reason Ketchum hadn't gone to the wedding was that the cook had asked him not to come.

"I know you, Ketchum—you'll bring your Browning knife and a twelve-gauge. You'll kill every Callahan you can identify, Katie included, and then you'll go to work on a couple of Danny's fingers with the Browning."

"I know you feel the same way I do, Cookie."

"Yes, I do," the cook admitted to his best friend, "and Carmella even agrees with us. But we've got to let Daniel do this his way. The Callahan whore is going to have *someone's* baby, and that baby will keep mine out of this disastrous war."

So Ketchum had stayed in Maine. The logger would later say it was a good thing Cookie had gone to the wedding. When Joe turned out to be tall, the cook might have been inclined to believe that his beloved Daniel couldn't have been the boy's father. After all, Katie fucked anyone she wanted to; she could easily have been knocked up by someone else and then married Daniel. But the wedding offered proof that there was a gene for tall men in the Callahan family, and Joe turned out to be the spitting image of Danny; it was just that the top of his dad's head came up only to the top of the young man's chest.

Joe had the body of an oarsman, but he wasn't a rower. For the most part, he'd grown up in Vermont—the boy was an experienced downhill skier. His dad didn't much care for the sport; as a runner, he preferred cross-country skiing, when he skied at all. Danny had continued to run; it still helped him to think, and to imagine things.

Joe was a wrestler at Northfield Mount Hermon, though he didn't have the body of a wrestler. It was probably Ketchum's influence that made Joe choose wrestling, the cook thought. (Ketchum was just a barroom brawler, but wrestling came closer to describing Ketchum's favorite kind of fight than boxing did. Usually, Ketchum didn't hit people until he got them down on the ground.)

The first time Ketchum had gone to one of Joe's wrestling matches at NMH, the barroom brawler hadn't understood the sport very well. Joe had scored a takedown, and his opponent lay stretched out on his side, when Ketchum shouted, "*Now* hit him—hit him *now!*"

"Ketchum," Danny said, "there's no hitting allowed—it's a wrestling match."

"Christ, that's the best time to hit a fella," Ketchum said, "when you've got him stretched out like that."

Later in that same match, Joe had his opponent in a near-pin position; Joe had sunk a half nelson around the other wrestler's neck and was tilting him toward his back.

"Joe's got his arm around the wrong side of the neck," Ketchum complained to the cook. "You can't choke someone with your arm around the *back* of a fella's neck—you've got to be on his fucking throat!"

"Joe's trying to pin that guy on his back, Ketchum—he's not trying to *choke* him!" Tony Angel told his old friend.

"Choking is illegal," Danny explained.

Joe won his match, and, after all the matches were over, Ketchum went to shake the boy's hand. That was when Ketchum stepped on a wrestling mat for the first time. When the woodsman felt the mat yield under his foot, he stepped quickly back to the hardwood floor of the gym; it was as if he'd stepped on something alive. "Shit, that's the first problem," Ketchum said. "The mat's too soft—you can't really hurt a guy on it."

"Ketchum, you're not trying to hurt your opponent—just pin him, or beat him on points," Danny tried to explain. But the next thing they knew, Ketchum was attempting to show Joe a better way to crank someone over on his back.

"You get him down on his belly, and pull one of his arms behind his back," Ketchum said with enthusiasm. "Then you get a little leverage under the fella's forearm, and you drive his right elbow till it touches his left ear. Believe me, he'll turn over—if he doesn't want to lose his whole shoulder!"

"You can't bend someone's arm past a forty-five-degree angle," Joe told the old logger. "Submission holds and choke holds used to be legal, but nowadays you can't make someone yield to pain—that's called a submission hold—and you can't choke anyone. Those things aren't legal—not anymore."

"Constipated Christ—it's like everything else!" Ketchum complained. "They take what was once a good thing and fuck it up with *rules*!"

But after Ketchum had seen a few more of Joe's matches, he grew to like high school wrestling. "Hell, to be honest with you, Cookie, when I first saw it, I thought it was a sissy way to fight. But once you get the idea of it, you can actually tell who would win the match if it was taking place in a parking lot and there was no referee."

Joe was surprised by how many matches Ketchum attended. The old woodsman drove all over New England to see Joe and the NMH team wrestle. They had a pretty good team in Joe's senior year. In Joe's four years at Northfield Mount Hermon, Ketchum definitely saw more of the boy's wrestling matches than his father or grandfather did.

The matches were on Wednesdays and Saturdays. Tony Angel's Brattleboro restaurant was closed Wednesday, so that Tony could see some of his grandson's wrestling matches. But the cook could never find the time to see Joe wrestle on a Saturday, and it seemed that the more important matches—the season-ending tournaments, for example—were on the weekends. Danny Angel got to see more than half of his son's matches, but the writer took a lot of publishing-related trips. It was Ketchum who went to almost all of Joe's "fights," as the logger was inclined to call them.

"You missed a good fight," Ketchum would say, when he called the cook or Danny to tell them the results of young Joe's wrestling matches.

UNTIL HE HAD A BESTSELLER with *The Kennedy Fathers,* Danny didn't know that publishing houses had publicity departments. Now that his publishers were promoting his books, Danny felt an obligation to do some traveling on the books' behalf. And the translations were published at different times, rarely simultaneously with the English-language editions. This meant that it was unusual for a year to go by without Danny going somewhere to do a book tour.

When it wasn't wrestling season and his dad was traveling, Joe often spent weekends at his grandfather's apartment in Brattleboro. Sometimes his friends from Northfield Mount Hermon would have their parents take them out to dinner at Tony Angel's Italian restaurant. Occasionally, Joe would help out in the kitchen. It was like old times, and *not* like them, the cook would think—seeing his grandson instead of his son in a working kitchen, or busing tables. Tony, né Dominic, was reminded that he'd not seen as much of Daniel in those prep-school years as he now saw of Joe. Because of this, there was something bittersweet about the cook's relationship with his grandson; almost magically, there were times when Tony Angel got to relax with Joe—without once judging the boy the way the cook had felt compelled to judge (and criticize) Daniel.

The other guys on Joe's wrestling team had grown fond of Ketchum. "Is he your uncle—that tough-looking man with the scar?" the wrestlers would ask Joe.

"No, Ketchum's just a friend of the family—he was a river driver," Joe would tell them.

One day, Joe's wrestling coach asked him, "Did that big man with the hard handshake ever wrestle? He kind of looks like he might have, or could have."

"Not officially," Joe answered.

"What about that scar?" the coach asked Joe. "That's a nasty one—better than your average head-butt, anyway."

"That was no head-butt—that was a bear," Joe told the coach.

"A *bear*!"

"Just don't ever ask Ketchum about it," Joe said. "It's a terrible story. Ketchum had to kill the bear, but he didn't want to. He *likes* bears, generally."

There was a bit of the writer Danny Angel in Joe Baciagalupo, clearly—a deeper ingredient than a physical resemblance. But Danny worried that there was something reckless about his son; it wasn't a Baciagalupo recklessness of the *imagination,* either. It also wasn't the wrestling, which was nothing Danny had ever wanted to do—and the cook couldn't have imagined doing it, not with that limp. In fact, the wrestling seemed safe enough—once Joe had learned a little about it. There was another element in young Joe that Danny didn't recognize as coming from himself or his dad.

If there was an active Katie Callahan gene in the boy, maybe it was his penchant for risk-taking. He skied too fast, he drove a car too fast, and he was more than fast with girls; it seemed to his writer father that Joe just took too many chances.

"Maybe that's the Katie in him," Danny had said to his dad.

"Maybe," the cook replied; Tony Angel didn't like to think that *anything* of that awful woman had gotten into his grandson. "Then again, it might be your mother, Daniel. Rosie was a risk-taker, after all—just ask Ketchum."

In the time he'd spent looking at those photographs of his mother, Danny could have written a novel—though he'd stopped looking at the photos, for a while, after he learned the truth about his mom and Ketchum and his father. He'd once tried to give the photos to his dad, but Tony Angel wouldn't take them. "No, they're yours—I can see her very clearly, Daniel." His father tapped his temple. "Up here."

"Maybe Ketchum would like the photos," Danny said.

"Ketchum has his own pictures of your mother, Daniel," the cook told him.

Over time, a few of those photos Danny had pressed flat between the pages of the novels left behind in Twisted River—some of them, but no way near all of them—had been sent to him by Ketchum. "Here, I found this picture in one of her books," the accompanying letter from Ketchum would say. "I thought you should have it, Danny."

Albeit reluctantly, Danny had kept the photos. Joe liked to look at them. Perhaps the cook was right: Maybe Joe got some of his risk-taking or reckless instincts from his grandmother, not from Katie. When Danny looked at his mom's pictures, he saw a pretty woman with intense blue eyes, but the drunken rebel who'd do-si-doed two drunken men on the black ice of Twisted River—well, that element of Rosie Baciagalupo, née Calogero, wasn't evident in the photos her son had kept.

"Just keep an eye on his drinking," the cook had told his son—he meant young Joe's drinking. (It was Tony Angel's way of inquiring if his eighteen-year-old grandson was drinking yet.)

"I suppose there's the occasional party," Danny told his dad, "but Joe doesn't drink around me."

"The kind of drinking Joe might do around you isn't the kind we need to worry about," the cook said.

Joe's drinking would bear watching, the writer Danny Angel imagined. As for his son's genetic package, Danny knew more than he cared to remember about the boy's mom, Katie Callahan; she'd had one whale of an alcohol problem. And in Katie's case, she'd done more than the "occasional" marijuana, when she and Danny had been a couple—she'd smoked more than a "little" pot, Danny knew.

IT COULD BE ARGUED that Windham College was in its death throes before the end of the Vietnam War. Decreasing enrollment and an inability to meet a loan repayment would force the college to close in 1978, but Danny Angel sensed that there were signs of trouble ahead for Windham well before then. The writer would resign from the college in 1972, when he accepted a teaching job back at the Writers' Workshop in Iowa. He'd not written *The Kennedy Fathers* yet; Danny still had to teach for a living, and for teaching-writing jobs, Iowa is as good as they get. (You have students who are serious, and busy with their own writing, which means you get lots of time to write.)

Danny Angel would publish his second novel and write his third when he was again in Iowa City. In those years, before Joe was a teenager, Iowa City was a great town for Danny's son, too—pretty good schools, as one would expect in a university town, and a semblance of neighborhood life. Iowa City wasn't the North End, to be sure—not when it came to restaurants, especially—but Danny had liked being back there.

The writer gave his dad a choice: Tony Angel could come to Iowa City or he could stay in Putney. Danny wanted to keep the Vermont farmhouse. He'd bought the rental property on Hickory Ridge Road, just before he accepted the Iowa offer and resigned from Windham, because he wanted his father to be able to stay in Windham County— if the cook wanted to.

In the cook's mind, Carmella was the question. For the five years Tony Angel ran the Benevento pizza place in Putney, he'd taken a lot of shopping trips to Boston. It was more than a two-hour drive each way—kind of far for "shopping." Danny's dad claimed that he had to buy his pizza sausages at the Abruzzese meat market in the North End—and while he was in his old neighborhood, he might as well stock up on his cheeses, his olives, and his olive oil. But Danny knew that his dad was trying to "stock up" on as much of Carmella as he could. They hadn't really been able to break things off cleanly.

The cook had invested very little in Benevento; compared to where he'd worked before, in both Coos County and Boston, a pizza place in a poor man's college town had been relatively easy. He'd bought the building from an aging hippie who'd called himself The Sign Painter; it had looked to Tony Angel like a failing small business, and there was a rumor in town that the sign painter was responsible for the mis-spelling of the *theatre* word on the Latchis Theatre in Brattleboro. (The word on the marquee of the Main Street movie house was spelled "Theater," not "Theatre"; for years, the Latchis had sought funds to correct the mistake.) It was no rumor that the sign painter's wife, an allegedly flaky potter, had recently run out on him. All she'd left the miserable sign painter was her kiln, which gave the cook the idea for his brick pizza oven.

At the time Danny invited him to come to Iowa City, Tony was a little tired of running his own restaurant—a pizza place wasn't quite the kind of restaurant the cook wanted to own, anyway—and things with Carmella had pretty much run their course. Seeing each other only occasionally, she'd told the cook, had made her feel she was in an illicit relationship instead of a legitimate one. The *illicit* word sounded to Tony like something that might have come up when Carmella had been confessing her sins—either at St. Leonard or St. Stephen's, wherever Carmella did her confessing. (Confessing one's sins was a Catholic thing that had never caught on with the cook.)

Why not just see what the Midwest was like? Tony Angel thought. If he sold it now, the cook could get a little money for Benevento—whereas, if he waited, and if Windham College was going under, which Danny said it was, what would anyone want with a pizza place in Putney?

"Why don't you just let a fire get out of control in your pizza oven, and then collect the insurance?" Ketchum had asked his old friend.

"Did you burn down Twisted River?" the cook asked Ketchum.

"Hell, it was a ghost town when it burned—it was nothing but an eyesore, Cookie!"

"Those buildings, my cookhouse among them, weren't *nothing*, Ketchum."

"Shit, if that's how you feel about a little fire, maybe you *should* just sell your pizza place," the cook's old friend told him.

It was hardly a "little" fire that took down what had been the town of Twisted River. Ketchum had planned the torching to perfection. He chose a windless night in March, before mud season; it was before Carl had stopped drinking, too, which was why Ketchum got away with it. No one was able to find the deputy sheriff; in all probability, you couldn't have woken up the cowboy if you'd found him.

If there'd been any wind, Ketchum would have had to light only one fire—to burn both the town and the cookhouse. But he might have started a forest fire in the process—even in what had been a typically wet month of March, when there was still a lot of snow on the ground. Ketchum wasn't taking any chances. He *liked* the forest—it was the town of Twisted River and the cookhouse that he hated. (The night Rosie died, Ketchum had almost cut off his left hand in the cookhouse kitchen; he'd heard Cookie crying himself to sleep while Jane had stayed upstairs with the cook and little Danny.)

The night Twisted River burned, Ketchum must have had three-quarters of a cord of firewood in his truck. He divided the wood between the two bonfires he built—one at the abandoned sawmill in town, the other in what had been the cookhouse kitchen. He set both fires within minutes of each other, and watched them burn to the ground before morning. He used some fancy pine-scented lamp oil to ignite the bonfires; either kerosene or gasoline might have left some residue of themselves, and surely both would have left a taint in the air. But there'd been nothing left of the lamp oil, with its innocent pine scent—not to mention the well-seasoned firewood he'd used to start both fires.

"You know anythin' 'bout that fire in Twisted River last night, Ketchum?" Carl asked him the following day, after the hungover deputy sheriff had driven to the site of the devastation. "The tire tracks back in there looked like your truck to me."

"Oh, I was back in there, all right," Ketchum told the cop. "It was a *helluva* fire, cowboy—you should have seen it! It burned damn-near all night! I just took a beer or two and drove back in there to watch it." (It was a pity that the deputy had stopped drinking, Ketchum would say in later years.)

They were not on friendlier terms these days—the cowboy and Ketchum—now that Carl knew the Baciagalupo boy had killed Injun Jane with a skillet, and all the rest of it. Jane's death had been an accident, the deputy sheriff understood; according to Ketchum, her death probably didn't matter all that much to Carl, though the cop was pissed at Ketchum for never telling him the truth. What really mattered to the cowboy was that Cookie had been fucking Jane—at a time when Jane "belonged" to Carl. That was why Carl wanted to kill the cook; the deputy had made himself clear to Ketchum on that point.

"I know you won't tell me where Cookie is, Ketchum, but you tell that little cripple for me—I'm gonna find him," the cowboy said. "And you better watch your back, if you know what's good for you."

"I'm always watching my back, Carl," Ketchum told him. The old woodsman didn't say a word about his dog, that "fine animal." If the cowboy came after Ketchum, the veteran logger wanted the dog to be a surprise. Naturally, everyone who lived year-round on the upper Androscoggin must have known that Ketchum had a dog—Carl included. The animal rode around in Ketchum's truck. It was the dog's ferocity that Ketchum had managed to keep secret. (Of course it couldn't have been the *same* fine animal protecting Ketchum for six-

teen years; the present watchdog had to have been the son or grandson of that *first* fine animal, the dog who'd replaced Six-Pack Pam.)

"I told you," Ketchum would say, to both Danny and his dad. "New
Hampshire is next to Vermont—that's too close for comfort, in my
opinion. I think it's a *terrific* idea for you both to go to Iowa. I'm sure
little Joe will love it out there, too. It's another Injun name, Iowa—isn't
it? Boy, those Injuns were once all over, weren't they? And just look
what this country did to them! It kind of makes you wonder about our
country's intentions, doesn't it? Vietnam wasn't the first thing that
made us look bad. And where this asshole country is *headed*—well,
maybe those Injuns lying underground in Iowa, and all over, might just
say that we're one day going to get what's coming to us."

HOW WOULD ONE describe Ketchum's politics? the cook was thinking, as he limped down Brattleboro's Main Street, making his slow
way back to his restaurant from The Book Cellar.

LIVE FREE OR DIE

That's what it said on the New Hampshire license plates; Ketchum
was clearly a live-free-or-die man, and he'd always believed that the
country was going to Hell, but Tony Angel was wondering if his old
friend had ever even voted. The woodsman was disinclined to trust
any government, or anyone who took part in it. In Ketchum's opinion,
the only justification for having laws—for abiding by any rules,
really—was that the assholes outnumbered the sensible fellas. (And of
course the laws didn't apply to Ketchum; he'd lived without rules, except those of his own making.)

The cook stopped walking and looked admiringly down the hill at
his very own restaurant—the one he'd always wanted.

AVELLINO
ITALIAN COOKING

Avellino was that other hill town (also a province) in the vicinity of
Naples; it had always been the second word Nunzi murmured in her
sleep. And the sign said COOKING, not CUISINE—for the same reason

that Tony Angel thought of himself and called himself a cook, not a chef. He would always be just a cook, Tony thought; he believed he wasn't good enough to be a chef. Deep in his bones, the former Dominic Baciagalupo—how he missed the *Dominic!*—was just a mill-town, logging-camp kind of cook.

Tony Molinari was a *chef,* the cook was thinking—Paul Polcari, too. Tony Angel had learned a lot from those two—more than Nunzi ever could have taught him—but the cook had also learned he would never be as good as Molinari or Paul.

"You have no feeling for fish, Gamba," Molinari had told him as sympathetically as possible. It was true. There was only one fish dish on the menu at Avellino, and sometimes the only seafood of the day was a pasta dish—if the cook could get calamari. (He stewed it slowly for a long time, in a spicy marinara sauce with black olives and pine nuts.) But in Brattleboro, the calamari he could get generally came frozen, which was all right, and the most reliable fresh fish was swordfish, which Tony Molinari had taught him to prepare with lemon and garlic and olive oil—either under the broiler or on a grill—with fresh rosemary, if the cook could get it, or with dried oregano.

He didn't do *dolci.* It was Paul Polcari who'd gently made the point that the cook had no feeling for desserts, either—more to the point, *Italian* desserts, Tony Angel was thinking. What he did do well was the regular mill-town and logging-camp fare—pies and cobblers. (In Vermont, you couldn't go wrong with blueberries and apples.) At Avellino, the cook served a fruit-and-cheese course, too; many of his regular customers preferred that to dessert.

The admiration of his very own restaurant had distracted Tony Angel from his thoughts about Ketchum's politics, which he returned to while he made his gimpy way downhill to Avellino. When it came to what other people called progress—most engines, and machinery of all sorts—Ketchum was a bit of a Luddite. Not only did he miss the river drives; he claimed he'd liked logging better before there were chainsaws! (But Ketchum was overly fond of guns, the cook was thinking—guns were in a category of *machinery* the old woodsman would approve of.)

Neither a liberal nor a conservative, Ketchum could best be described as a libertarian—well, the logger was a libertine, too, Tony

Angel considered, and (in the woodsman's younger days) something of a rake and a profligate. Why was it that every time he thought of Ketchum, the cook couldn't help thinking of the logger in *sexual* terms? (The former Dominic Baciagalupo knew why that was, of course; it just always depressed him when his thoughts about Ketchum went there.)

Ketchum had been furious when father and son and grandson all came back to Vermont from Iowa, but the Writers' Workshop had been generous to let Danny teach there for as long as they did. They'd offered him only a two-year contract; Danny had asked to stay a third year, and they let him, but in the summer of '75, when Joe was ten, the family returned to Windham County. Danny loved his old farmhouse in Putney. His father would have nothing to do with living there. The Vietnam War was over; Windham College's death throes were more apparent. Besides, Tony Angel had never liked Putney.

While neither Danny's second nor third novel would make him any money, the cook had increased his savings in Iowa—enough to buy the old storefront space with the apartment above it on Brattleboro's Main Street. That was the year Avellino was born—when Danny was commuting to Mount Holyoke College in South Hadley, Massachusetts. It was the closest college-teaching job that the writer could find, but the distinguished and somewhat staid women's college was well over an hour's drive (nearly two) from Putney—a long commute in the winter months, if it was snowing. Still, living in Putney mattered to Danny. No small part of it was his high opinion of the Grammar School—within walking distance of home—where Joe would finish the eighth grade before going off to Northfield Mount Hermon.

The cook was shaking his head as he limped into his restaurant, because he was thinking that Daniel truly must love living in the country. Tony Angel didn't; the North End had made a city man out of him, or at least he was a neighborhood kind of guy. But not Daniel. He'd made the commute to that women's college for three years, before *The Kennedy Fathers* was published in '78; the novel's success had freed him from ever having to teach again.

Of course there'd been more money suddenly, and the cook had worried—he *still* worried—about what effect it might have on young

Joe. Daniel was old enough (thirty-six) when the bestseller business found him to not be affected by either the fame or the good fortune. But when Joe was only thirteen, the boy woke up one morning with a famous father. Couldn't this have made an unwelcome mark on any kid that age? And then there were the women Daniel went through— both before and after he was famous.

The writer had been living with one of his former Windham College students when he, Tony, and Joe moved to Iowa City. The girl with a boy's name—"It's Franky, with a *y*," she liked to say with a pout—hadn't made the move with them.

Thank God for that, the cook thought at the time. Franky was a feral-looking little thing, a virtual wild animal.

"She wasn't my student when I began to sleep with her," Danny had argued with his dad. No, but Franky had been one of his writing students only a year or two before; she was one of many Windham College students who never seemed to leave Putney. They went to Windham, they graduated, or they quit school but continued to hang around—they wouldn't leave.

The girl had dropped in on her former teacher one day, and she'd simply stayed.

"What does Franky do all day?" his dad had asked Danny.

"She's trying to be a writer," Danny said. "Franky likes hanging around, and she's nice to Joe—*he* likes her."

Franky did some housecleaning, and a little cooking—if you could call it that, the cook thought. The wild girl was barefoot most of the time—even in that drafty old farmhouse in the winter months, when Daniel heated the whole place with a couple of woodstoves. (Putney was the kind of town that worshipped woodstoves, Tony Angel had observed; there was even an *alternative* to heating in that town! The cook simply hated the place.)

Franky was a dirty-blonde with lank hair and a slouchy posture. She wore funny old-fashioned dresses of the kind the cook remembered Nunzi wearing, except Franky never wore a bra, and her underarms—what the cook saw of them—were unshaven. And Franky couldn't have been more than twenty-two or twenty-three when she'd lived with Daniel and little Joe. Daniel had just turned thirty when they went to Iowa.

There'd been more young women in the writer's life in Iowa City, one of his workshop students among them, and while there was no one special now—nor had there been anyone long-lasting since Danny Angel became famous—Joe, by the time he was a teenager, had seen his dad with numerous young women. (And three or four notably older women, the cook was remembering; two of those ladies were among Daniel's foreign publishers.)

The Putney property was a virtual compound these days. The writer had turned the old farmhouse into his guesthouse; he'd built a new house for himself and Joe, and there was a separate building where Danny did his writing. His "writing shack," Daniel called it. Some *shack*! Tony Angel thought. The building was small, but it had a half-bathroom in it; there was also a phone, a TV, and a small fridge.

Danny may have liked living in the country, but he wasn't exactly reclusive—hence the guesthouse. In his life as a writer, he'd gotten to know a number of city people, and they came to visit him—the occasional women included. Had Joe's exposure to his famous father's casual relationships with women made the teenager something of a playboy at prep school? Tony Angel wondered. He worried about his grandson—as much as, if not more than, the boy's dad did. Yes, the eighteen-year-old's drinking would bear watching, the cook knew. Joe had the mischievous insouciance of a boy who liked to party.

With the war in Vietnam, they would lower the drinking age in many states to eighteen, the logic being that if they could send mere boys off to die at that age, shouldn't the kids at least be allowed to drink? After the war was over, the drinking age would go back up to twenty-one again—but not until 1984—though nowadays, Tony knew, many kids Joe's age had fake I.D.'s. The cook saw them all the time at Avellino; he knew his grandson had one.

It was how Joe was more than fast with girls that *really* worried Tony Angel. Going too fast too soon with girls could get you in as much trouble as drinking, the former Dominic Del Popolo, né Baciagalupo, knew. It had gotten the cook in trouble, in his opinion—and Daniel, too.

Despite Carmella's best efforts, Tony knew all about her catching her niece Josie with Daniel; the cook was sure that his son had banged more than one of those DiMattia girls, and even a Saetta and a

Calogero or two! But young Joe had at least seen, if not actually overheard, his father in a few more *adult* relationships than whatever foolishness Daniel had been up to with his kissing cousins. And his
grandfather knew that Joe had spent more than a few nights in the
girls' dorms at NMH. (It was a wonder the boy hadn't been caught
and kicked out of school; now, in the spring term of his senior year,
maybe he *would* be!) There were things Joe's dad didn't know, but his
grandfather did.

In his frantic last night in Twisted River, the cook had prayed—for
the first and only time, until now. Please, God, give me *time*, Tony
Angel had prayed, long ago—seeing his twelve-year-old's small face
behind the water-streaked windshield of the Chieftain Deluxe.
(Daniel had been waiting in the passenger seat, as if he'd never lost
faith that his father would safely return from leaving Injun Jane's body
at Carl's.)

For all the talking the cook and Ketchum did about Danny Angel's
novels—not only about what was in them but, more important, what
the writer seemed to be purposely leaving out—the one thing the men
noticed without fail was how much the books were about what Danny
feared. Maybe the imagination does that, Tony thought, as he peeked
under the damp towels covering his pizza dough; the dough hadn't
risen enough for him to punch it down. Danny Angel's novels had
much to do with what the writer feared *might* happen. The stories
often indulged the nightmarish—namely, what every parent fears
most: losing a child. There was always something or someone in a
Danny Angel novel that was ominously threatening to children, or to
a child. Young people were in peril—in part, *because* they were young!

Tony Angel wasn't much of a reader anymore—though he'd
bought innumerable novels (on his son's and Ketchum's recommendations) at The Book Cellar. He'd read a lot of first chapters and had just
stopped. Something about Ketchum's relationship with Rosie had
kicked the reading right out of the cook. The *only* novels he actually
finished—and he read every word—were his son's. Tony wasn't like
Ketchum, who'd read (or heard) everything.

The cook knew his son's worst fears: Daniel was absolutely terrified of something happening to his loved ones; he simply *obsessed*
about that subject. That was where the writer's fearful imagination

came from—childhood terrors. The writer Danny Angel seemed driven to imagine the worst things that could happen in any given situation. In a way, as a writer—that is to say, in his *imagination*—the cook's son (at forty-one) was still a child.

IN HIS QUIET KITCHEN, in his cherished Avellino, the cook prayed that he be allowed to live a little longer; he wanted to help his grandson survive being a teenager. Maybe boys aren't out of the woods until their late twenties, Tony considered—after all, Daniel had been twenty-two when he married Katie. (Certainly that had been taking a risk!) What if Joe had to be *thirty* before he was safe? And if anything did happen to Joe, the cook prayed he would still be alive to look after Daniel; he knew how much help his son would need then.

Tony Angel looked at the silent radio; he almost turned it on, just to help him banish these morbid thoughts. He considered writing a letter to Ketchum instead of turning on the radio, but he didn't do either of these things; he just kept praying. It seemed that the praying had come to him out of nowhere, and he wished he could stop doing it.

There in his kitchen, next to his cookbooks, were various editions of Danny Angel's novels, which the cook kept in chronological order. There was no more revered place for those novels than among his dad's cookbooks, Danny knew. But it didn't calm the cook down to look at his famous son's books.

After *Family Life in Coos County,* the cook knew that Daniel had published *The Mickey,* but was that in 1972 or '73? The first novel had been dedicated to Mr. Leary, but the second one should have been, given its subject matter. As he'd more or less promised, however, Danny had dedicated his second novel to his dad. "For my father, Dominic Baciagalupo," the dedication read, which was a little confusing, because the author's name was Danny Angel—and Dominic was already called Tony, or *Mr.* Angel.

"Isn't that sort of like letting the nom-de-plume cat out of the nom-de-plume bag?" Ketchum had complained, but it had turned out for the better. When Danny became famous for his fourth novel, the issue of him writing under a nom de plume had long been defused. Almost everyone in the literary world knew that Danny Angel was a nom de plume, but very few people remembered what his real name was—or they didn't care. (Mr. Leary had been right to suggest that there were easier names to remember than Baciagalupo, and how many people—even in the literary world—know what John Le Carré's real name is?)

Danny, not surprisingly, had defended his decision to Ketchum by saying that he doubted the deputy sheriff was very active in the literary world; even the logger had to acknowledge that the cowboy wasn't a reader. Besides, very few people read *The Mickey* when it was originally published. When his fourth novel made Danny famous, and readers went back to the earlier books, that was when everyone read *The Mickey*.

A secondary but major character in *The Mickey* is a repressed Irishman who teaches English at the Michelangelo School; the novel focuses on the main character's last encounter with his former English teacher at a striptease show in the Old Howard. To the cook, it seemed a slight coincidence to build a whole book around—the mutual shame and embarrassment of the former student (now an Exeter boy, with a bunch of his Exeter friends) and the character who was clearly modeled on Mr. Leary. Probably, the episode at the Old Howard had actually happened—or so the novelist's father believed.

The third novel came along in '75, just after they'd all moved back to Vermont from Iowa. The cook would wonder if his was the only family to have mistakenly assumed that "kissing cousins" meant cousins who were sexually interested in, or involved with, one another. Danny's third novel was called *Kissing Kin*. (Originally, so-called kissing kin meant *any* distant kin who were familiar enough to be greeted with a kiss; it *didn't* mean what Danny's dad had always thought.)

The cook was relieved that his son's third book *wasn't* dedicated to Danny's cousins in the Saetta and Calogero families, because the irony of such a dedication might not have been appreciated by the male members of those families. The story concerns a young boy's sexual initiation in the North End; he is seduced by an older cousin who works as a waitress in the same restaurant where the boy has a part-time job as a busboy. The older cousin in the novel was clearly modeled, the cook knew, on that slut Elena Calogero—better said, the physical description of the character was true to Elena. Yet both Carmella and the cook were pretty sure that Daniel's first sexual experience had been with Carmella's niece Josie DiMattia.

The novel might have been pure fantasy, or wishful thinking, the cook supposed. But there were details that particularly bothered the writer's dad—for example, how the older cousin breaks off the relationship with the young boy when he's going off to boarding school. The waitress tells the kid that all along, she *wanted* to be fucking the boy's father—not the boy. (Little is written about the character of the dad; he's rather distantly described as the "new cook" in the restaurant where his son is a busboy.) The rejected boy goes off to school hating his father, because he imagines that the older cousin will eventually seduce his dad.

Surely this couldn't be true—this was outrageous! Tony Angel was thinking, as he searched in the book for that passage where the train is pulling out of North Station, and the boy is looking out the window of the train at his father on the station platform. The boy suddenly can't bear to look at his dad; his attention shifts to his stepmother. "I knew that the next time I saw her she would probably have put on a few more pounds," Danny Angel wrote.

"How could you write that about Carmella?" the cook had yelled at his writer son when he'd first read that hurtful sentence.

"It's not Carmella, Dad," Daniel said. (Okay—maybe the character of the stepmother in *Kissing Kin* wasn't Carmella, but Danny Angel dedicated the novel to her.)

"I suppose it's just tough luck being in a writer's family," Ketchum had told the cook. "I mean, we get mad if Danny writes about us, or someone we know, but we also get mad at him for *not* writing about us, or for not really writing about himself—his *true* self, I mean. Not to mention that he made his damn ex-wife a better person than she ever was!"

All that was true, the cook thought. Somehow what struck him about Daniel's fiction was that it was both autobiographical and *not* autobiographical at the same time. (Danny disagreed, of course. After his schoolboy attempts at fiction writing, which he'd shown only to Mr. Leary—and those stories were nothing but a confusing mix of memoir and fantasy, both exaggerated, and nearly as "confusing" to Danny as they were to the late Michael Leary—the young novelist had not *really* been autobiographical at all, not in his opinion.)

The cook couldn't find the passage he was searching for in *Kissing*

Kin. He put his son's third novel back on the bookshelf, his eyes passing quickly over the fourth one—"the fame-maker," Ketchum called it. Tony Angel didn't even like to look at *The Kennedy Fathers*—the one with the fake Katie in it, as he thought of it. The novel had not only made his son famous; it was an international bestseller and the first one of Daniel's books to be made into a movie.

Almost everyone said that it wasn't a bad movie, though it was not nearly as successful as the novel. Danny didn't like the film, but he said he didn't hate it, either; he just wanted nothing to do with the moviemaking process. He said that he never wanted to write a screenplay, and that he wouldn't sell the film rights to any of his other novels—unless someone wrote a halfway decent adaptation first, and Danny got to read the screenplay *before* he sold the movie rights to the novel.

The writer had explained to his dad that this was not the way the movie business worked; generally speaking, the rights to make a film from a novel were sold before a screenwriter was even attached to the project. By demanding to see a finished screenplay before he would consider selling the rights to his novel, Danny Angel was pretty much assuring himself that no one would ever make another movie of one of his books—not while he was alive, anyway.

"I guess Danny *did* hate the movie of *The Kennedy Fathers*, after all," Ketchum had said to the cook.

But the logger and the author's dad had to be careful what they said about *The Kennedy Fathers* around young Joe. Danny had dedicated the novel to his son. Ketchum and the cook were at least pleased to see that the book *wasn't* dedicated to Katie. Naturally, Danny was aware that the two old friends weren't exactly fans of his famous fourth novel.

It was only natural, one of Daniel's publishers had told the cook—she was one of the foreign ones, one of the older women the writer had slept with—that whatever novel Danny Angel wrote after *The Kennedy Fathers* was going to get criticized for not living up to the breakthrough book and runaway bestseller that the famous fourth novel was. Even so, Danny didn't help himself by writing a fifth novel that was both dense and sexually disturbing. And, as more than one critic wrote, the writer loved semicolons to excess; he'd even put one in the *title*!

It was simply stupid, that title—*The Spinster; or, The Maiden Aunt*, Daniel had called it. "Constipated Christ!" Ketchum had shouted at the bestselling author. "Couldn't you have called it one thing or the other?"

In interviews, Danny always said that the title reflected the old-fashioned nineteenth-century kind of story that the novel was. "Bull-shit," the cook had said to his son. "That title makes you look like you can't make up your mind."

"Whatever you call them, they look like someone smashed a fly over the comma," Ketchum said to Danny, about all the semicolons. "The only writing I do are letters to you and your dad, but I've written rather a lot of them, and in all those letters, I don't believe I've ever used as many of those damn things as you use on any one fucking page of this novel."

"They're called semicolons, Ketchum," the writer said.

"I don't care what they're called, Danny," the old woodsman said. "I'm just telling you that you use too damn many of them!"

But of course what really pissed off Ketchum and the cook about Danny Angel's fifth novel was the fucking dedication—"Katie, in memoriam."

All Tony Angel could say about it to Ketchum was: "That Calla-han cunt broke my son's heart and abandoned my grandson." (It was not a good time, Ketchum knew, to point out to his old friend that she'd also kept his son out of the war and had *given* him the grand-son.)

Not to mention what *The Spinster; or, The Maiden Aunt* was about, the cook was thinking, as he looked with suspicion at the novel on his kitchen bookshelf. It's another North End story, but this time the boy who is coming of age is sexually initiated by one of his *aunts*—not an older cousin—and the maiden aunt and spinster is a dead ringer for Rosie's youngest sister, the unfortunate Filomena Calogero!

Surely *this* hadn't happened! the cook hoped, but had Daniel once wished that it had—or had it *almost* happened? Once again (as in any Danny Angel novel) the graphic detail was quite convincing, and the sexual descriptions of the boy's petite aunt—she was such a pathetic, self-pitying woman!—were painful for the cook, though he'd read every word.

Critics also made the point that "the perhaps overrated writer" was "repeating himself"; Daniel had been thirty-nine when his fifth novel was published in 1981, and all the criticism must have stung him, though you wouldn't know it. If the cousin in *Kissing Kin* tells the boy she's breaking up with that she always wanted to sleep with his father instead, in the novel about the neurotic aunt, *she* tells the boy that she *imagines* she's having sex with his father whenever she has sex with the son! (What manifestation of self-torture is this? the cook had wondered, when he'd first read *The Spinster; or, The Maiden Aunt.*)

Maybe it *did* happen, the man who missed the Dominic in himself now imagined. He'd always thought that Rosie's sister Filomena was completely crazy. He couldn't look at her without feeling she was a grotesque mask of Rosie—"a Rosie imposter," he'd once described her to Ketchum. But Daniel had seemed improbably infatuated with Filomena; the boy couldn't stop himself from staring at her, and it was not *as an aunt* that he appeared to be regarding her. Had the flighty Filomena, who was *still* miserable and unmarried (or so the cook assumed), actually accepted or even encouraged her smitten young nephew's adoration?

"Why don't you just *ask* Danny if the crazy aunt popped his cherry?" Ketchum had inquired of the cook. That was a vulgar Coos County expression, and the cook hated it. (If he'd paid closer attention to the conversations around him in Boston, the cook might have realized that "cherry-popping" was a vulgar North End expression, too.)

There was one part of *The Spinster; or, The Maiden Aunt* that both Tony Angel and Ketchum had loved: the wedding at the end. The boy has grown up and he's marrying his college sweetheart—an indifferent bride, if you ever met one, and closer to a real-life Katie character than Caitlin in *The Kennedy Fathers* ever was. Also, Danny had nailed those ice-cube-sucking Callahan men dead between their eyes— those tight-assed patrician Republicans who, Danny believed, had made Katie the anarchist rule-breaker she was. She was a trust-fund kid who'd reinvented herself as a radical, but she'd been a faux revolutionary. Katie's only revolution had been a small, sexual one.

THERE WAS ONE BOOK Danny Angel had written that was not on the kitchen bookshelf in Avellino. That was his sixth novel, which had not yet been published. But the cook had almost finished reading it. A copy of the galleys was upstairs in Tony Angel's bedroom. Ketchum also had a copy. Both men felt ambivalent about the novel, and neither was in any hurry to finish it.

East of Bangor was set in an orphanage in Maine in the 1960s—when abortion was still illegal. Virtually the same damn boy from those earlier Danny Angel novels—a boy from Boston who ends up going away to boarding school—gets *two* of his North End cousins pregnant, one when he's still a student at Exeter (before he's learned to drive) and the second after he's gone off to college. He goes to the University of New Hampshire, naturally.

There's an old midwife in the Maine orphanage who performs abortions—a deeply sympathetic woman who struck the cook as being modeled on the unlikely fusion of sweet, gentle Paul Polcari ("the fuck-ing *pacifist!*" as Ketchum insisted on calling him) and Injun Jane.

The first cousin who goes off to Maine has the baby and leaves it behind; she is so devastated by having a child and not knowing what has become of it that she tells the *other* pregnant cousin not to do what she did. The second pregnant cousin also goes to Maine—to the very same orphanage, but to have an abortion. The problem is that the old midwife might not live long enough to perform the procedure. If the young midwife-in-training ends up doing the D & C, the cousin might suffer the consequences. The young midwife doesn't know enough about what she's doing.

Both Ketchum and the cook were hoping that the novel was going to turn out well, and that nothing too bad would happen to the second pregnant cousin. But, knowing Danny Angel's novels, the two old readers had their fears—and something else was worrying them.

Over a year ago, Joe had gotten a girl in trouble at Northfield Mount Hermon. Because his father was famous—for a writer, Danny Angel was very recognizable—and because Joe already knew something about the subject of the novel his dad was writing, the boy hadn't asked for his father's help. Those anti-abortion people picketed most clinics or doctors' offices where you could get an abortion; Joe didn't want his dad taking him and the unfortunate girl to one of those places where the protesters were. What if some so-called right-to-lifer recognized his famous father?

"Smart boy," Ketchum said to Joe, when Danny's son had written him. Young Joe hadn't wanted to tell his grandfather, either, but Ketchum insisted that the cook come along with them.

They'd driven to an abortion clinic in Vermont together. Ketchum and the cook sat up front, in the cook's car; Joe and the sad, frightened girl were in the backseat. It had been an awkward situation because the couple were no longer boyfriend and girlfriend. They'd broken up almost a month before the girl discovered she was pregnant, but they both knew Joe was the baby's father; they were doing the right thing (in the cook and Ketchum's opinion), but it was difficult for them.

Ketchum tried to console them, but—Ketchum being Ketchum—it came out a little clumsily. The logger said more than he meant to. "There's one thing to be happy about," he told the miserable-looking couple in the backseat. "When the same thing happened to your dad and a girl he knew, Joe, abortion wasn't legal—and it wasn't necessarily safe."

Had the old woodsman forgotten the cook was in the car?

"So that's why you took Danny and that DiMattia girl to *Maine*!" Tony Angel cried. "I always *thought* so! You said you wanted to show them the Kennebec—'the last great river-driving river,' you called it, or some such bullshit. But that DiMattia girl was so dumb—she told Carmella you'd driven her and Danny somewhere east of *Bangor*. I *knew* Bangor was nowhere near the Kennebec!"

Ketchum and the cook had argued the whole way to the abortion clinic, where there'd been picketers; Joe had been right not to involve his famous father with the protesters. And all the way home—the ex-girlfriend and Joe were spending the weekend in Brattleboro with the boy's grandfather—Joe had held the girl in the backseat, where she sobbed and sobbed. She couldn't have been older than sixteen—seventeen, tops. "You're going to be all right," Joe, who was not yet seventeen, kept saying to the poor kid. Ketchum and the cook hoped so.

And now the two older men had stopped themselves in the last chapter of *East of Bangor*—Danny Angel's abortion novel, as it would be called. The cook could see that there was something of Ketchum in the character who drove the boy (and his first pregnant cousin) to Maine. By the description, the friendly older man also reminded the cook of Tony Molinari; Danny Angel calls him the principal chef in the North End restaurant where the two pregnant cousins work as waitresses. It's the way the man handles the truck they drive to Maine in—that was what led Tony Angel to see the so-called chef as "the Ketchum character." The Molinari likeness was a disguise Danny gave to the character, because of course the writer didn't know, when he was finishing the final draft of his abortion novel, that Ketchum had already told his dad about Danny getting the DiMattia girl pregnant—and how the logger drove the two of them to an orphanage somewhere east of Bangor, Maine.

The book was dedicated to those two chefs Danny Angel and his dad both loved, Tony Molinari and Paul Polcari—"*Un abbràccio* for Tony M. and Paul P.," the author had written, allowing the two men some measure of privacy. ("An embrace" for them from the former busboy/waiter/substitute pizza and sous chef in Vicino di Napoli.) Both those chefs, the cook knew, were retired; Vicino di Napoli was gone, and another restaurant with another name had taken its place in North Square.

Tony Angel still drove periodically to the North End to do a little shopping. He would meet Molinari and Paul at the Caffè Vittoria for some espresso. They always assured him that Carmella was doing well; she seemed reasonably content with another fella. It came as no surprise to the cook that Carmella would end up with someone; she was both beautiful and lovable.

East of Bangor might be a difficult novel for young Joe to read, whenever he got around to it; Joe had no time to read his father's novels when he was at Northfield Mount Hermon. To the cook's knowledge, his grandson had read only one of his dad's books: *The Kennedy Fathers,* of course—if only in the hope he would learn a little about what his mother had been like. (Given Ketchum's opinion of the Katie character, what young Joe would learn about his mother from that novel "wasn't worth a pinch of coon shit"—according to the logger.)

WELL, HERE I AM—back to worrying about young Joe again, and all that *that* leads to—the cook was thinking. He looked under the damp dish towels covering his pizza dough; the dough was ready to punch down, which the cook did. Tony Angel wet the dishcloths once more;

he wrung them only partially dry before re-covering the bowls for his pizza dough's second rise.

He thought his next letter to Ketchum might begin, "There's so much to worry about, I can't seem to stop myself from doing it. And you'd laugh at me, Ketchum, because I've even been praying!" But the cook didn't begin that letter. He felt strangely exhausted, and he'd shot the whole morning doing almost nothing—just starting his pizza dough and limping to the bookstore and back. It was already time to go shopping. Avellino wasn't open for lunch—just dinner. Tony Angel shopped at midday; his staff showed up in the early afternoon.

As for worrying, the cook wasn't alone; Danny worried a lot, too. And neither of them was as worried as Ketchum, even though it was almost June—way past mud season in southern Vermont, and they'd been mud-free for several weeks in northern New Hampshire. Ketchum had been known to feel almost exhilarated in those first few weeks after mud season had passed. But not now, and truly not since the cook had come back to Vermont from Iowa with his son and grandson. Ketchum didn't like them to be anywhere near New Hampshire—particularly not his old friend with the new and hard-to-get-used-to name.

The funny thing was that the cook, for all his worrying, didn't give the slightest thought to that. So much time had passed; it had been sixteen years since he'd moved out of Boston, and twenty-nine since his last, eventful night in Twisted River. Dominic Del Popolo, né Baciagalupo, who was now Tony Angel, wasn't as worried about an angry old cowboy in Coos County as he was about other things.

The cook *should* have been more worried about Carl, because Ketchum was right. Vermont was next door to New Hampshire—too close for comfort. And the deputy sheriff, who was sixty-six, had retired; he had lots of time on his hands, and that cowboy was still looking for the little cripple who'd stolen his Injun Jane.

CHAPTER 8

DEAD DOG; REMEMBERING MAO'S

F ROM THE FAMOUS WRITER'S "COMPOUND"—AS THE PUTNEY locals (and the writer's own father) were inclined to call it—Hickory Ridge Road climbed for over a mile, the road both crossing the brook and running parallel to the water. The so-called back road from Putney to Westminster West was dirt, and at a point less than midway between Danny Angel's property in Putney and his best friend's house in Westminster West, there was quite a pretty farm, with horses, at the end of a long, steep driveway. In the warm weather—after he'd opened his swimming pool in May, and before he winterized the pool every October—Danny called his friend in Westminster West and told him when he was starting out on a run. It was four or five miles, maybe six or seven; Danny was such a daydreamer that he didn't keep track of the distance of his runs anymore.

The pretty farm at the end of the long, uphill driveway seemed to focus the writer's reveries, because an older woman with snow-white hair (and the body of a dancer in her twenties) lived there. Danny had had an affair with her some years ago—her name was Barrett. She wasn't married, and hadn't been at the time; there was no scandal attached to their relationship. Nevertheless, in the writer's imagination—at about the two-mile mark of his run—Danny always foresaw his own murder at the place where this woman's steep driveway met the road.

He would be running on the road, just a half-second past her driveway, and Barrett would come gliding down the hill, her car coasting in neutral, with the engine off, so that by the time he heard her tires scattering the loose gravel on the road, it would be too late for him to get out of the almost-silent car's path.

A spectacular way for a storyteller to die, Danny had imagined—a vehicular homicide, with the famous novelist's ex-lover at the wheel of the murder weapon!

That Barrett had no such designs on ending the writer's life didn't matter; it would have been a good story. In fact, she'd had many affairs, and (in Danny's estimation) Barrett harbored no homicidal feelings for her ex-lovers; the writer doubted that Barrett would go out of her way to run over any of them. She was exclusively focused on caring for her horses and maintaining her youthful physique.

When there was a conceivably interesting movie playing at the Latchis in Brattleboro, Danny would often ask Barrett to see the film with him, and they would have dinner at Avellino. That Barrett was much closer in age to Danny's dad than she was to Danny had provided the cook with grounds for complaining to his writer son. Nowadays, Danny frequently found it necessary to remind his father that he and Barrett were "just friends."

Danny could run five or six miles at a pace of seven minutes per mile, usually running the last mile in closer to six minutes. At forty-one, he'd had no injuries and was still slight of build; at five feet seven, he weighed only 145 pounds. (His dad was a little smaller, and perhaps the limp made him seem shorter than he was.) Because of the occasional bad dog on the back road to Westminster West, Danny ran with a couple of sawed-off squash racquets—just the handles. If a dog attacked him when he was running, Danny would stick one of the racquet handles in the dog's face—until the dog chomped on it. Then, with the other sawed-off handle, he would hit the dog—usually on the bridge of the nose.

Danny didn't play squash. His friend in Westminster West was the squash player. When Armando DeSimone broke one of his racquets, he gave it to Danny, who sawed off the racquet head and kept the handle. Armando had grown up in the North End about a decade before Danny and his dad moved there; like the cook, Armando still drove to his beloved Boston, periodically, to shop. Armando and Danny enjoyed cooking for each other. They'd been colleagues in the English department at Windham, and when the college folded, Armando took a job teaching at the Putney School. His wife, Mary, had been Joe's English and history teacher at the Grammar School.

When Danny Angel became rich and famous, he lost a few of the old friends he'd had, but not the DeSimones. Armando had read all but the first of Danny Angel's novels in manuscript. For five out of six novels, he'd been Danny's earliest reader. You don't lose a friend like that.

Armando had built a squash court in an old barn on his Westminster West property; he talked about building a swimming pool next, but in the meantime he and Mary swam in Danny's pool. Nearly every afternoon, when it wasn't raining, the writer would run to the DeSimones' house in Westminster West; then Armando and Mary would drive Danny back to Putney, and they'd all swim in the pool. Danny would make drinks for them and serve the drinks at the pool after they swam.

Danny had stopped drinking sixteen years ago—long enough so that he had no problem having alcohol in his house, or fixing drinks for his friends. And he wouldn't dream of having a dinner party and *not* serving wine, though he could remember that when he'd first stopped drinking, he was unable to be around people who were drinking anything alcoholic. At the time, in Iowa City, that had been a problem.

As for the writer's second life in Iowa City, with his dad and little Joe—well, that had been a peaceful interlude, for the most part, except for the unwelcome reminders of Danny's earlier time in that town with Katie. In retrospect, Danny thought, those last three years in Iowa—in the early seventies, when Joe had been in the second, third, and fourth grades, and the greatest danger the boy faced was what might happen to him on his *bicycle*—seemed almost blissful. Iowa City had been *safe* in those years.

Joe was seven when he'd gone back to Iowa with his dad and grandfather, and was still only ten when they'd returned to Vermont. Maybe those ages were the safest ages, the writer was imagining as he ran; possibly, Iowa City had had nothing to do with it.

—

CHILDHOOD, AND HOW IT FORMS YOU—moreover, how your childhood is relived in your life as an adult—that was his subject (or his obsession), the writer Danny Angel daydreamed as he ran. From the age of twelve, he had become afraid for his father; the cook was still a hunted man. Like his dad, but for different reasons, Danny had been a young father—in reality, he'd also been a single parent (even before Katie left him). Now, at forty-one, Danny was more afraid for young Joe than he was for his dad.

Maybe it was more than the Katie Callahan gene that put Joe at risk; nor did Danny necessarily believe that the source of the wildness in his son was the boy's free-spirited grandmother, that daring woman who'd courted disaster on the late-winter ice of Twisted River. No, when Danny looked at young Joe at eighteen, it was *himself* at that dangerous age he saw. From all they'd read into (and had misread in) Danny Angel's novels, the cook and Ketchum couldn't have fathomed the perilous configuration of the various bullets Danny had dodged—not only in his life with Katie, but long before her.

It hadn't been Josie DiMattia who'd sexually initiated Danny at the age of fifteen, before he went off to Exeter; furthermore, Carmella may have caught them at it, but Josie wasn't the one who got pregnant. Ketchum had indeed driven Danny to that orphanage with the obliging midwife in Maine, but with the *oldest* DiMattia girl, Teresa. (Perhaps Teresa had given so many condoms to her younger sisters that she'd forgotten to save some for herself.) And neither Teresa nor Danny's equally older cousin Elena Calogero had provided Danny with his *first* sexual experience—though the boy was much more attracted to those older girls than he was to any girl his own age, including Josie, who'd been only a *little* older. There'd also been an older Saetta cousin, Giuseppina, who'd seduced young Dan, but Giuseppina wasn't his first seducer.

No, indeed—that instructive and most formative experience had been with the boy's aunt Filomena, his mother's youngest sister, when Danny had been only fourteen. Had Filomena been in her late twenties, or might she already have turned thirty when the assignations with her young nephew began? Danny was wondering as he approached the final two miles of his run.

It was still May; the blackflies were bad, but not at the pace he was running, which he began to pick up. As he ran, he could hear his heart and his own breathing, though these elevated functions didn't seem to Danny as loud or urgent as the beating of his heart or his gasps for breath whenever the boy had been with his insane aunt Filomena. What had she been thinking? It was Danny's dad she'd adored, and the cook wouldn't look at her. Had the way her nephew doted on her—Danny couldn't take his eyes off her—seemed a sufficient consolation prize to Filomena?

She'd been only the second woman in the Saetta and Calogero clans to attend college, but Filomena had shared another distinction with her older sister Rosie—namely, a certain lawlessness with men. Filomena might have been only a preteen—at most, thirteen or fourteen—when Rosie had been sent away to the north country. She'd loved Rosie, and had looked up to her—only to see her disgraced, and displayed as a bad example to the younger girls in the family. Filomena had been sent to Sacred Heart, an all-girls' Catholic school near the Paul Revere House on North Square. She'd been kept as safe from boys as was humanly *and* spiritually possible.

As Danny Angel picked up the pace in his long run, he considered that this might have been why his aunt Filomena had been more interested in him, a boy, than she appeared to be interested in *men*. (Her sacred sister's widower excluded—yet Filomena must have known that the cook was a closed door to her, an unfulfilled fantasy, whereas Danny, who had not yet started to shave, had his father's long eyelashes and his mother's fair, almost fragile skin.) And it must have made an impression on Filomena that, at fourteen, the boy worshipped his small, pretty aunt. According to Danny's dad, Filomena's eyes weren't the same *lethal* blue as Rosie's, but his aunt's eyes, and all the rest of her, were dangerous enough to do Danny some long-lasting harm. For one thing, Filomena managed to make *all* girls Danny's age uninteresting to him—that is, until he met Katie.

The cook and Ketchum had jumped to the conclusion that young Daniel had seen something of his mother in Katie. What the boy had seen, perhaps, was that combination of a repressed girlhood in an angry young woman of wanton self-destructiveness; Katie had been a younger, more political version of his aunt Filomena. The difference between them was that Filomena had been devoted to the boy, and her sexual efforts to outdo the mere girls in Danny's life were entirely successful. Denied any demonstrable expression of her sexuality as a girl, Filomena (in her late twenties, and well into her thirties) was a woman possessed. By the time Danny met her, Katie Callahan was almost indifferent to sex; that she'd had a lot of sex didn't mean that she actually *liked* it. By the time Danny met her, Katie already thought of sex as a way of *negotiating*.

In Danny's prep-school years, his aunt Filomena would book a room at the Exeter Inn almost every weekend. The boy's trysts in that musty brick building were the unparalleled pleasures of his life at Exeter, and a contributing reason why he spent so few of his Exeter weekends at home in the North End. Carmella and the cook always worked hardest at Vicino di Napoli on Friday and Saturday nights, while the boy banged his youthful aunt—often in a Colonial four-poster bed, beneath a gauzy-white canopy. (He was a runner; runners have stamina.) With Filomena's considerable and licentious assistance, Danny had achieved an adult independence—from both his actual and his Exeter families.

How could the boy possibly have had any interest in Exeter's dances with various girls' schools? How could a closely chaperoned and chaste hug on the dance floor ever compete with the ardent, sweat-slicked contact he'd maintained with Filomena on an almost weekly basis—not only throughout his Exeter years but including Danny's first two years of college in Durham?

And all the while, those Calogeros and Saettas took pity on "poor" Filomena; pretty as she was, she struck them as an eternal wallflower, both a maiden aunt and a spinster-in-the-making. Little did they know that, for seven hungry years, the woman was indulging the ceaseless sexual appetites of a teenage boy on his way to becoming a young man. In those seven years that his aunt Filomena dominated Danny's sexual life, she more than made up for lost time. That she was a teacher at Sacred Heart—in the same Catholic and all-girls' environment where the *younger* Filomena had been held down—was a perfect disguise.

All those other Calogeros, and the Saettas, thought of Filomena as "pathetic"—those were his father's very words for her, Danny remembered, as he ran harder and harder. Outwardly, Filomena had seemed the picture of propriety and Catholic repression, but—oh!—not when she shed her clothes!

"Let's just say I keep them busy at confession," she told her spell-bound nephew, for whom Filomena had set a standard; the young women who followed Filomena in Danny's life couldn't match his aunt's erotic performance.

Filomena was in her mid- to late thirties—too old to have a baby, in her estimation—when the issue of Danny going to Vietnam (or not) was raised. She might have been happier with Ketchum's solution; if Danny had lost a finger or two, he might have stayed with his aunt a little longer. Filomena was insane, but she was no fool; she knew she wouldn't get to keep her beloved young Dan forever. She liked the sound of Katie Callahan's idea better than she ever warmed to Ketchum's plan—after all, in her own odd way, Filomena loved her nephew, and she had not met Katie.

Had Filomena met that most vulgar young woman, she might have opted for Ketchum's Browning knife instead, but ultimately that decision wasn't hers. Filomena felt fortunate to have captured such a vital young man's almost complete attention for the seven years she'd held him in her thrall. Danny's dalliances with those DiMattia girls, or several of his kissing cousins, didn't bother her. Filomena knew that Danny would always come back to her, with renewed vigor. Those clumsy sluts couldn't hold a candle to her—not in the boy's fond esti-mation, anyway. Nor would Katie ever become the *younger* Filomena Danny may have desired—or, once upon a time, wished her to be.

Filomena would be in her mid- to late fifties now, the writer knew—running harder. Filomena had never married; she was no longer at Sacred Heart, but she was still teaching. His novel with the semicolon in the title—the one everyone had scorned (*The Spinster; or, The Maiden Aunt*)—had received one favorable review, which the writer Danny Angel appreciated.

In her letter, Filomena wrote: "I warmly enjoyed your novel, as you no doubt intended—a generous amount of homage with a justifiable measure of condemnation. Yes, I took advantage of you—if only in the beginning. That you stayed with me so long made me proud of myself, as I am proud of you now. And I'm sorry if, for a time, I made it hard for you to appreciate those inexperienced girls. But you must learn to choose more wisely, my dear—now that you're a little older than I was when we went our separate ways."

She'd written that letter two years ago—*The Spinster; or, The Maiden Aunt* had been published in '81. He'd often thought of seeing her again, but how could Danny revisit Filomena without having unrealistic expectations? A man in his early forties, his unmarried aunt in her mid- to late fifties—well, what sort of relationship could exist between them *now*?

Nor had he learned to choose more wisely, as Filomena had recommended; perhaps he'd purposely decided against choosing to be with anyone who so much as hinted at the promise of permanence. And the writer knew he was too old to *still* hold his aunt accountable for introducing him to sex when he was too young. Whatever reluctance Danny felt for involving himself in a permanent relationship couldn't be blamed on Filomena—certainly not anymore.

IT WAS THE BAD-DOG PART of Danny's run; if there was going to be trouble, it would happen here. Danny was looking for the different-eyed dog in the narrow, flat driveway lined with abandoned vehicles—dead cars, some minus tires, trucks without engines, a motorcycle on its side and missing its handlebars—when the big male dog emerged from a Volkswagen bus without any doors. A husky-shepherd mix, he came into the road on a dead run—no bark, not a growl, all business. The patter of the pads of his paws on the dirt road was the only sound the dog made; he hadn't yet begun to breathe hard.

Danny had had to beat him off with the squash-racquet handles before, and he'd had words with the animal's no-less-aggressive owner—a young man in his twenties, possibly one of those former Windham College students who wouldn't move away. The guy had a hippie appearance but was no pacifist; he might have been one of the countless young men living in the Putney area who called themselves "carpenters." (If so, he was a carpenter who either didn't work or was always at home.)

"Mind your dog!" Danny had called up the driveway to him, that previous time.

"Fuck you! Run somewhere else!" the hippie carpenter had yelled back.

Now here was the unchained dog again, snapping at the runner. Danny moved to the far-right side of the road and tried to outrun the dog, but the husky-shepherd quickly gained on him. Danny stopped diagonally across the road from the hippie carpenter's driveway, and the dog stopped, too—circling him, his head low to the ground, his teeth bared. When the dog lunged at his thigh, Danny jabbed him in the ear with one of the sawed-off squash racquets; when the husky-shepherd seized the racquet handle in his teeth, Danny hit the animal as hard as he could with the other handle, both on the bridge of the nose and between the eyes. (One of his eyes was the light-blue color of a Siberian husky's eyes, and the other was the dark-brown, more penetrating eye of a German shepherd.) The dog yelped and let go of the first racquet handle. Danny hit him on one ear, then the other, as the animal momentarily retreated.

"Leave my dog alone, you son of a bitch!" the hippie carpenter yelled. He was walking down his driveway between the rows of wrecked vehicles.

"Mind your dog," was all Danny told him. He had started to run again before he saw the second dog—so similar-looking to the first that Danny thought, for a moment, it was the same dog. Then, suddenly, he had *two* dogs snapping at him; the second one was always at his back. "Call your dogs!" Danny shouted to the hippie carpenter.

"Fuck you. Run somewhere else," the guy said. He was walking back up his driveway; he didn't care if his dogs bit Danny, or not. The dogs tried hard to bite him, but Danny managed to jam one of the racquet handles deep down the throat of the first dog, and a lucky backhand swing caught the second dog in the face—lashing one of its eyes, as it was about to bite Danny in the calf. He kicked the dog choking on the squash-racquet handle in the throat. As the dog turned to run, Danny struck him behind one ear; the dog fell but quickly got up again. The second dog was slinking away. The hippie carpenter was nowhere to be seen, now that his dogs drew back to their territory in the driveway.

When Danny had first moved to Windham County, there'd been a bad dog on the back road between Dummerston and the Putney School. Danny had called the state police; it was a similar hostile-dog-owner situation. A state trooper had driven out there, just to talk to the dog owner, and when the dog attacked the trooper, he'd shot it dead—right in the driveway. "What did you say to the dog owner?" Danny had asked the trooper. (His name was Jimmy; they'd since become friends.)

"I told him to mind his dog," Jimmy had answered.

Danny had been saying that ever since, but with less authority than a state trooper—clearly. Now, without further incident, he ran to the DeSimones' house, but Danny didn't like it when he'd had to break the pace he'd picked up in his last couple of miles. He told Armando about the two dogs and the hippie carpenter. "Call your friend Jimmy," Armando said, but Danny explained that the state trooper would probably be forced to shoot both dogs.

"Why don't we kill just one of them?" Armando suggested. "Then maybe the hippie carpenter will get the idea."

"That seems harsh," Danny said. He'd understood what Armando's proposed method of killing one of the husky-shepherds would entail. The DeSimones' dog was a purebred German shepherd male named Rooster. Even as a puppy, Rooster had stuck out his chest and strutted, stiff-legged and threatening, in the presence of other male dogs—hence his name. But Rooster hadn't been bluffing. Full-grown, he was a dog-killer—Rooster hated other male dogs. At least one of the dogs who'd attacked Danny was a male; the writer couldn't be sure about the second dog, because it had come at him from behind.

Armando DeSimone was more than what amounted to Danny Angel's only "literary" friend in Putney; Armando was a real reader, and he and Danny argued about what they read in a reasonably constructive way. But there was something innately confrontational in Armando, who reminded Danny of a more civilized version of Ketchum.

Danny had a tendency to avoid confrontation, which he often regretted. People who picked an argument or a fight with the writer got the idea that he would never fight back; they were surprised, or their feelings were hurt, when Danny *did* come back at them—though not until the third or fourth provocation. What Danny had learned was that these people who'd grown used to baiting or goading him were always indignant to discover that the writer had been keeping score.

Armando didn't keep score. When attacked, he attacked back—the first time. Danny believed this was healthier—for a writer, especially—but it was not in his nature to be like Armando. In the disturbing case of the undisciplined dogs, it was only because he believed Armando's way was better that Danny Angel allowed himself to be persuaded. ("Then maybe the hippie carpenter will get the idea," Armando had reasoned.)

The only way that would happen, the writer should have known, was if Rooster bit the hippie carpenter. Yet Rooster wasn't wired that way; Rooster never bit *people*.

"Just *one* dog, Armando—you promise," his wife, Mary, said, when they were all in the car with Rooster, driving back to Danny's house.

"Tell Rooster—make *him* promise," Armando said; he'd been a boxer, back when colleges and universities had boxing teams. Armando drove, with Danny up front in the passenger seat of the VW Beetle. Seemingly long-suffering Mary sat in the back with the panting German shepherd. Mary often seemed at odds with, or put out by, her husband's combativeness, but Danny knew that Armando and Mary were a formidable couple—at heart, they were unassailably supportive of each other. Maybe Mary was more like Armando than Armando. Danny remembered her remark when a fellow teacher had been fired—a former colleague of Mary's at the Grammar School, and later of Armando's at the Putney School.

"Because justice is so rare, it's such a delight," Mary had remarked. (Now, Danny wondered, did Mary only *seem* to disapprove of her husband appointing Rooster as executioner?)

In the end, Danny Angel could only have said (in his own defense) that he did not acquiesce to the assassination of the dog—even a dog who'd attacked him—lightly. Yet, somehow, whenever Armando was involved—on matters of moral authority, especially—Danny *did* acquiesce.

"Oh, you mean *this* asshole," Armando said, when Danny indicated the driveway with the dead cars.

"You know him?" Danny asked.

"*You* know him!" Armando said. "I'm sure he was one of your students."

"At Windham?"

"Of *course* at Windham," Armando said.

"I didn't recognize him. I don't think he was ever a student of mine," Danny told his friend.

"Do you remember all your mediocre students, Danny?" Mary asked him.

"He's just another hippie carpenter—or noncarpenter, as the case may be," Danny said, but (even to himself) he didn't sound too sure about it.

"Perhaps he's a *writer* carpenter," Armando suggested. Danny hadn't considered that the young man might have known who Danny Angel was. There were almost as many would-be writers in Putney as there were hippies calling themselves carpenters. (The animosity, or envy, you encountered as a writer in Vermont was often of a back-road mentality.)

A HUSKY-SHEPHERD MIX is generally no match for a purebred German shepherd, but there were two of them. Then again, maybe no two dogs were ever a match for Rooster. Danny got out of the VW and pulled his seat-back out of the way to let Rooster out of the rear of the car. The German shepherd had hardly touched the ground with his forepaws when the two mixed breeds attacked him. Danny just got back in the Volkswagen and watched. Rooster killed one dog so quickly that neither Danny nor the DeSimones could ascertain if the second dog was male or female; it had crawled under the VW Beetle, where Rooster couldn't get it. (The German shepherd had seized the first dog by the throat, and had snapped his neck with a couple of shakes.)

Armando called Rooster, and Danny let the German shepherd back into the Beetle. The hippie or writer carpenter had come out of his house and was staring at his dead dog; he hadn't yet figured out that his other dog was cringing under the little car. "Mind your dog," Danny said to him—as Armando slowly backed up, over the remaining husky-shepherd mix. There was just a bump when one of the front wheels rolled over the dog, and a corresponding grunt from the dog. The shepherd-husky got up stiffly and shook itself; it was another male, Danny could see. He saw the dog walk over to his dead mate, sniffing the body while the asshole hippie watched the Volkswagen

Beetle back out of his driveway. But was this what Mary (or Armando) meant by "justice"? Maybe calling Jimmy would have been a better idea, Danny thought—even if the state trooper had wound up killing both dogs. It was the dog owner someone should have shot and killed, the writer believed; that would have been a better story.

THERE ARE THINGS I'LL MISS about Vermont, if I ever have to leave, Danny Angel was thinking, but most of all he would miss Armando and Mary DeSimone. He admired their certainty.

As the three friends swam in the pool at Danny's Putney property, the dog-killer German shepherd watched over them. Rooster didn't swim, but he did drink from a large bowl of cold water that Danny had given him, while the writer made gin and tonics for Armando and Mary. Looking back, it would be Danny's sharpest memory of Rooster—the dog was panting with apparent satisfaction near the deep end of the pool. The big shepherd loved little children but hated other male dogs; something in the animal's history must have made this so, something neither Danny nor the DeSimones ever knew.

Rooster would one day be killed on a back road—struck by a car while he was mindlessly chasing a schoolbus. Violence begets violence, as Ketchum and the cook already knew, as one nearly forgotten hippie carpenter, with one dead dog and one momentarily alive, might one day figure out.

Danny didn't know it, but he'd taken his last run on the back road between Putney and Westminster West. It was a world of accidents, right? Perhaps it was wise not to be too confrontational in such a world.

BOTH THEIR HUSBANDS had retired from the spruce mill in Milan. A world of small engine repair, and other tinkering, lay ahead of them. The fat sawmill workers' wives—Dot and May, those bad old broads—took every occasion that presented itself, no matter how much driving was involved, to leave town and their tiresome husbands. Retired men made a nuisance of themselves, the two old ladies had discovered; Dot and May preferred their own company to anyone else's. Now that May's younger children (and her older grandchildren) were producing *more* children, she used the excuse of being needed when whatever mother (and whoever's new baby) came home from the hospital. Wherever "home" was, it was a way to get out of Milan. Dot was always the driver.

They were both sixty-eight, a couple of years older than Ketchum, whom they spotted occasionally—Ketchum lived in Errol, farther up the Androscoggin. The old logger never recognized Dot or May, nor would he have paid them any attention if he did recognize them, but everyone noticed Ketchum; the woodsman's reputation as a wild man had marked him, as surely as the scar on his forehead was a vivid advertisement of his violent history. But Dot had put on another sixty pounds, or so, and May another eighty; they were white-haired, with those weatherworn faces you see in the north country, and they ate their way through every day, the way some people in cold climates do, as if they were constantly starving.

They'd come across northern New Hampshire on the Groveton road, through Stark—much of the way, they were following the Ammonoosuc—and in Lancaster they crossed the Connecticut, into Vermont. They intersected I-91 just below St. Johnsbury, and followed the interstate south. They had a long drive ahead of them, but they were in no hurry to get there. May's daughter or granddaughter had given birth in Springfield, Massachusetts. If Dot and May arrived in time for supper, they would necessarily get themselves involved in feeding a bunch of little kids and cleaning up after them. The two old ladies were smarter than that—they'd decided they would stop somewhere for supper en route. That way, they could have a nice big meal by themselves and arrive in Springfield well after suppertime; with any luck, someone else would have done the dishes and put the littlest kids to bed.

About the time those bad old broads were passing McIndoe Falls on I-91, the cook and his staff were finishing their midafternoon meal at Avellino. To have fed his staff a good meal, and to watch everyone cleaning up and readying themselves for the evening's dinner service, always made Tony Angel nostalgic. He was thinking about those years in Iowa City in the seventies—that interlude from their life in Vermont, as both the cook and his son remembered it.

In Iowa City, Tony Angel had worked as a sous chef in the Cheng brothers' Chinese restaurant out on First Avenue—what the cook called the Coralville strip. The Cheng brothers might have had more business if they'd been closer to downtown; they were too upscale for Coralville, overlooked among its fast-food joints and cheap motels, but the brothers liked their proximity to the interstate, and on those Big Ten sports weekends when an Iowa team was competing at home, the restaurant attracted lots of out-of-towners. It was too expensive for most students, anyway—unless their parents were paying—and the university faculty, whom the Chengs considered their target clientele, all had cars and weren't limited to the bars and restaurants nearer the center of the campus, downtown.

In Tony Angel's opinion, the name of the Chengs' restaurant was another questionable business decision—*Mao's* might have worked better with politically disenchanted students than it did with their parents, or the out-of-town sports fans—but the Cheng brothers were completely caught up in the anti-war protests of the time. Public opinion, especially in a university town, had turned against the war; from '72 till '75, there were many demonstrations outside the Old Capitol on the Iowa campus. Admittedly, Mao's might have worked better in Madison or Ann Arbor. Out on the Coralville strip, a passing patriot—in a quickly disappearing car or pickup truck—would sometimes lob a brick or a rock through the restaurant's window.

"A warrior farmer," said Ah Gou Cheng, dismissively; he was the elder brother. *Ah Gou* was Shanghai dialect for "Big Brother."

He was a terrific chef; he'd gone to cooking school at the Culinary Institute of America, and he'd grown up working in Chinese restaurants. Born in Queens, he'd moved to Long Island and then to Manhattan. A woman he'd met in a karate class had lured Ah Gou to Iowa, but she'd left him there. By then, Ah Gou was convinced that Mao's could make it in Iowa City.

Ah Gou was just old enough to have missed the Vietnam War but not the U.S. Army; he'd been an army cook in Alaska. ("No authentic ingredients there, except the fish," he'd told Tony Angel.) Ah Gou had a Fu Manchu mustache and a black ponytail with a dyed orange streak in it.

Ah Gou had coached his younger brother on how to stay out of the Vietnam War. In the first place, the little brother hadn't waited to be drafted—he'd volunteered. "Just say you won't kill other Asians," Ah Gou had advised him. "Otherwise, sound gung ho."

The younger brother had said he would drive any vehicle anywhere, and cook for anyone. ("Show me the combat! I'll drive into an ambush, I'll cook in a mortar attack! I just won't kill other Asians.")

It was a gamble, of course—the army still might have taken him. Good coaching aside, Tony Angel considered, the younger brother didn't have to pretend to be crazy—he was certifiable. That he'd saved his little brother from the Vietnam War—and from killing, or being killed by, other Asians—gave Ah Gou a certain chip on his shoulder.

MAO'S DID CLASSIC French or a mix of Asian styles, but Ah Gou kept the Asian and French food separated—with some exceptions. Mao's version of oysters Rockefeller was topped with panko, Japanese bread crumbs, and Ah Gou used grapeseed oil and shallots to make the mayonnaise for his crabcakes. (The crab was tossed in the Japanese bread crumbs with some chopped tarragon; the panko didn't get soggy in the fridge, the way other bread crumbs did.)

The problem was, they were in *Iowa*. Where was Ah Gou going to get panko—not to mention oysters, grapeseed oil, and crabs? That was where the crazy younger brother came in. He was a born driver. *Xiao Dee* meant "Little Brother" in Shanghai dialect; the *Xiao* was pronounced like *Shaw*. Xiao Dee drove the Cheng brothers' refrigerated truck—complete with two freezer units—to Lower Manhattan, and back, once a week. Tony Angel made the ambitious road trips with him. It was a sixteen-hour drive from Iowa City to Chinatown— to the markets on Pell and Mott streets, where the cook and Xiao Dee shopped.

If a woman in a karate class had lured Ah Gou to Iowa, Xiao Dee had *two* women driving him nuts—one in Rego Park, the other in Bethpage. The cook didn't really care which woman Little Brother was seeing. Tony Angel missed the North End, and he was equally fond of the small Chinese communities in Queens and on Long Island; the people were friendly to him and affectionate with one another. (Personally, the cook would have preferred the Rego Park girlfriend, whose name was Spicy, to the one in Bethpage, whose name he could neither remember nor pronounce.) And Tony loved the shopping in Chinatown—even the long drive back to Iowa on I-80. The cook shared the driving on the interstate with Little Brother, but he let Xiao Dee do the driving around New York City.

They would leave Iowa on a Tuesday afternoon, driving all night till dawn; they emerged from the Holland Tunnel onto Hudson and Canal streets before the Wednesday morning rush hour. They were parked in the Pell Street or Mott Street area of Chinatown when the markets opened. They spent Wednesday night in Queens, or on Long Island, and left before the morning rush hour on Thursday. They would drive all day back to Iowa City, and unload the new goods at Mao's after dinnertime Thursday evening. The weekends were big at Mao's. Even the oysters and mussels and fresh fish from Chinatown would still be fresh on Friday night—if they were lucky, on Saturday night, too.

The cook had never felt stronger; he'd been forty-eight, forty-nine, and fifty in those Iowa years, but loading and unloading Xiao Dee's refrigerated truck gave him the muscles of a professional mover. There was a lot of heavy stuff on board: the cases of Tsingtao beer, the vat of salt water with the smoking blocks of dry ice for the mussels, the tubs of crushed ice for the oysters. On the way back, they would usually stop for more ice at a discount-liquor store in Indiana or Illinois. They kept the flounder, the monkfish, the sea bass, the Scottish salmon, the scallops, the shrimp, the *lap xuong* sausage, and all the crabs on ice, too. The whole way west, the truck melted and sloshed. One of the freezers always smelled like squid; they kept the calamari frozen. The big brown crocks of Tianjin preserved vegetable (from China) had to be wrapped in newspaper or they would crack against themselves and break. It was "asking for bad luck" to pack the Japanese dried anchovies anywhere near the Chinese preserved duck eggs, Xiao Dee said.

Once, when they were crossing the bridge over the Mississippi, at East Moline, they swerved to avoid a bus with a blown-out tire, and all the scents of Asia followed them home: the broken jars of Golden Boy fish sauce for the green Thai curry; the shattered remains of the Chinese soybean sauce (fermented bean curd) and Formosa pork sung; the many jagged edges from the Thai Mae Ploy bottles of sweet

chili sauce, and red and green curry paste. The truck was awash with
sesame oil and soy sauce, but it was mainly the Hong Kong chili garlic sauce that had endured. The aura of garlic was somehow perme-
ated with the lasting essence of Japanese bonito tuna flakes and dried
Chinese shrimp. Black shiitake mushrooms turned up everywhere, for
weeks.

The cook and Xiao Dee had pulled off I-80 immediately west of
Davenport—just to open the rear door of the truck and survey the
spillage from the near-collision over the Mississippi—but an inde-
scribable odor forewarned them not to risk opening the truck until
they were back at Mao's. Something undefined was leaking under the
truck's rear door.

"What does it smell like?" Xiao Dee asked the cook. It was a
brownish liquid with beer foam in it—they could both see that much.

"*Everything,*" Tony Angel answered, kneeling on the pavement and
sniffing the bottom of the door.

A motorcycle cop drove up and asked them if they needed assistance. Little Brother kept all the receipts from their shopping in the
glove compartment in case they were ever stopped and suspected of
transporting stolen goods. The cook explained to the policeman how
they'd swerved on the bridge to avoid the incapacitated bus.

"Maybe we should just keep going, and inspect the damage when
we get to Iowa City," Tony said. The baby-faced, clean-shaven Xiao
Dee was nodding his head, his glossy black ponytail tied with a pink
ribbon, some trifle of affection either Spicy or the other girlfriend had
given him.

"It smells like a Chinese restaurant," the motorcycle cop commented to the cook.

"That's what it *is*," Tony told him.

Both Little Brother and the cook could tell that the cop wanted to
see the mess inside; now that they'd stopped, they had no choice but
to open the truck's rear door. There was Asia, or at least the entire
continent's culinary aromas: the pot of lychee nuts with almond-milk
gelée, the pungent shock of the strewn fresh ginger, and the Mitoku
Trading Company's brand of miso leaves—the latter giving a fungal
appearance to the walls and ceiling of the truck. There was also a
ghoulish monkfish staring at them from a foul sea of soy sauce and

dark-brown ice—a contender for the title of Ugliest Fish in the World, under the best of circumstances.

"Sweet Jesus, what's *that*?" the motorcycle cop asked.

"Monkfish, the poor man's lobster," Xiao Dee explained.

"What's the name of your restaurant in Iowa City?" the cop asked.

"Mao's," Xiao Dee answered proudly.

"*That* place!" the motorcycle cop said. "You get the drive-by vandalism, right?"

"Occasionally," the cook admitted.

"It's because of the war," Xiao Dee said defensively. "The farmers are hawks."

"It's because of the *name*!" the cop said. "*Mao's*—no wonder you get vandalized! This is the Midwest, you know. Iowa City isn't *Berkeley*!"

Back in the truck that would forever smell like all of Pell and Mott streets on a bad morning (such as when there was a garbage strike in Lower Manhattan), the cook said to Little Brother, "The cop has a point, you know. About the *name*, I mean."

Xiao Dee was hopped up on chocolate-espresso balls, which he kept in the glove compartment with all the receipts and ate nonstop when he drove—just to keep himself fanatically awake. If the cook had more than two or three on the sixteen-hour drive, his heart would race until the following day—his bowels indicating the pending onset of explosive diarrhea—as if he'd had two dozen cups of double espresso.

"What's the matter with this country? Mao is just a *name*!" Xiao Dee cried. "This country has been getting its balls cut off in Vietnam for ten years! What does *Mao* have to do with it—it's just a *name*!" The provocative pink ribbon Spicy (or the other girl) had tied around his ponytail had come undone; Xiao Dee resembled a hysterical woman weightlifter driving an entire Chinese restaurant, where you would surely be food-poisoned to death.

"Let's just get home and unload the truck," the cook proposed, hoping to calm Little Brother down. Tony Angel was trying to forget the image of the monkfish swimming through sesame oil, and everything else that was afloat in the back of the truck.

The vat of sea water had spilled; they'd lost all the mussels. There would be no sake-steamed mussels in black-bean sauce that weekend.

No oysters Rockefeller, either. (To add insult to injury, by the time Xiao Dee and the cook got back to Iowa City, Ah Gou had already chopped the spinach and diced the bacon for the oysters Rockefeller.) The sea bass had perished en route, but the monkfish was salvageable—the tail was the only usable part, anyway, and Ah Gou served it sliced in medallions.

The cook had learned to test the freshness of the Scottish salmon by deboning it; if the bones were hard to pull out, Ah Gou said the fish was still pretty fresh. The *lap xuong* sausage, the fresh flounder, and the frozen squid had survived the near collision with the bus, but not the shrimp, the scallops, or the crabs. Ah Gou's favorite mascarpone and the Parmesan were safe, but the other cheeses had to go. The bamboo mats, or *nori* rolls—for rolling out the sushi—had absorbed too much sesame oil and Tsingtao beer. Xiao Dee would hose out the truck every day for *months*, but it would always smell of that near accident over the Mississippi.

HE'D LOVED THAT TIME in Iowa City—including those road trips with Xiao Dee Cheng, Tony Angel was thinking. Every night, on the menu at Avellino, was an item or two the cook had acquired from working with Ah Gou at Mao's. At Avellino, the cook indicated the French or Asian additions to his menu by writing simply, "Something from Asia" or "Something from France"; he'd learned this from Ah Gou at Mao's. In an emergency, when *all* the fish (and the oysters and mussels) had perished before Saturday night, Ah Gou asked the cook to do a pasta special or a pizza.

"Something from Italy," the menu at Mao's would then say.

The long-distance truckers who stopped off the interstate would invariably complain. "What's this fucking 'Something from *Italy*' about? I thought this was a Chinese place."

"We're a little of everything," Xiao Dee would tell them—Little Brother was usually the weekend maître d', while the cook and Ah Gou slaved away in the kitchen.

The rest of the staff at Mao's was a fiercely intelligent and multicultural collection of Asian students from the university—many of them not from Asia but from Seattle and San Francisco, or Boston, or New York. Tzu-Min, Ah Gou's relatively new girlfriend, was a Chinese law-school student who'd been an undergraduate at Iowa just a couple of years before; she'd decided to stay in Iowa City (and not go back to Taiwan) because of Mao's and Ah Gou *and* the law school. On Thursday nights, when Xiao Dee was still suffering the jazzed-up aftereffects of the chocolate-espresso balls, Tzu-Min would sub as the maître d'.

They didn't have a radio at Mao's, Tony Angel was remembering as he surveyed the place settings at Avellino, which on that late-spring '83 night was not quite open for business but soon would be. At Mao's, Ah Gou had kept a TV in the kitchen—the cause of many cut fingers, and other knife or cleaver accidents, in the cook's opinion. But Ah Gou had liked sports and news; sometimes the Iowa football or basketball games were televised, and that way the kitchen knew in advance whether to expect a celebratory or dejected crowd after the game.

In those years, the Iowa wrestling team rarely lost—least of all, at home—and those dual meets brought an especially fired-up and hungry crowd to Mao's. Daniel had taken young Joe to most of the home matches, the cook suddenly remembered. Maybe it had been the success of the Iowa wrestling team that made Joe want to wrestle when he went off to Northfield Mount Hermon; quite possibly, Ketchum's reputation as a barroom brawler had had nothing to do with it.

Tony Angel had a Garland eight-burner stove, with two ovens and a broiler, in his kitchen at Avellino; he had a steam table for his chicken stocks, too. At Mao's, at their busiest, they could seat eighty or ninety people in an evening, but Avellino was smaller. Tony rarely fed more than thirty or forty people a night—fifty, tops.

Tonight the cook was working on a red-wine reduction for the braised beef short ribs, and he had both a light and a dark chicken stock on the steam table. In the "Something from Asia" category, he was serving Ah Gou's beef *satay* with peanut sauce and assorted tempura—just some shrimp, haricots verts, and asparagus. There were the usual pasta dishes—the calamari with black olives and pine nuts, over penne, among them—and two popular pizzas, the pepperoni with marinara sauce and a wild-mushroom pizza with four cheeses. He had a roast chicken with rosemary, which was served on a bed of arugula and grilled fennel, and a grilled leg of spring lamb with garlic, and a wild-mushroom risotto, too.

Greg, the cook's young sous chef, had been to cooking school on Ninety-second Street in Manhattan and was a fast learner. Tony was letting Greg do a sauce *grenobloise*, with brown butter and capers, for the chicken paillard—that was the little "Something from France" for the evening. And Tony's two favorite waitresses were on hand, a single mother and her college-student daughter. Celeste, the mom, had worked for the cook since '76, and the daughter, Loretta, was more mature than the usual Brattleboro high school kids he hired as waitresses, busboys, and dishwashers.

Loretta was older than most college students; she'd had a baby her senior year in high school. Loretta was unmarried and had cared for the child in her mom's house until the little boy was old enough (four or five) to not drive Celeste crazy. Then Loretta had gotten into a nearby community college—not the easiest commute, but she'd arranged all her classes on a Tuesday–Thursday schedule. She was back home in Brattleboro, still living with her mom and young son, from every Thursday night till the following Tuesday morning.

Since the cook had been sleeping with Celeste—only for the last year, going on eighteen months—the arrangement had worked well for Tony Angel. He stayed in Celeste's house, with Celeste and her first-grade grandson, only two nights a week—on one of which, every Wednesday, the restaurant was closed. The cook moved back into his apartment whenever Loretta came home to Brattleboro. It had been more awkward last summer, when Celeste moved into Tony's small apartment above Avellino for upwards of three or four nights at a time. A redhead, with very fetching freckles on her chest, she was a big woman, though not nearly the size of either Injun Jane or Carmella. Celeste (at fifty) was as many years older than the cook's son, Danny, as she was younger than the cook.

There was no hanky-panky between them in the kitchen at Avellino—at their mutual insistence—though everyone on the staff (Loretta, of course, included) knew that Tony Angel and Celeste were a couple. The lady friends the cook had met at The Book Cellar had since moved on, or they were married now. The old joke Tony cracked to the bookseller was no longer acted upon; it was an *innocent* joke when the cook asked the bookseller if she knew any women to introduce him to. (She either didn't or she *wouldn't*, not with Celeste in the picture. Brattleboro was a small town, and Celeste was a popular presence in it.)

It had been easier to meet women in Iowa, Tony Angel was remembering. Granted, he was older now, and Brattleboro was a *very* small town compared to Iowa City, where Danny had invited his dad to all the Writers' Workshop parties; those women writers knew how to have a good time.

Danny had treated his workshop students to an evening at Mao's on many occasions—not least the celebration of the Chinese New Year, every January or February, when Ah Gou had presented a ten-course prix-fixe menu for three nights in a row. Just before the Chinese New Year in '73—it was the Year of the Ox, the cook remembered—Xiao Dee's truck had broken down in Pennsylvania, and Tony Angel and Little Brother almost hadn't made it back to Iowa City with the goods in time.

In '74—the Year of the Tiger, Tony thought—Xiao Dee had convinced Spicy to ride along to Iowa City with them, all the way from Queens. Spicy was fortunately small, but it was still a tight squeeze in the truck's cab, and somewhere in Indiana or Illinois, Spicy figured out that Xiao Dee had been seeing a woman in Bethpage—"that Nassau County cunt," Spicy called her. The cook had listened to them argue the rest of the way.

Somehow, thinking of Iowa City and Mao's had made Tony Angel consider that Avellino lacked *ambition*, but one of the things the cook loved about his Brattleboro restaurant was that it was relatively easy to run; real chefs, like Ah Gou Cheng and Tony Molinari and Paul Polcari, might find Avellino unambitious, but the cook (at fifty-nine) wasn't trying to compete with them.

One sadness was that Tony Angel wouldn't invite his old friends and mentors to come visit him in Vermont, and have a meal at Avellino. The cook felt that his Brattleboro restaurant was unworthy of these superior chefs, who'd taught him so much, though they probably would have been touched and flattered to have seen their obvious good influences on the menu at Avellino, and they surely would have supported the cook's pride in having his very own restaurant, which—albeit only in Brattleboro—was a local success. Since Molinari and Polcari were retired, they could have come to Vermont at their convenience; it might have been harder for the Cheng brothers to find the time.

Ah Gou and Xiao Dee had moved back East, this on the good counsel of Tzu-Min, the young Chinese lawyer who'd married Big Brother—she'd given him some solid business advice, and had never gone back to Taiwan. Connecticut was closer to Lower Manhattan, where Little Brother needed to shop; it made no sense for the Chengs to kill themselves while striving for authenticity in Iowa. The first name of their new restaurant, Baozi, meant "Wrapped" in Chinese. (The cook remembered the golden pork spring rolls and braised pork *baozi* that Ah Gou made every Chinese New Year. The steamed dough balls were split, like a sandwich, and filled with a braised pork shoulder that had been shredded and mixed with Chinese five-spice powder.) But Tzu-Min was the businessperson in the Cheng family; she changed the name of the restaurant to Lemongrass, which was both more marketable and more comprehensible in Connecticut.

One day, Tony Angel thought, maybe Daniel and I can drive down to Connecticut and eat at Lemongrass; we could spend the night somewhere in the vicinity. The cook missed Ah Gou and Xiao Dee, and he wished them well.

"What's the matter, Tony?" Celeste asked him. (The cook was crying, though he'd not been aware of it.)

"Nothing's the matter, Celeste. In fact, I'm very happy," Tony said. He smiled at her and bent over his red-wine reduction, savoring the smell. He'd blanched a sprig of fresh rosemary in boiling water, just to draw out the oil before putting the rosemary in the red wine.

"Yeah, well, you're *crying*," Celeste told him.

"Memories, I guess," the cook said. Greg, the sous chef, was watching him, too. Loretta came into the kitchen from the dining room.

"Are we going to unlock the place tonight, or make the customers find a way to break in?" she asked the cook.

"Oh, is it time?" Tony Angel asked. He must have left his watch upstairs in the bedroom, where he'd not yet finished the galleys of *East of Bangor.*

"What's he crying about?" Loretta asked her mother.

"I was just asking him," Celeste said. "Memories, I guess."

"*Good* ones, huh?" Loretta asked the cook; she took a clean dish towel from the rack and patted his cheek. Even the dishwasher and the busboy, two Brattleboro high school kids, were watching Tony Angel with concern.

The cook and his sous chef were not rigid about sticking to their stations, though normally Greg did the grilling, roasting, and broiling, while Tony watched over the sauces.

"You want me to be the *saucier* tonight, boss?" Greg asked the cook.

"I'm fine," Tony told them all, shaking his head. "Don't you ever have memories?"

"Danny called—I forgot to tell you," Loretta said to the cook. "He's coming in tonight."

"Yeah, Danny sounds like he had an exciting day—for a writer," Celeste told Tony. "He got attacked by two dogs. Rooster killed one. He wanted a table at the usual time, but just for one. He said that Barrett wouldn't appreciate the dog story. He said, 'Tell Pop I'll see him later.' "

The "Pop" had its origins in Iowa City—the cook liked it.

Barrett was originally from England; though she'd lived in the United States for years, her English accent struck Tony Angel as sounding more and more English every time he heard it. People in America were overly impressed by English accents, the cook thought. Perhaps English accents made many Americans feel uneducated.

Tony knew what his son had meant by Barrett not appreciating the dog story. Although Danny had been bitten by dogs when he was running, Barrett was one of those animal lovers who always took the dog's side. (There were no "bad" dogs, only bad dog owners; the Vermont State Police should *never* shoot anyone's dog; if Danny didn't run with the squash-racquet handles, maybe the dogs wouldn't *try* to bite him, and so forth.) But the cook knew that his son ran with the racquet handles *because* he'd been bitten when he ran without them—he'd needed stitches twice but the rabies shots only once.

Tony Angel was glad that his son wasn't coming to dinner with Barrett. It bothered the cook that Daniel had *ever* slept with a woman almost as old as his own *father*! But Barrett's Englishness and her belief that there were no bad dogs bothered Tony more. Well, wasn't an unexamined love of dogs to be expected from a *horse* person? the cook asked himself.

Tony Angel used an old Stanley woodstove from Ireland for his pizzas; he knew how to keep the oven at six hundred degrees without making the rest of the kitchen too hot, but it had taken him two years to figure it out. He was refilling the woodbox in the Stanley when he heard Loretta unlocking the front door and inviting the first customers into the dining room.

"There was another phone call," Greg told the cook.

Tony hoped that Daniel hadn't changed his mind about coming to dinner, or that his son hadn't decided to bring Barrett with him, but the other message was from Ketchum.

The old logger had gone on and on to Greg about the miraculous invention of the fax machine. God knows for how long fax machines had been invented, the cook thought, but this was not the first he'd heard about Ketchum wanting one. Danny had been to New York and seen some rudimentary fax machine in operation in the production department of his publishing house; in Daniel's estimation, his father recalled, it had been a bulky machine that produced oily scraps of paper with hard-to-read writing, but this didn't deter Ketchum. The formerly illiterate woodsman wanted Danny and his dad to have fax machines; then Ketchum would get one, and they could all be instantly in contact with one another.

Dear God, the cook was thinking, there would be no end of faxes; I'll have to buy *reams* of paper. And there will be no more peaceful mornings, Tony Angel thought; he loved his morning coffee and his favorite view of the Connecticut. (Like the cook, Ketchum was an early riser.)

Tony Angel had never seen where Ketchum lived in Errol, but he'd envisioned something from the wanigan days—a trailer maybe, or several trailers. Formerly mobile homes, perhaps, but no longer mobile—or a Volkswagen bus with a woodstove inside it, and without any wheels. That Ketchum (at sixty-six) had only recently learned to read but now wanted a fax machine was unimaginable. Not that long ago, Ketchum hadn't even owned a *phone*!

THE COOK KNEW WHY he had cried; his "memories" had nothing to do with it. As soon as he'd thought of taking a trip with his son to see the Chengs in their Connecticut restaurant, Tony Angel had known that Daniel would never do it. The writer was a workaholic; to the cook's thinking, a kind of logorrhea had possessed his son. That Daniel was coming to dinner at Avellino alone was fine with Tony Angel, but that his son *was* alone (and probably would remain so) made the cook cry. If he worried about his grandson, Joe—for all the obvious dangers any eighteen-year-old needed to be lucky to escape— the cook was sorry that his son, Daniel, struck him as a terminally lonely, melancholic soul. He's even lonelier and more melancholic than *I* am! Tony Angel was thinking.

"Table of four," Loretta was saying to Greg, the sous chef. "One wild-mushroom pizza, one pepperoni," she told the cook.

Celeste came into the kitchen from the dining room. "Danny's here, alone," she said to Tony.

"One calamari with penne," Loretta went on, reciting. When it was busy, she just left the two cooks her orders in writing, but when there was almost no one in Avellino, Loretta seemed to enjoy the drama of an out-loud presentation.

"The table of four doesn't want any first courses?" Greg asked her.

"They all want the arugula salad with the shaved Parmesan," Loretta said. "You'll love this one." She paused for the full effect. "One chicken paillard, but hold the capers."

"Christ," Greg said. "A sauce *grenobloise* is all about the capers."

"Just give the bozo the red-wine reduction with rosemary—it's as good on the chicken as it is on the braised beef," Tony Angel said.

"It'll turn the chicken *purple*, Tony," his sous chef complained.

"You're such a purist, Greg," the cook said. "Then give the bozo the paillard with a little olive oil and lemon."

"Danny says to surprise him," Celeste told Tony. She was watching the cook closely. She'd heard him cry in his sleep, too.

"Well, that will be fun," the cook said. (Finally, there's a smile— albeit a small one—Celeste was thinking.)

MAY WAS A TALKATIVE PASSENGER. While Dot drove—her head nodding, but usually not in rhythm to whatever junk was playing on the radio—May read most of the road signs out loud, the way children who've only recently learned to read sometimes do.

"Bellows Falls," May had announced, as they'd passed that exit on

I-91—maybe fifteen or more minutes ago. "Who would want to live in Bellows Falls?"

"You been there?" Dot asked her old friend.

"Nope. It just sounds awful," May said.

"It's beginnin' to look like suppertime, isn't it?" Dot asked.

"I could eat a little somethin'," May admitted.

"Like what?" Dot asked.

"Oh, just half a bear or a whole cow, I guess," May said, cackling. Dot cackled with her.

"Even *half* a cow would hit the spot," Dot more seriously proposed.

"Putney," May read out loud, as they passed the exit sign.

"What kinda name is that, do you suppose? Not Injun, from the sound of it," Dot said.

"Nope. Not Injun," May agreed. The three Brattleboro exits were coming up.

"How 'bout a pizza?" Dot said.

"BRAT-el-burrow," May enunciated with near perfection.

"Definitely not an Injun name!" Dot said, and the two old ladies cackled some more.

"There's gotta be a pizza place in Brattleboro, don'tcha think?" May asked her friend.

"Let's have a look," Dot said. She took the second Brattleboro exit, which brought her onto Main Street.

"The Book Cellar," May read out loud, as they drove slowly past the bookstore on their right.

When they got to the next traffic light, and the steep part of the hill, they could see the marquee for the Latchis Theatre. A couple of the previous year's movies were playing—a Sylvester Stallone double feature, *Rocky III* and *First Blood.*

"I saw those movies," Dot said proudly.

"You saw them with *me,*" May reminded her.

The two ladies were easily distracted by the movie marquee at the Latchis, and Dot was driving; Dot couldn't drive and look at both sides of the street at the same time. If it hadn't been for May, her hungry passenger and compulsive sign-reader, they might have missed seeing Avellino altogether. The *Avellino* word was a tough one for May; she stumbled over it but managed to say, "Italian cooking."

"Where?" Dot asked; they had already driven past it.

"Back there. Park somewhere," May told her friend. "It said 'Italian'—I know it did."

They ended up in the supermarket parking lot before Dot could gather her driving wits about her. "Now we'll just have to hoof it," she said to May.

Dot didn't like to *hoof it*; she had a bunion that was killing her and caused her to limp, which made May recall Cookie's limp, so that Cookie had been on the bad old broads' minds lately. (Also, the *Injun* conversation in the car might have made them remember their long-ago time in Twisted River.)

"I would walk a mile for a pizza, or two," May told her old friend.

"One of *Cookie's* pizzas, anyway," Dot said, and that did it.

"Oh, weren't they *good*!" May exclaimed. They had waddled their way to the Latchis, on the wrong side of the street, and were nearly killed crossing Main Street in a haphazard fashion. (Maybe Milan was more forgiving to pedestrians than Brattleboro.) Both Dot and May gave the finger to the driver who'd almost hit them.

"What was it Cookie wanted to put in his pizza dough?" Dot asked May.

"Honey!" May said, and they both cackled. "But he changed his mind about it," May remembered.

"I wonder what his secret ingredient was," Dot said.

"Didn't have one, maybe," May replied, with a shrug. They had stopped in front of the big picture window at Avellino, where May struggled out loud to say the restaurant's name.

"It sure sounds like real Italian," Dot decided. The two women read the menu that was posted in the window. "Two different pizzas," Dot observed.

"I'm stickin' to the pepperoni," May told her friend. "You can die eatin' wild mushrooms."

"The thing about Cookie's crust was that it was really thin, so you could eat a lot more pizza without gettin' filled up," Dot was remembering.

Inside, a family of four was finishing their meal—Dot and May could see that the two kids had ordered pizzas. There was a good-looking man, maybe fortyish, sitting alone at a table near the swinging doors to the kitchen. He was writing in a notebook—just a lined notebook of the kind students use. The old ladies didn't recognize Danny, of course. He'd been twelve when they'd last seen him, and now he was a whole decade older than his father was when Dot and May had last seen the cook.

Danny had looked up when the old ladies came in, but he'd quickly turned his attention back to whatever he was writing. He might not even have remembered what Dot and May looked like in 1954; twenty-nine years later, Danny didn't have the slightest idea who those bad old broads were.

"Just the two of you, ladies?" Celeste asked them. (It always amused Dot and May when anyone thought of them as "ladies.")

They were given a table near the window, under the old black-and-white photograph of the long-ago logjam in Brattleboro. "They used to drive logs down the Connecticut," Dot said to May.

"This must have been a mill town, in its day," May remarked. "Sawmills, paper, maybe—textiles, too, I suppose."

"There's an insane asylum in this town, I hear," Dot told her friend. When the waitress came to pour them water, Dot asked Celeste about it. "Is the loony bin still operatin' here?"

"It's called the *retreat*," Celeste explained.

"That's a sneaky fuck of a name for it!" May said. She and Dot were cackling again when Celeste went to get them menus. (She'd forgotten to bring the old biddies menus when she brought them their water. Celeste was still distracted by the cook's crying.)

A young couple came in, and Dot and May observed a younger waitress—Celeste's daughter, Loretta—showing them to their table. When Celeste came back with the menus, Dot said, "We'll both have the pepperoni pizza." (She and May had already had a look at the menu in the window.)

"One each or one to share?" Celeste asked them. (Just looking at these two, Celeste knew the answer.)

"One *each*," May told her.

"Would you like a salad, or a first course?" Celeste asked the old ladies.

"Nope. I'm saving room for the apple pie," May answered.

Dot said: "I imagine I'll be havin' the blueberry cobbler."

They both ordered Cokes—"*real* ones," May emphasized to Celeste. For the drive ahead, not to mention the slew of children and grandchildren, Dot and May wanted all the caffeine and sugar they could get.

"I swear," May said to Dot, "if my kids and grandkids keep havin' *more* kids, you can check me into that so-called retreat."

"I'll come visit you," her friend Dot told her. "If the pizza's any good," she added.

In the kitchen at Avellino, maybe the cook had heard the old ladies cackling. "Two pepperoni pizzas," Celeste told him. "Two *probable* pie and cobbler customers."

"Who are they?" the cook asked her; he wasn't usually so curious. "A couple of locals?"

"A couple of bad old broads, if you ask me—locals or otherwise," Celeste said.

It was almost time for the Red Sox game on the radio. Boston was playing at home, in Fenway Park, but Greg was listening to some sentimental crap called *The Oldie-But-Goldie Hour* on another station. The cook hadn't really been paying attention, but the featured recording, from 1967, was *Surrealistic Pillow*—the old Jefferson Airplane album.

When Tony Angel recognized Grace Slick's voice singing "Somebody to Love," he spoke with uncharacteristic sharpness to his sous chef.

"Time for the game, Greg," the cook said.

"Just lemme hear—" the sous chef started to say, but Tony abruptly switched stations. (Everyone had heard the impatience in his voice and seen the angry way he'd reached for the radio.)

All the cook could say for himself was: "I don't like that song."

With a shrug, Celeste said to them all: "Memories, I guess."

Just one thin wall and two swinging doors away were two more old *memories*. Unfortunately, the cook would not get rid of Dot and May as easily as he'd cut off that song on the radio.

CHAPTER 9

THE FRAGILE, UNPREDICTABLE NATURE OF THINGS

OUT ON THE CORALVILLE STRIP, WITHIN SIGHT OF MAO'S, there'd been a pizza place called The Greek's; kalamata olives and feta cheese was the favorite topping. (As Danny's dad had said at the time, "It isn't bad, but it isn't pizza.") In downtown Iowa City was an imitation Irish pub called O'Rourke's—pool tables, green beer every St. Patrick's Day, bratwurst or meatball sandwiches. To Danny, O'Rourke's was strictly a student hangout—an unconvincing copy of those Boston pubs south of the Haymarket, in the vicinity of Hanover Street. The oldest of these was the Union Oyster House, a clam bar and restaurant, which would one day be across the street from a Holocaust commemoration site, but there was also the Bell in Hand Tavern on the corner of Union and Marshall streets—a pub where the underage Daniel Baciagalupo had gotten drunk on beer with his older Saetta and Calogero cousins.

Those taverns had not been far enough out of the North End to have escaped the cook's attention. One day he'd followed Daniel and his cousins to the Bell in Hand. When the cook saw his young son drinking a beer, he'd pulled the boy out of the tavern by his ear.

As the writer Danny Angel sat working away in his notebook at Avellino—waiting for his dad, the cook, to surprise him—he wished that his humiliation in the Bell in Hand, in front of his older cousins, had been sufficient to make him stop drinking before he really got started. But in order to stop himself, Danny had needed a greater fright and subsequent humiliation than that earlier misadventure in a Boston bar. It would come, but not before he was a father. ("If becoming a parent doesn't make you responsible," the cook had once said to his son, "nothing will.")

Had Danny been thinking *as a father* when he'd typed a one-page message to the hippie carpenter, and had driven out the back road to Westminster West in order to put the message in the asshole dog owner's mailbox, before driving to Brattleboro and his surprise dinner at Avellino? Was this what the writer would have wanted young Joe to do, if his son were to find himself in a similarly hostile situation?

"I am truly sorry your dog is dead," Danny had typed. "I was angry. You take no responsibility for your dogs, and you won't acknowledge that a public road is not your dogs' territory. But I should have held my temper better than I did. I'll run somewhere else. You've lost a dog; I'll give up my favorite run. Enough is enough, okay?"

It was just a plain piece of typing paper. The writer didn't include his name. If Armando was right—if the asshole was a *writer* carpenter, and/or one of Danny's former students at Windham—then of course the infuriating dog owner already knew that the runner with the squash-racquet handles was the writer Danny Angel. But Danny saw no reason to advertise this. He didn't put the piece of paper in an envelope, either; he'd just folded it twice and put it in the dog owner's mailbox, out where the driveway lined with dead vehicles met the road.

Now, as he sat writing in Avellino, Danny knew what Armando would say: "You don't try to make peace with assholes," or words to that effect. But Armando didn't have children. Did that make Armando more unafraid? The very idea of an altercation escalating out of control—well, wasn't that high on the list of things to protect your children from? (In the notebook, where Danny was scribbling to himself, the phrase "a nameless fear" stood out with an identifying awkwardness in several unfinished sentences.)

As a boy, and as a young man, Danny had always assumed that his dad and Ketchum were different, chiefly because his dad was a cook and Ketchum was a river driver—a logger, tougher than his caulk boots, an intemperate woodsman who would never back down from a fight.

But Ketchum was estranged from his children; he'd already lost them. It wasn't necessarily true that Ketchum was braver, or more bold, than the cook. Ketchum wasn't a father, not anymore; he didn't have as much to lose. Danny only now understood that his dad had been doing his best to look out for him. Leaving Twisted River had been a *father's* decision. And the cook and his son were both trying to look out for young Joe; their mutual fear for the boy had brought Danny and his dad closer together.

He'd felt close to his father in Iowa City, too, the writer was remembering. (Their *Asian* interlude, as Danny thought of Iowa that second time around.) His dad's steadiest girlfriend those years in Iowa City had been an ER nurse at Mercy Hospital—Yi-Yiing was Chinese. She was Danny's age—in her early thirties, almost twenty years younger than the cook—and she had a daughter, who was Joe's age, back in Hong Kong. Her husband had left her upon the daughter's birth—he'd wanted a son—and Yi-Yiing had trusted her mother and father to care for her child while she'd made a new life for herself in the Midwest. The nursing career had been a good choice, and so had Iowa City. The doctors at Mercy Hospital had declared that Yi-Yiing was indispensable. She had her green card and was on track to become a U.S. citizen.

Of course Yi-Yiing would hear the occasional *gook* word—the most common insult from a prejudiced patient in the emergency room, and from an unseen driver or passenger in a moving car. But it didn't faze her to be mistaken for the war bride of a Vietnam vet. She had a harder, uphill task ahead of her—namely, moving her daughter and her parents to the United States—but she was well on her way to unraveling the red tape that was involved. Yi-Yiing had her own reasons for remaining undistracted from achieving her goal. (She'd been assured it would be easier to bring her family to the United States once the war in Vietnam was over; it was "only a matter of time," a reliable authority had told her.)

What Yi-Yiing had said to Tony Angel was that it wasn't the time for her to be "romantically involved." Maybe this was music to his dad's ears, Danny had thought at the time. Quite possibly, given Yi-

Yiing's heroic undertaking, the cook was a consoling and undemanding partner for her; with so much of his life lost to the past, Tony Angel wasn't exactly seeking so-called romantic involvement, either. Moreover, that the cook's grandson was the same age as Yi-Yiing's daughter gave the nurse a motherly affection for young Joe.

Danny and his dad always had to think about Joe before including new women in their lives. Danny had liked Yi-Yiing—no small part of the reason being how sincerely she'd paid attention to Joe—though it was awkward that Yi-Yiing was Danny's age, and that the writer was attracted to her.

In those three years, Danny and his dad had rented three different houses on Court Street in Iowa City—all from tenured faculty on sabbaticals. Court Street was tree-lined with large, three-story houses; it was a kind of residential faculty row. The street was also within safe walking distance of the Longfellow Elementary School, where Joe would attend second, third, and fourth grades. Court Street was somewhat removed from downtown Iowa City, and Danny never had to drive on Iowa Avenue, where he'd earlier lived with Katie—not, in any case, on his way to and from the English-Philosophy Building on the Iowa River. (The EPB, as it was called, was where Danny's office at the Writers' Workshop was.)

As big as the rental houses on Court Street were, Danny didn't write at home—largely because Yi-Yiing worked irregular hours in the ER at Mercy Hospital. She often slept in the cook's bedroom until midday, when she would come down to the kitchen and fix herself something to eat in her silk pajamas. When she wasn't working at the hospital, Yi-Yiing lived in her slinky Hong Kong pajamas.

Danny liked walking Joe to school, and then going to write at the English-Philosophy Building. When his office door was closed, his students and the other faculty knew not to bother him. (Yi-Yiing was small of stature, short but surprisingly heavyset, with a pretty face and long, coal-black hair. She had many pairs of the silk pajamas, in a variety of vibrant colors; as Danny recalled, even her black pajamas appeared to vibrate.) This parenthetical non sequitur, long after he'd begun his morning's writing—an alluring image of Yi-Yiing in her vibrating pajamas, asleep in his father's bed—was a lingering distraction. Yi-Yiing and her pajamas, or their enticing presence, traveled to the English-Philosophy Building with Danny.

"I don't know how you can write in such a sterile building," the writer Raymond Carver said of the EPB. Ray was a colleague of Danny Angel's at the workshop in those years.

"It's not as . . . sterile as you may think," Danny said to Ray.

Another writer colleague, John Cheever, compared the EPB to a hotel—"one catering to conventioneers"—but Danny liked his fourth-floor office there. Most mornings, the offices and classrooms of the Writers' Workshop were deserted. No one but the workshop's administrative assistant was ever there, and she was good about taking messages and not putting through any phone calls—not unless there was a call from young Joe or Danny's dad.

The aesthetics of a given workplace notwithstanding, writers tend to love where they work well. For as much of the day as Joe was safe in school, Danny grew to love the EPB. The fourth floor was silent, a virtual sanctuary—provided he left by midafternoon.

Usually, writers don't confine their writing to the *good* things, do they? Danny Angel was thinking, as he scribbled away in his notebook at Avellino, where Iowa City was foremost on his mind. "The Baby in the Road," he had written—a chapter title, possibly, but there was more to it than that. He'd crossed out the *The* and had written, "A Baby in the Road," but neither article pleased him—he quickly crossed out the *A,* too. Above where he was writing, on the same page of the notebook, was more evidence of the writer's reluctance to use an article—"The Blue Mustang" had been revised to "Blue Mustang." (Maybe just "Baby in the Road" was the way to go?)

To anyone seeing the forty-one-year-old writer's expression, this exercise was both more meaningful and more painful than a mere title search. To Dot and May, the troubled-looking young author seemed strangely attractive and familiar; waiting for their food, they both watched him intently. In the absence of signs to read out loud, May was at a momentary loss for words, but Dot whispered to her friend: "Whatever he's writin', he's not havin' any fun doin' it."

"I could give him some fun *doin' it*!" May whispered back, and both ladies commenced to cackling, in their inimitable fashion.

At this moment in time, it took a lot to distract Danny from his writing. The blue Mustang and the baby in the road had seized the writer's attention, almost completely; that one or the other might make a good title was immaterial. Both the blue Mustang and the baby in the road were triggers to Danny's imagination, and they meant much more to him than titles. Yet the distinctive cackles of the two old ladies caused Danny to look up from his notebook, whereupon Dot and May quickly looked away. They'd been staring at him—that much was clear to Danny, who would have sworn that he'd heard the fat women's indelible and derisive laughter before. But where, and when?

Too long ago for Danny to remember, obviously, seized as he was by those fresher, more memorable details, the speeding blue Mustang and that helpless baby in the road. Danny was a far distance from the twelve-year-old he'd been in the cookhouse kitchen, where (and when) Dot and May's cackling had once been as constant as punctuation. The writer returned his attention to his notebook; he was imagining Iowa City, but he was closer to that time in Twisted River than he could have known.

THEIR FIRST YEAR ON COURT STREET, Danny and his dad and Joe gradually grew used to sharing the house with Yi-Yiing and her vibrant pajamas. She'd arranged her schedule at the hospital so that she was usually in the house when Joe came home from school. This was before Joe's bike-riding began in earnest, and what girlfriends Danny had were transient; the writer's passing acquaintances rarely spent the night in the Court Street house. The cook left for the kitchen at Mao's every midafternoon—that is, when he wasn't driving to Lower Manhattan and back with Xiao Dee Cheng.

Those two nights a week when Tony Angel was on the road, Yi-Yiing didn't stay in the Court Street house. She'd kept her own apartment, near Mercy Hospital; maybe she knew all along that Danny was attracted to her—Yi-Yiing did nothing to encourage him. It was the cook and young Joe who received all her attention, though she'd been the first to speak to Danny when Joe started riding his bike to school. By then, they'd all moved into the second house on Court Street; it was nearer the commuter traffic on Muscatine Avenue, but there were only small backstreets between Court Street and the Longfellow Elementary School. Even so, Yi-Yiing told Danny that he should make Joe ride his bike on the sidewalk—and when the boy had to cross a street, he should *walk* his bike, she said.

"Kids on bikes get hit by cars all the time in this town," Yi-Yiing told Danny. He tried to overlook whichever pair of pajamas she was wearing at the moment; he knew he should focus on her experience as an emergency-room nurse. "I see them all the time—there was one in the ER last night," she said.

"Some kid was riding his bike at night?" Danny asked her.

"He got hit on Dodge Street when it was still daylight, but he was in the ER all night," Yi-Yiing said.

"Is he going to be all right?" Danny asked.

Yi-Yiing shook her head; she was making tea for herself in the kitchen of the second Court Street house, and a thin piece of toast dangled like a cigarette from her lower lip. Joe was home sick from school, and Danny had been writing at the kitchen table. "Just make Joe ride his bike on the sidewalk," Yi-Yiing said, "and if he wants to go downtown—or to the pool, or the zoo, in City Park—for God's sake, make him walk or take the bus."

"Okay," Danny told her. She sat down at the table with him, with her tea and the rest of her toast.

"What are you doing home?" Yi-Yiing asked him. "I'm here, aren't I? I'm awake. You should go write in your office. I'm a *nurse*, Danny— I can look after Joe."

"Okay," Danny said again. Just how safe could Joe get? the writer was wondering. The boy had an ER nurse taking care of him, not to mention *two* Japanese babysitters.

Most nights, both the cook and his emergency-room nurse were working; either Danny stayed home with Joe, or one of the Japanese twins looked after the boy. Sao and Kaori's parents were from Yoko-hama originally, but the twins had been born in San Francisco and they'd grown up there. One night the cook had brought them home from Mao's; he'd woken up Danny to introduce him to the twins, and he'd taken Sao and Kaori into Joe's room to allow them to observe the sleeping boy. "See?" Tony whispered to the twins, while Danny lay be-wildered and barely awake in his bed. "This child is an angel—he's easy to look after."

The cook had disapproved of Danny asking his workshop students to babysit for Joe. Danny's students were writers—hence easily distracted, or preoccupied, in Tony Angel's opinion. Young writers lived in their imaginations, didn't they? the cook had asked his son. (Danny knew that his dad had always distrusted imagination.) Furthermore, these young writers were *graduate* students; many of them were older than the usual graduate students, too. "They're too *old* to be competent babysitters!" the cook had said. His dad's theory was new to Danny, but he liked Sao and Kaori, the identical twins—though he could never tell them apart. (Over time, Joe could, and wasn't that all that mattered?)

"The Yokohamas," as Danny thought of the twins—as if Yokohama were their family name—were undergraduates and part-time waitresses at Mao's. Therefore, Iowa City had a decidedly Asian flavor not only for the cook but for Danny and young Joe. The twins spoke Japanese to each other, which Joe loved but Danny found distracting. Most nights, when Sao worked at Mao's, Kaori was Joe's babysitter—or vice versa. (In which case, no Japanese was spoken.)

The Yokohamas had at first maintained a distant respect for Yi-Yiing, whose ER schedule did not often allow her to coincide in the house with either Sao or Kaori. They were more likely to run into one another at Mao's, where Yi-Yiing occasionally came late (and by herself) to dinner—though she preferred the all-night shift in the emergency room to working daytime hours.

One night, when Xiao Dee was the maître d', he mistook Yi-Yiing for one of the waitresses who worked at Mao's. "You're late!" he told her.

"I'm a customer—I have a reservation," Yi-Yiing told Little Brother.

"Oh, shit—you're Tony's nurse!" Xiao Dee said.

"Tony's too young to need a nurse yet," Yi-Yiing replied.

Later, the cook tried to defend Xiao Dee. ("He's a good driver—he's just a shitty maître d'.") But Yi-Yiing was sensitive.

"The Americans think I'm Vietnamese, and some Shanghai clown from Queens thinks I'm a *waitress*!" she told Tony.

Unfortunately, one of the Japanese twins, who *was* a waitress—at this moment, she was also young Joe's babysitter—overheard Yi-Yiing say this. "What's so bad about being a *waitress*?" Sao or Kaori asked the nurse.

The Japanese twins had also been mistaken for Vietnamese war brides in Iowa City. Most people in their native San Francisco, either Sao or Kaori had explained to Danny, could tell the Japanese and Vietnamese apart; apparently this was not the case in the Midwest. To this shameful lumping together, what could Danny truthfully say? After all, *he* still couldn't tell Sao and Kaori apart! (And, after Yi-Yiing used the *waitress* word as an epithet, the Yokohamas' formerly distant respect for the nurse from Hong Kong grew *more* distant.)

"We're all one happy family," Danny would later try to explain to one of his older workshop students. Youn was a writer from Seoul; she came into Danny's fiction workshop the second year he was back in Iowa City. There were some Vietnam vets among the workshop students in those years—they, too, were older. And there were a few women writers who'd interrupted their writing lives to get married and have children, and get divorced. These older graduate students had an advantage over the younger writers who'd come to the Writers' Workshop right out of college; the older ones had something to write about.

Youn certainly did. She'd been a slave to an arranged marriage in Seoul—"*virtually* arranged," was how she first described the marriage in the novel she was writing.

Danny had criticized the *virtually*. "Either it was an arranged marriage or it wasn't, right?" he'd asked Youn.

Her skin was as pale as milk. Her black hair was cut short, with bangs, under which her big dark-brown eyes made her appear waifish, though Youn was over thirty—she was exactly Danny's age—and her efforts to get her real-life husband to divorce her, so she wouldn't be dragged through "the Korean rigmarole" of trying to divorce him, gave her novel-in-progress a labyrinthine plot.

If you could believe either her actual story or her novel, the writer Danny Angel had thought. When he'd first met her, and had read the early chapters, Danny didn't know if he could trust her—either as a woman or as a writer. But he'd *liked* her from the beginning, and Danny's developing attraction to Youn at least alleviated his inappropriate fantasizing about his father's girlfriend in her countless pairs of pajamas.

"Well," the cook had said to his son, after Danny introduced him to Youn, "if there's a Chinese nurse and two Japanese girls in the house, why not a Korean writer, too?"

But they were all hiding something, weren't they? Certainly, the cook and his son were in hiding—they were fugitives. His dad's Chinese nurse gave Danny the impression that there was something she wasn't saying. As for Danny's Korean writer, he knew she exhibited a seemingly willful lack of clarity—he didn't mean only in her prose.

There was no fault to be found with the Japanese babysitters, whose affection for young Joe was genuine, and whose fondness for the cook stemmed from the camaraderie of them all working together in the ambitious chaos of Asian and French cuisine at Mao's.

Not that Yi-Yiing's rapt attention to Joe was insincere; the ER nurse was a truly good soul. It was her relationship with the cook that amounted to a compromise, perhaps to them both. But Tony Angel had long been wary of women, and he was used to hedging his bets; it was Yi-Yiing who shouldn't have tolerated Tony's short-term flings with those traveling women he met at the Writers' Workshop parties, but the nurse accepted even this from the cook. Yi-Yiing liked living with a young boy the same age as her missing daughter; she liked being a mother to *someone.* Being a part of the cook's all-male family may also have struck Yi-Yiing as a bohemian adventure—one she might not find so easy to slip into once her daughter and parents finally joined her in America.

To those bold young doctors at Mercy Hospital who would inquire as to her *status*—was she married, or did she have a boyfriend? they wanted to know—Yi-Yiing always said, to their surprise, "I live with the writer Danny Angel." She must have liked saying this, for reasons beyond it being a conversation-stopper, because it was only to her closer friends and acquaintances that Yi-Yiing would bother to add: "Well, actually, I'm dating Danny's *father.* He's a cook at Mao's—not the Chinese one." But the cook understood that it was complicated for Yi-Yiing—a woman in her thirties with an unsettled life, living so far away from her native land, and with a daughter she knew only from photographs.

Once, at a party, someone who worked at Mercy Hospital said to Danny, "Oh, I know your girlfriend."

"*What* girlfriend?" Danny had asked; this was before Youn came into his fiction workshop, and (before long) had moved into the second house on Court Street.

"Yi-Yiing—she's Chinese, a nurse at—"

"She's my *dad's* girlfriend," the writer quickly said.

"Oh—"

"What's going on with Yi-Yiing?" Danny had later asked his father. "Some people think she's living with *me*."

"I don't question Yi-Yiing, Daniel. She doesn't question me," the cook pointed out. "And isn't she terrific with Joe?" his dad asked him. Both of them knew very well that this was the same point Danny had made to his father about his former Windham College student Franky, back in Vermont—yet it was strange, nonetheless, Danny thought. Was the cook, who was turning fifty, more of a bohemian than his writer son (at least until Youn moved into that second Court Street house)?

And what was it that was wrong about that house? It had been big enough for them all; that wasn't it. There were enough bedrooms so that everyone could have slept separately; Youn used one of the extra bedrooms as a place to write, and for all her things. For a woman over thirty who'd had no children and endured an incomprehensible Korean divorce—at least it was "incomprehensible" in her novel-in-progress, or so Danny thought—Youn had remarkably few things. Had she left everything behind in Seoul, not just her truly terrifying-sounding former husband?

"I'm a *student*," she'd said to Danny. "That is what is so liberating about being a student again—I don't have any *things*." It was a smart answer, the writer thought, but Danny didn't know if he believed her.

IN THE FALL OF '73, when Joe was starting third grade, the cook kept a crate of apples on the back porch of their Iowa City house. The porch overlooked a narrow, paved alley; it ran the length of the long row of houses that fronted Court Street. The alley didn't appear to be used for anything, except for picking up garbage. Only an occasional slow-moving car passed, and—more often, even constantly—kids on bicycles. There was some loose sand or gravel on the little-used pavement, which meant the kids could practice skids on their bikes. Joe had fallen off his bike in that back alley. Yi-Yiing had cleaned the scrape on the boy's knee.

A porch, off the kitchen, faced the alley, and something was eating the apples that the cook left out on the porch—a raccoon, Danny at first suspected, but it was a possum, actually, and one early evening when young Joe went out on the porch to fetch an apple for himself, he put his hand in the crate and the possum scared him. It growled or hissed or snarled; the boy was so scared that he couldn't even say for sure if the primitive-looking animal had bitten him.

All Danny kept asking was, "Did it *bite* you?" (He couldn't stop examining Joe's arms and hands for bite marks.)

"I don't *know*!" the boy wailed. "It was white and pink—it looked *awful*! What *was* it?"

"A possum," Danny kept repeating; he'd seen it slink away. Possums were ugly-looking creatures.

That night, when Joe fell asleep, Danny went into the boy's bedroom and examined him all over. He wished Yi-Yiing was home, but she was working in the ER. She would know if possums were occasionally rabid—in Vermont, raccoons often were—and the good nurse would know what to do if Joe had been bitten, but Danny couldn't find a bite mark anywhere on his son's perfect body.

Youn had stood in the open doorway of the boy's bedroom; she'd watched Danny looking for any indication of an animal bite. "Wouldn't Joe *know* if he was bitten?" she asked.

"He was too startled and too scared to know," Danny answered her. Youn was staring at the sleeping boy as if he were a wild or unknown animal to her, and Danny realized that she often looked at Joe with this puzzled, from-another-world fascination. If Yi-Yiing doted on Joe because she longed to be with her daughter of that same age, Youn looked at Joe with what appeared to be incomprehension; it was as if she'd never been around children of *any* age before.

Then again, if one could believe her story (*or* her novel), her success in obtaining a divorce from her husband—most important, in getting him to initiate the allegedly complicated procedure—was due to her failure to get pregnant and have a child. That was her novel's tortuous plot: how her husband presumed she was *trying* to get pregnant, when all along she'd been taking birth-control pills *and* using a diaphragm—she was doing all she could *not* to get pregnant, and to *never* have a child.

Youn was writing her novel in English, not Korean, and her English was excellent, Danny thought; her *writing* was good, though certain Korean elements remained mystifying. (What *was* Korean divorce law, anyway? Why was the charade of *pretending* to try to get pregnant necessary? And, according to Youn, she'd hated taking birth-control pills.)

The husband—ultimately, Danny assumed, the *ex*-husband—in Youn's novel was a kind of gangster businessman. Perhaps he was a well-paid assassin, or he hired lesser hit men to do his dirty work; in Danny's reading of Youn's novel-in-progress, this wasn't clear. That the husband was dangerous—in both Youn's real life *and* her novel—seemed obvious. Danny could only wonder about the sexual detail. There was something sympathetic about the husband, despite Youn's efforts to demonize him; the poor man imagined it was *his* fault that his scheming wife couldn't get pregnant.

It didn't help that, in bed at night, Youn told Danny the *worst* details of her miserable marriage—her husband's tireless need for sex included. (But he was trying to get you *pregnant*, wasn't he? Danny wanted to ask, though he didn't. Maybe sex had felt like a duty to Youn's unfortunate husband *and* to Youn. The things she told Danny in the dark and the details of her novels were becoming blurred—or were they interchangeable?)

Shouldn't the fictional husband, the cold-blooded-killer executive in her novel, have a *different* name from her actual ex-husband? Danny had asked Youn. What if her former husband ever read her novel? (Assuming she could get it published.) Wouldn't he then know how she'd deceived him—by deliberately trying *not* to get pregnant when they were married?

"My previous life is *over*," Youn answered him darkly. She did not seem to associate sex with duty now, though Danny couldn't help but wonder about that, too.

Youn was extraordinarily neat with her few belongings. She even kept her toilet articles in the small bathroom attached to the unused bedroom where she wrote. Her clothes were in the closet of that bedroom, or in the lone chest of drawers that was there. Once, when Youn was out, Danny had looked in the medicine cabinet of the bathroom she used. He saw her birth-control pills—it was an Iowa City prescription.

Danny always used a condom. It was an old habit—and, given his history of occasionally having more than one sexual partner, not a bad one. But Youn had said to him one time, almost casually, "Thank you for using a condom. I've taken a lifetime of birth-control pills. I don't ever want to take them again."

But she *was* taking them, wasn't she? Well, if Danny's dad didn't question Yi-Yiing, why should Danny expect answers to everything from Youn? Hadn't her life been complicated, too?

It was into this careless world of unasked or unanswered questions—not only of an Asian variety, but including some long-standing secrets between the cook and his writer son—that a blue Mustang brought them all to their senses (albeit only momentarily) regarding the fragile, unpredictable nature of things.

ON SATURDAY MORNINGS in the fall, when there was an Iowa home football game, Danny could hear the Iowa band playing—he never knew where. If the band had been practicing in Kinnick Stadium, across the Iowa River and up the hill, could he have heard the music so far away, on Court Street, on the eastern side of town?

That Saturday it was bright and fair, and Danny had tickets to take Joe to the football game. He'd gotten up early and had made the boy pancakes. Friday had been a late night for the cook at Mao's, and the Saturday night following a home football game would be later. That morning, Danny's dad was still in bed; so was Yi-Yiing, who'd finished her usual night shift at Mercy Hospital. Danny didn't expect to see the Pajama Lady before noon. It was Joe's neighborhood friend Max, an Iowa faculty kid in Joe's third-grade class at Longfellow Elementary, who'd first referred to Yi-Yiing as the Pajama Lady. (The eight-year-old couldn't remember Yi-Yiing's name.)

Danny was washing his and Joe's breakfast dishes while Joe was playing outside with Max. They were riding their bicycles in the back alley again; they'd taken some apples from the crate on the porch, but not to eat them. The boys were using the apples as slalom gates, Danny would later realize. He liked Max, but the kid rode his bike all over town; it was a source of some friction between Danny and Joe that Joe wasn't allowed to do this.

Max was a fanatical collector of posters, stickers, and sew-on insignia, all advertising brands of beer. The kid had given dozens of these to Joe, who had Yi-Yiing sew the various insignia on his jean jacket; the stickers were plastered to the fridge, and the posters hung in Joe's bedroom. It was funny, Danny thought, and totally innocent; after all, the eight-year-olds weren't *drinking* the beer.

What Danny would remember foremost about the car was the sudden screech of tires; he saw only a blue blur pass by the kitchen window. The writer ran out on the back porch, where he'd previously thought the only threat to his son was a possum. "Joe!" Danny called, but there was no answer—only the sound of the blue car hitting some trash barrels at the farthest end of the alley.

"Mr. Angel!" Danny heard Max calling; the boy was almost never off his bike, but this time Danny saw him running.

Several of the apples, placed as slalom gates, had been squashed flat in the alley. Danny saw that both boys' bikes were lying on their sides, off the pavement; Joe lay curled up in a fetal position next to his bike.

Danny could see that Joe was conscious, and he appeared more frightened than hurt. "Did it hit you? Did the car *hit* you?" he asked his son. The boy quickly shook his head but otherwise wouldn't move; he just stayed in a tight ball.

"We crashed, trying to get out of the way—the Mustang was coming right at us," Max said. "It was the blue Mustang—it always goes too fast," Max told Danny. "It's gotta be a customized job—it's a funny blue."

"You've seen the car before?" Danny asked. (Clearly, Max knew cars.)

"Yeah, but not here—not in the alley," the boy said.

"Go get the Pajama Lady, Max," Danny told the kid. "You can find her. She's upstairs, with my pop." Danny had never called his dad a "pop" before; where the word came from must have had something to do with the fright of the moment. He knelt beside Joe, almost afraid to touch him, while the boy shivered. He was like a fetus willing himself back to the womb, or trying to, the writer thought. "Joe?" his father said. "Does anything hurt? Is anything broken? Can you *move*?"

"I couldn't see a driver. It was just a car," the boy said—still not moving, except for the shivering. Probably the sunlight had been reflecting off the windshield, Danny thought.

"Some teenager, I'll bet," Danny said.

"There was no driver," Joe insisted. Later Max would claim to have *never* seen the driver, though he'd seen the speeding blue Mustang in the neighborhood before.

"Pajama Lady!" Danny heard Max calling. "Pop!"

The cook had sat up in bed beside the drowsy Yi-Yiing. "Who's 'Pop,' do you suppose?" he asked her.

"I'm guessing that *I'm* the Pajama Lady," Yi-Yiing answered sleepily. "*You* must be Pop."

Quite a commotion ensued when Yi-Yiing and the cook learned that Joe had fallen off his bike and there'd been a car involved. Max would probably take to his grave the image of how fast the Pajama Lady ran barefoot to the scene of the accident, where Joe was now sitting up—rocking back and forth in his father's arms. The cook, with his limp, was slower to arrive; by then, Youn had interrupted her novel-in-progress to see what was the matter.

The elegantly dressed dame at the farthest end of the alley—her trash barrels had been knocked over by the vanishing blue Mustang—approached fearfully. She was elderly and frail, but she wanted to see if the boys on their bicycles were all right. Like Max, the regal old woman had seen the blue Mustang in the neighborhood before—but never the driver.

"What kind of blue?" Danny asked her.

"Not a common blue—it's *too* blue," the old dame said.

"It's a customized job, Mr. Angel—I told you," Max said.

"You're all right, you're all right," Yi-Yiing kept saying to Joe; she was feeling the boy all over. "You never hit your head, did you?" she asked him; he shook his head. Then she began to tickle him, maybe to relieve them both. Her Hong Kong pajamas this morning were an iridescent fish-scale green.

"Everything's fine, isn't it?" Youn asked Danny. The Korean divorcée probably wanted to get back to her writing.

No, everything isn't "fine," the writer Danny Angel was thinking—not with the driverless blue Mustang on the loose—but he smiled at her (Youn was also barefoot, wearing a T-shirt and jeans) and at his worried-looking father. The cook must have limped naked into the upstairs hall before he realized he lacked clothes, because he was wearing just a pair of Danny's running shorts; Danny had left them on the railing at the top of the stairs.

"Are you taking a run, Pop?" Danny asked his dad, the new word seeming strangely natural to them both—as if a bullet dodged marked a turning point, or a new beginning, in both their lives and young Joe's. Maybe it did.

COLBY WAS THE COP'S NAME. "*Officer* Colby," the cook kept calling him, in the kitchen of the Court Street house—perhaps in mock respect of that other, long-ago policeman in his life. Except for the bad haircut, the young Iowa City cop in no way resembled Carl. Colby was fair-skinned with Scandinavian-blue eyes and a neatly trimmed blond mustache; he apologized for not responding sooner to Danny's call about the dangerous driver, but those weekends when the Iowa football team played at home kept the local police busy. The policeman's demeanor was at once friendly and earnest—Danny liked him immediately. (The writer could not help but observe how observant the policeman was; Colby had an eye for small details, such as those beer stickers on the fridge.) Officer Colby told Danny and his dad that he'd received previous reports of a blue Mustang; as Max had said, the car was probably a customized job, but there were some inconsistencies in the various sightings.

The hood ornament was either the original mustang or—according to a hysterical housewife in the parking lot of a supermarket near Fairchild and Dodge—an obscene version of a centaur. Other witnesses identified a nonspecific but clearly out-of-state license plate, while a university student who'd been run off Dubuque Street on his motorcycle said that the blue Mustang definitely had Iowa plates. As Officer Colby told the cook and his writer son, there were no descriptions of the driver.

"The boys will be home from school any minute," Danny said to the cop, who'd politely glanced at his watch. "You can talk to them. I saw nothing but an unusual shade of blue."

"May I see your son's room?" the officer asked.

A curious request, Danny thought, but he saw no reason to object. It took only a minute, and Colby made no comment on the beer posters; the three men returned to the kitchen to wait for the kids. As for the back alley, where the blue Mustang had almost hit the boys on their bikes, Officer Colby pronounced it safe for bike-riding "under normal circumstances." However, the officer seemed to share Yi-Yiing's overall feelings about kids on bicycles in Iowa City. It was better for the kids to walk, or take the bus—certainly they should avoid riding their bikes downtown. There were more and more students driving, many of them newcomers to the university town—not to mention the out-of-towners on the big sports weekends.

"Joe doesn't ride his bike downtown—only in this neighborhood—and he always walks his bike across the street," Danny told the policeman, who looked as if he doubted this. "No, really," the writer said. "I'm not so sure about Max, our neighbor's eight-year-old. I think Max's parents are more liberal—I mean concerning where Max can ride his bike."

"Here they are," the cook said; he'd been watching the back alley for Joe and Max to appear on their bicycles.

The eight-year-olds seemed surprised to see Officer Colby in the kitchen; like the third graders they were, and almost as if they were passing a secret message in class, they looked quickly at each other and then stared at the kitchen floor.

"The beer-truck boys," Colby said. "Maybe you boys should keep in mind that the blue Mustang has been seen all over town." The officer turned his attention to Danny and his dad. "They're good kids, but they like getting beer stickers and posters and those sew-on badges from the beer-truck drivers. I see these boys at the bars downtown. I just remind them that they can't go *inside* the bars, and I occasionally have to tell them not to follow the beer trucks from bar to bar—not on their bikes. Clinton and Burlington streets are particularly bad for bikes."

Joe couldn't look at his dad or grandfather. "The beer-truck boys," the cook repeated.

"I gotta go home," Max said; he was that quickly gone.

"When I see these boys in City Park," Colby went on, "I tell them I hope they're not riding their bikes on Dubuque Street. It's safer to take the footbridge behind the student union, and ride their bikes along the Hancher side of the river. But I suppose it takes you longer to get to the park or the zoo that way—doesn't it?" Officer Colby asked Joe. The boy just nodded his head; he knew he'd been busted.

Very early the next morning, when Youn was sound asleep and Yi-Yiing hadn't yet come home from her night shift at Mercy Hospital, Danny went into Joe's bedroom and observed the eight-year-old asleep in what amounted to a shrine to various brands of beer. "Wake up," he said to his son, shaking him gently.

"It's too early for school, isn't it?" Joe asked.

"Maybe you'll miss school this morning," his father said. "We'll just tell the school you're sick."

"But I feel fine," the boy said.

"Get up and get dressed, Joe—you're *not* fine," his dad told him. "You're dead—you've already died."

They left the house without having any breakfast, walking down to Muscatine Avenue. In the early morning, there was always traffic on Muscatine, which turned into Iowa Avenue, a divided highway with a grassy median strip separating the driving lanes of the two-way street.

When Joe had been a baby and a toddler, and Danny had lived with Katie in a duplex apartment on Iowa Avenue, the young couple had complained about the noise of the traffic on the street; the residences (among them, an especially rowdy sorority house nearer the campus and downtown) were then slightly upscale off-campus housing for graduate students or well-to-do undergraduates. But in the fall of '73, when Danny walked to Iowa Avenue with his third-grade son, the houses along the divided, tree-lined street were even more pricey; junior faculty, and probably some tenured faculty, lived there. "Isn't this the street where you lived with Mom?" Joe asked his dad, as they walked toward the campus and downtown.

"Where *we* lived with Mom, you mean—yes, it is," Danny said. Somewhere between the intersections with Johnson and Gilbert streets, the writer recognized the gray-clapboard, two-story house— the bottom floor of which had been the apartment he'd shared with Katie and their little boy. The house had since been repainted— there'd been pale-yellow clapboards in the late sixties—and it was probably a single-family dwelling now.

"The gray one?" Joe asked, because his dad had stopped walking on the sidewalk in front of the house, which was on the downtown-heading-traffic side of the street. The cars veering off Muscatine onto Iowa Avenue were more numerous now.

"Yes, the gray one," Danny said; he turned his back on the house and faced the avenue. He noticed that the plantings in the median strip had been prettified in the six years since he'd moved away from Iowa Avenue.

"Grandpa said you didn't like Iowa Avenue—that you wouldn't even drive on the street," Joe said to his dad.

"That's right, Joe," Danny said. Standing close together, they just watched the traffic going by.

"What's wrong? Am I grounded?" the boy asked his dad.

"No, you're not grounded—you're already dead," his father told him. Danny pointed to the street. "You died out there, in the road. It was the spring of '67. You were still in diapers—you were only two."

"Was I hit by a car?" Joe asked his dad.

"You should have been," his father answered. "But if you'd really been hit by a car, I would have died, too."

There was one driver in the outbound lane who would see them standing on the other side of Iowa Avenue—Yi-Yiing, on her way back to Court Street from Mercy Hospital. In the incoming lane, one of Danny's colleagues at the Writers' Workshop, the poet Marvin Bell, drove by them and honked his horn. But neither father nor son acknowledged him.

Perhaps Danny and Joe weren't really standing on the sidewalk, facing the traffic; maybe they were back in the spring of 1967. At least the writer Daniel Baciagalupo, who'd not yet chosen a nom de plume, was back there. It often seemed to Danny that he'd never really left that moment in time.

IN AVELLINO, LORETTA BROUGHT the writer his surprise first course. In the something-from-Asia category, the cook had prepared Ah Gou's beef *satay* with peanut sauce for his son; the beef was grilled on wooden skewers. There was assorted tempura, too—shrimp, haricots verts, and asparagus. Loretta also brought Danny chopsticks, but she hesitated before handing them over. "Do you use these? I can't remember," she said. (The writer knew she was lying.)

"Sure, I use them," he told her.

Loretta still held on to the chopsticks. "You know what? You're alone too much," she told him.

"I *am* alone too much," Danny said. They flirted with each other, but that was as far as it ever went; it was simply awful, for both of them, to contemplate sleeping with each other when Loretta's mom and Danny's dad were sleeping together, too.

Whenever Danny had considered it, he'd imagined Loretta saying, "That would be too much like being brother and sister, or something!"

"What are you writing?" Loretta asked him; as long as she held the chopsticks, he would keep looking at her, she thought.

"Just some dialogue," Danny told her.

"Like we're having?" she asked.

"No, it's . . . different," he said. Loretta could tell when she'd lost his attention; she gave him the chopsticks. The way the notebook was open on the table, Loretta could have read the dialogue Danny was writing, but he seemed edgy about it, and she decided not to be pushy.

"Well, I hope you like the surprise," she told him.

The cook knew it was what Danny had ordered at Mao's—maybe a hundred times. "Tell Dad it's the perfect choice," Danny said, as Loretta was leaving.

He glanced once at the dialogue he had written in the notebook. Danny wanted the line to be very *literal*—the way an eight-year-old would phrase a question to his father, carefully. ("Why would you have died, too—if I'd really been hit by a car?" the writer had written.)

Dot and May, who were still waiting for their pizzas, had watched everything between Danny and Loretta. It totally killed them that they hadn't been able to hear *their* dialogue. "The waitress wants to fuck him, but there's a problem," Dot said.

"Yeah, he's more interested in what he's *writin'*!" May said.

"What's he eatin'?" Dot asked her old friend.

"It's somethin' on a stick," May said. "It doesn't look very *appetizin'.*"

"I get the feelin' our pizzas are gonna be disappointin'," Dot told her.

"Yeah, I wouldn't be surprised," May said.

"Now look at him!" Dot whispered. "He's got food in front of him, and he *still* can't stop writin'!"

But the food was good; Danny liked most of his memories of Mao's, and he'd liked *all* the food there. The dialogue he'd written was also good—it would work fine, Danny had decided. It was just that the timing was wrong, and he wanted to remind himself of the right time to use the line. Before turning his attention to the beef *satay,* the writer simply circled the dialogue and wrote a note to himself in the margin of the notebook.

"Not now," Danny wrote. "Tell the part about the pig roast first."

CHAPTER 10

LADY SKY

SPRING WAS A BIG DEAL IN IOWA; THE FIELDS WERE A SPECIAL green. Pig roasts were the rage with the art-department types and the writing students. Danny had avoided most of the Writers' Workshop parties when he'd been a student, but Katie dragged him to the artists' parties, which in Danny's opinion were worse than whatever trouble the writers managed to cause themselves. Katie knew everyone in the Iowa art department, because of her modeling for the life-drawing classes; though he'd been a life-drawing model in New Hampshire, Danny hadn't been married at the time. In Iowa, it made him uncomfortable to know that many of the graduate students in art—not to mention some of the faculty—had seen his wife naked. Danny didn't know most of their names.

This particular pig roast had been hard to find. Little Joe cried the whole way to Tiffin on U.S. 6, but Danny, who was driving, wouldn't let Katie take the two-year-old out of his car seat. They left the highway in Tiffin but were nearer to North Liberty when they got lost; either Buffalo Creek Road didn't exist, or it wasn't marked, and by the time they found the dilapidated farmhouse, Danny had spoken sarcastically on the subject of art students. (They were either too nonverbal or too abstract to give good directions, in his opinion.)

"What do you care if we can't find the stupid farm?" Katie had asked him. "You never want to go to the parties I'm invited to, anyway."

"I never want to go to the parties *I'm* invited to, either," he pointed out to her.

"Which makes you loads of fun, fuckhead," Katie said.

The farmer tended to his pigs in the early morning, and once again in the late afternoon; he lived in one of those motel-looking but expensive ranch houses on Rochester Avenue in Iowa City, and he rented his falling-apart farmhouse to four scruffy young men who were graduate students in art. Katie called them artists—as if they'd already achieved something.

The writer was more cynically inclined; Danny thought of the male graduate students on the pig farm as three half-assed painters and one pretentious photographer. Though Danny did know that the half-assed painters had all drawn Katie in one or another life-drawing class, he hadn't known that the pretentious photographer had photographed her in the nude—this unwelcome news had emerged in the car, when they got lost on their way to the pig roast—and Danny had been unprepared for the drawings *and* photos of his naked wife in the graduate students' untidy farmhouse.

Joe didn't seem to recognize his mother in the first of the sketches the two-year-old saw; in the farmhouse kitchen and dining room, some smudged charcoal drawings of Katie were taped to the walls. "Nice decor," Danny said to his wife. Katie shrugged. Danny saw that someone had already given her a glass of wine. He hoped there was beer; Danny was always the driver, and he drove a little better on beer.

In the car, he'd said to his wife: "I didn't know that the life-drawing classes were open to photographers."

"They aren't," Katie had told him. "It was arranged outside class."

"Arranged," he'd repeated.

"God, now you're repeating everything," she'd said, "like your fucking father."

While Danny looked in vain for a beer in the refrigerator, Joe told him that he needed to go to the bathroom. Danny knew that Joe wasn't yet toilet-trained. When the boy said he needed to go to the bathroom, he meant that it was time for someone to change his diaper.

Katie usually resented carrying diapers in her purse, but she had wanted to go to the pig roast badly enough that she hadn't complained—until now. "It's about time the two-year-old was house-broken, isn't it?" she said to Danny, handing him a clean diaper. Katie called Joe *the two-year-old* as if the boy's age condemned him to denigration.

In the downstairs bathroom of the farmhouse, there was no curtain for the shower stall, and the bathroom floor was wet. Father and son both washed their hands in the grimy sink, but finding a towel was no more successful an endeavor than Danny's search for a beer. "We can *wave* our hands dry," Danny said to the boy, who waved to his dad as if he were saying good-bye—the standard one-handed wave.

"Try waving *both* hands, Joe."

"Look—*Mommy!*" the boy said. He was pointing to the photographs on the wall behind his father. There was a black-and-white contact sheet and half a dozen enlargements thumbtacked to the wall above the empty towel rack. Katie was naked with her hands hiding her small breasts, but her crotch was fully exposed; it looked as if her modesty had been purposely manipulated or misplaced. Someone's conscious idea, clearly—a deliberate statement, but of what? Danny wondered. And had it been Katie's idea or the photographer's? (His name was Rolf—he was one of the bearded ones, Danny only now remembered.)

"Yes, the lady looks a lot like Mommy," Danny said, but this strategy backfired. Joe looked more closely at the photos, frowning.

"It *is* Mommy," the boy said.

"You think?" his dad asked. He'd taken his son's small hand and was leading him out of the filthy bathroom.

"Yes, it's really Mommy," Joe answered gravely.

Danny poured himself a glass of red wine; there were no wine-glasses left, so he used a milk glass. There were no plastic cups, either. In one of the kitchen cabinets, he found a coffee mug that looked sturdy enough—if not completely childproof—and he gave Joe some ginger ale. Danny wouldn't have trusted any milk in the fridge, if he'd been able to find some, and the ginger ale was the only mixer there that could possibly appeal to a child.

The party was outside on the lawn, near the pigpen. Given the late-afternoon, early-evening time of day, Danny assumed that the farmer had already fed his pigs for the day and departed. At least the pigs looked contented, though they watched the assembled partygoers with almost human curiosity; on an average day, the pigs probably didn't get to observe a dozen or more *artists.*

Danny noted that there were no other children at the party—not too many married couples, either. "Are there any faculty here?" he asked Katie, who'd already refilled her wineglass—or someone had. He knew Katie had been hoping that Roger would come. Roger was the faculty member who taught the graduate classes in life drawing; he was the life-drawing instructor Katie was sleeping with at the time. Katie would still be sleeping with Roger when she told Danny she was leaving, but that event was a couple of days away.

"I thought Roger would be here, but he isn't," Katie said with disappointment. She was standing next to Rolf, the bearded photographer; Danny realized she'd actually been speaking to him, not Danny. Roger also had a beard, Danny recalled. He knew Katie was sleeping with Roger, but it only now occurred to him that she might be sleeping with Rolf, too. Maybe she was going through a *beard* phase, the writer imagined. Looking at Rolf, Danny wondered how and where they had *arranged* the photographs.

"Nice pictures," Danny told him.

"Oh, you saw them," Rolf said casually.

"You're all over the place," Danny said to Katie, who just shrugged.

"Did you see your mom?" Rolf asked Joe, bending down to the boy, as if he thought the child were hard of hearing.

"He barely talks," Katie said, which was totally untrue; Joe was exceptionally articulate for a two-year-old, as only children tend to be. (Maybe because he was a writer, Danny talked to the boy all the time.)

"Mommy's right there," the boy said, pointing at her.

"No, I meant the pictures," Rolf explained. "They're in the bathroom."

"*That's* Mommy," Joe insisted, pointing to his mother again.

"See what I mean?" Katie asked the photographer.

Danny didn't yet know about Katie's plan to save another stupid boy from the war in Vietnam; that revelation was also a couple of days away. But when Danny did learn of Katie's intentions, he would remember Rolf's attempt to communicate with little Joe that day at the pig farm. While Rolf certainly seemed stupid enough to need saving, the beard didn't fit with Danny's image of the *boy* word. Danny would never know the boy who became Katie's next Kennedy father, but the writer somehow didn't picture him with a beard.

The three graduate-student painters were circling the fire pit, where the pig was roasting. Danny and Joe were standing nearby.

"We started the fucking fire before dawn," one of the painters said to Danny.

"The pig isn't done yet," another painter said; he also had a beard, which made Danny regard him closely.

They had built a wood fire—according to the bearded painter, "a roaring big one"—and when it was reduced to coals, they'd lowered the springs for a double-bed mattress into the pit. (They'd found the bedsprings in the barn, and the farmer had assured them that the stuff in the barn was junk.) They'd put the pig on the red-hot bedsprings, but now they had no way of getting more wood under the bedsprings and the pig. When they'd tried to raise the bedsprings, the pig started to fall apart. Because of how utterly destroyed the roasting pig looked, Danny thought better of calling it to little Joe's attention—not when there were *live* pigs present. (Not that the mess on the smoking bedsprings remotely resembled an *actual* pig—not anymore. Joe didn't know what it was.)

"We'll just have to wait until the pig is done," the third painter told Danny philosophically.

Joe held tightly to his dad's hand. The boy didn't venture near the smoldering fire pit; it was bad enough that there was a hole in the ground with smoke coming out of it.

"Want to look at the pigs?" Joe asked, pulling on his father's hand.

"Okay," Danny said.

It seemed that the pigs in the pen were unaware that one of their own was roasting; they just kept staring through the slats of the fence at all the people. Every Iowan Danny had met said you had to watch yourself around pigs. Supposedly, pigs were very smart, but the older ones could be dangerous.

The writer wondered how you could tell the older pigs from the younger ones—just by their size, perhaps. But all the pigs in the pen seemed huge. That must have been a suckling pig in the fire pit, Danny thought, a relatively small one, not one of these enormous creatures.

"What do you think of them?" Danny asked little Joe.

"Big pigs!" the boy answered.

"Right," his dad said. "*Big* pigs. Don't touch them, because they bite. Don't stick your hands through the fence, okay?"

"They bite," the boy repeated solemnly.

"You won't get close to them, okay?" his father asked.

"Okay," Joe said.

Danny looked back at the three painters standing around the smoldering fire pit. They weren't watching the cooking pig—they were staring at the sky. Danny glanced up at the sky, too. A small plane had appeared on the horizon to the north of the pig farm. It was still gaining altitude—the sound probably wouldn't reach them for a little while. The pig farm was due south of Cedar Rapids, where there was an airport; perhaps the plane had taken off from there.

"Plane. Not a bird," Danny heard Joe say; the boy was also watching the sky.

"A plane, yes. Not a bird," his dad repeated.

Rolf passed by, refilling Danny's milk glass with red wine. "There's beer, you know—I saw some in a tub of ice somewhere," the photographer said. "You drink beer, don't you?"

Danny wondered how Rolf knew that; Katie must have told him. He watched the photographer bring the bottle of wine over to Katie. Without looking up at the airplane, Rolf pointed at the sky with the wine bottle, and Katie began to watch the small plane. Now you could hear it, though it was very high in the sky—too high to be a crop duster, Danny was guessing.

Rolf was whispering in Katie's ear while Katie watched the plane. Something's going on, the writer thought, but Danny was thinking that something was going on with Katie and Rolf—he wasn't thinking about the plane. Then Danny noticed that the three painters at the fire pit were whispering to one another; they were all watching the plane, too.

Joe wanted to be picked up—maybe the size of the pigs had intimidated him. Two of the pigs were a muddy pink, but the rest had black splotches. "They look like pink-and-black cows," Danny said to Joe.

"No, they're *pigs*. Not cows," the boy told him.

"Okay," Danny said. Katie was coming over to them.

"Look at the pigs, Mommy," Joe said.

"Yuck," she said. "Keep watching the plane," Katie told her husband. She was going away again, but not before Danny caught the scent of marijuana; the smell must have clung to her hair. He'd not seen her smoking any pot—not even one toke—but while he'd been changing Joe's diaper, she must have had some. "Tell the kid to keep his eyes on the airplane," Katie said, still walking away. It sounded wrong, how Katie called Joe *the kid*, Danny was thinking. It was as if the boy were someone else's kid—that's how it sounded.

THE LITTLE PLANE wasn't climbing anymore; it had leveled off and was now directly above the farm, but still high in the sky. It appeared to have slowed down, perfectly suspended above them, almost not moving. "We're supposed to watch the airplane," Danny told his small son, kissing the boy's neck, but Danny watched his wife instead. She had joined the painters at the smoking fire pit; Rolf was with them. They were watching the plane with anticipation, but because Danny was watching them, he missed the moment.

"Not a bird," he heard little Joe say. "Not flying. *Falling!*"

By the time Danny looked up, he couldn't be sure—at such a height—exactly what had fallen from the plane, but it was dropping down fast, straight at them. When the parachute opened, the painters and Rolf cheered. (The asshole artists had hired a skydiver for entertainment, Danny was thinking.)

"What's coming down?" Joe asked his dad.

"A skydiver," Danny told the boy.

"A *what* in the sky?" the two-year-old said.

"A person with a parachute," Danny said, but this made no sense to little Joe.

"A *what*?"

"A parachute keeps the person from falling too fast—the person is going to be all right," Danny was explaining, but Joe clung tightly to his father's neck. Danny smelled the marijuana before he realized that Katie was standing next to them.

"Just wait—keep watching," she said, floating away again.

"A *sky* something," Joe was saying. "A para-*what*?"

"A skydiver, a parachute," Danny repeated. Joe just stared, open-mouthed, as the parachute drifted down to them. It was a big parachute, the colors of the American flag.

The skydiver's breasts were the first giveaway. "It's a lady," little Joe said.

"Yes, it is," his father replied.

"What happened to her clothes?" Joe asked.

Now everyone was watching, even the pigs. Danny hadn't noticed when the pigs began to be aware of the parachutist, but they were aware of her now. They must not have been used to flying people dropping down on them—or used to the giant descending parachute, which now cast a shadow over their pigpen.

"Lady Sky!" Joe screamed, pointing up at the naked skydiver.

When the first pig squealed and started to run, the other pigs all snorted and ran. That may have been when Lady Sky saw where she was going to land—in the pigpen. The angry skydiver began to swear.

By then, even the drunk and the stoned could see that she was naked. Fucking art students! Danny was thinking. Of course they couldn't just hire a skydiver; naturally, she had to be a nude. Katie looked unconcerned—quite possibly, she was jealous. Once she realized the skydiver was naked, maybe Katie wished that *she* could be the skydiver. Katie probably didn't like having another nude model at the art students' pig roast.

"Christ, she's going to end up in the fucking pigpen!" Rolf was saying. Had he only now noticed? He must have been the one who was smoking dope with Katie. (Rolf was definitely *stupid* enough to need saving—if not from the war in Vietnam, Danny would one day find himself thinking.)

"Hold him," Danny said to his wife, handing little Joe to Katie.

The furious naked woman passed overhead. Danny jumped and tried to grab her feet, but she drifted just above and beyond his reach, swearing as she went. For all of them on the ground, people and pigs, a traveling vagina had hovered over them—descending.

"Someone should tell her that's an unflattering angle, if you're a woman and you're naked," Katie was saying. Probably to Rolf—her remark wouldn't have made any sense to Joe. (Katie never had much to say to *the kid*, anyway.)

It was very muddy in the pigpen, but Danny had run in mud before—he knew you had to keep your feet moving. He paid no attention to where the pigs were; he could tell by the way the ground shook that they were also running. Danny just followed the drifting woman. When her heels struck the ground, she slid through the shitty mud with her chute collapsing after her. She fell on one hip and the chute dragged her sideways, on her stomach, before Danny could catch up to her. She was almost as surprised to see him as they both were shocked by the awful smell, and by how big the pigs were when they were this close to them. There was also the constant grunting. One of the pigs trampled over the parachute, but the feel of the chute, under its hooves, appeared to panic the animal; it veered, squealing, away from them.

She was a big skydiver, of Amazonian proportions—a virtual giantess. Danny couldn't have carried her out of the pen, but he saw how she was trying to free herself from the harness that attached her to the parachute, which was hard to drag through the muck, and Danny was able to help her with that. The naked skydiver was covered with pig shit and mud. The back of one of Danny's hands brushed against her dirty nipple as he struggled with the strap of the harness that divided her breasts. Danny only then realized that he'd fallen a few times; he was spattered with pig shit and mud, too.

"No one told me it was a fucking *pig* farm!" the skydiver said. She had closely cropped hair, and she'd shaved her pubic hair, leaving just a vertical strip, but she was a strawberry blonde, top to bottom.

"They're a bunch of asshole artists—I had nothing to do with this," Danny told her.

From her scar, he could see she'd had a cesarean section. She looked a decade older than Danny, in her thirties, maybe. Evidently, she'd been a bodybuilder. Her tattoos were indiscernible in the muck, but she was definitely not the nude the art students had been imagining; maybe she was more than they'd bargained for, the writer hoped.

"My name's Danny," he told her.

"Amy," she said. "Thanks."

When she was freed from the chute, Danny put his hand on the small of her back and pushed her ahead of him. "Run to the fence— just keep running," he told her. He kept his hand against her damp skin the whole way. A pig blundered past them as if it were racing them, not chasing them. Possibly it was running away from them. They almost collided with another pig, this one running in the opposite direction. Perhaps it was the parachute that had upset the pigs— not the naked lady.

"Lady Sky!" Danny could hear Joe shouting.

Someone else started yelling it: "Lady Sky!"

"Be sure you show me the asshole artists," Amy said, when they reached the perimeter of the pigpen. She needed no help getting over the fence. Danny was looking all around for Joe, but the little boy wasn't with Katie; he saw his wife standing with Rolf and the three painters.

"Those are the four guys you want," Danny told Amy, pointing to them. "The ones with the small woman, but *not* the woman—she wasn't in on it. Just the two guys with the beards, and the two without."

"*This* pig doesn't bite," Danny thought he heard his son say in a quiet, contemplative voice.

"Joe!" the writer called.

"I'm right here, Daddy."

That was when Danny realized that little Joe was in the pigpen with him. The boy stood next to one of the pink-and-black pigs; it must have been running, because it was clearly out of breath, though it stood very still. Only its harsh breathing made the big pig move at all—except for the way it inclined its head toward the boy, who had hold of the animal's ear. Maybe it felt good to a pig to have its ear rubbed or gently pulled. In any case, the more the two-year-old stroked its ear, the more the pig tilted its head and lowered its long ear in Joe's direction.

"Pigs have funny ears," the boy said.

"Joe, get out of the pen—right now," his dad said. He must have raised his voice more than he'd meant to; the pig snapped its head in Danny's direction, as if it deeply resented the ear-rubbing interruption. Only a low-to-the-ground feeding trough separated them, and the pig hunched its shoulders on either side of its huge head and squinted at him. Danny stood his ground until he saw Joe climb safely through the slats in the fence.

The drama with the skydiver, and then with Joe, prevented Danny from seeing how low in the sky the small plane had circled. The pilot and copilot probably wanted to be sure that Amy had touched down without mishap, but Amy gave the plane the finger—*both* fingers, in fact—and the plane dipped a wing to her, as if in salutation, then flew off in the direction of Cedar Rapids.

"Welcome to Buffalo Creek Farm," Rolf had said to the skydiver. Regrettably, Danny missed seeing this part, too—how Amy had grabbed the photographer by both his shoulders, snapped him toward her, and head-butted him in his forehead and the bridge of his nose. Rolf staggered backward, falling several feet from the spot where Amy had made contact.

She knocked down the painter with the beard with a left jab followed by a right hook. "I don't jump into *pigs*!" she shouted at the two painters left standing.

Both Danny and Joe saw the next bit. "Which one of you *artists* is going to get my parachute?" she asked them, pointing to the pigpen. By now, the pigs had calmed down; they'd returned to the fence and were once more observing the artistic crowd, their snouts poking through the slats. The pig whose ear had been stroked, to its apparent satisfaction, was now indistinguishable from the others. Way out in the muck, the trampled red-white-and-blue parachute lay like a flag fallen in battle.

"The farmer told us never to go in the pigpen," one of the graduate-student painters began.

Danny carried Joe over to Katie. "You were supposed to hold him," he said to her.

"He peed all over me when you went into the pigpen," Katie said.

"He has a diaper on," Danny told her.

"I could still feel how wet he was," she said.

"You weren't even *watching* him," Danny told her.

Amy had the painter who'd spoken up in a headlock. "I'll get your fucking parachute," Katie suddenly told her.

"You can't go in there," Danny said.

"Don't tell me what I can't do, *hero*," she said.

Katie had always been competitive that way. First the nude sky-diver had taken the art students' attention away from her; then her husband's act of bravado had upstaged her. But of course what Katie really wanted to do was undress. "I'll just keep the pig shit off my clothes, if you don't object," she said to Danny; she began handing her clothes to the one painter who'd been untouched by the shit-smeared skydiver. "I would give them to you," she told Danny, "but you're covered with shit—you should see yourself."

"It wouldn't be good if something happened to you in front of Joe," Danny started to tell her.

"Why?" she asked him. "A two-year-old won't remember it. Only you will—you fuckhead *writer*."

Seeing her naked and defiant made Danny realize that what had once attracted him to Katie now repelled him. He'd mistaken what was brazen about her for a kind of sexual courage; she'd seemed both sexy and progressive, but Katie was merely vulgar and insecure. What Danny had desired in his wife only filled him now with revulsion— and this had taken a mere two years to transpire. (The loving-her part would last a little longer; neither Danny nor any other writer could ever explain that.)

HE'D CARRIED JOE BACK to the downstairs bathroom so that they could clean up, or try to. (Danny didn't want Joe to see his naked mother devoured by a pig; surely the two-year-old would remember *that*, if only for a little while.)

"Is Mommy giving Lady Sky her clothes?" Joe asked.

"Mommy's clothes wouldn't fit Lady Sky, sweetie," Danny answered his son.

Amy didn't want any clothes; she told the asshole artists that all she wanted was a bath. The pilot and copilot were bringing her clothes—"or they better be," the skydiver said.

"I hope your bathroom is cleaner than ours," Danny said to Amy, as she was following the unassaulted painter up the farmhouse stairs.

"I'm not counting on it," Amy told him. "Was that your wife—that little thing who was going to fetch my parachute?" the skydiver called down the stairs to Danny.

"Yes," he answered her.

"She's got balls, hasn't she?" Amy asked him.

"Yes—that's Katie," Danny said.

He'd forgotten that there wasn't a towel in the downstairs bathroom, but getting the pig shit off himself and little Joe was what mattered. Who cared if they were wet? Besides, the boy's clothes had somehow managed to stay clean; Joe's pants were a little damp, because he'd really peed like crazy in his diaper.

"I guess you liked that ginger ale, huh?" Danny asked the boy. He'd also forgotten to ask Katie for a dry diaper, but that didn't really matter as much as getting the pig shit off little Joe's hands. There was shit all over Danny *and* his clothes—his running shoes were ruined. If his wife could take off all her clothes, Danny guessed that no one would mind if he wore just his boxers for the remainder of the artists' party. It was a sunny spring day—April in Iowa—warm enough to be wearing only a pair of boxers.

"You call this a *clean* towel?" the skydiver was shouting.

Danny undressed himself and little Joe, and they both got into the shower. There was no soap, but they used a lot of shampoo instead. They were still in the shower when Katie came into the downstairs bathroom, carrying her clothes and a towel. She was not as shit-spattered as Danny had expected.

"If you don't try to run in that muck, you don't fall down, *fuckhead*."

"So you just walked out to the parachute, and walked back?" Danny asked her. "The pigs didn't bother you?"

"The pigs were spooked by the chute," Katie said. "Move over—both of you." She got into the shower with them, and Danny shampooed her hair.

"Mommy got pig poo on her, too?" Joe asked.

"*Everyone's* got pig poo on them somewhere," Katie said.

They took turns with the towel, and Danny put a dry diaper on Joe. He dressed the little boy before putting on his boxers. "That's all you're wearing?" Katie asked him.

"I'm donating the rest of my clothes to the farm," Danny told her. "In fact, I'm not touching them—they're staying right there," he said, pointing to the pile of clothes on the wet floor. Katie threw her bra and panties on the pile. She slipped into her jeans; you could see her breasts through the white blouse she was wearing—her nipples, especially.

"Is that all *you're* wearing?" Danny asked her.

Katie shrugged. "I guess I can donate my underwear to the farm, if I want to," she said.

"Is everything a contest, Katie?"

But she didn't answer him. She opened the bathroom door and left them with the pile of clothes and Danny's discarded running shoes. "I lost my sandals somewhere," she told them.

Outside, the skydiver was wearing just a towel around her waist and was drinking a beer. "Where'd you find the beer?" Danny asked her. He'd already had too much wine on an empty stomach.

Amy showed him the tub of ice. Rolf was sitting on the ground beside the tub, repeatedly dunking his face in the icy water. There was blood from his nose everywhere. He had a pretty good gash on one eyebrow, too—all from the head-butt. Danny took out two beers, wiping the necks of the bottles on his boxers. "That was a terrific idea, Rolf," Danny told the photographer. "Too bad she didn't land in the fire pit."

"Shit," Rolf said, standing up. He looked a little unsteady on his feet. "No one's watching the pig in the pit—we got distracted by all the heroics."

"Is there an opener?" Danny asked him.

"There's one in the kitchen somewhere," Rolf answered. The bearded painter who'd been hit with Amy's jab and hook was holding a wet T-shirt to his face. He kept dipping the T-shirt in the icy water and then putting it back on his face.

"How's the roast pig coming along?" Danny asked him.

"Oh, Christ," the painter said; he hurried after Rolf in the direction of the smoking hole.

There was potato salad and a green salad and some kind of cold pasta on the dining-room table, together with the wine and the rest of the booze.

"Does any of this food look interesting to you?" Danny asked Joe. The writer hadn't been able to find an opener in the farmhouse kitchen, but he'd used the handle on one of the kitchen drawers to open both beers. He drank the first beer very fast; he was already halfway through the second.

"Where's any meat?" Joe asked.

"I guess it's still cooking," his dad said. "Let's go look at it."

Someone had turned on a car radio, so they could have music outdoors. Donovan's "Mellow Yellow" was playing. Rolf and the painter with the beard had managed to lift the bedsprings out of the fire pit; the painter with the beard had burned his hands, but Rolf had taken off his jeans and used them as pot holders. Rolf's nose and the cut on his eyebrow were still bleeding as he put his jeans back on. Some of the roast pig had fallen off the bedsprings into the fire, but there was plenty to eat and it was certainly cooked enough—it looked very well done, in fact.

"What is it?" Joe asked his dad.

"Roast pork—you like pork," Danny told the boy.

"Once upon a time it was a pig," Rolf explained to the two-year-old.

"A pretty small one, Joe," Danny told his son. "Not one of your big friends in the pen."

"Who killed it?" Joe asked. No one answered him, but Joe didn't notice—he was distracted. Lady Sky was standing over the blackened pig on the bedsprings; little Joe was clearly in awe of her, as if he expected her to take flight again and fly away.

"Lady Sky!" the boy said. Amy smiled at him. "Are you an angel?" Joe asked her. (She was beginning to look like one, to Danny.)

"Well, *sometimes*," Lady Sky said. She was distracted, too. A car was turning in to the long driveway of the pig farm—probably the little plane's pilot and copilot, Danny was thinking. Amy took another look at the roast pig on the bedsprings. "But there are other times when I'm just a vegetarian," she said to Joe. "Like today."

Merle Haggard was singing "I'm a Lonesome Fugitive" on the car radio; probably someone had changed the station. Out on the lawn, Katie had been dancing by herself—or with her glass of wine—but she stopped now. Everyone was curious about the pilot and the copilot, if only to see what would happen when they arrived. Amy walked over to the car before the two men could get out.

"Fuck you, Georgie—fuck you, Pete," the skydiver greeted them.

"We were too high up to see the pigs, Amy—we couldn't see them when you jumped," one of the men told her; he handed her some clothes.

"Fuck you, Pete," Amy told him again. She took off her towel and threw it at him.

"Calm down, Amy," the other man said. "The guys on the farm should have told us there were pigs."

"Yeah, well—I made that point to them, Georgie," the skydiver told him.

Georgie and Pete were surveying the artists in the pig-roast crowd. They must have noticed that Rolf was bleeding, and the painter with the beard still held a wet T-shirt to his face; the pilot and copilot surely knew this was Amy's work.

"Which one ran into the pigpen to help you?" Pete asked her.

"See the small guy in the boxers? The little boy's daddy—that's the one," Amy said. "My *rescuer*."

"Thanks," Pete said to Danny.

"We appreciate it," Georgie told the writer.

Lady Sky was only slightly less formidable-looking when she was dressed, in part because she dressed like a man—except for her underwear, which was black and skimpy. Amy wore a blue denim workshirt, tucked in, and jeans with a belt with a big buckle; her cowboy boots had a rattlesnake pattern. She walked over to where Danny was holding little Joe. "If you're ever in trouble, I'll be back," Lady Sky told the boy; she bent over him, kissing his forehead. "Meanwhile, you take care of your daddy," she said to Joe.

Katie was dancing by herself again, but she was watching how the skydiver made a fuss over her husband and little boy; Katie never took her eyes off the big woman. There was a song from The Rolling Stones' album *Between the Buttons* on the radio, but Danny could never remember which song it was. By then, he'd had a third beer and was working on his fourth—this was on top of the red wine, and he still hadn't eaten. Someone had once again changed the station on the car radio, the writer had noticed. He'd watched Lady Sky kiss his son, sensing that the kiss was meant for him; Amy must have known there was no better way to make an impression on a parent than to be nice to the beloved child. But who *was* she? Danny wanted to know. The scar from her cesarean section must have made her someone's mother, but Danny wondered if one of the stooges with her was her husband or boyfriend.

"Can we get anything to eat here?" Georgie was asking.

"Believe me, Georgie, we don't want to eat here," Amy told him. "Not even Pete," she added, without looking at him—as if Pete couldn't be trusted to make his own food decisions. Danny didn't think she was sleeping with either of them.

The pilot and copilot tried to be careful how they stuffed the parachute and the skydiver's harness into the trunk of the car, but it was impossible not to get some pig shit on themselves in the process. Amy got into the driver's seat of the car.

"You driving, Amy?" Georgie asked her.

"It looks like it," she told him.

"I'll get in the back," Pete said.

"You'll *both* get in the back," Amy told them. "I've smelled enough pig shit today." But before the men could get into the car, the skydiver said: "You see that pretty little woman, the dancer, over there? You can see her tits through her shirt—that one."

Danny knew that both Georgie and Pete had already noticed Katie; most men did.

"Yeah, I see her," Georgie said.

"What about her, Amy?" Pete asked.

"If you ever lose me—if my chute doesn't open, or something—you can ask her to do anything. I'll bet you she'd do it," the skydiver said.

The pilot and copilot looked uneasily at each other. "What do you mean, Amy?" Pete asked.

"You mean she'd jump out of an airplane without any clothes on—you mean that kind of thing?" Georgie asked the skydiver.

"I mean she'd jump out of an airplane without a *parachute*," Amy told them. "Wouldn't you, honey?" she asked Katie.

Danny would remember this—how Katie liked it when the attention came to her, for whatever reason. He saw that his wife had found her sandals, though she wasn't wearing them. She held the sandals in one hand, her wineglass in the other, and she just kept moving her feet—she was still dancing. "Well, that would depend on the circum-stances," Katie said, lolling her head and neck to the music, "but I wouldn't rule it out—not categorically."

"See what I mean?" Amy asked Georgie and Pete, as the two men got into the backseat. Then the skydiver drove away, giving the artists the finger out the window of the car. Patsy Cline was singing on the radio, and Katie had stopped dancing; someone must have changed the station again.

"I don't want to eat the pig," Joe told his dad.

"Okay," Danny said. "We'll try to eat something else."

He carried the boy over to where his mother had stopped dancing; Katie was just swaying in place, as if waiting for the music to change. She was drunk, Danny could tell, but she didn't smell like marijuana anymore—he'd shampooed every trace of the pot out of her hair. "Under what circumstances would you *ever* jump out of an airplane without a parachute?" the writer asked his wife.

"To get out of a boring marriage, maybe," Katie answered him.

"Since I'm the driver, I'd like to leave before dark," he told her.

"Lady Sky is an *angel,* Mommy," Joe said.

"I doubt it," Katie said to the boy.

"She told us she was an angel *sometimes,*" Danny said.

"That woman has never been an angel," Katie told them.

JOE WAS SICK in his car seat on their way into Iowa City. A Johnson County sheriff's car had followed them the whole way on U.S. 6. Danny was afraid he might have a taillight out, or that he'd been driv-ing erratically; he was thinking about how much to say he'd had to drink if the police car pulled them over, when the sheriff turned north on the Coralville strip, and Danny kept driving into downtown Iowa City. He couldn't remember how much he'd *actually* had to drink. In his boxer shorts, Danny knew he wouldn't have been very convincing to the sheriff.

Danny was thinking he was home free when Joe threw up. "It was probably the potato salad," he told the boy. "Don't worry about it. We'll be home in just a couple of minutes."

"Let me out of the fucking car," Katie said.

"Here?" Danny asked her. "You want to walk home from here?" He saw she'd already put on her sandals. They were still downtown.

"Who said I was coming home?" she asked him.

"Oh," Danny said.

Just before dark, he'd seen her talking to someone on the phone in the farmhouse kitchen—probably Roger, Danny now decided. He pulled over at the next red light, and Katie got out of the car.

"Lady Sky really is an angel, Mommy," Joe said to her.

"If you say so," Katie said, shutting the door.

Danny knew she didn't have any underwear on, but if it was Roger she was seeing, what did that matter?

SIX YEARS LATER, the early-morning traffic had subsided on Iowa Avenue. Yi-Yiing had long been back on Court Street—she was home from the hospital. (She'd probably told the cook about seeing Danny and young Joe on Iowa Avenue at such an early hour of the morning.)

"Why would you have died, too—if I'd really been hit by a car?" the eight-year-old asked his father.

"Because you're supposed to outlive me. If you die before I do, that will kill me, Joe," Danny told his son.

"Why don't I remember her?" the boy asked his dad.

"You mean your mom?" Danny asked.

"My mom, the pigs, what happened next—I don't remember any of it," Joe answered.

"What about Lady Sky?" his father asked.

"I remember someone dropping from the sky, like an angel," the boy told him.

"Really?" Danny asked.

"I think so. You haven't told me about her before, have you?" Joe asked.

"No, I haven't," Danny said.

"*Then* what happened?" Joe asked his dad. "I mean, after Mom got out of the car downtown."

Naturally, the writer had told young Joe an *edited* version of the pig roast. After he drove the two-year-old home from the farm, there was less that the storyteller had to censor from the tale. (No doubt because Katie hadn't come home with them.)

In the early evening—it was just after dark—only the occasional passerby, and not one of Danny's neighbors, had seen the writer in his boxer shorts carrying his two-year-old into the ground-floor apartment of the duplex on Iowa Avenue.

"Can you still smell the pigs?" little Joe had asked his dad, as they came inside.

"Only in my mind," the writer answered.

"I can smell them, but I don't know where they are," the boy said.

"Maybe it's the throw-up you smell, sweetie," Danny said. He gave the boy a bath, and washed his hair again.

It was warm in the apartment, though the windows were open. Danny put little Joe to bed wearing just a diaper. If it got cooler in the night, he could put the boy's pajamas on then. But after Joe had fallen asleep, Danny imagined he could still smell the pigs or the puke. He put on a pair of jeans and went out to the car; he brought the car seat into the kitchen and washed the vomit off it. (It probably would have been safer for little Joe to have eaten the pig instead of the potato salad, his dad was thinking.)

Later, Danny took a shower and had another shampoo. It was likely he'd had five beers, on top of the wine. Danny didn't feel like another beer, but he didn't want to go to bed, either, and he'd had too much to drink to even think about writing. Katie was gone for the night, he felt certain.

There was some vodka—it was what Katie drank when she didn't want her breath to smell like she'd been drinking—and some rum from Barbados. Danny found a lime in the fridge; he cut a chunk out of the lime and put it in a tall glass with ice, and filled the glass with rum. He was wearing a clean pair of boxers when he sat for a while in the darkened living room by an open window, watching the diminishing traffic on Iowa Avenue. It was that time in the spring when the frogs and toads seemed especially loud—maybe because we have missed them all winter, the writer was thinking.

He was wondering what his life might have been like if he'd met someone like Lady Sky instead of Katie. Possibly, the skydiver had been closer to Danny's age than he'd first thought. Maybe some bad stuff had happened to her—things that made her look older, the writer imagined. (Danny didn't mean the scar from her cesarean section; he meant worse things.)

Danny woke up on the toilet, where he'd fallen asleep with a magazine on his lap; the empty glass with the chunk of lime stared up at him from the bathroom floor. It was cooler. Danny turned the light off in the kitchen, where he saw that he'd had more than one glass of rum—the bottle was nearly empty—though he didn't remember pouring himself a second (or a third) drink. He wouldn't remember what he did with the near-empty bottle, either.

He thought he'd better have a look at Joe before he staggered off to bed, and perhaps he should put some pajamas on the boy, but Danny felt he lacked the necessary dexterity to dress the sleeping child. Instead, he closed the windows in the boy's bedroom and checked to be sure the rails on the child bed were secure.

Joe couldn't have fallen out of bed with the rails in the lowered position, and the boy was that age when he could climb out of the bed if the rails were in either the raised or the lowered position. Sometimes the rails weren't securely latched in either position; then the rails could slip, pinching the boy's fingers. Danny checked to be sure the rails were locked fast in the raised position. Joe was sleeping soundly on his back, and Danny leaned over to kiss him. This was awkward to do when the bed rails were raised, and Danny had had enough to drink that he couldn't manage to kiss his son without losing his balance.

He left Joe's bedroom door open, to be sure he would hear the boy if he woke up and cried. Danny left the door to the master bedroom open, too. It was after three in the morning. Danny noted the time on the alarm clock on the night table as he got into bed. Katie wasn't back from seeing Roger, if that's who she was seeing.

Whenever Danny closed his eyes, the bedroom began to spin. He fell asleep with his eyes open—or he imagined that he did, because his eyes were open, and they felt very dry, when he was awakened in the morning by a man shouting.

"There's a baby in the road!" some idiot was yelling.

Danny could smell the marijuana; he must have been half asleep, or only half awake, because he imagined that the shouting man was stoned. But the smell of the pot was beside Danny, on the nearest pillow. Katie was sleeping naked there, the covers thrown off and her hair redolent of marijuana. (It was Danny's impression that Roger smoked dope all the time.)

"Whose baby is this?" the man was shouting. "This baby's gotta belong to *someone*!"

Maniacal shouting would occasionally reach them from the noisy sorority house farther west on Iowa Avenue, or from the downtown area, but not during what amounted to the morning rush hour.

"Baby in the road!" the maniac kept repeating. It was cold in the bedroom, too, Danny only now realized; he'd passed out with the windows open, and whenever Katie had come home, she'd not bothered to close them.

"It's not our fucking baby," Katie said; her voice was slurred, or she spoke into her pillow. "Our baby's in bed with us, fuckhead!"

"He *is*?" Danny asked, sitting up; his head was pounding. Little Joe wasn't in the tousled bed with them.

"Well, he *was*," Katie said; she sat up in bed, too. Her cheeks were a little roughed up, or red-looking—the way your face can get when you're kissing someone with a scratchy beard, the writer supposed. "The kid was fussing about something, so I brought him into bed with us," Katie was saying.

Danny had already headed down the hall. He saw that Joe's bed was empty, with the rails in the lowered position; Katie was so short, she could never lift the boy out of his bed without first lowering the rails.

The traffic was backed up on Iowa Avenue—all the way east, to the bend on Muscatine—as if there'd been an accident in the avenue, directly in front of Danny's ground-floor apartment. Danny ran out the front door of the duplex in his boxer shorts. Given his state of undress, the writer must have struck the driver of the dirty-white van, which was blocking the incoming traffic to town, as a likely candidate for the neglectful parent.

"Is this *your* baby?" the van driver screamed at Danny. The handlebar mustache and bushy sideburns may have frightened little Joe as much as the man's ceaseless shouting—that and the fact that the van driver had managed to corral Joe on the grassy median strip in the middle of Iowa Avenue without actually picking the boy up, or even touching him. Joe stood uncertainly on the grass in his diaper; he'd wandered out of the house and across the sidewalk, into the lane of incoming traffic, and the dirty-white van had been the first vehicle to almost hit him.

Now a woman from the car that was stopped behind the white van ran into the median and scooped the baby into her arms. "Is *that* your daddy?" she asked Joe, pointing to Danny in his boxer shorts. Joe started to cry.

"He's mine—I was asleep," Danny told them. He crossed the pavement into the median strip, but the woman—middle-aged, glasses, a pearl necklace (Danny would remember nothing more definitive about her)—seemed reluctant to give the baby up.

"Your baby was in the street, pal—I almost ran over him," the van driver told Danny. "The fucking diaper, its whiteness, just caught my eye."

"It doesn't appear that you were looking for this baby, or that you even knew he was missing," the woman said to Danny.

"Daddy," Joe said, holding out his arms.

"Does this child have a mother?" the woman wanted to know.

"She's asleep—we were both asleep," Danny told her. He took little Joe from the woman's tentatively outstretched arms. "Thank you," Danny said to the van driver.

"You're still wasted, man," the driver told him. "Is your wife wasted, too?"

"Thank you," Danny told him again.

"You should be reported," the woman said to him.

"Yes, I should be," Danny told her, "but please don't."

Now cars were honking their horns, and Joe started to cry again. "I couldn't see the sky from the house," the boy was sobbing.

"You couldn't see the sky?" his dad asked. They crossed the pavement to the sidewalk, and went into the house to the continuous honking of horns.

"I couldn't see if Lady Sky was coming down," Joe said.

"You were looking for Lady Sky?" his father asked.

"I couldn't see her. Maybe she was looking for me," the boy said.

The divided avenue was wide; from the middle of the road, or from the median strip, Danny realized that his two-year-old had been able to see the sky. The boy had been hoping that Lady Sky would descend again—that was all there was to it.

"Mommy's home," Joe told his dad, as they came into the apartment, which the two-year-old called the *um*partment; from the moment he'd begun to talk, an apartment was an *um*partment.

"Yes, I know Mommy's home," Danny said. He could see that Katie had fallen back to sleep. On the kitchen table, the writer also noticed that the rum bottle was empty. Had he finished it before going to bed, or had Katie downed what was left in the bottle when she'd come home? (It was probably *me*, Danny thought; he knew that Katie didn't like rum.)

He took Joe into the boy's room and changed his diaper. He had trouble looking at his son's eyes—imagining them open and staring, unseeing, as the two-year-old in his bright-white diaper lay dead in the road.

"AND THEN YOU stopped drinking, right?" young Joe asked his father. For the duration of the long story, they'd kept their backs to the house they had lived in with Katie.

"The last of that rum was the end of it," Danny said to the eight-year-old.

"But Mom didn't stop drinking, did she?" Joe asked his dad.

"Your mom couldn't stop, sweetie—she probably still hasn't stopped," Danny told him.

"And I *am* grounded, right?" young Joe asked.

"No, you're not grounded—you can go anywhere you want, on foot or on the bus. It's your *bicycle* that's grounded," Danny said to the boy. "Maybe we'll give your bike to Max. I'll bet he could use it for a backup, or for spare parts."

Joe looked up at the brilliant blue of the fall sky. No descending angel was going to get him out of this predicament. "You never thought Lady Sky was an angel, did you?" the boy asked his dad.

"I believed her when she said she was an angel *sometimes*," Danny said.

The writer would drive all over Iowa City looking for the blue Mustang, but he wouldn't find it. The police would never spot the rogue car, either. But, back on Iowa Avenue, all Danny did was put his arm around the eight-year-old's shoulders. "Think of it this way," he said to his son. "That blue Mustang is still looking for you. Six years ago, when you stood in this street—with nothing but a diaper on—maybe the blue Mustang was stuck in traffic. It might have been several cars behind the white van; that blue Mustang might have been trying to get you even then."

"It's not really looking for me, is it?" Joe asked.

"You better believe it is," his dad told him. "The blue Mustang *wants* you—that's why you've got to be careful."

"Okay," the eight-year-old told his father.

"Do you know any two-year-olds?" Danny asked his son.

"No," the boy answered, "not that I can think of."

"Well, it would be good for you to meet one," his dad said, "just so you can see what you looked like in the road."

That was when the cook drove down Iowa Avenue, in the incoming lane, and pulled over to the curb, where the father and son were standing. "Get in, you two," Tony Angel told them. "I'll drop Joe at school, then I'll take you home," the cook said.

"Joe hasn't had any breakfast," Danny told his dad.

"I made him a big lunch—he can eat half of it on the way to school, Daniel. Get in," he repeated. "We have a . . . *situation*."

"What's wrong, Pop?" the writer asked.

"It seems that Youn is still married," the cook replied, as Danny and Joe got into the car. "It seems that Youn has a two-year-old daughter, and that her husband and daughter have come to visit her—just to see how all the *writing* is going."

"They're at the house?" Danny asked.

"It's good that they came after Youn was up. She was already in *her* room—writing," the cook said.

Danny could imagine how she'd left their bedroom—meticulously, without a trace of herself remaining, just that pearl-gray nightie tucked under her pillow, or maybe it was the beige one. "Youn has a two-year-old?" Danny asked his dad. "I want Joe to see the daughter."

"Are you crazy?" the cook said to his son. "Joe should go to school."

"Youn is married?" Joe asked. "She has a *kid*?"

"It appears so," Danny said; he was thinking about the novel Youn was writing—how it was so exquisitely written but not everything added up. The usually limpid prose notwithstanding, something had always been unclear about the book.

"I think you should go to school, sweetie," Danny said. "You can meet a two-year-old another time."

"But you want me to meet one, right?" Joe asked.

"What's this about?" the cook inquired; he was driving to Joe's school, not waiting for contradictory directions.

"It's a long story," Danny told him. "What's the husband like? Is he a gangster?"

"He's a surgeon in Korea, he told me," Tony Angel replied. "He's attending a surgical conference in Chicago, but he brought his daughter along, and they thought they'd surprise Mommy—and let Youn look after the two-year-old for a couple of days, while Kyung is in meetings. Some surprise, huh?" the cook asked.

"His name is *Kyung*?" Danny said. In the book Youn was writing, the gangster husband was named Jinwoo; Danny guessed that wasn't the only element of her story she'd made up, and all along he'd thought her novel was too autobiographical!

"Her husband seems like a nice guy," Tony Angel said.

"So I'm going to meet Youn's two-year-old daughter?" Joe asked, as he was getting out of the car.

"Eat something," the cook told his grandson. "I already called the school and told them you were coming late."

"It sounds like you *may* meet the little girl, yes," Danny told the boy. "But what are you on the lookout for?" he asked Joe, as the boy opened his lunch box and peered inside.

"The blue Mustang," Joe answered, without hesitation.

"Smart boy," his father said.

They were almost back at the Court Street house before the cook told his son, "Yi-Yiing and I decided that it should appear you two are a couple."

"Why should Yi-Yiing and I be a *couple*?" Danny said.

"Because you're the same age. While the husband from Korea is around, you should just pretend that you're *together*. Not even a Korean surgeon is going to suspect that *I'm* sleeping with his wife," the cook said. "I'm too old."

"How do we *pretend*?" Danny asked his dad.

"Let Yi-Yiing do the pretending," his father said.

In retrospect, the writer was thinking, the pretending hadn't been the most difficult part of the impromptu deception. Yi-Yiing did a good job of acting as Danny's girlfriend—that is, while Youn's husband was there in the Court Street house. The surgeon from Seoul struck Danny as a sweet man, both proud of himself and embarrassed for "surprising" his writer wife. Youn, for her part, could not conceal how happy she was to see her daughter, Soo. The Korean writer's eyes had sought Danny for some reassurance, and Danny hoped he'd provided it; he felt relieved, actually, because he'd been looking ahead to their inevitable parting with more than the usual guilt.

Yes, he would definitely be in Iowa City through this academic year—he'd already asked the Writers' Workshop if he could stay another year after that—but Danny knew that he probably wouldn't be staying in town long enough for Youn to finish her novel. (And when Danny went back to Vermont, he had all along been assuming that Youn would go back to Seoul.)

The surgeon, who would be in Chicago for only a few days, kissed his wife and daughter good-bye. All the introductions and good-byes had happened in the Court Street kitchen, where the cook acted as if he owned the place, and Yi-Yiing had two or three times slipped behind Danny and encircled him with her arms—drawing him to her, once kissing the back of his neck. It being a warm fall day, the writer wore only a T-shirt and jeans, and he could feel Yi-Yiing's silky pajamas brushing against his back. These hugs conveyed a coziness between them, the writer supposed—not knowing what Youn might have made of this intimate contact, or if Yi-Yiing and the cook had informed the Korean adulteress of their plan that Danny and the Hong Kong nurse should "pretend" to be a couple.

The daughter, Soo, was a little jewel. "She's not wearing a diaper?" Danny asked the surgeon, remembering Joe at that age.

"Girls are toilet-trained before boys, *honey*," Yi-Yiing told him, with what struck the writer as an overacted emphasis on the *honey* word—but the cook had laughed, and so had Youn. Danny would wonder, later, if perhaps Youn had also been relieved that her relationship with her fiction teacher was so efficiently ended. (What need was there for any further explanation?)

The days when the Korean doctor was in Chicago were easy enough, and Joe could see with his own eyes how innocent a two-year-old really was—about dangers in the road, obviously, but about angels falling from the sky, too. The eight-year-old could observe for himself that little Soo was capable of believing anything.

The fragrant nightie under the pillow on Youn's side of the bed turned out to be the beige one, and Danny found a discreet moment to give it back to her. Now *no* evidence of her remained in his bedroom. Youn slept with her tiny daughter in her writing room; they were both small enough to fit in the bed in that extra bedroom, although Danny had suggested to Youn that she could put Soo in the *extra* extra bedroom. (He'd noticed that Youn's husband had slept in that room, alone.)

"A two-year-old shouldn't sleep *unattended,*" Youn had told Danny, who realized that he'd misread the curiosity with which Youn had scrutinized Joe; she'd simply been wondering what changes to expect in her daughter between the ages of two and eight. (As for what she'd written about, and why, there would never be a satisfactory explanation, Danny supposed.)

When Kyung came back from Chicago, and the doctor soon left again with his little girl—they went home to Seoul together—Youn wasted no time in finding a place of her own to live, and by the next semester she had transferred to someone else's fiction workshop. Whether she ever finished her novel-in-progress was immaterial to the writer Danny Angel. Whether Youn would one day become a published novelist also mattered little to Danny, who knew firsthand that—in Youn's time in Iowa City—her fiction had been an almost complete success.

It was Yi-Yiing's success, at pretending to be Danny's girlfriend, that would linger a little longer. The ER nurse was not naturally flirtatious, but for months after the need to pretend she and Danny were a couple, Yi-Yiing would occasionally brush against the writer, or trail her fingers, or the back of her hand, against Danny's cheek. It seemed she had sincerely forgotten herself, for she would instinctively stop—as soon as she'd started something. Danny doubted that the cook ever saw her do this; if Joe saw, the eight-year-old took no notice.

"Would you prefer it if I dressed normally around the house?" Yi-Yiing would one day ask the writer. "I mean, maybe it's 'enough already' with the pajamas."

"But you're the Pajama Lady—that's just who you are," Danny told her evasively.

"You know what I mean," Yi-Yiing said to him.

She stopped wearing them—or, perhaps, she only slept in them. Her normal clothes were a safer barrier between them, and what had amounted to the occasional contact—the brush of her passing behind his back, the touch of her fingertips or the knuckles on her small hands—stopped soon after as well.

"I miss Yi-Yiing's pajamas," Joe said to his dad one morning, when they were walking to the boy's school.

"I do, too," Danny told him, but by then the writer was seeing someone else.

WITH YOUN GONE FROM their lives—especially later, in their last year in Iowa City, when they were living in the third house on Court Street—their regular habits resumed as if uninterrupted. The third house was on the other side of Court Street, near Summit, where Danny conducted a discreet daytime affair with an unhappy faculty wife whose husband was cheating on her. The back alley, where Joe had been tempted to pity himself—while he watched Max practice skids on his "backup" bike—was also gone from their lives, as was the possum. The Yokohamas, Sao and Kaori, still took turns babysitting for Joe, and everyone—all of them—gathered with a seemingly increasing need (or desperation) at Mao's.

The cook knew in advance how much he would miss the Cheng brothers—almost as much as he would miss Yi-Yiing. It was never knowing what it might have been like to be with the Hong Kong nurse that Danny would miss, though his return to Vermont was preceded by another kind of closure.

As their Iowa adventure was concluding, so was—at long last—the war in Vietnam. The mood at Mao's was not predisposed to a happy ending. "Operation Frequent Wind," as the helicopter evacuation of Saigon was called—"Operation More Bullshit," Ketchum had called it—turned out to be a devastating distraction from the dinnertime preparations at the Asian and French restaurant. The TV in the little kitchen off the Coralville strip proved to be a magnet for discontent.

April 1975 had been a bad month for business at Mao's. There were four drive-by brick-throwings—one of the restaurant's window-breakers was actually a chunk of cement the size of a cinder block, and one was a rock. "Fucking patriot farmers!" Xiao Dee had called the vandals. He and the cook had canceled a shopping trip to Chinatown because Xiao Dee was convinced that Mao's was under attack—or, as Saigon fell, the restaurant would come under heavier siege. Ah Gou was running short of his favorite ingredients. (With Tony Angel's help, there were a few more items from Italy on the menu than usual.)

All that year, the South Vietnamese soldiers were deserting in droves. The runaway soldiers had been rounding up their families and converging on Saigon, where they must have believed the Americans would help them escape the country. In the last two weeks of April, the U.S. had airlifted sixty thousand foreigners and South Viet-namese; hundreds of thousands more would soon be left to find their own way out. "It will be sheer chaos," Ketchum had predicted. ("What did we expect would happen?" the logger would say later.)

Did we *care* what would happen? Danny was thinking. He and Joe had a table to themselves at Mao's, and Yi-Yiing had joined them for dinner. She'd skipped her shift in the emergency room because she had a cold; she didn't want to make a lot of sick or injured people any worse, she'd told Danny and Joe. "I'm *already* going to make you two sick—you two *and* Pop," she said to them, smiling.

"Thanks a lot," Danny told her. Joe was laughing; he adored Yi-Yiing. The boy would miss having his own nurse when he was back in Vermont. (And I'll miss having a nurse for him, the writer was thinking.)

There were two couples at one table, and three businessmen types at another. It was a quiet night for Mao's, but it was still early. The boarded-up window didn't improve the looks of the front entrance, Danny was thinking, when one of the Yokohamas came out of the kitchen, her face as white as her apron and her lower lip trembling. "Your dad says you should see what's on television," the Japanese girl said to the writer. "The TV's in the kitchen."

Danny got up from the table, but when Joe tried to go with him, Yi-Yiing said, "Maybe you should stay with me, Joe."

"Yes, you *stay!*" Sao or Kaori told the boy. "You shouldn't see!"

"But I want to see what it is," Joe said.

"Do what Sao says, Joe—I'll be right back," his dad told him.

"I'm Kaori," the Japanese twin said to Danny. She burst into tears. "Why am I getting the feeling that all 'gooks' are the same to you Americans?"

"What's on the TV?" Yi-Yiing asked her.

The two couples had been laughing about something; they hadn't heard Kaori's outburst. But the businessmen types had frozen; the *gooks* word held them poised over their beers.

Ah Gou's smart girlfriend, Tzu-Min, was the maître d' that night. Xiao Dee was too agitated by the brick-throwing patriot farmers to be safely allowed out of the kitchen.

"Go back in the kitchen, Kaori," Tzu-Min told the sobbing girl. "No crying permitted out here."

"What's on the TV?" Yi-Yiing asked the maître d'.

"Joe shouldn't see it," Tzu-Min told her. Danny had already disappeared into the kitchen.

It was bedlam back there. Xiao Dee was shouting at the television. Sao, the other Japanese twin, was throwing up in the big sink—the one the dishwasher scrubbed the pots and pans in.

Ed, the dishwasher, stood aside; a recovering alcoholic, he was a World War II vet with several faded tattoos. The Cheng brothers had given Ed a job at a time when no one else would, and Ed felt loyal to them, though the small Coralville kitchen made him feel claustrophobic at times, and the political talk at Mao's was a foreign country to him. Ed had no use for foreign countries; that we were getting out of Vietnam was good enough for him. He'd been in the navy, in the Pacific. Now one of the Japanese twins was vomiting in his sink and the other one was in tears. (Ed might have been thinking that he had killed their relatives; if so, he was not sorry about it.)

"How's it going, Ed?" Danny said to the dishwasher.

"It's not going too good right now," Ed told him.

"Kissinger is a war criminal!" Xiao Dee was screaming. (Henry Kissinger had appeared, albeit briefly, on the television.) Ah Gou, who was chopping scallions, brandished his cleaver at the mere mention of the hated Kissinger, but now the TV returned to that image of enemy tanks rolling through the streets of Saigon; the tanks were closing in on the U.S. Embassy there, or so some nameless voice said. It was almost the end of April—these were the last airlifts, the day before Saigon surrendered. About seventy American helicopters had been shuttling between the walled-off courtyard of the embassy and the U.S. warships off the coast; as many as sixty-two hundred people were rescued that day. The last two helicopters to leave Saigon carried away the U.S. ambassador and the embassy's marine guards. Hours later, South Vietnam surrendered.

But that wasn't what was hard to watch on the little TV in the kitchen at Mao's. There were more people who wanted to leave Saigon than there were helicopters. Hundreds would be left behind in the embassy's courtyard. Dozens of Vietnamese clung to the skids of the last two helicopters to leave; they fell to their deaths as the choppers lifted away. The television just kept showing it. "Those poor people," the cook had said, seconds before Sao threw up in Ed's sink.

"They're not *people,* not to most Americans—they're *gooks!*" Xiao Dee was shouting.

Ah Gou was watching the TV instead of the scallions; he chopped the first digit off the index finger of his left hand. Kaori, still in tears, fainted; the cook dragged her away from the stove. Danny took a dish towel and began to twist it, tightly, around Ah Gou's upper arm. The tip of Big Brother's finger lay in a pool of blood with the chopped scallions.

"Go get Yi-Yiing," the cook said to Sao. Ed took a wet towel and wiped the girl's face. Sao was as insubstantial-looking as her fainted twin, but she had stopped throwing up, and, like a ghost, she drifted away to the dining room.

When the swinging door to the dining room opened, Danny heard one of the businessmen say, "What kind of crazy, fucked-up place is this, anyway?"

"Ah Gou cut off his finger," he heard Sao say to Yi-Yiing.

Then the door swung closed and Danny didn't hear how Sao or Tzu-Min or Yi-Yiing answered the businessman, or if any of the women had tried. (Mao's *was* a crazy, fucked-up place that night when Saigon was falling.)

The door to the dining room swung open again, and they all came into the kitchen—Yi-Yiing with young Joe, Tzu-Min and Sao. Danny was mildly surprised that the three businessmen types and the two couples weren't with them, though there was no room for anyone else in the chaotic kitchen.

"Thank God they all ordered the guinea hen," the cook was saying.

Kaori had sat up on the floor. "The two couples are having the guinea hen," she said. "The business guys ordered the ravioli."

"I just meant the couples," Tony Angel said. "I'm feeding them first."

"The business guys are ready to walk out—I'm warning you," Tzu-Min told them.

Yi-Yiing found the tip of Ah Gou's finger in the scallions. Xiao Dee wrapped his arms around Ah Gou while the cook poured vodka on the stump of his left index finger. Big Brother was still screaming when Yi-Yiing held out the fingertip, and Tony Angel poured more vodka on it; then she put the fingertip back where it belonged. "Just hold it on," she told Big Brother, "and stop screaming."

Danny was sorry that Joe was watching the television; the ten-year-old seemed transfixed by that image of the people clinging to the helicopters' skids, and then falling off. "What's happening to them?" the boy asked his dad.

"They're dying," Danny said. "There's no room for them on the helicopters."

Ed was coughing; he went out the kitchen door. There was an alley back there—it was used for deliveries, and for picking up the trash—and they all thought that Ed was just stepping out for a cigarette. But the dishwasher never came back.

Yi-Yiing took Ah Gou out the swinging door and through the dining room; he held his severed fingertip in place, but now that Danny was no longer tightening the towel around his upper arm, Big Brother was bleeding profusely. Tzu-Min went with them. "I guess I'm going to give everyone in the emergency room my cold, after all," Yi-Yiing was saying.

"What the fuck is going on?" one of the businessmen shouted. "Is there anyone working here, or what?"

"Racists! War criminals! Fascist pigs!" Ah Gou yelled at them, still bleeding.

In the kitchen, the cook said to his son and grandson, "You're my sous chefs now—we better get started."

"There are only two tables to deal with, Pop—I think we can manage this," Danny told him.

"If we just ignore the business guys, I think they'll leave," Kaori said.

"Nobody leaves!" Xiao Dee shouted. "I'll show them what kind of crazy, fucked-up place this is—and they better like it!"

He went out into the dining room through the swinging door—his ponytail in that absurd pink ribbon possibly belonging to Spicy—and even after the door swung shut, they could still hear Little Brother from the kitchen. "You want to eat the best food you ever had, or do you want to *die*?" Xiao Dee was yelling. "*Asians* are dying, but you can eat well!" he screamed at the businessmen.

"The guinea hen is served with asparagus, and a risotto of oyster mushrooms and sage *jus*," the cook was explaining to Danny and young Joe. "Don't *slop* the risotto on the plates, please."

"Where are the guinea hens from, Pop?" Danny asked.

"From Iowa, of course—we're out of almost everything that *isn't* from Iowa," the cook told him.

"You want to see how your mushroom and mascarpone ravioli gets made?" Xiao Dee was asking the businessmen types. "It's done with Parmesan and white truffle oil! It's the best fucking ravioli you'll ever have! You think white truffle oil comes from *Iowa*?" he asked them. "You want to come out in the kitchen and see a bunch of Asians *dying*? They are dying on TV right now—if you want to see!" Little Brother was shouting.

Tony Angel turned to the Japanese twins. "Go rescue the business guys from Xiao Dee," he told them, "*both* of you."

The cook accompanied the Yokohamas to the dining room, where they served the two couples the guinea hens. "Your pasta will be coming right along," Tony told the businessmen; he'd wondered why the business guys had so quietly listened to Xiao Dee's tirade. Now he saw that Little Brother had taken the bloody cleaver with him into the dining room.

"We need you back in the kitchen—we want you like *crazy* back there! We're *dying* for you!" the Japanese twins were telling Xiao Dee; they had draped themselves on him, being careful not to touch the bloody cleaver. The businessmen types just sat there, waiting, even after the cook (and Xiao Dee, with Kaori and Sao) had gone back into the kitchen.

"What are the fascist pigs drinking?" Xiao Dee was asking the Yokohamas.

"Tsingtao," Kaori or Sao answered him.

"Bring them more—keep the beer coming!" Little Brother told them.

"What goes with the ravioli, Pop?" Danny asked his dad.

"The peas," the cook told him. "Use the slotted spoon, or there will be too much oil on them."

Joe couldn't get interested in being a sous chef, not while the television kept showing the helicopters. When the phone rang, Joe was the only one whose hands weren't busy doing something; he answered it. They all knew there was no maître d' in the dining room, and they thought it might be Yi-Yiing or Tzu-Min calling from Mercy Hospital with a report on whether or not they could save Ah Gou's finger.

"It's collect, from Ketchum," Joe told them.

"Say that you accept," his grandfather told him.

"I accept," the boy said.

"*You* talk to him, Daniel—I'm busy," the cook said.

But in the passing of the telephone, they could all hear what Ketchum had to say—all the way from New Hampshire. "This asshole country—"

"Hi, it's me—it's Danny," the writer told the old logger.

"You still sorry you didn't get to go to Vietnam, *fella*?" Ketchum roared at him.

"No, I'm not sorry," Danny told him, but it took him too long to say it; Ketchum had already hung up.

There was blood all over the kitchen. On the TV, the desperate Vietnamese dangled from, and then fell off, the skids of the helicopters. The debacle would be replayed for days—all over the world, the writer supposed, while he watched his ten-year-old watching the end of the war his dad hadn't gone to.

The Japanese twins were placating the business guys with more beer. Xiao Dee was standing in the walk-in refrigerator with the door open. "We're almost out of Tsingtao, Tony," Little Brother was saying. He walked out of the fridge and closed the door; then he noticed that the door to the alley was still open. "What happened to Ed?" Xiao Dee asked. He stepped cautiously into the alley. "Maybe some fucking patriot farmer mistook him for one of us 'gooks' and killed him!"

"I think poor Ed just went home," the cook said.

"I threw up in his sink—maybe that's why," Sao said. She and Kaori had come back to the kitchen to bring the business guys their pasta order.

"Can I turn the TV off?" Danny asked them all.

"Yes! Turn it off, please!" one of the Yokohamas told him.

"Ed is *gone!*" Xiao Dee was shouting from the alley. "The fucker-patriots have *kidnapped* him!"

"I can take Joe home and put him to bed," the other twin said to Danny.

"The boy has to eat first," the cook said. "You can be the maître d' for a little while, can't you, Daniel?"

"Sure, I can do it," the writer told him. He washed his hands and face, and put on a clean apron. When he went into the dining room, the businessmen types seemed surprised that he wasn't Asian—or especially angry-looking.

"What's going on in the kitchen?" one of the men asked him tentatively; he definitely didn't want Xiao Dee to overhear him.

"It's the end of the war, on the television," Danny told them.

"The pasta is terrific, in spite of everything," another of the businessmen types said to Danny. "Compliments to the chef."

"I'll tell him," Danny said.

Some faculty types showed up later, and a few proud parents taking their beloved university students out to dinner, but if you weren't back in the kitchen at Mao's with the angry Asians, you might not have known that the war was over, or how it ended. (They didn't show that television footage everywhere, or for very long—not in most of America, anyway.)

Ah Gou would get to keep his fingertip. Kaori or Sao took young Joe home and put him to bed that night, and Danny drove home with Yi-Yiing. The cook would drive himself home, after Mao's had closed.

There was an awkward moment—after the Japanese babysitter had gone, and before the cook came home—when Joe was asleep upstairs, and Danny was alone in the third Court Street kitchen with the nurse from Hong Kong. Like Danny and his dad, Yi-Yiing didn't drink. She was making tea for herself—something allegedly good for her cold.

"So, here we are, alone at last," Yi-Yiing said to him. "I guess we're *almost* alone, anyway," she added. "It's just you and me and my damn cold."

The kettle had not yet come to boil, and Yi-Yiing folded her arms on her breasts and stared at him.

"What?" Danny asked her.

"You know what," she said to him. He was the first to lower his eyes.

"How's it going with that tricky business of moving your daughter and your parents here?" he asked her. Finally, she turned away.

"I'm very slowly changing my mind about that," Yi-Yiing told him.

Much later, the cook would hear that she'd gone back to Hong Kong; she was working as a nurse there. (None of them ever heard what happened to the Yokohamas, Kaori and Sao.)

That night the war ended, Yi-Yiing took her tea upstairs with her, leaving Danny alone in the kitchen. The temptation to turn on the TV was great, but Danny wandered outside to the Court Street sidewalk instead. It wasn't very late—not nearly midnight—but most of the houses on the street were dark, or the only lights that were on were in the upstairs of the houses. People reading in bed, or watching television, Danny imagined. From several of the nearby houses, Danny could recognize that sickly light from a TV set—an unnatural blue-green, blue-gray shimmer. There was something wrong with that color.

It was warm enough in Iowa at the end of April for some windows to be open, and while he couldn't make out the exact language on the television, Danny recognized the drone as the disembodied voice of the news—or so the writer imagined. (If someone had been watching a love story or another kind of movie, how would Danny have known?)

If the stars were out, Danny couldn't see them. He'd lived on Court Street for three years; there'd been nothing ominous about living there, except for the driverless blue Mustang, and now the writer and his family were about to go back to Vermont. "This asshole country—" Ketchum had started to say; he'd been too angry or too drunk, or both, to even finish his thought. Wasn't it too harsh an assessment, anyway? Danny hoped so.

"Please look after my dad and my little boy," the writer said aloud, but to what was he speaking—or to whom? The starless night above Iowa City? The one alert and restless soul on Court Street who might have heard him? (Yi-Yiing—if she was still awake—maybe.)

Danny stepped off the sidewalk and into the empty street, as if daring the blue Mustang to take notice of him. "Please don't hurt my father or my son," Danny said. "Hurt *me,* if you have to hurt someone," he said.

But who was out there, under the unseen heavens, to either look after them or hurt them? "Lady Sky?" the writer asked out loud, but Amy had never said she was a full-time angel, and he'd not seen her for eight years. There was no answer.

CHAPTER 11

HONEY

WHERE HAS MY MEMORY GONE? THE COOK WAS THINKING; he was almost sixty, his limp more pronounced. Tony Angel was trying to remember those markets Little Brother had taken him to in Chinatown. Kam Kuo was on Mott Street, Kam Man on the Bowery—or was it the other way around? It didn't matter, the cook concluded; he could still recall the more important things.

How Xiao Dee had hugged him when they'd said good-bye—how Ah Gou had twisted the reattached tip of his left index finger, to make himself cry. *"She bu de!"* Xiao Dee had shouted. (The Cheng brothers pronounced this SEH BOO DEH.)

"She bu de!" Ah Gou cried, bending that scarred and slightly crooked first digit.

Chinese immigrants said *she bu de* to one another, Xiao Dee had explained to the cook during one of their sixteen-hour marathons to or from Chinatown, somewhere out on I-80. You said *she bu de* when you were leaving your Chinese homeland, for New York or San Francisco—or for anywhere far away, where you might not see your childhood friends or members of your own family ever again. (Xiao Dee had told Tony Angel that *she bu de* meant something like "I can't bear to let go." You say it when you don't want to give up something you have.)

"She bu de," the cook whispered to himself in his cherished kitchen at Avellino.

"What's that, boss?" Greg, the sous chef, asked him.

"I was talking to my calamari," Tony told him. "The thing with squid, Greg, is either you cook it just a little or you cook it forever— anything in between, and it's rubber."

Greg had certainly heard this soliloquy on squid before. "Uh-huh," the sous chef said.

The calamari the cook was preparing for his son, Daniel, was the *forever* kind. Tony Angel slowly stewed it with canned tomatoes and tomato paste—and with garlic, basil, red pepper flakes, and black olives. The cook added the pine nuts and chopped parsley only at the end, and he served the squid over penne, with more chopped parsley on the side. (Never with Parmesan—not on calamari.) He would give Daniel just a small arugula salad after the pasta dish, maybe with a little goat cheese; he had a local Vermont chèvre that was pretty good.

But right now the pepperoni pizzas were ready, and the cook pulled them from the oven of his Stanley woodstove. (*"She bu de,"* he whispered to the old Irish stove, and Greg once more glanced in his direction.)

"You're crying again—you know that, don't you?" Celeste said to Tony. "You want to talk about it?"

"It must be the onions," the cook told her.

"Bullshit, Tony," she said. "Are those my two pepperonis for the old broads out there?" Without waiting for an answer, Celeste said: "They better be my pizzas. Those old girls are looking hungry enough to eat Danny for a first course."

"They're all yours," Tony Angel told Celeste. He'd already put the penne in the pot of boiling water, and he took one out with a slotted spoon and tasted it while he watched every step of Celeste's dramatic exit from the kitchen. Loretta was looking at him as if she were trying to decipher a code. "What?" the cook said to her.

"Mystery man," Loretta said. "Danny's a mystery man, too—isn't he?"

"You're as dramatic as your mother," the cook told her, smiling.

"Is the calamari ready, or are you telling it your life story?" Loretta asked him.

Out in the dining room, Dot exclaimed: "My, that's a thin-lookin' crust!"

"It's thin, all right," May said approvingly.

"Our cook makes great pizzas," Celeste told them. "His crusts are always thin."

"What's he put in the dough?" Dot asked the waitress.

"Yeah, what's his secret ingredient?" May asked Celeste.

"I don't know if he has one," Celeste said. "I'll ask him." The two old broads were digging in—they ignored her. "I hope you ladies are hungry," Celeste added, as she turned to go back to the kitchen. Dot and May just kept eating; this was no time to talk.

Danny watched the women eat with growing wonder. Where had he seen people eat like that? he was thinking. Surely not at Exeter, where table manners didn't matter but the food was awful. At Exeter, you picked over your food with the greatest suspicion—and you talked nonstop, if only to distract yourself from what you were eating.

The old women had been talking and whispering (and *cackling*) together (like a couple of crows); now there wasn't a word between them, and no eye contact, either. They rested their forearms on the table and bent over their plates, heads down. Their shoulders were hunched, as if to ward off an attack from behind, and Danny imagined that if he were closer to them, he might hear them emit an unconscious moan or growl—a sound so innately associated with eating that the women were unaware of it and had long ceased to hear it themselves.

No one in the North End had ever eaten that way, the writer was remembering. Food was a celebration at Vicino di Napoli, an event that inspired conversation; people were engaged with one another when they ate. At Mao's, too, you didn't just talk over a meal—you *shouted.* And you shared your food—whereas these two old broads appeared to be protecting their pizzas from each other. They wolfed their dinners down like dogs. Danny knew they wouldn't leave a scrap.

"The Red Sox just aren't reliable," Greg was saying, but the cook was concentrating on the surprise squid dish for his son; he'd missed what had happened in the game on the radio.

"Daniel likes a little extra parsley," he was saying to Loretta, just as Celeste came back into the kitchen.

"The two old broads want to know if there's a secret ingredient in your pizza dough, Tony," Celeste said to the cook.

"You bet there is—it's *honey*," Tony Angel told her.

"I would never have guessed that," Celeste said. "That's some secret, all right."

Out in the dining room, it suddenly came to the writer Danny Angel where he'd seen people eat as if they were animals, the way these two old women were eating their pizzas. The woodsmen and the sawmill workers had eaten like that—not only in the cookhouse in Twisted River, but also in those makeshift wanigans, where he and his father had once fed the loggers during a river drive. Those men ate without talking; sometimes even Ketchum hadn't spoken a word. But these tough-looking broads couldn't have been *loggers*, Danny was thinking, when Loretta interrupted his thoughts.

"Surprise!" the waitress said, as she put the squid dish in front of him.

"I was hoping it was going to be the calamari," Danny told her.

"Ha!" Loretta said. "I'll tell your dad."

May had finished her pepperoni pizza first, and anyone seeing the way she eyed the last piece on Dot's plate might have had reason to warn Dot that she should never entirely trust her old friend. "I guess I liked mine a little better than you're likin' yours," May said.

"I'm likin' mine just fine," Dot answered with her mouth full, her thumb and index finger quickly gripping the crust of that precious last slice.

May looked away. "That writer is finally eatin' somethin', and it looks pretty appetizin'," she observed. Dot just grunted, finishing her pizza.

"Would you say it's *almost* as good as Cookie's?" May asked.

"Nope," Dot said, wiping her mouth. "Nobody's pizza is as good as Cookie's."

"I said *almost*, Dot."

"*Close*, maybe," Dot told her.

"I hope you ladies left room for dessert," Celeste said. "It looks like those pizzas hit the spot."

"What's the secret ingredient?" May asked the waitress.

"You'll never guess," Celeste said.

"I'll bet it's *honey*," Dot said; both she and May cackled, but they stopped cackling when they saw how the waitress was staring at them. (It didn't happen often that Celeste was speechless.)

"Wait a minute," May said. "It *is* honey, isn't it?"

"That's what the cook said—he puts honey in his dough," Celeste told them.

"Yeah, and the next thing you're gonna tell us is that the cook *limps*," Dot said. That really cracked up the two old broads; Dot and May couldn't stop cackling over that one, not that they missed the message in Celeste's amazed expression. (The waitress might as well have told them outright. Yes, indeed, the cook limped. He limped up a storm!)

But Danny had overheard snippets of their conversation before the ladies' cackling got out of control. He'd heard Celeste say something about his dad putting honey in the pizza dough, and one of the old broads had joked about the cook's limp. Danny was sensitive about his father's limp; he'd heard enough jokes on that subject to last a lifetime, most of them from those West Dummer dolts at that piss-poor Paris Manufacturing Company School. And why did Celeste look so stricken suddenly? the writer was wondering.

"Weren't you ladies interested in the pie and the cobbler?" the waitress asked them.

"Wait a minute," May said again. "Are you sayin' your cook's got a limp?"

"He limps a *little*," Celeste hesitated to say, but in effect she'd already said it.

"Are you shittin' us?" Dot asked the waitress.

Celeste seemed offended, but she also looked afraid; she knew something was wrong, but she didn't know why or what it was. Neither did Danny, but to anyone seeing him, the writer appeared to be frightened, too.

"Look, our cook's got a limp, and he puts honey in his pizza dough—it's no big deal," Celeste said to them.

"Maybe it's a big deal to *us*," May told the waitress.

"Is he a little fella?" Dot asked.

"Yeah . . . and what's his name?" May asked.

"I would say our cook is . . . slightly built," Celeste answered carefully. "His name's Tony."

"Oh," Dot said, disappointed.

"Tony," May repeated, shaking her head.

"You can bring us one apple pie and one blueberry cobbler," Dot told the waitress.

"We'll share 'em," May said.

It might have ended there, if Danny hadn't spoken; it was his voice that made Dot and May look at him more closely. When they'd first seen him, they must have missed the writer's physical resemblance to his father as a young man, but it was how well-spoken Danny was that reminded both Dot and May of the cook. In a town like Twisted River, the cook's enunciation—and his perfect diction—had stood out.

"Might I inquire if you two ladies are from around here?" Danny asked those bad old broads.

"Sweet Jesus, May," Dot said to her friend. "Don't that voice kinda take you back?"

"*Way* back," May said, looking hard at Danny. "Don't he look just like Cookie, too?"

The *Cookie* word was enough to tell Danny where these old ladies were from, and why they might have been badgering Celeste about honey in pizza dough and a little fella of a cook—one who limped.

"Your name was Danny," Dot said to him. "Have you changed your name, too?"

"No," the writer told them too quickly.

"I gotta meet this here cook," May said.

"Why don'tcha tell your dad to come say hello to us, will ya?" Dot asked Danny. "It's been so long since we seen one another, we got some serious catchin' up to do."

Celeste came back with the ladies' desserts, which Danny knew would be only a temporary distraction.

"Celeste," Danny said. "Would you please tell Pop that there are two old friends who want to see him? Tell him they're from Twisted River," Danny told her.

"Our cook's name is *Tony*," Celeste said a little desperately to the bad old broads. She'd heard enough about Twisted River to make her hope she would never hear anything more about it. (The cook had told her it would be all over on the day Twisted River caught up to him.)

"Your cook's name is *Cookie*," Dot said to the waitress.

"Just tell him we're *chokin'*," May told Celeste. "That'll bring him runnin'."

"*Limpin'*, you mean," Dot corrected her, but now their cackles were suppressed. If the writer had to guess, it seemed that these women had a score to settle with his father.

"You got the same superior-soundin' voice as your daddy," May said to Danny.

"Is the Injun around?" Dot asked him.

"No, Jane is . . . long gone," Danny told them.

In the kitchen, Celeste was still dry-eyed when she walked past her daughter. "I could have used a little help with the party of eight, Mom," Loretta was saying to her, "and then those three couples came in, but you just kept talking away to those two old biddies."

"Those old biddies are from Twisted River," Celeste told the cook. "They said to tell you they were *chokin'* . . . Cookie." Celeste had never seen such an expression on Tony Angel's face—none of them had— but of course she'd never called him "Cookie" before.

"Is there a problem, boss?" the sous chef asked.

"It was the honey in the pizza, wasn't it?" Celeste was saying. "The honey gave it away, I guess."

"Dot and May. It's finished, sweetheart," Tony Angel said to Celeste; she started to cry.

"Mom?" Loretta said.

"You don't know me," the cook told them all. "You won't ever know where I go from here." He took off his apron and let it fall on the floor. "You're in charge, Greg," he said to the sous chef.

"They don't know your last name, not unless Danny tells them," Celeste managed to say; Loretta was holding her while she sobbed.

The cook walked out into the dining room. Danny was standing between him and the two tough broads. "They don't know the *Angel* name, Pop," his son whispered to him.

"Well, that's something to be thankful for," his dad said.

"I wouldn't call that a *little* limp—would you, May?" Dot asked her old friend.

"Hello, ladies," the cook said to them, but he didn't come any closer.

"The limp's gotten *worse,* if you ask me," May replied to Dot.

"Are you just traveling through?" the cook asked them.

"How come you changed your name, Cookie?" Dot asked him.

"Tony was easier to say than Dominic," he answered them, "and it still sounds Italian."

"You look awful, Cookie—you're as white as flour!" May told him.

"I don't get a lot of sunshine in the kitchen," the cook said.

"You look like you been hidin' under a rock," Dot said to him.

"How come you and Danny are so spooked to see us?" May asked him.

"They were always *superior* to us," Dot reminded her friend. "Even as a kid, you were a superior little snot," she said to Danny.

"Where are you living nowadays?" the cook asked them. He was hoping they lived close by—somewhere in Vermont, or in New York State—but he could tell by their accents, and by just looking at them, that they were still living in Coos County.

"Milan," May answered. "We see your pal Ketchum, from time to time."

"Not that Ketchum would say hello to us, or nothin'," Dot said. "You was all so superior—the three of you *and* the Injun!"

"Well . . ." the cook began; his voice trailed away. "I have a lot to do, in the kitchen."

"First you was gonna put honey in the dough, and the next minute you wasn't. Then you changed your mind about it *again,* I guess," May said to him.

"That's right," the cook said.

"I'm havin' a look in the kitchen," Dot suddenly said. "I don't believe a fuckin' word these two are tellin' us. I'm gonna see for myself if Jane's still with him!" Neither Danny nor his dad did anything to stop her. May just waited with them while Dot went into the kitchen.

"There's the two waitresses, both of 'em cryin', and a young cook, and what looks like a busboy, and some kid doin' the dishes—no Injun," Dot announced, when she came back.

"Boy, do you look like you're puttin' your pecker somewhere you shouldn't, Cookie!" May told him. "You, too," she said to Danny. "You got a wife and kids, or anythin'?"

"No wife, no children," Danny told them—again, too quickly.

"Bullshit," Dot said. "I don't believe a fuckin' word!"

"And I suppose you're not bangin' anybody, either?" May asked the cook. He didn't answer her; he just kept looking at his son, Daniel. Their minds were racing far ahead of this moment in Avellino. How soon could they leave? Where would they go this time? How long before these bad old broads crossed paths with Carl, and what would they tell the cowboy when they ran into him? (Carl lived in Berlin; Ketchum lived in Errol. Milan was between them.)

"If you ask me, Cookie's humpin' our waitress—that older one," Dot said to May. "She's the one doin' most of the cryin'."

The cook just turned and walked back into the kitchen. "Tell them their dinners are on me, Daniel—free pizzas, free desserts," he said as he was leaving.

"You don't need to tell us—we heard him," May said to Danny.

"You coulda just been *nice* to us—glad to see us, or somethin'!" Dot called after the cook, but he was gone. "You don't hafta buy us supper, Cookie!" Dot hollered into the kitchen, but she didn't go after him.

May was putting money on Danny's table—too much money for their dinners, but Danny wouldn't try to stop her. "And we didn't even eat our pie and cobbler!" she said to the writer. May pointed to his notebook on the table. "What are you, the friggin' bookkeeper or somethin'? You keepin' the accounts, huh?"

"That's right," he told her.

"Fuck you and your dad," Dot told him.

"Cookie was always holier-than-thou, and you were always a holier-than-thou *kid*!" May said to him.

"Sorry," Danny said. He just wanted them to leave so that he could concentrate on all that he and his dad had to do, and how much or little time they had to do it—beginning with telling Ketchum.

Meanwhile, there was an unserved party of eight and another table with three astonished-looking couples. Everyone had been paying close attention to the confrontation, but it was over now. Dot and May were leaving. The women both gave Danny the finger as they went out the door. For a bewildering moment—it was almost as if the sawmill workers' wives weren't real, or they had never found their way to Avellino—the old ladies didn't appear to know which way to turn on Main Street. Then they must have remembered that they'd parked downhill, past the Latchis Theatre.

When the bad old broads were gone, Danny spoke to the restaurant's uneasy, unattended patrons. "Someone will be right with you," he told them, not knowing if this was even remotely true; he knew it wouldn't be true if both Loretta and Celeste were still in tears.

Back in the kitchen, it was worse than Danny had expected. Even the kid doing dishes and the busboy were crying. Celeste had slumped to the floor, where Loretta was kneeling beside her. "Stop *shouting* at me!" the cook yelled into the telephone. "I should never have called you—then I wouldn't have to *listen* to you!" (His father must have called Ketchum, Danny realized.)

"Tell me what to say, Greg, and I'll say it," Danny said to the sous chef. "You've got a table of eight and a table of six out there. What do I tell them?"

Greg was weeping into the rosemary and red-wine reduction. "Your dad said Avellino is finished," Greg told him. "He said this is his last night. He's putting the place up for sale, but we can run the restaurant ourselves until it sells—if we can manage, somehow."

"Greg, just how the fuck do we *manage*?" Celeste cried out.

"I didn't say we *could*," Greg blubbered.

"Get rid of the Red Sox, for starters," Danny said, changing the radio station. "If you're going to be hysterical, you ought to play some music back here—everyone in the restaurant can hear you."

"Yes, I *know* you were always of the opinion that Vermont was too fucking close to New Hampshire, Ketchum!" the cook was shouting into the phone. "Why don't you tell me something *useful*?"

"Tell me what to say to the customers, Greg," Danny said to the blubbering sous chef.

"Tell them they better keep their orders simple," Greg told him.

"Tell them to go home, for Christ's sake!" Loretta said.

"No, goddamn it—tell them to *stay*!" the sous chef said angrily. "We can manage."

"Don't be an asshole, Greg," Celeste told him; she was still sobbing.

Danny went back into the dining room, where the party of eight was already arguing with one another—about whether to stay or leave, no doubt. The three couples at the table for six seemed more resigned to their fate, or at least more willing to wait. "Listen," Danny said to them all, "there's a crisis in the kitchen—I'm not kidding. I would advise you either to leave now or to order something basic. The pizzas, maybe, or a pasta dish. By the way, the beef *satay* is excellent. So is the calamari."

He went to the wine rack and picked out a couple of good reds; Danny Angel may have stopped drinking sixteen years ago, when he was still Daniel Baciagalupo, but the writer knew the names of the better bottles. "The wine is on me," he told them, bringing them glasses, too. He had to go back to the kitchen to get a corkscrew from either Loretta or Celeste, and one of the party of eight asked him timidly for a beer. "Sure," Danny said. "A beer's no problem. You should try a Moretti."

At least Celeste was standing, though Loretta looked in better shape. "One Moretti for the party of eight. I gave wine to everyone else—on me," Danny said to Loretta. "Can you pull the corks?"

"Yeah, I guess I'm okay," Loretta told him.

"I can work," Celeste said unconvincingly.

"You better get your dad off the phone before he has a heart attack," Greg said to Danny.

"I'm not changing my name *again!*" the cook was screaming into the phone. "I'm not leaving my country, Ketchum! Why do I have to leave the entire *country?*"

"Let me speak to him, Pop," Danny said; he kissed his father on the forehead, taking the telephone from him. "It's me, Ketchum," the writer began.

"Dot and May!" Ketchum hollered. "For Christ's sake, Danny—those two would talk their heads off to a pinch of coon shit! The first time those bitches run into Carl, the cowboy's going to know where to find you!"

"How long do we have, Ketchum?" Danny asked. "Just give me an educated guess."

"You should have left yesterday," Ketchum told him. "You have to leave the country as soon as possible!"

"The *country?*" Danny asked.

"You're a famous writer! What do you have to live in this asshole country for?" Ketchum asked him. "You can write anywhere, can't you? And how long before Cookie retires? For that matter, he can *cook* anywhere—can't he? Just don't let it be an *Italian* place! That's what the cowboy will be looking for. And Cookie needs a new name."

"Dot and May never heard the *Angel* name," Danny told the old logger.

"Carl could hear it—when he comes looking for you two, Danny. No matter how long after you're gone, someone could say the *Angel* name to the cowboy."

"So I'm supposed to change my name, too? For God's sake, Ketchum—I'm a *writer!*"

"Keep it, then," Ketchum said morosely. "The cowboy's no reader, I'll grant you that. But Cookie can't keep the Tony Angel—he'd be better off being Dominic Baciagalupo again! Danny, don't you dare let him cook in any restaurant with an Italian name—not even if it's out of the country."

"I have a son, Ketchum—he's *American*, remember?" Danny said to the old woodsman.

"Joe is going to be in college in *Colorado*," Ketchum reminded him. This was a sore point with Danny: That Joe would be going to the University of Colorado, in Boulder, was something of a disappointment to his dad. In Danny's opinion, his son had gotten into better schools. Danny believed that Joe was going to Colorado for the *skiing*, not an education; the writer had also read that Boulder was a big party town. "Carl doesn't even know you have a child," Ketchum also reminded Danny. "If you're out of the country, *I'll* look after Joe."

"In Colorado?" Danny asked.

"First things first, Danny," Ketchum said. "Get the fuck out of Vermont—both you and your dad! I can look after your boy in the interim—before he goes off to Colorado, anyway."

"Maybe Pop and I could go to Colorado, too," Danny suggested. "It's a little like Vermont, I imagine—there are mountains, just bigger ones. Boulder is a university town, and we all liked Iowa City. Writers can fit in, in a university town. A cook could fit in, in Boulder—couldn't he? It wouldn't have to be *Italian*—"

Ketchum cut him off. "You must be as simple-minded as a pinch of coon shit, Danny! You guys ran the first time—now you have to keep running! Do you think Carl cares that you're a *family*? The cowboy doesn't have a family—he's a fucking *killer*, Danny, and he's on a *mission*!"

"I'll let you know our plans, Ketchum," the writer told his father's old friend.

"Carl doesn't know shit about foreign countries," Ketchum said. "Hell, Boston wasn't foreign enough for him. You think Colorado would be too far away for the cowboy to find you? Colorado's a lot like New Hampshire, Danny—they have *guns* out there, don't they? You could be carrying a gun in Colorado, and no one would look at you twice—isn't that right?"

"I suppose so," Danny said. "I know you love us, Ketchum."

"I promised your mom I would look after you!" Ketchum shouted, his voice breaking.

"Well, I guess you're doing it," Danny told him, but Ketchum had hung up. The writer would remember the song that was playing on the radio; it was Neil Young's "After the Gold Rush," a song from the seventies. (When Danny had switched stations from the Red Sox game, he'd inadvertently found Greg's *Oldie-But-Goldie* music.)

> *I was thinking about what a*
> *Friend had said.*
> *I was hoping it was a lie.*

Danny saw that his father was once more stirring his sauces; the cook then started rolling out the dough for what looked like three or four more pizzas. Greg was grilling something, but the sous chef paused to take a dish out of the oven. Neither waitress was in the kitchen, but the busboy was busy filling a couple of bread baskets.

The dishwasher was waiting for more dirty dishes; an earnest-looking boy, he was reading a paperback. Probably an assignment for school, Danny thought; nowadays, kids didn't read much on their own. Danny asked the boy what he was reading. The young dishwasher smiled shyly, showing the author a dog-eared mass-market edition of a Danny Angel novel. But that was such a tough night, when Dot and May made their disruptive appearance in Avellino, the writer would never remember which book the kid was reading.

And the bad night was far from over; for Danny, it was just beginning.

"YOU'LL FIND SOMEONE," Kurt Vonnegut had said to Danny when the young writer was leaving Iowa City the first time; Katie had only recently left him. But it hadn't happened—not yet. Danny supposed there was still time for him to find someone; he was only forty-one, and he never would have claimed that he'd sincerely been *trying*. Did he think Lady Sky was going to drop into his life again, just because he couldn't forget her?

As for what Vonnegut also said to the then-unpublished writer—the part about "maybe capitalism will be kind to you"—well, Danny was wondering (as he drove home to Putney from Brattleboro) how Kurt had known.

On the night of Dot and May's visit to Avellino, when Danny and his dad would soon be on the move again, the famous writer's compound in Putney was ablaze with lights. To anyone driving by on Hickory Ridge Road, the lights that were on—in every room, in each building—seemed to advertise just *how* kind capitalism had been to the bestselling author Danny Angel.

Was the compound overrun with revelers? Was every last room of the old farmhouse (now the guesthouse) *occupied*—as was, evidently, the new house that Danny had built for himself and Joe? The lights were also on in the famous writer's so-called writing shack, as if the partygoers were even partying there.

But Danny had left only the kitchen light on, in the new building; he'd left the other rooms (and the other buildings) dark. The music was loud and conflicting—it was coming from both the new building *and* the guesthouse, and every window must have been open. It was a wonder that someone hadn't called the police about the noise; though the writer's compound had no near neighbors, almost anyone driving by had to have heard the clashing music. Danny heard it, and saw all the lights ablaze even before he turned in to his driveway, where he stopped his car and turned off the engine and his headlights. There were no other cars around, except Joe's. (It was parked in the open garage, where Joe had left it the last time the boy had been home from school.) From the far end of his driveway, Danny could see that even the lights in the garage were on. If Amy were ever to forgo arriving via parachute, the writer was thinking, maybe this was how she would announce herself.

Or was it a prank? Pranks weren't Armando DeSimone's style. Other than Armando, Danny had no close friends in the Putney area—certainly no one who would have felt comfortable coming on the writer's property uninvited. Had Dot and May already called Carl? But those bad old broads didn't know where Danny lived, and if the cowboy had somehow managed to find Danny Angel, wouldn't the retired deputy have preferred the dark? Surely, the former constable and deputy sheriff wouldn't have turned on all the lights and the music; why would Carl have wanted to *announce* himself?

Furthermore, there was no occasion for a surprise party—not that the writer could think of. Maybe it *was* Armando, Danny was reconsidering, but the choice of music couldn't have been Armando's or Mary's. The DeSimones liked to dance; they were Beatles people. This sounded like *eighties'* music—the stuff Joe played when he was home. (Danny didn't know what the music was, but there were two separate sounds—both of them terrible, at war with each other.)

The *tap-tap* of the flashlight on the driver's-side window made Danny jump in the seat. He saw it was his friend Jimmy, the state trooper. Jimmy must have turned off the headlights of his patrol car when he'd slipped into the driveway and had parked broadside, behind Danny's car; he'd cut the police car's engine, too, not that Danny could possibly have heard the trooper's arrival over the music.

"What's with the music, Danny?" Jimmy asked him. "It's a little loud, isn't it? I think you should turn it down."

"I didn't turn it *on*, Jimmy," the writer said. "I didn't turn on the lights *or* the music."

"Who's in your house?" the trooper asked.

"I don't know," Danny said. "I didn't invite anyone."

"Maybe they've come and gone—shall I have a look?" Jimmy asked him.

"I'll come with you," Danny told the trooper.

"Have you had any letters from a crazy fan lately?" Jimmy asked the writer. "Or any hate mail, maybe?"

"Nothing like that for a while," Danny told him. There'd been the usual religious nuts, and the assholes who constantly complained about the writer's "unseemly" language or the "too-explicit" sex.

"Everyone's a fucking censor nowadays," Ketchum had said.

Once he published *East of Bangor*—his so-called abortion novel—the hate mail might heat up for a while, Danny knew. But there'd been nothing of a threatening nature recently.

"There's nobody out to get you—no one you know about, right?" Jimmy asked.

"There's someone who thinks he has a score to settle with my dad—someone dangerous," Danny said. "But this can't be about that," the writer said.

Danny followed the trooper into the kitchen of the new house first. Little things were amiss: The oven door was open; a bottle of olive oil lay on its side on the counter, but the cap was screwed on tight and the oil hadn't leaked. Danny walked into the living room, where he could shut off the loudest of the head-pounding music, and he noted that a coffee-table lamp now lay on the couch, but nothing appeared to have been damaged. The deliberate but small disturbances signified mischief, not vandalism; the television had been turned on, but without sound.

Though Danny had walked through the dining room on his way to the living room, which was the source of half the music, he'd noticed only that one of the chairs at the dining-room table had been up-ended. But Jimmy had lingered there, at the table. When Danny turned the music off, Jimmy said, "Do you know whose dog this is, Danny? I believe it's one of a pair of dogs I know out on the back road to Westminster West. The dogs belong to Roland Drake. Maybe you know him—he went to Windham."

The dead dog had stiffened since Danny last saw him—he was the husky-shepherd mix, the one Rooster had killed. The dog lay fully extended, with a frozen snarl, on the dining-room table. One of the dog's paws, contorted by rigor mortis, pressed flat the note Danny had composed to the hippie carpenter. Where Danny had typed, "Enough is enough, okay?" the hippie had replied in longhand.

"Don't tell me—let me guess," the writer said to the state trooper. "I'll bet the asshole wrote, 'Fuck you!'—or words to that effect."

"That's what he wrote, Danny," Jimmy said. "I guess you know him."

Roland Drake—*that* asshole! Danny was thinking. Armando DeSimone had been right. Roland Drake had been one of Danny's writing students at Windham College, albeit briefly. Drake had dropped the course after his first teacher's conference, when Danny told the arrogant young fuck that good writing could rarely be accomplished without revision. Roland Drake wrote first-draft gibberish—he had a halfway decent imagination, but he was sloppy. He paid no attention to specific details, or to the language.

"I'm into writing, not rewriting," Drake had told Danny. "I only like the *creative* part."

"But rewriting *is* writing," Danny said to the young man. "Sometimes, rewriting is the *most* creative part."

Roland Drake had sneered and walked out of Danny's office. That had been their only conversation. The boy hadn't been as hairy then; perhaps Drake hadn't been as drawn to the hippie persuasion when he was younger. And Danny had trouble recognizing people he previously knew. That was a real problem with being famous: You were always meeting people for what you thought was the first time, but they would remember that they'd already met you. It was probably an additional insult to Drake that Danny hadn't remembered him—not just that Danny had told Drake to mind his dog (or dogs).

"Yes, I know Roland Drake," Danny said to Jimmy. He told the state trooper the story—including the part about Rooster killing the dog that now lay stiffly on the dining-room table. From Danny's typed note, Jimmy could see for himself how the writer had tried to make peace with the asshole hippie. The *writer* carpenter, as Armando had called him, didn't know when enough was enough—no more than Roland Drake knew that rewriting *was* writing, and that it could be the most creative part of the process.

Danny and Jimmy went through the rest of the main house, turning off lights, putting things in order. In Joe's bathroom, the bathtub had been filled. The water was cold, but there was no mess; there'd been no spills. In Joe's bedroom, one of the boy's wrestling-team photos had been removed from the picture hook on the wall and was propped up (by a pillow) against the headboard of the bed. In Danny's bathroom, one of his suit jackets (on a coat hanger) had been hung on the shower-curtain rod; his electric razor and a pair of dress shoes were in the otherwise-empty bathtub. All the bath towels were piled at the foot of the bed in the master bedroom.

"Drake is just a shit-disturber, Danny," the trooper told him. "He's a little trust-fund fuck—they never dare to do any real damage, because they know their parents would end up having to pay for it."

The same small nuisances were everywhere, throughout the house. When they went to turn the lights out in the garage, Danny discovered a tube of toothpaste on the driver's seat of Joe's car; a toothbrush was tucked under the driver's-side sun visor.

There was more of the same juvenile mischief in the guesthouse— the original farmhouse—where the music had been cranked up as loud as it would go and the soundless TV was on. Lamps were tipped on their sides, a pyramid of lampshades decorated the kitchen table, several pictures had been rehung (upside down), and the beds were unmade—in a manner that made you think someone had slept in them.

"This is irritating, but it's mainly childish," Danny said to the trooper.

"I agree," Jimmy said.

"I'm selling the whole property anyway," Danny told him.

"Not because of *this*, I hope," the state trooper said.

"No, but this makes it easier," the writer answered. Because Danny knew he was moving away, and the Putney property would have to be sold, maybe Roland Drake's violation of the writer's personal effects felt like less of an invasion than it truly was—that is, until Danny and Jimmy came to the famous author's writing shack. Yes, all the lights were on, and some papers had been misplaced, but Drake had overstepped; he'd done some actual harm.

Danny had been proofreading the galleys of *East of Bangor.* As testimony to the novelist's ceaseless need to *re*write—to tamper with, to endlessly revise—Danny had written more than the usual number of notes and queries in the margins of the galleys. This demonstration— namely, that Danny Angel was both a writer and a rewriter—must have been too much to take for a *failed* writer (a writer *carpenter*) like Roland Drake. The evidence of rewriting in the galleys of Danny's soon-to-be-published next novel had pushed Drake over the edge.

With a Sharpie permanent marker, in deep black, Roland Drake had scrawled on the cover of the uncorrected proofs of *East of Bangor,* and inside the galleys, on every page, Drake had written his comments with a Sharpie fine-point red pen. Not that the writer carpenter's commentary was either insightful or elaborate, but Drake had taken the time to defile every page; there were more than four hundred pages in the galleys of *East of Bangor.* Danny had proofread three quarters of the novel, and—notwithstanding what a rewriter he was—he'd written notes or queries on only about fifteen or twenty of the pages. Roland Drake had crossed out Danny's notes and queries; he'd rendered the author's revisions unreadable. Drake had purposely made a mess of the galleys, but it needn't have cost Danny more than two weeks' additional work—not even that, under normal circumstances, though Drake's destruction of the writer's uncorrected proofs seemed greater than a merely symbolic assault.

But at a time when the cook and his son were confronted with the chaos of going on the run again, Roland Drake's attack on Danny's sixth novel might delay the publication of *East of Bangor* by several months—conceivably, for as long as half a year. The novel was scheduled to be published in the fall of '83. (Maybe not now—possibly, the book wouldn't be published until the winter of '84. With all that was newly happening in Danny's life, it would take the author a while to remember the revisions he'd already made in the galleys—and to find the time to proofread the last quarter of the novel.)

"Revise the chickenshit title!" Drake had scribbled on the cover of *East of Bangor,* in deep black. "Change the author's fake name!"

And in red, throughout the novel, while the writer carpenter's criticism demonstrated no great range or in-depth perception, Drake had underlined a phrase or circled a word—on four-hundred-plus pages— and he'd added a cryptic comment, albeit only one per page. "This sucks!" and "Rewrite!" were the most repeated, along with "Cut!" and "Dog-killer!" Less common were "Lame!" and "Feeble!" More than once, "Lengthy!" had been scrawled across the entire page. Only twice, but memorably, Drake had written, "I fucked Franky, too!"

(Perhaps Drake *had* slept with Franky, Danny only now considered; that might have contributed to the onetime writing student's animosity toward the bestselling author.)

"Have a look, Jimmy," Danny said to the trooper, handing him the desecrated copy of the galleys.

"Gee . . . this makes more work for you, I suppose," Jimmy said, turning the pages. " '*Year of the Dog* wouldn't publish this shit!' " the state trooper read aloud, with deadpan puzzlement. Jimmy always looked pained by what he didn't understand—at once heartbroken and baffled. For a cop who'd shot his share of dogs, Jimmy had the sad, droopy eyes of a Labrador retriever; tall and thin, with a long face, the trooper looked questioningly at Danny for some explanation of Roland Drake's ravings.

"*Year of the Dog* was a small literary magazine," Danny explained. "Either Windham College published it, or it was independently published by some Windham College students—I can't remember."

"Franky is a girl?" Jimmy asked, reading further.

"Yes," the writer answered.

"That young woman who lived here for a while—that one, right?" the trooper asked.

"That's her, Jimmy."

" 'You write with a limp!' " Jimmy read aloud. "Gee . . ."

"Drake should bury his own dog—don't you think, Jimmy?" Danny asked the trooper.

"I'll take Roland's dog back to him. We'll have a little talk," Jimmy said. "You could get a restraining order—"

"I don't need one, Jimmy—I'm leaving, remember?" Danny said.

"I know how to talk to Roland," the trooper said.

"Just watch out for the other dog, Jimmy—he comes at you from behind," Danny warned him.

"I won't shoot him if I don't have to, Danny—I only shoot them when I have to," the trooper said.

"I know," Danny told him.

"It's hard to imagine anyone out to get your dad," Jimmy ventured. "I can't conceive of someone having a score to settle with the cook. You want to tell me about that, Danny?" the cop asked.

Here was another intersection in the road, the writer thought.

What were these junctions, where making a sharp-left or sharp-right turn from the previously chosen path presented a tempting possibility? Hadn't there been an opportunity for Danny and his dad to go back to Twisted River, as if nothing had ever happened to Injun Jane? And of course there was the case of putting Paul Polcari back in the kitchen at Vicino di Napoli with Ketchum's single-shot 20-gauge— instead of putting someone back there who might have pulled the fucking trigger!

Well, wasn't this another opportunity to escape the conundrum? Just tell Jimmy *everything*! About Injun Jane, about Carl and Six-Pack Pam—about the retired deputy with his long-barreled Colt .45, that fucking cowboy! Short of asking Ketchum to kill the bastard, what other way out was there? And Danny knew that if he or his dad asked Ketchum outright, Ketchum would kill the cowboy. The old logger hadn't murdered Lucky Pinette in his bed with a stamping hammer; Lucky was probably asleep at the time, but the killer couldn't have been Ketchum, or there would be nothing holding Ketchum back from killing Carl.

But all Danny said to his state-trooper friend was, "It's about a woman. A long time ago, my dad was sleeping with a logging-camp constable's girlfriend. Later, the camp constable became a county deputy sheriff—and when he found out what had happened to his girlfriend, he came looking for my dad. The deputy is retired now, but we have reason to believe he might still be looking—he's crazy."

"A crazy ex-cop . . . that's not good," Jimmy said.

"The former deputy sheriff is getting old—that's the good part. He can't keep looking much longer," Danny told the trooper, who looked thoughtful; Jimmy also seemed suspicious.

There was more to the story, of course, and the state trooper probably could discern this in the writer's atypically vague telling of the tale. (And what trouble could Danny have gotten into for killing a woman he mistook for a bear when he'd been a twelve-year-old?) But Danny didn't say more about it, and Jimmy could tell that his friend was content to keep the matter to himself and his dad. Besides, there was a dead dog to deal with; the business at hand, giving Roland Drake a good talking-to, must have seemed more pressing to the state trooper.

"Have you got some of those large green garbage bags?" Jimmy asked. "I'll take care of that dog for you. Why don't you get a little sleep, Danny? We can talk more about the crazy old ex-cop when you want to."

"Thanks, Jimmy," Danny told his friend. Just like that, the writer was thinking, he'd driven past the intersection in the road. It hadn't even been in the category of a decision, but now the cook and his son could only keep driving. And how old was the cowboy, anyway? Carl was the same age as Ketchum, who was the same age as Six-Pack Pam. The retired deputy sheriff was sixty-six, not too old to squeeze a trigger—not yet.

From his driveway, Danny watched the taillights of the state-police patrol car as Jimmy drove off on Hickory Ridge Road. It wouldn't take the trooper long to get to Roland Drake's driveway of abandoned vehicles, and Drake's surviving husky-shepherd mix. Suddenly, it meant a lot to Danny to know what was going to happen when Jimmy brought the dead dog back to the asshole hippie. Would that really be the end of it? Was enough *ever* enough, or did the violence just perpetuate—that is, whenever something began violently?

Danny had to know. He got in his car and drove up Hickory Ridge Road until he spotted the trooper's taillights flickering ahead of him; then Danny slowed down. He could no longer keep the squad car's taillights in sight, but he kept following at a distance. Jimmy had probably seen Danny's headlights, albeit briefly. Surely the state policeman would have known he was being followed; knowing Jimmy, he would have guessed it was Danny, too. But Danny knew that he didn't need to *see* what happened when the trooper pulled into Roland Drake's salvage yard of a driveway. The writer knew he needed only to be near enough to hear the shot, if there was a shot.

IT TURNED OUT THAT Danny and his dad had more time than they knew, but they were wise not to count on it. They listened to Ketchum this time. For hadn't Ketchum been right the last time? Vermont *wasn't* far enough away from New Hampshire, as the old woodsman had told them. Would Dot and May have wandered into Mao's, in Iowa City? Not likely. For that matter, Danny wondered whether anyone from Coos County ever would have found the cook and his son in

Boulder, Colorado, where Joe would soon be going to school. Also unlikely, but the writer was persuaded not to take that chance, though leaving the country wouldn't be easy—not the way Ketchum meant it, because the logger had something *permanent* in mind. (Ketchum also had an idea about *where.*)

Ketchum had called the cook and his son, in the logger's hungover or fragile sobriety of the morning following Dot and May's calamitous visit to Avellino. Of course Ketchum phoned them individually, but it was irritating how the woodsman spoke to each of them as if both Danny and his dad were there.

"For thirteen years, the cowboy believed you two were in Toronto—because Carl thought that was where Angel was from, right? You *bet* I'm right!" Ketchum bellowed.

Dear God, the cook was thinking in his beloved kitchen at Avellino, where he'd made himself a very strong espresso and was wondering why Ketchum couldn't resist shouting to make himself heard. According to Ketchum, Dot and May had sizably less imagination than a pinch of coon shit; while "the gossip-feeding bitches" would definitely tell the cowboy what they knew, they wouldn't agree with each other about how to tell him, or when. Dot would be in favor of waiting until the retired deputy did something particularly obnoxious, or he was behaving in a superior fashion, whereas May would want to *insinuate* that she knew something—until Carl was crazy to know what it was. In short, the old broads' habits of mean-spirited manipulation might buy Danny and his dad a little time.

On the phone to Danny, Ketchum was more exact: "Here's the point, you two. Now that Carl knows you went to Boston, not Toronto—and he'll know soon enough that you then went to Vermont—the cowboy would never believe that you're in Toronto. That's the last place he'd look—that's where you should go! They speak English in Toronto. You've got a publisher there, don't you, Danny? And I imagine there's lots of jobs for a cook—something not Italian, Cookie, or I swear I'll come shoot you myself!"

I'm not Cookie, Danny almost said, but he just held the phone.

Toronto wasn't such a bad idea, the writer Danny Angel was thinking, as he waited out the mounting hysteria of Ketchum's phone call. Danny had been there on a book tour or two. It was a good city, he was thinking—to the degree that Danny thought about cities at all. (The cook was more of a city guy than his son.) Canada was a foreign country, thus satisfying Ketchum's criterion, but Toronto was near enough to the States to make keeping in touch with Joe possible; Colorado would be easy to get to from Toronto. Of course, Danny wanted to know what Joe might think of the idea—not to mention what the cook thought of Ketchum's suggestion.

After Ketchum ended his call to Danny, the writer's telephone rang almost immediately. Naturally, it was Danny's dad.

"There will be no peace while that lunatic has his own phone, Daniel," the cook said to his son. "And if he ever gets a fax machine, we will be doomed to be addressed in capital letters and exclamation points for the rest of our lives."

"But what do you think of Ketchum's idea, Dad? What about Toronto?" Danny asked.

"I don't care where we go—I'm just sorry to have dragged you into this. I was only trying to keep you *safe*!" his father said; then the cook started to cry. "I don't want to go *anywhere*," Tony Angel said. "I love it *here*!"

"I know you do—I'm sorry, Pop. But we'll be okay in Toronto—I know we will," the writer told his father.

"I can't ask Ketchum to kill Carl, Daniel—I just can't do it," the cook told his son.

"I know—I can't ask him, either," Danny said.

"You *do* have a publisher in Canada, don't you, Daniel?" his dad asked. For the first time, Danny could hear something old—something approaching *elderly*—in his father's voice. The cook was almost sixty, but what Danny had heard in his dad's voice sounded older than that; he'd heard something more than anxious, something almost frail. "If you have a publisher in Toronto," his father was saying, "I'm sure he'll help us get settled in there, won't he?"

"*She*—my Canadian publisher is a *she*," Danny told his dad. "I know she'll help us, Pop—it'll be easy there. And we'll get a place in Colorado, where we can visit Joe—and Joe can come visit us. We don't have to think of this move as necessarily *permanent*—not for a while, anyway. We'll just see how we like it in Canada, okay?"

"Okay," the cook said, but he was still crying.

I could leave Vermont *today,* the writer was thinking. Danny did not feel an attachment to his Putney property that nearly approximated his dad's love of Avellino in Brattleboro, or his father's life there. After Dot and May's appearance in the restaurant—not to mention Roland Drake's visit, and Drake's dead dog on the dining-room table—Danny felt that he could leave Vermont forever, and never look back.

When Carl eventually encountered those bad old broads Dot and May, the cowboy would get to Vermont too late. With Armando and Mary DeSimone's help, Danny had sold the Putney property by then; there was no writer's compound remaining on Hickory Ridge Road. And Windham College, where the writer Danny Angel had taught, was a college with a different name (and purpose) now—Landmark College, a leading institution for learning-disabled students. By the time the cowboy showed up in Brattleboro, Avellino itself would be gone—and wherever Greg, the sous chef, went, Carl wouldn't find him. At the cook's urging, Celeste and her daughter, Loretta (and Loretta's kid), left town. The cowboy would come up empty, once again, but there was no question that Dot and May had blabbed their best to him.

Was it possible that Carl was as much of an imbecile as Ketchum had, at times, maintained? Did the cowboy possess no better detective skills than those of Ketchum's much-maligned pinch of coon shit? Or was it simply that, throughout the retired deputy's investigations in Vermont, the *Angel* name had not come up? In Brattleboro, evidently, the cowboy had not inquired about the cook and his son at The Book Cellar!

"You knew Cookie was in Vermont—you knew it all along, didn't you, Ketchum?" Carl would one day ask the old logger.

"Cookie? Is *he* still around?" Ketchum said to the cowboy. "I wouldn't have figured that a little fella with a limp like his would be so long-lasting—would you, Carl?"

"Keep it up, Ketchum—you just keep it up," Carl said.

"Oh, I will—I'll keep it up, all right," Ketchum told the cowboy.

But Danny couldn't wait to leave Vermont; after the night he and Jimmy found the dead dog on the writer's dining-room table, Danny Angel wanted to be gone.

That night he'd driven no farther out the back road to Westminster West than the bottom of Barrett's long, uphill driveway. He had backed his car onto the animal lover's property. Danny knew that Barrett went to bed early, and that she wouldn't be aware of a car parked in her driveway—so far away from her horse farm that not even her horses would be disturbed by its presence. Besides, Danny had turned off the engine and his headlights. He just sat in the car, which was facing Westminster West with all the windows open.

It was a warm, windless night. Danny knew he could hear a gunshot for a couple of miles on such a night. What he didn't know at first was: Did he really want to hear it? And what would hearing or not hearing that gunshot signify, exactly? It was more than the survival or the death of Roland Drake's bite-you-from-behind husky-shepherd mix that the writer was listening for.

At forty-one, Danny felt like a twelve-year-old all over again; it didn't help that it had started to rain. He remembered the misty night he and his dad had left Twisted River in the Pontiac Chieftain—how he'd sat waiting in the station wagon, which was parked near Six-Pack Pam's. Danny had been listening for the discharge of Carl's Colt .45, which would mean his dad was dead. Upon the sound of that shot, the boy would have run up the stairs to Six-Pack's place; he would have begged her to let him in, and then Ketchum would have taken care of him. That had been the plan, and Danny had done his part; he'd sat in the car, in the falling rain, waiting to hear the gunshot that never came, though there were times when Danny felt he was still waiting to hear it.

On the back road to Westminster West—at the foot of his former lover's driveway—the writer Danny Angel was listening as alertly as he could. He was hoping he would never hear *that* shot—the earsplitting discharge of the cowboy's Colt .45—but it was with that shot in mind that the writer began to indulge the dangerous, *what-if* side of his imagination. *What if* the state trooper didn't have to shoot Roland Drake's other dog—*what if,* somehow, Jimmy could persuade the writer carpenter *and* his shepherd-husky mix that, truly, enough was enough? Might that signify an end to the violence, or to the threat of violence?

It was then that the writer was aware of what he was listening for:

nothing. It was nothing that he hoped he would hear. It was the *no-shot* that might mean his dad would be safe—that the cowboy, like Paul Polcari, might never pull the trigger.

Danny was trying not to think about what Jimmy had told him—this was concerning the tube of toothpaste and the toothbrush in Joe's car. Possibly, they'd not been put there by Roland Drake; maybe the toothpaste and the toothbrush hadn't been part of Drake's mischief.

"I hate to tell you this, Danny, but I've busted lots of kids who've been drinking in their cars," the trooper had said. "The kids often have toothpaste and a toothbrush handy—so their parents don't smell what they've been drinking on their breath, when they come home." But Danny preferred to think that the toothpaste and the toothbrush had been more of Drake's childish business. The writer didn't like to think about his son drinking and driving.

Was Danny superstitious? (Most writers who believe in plot are.) Danny didn't like to think about what Lady Sky had said to Joe, either. "If you're ever in trouble, I'll be back," she'd said to the two-year-old, kissing his forehead. Well, not on a night as dark as this one, the writer thought. On a night as dark as this one, no skydiver—not even Lady Sky—could see where to land.

Now the rain had blotted out what little moonlight there was; the rain was coming in the open windows of Danny's car, and the water had beaded on the windshield, which made the darkness more impenetrable.

Surely, the state trooper had already arrived in Drake's junkyard of a driveway. And what would Jimmy do then? Danny was wondering. Just sit in the patrol car until Drake had noticed the car was there and came outside to talk to him? (And would Roland have come out alone, or would he have brought the back-biting dog with him?) Then again, it was raining; out of consideration for the hippie carpenter, and because it was late, the trooper might have gotten out of his car and knocked on Drake's door.

At that thought came a knocking on the passenger-side door of Danny's car; a flashlight shone in the writer's face. "Oh, heart be still—it's just you," he heard Barrett say. His former lover, who was carrying a rifle, opened the car door and slipped inside to sit beside him. She was wearing her knee-high rubber stable boots and an oilskin poncho. She'd pushed back the hood when she got into the car, and her long white hair was unbraided—as if she'd gone to bed hours ago, and had suddenly been woken up. Barrett's thighs were bare; under the poncho, she was wearing nothing. (Danny knew, of course, that Barrett slept naked.) "Were you missing me, Danny?" she asked him.

"You're up late, aren't you?" Danny asked her.

"About an hour ago, I had to put one of my horses down—it was too late to call the bloody vet," Barrett told him. She sat like a man, with her knees spread apart; the carbine, with the barrel pointed to the floor, rested between her pretty dancer's legs. It was an old bolt-action Remington—a .30-06 Springfield, she'd explained to him, some years ago, when she'd shown up on his Putney property, where she was hunting deer. Barrett still hunted deer there; there was an untended apple orchard on the land, and Barrett had shot more than one deer in that orchard. (What had the cook called her—a "selective" animal lover, was it? Danny knew more than a few like her.)

"I'm sorry about your horse," he told her.

"I'm sorry about the gun—I know you don't like guns," she said. "But I didn't recognize your car—it's new, I guess—and one should take some precaution when there are strange men parked in one's driveway."

"Yes, I was missing you," Danny lied. "I'm leaving Vermont. Maybe I was just trying to remember it, before I go." This last bit was true. Besides, the fiction writer couldn't tell such a *selective* animal lover the dead-dog story—not to mention that he was waiting to hear the fate of a second dog—not on such a gloomy night as the one Dot and May had created, anyway.

"You're leaving?" Barrett asked him. "Why? I thought you liked it here—your dad *loves* his place in Brattleboro, doesn't he?"

"We're both leaving. We're . . . lonely, I guess," Danny told her.

"Tell me about it," Barrett said; she let the butt of the gun rest against her thigh while she took one of Danny's hands and guided it under the poncho, to her breast. She was so small—as petite as Katie had been, the writer realized—and in the silvery light of the blotted-out moon, in the near-total darkness of the car's interior, Barrett's white hair shone like the hair of Katie's ghost.

"I must have wanted to say good-bye," Danny said to her. He meant it, actually—this wasn't untrue. Might it not be a comfort to lie in the lithe, older woman's warm arms, and not think about anything else?

"You're sweet," Barrett said to him. "You're much too sad for my taste, but you're very sweet."

Danny kissed her on the mouth, the shock of her extremely white hair casting a ghostly glow on her narrow face, which she'd turned up to him while she closed her pale-gray, ice-cold eyes. This allowed Danny to look past her, out the open window of the car; he wanted to be sure he saw Jimmy's state-police cruiser if it passed by on the road.

How long did it take to deliver a dead dog to the animal's owner, and to deliver whatever lecture Jimmy had in mind for the asshole hippie? Danny was wondering. Almost certainly, if the trooper was going to be forced to shoot Drake's other dog, Danny would already have heard the shot; he'd been listening and listening for it, even over his conversation with Barrett. (It was better to kiss her than to talk; the kissing was quiet. There would be no missing the gunshot, if there was one.)

"Let's go up to my house," Barrett murmured to him, breaking away from the kiss. "I just shot my horse—I want to take a bath."

"Sure," Danny said, but he didn't reach for the key in the ignition. The squad car hadn't driven past Barrett's driveway, and there'd been no shot.

The writer tried to imagine them—Jimmy and the writer carpenter. Maybe the trooper and Roland Drake, that trust-fund fuck, were sitting at the hippie's kitchen table. Danny tried to envision Jimmy patting the husky-shepherd mix, or possibly scratching the dog's soft ears—most dogs liked it when you did that. But Danny had trouble seeing such a scene; that was why he hesitated before starting his car.

"What is it?" Barrett asked him.

The shot was louder than he'd expected; though Drake's driveway was two or three miles away, Danny had underestimated the sound of Jimmy's gun. (He'd been thinking that the trooper carried a .38, but—not knowing guns, handguns especially—Danny didn't know that Jimmy liked a .475 Wildey Magnum, also known as the Wildey Survivor.) There was a muffled bang—even bigger than the cowboy's

Colt .45, Danny only realized as Barrett flinched in his arms, her fingers locating but scarcely touching the trigger of her Remington.

"Some bloody poacher—I'll give Jimmy a call in the morning," Barrett said; she had relaxed again in his arms.

"Why call Jimmy?" Danny asked her. "Why not the game warden?"

"The game warden is worthless—the bloody fool is afraid of poachers," Barrett said. "Besides, Jimmy knows who all the poachers are. They're all afraid of him."

"Oh," was all Danny could say. He didn't know anything about poachers.

Danny started the engine; he turned on his headlights and the windshield wipers, and he and Barrett put up the windows of the car. The writer turned around in the road and headed up the long driveway to the horse farm—not knowing which piece of the puzzle was missing, and not sure what part of the story was still ongoing.

One thing was clear, as Barrett sat beside him with the carbine now across her lap, the short barrel of the lightweight rifle pointed at the passenger-side door. Enough was never enough; there would be no stopping the violence.

IV.

TORONTO, 2000

—

THE BLUE MUSTANG

IT WAS NOT FAR FROM THEIR ROSEDALE NEIGHBORHOOD, WHERE the cook shared a three-story four-bedroom house with his writer son, to the restaurant on Yonge Street. But at his age—he was now seventy-six—and with his limp, which had noticeably worsened after seventeen years of city sidewalks, Dominic Baciagalupo, who'd reclaimed his name, was a slow walker.

The cook now limped along the slippery sidewalk; winter had never been his friend. And today Dominic was worrying about those two new condominiums under construction, virtually in their backyard. What if one or the other of these eclipsed Daniel's writing-room view of the clock tower on the Summerhill liquor store?

"When I can no longer see the clock tower from my desk, it's time for us to move," Danny had told his dad.

Whether his son was serious or not, the cook was no fan of moving; he'd moved enough. The view from the house on Cluny Drive was of no concern to Dominic. He'd not had any alcohol for more than fifty-six years; the cook couldn't have cared less that a couple of condominiums-in-progress might keep him from seeing the Summerhill liquor store.

Was it because Daniel was drinking again that he cared about losing his view of the liquor store? Dominic wondered. And for how long would the construction sites be an eyesore? the cook was fretting. (Dominic was of an age when anything that made a mess bothered him.) Yet he liked living in Rosedale, and he loved the restaurant where he worked.

Dominic Baciagalupo also loved the sound of tennis balls, which he could hear in the warm-weather months, when the windows were open in the house on Cluny Drive, because the cook and his son lived within sight and sound of the courts belonging to the Toronto Lawn Tennis Club, where they could also hear the voices of children in the swimming pool in the summer. Even in the winter months, when all the windows were closed, they slept to the sound of the slowly moving trains that snaked through midtown Toronto and crossed Yonge Street on the trestle bridge, which the cook now saw was adorned with Christmas lights, enlivening the dull, gray gloom of early afternoon.

It was December in the city. The festive lights, the decorations, the shoppers were all around. As he stood waiting for the crossing light on Yonge Street to change, it was a mild shock to Dominic to suddenly remember that Ketchum was coming to Toronto for Christmas; while this wasn't a recent phenomenon, the cook couldn't get used to the unnaturalness of the old logger being in the city. It had been fourteen years since the writer Danny Angel and his dad had spent their Christmases in Colorado with Joe. (Ketchum had not made those trips. It was too long a drive from New Hampshire to Colorado, and Ketchum steadfastly refused to fly.)

In those winters when Joe went to the university in Boulder, Daniel had rented a ski house in Winter Park. The road out of Grand Lake, through Rocky Mountain National Park, was closed in the wintertime, so it took about two hours to drive from Boulder—you had to take I-70, and U.S. 40 over Berthoud Pass—but Joe loved the skiing in Winter Park, and his dad had spoiled him. (Or so the cook reflected, as he waited for the long light on Yonge Street to change.)

Those Christmases in Colorado were beautiful, but the house in Winter Park had been too much of a temptation for Joe—especially during the remainder of the ski season, when the young college student's father and grandfather were back in Toronto. Naturally, the boy was going to cut some classes—if not every time there was fresh snow in the ski area. The nearby skiing alone would have tempted any college kid in Boulder, but having a house in Winter Park at his disposal—it was within walking distance of the ski lifts—was almost certainly Joe's undoing. (Oh, Daniel, what were you thinking? Dominic Baciagalupo thought.)

At last, the light changed and the cook limped across Yonge Street, mindful of those harebrained city drivers who were desperate to find a parking place at the Summerhill liquor store or The Beer Store. What had his writer son once called the neighborhood? the cook tried to remember. Oh, yes, Dominic recalled. "Shopping for hedonists," Daniel had said.

There were some fancy markets there; it was true—excellent produce, fresh fish, great sausages and meats, but ridiculously expensive, in the cook's opinion—and now, in the holiday season, it seemed to Dominic that every bad driver in town was buying booze! (He did not fault his beloved Daniel for drinking again; the cook understood his son's reasons.)

The icy wind whipped the long way up Yonge Street from Lake Ontario as Dominic fumbled with his gloves and the key to the restaurant's locked door. The waitstaff and most of the kitchen crew entered the kitchen from Crown's Lane—the alleyway parallel to Yonge Street, behind the restaurant—but the cook had his own key. Turning his back to the wind, he struggled to let himself in the front door.

The winters had been colder in Coos County—and in Windham County, Vermont, too—but the damp, penetrating cold of the wind off the lake reminded Dominic Baciagalupo of how cold he'd been in the North End of Boston. Though he'd had Carmella to keep him warm, the cook was remembering. He missed her—her alone, *only* Carmella—but Dominic strangely *didn't* miss having a woman in his life. Not anymore, not at his age.

Why was it that he didn't miss Rosie? the cook caught himself thinking. "Nowadays, Cookie," Ketchum had said, "I sometimes find myself *not* missing her. Can you imagine that?" Yes, he could, Dominic had to admit. Or was it the tension among the three of them—or Jane's harsh judgment, or keeping Daniel in the dark—that Ketchum and the cook didn't miss?

—

INSIDE THE RESTAURANT, Dominic was greeted by the smell of what Silvestro, the young chef, called "the mother sauces." The veal *jus*—the mother of all mother sauces—had been started during the dinner service last night. It underwent both a first and a second boil before a final reduction. Silvestro's other mother sauces were a tomato sauce and a béchamel. The cook, as he hung up his coat and scarf—and halfheartedly attempted to rearrange what Joe's favorite ski hat had done to his hair—could somehow smell *all* the mother sauces at once.

"The old pro," they called him in the kitchen, although Dominic was content with the role of sous chef to the masterful Silvestro, who was the *saucier* and did all the meats. Kristine and Joyce did the soups and the fish—they were the first women chefs the cook had worked with—and Scott was the bread and dessert guy. Dominic, who was semiretired, was the odd-job man in the kitchen; he did start-up and finish-up jobs from each station, which included spelling Silvestro with the sauces and the meats. "Jack of all trades," they called the cook in the kitchen, too. He was older than any of them, by far—not just Silvestro, their hotshot young chef, whom Dominic adored. Silvestro was like a second son to him, the cook thought—not that he ever would have said so to his beloved Daniel.

Dominic had also been careful not to mention the filial nature of his feelings for young Silvestro to Ketchum—partly because the woodsman was now a veteran and bullying faxer. Ketchum's faxes to the cook and his son were ceaseless and indiscriminate. (You could sometimes read a page or more without knowing who the fax was for!) And Ketchum's faxes arrived at all hours of the day and night; for the sake of a good night's sleep, Danny and his dad had been forced to keep the fax machine in the kitchen of their house on Cluny Drive.

More to the point, Ketchum had issues regarding Silvestro; the young chef's name was too Italian for the old logger's liking. It wouldn't be good if Ketchum knew that his pal Cookie thought of Silvestro as "a second son"—no, Dominic didn't want to receive a slew of faxes from Ketchum complaining about that, too. Ketchum's *usual* complaints were more than enough.

I THOUGHT THIS WAS A FRENCH PLACE—WHERE YOU
WERE WORKING IN YOUR SEMIRETIRED FASHION,
COOKIE. YOU WOULDN'T BE THINKING OF CHANGING
THE RESTAURANT'S NAME, WOULD YOU? NOT TO ANY-
THING ITALIAN, I PRESUME! THAT NEW FELLA, THE
YOUNG CHEF YOU SPEAK OF—SILVESTRO? IS THAT HIS
NAME? WELL, HE DOESN'T SOUND VERY FRENCH TO ME!
THE RESTAURANT IS STILL CALLED <u>PATRICE</u>, RIGHT?

Yes and no, the cook was thinking; there was a reason he hadn't answered Ketchum's most recent fax.

THE OWNER AND maître d' of the restaurant, Patrice Arnaud, was
Daniel's age—fifty-eight. Arnaud had been born in Lyon but grew up
in Marseilles—at sixteen, he went to hotel school in Nice. In the
kitchen at Patrice, there was an old sepia-toned photograph of Arnaud as a teenager in chef's whites, but Arnaud's future would lie in
management; he had impressed the guests in the dining room of a
beach club in Bermuda, where he'd met the proprietor of Toronto's
venerable Wembley Hotel.

When the cook had first come to Toronto, in '83, Patrice Arnaud
was managing Maxim's—a favorite café rendezvous in the Bay and
Bloor area of the city. At the time, Maxim's was the third transformation of a café-restaurant in the tired old Wembley. To Dominic Baciagalupo, who was still quaking from Ketchum's dire warning that he
totally detach himself from the world of Italian restaurants, Patrice
Arnaud and Maxim's were clearly first-rate—better yet, they were not
Italian. In fact, Patrice had enticed his brother, Marcel, to leave Marseilles and become the chef at Maxim's, which was very French.

"Ah, but the ship is sinking, Dominic," Patrice had warned the
cook; he meant that Toronto was rapidly changing. The restaurant-
goers of the future would want to venture beyond the staid hotel
restaurants. (After Arnaud and his brother left Maxim's, the old
Wembley Hotel became a parking garage.)

For the next decade, the cook worked with the Arnaud brothers at
their own restaurant on Queen Street West—a neighborhood in tran-

sition, and somewhat seedy for much of that time, but the restaurant, which Patrice named Bastringue, prospered. They were doing fifty covers at lunch and dinner; Marcel was the master chef then, and Dominic loved learning from him. There was foie gras, there were fresh Fine de Claire oysters from France. (Once again, the cook failed to teach himself desserts; he never mastered Marcel's tarte tatin with Calvados sabayon.)

Bastringue—Parisian *argot* for a popular dance hall and bar that served food and wine—would even weather the 1990 recession. They put waxed paper over the linen tablecloths and turned the restaurant into a bistro—steak frites, steamed mussels with white wine and leeks—but their lease ran out in '95, after Queen Street West had gone from seedy to hip to dull mainstream in the space of a decade. (Bastringue became a shoe store; Marcel went back to France.)

The cook and Patrice Arnaud stuck together; they went to work at Avalon for a year, but Arnaud told Dominic that they were "just biding time." Patrice wanted another place of his own, and in '97 he bought what had been a failed restaurant on Yonge Street at Summerhill. As for Silvestro, he originally came from Italy, but he was a Calabrese who'd worked in London and Milan; travel was important to Arnaud. ("It means you can learn new things," Patrice told Dominic, when he decided on young Silvestro as his next master chef.)

As for the new restaurant's name, *Patrice*—well, what else would Arnaud have called it? "You earned it," Dominic told Patrice. "Don't be embarrassed by your own name."

For the first few years, Patrice—the name and, to a lesser extent, the restaurant—had worked. Arnaud and the cook taught Silvestro some of Marcel's standbys: the lobster with mustard sabayon, the fish soup from Brittany, the duck foie-gras terrine with a spoonful of port jelly, the halibut *en papillote*, the *côte de boeuf* for two, the grilled calf's liver with lardons and pearl onions and a balsamic demi-glace. Naturally, Silvestro added his own dishes to the menu—ravioli with snails and garlic-herb butter, veal scallopini with a lemon sauce, house-made tagliatelle with duck confit and porcini mushrooms, rabbit with polenta gnocchi. (Dominic made a few familiar contributions to the menu, too.) The restaurant at 1158 Yonge Street was new, but it wasn't entirely French—nor was it as big a hit in the neighborhood as Arnaud had hoped.

"It's not just the name, but the name sucks, too," Patrice told Dominic and Silvestro. "I have totally misread Rosedale—this neighborhood doesn't need an expensive French restaurant. We need to be easygoing, and *cheaper*! We want our clientele to come two or three times a week, not every couple of months."

Over the Christmas break, Patrice was normally closed—this year from December 24 until January 2, enough time for the renovations Arnaud had planned. The banquettes would be brightened, completely recovered; the lemon-yellow walls were to be freshly spackled. Posters from the old French Line would be hung. "Le Havre, Southampton, New York—Compagnie Générale transatlantique!" Patrice had announced, and he'd found a couple of Toulouse-Lautrec posters of the Moulin Rouge dancer La Goulue and singer Jane Avril. Fish and chips were going to be added to the menu, and steak tartare with frites; the prices for both food and wine would drop 25 percent. It would be back to bistro, again—like those fabulous recession days at Bastringue—though Patrice wouldn't use the *bistro* word anymore. ("*Bistro* is so overused—it has become meaningless!" Arnaud declared.)

Reinvention was the essential game with restaurants, Arnaud knew.

"But what about the *name*?" Silvestro had asked his boss. The Calabrese had his own candidate, Dominic knew.

"I think *Patrice* is too French," Patrice had answered. "It's too old-school, too old-money. It has to go." Arnaud was smart and suave; his style was casual but debonair. Dominic loved and admired the man, but the cook had been dreading this part of the changeover—all to accommodate the preening Rosedale snobs.

"You guys know what I think," Silvestro said, with an insincere, insouciant shrug; he was handsome and confident, the way you would want your son to be.

The young chef had been struck by the effect of the frosted glass on the lower half of the restaurant's large front window, facing Yonge Street. Passersby on the street could not see through the clouded glass;

the customers, seated at their tables, were not in view from the sidewalk. But the top half of the big pane of glass was clear; diners could see the red maple leaf on the Canadian flag above the Summerhill liquor store, across Yonge Street, and (eventually) those two high-rise condominiums under construction in what would be called Scrivener Square. The lower, frosted portion of the windowpane had the effect of a curtain—such was Silvestro's convoluted reasoning for the restaurant's new name.

"La Tenda," Silvestro said, with feeling. " 'The Curtain.' "

"It sounds ominous to me," Dominic had told the young chef. "I wouldn't want to eat in a place with that name."

"I think, Silvestro, you should save this name for the very first restaurant you own—when you become an owner-chef, which you certainly will!" Arnaud said.

"La Tenda," Silvestro repeated, fondly, his warm brown eyes watering with tears.

"It's too Italian," Dominic Baciagalupo told the emotional young man. "This restaurant may not be strictly French, but it's not Italian, either." If the former Patrice were given an Italian name, what would Ketchum say? the cook was thinking, while at the same time he saw the absurdity of his argument—he whose Sicilian meat loaf and penne *alla puttanesca* would, after the Christmas holiday, be added to the more low-key menu.

The baffled Patrice and the shocked Silvestro stared at the cook in disbelief. They were all at a standstill. Dominic thought: I should ask Daniel to come up with a name—he's the writer! That was when Silvestro broke the silence. "What about *your* name, Dominic?" the young chef said.

"Not *Baciagalupo*!" the cook cried, alarmed. (If the cowboy didn't kill him, Dominic knew that Ketchum would!)

"Talk about *too Italian*!" Arnaud said affectionately.

"I mean what your name *means*, Dominic," Silvestro said. Patrice Arnaud hadn't guessed Baciagalupo's *meaning*, though the words were similar in French. " 'Kiss of the Wolf,' " Silvestro said slowly—the emphasis equally placed on both the *Kiss* and the *Wolf*.

Arnaud shuddered. He was a short, strongly built man with closely cropped gray hair and a sophisticated smile—he wore dark trousers, sharply pressed, and always an elegant but open-necked shirt. He was a man who made ceremony seem natural; at once polite and philosophical, Patrice was a restaurateur who understood what was worthwhile about the old-fashioned while knowing instantly when change was good.

"Ah, well—Kiss of the Wolf!—why didn't you tell me, Dominic?" Arnaud impishly asked his loyal friend. "Now *there's* a name that is seductive and modern, but it also has an *edge!*"

Oh, Kiss of the Wolf had an *edge*, all right, the cook was thinking—though that wouldn't be the most salient response Ketchum might make to the restaurant's new name. Dominic didn't want to imagine what the old logger would say when he heard about it. "Mountains of moose shit!" Ketchum might declare, or something worse.

Wasn't it risky enough that the cook had taken back his real name? In an Internet world, what danger did it present that there was a Dominic Baciagalupo back in action? (At least Ketchum was somewhat relieved to learn that, at the height of her phonetic sensibilities, Nunzi had misspelled the *Baciacalupo* word!)

But, realistically thinking, how would it be possible for a retired deputy sheriff in Coos County, New Hampshire, to discover that a restaurant called Kiss of the Wolf in Toronto, Ontario, was the English translation of the phonetically made-up name of Baciagalupo? And don't forget, the cook reassured himself—the cowboy is as old as Ketchum, who's *eighty-three!*

If I'm not safe now, I never will be, Dominic was thinking as he came into the narrow, bustling kitchen of Patrice—soon to be renamed Kiss of the Wolf. Well, it's a world of accidents, isn't it? In such a world, more than the names would keep changing.

DANNY ANGEL WISHED with all his heart that he had never given up the name Daniel Baciagalupo, not because he wanted to be the more innocent boy and young man he'd once been—or even because Daniel Baciagalupo was his one true name, the only one his parents had given him—but because the fifty-eight-year-old novelist believed it was a better name for a writer. And the closer the novelist came to sixty, the less he felt like a Danny or an Angel; that his father had all along insisted on the *Daniel* name made more and more sense to the son. (Not that it was always easy for a stay-at-home, work-at-home writer, who was almost sixty, to share a house with his seventy-six-year-old dad. They could be a contentious couple.)

Given the disputed presidential election in the United States—"the Florida fiasco," as Ketchum called George W. Bush's "theft" of the presidency from Al Gore, the result of a 5–4 Supreme Court vote along partisan lines—the faxes from Ketchum were often incendiary. Gore had won the popular vote. The Republicans stole the election, both Danny and his dad believed, but the cook and his son didn't necessarily share Ketchum's more extreme beliefs—namely, that they were "better off being Canadians," and that America, which Ketchum obdurately called an "asshole country," deserved its fate.

WHERE ARE THE ASSASSINS WHEN YOU WANT ONE?

Ketchum had faxed. He didn't mean George W. Bush; Ketchum meant that someone should have killed Ralph Nader. (Gore would have beaten Bush in Florida if Nader hadn't played the *spoiler* role.) Ketchum believed that Ralph Nader should be bound and gagged—"preferably, in a child's defective car seat"—and sunk in the Androscoggin.

During the second Bush-Gore presidential debate, Bush criticized President Clinton's use of U.S. troops in Somalia and the Balkans. "I don't think our troops ought to be used for what's called nation-building," the future president said.

YOU WANT TO WAIT AND SEE HOW THAT LYING LITTLE FUCKER WILL FIND A WAY TO USE OUR TROOPS? YOU WANT TO BET THAT "NATION-BUILDING" WON'T BE PART OF IT?

Ketchum had faxed.

But Danny didn't relish America's impending disgrace—not from the Canadian perspective, particularly. He and his dad had never wanted to leave their country. To the extent it was possible for an internationally bestselling author to *not* make a big deal of changing his citizenship, Danny Angel had tried to play down his politics, though this had been harder to do after *East of Bangor* was published in '84; his abortion novel was certainly political.

The process of Danny and his dad being admitted to Canada as new citizens was a slow one. Danny had applied as self-employed; the immigration lawyer representing him had categorized the writer as "someone who participates at a world-class level in cultural activities." Danny made enough money to support himself and his father. They'd both passed the medical exam. While they were living in Toronto on visitors' visas, it had been necessary for them to cross the border every six months to have their visas validated; also, they'd had to apply for Canadian citizenship at a Canadian consulate in the United States. (Buffalo was the closest American city to Toronto.)

An assistant to the Minister of Immigration and Citizenship had discouraged them from a so-called fast-track application. In their case, what was the hurry? The famous writer wasn't *rushing* to change countries, was he? (The immigration lawyer had forewarned Danny that Canadians were a little suspicious of success; they tended to punish it, not reward it.) In fact, to escape undue attention, the cook and his son had made the slowest possible progress in their application for Canadian citizenship. The process had taken four, almost five years. But now, with the Florida fiasco, there'd been comments in the Canadian media about the writer Danny Angel's "defection"; his "giving up on the United States" when he did, more than a decade ago, made the author appear "prescient"—or so the Toronto *Globe and Mail* had said.

It didn't help that the film adapted from *East of Bangor* had released in theaters only recently—in '99—and the movie had won a couple of Academy Awards in 2000. Early in the New Year, 2001, a joint session of Congress would meet to certify the electoral vote in the States; now that there was going to be a U.S. president who opposed abortion rights, it came as no surprise to Danny and his dad that the writer's liberal abortion politics were back in the news. And writers were more in the news in Canada than in the United States—not only for what they wrote but for what they said and did.

Danny was still sensitive to what he read about himself in the American media, where he was frequently labeled "anti-American"—both for his writing and because of his expatriation to Toronto. In other parts of the world—without fail, in Europe and in Canada—the author's alleged anti-Americanism was viewed as a *good* thing. It was written that the expatriate writer "vilified" life in the United States—that is, in his novels. It had also been reported that the American-born author had moved to Toronto "to make a statement." (Despite Danny Angel's commercial success, he had accepted the fact that his Canadian taxes were higher than what he'd paid in the States.) But, as a novelist, Danny was increasingly uncomfortable when he was condemned *or* praised for his perceived anti-American politics. Naturally, he couldn't say—most of all, not to the press—why he had *really* moved to Canada.

What Danny *did* say was that only two of his seven published novels could fairly be described as political; he was aware that he sounded defensive in saying this, but it was notably true. Danny's fourth book, *The Kennedy Fathers,* was a Vietnam novel—it was read as a virtual protest of that war. The sixth, *East of Bangor,* was a didactic novel—in the view of some critics, an abortion-rights polemic. But what was political about the other five books? Dysfunctional families; damaging sexual experiences; various losses of innocence, all leading to regret. These stories were small, domestic tragedies—none of them condemnations of society or government. In Danny Angel's novels, the villain—if there was one—was more often human nature than the United States. Danny had never been any kind of activist.

"All writers are outsiders," Danny Angel had once said. "I moved to Toronto because I like being an outsider." But no one believed him. Besides, it was a better story that the world-famous author had rejected the United States.

Danny thought that his move to Canada had been sensationalized in the press, the presumed politics of their entirely personal decision magnified out of proportion. Yet what bothered the novelist more was that his novels had been trivialized. Danny Angel's fiction had been ransacked for every conceivably autobiographical scrap; his novels had been dissected and overanalyzed for whatever could be construed as the virtual memoirs hidden inside them. But what did Danny expect?

In the media, real life was more important than fiction; those elements of a novel that were, at least, based on personal experience were of more interest to the general public than those pieces of the novel-writing process that were "merely" made up. In any work of fiction, weren't those things that had *really happened* to the writer—or, per-haps, to someone the writer had intimately known—more authentic, more verifiably true, than anything that anyone could imagine? (This was a common belief, even though a fiction writer's job was imagin-ing, truly, a whole story—as Danny had subversively said, whenever he was given the opportunity to defend the *fiction* in fiction writing—because real-life stories were never whole, never complete in the ways that novels could be.)

Yet who was the audience for Danny Angel, or any other novelist, defending the *fiction* in fiction writing? Students of creative writing? Women of a certain age in book clubs, because weren't most book-club members usually women of a certain age? Who else was more in-terested in fiction than in so-called real life? Not Danny Angel's interviewers, evidently; the first question they always asked had to do with what was "real" about this or that novel. Was the main character based on an *actual* person? Had the novel's most memorable (meaning most catastrophic, most devastating) outcome *actually* happened to anyone the author knew or had known?

Once again, what did Danny expect? Hadn't he begged the ques-tion? Just look at his last book, *Baby in the Road;* what did Danny think the media would make of it? He had begun that book, his sev-enth novel, before he'd left Vermont. Danny was almost finished with the manuscript in March '87. It was late March of that year when Joe died. In Colorado, it was not yet mud season. ("Shit, it was *almost* mud season," Ketchum would say.)

It was Joe's senior year in Boulder; he had just turned twenty-two. The irony was that *Baby in the Road* had always been about the death of a beloved only child. But in the novel Danny had almost finished, the child dies when he's still in diapers—a two-year-old, run over in the road, much as what *might* have happened to little Joe that day on Iowa Avenue. The unfinished novel was about how the death of that child destroys what the cook and Ketchum would no doubt have de-scribed as the Danny character and the Katie character, who go their separate but doomed ways.

Naturally, the novel would change. After the death of his son, Danny Angel didn't write for more than a year. It was not the writing that was hard, as Danny said to his friend Armando DeSimone; it was the *imagining*. Whenever Danny tried to imagine anything, all he could see was how Joe had died; what the writer also endlessly imagined were the small details that might have been subject to change, those infinitesimal details that could have kept his son alive. (If Joe had only done this, not that . . . if the cook and his son had not been in Toronto at that time . . . if Danny had bought or rented a house in Boulder, instead of Winter Park . . . if Joe had not learned to ski . . . if, as Ketchum had advised, they'd never lived in Vermont . . . if an avalanche had closed the road over Berthoud Pass . . . if Joe had been too drunk to drive, instead of being completely sober . . . if the passenger had been another boy, not that girl . . . if Danny hadn't been in love. . . .) Well, was there anything a writer *couldn't* imagine?

What *wouldn't* Danny have thought of, if only to torture himself? Danny couldn't bring Joe back to life; he couldn't change what had happened to his son, the way a fiction writer could revise a novel.

When, after that year had passed, Danny Angel could finally bear to reread what he'd written in *Baby in the Road*, the accidental killing of that two-year-old in diapers, which once began the book, not to mention the subsequent tormenting of the dead toddler's parents, seemed almost inconsequential. Wasn't it worse to have a child escape death that first time, and grow up—only to die later, a young man in his prime? And to make the story *worse* in that way, in a novel—to make what happens more heartbreaking, in other words—well, wasn't that actually a *better* story? Doubtless, Danny believed so. He'd rewritten *Baby in the Road* from start to finish. This had taken another five, almost six years.

Not surprisingly, the theme of the novel didn't change. How could it? Danny had discovered that the devastation of losing a child stayed very much the same; it mattered little that the details were different.

BABY IN THE ROAD WAS FIRST PUBLISHED IN 1995, eleven years after the publication of *East of Bangor* and eight years after Joe had died. In the revised version, the former two-year-old grows up to be a risk-taking young man; he dies at Joe's age, twenty-two, when he's still a college student. The death is ruled an accident, though it might have been a suicide. Unlike Joe, the character in Danny's seventh novel is drunk at the time of his death; he has also swallowed a shitload of barbiturates. He inhales a ham sandwich and chokes to death on his own vomit.

In truth, by the time he was a senior in college, Joe seemed to have outgrown his recklessness. His drinking—what little he did of it— was in control. He skied fast, but he'd had no injuries. He appeared to be a good driver; for four years, he drove a car in Colorado and didn't get a single speeding ticket. He'd even slowed down with the girls a little—or so it had seemed to his grandfather and his dad. Of course the cook and his son had never stopped worrying about the boy; throughout his college years, however, Joe had honestly given them little cause to be concerned. Even his grades had been good—better than they'd been at Northfield Mount Hermon. (Like many kids who'd gone away from home to an independent boarding school, Joe always claimed that college was easier.)

As a novelist, Danny Angel had taken pains to make the arguably suicidal character in *Baby in the Road* as unlike Joe as possible. The young man in the book is a sensitive, artistic type. He's in delicate health—from the beginning, he seems fated to die—and he's no athlete. The novel is set in Vermont, not in Colorado. Revised, the boy's wayward mother isn't wayward enough to be a Katie character, although, like her doomed son, she has a drinking problem. In the rewrite, the Danny character, the boy's grieving father, doesn't give up drinking, but he's not an alcoholic. (He is never compromised or incapacitated by what he drinks; he's just depressed.)

In the first few years after Joe died, the cook would occasionally try to talk his son out of drinking again. "You'll feel better if you don't, Daniel. In the long run, you'll wish you hadn't gone back to it."

"It's for research, Pop," Danny would tell his dad, but that answer no longer applied—not after he'd rewritten *Baby in the Road,* and the book had been finished for more than five years. In the new novel that Danny was writing, the main characters weren't drinkers; Danny's drinking wasn't for "research"—not that it ever was.

But the cook could see that Danny didn't drink to excess. He had a couple of beers before dinner—he'd always liked the taste of beer—

and not more than a glass or two of red wine with his meal. (Without the wine, he didn't sleep.) It was clear that Dominic's beloved Daniel hadn't gone back to being the kind of drinker he used to be.

Dominic could also see for himself that his son's sadness had endured. After Joe's death, Ketchum observed that Danny's sadness had a look of permanence about it. Even interviewers, or anyone meeting the author for the first time, noticed it. Not surprisingly, in many of the interviews Danny had done for various publications of *Baby in the Road*, the questions about the novel's main subject—the death of a child—had been personal. In every novel, there are parts that hit uncomfortably close to home for the novelist; obviously, these are areas of emotional history that the writer would prefer not to talk about.

Wasn't it enough that Danny had made every effort to detach himself from the personal? He'd enhanced, he'd exaggerated, he'd stretched the story to the limits of believability—he'd made the most awful things happen to characters he had imagined as completely as possible. ("So-called real people are never as complete as wholly imagined characters," the novelist had repeatedly said.) Yet Danny Angel's interviewers had asked him almost nothing about the story and the characters in *Baby in the Road;* instead they'd asked Danny how he was "dealing with" the death of his son. Had the writer's "real-life tragedy" made him reconsider the importance of fiction—meaning the weight, the gravity, the relative value of the "merely" make-believe?

That kind of question drove Danny Angel crazy, but he expected too much from journalists; most of them lacked the imagination to believe that anything credible in a novel had been "wholly imagined." And those former journalists who later turned to writing fiction subscribed to that tiresome Hemingway dictum of writing about what you know. What bullshit was this? Novels should be about the people you know? How many boring but deadeningly realistic novels can be attributed to this lame and utterly uninspired advice?

But couldn't it be argued that Danny should have anticipated the personal nature of his interviewers' questions concerning *Baby in the Road*? Even nonreaders had heard about the accident that killed the famous writer's son. (To Ketchum's relief, the cowboy seemed to have missed it.) There'd also been the predictable pieces about the calamitous lives of celebrities' children—unfair in Joe's case, because the accident didn't appear to have been Joe's fault, and he hadn't been drinking. Yet Danny should have anticipated this, too: Before there was verification that alcohol wasn't a factor, there would be those in the media who too quickly assumed it had been.

At first, after the accident—and again, when *Baby in the Road* was published—Dominic had done his best to shield his son from his fan mail. Danny had let his dad be a first reader, understanding that the cook would decide which letters he should or shouldn't see. That was how the letter from Lady Sky was lost.

"You have some weird readers," the cook had complained one day. "And so many of your fans address you by your first name, as if they were your *friends*! It would unnerve me—how you have all these people you don't know presuming that they know you."

"Give me an example, Pop," Danny said.

"Well, I don't know," Dominic said. "I throw out more mail than I show you, you know. There was one letter last week—she might have been a *stripper,* for all I know. She had a stripper's *name.*"

"Like what?" Danny had asked his dad.

" 'Lady Sky,' " the cook had said. "Sounds like a stripper to me."

"I think her real name is Amy," Danny said; he tried to remain calm.

"You *know* her?"

"I know only one Lady Sky."

"I'm sorry, Daniel—I just assumed she was a *wacko.*"

"What did she say, Pop—do you remember?"

Naturally, the cook couldn't remember all the details—just that the woman seemed presumptuous and deranged. She'd written some gibberish about protecting Joe from pigs; she'd said she was no longer flying, as if she'd once been able to fly.

"Did she want me to write her back?" Danny asked his dad. "Do you remember where her letter was from?"

"Well, I'm sure there was a return address—they *all* want you to write them back!" the cook cried.

"It's okay, Pop—I'm not blaming you," Danny said. "Maybe she'll write again." (He didn't really think so, and his heart was aching.)

"I had no idea you *wanted* to hear from someone named Lady Sky, Daniel," the cook said.

Something must have happened to Amy; Danny wondered what it could have been. You don't jump naked out of airplanes for no reason, the writer thought.

"I was sure she was a crazy person, Daniel." With that, the cook paused. "She said she had lost a child, too," Dominic told his son. "I thought I would spare you those letters. There were quite a lot of them."

"Maybe you should show me those letters, Dad," Danny said.

After the discovery that Lady Sky had written to him, Danny received a few more letters from his fans who'd lost children, but he'd been unable to answer a single one of those letters. There were no words to say to those people. Danny knew, since he was one of them. He would wonder how Amy had managed it; in his new life, without Joe, Danny didn't think it would be all that hard to jump naked out of an airplane.

IN DANNY ANGEL'S WRITING ROOM, on the third floor of the house on Cluny Drive, there was a skylight in addition to the window with the view of the clock tower on the Summerhill liquor store. This had once been Joe's bedroom, and it occupied the entire third floor and had its own bathroom, with a shower but not a tub. The shower was adequate for a college kid like Joe, but the cook had questioned the extravagant size of the bedroom—not to mention the premier view. Wasn't this wasted on a young man attending school in the States? (Joe would never get to spend much time in Toronto.)

But Danny had argued that he wanted Joe to have the best bedroom, because maybe then his son would be more inclined to come to Canada. The room's isolation on the third floor also made it the most private bedroom in the house, and—for safety's sake—no third-floor bedroom should be without a fire escape, so Danny had built one. The room, therefore, had a private entrance. When Joe died, and Danny converted the boy's bedroom into a *writing* room, the novelist left his son's things as they were; only the bed had been removed.

Joe's clothes stayed in the closet and in the chest of drawers—even his shoes remained. All the laces were untied, too. Joe had not once taken off a pair of shoes by untying the laces first. He'd kicked off his shoes with the laces tied, and they were always tightly tied, with a

THE BLUE MUSTANG 379

double knot, as if Joe were still a little boy whose shoes often came un-tied. Danny had long been in the habit of finding his son's double-knotted shoes and untying the laces for him. It was a few months, or more, after Joe died before Danny had untied the last of Joe's shoelaces.

What with Joe's wrestling and skiing photographs on the walls, the so-called writing room was a virtual *shrine* to the dead boy. In the cook's mind, it was masochistic of his son to choose to write there, but a limp like Dominic's would keep him from investigating that third-floor writing room with any regularity; Dominic rarely ventured there, even when Daniel was away. With the bed gone, no one else would sleep there—apparently, that was what Danny wanted.

When Joe had been with them in Toronto, both the cook and his son could hear the boy's kicked-off shoes drop (like two rocks) above them—or the more subtle creaking of the floorboards whenever Joe was walking around (even barefoot, or in his socks). You could also hear that third-floor shower from the three bedrooms on the second floor. Each of the second-floor bedrooms had its own bath, with the cook's bedroom being at the opposite end of the long hall from his beloved Daniel's bedroom—hence father and son had some measure of privacy, because the guest room was between them.

That guest room and its bathroom had recently been spruced up—in readiness for Ketchum's expected arrival, the woodsman's now-annual Christmas visit—and because the bedroom door was open, both Danny and his dad couldn't help but notice that the cleaning woman had prominently placed a vase of fresh flowers atop the guest room's dresser. The bouquet was reflected in the dresser's mirror, mak-ing it appear, from the second-floor hall, as *two* vases of flowers. (Not that Ketchum would have noticed or acknowledged a *dozen* vases of flowers in his room, the writer thought.)

Danny guessed that the cleaning woman probably had a crush on Ketchum, though the cook claimed that Lupita must have pitied the logger for how old he was. The flowers were in anticipation of how near death Ketchum was, Dominic absurdly said—"the way people put flowers on a grave."

"You don't really believe that," Danny told his dad.

But the flowers and Lupita were a mystery. The Mexican cleaning woman never put a vase of flowers in the guest room for any other visitor to the Rosedale residence, and that guest room in the house on Cluny Drive was more than occasionally occupied—not only at Christmas. Salman Rushdie, the author with a death threat against him, sometimes stayed there when he was in Toronto; Danny Angel's other writer friends, both from Europe and the United States, often came to visit. Armando and Mary DeSimone were visitors to the city at least twice a year, and they always stayed with Danny and his dad.

Many of Danny's foreign publishers had slept in that guest room, which reflected the author's international reputation; the majority of the books in the room were translations of Danny Angel's novels. Hanging in that guest bedroom, too, was a framed poster of the French edition of *Baby in the Road—Bébé dans la rue.* (In the connecting bathroom, there was an oversize poster of the German translation of that same novel—*Baby auf der Strasse.*) Yet, in the mind of the Mexican cleaning woman, only Ketchum merited flowers.

Lupita was a wounded soul, and she certainly recognized the damage done to others. She could not clean Danny's third-floor writing room without weeping, though Lupita had never met Joe; in those years when he'd come to Canada from Colorado, Joe never stayed for long, and Danny and his dad had not yet met what the cook called "the Mexican marvel." They'd had a host of unsatisfactory cleaning women in those years.

Lupita was a relatively recent find, but she was visibly moved by these two saddened gentlemen who'd lost, respectively, a son and a grandson. She'd told the cook that she was worried about how Danny was doing, but to Danny she would only say: "Your boy is in Heaven—higher up than the third floor, Señor Angel."

"I'll take your word for it, Lupita," Danny had replied.

"*¿Enfermo?*" Lupita was always inquiring—not of the seventy-six-year-old cook but of his depressed fifty-eight-year-old son.

"No, I am not sick, Lupita," Danny never failed to answer her. "*Yo sólo soy un escritor.*" ("I am merely a writer"—as if that explained how miserable he must have looked to her.)

Lupita had lost a child, too; she couldn't speak of it to Danny, but she'd told the cook. There were no details, and there was scant mention of the child's father, a Canadian. If Lupita had ever had a husband, she'd also lost him. Danny didn't think there were many Mexicans in Toronto, but probably more would be coming soon.

Lupita seemed ageless, with her smooth brown skin and long black hair, though Danny and his dad guessed that she was somewhere between their ages, in her sixties, and while she wasn't a big woman, she was heavy—noticeably overweight, if not fat in a condemnatory way.

Because Lupita had a pretty face, and she was in the habit of leaving her shoes on the ground floor of the house (she crept about the upstairs barefoot, or in her socks), Danny once said to his father that Lupita reminded him of Injun Jane. The cook couldn't agree that there was any resemblance; Dominic had sternly shaken his head at the suggestion. Either Danny's dad was in denial regarding the obvious likeness Lupita shared with Jane, or else Danny's memory of the Indian dishwasher was misleading him—the way fiction writers are often misled by their memories.

IN THE LATE AFTERNOON, when the cook was busy with the dinner prep at Patrice, Danny often left his writing room on the third floor—just as the last of the sun, if there was any to speak of, was glimmering through the skylight. There was no visible sun on this gray December afternoon, which made it easier for the novelist to tear himself away from his desk. Whatever remaining light there was from the west barely managed to penetrate the second-floor hall. In his socks, Danny padded to his father's bedroom. When the cook was out, his son often went into that room to see the snapshots Dominic had pinned to the five bulletin boards hanging from the bedroom's walls.

There was an old-fashioned desk, with drawers, in his dad's bedroom, and Danny knew there were hundreds more photographs in those drawers. With Lupita's help, Dominic constantly rearranged the snapshots on his bulletin boards; the cook never threw a photo away, but instead returned each removed picture to one of the desk drawers. That way, twice-used (or thrice-used) photos became new again— once more displayed on the bulletin boards, the only telltale signs of their previous use being the excessive number of almost invisible pinpricks.

On the bulletin boards, the snapshots were intricately overlapped in a confusing but possibly thematic pattern—either of Dominic's de-sign or of Lupita's, because Danny knew that without the Mexican cleaning woman's assistance, his dad could not have managed to unpin and repin the photographs with such evident ardor and repetition. It was hard work, and because of where the bulletin boards were mounted on the walls, it was necessary to perch on the arm of a couch, or stand on a chair, in order to reach the uppermost sections—not a labor that the cook, with his limp, could easily perform. (Given what she weighed, and her estimated age, Danny worried about Lupita un-dertaking such a balancing act on a couch or a chair.)

In spite of his considerable imagination, Danny Angel couldn't fathom his father's logic; the overlapping snapshots defied either a historical or a visual interpretation. In an ancient black-and-white photograph, a surprisingly young-looking Ketchum appeared to be dancing with Injun Jane in what Danny clearly remembered was the cookhouse kitchen in Twisted River. That this old photo was juxta-posed with one (in color) of Danny with Joe (as a toddler) in Iowa was inexplicable—except that Danny recalled Katie being in that photo-graph, and the cook had cleverly overlapped her entirely with a photo of Carmella with Paul Polcari, standing in front of the pizza oven in Vicino di Napoli; either Tony Molinari or old Giusé Polcari must have snapped the picture.

Thus Vermont overlapped Boston, or vice versa—Avellino and Mao's were apparently interchangeable—and the Asian faces of the cook's own Iowa interlude appeared alongside more current Toronto-nians. The early days at Maxim's, which gave way to Bastringue on Queen Street West, would be captured next to Ketchum in one or an-other of his virtual wanigans of a pickup truck, or beside Joe as a col-lege student in Colorado—often on skis, or in a mountain-bike race—and there was even one of Joe's Iowa City friend Max, who (to-gether with Joe) had come close to being killed in that alleyway be-hind the Court Street house by the speeding blue Mustang. The portrait of the two eight-year-olds was bafflingly pinned next to one of the young culinary maestro Silvestro, being kissed on both cheeks by his female sous chefs, Joyce and Kristine.

Was it possible, Danny wondered, that most of the photographs had been pinned to the bulletin boards not only by Lupita's plump

hands but according to *her* artless plan? That would explain the seeming randomness of the arrangements—if the collages of snapshots had
been almost entirely up to Lupita, if the cook had played next to no
part in the overall design. (That might also explain, the writer
thought, why no picture of Ketchum was returned to the desk
drawers—not since Lupita had come to work for Danny and his dad.)

How had the eighty-three-year-old logger managed to make such
a romantic impression on the sixty-something Mexican cleaning
woman? Danny was thinking. The cook seemed to be nauseated by
the very idea; Lupita couldn't have encountered Ketchum more than
two or three times. "It must be because of Lupita's ardent Catholi-
cism!" Dominic had exclaimed.

To his dad's thinking, Danny knew, there could only be superstitious or nonsensical reasons for any woman in her right mind to be attracted to Ketchum.

NOW, IN HIS OWN BEDROOM, Danny changed into his workout
clothes. There were no photographs of Joe in Danny's bedroom;
Danny Angel had enough trouble sleeping without pictures of his
dead son. Except in the evenings—when he went out for dinner, or to
see a movie—Danny rarely left the house on Cluny Drive, and most
evenings his dad was working. Dominic's idea of semiretirement was
that he usually left the restaurant and took himself home to bed by
10:30 or 11:00 every night, even when Patrice was packed; that was retired enough for him.

When Danny was on a book tour, or otherwise out of town, the
cook went into his son's bedroom—just to remind himself of what
might have been, if Joe hadn't died. It grieved Dominic Baciagalupo
that the only photographs in his beloved Daniel's bedroom were of
the screenwriter Charlotte Turner, who was fifteen years younger than
his son—and, boy, did she look it. Charlotte was just twenty-seven
when she'd met Daniel—in '84, when he'd been forty-two. (This was
shortly after the cook and his son had come to Canada. *East of Bangor*
had just been published, and Joe was finishing his freshman year at
Colorado.) Charlotte was only eight years older than Joe, and she'd
been a very *young*-looking twenty-seven.

She was a young-looking forty-three now, the cook reflected. It

pained Dominic to see Charlotte's pictures, and to reflect on how fond
he was of the young woman; the cook believed that Charlotte would
have been the perfect wife for his lonely son.

But a deal is a deal. Charlotte had wanted children—"Just one
child, if that's all you can handle," she'd told Danny—and Danny had
promised her that he would get her pregnant and give her a child.
There was only one condition. (Well, perhaps the *condition* word was
wrong—maybe it was more of a *request.*) Would Charlotte wait to get
pregnant until after Joe had graduated from college? At the time, Joe
had three years to go at the University of Colorado, but Charlotte
agreed to wait; she would only be thirty when Joe got his undergraduate degree. Besides, as the cook recalled, she and Daniel had loved
each other very much. They'd been very happy together; those three
years hadn't seemed like such a long time.

At twenty-seven, Charlotte Turner was fond of saying, dramati-
cally, that she had lived in Toronto her "whole life." More to the point,
she'd never lived with anyone—nor had she ever kept a boyfriend for
longer than six months. When she met Danny, she was living in her
late grandmother's house in Forest Hill; her parents wanted to sell the
house, but she'd persuaded them to allow her to rent it. The house had
been a cluttered, messy place when her grandmother lived there, but
Charlotte had auctioned off the old furniture, and she'd turned the
downstairs into her office and a small screening room; upstairs, where
there was only one bathroom, she'd made a big bedroom out of three
smaller, practically useless rooms. Charlotte didn't cook, and the
house was unsuitable for entertaining; she'd left her grandmother's
antiquated kitchen as it was, because the kitchen was sufficient for
her. None of Charlotte's short-term boyfriends had ever spent the
night in that house—Danny would be the first—and Charlotte never
exactly moved in with Danny in the house on Cluny Drive.

The cook had offered to move out. He saw himself as a potential
invasion of his son's privacy, and Dominic desperately wanted Daniel's
relationship with Charlotte to succeed. But Charlotte wouldn't hear
of "evicting" Danny's dad, as she put it—not until after the wedding,
which was planned (more than two years in advance) for June '87, following Joe's college graduation. Joe would be Danny's best man.

At the time, it had seemed wise to wait on the wedding—and on Charlotte getting pregnant, and on having a new baby in the house. Danny had wanted to "shepherd" Joe through the boy's college years— that was the writer's word for it. But there were those in Toronto who knew Charlotte's history with men; they might have bet that a wedding as much as two years in the offing was unlikely, or that after leaving for one of her many trips to L.A., the young screenwriter simply wouldn't come back. In the short three years they'd been together, Charlotte had kept scarcely any clothes in Danny's bedroom closet, though she more often spent the night in that Cluny Drive house than Danny would at her place in Forest Hill. She did keep her share of toiletries in Danny's bathroom, and her considerable cosmetics.

Both Charlotte and Danny were early risers, and while Charlotte was attending to her hair and her skin—she had the most beautiful skin, the cook suddenly remembered—Danny made them breakfast. Then Charlotte would take the Yonge Street subway to St. Clair, where she would walk to her place in Forest Hill; she did a long day's work there.

Even after they were married, Charlotte always said, she planned to have an office outside the house on Cluny Drive. ("Besides, there isn't room here for all my clothes," she'd told Danny. "Even after your dad moves out, I'll need at least an office—if not an entire house—for my clothes.")

The clothes could mislead you about Charlotte, Dominic often recalled—especially when he saw pictures of her. However, like Danny with his novels, Charlotte was a workaholic with her scripts— no less so in the case of her proposed adaptation of *East of Bangor,* which was the reason she and Danny had met.

Charlotte knew all about Danny Angel's nonnegotiable rules regarding the sale of film rights to his novels; she'd seen the interviews, where Danny had said that someone would have to write a "halfway decent" adaptation *before* he would part with the movie rights to this or that book.

The tall twenty-seven-year-old—she was a head taller than Daniel, the cook would remember, which made Charlotte closer in height *and* age to Joe than she was to Danny or his dad—had agreed to write the first draft of a screenplay of *East of Bangor* "on spec." No money would change hands, no film rights would pass; if Danny didn't like her script, Charlotte would simply be out of luck.

"You must already see a way to make a movie out of this novel," Danny had said when they first met. (He didn't do lunch, he'd told her. They met for dinner at Bastringue, where—in those days—Danny must have eaten three or four nights a week.)

"No, I just want to do this—I have no idea how," Charlotte said. She wore dark-framed glasses, and was very studious-looking, but there was nothing bookish about her body; she was not only tall but had a voluptuous figure. (She must have outweighed Daniel by a few pounds, as the cook recalled.) She was a big girl to wear a pink dress, Danny had thought that first night, and her lipstick was a matching pink, but Charlotte did a lot of business in L.A.; even in '84, she looked more like Los Angeles than Toronto.

Danny had really liked the first draft of her screenplay of *East of Bangor*—he'd liked it well enough to sell Charlotte Turner the movie rights to his novel for one dollar, Canadian, which at the time was worth about seventy-five cents, U.S. They'd worked together on subsequent drafts of the script, so Danny had seen for himself how hard Charlotte worked. In those days, Danny's writing room was on the ground floor of the house on Cluny Drive—where his gym was now. He and Charlotte had worked there, and in her grandmother's house in Forest Hill. It would take fifteen years to get the film made, but the screenplay of *East of Bangor* was pulled together in four months' time; by then, Charlotte Turner and Danny Angel were already a couple.

In Danny's bedroom, which was as much a memorial to Charlotte as the third-floor writing room was a shrine to Joe, the cook had often marveled at how well dusted and sparkling clean Lupita maintained all the framed photographs of the successful screenwriter. Most of the photos had been taken during the three years Daniel and Charlotte were together; many of these pictures were from their brief summer months on Lake Huron. Like some other Toronto families, Charlotte's parents owned an island in Georgian Bay; Charlotte's grandfather was alleged to have won the island in a poker game, but there were those who said he'd traded a car for it. Since Charlotte's father was terminally ill, and her mother (a doctor) would soon be retiring,

Charlotte stood to inherit the island, which was in the area of Pointe au Baril Station. Daniel had loved that island, the cook would remember. (Dominic had visited Georgian Bay only once; he'd hated it.)

The only snapshots of Charlotte that the cook continued to recycle on the bulletin boards in his bedroom were those of her with Joe, because Daniel couldn't sleep with pictures of the dead boy in his bedroom. The cook admired how Charlotte had been unjealously fond of Joe, and Joe could see for himself how happy his father was with her; Joe had liked Charlotte from the start.

Charlotte wasn't a skier, yet she tolerated those winter weekends and the Christmas holiday in Winter Park, where the cook had made fabulous dinners in the ski house at the base of the mountain. The restaurants in Winter Park weren't bad, or they were good enough for Joe and his college friends, but they were beneath the cook's standards, and Dominic Baciagalupo relished the opportunity to cook for his grandson; the boy didn't come to Canada often enough, not in Dominic's opinion. (Not in the writer Danny Angel's opinion, either.)

NOW WHAT LIGHT HAD LINGERED in the late December afternoon was entirely gone; both the darkness and the contrasting lights of the city were visible in the windows as Danny stretched out on the mat in his gym. Because it had been his writing room before it became his gym—and Danny wrote only in the daylight hours, since he'd gotten older—there were no curtains on the windows. In the winter months, it was often dark by the time he worked out, but Danny didn't care if anyone in the neighborhood saw him using the aerobic machines or the free weights. Both when it was his office *and* since it had become his gym, he'd been photographed in that room; he'd been interviewed there, too, because he never allowed any journalists in his writing room on the third floor.

As soon as they were married, Charlotte had said, she was going to put curtains or window shades in the gym, but because the wedding was canceled—with all the rest of it—the windows in that room had remained as they were. It was an odd gym, because it was still surrounded by bookshelves; even after he'd moved his work to Joe's former bedroom on the third floor, Danny had left many of his books in that ground-floor room.

When Danny and his dad had dinner parties in that house on Cluny Drive, everyone put their coats in the gym; they draped them on the handrails of the treadmill, or over the StairMaster machine, or on the stationary bike, and they piled them on the weight bench, too. Moreover, there were always a couple of clipboards in that room, and a ream of blank typing paper with lots of pens. Sometimes Danny made notes to himself when he rode the stationary bike in the late afternoon, or when he walked on the treadmill. His knees were shot from all the running, but he could still walk pretty fast on the treadmill, and riding the stationary bike or using the StairMaster didn't bother his knees.

For a fifty-eight-year-old man, Danny was in halfway decent physical shape; he was still fairly slight of build, though he had put on a few pounds since he'd starting drinking beer and red wine again—even in moderation. If Injun Jane had been alive, she would have told Danny that for someone who weighed as little as he did, even a couple of beers and one or two glasses of red wine were too much. ("Well, the Injun was harsh on the firewater subject," Ketchum had always said; he was not a man who put much stock in moderation, even at eighty-three.)

There was no telling when Ketchum would come for Christmas, Danny was thinking, as he settled into a comfortable pace on the StairMaster; for Christmas, Ketchum just showed up. For someone who fanatically faxed Danny or his dad a dozen times a week, and who still spontaneously phoned at all hours of the day and night, Ketchum was extremely secretive about his road trips—not only his trips to Toronto for Christmas but his hunting trips elsewhere in Canada. (The hunting trips—not to Quebec, but the ones up north in Ontario—occasionally brought Ketchum to Toronto, too.)

Ketchum started his hunting in September, the beginning of bear season in Coos County. The old woodsman claimed that the black bear population in New Hampshire was well over five thousand animals, and the annual bear harvest was "only about five or six hundred critters"; most of the bears were killed in the north and central regions of the state, and in the White Mountains. Ketchum's bear hound, that aforementioned "fine animal"—by now the grandson (or great-grandson!) of that first fine animal, one would guess—was allowed to hunt with him from the second week of September till the end of October.

The dog was a crossbreed, what Ketchum called a Walker bluetick. He was tall and rangy, like a Walker foxhound, but with the bluetick's white coat—blotched and flecked with bluish gray—and with the bluetick's superior quickness. Ketchum got his Walker blueticks from a kennel in Tennessee; he always chose a male and named him Hero. The dog never barked, but he growled in his sleep—Ketchum claimed that the dog *didn't* sleep—and Hero let loose a mournful baying whenever he was chasing a bear.

In New Hampshire, the end of the bear season overlapped with the muzzle-loader season for deer—a short time, only from the end of October through the first week of November. The regular firearm season for deer ran the rest of the month of November, into early December, but as soon as Ketchum killed a deer in Coos County (he always dropped one with his muzzle loader), he headed up north to Canada; the regular firearm season for deer ended earlier there.

The old logger had never been able to interest the cook in deer hunting; Dominic didn't like guns, or the taste of venison, and his limp was no fun in the woods. But after Danny and his dad moved to Canada, and Danny met Charlotte Turner, Ketchum was invited to Charlotte's island in Lake Huron; it was the first summer she and Danny were a couple, when the cook was also invited to Georgian Bay. That was where and when—on Turner Island, in August 1984—Ketchum talked Danny into trying deer hunting.

DOMINIC BACIAGALUPO DESPISED the imposed rusticity of the summer-cottage life on those Georgian Bay islands—in '84, Charlotte's family still used an outhouse. And while they had propane lights and a propane fridge, they hauled what water they needed (by the bucket method) from the lake.

Furthermore, Charlotte's family seemed to have furnished the main cottage and two adjacent sleeping cabins with the cast-off couches, chipped dishes, and mortally uncomfortable beds that they'd long ago replaced in their Toronto home; worse, the cook surmised, there was a tradition among the Georgian Bay islanders that upheld such stingy behavior. Anything new—such as electricity, hot water, or a flush toilet—was somehow contemptible.

But what they *ate* was what the cook most deplored. The mainland provisions at Pointe au Baril Station—in particular, the produce and anything that passed for "fresh"—were rudimentary, and everyone burned the shit out of what they blackened beyond recognition on their outdoor barbecues.

In his first and only visit to Turner Island, Dominic was polite, and he helped out in the kitchen—to the degree this was tolerable—but the cook returned to Toronto at the end of a long weekend, relieved by the knowledge that he would never again test his limp on those unwelcoming rocks, or otherwise set foot on a dock at Pointe au Baril Station.

"There's too much of Twisted River here—it's not Cookie's kind of place," Ketchum had explained to Charlotte and Danny, after Dominic went back to the city. While the logger said this in forgiveness of his old friend, Danny was not entirely different from his dad in his initial reaction to island life. The difference was that Danny and Charlotte had talked about the changes they would make on the island—certainly after (if not before) her father passed away, and her mother was no longer able to safely get into or out of a boat, or climb up those jagged rocks from the dock to the main cottage.

Danny still wrote on an old-fashioned typewriter; he owned a half-dozen IBM Selectrics, which were in constant need of repair. He wanted electricity for his typewriters. Charlotte wanted hot water—she'd long dreamed of such luxuries as an outdoor shower and an oversize bathtub—not to mention *several* flush toilets. A little electric heat would be nice, too, both Danny and Charlotte had agreed, because it could get cold at night, even in the summer—they were that far north—and, after all, they would soon be having a baby.

Danny also wanted to construct "a writing shack," as he called it—he was no doubt remembering the former farmhouse shed he'd written in, in Vermont—and Charlotte wanted to erect an enormous screened-in verandah, something large enough to link the main cottage to the two sleeping cabins, so that no one would ever have to go out in the rain (or venture into the mosquitoes, which were constant after nightfall).

Danny and Charlotte had plans for the place, in other words—the way couples in love do. Charlotte had cherished her summers on the island since she'd been a little girl; perhaps what Danny had adored were the possibilities of the place, the life with Charlotte he'd imagined there.

OH, PLANS, PLANS, PLANS—how we make plans into the future, as if the future will most certainly be there! In fact, the couple in love wouldn't wait for Charlotte's father to die, or for her mother to be physically incapable of handling the hardships of an island in Lake Huron. Over the next two years, Danny and Charlotte would put in the electricity, the flush toilets, and the hot water—even Charlotte's outdoor shower *and* her oversize bathtub, not to mention the enormous screened-in verandah. And there were a few other "improvements" that Ketchum suggested; the old woodsman had actually used the *improvements* word, on his very first visit to Georgian Bay and Turner Island. In the summer of '84, Ketchum had been a spry sixty-seven—young enough to still have a few plans of his own.

That summer, Ketchum had brought the dog. The fine animal was as alert as a squirrel from the second he put his paws on the island's main dock. "There must be a bear around here—Hero knows bears," Ketchum said. There was a stiff-standing ridge of fur (formerly, loose skin) at the back of the hound's tensed neck; the dog stayed as close to Ketchum as the woodsman's shadow. Hero wasn't a dog you were inclined to pat.

Ketchum wasn't a summer person; he didn't fish, or screw around with boats. The veteran river driver was no swimmer. What Ketchum saw in Georgian Bay, and on Turner Island, was what the place must be like in the late fall and the long winter, and when the ice broke up in the spring. "Lots of deer around here, I'll bet," the old logger remarked; he was still standing on the dock, only moments after he'd arrived and before he picked up his gear. He appeared to be sniffing the air for bear, like his dog.

"Injun country," Ketchum said approvingly. "Well, at least it *was*—before those damn missionaries tried to *Christianize* the fucking woods." As a boy, he'd seen the old black-and-white photographs of a pulpwood boom afloat in Gore Bay, Manitoulin Island. The lumber business around Georgian Bay would have been at its height about 1900, but Ketchum had heard the history, and he'd memorized the yearly cycles of logging. (In the autumn months, you cut your trees, you built your roads, and you readied your streams for the spring drives—all before the first snowfall. In the winter, you kept cutting trees, and you hauled or sledded your logs over the snow to the edge of the water. In the spring, you floated your logs down the streams and the rivers into the bay.)

"But, by the nineties, all your forests went rafting down to the States—isn't that right?" Ketchum asked Charlotte. She was surprised by the question; she didn't know, but Ketchum did.

It was like logging everywhere, after all. The great forests had been cut down; the mills had burned down, or they'd been torn down. "The mills perished out of sheer neglect," as Ketchum liked to put it.

"Maybe that bear's on a nearby island," Ketchum said, looking all around. "Hero's not agitated enough for there to be a bear on *this* island." (To Danny and Charlotte, the lean hound looked agitated enough for there to be a bear on the *dock*.)

It turned out that there was a bear on Barclay Island that summer. The water between the two islands was a short swim for a bear—both Danny and Ketchum discovered they could *wade* there—but the bear never showed up on Turner Island, perhaps because the bear had smelled Ketchum's dog.

"Burn the grease off the grill on the barbecue, after you've used it," Ketchum advised them. "Don't put the garbage out, and keep the fruit in the fridge. I would leave Hero with you, but I need him to look after me."

There was an uninhabited log cabin, the first building to be assembled on Turner Island, near the back dock. Charlotte gave Ketchum a tour of it. The screens were a little torn, and a pair of bunk beds had first been separated and then nailed together, side by side, where they were covered with a king-size mattress that overhung the bed frames. The blanket on the bed was moth-eaten, and the mattress was mildewed; no one had stayed there since Charlotte's grandfather stopped coming to the island.

It had been his cabin, Charlotte said, and after the old man died, no other member of the Turner family went near the run-down building, which Charlotte said was haunted (or so she'd believed as a girl).

She pulled aside a well-worn, dirty rug; she wanted to show Ketchum the hidden trapdoor in the floor. The cabin was set on cement posts, not much taller than cinder blocks—there was no foundation—and under the trapdoor was nothing but bare ground, about three feet below the floor. With the pine trees all around, pine needles had blown under the cabin, which gave the ground a deceptively soft and comfortable appearance.

"We don't know what Granddaddy used the trapdoor for," Charlotte explained to Ketchum, "but because he was a gambling man, we suspect he hid his money here."

Hero was sniffing the hole in the floor when Ketchum asked: "Was your granddaddy a *hunting* man, Charlotte?"

"Oh, yes!" Charlotte cried. "When he died, we finally threw away his guns." (Ketchum winced.)

"Well, this here's a *meat* locker," Ketchum told her. "Your granddaddy came up here in the winter, I would bet."

"Yes, he *did*!" Charlotte said, impressed.

"Probably after deer season, when the bay was frozen," Ketchum considered. "I'm guessing that when he shot a deer—and your Mounties would have known when someone was shooting, given how quiet it would be here in the winter, with all the snow—and when the Mounties came and asked him what he was shooting, I expect your granddaddy told them some story. Like he was shooting over a red squirrel's head, because the squirrel's chattering was driving him crazy, or that a herd of deer had been feeding on his favorite cedars, and he shot over *their* heads so they would go eat all the cedars on someone else's island—when the whole time he was talking, the deer, which Granddaddy would have gutted over this hole, so there wouldn't be any blood in the snow, and where he was keeping the meat cold . . . well, do you see what I'm getting at, Charlotte?" Ketchum asked her. "This here hole is a *poacher's* meat locker! I told you—there's lots of deer around here, I'll bet."

Ketchum and Hero had stayed in that run-down log cabin, haunted or not. ("Hell, most places I've lived are haunted," Ketchum had remarked.) The newer sleeping cabins were not to the old woods-man's liking; as for the torn screens in Granddaddy's cabin, Ketchum said, "If you don't get bitten by a mosquito or two, you can hardly tell you're in the woods." And there was more loon activity in that back bay, because there were fewer boats; Ketchum had figured that out on the first day, too. He liked the sound of loons. "Besides, Hero farts something awful—you wouldn't want him stinking up your sleeping cabins, Charlotte!"

At the end of the day, Charlotte wasn't shocked by the idea that her granddaddy had been a poacher. He'd died destitute and alcoholic; gambling debts and whiskey had done him in. Now, at least, the trap-door in the floor had been given a reason for its existence, and this rather quickly led Ketchum to his suggested *improvements*. It never occurred to the old river driver that Charlotte had not once been in-terested in living on her beloved island in the frigid winter months, when the prevailing wind had permanently bent the trees—when the bay was frozen and piled high with snow, and there wasn't a human soul around, except the occasional ice fisherman and those madmen who rode their snowmobiles over the lake.

"It wouldn't take a whole lot to winterize the main cottage," Ketchum began. "When you put in your flush toilets, you just want to be sure you install two septic systems—the main one, and a smaller one that nobody has to know about. Forget about using the sleeping cabins; it would be too expensive to heat them. Just stick to the main cottage. A little electric heat will be enough to keep the toilet and the sink—and the big bathtub you want, Charlotte—from freezing. You just have to heat-wrap the pipes to the small septic tank. That way, you can flush the toilet and drain the dishwater out of the sink—and empty the bathtub, too. You just can't pump water up from the lake, or heat any water—not in a propane hot-water heater, anyway. You'll have to cut a hole in the ice, and bring your water up by bucket; you heat the water on the gas stove for your baths, and for washing the dishes. You would sleep in the main cottage, of course—and most of your heat would come from the woodstove. You'll need a woodstove in your writing shack, too, Danny—but that's all you'll need. The back bay nearest the mainland will freeze first; you can haul in your gro-ceries on a sled towed by a snowmobile, and take your trash to town the same way. Hell, you could ski or snowshoe here from the mainland," Ketchum said. "You just might be better off staying away from the main channel out of Pointe au Baril Station. I don't imagine that channel freezes over too safely."

"But why would we want to come here in the *winter*?" Danny asked the old woodsman; Charlotte just stared at Ketchum, uncomprehending.

"Well, why don't we come up here this winter, Danny?" Ketchum asked the writer. "I'll show you why you might like it."

Ketchum didn't mean "winter"—not exactly. He meant deer season, which was in November. The first deer season that Danny met up with Ketchum at Pointe au Baril Station, the ice hadn't thickened sufficiently for them to cross the back bay from the mainland to Turner Island; not even snowshoes or cross-country skis would have been safe, and Ketchum's snowmobile surely would have sunk. In addition to the snowmobile, and a vast array of foul-weather gear, Ketchum had brought the guns, but he'd left Hero at home—actually, he'd left that fine animal with Six-Pack Pam. Six-Pack had dogs, and Hero "tolerated" her dogs, Ketchum said. (Deer hunting was "unsuitable" for dogs, Ketchum also said.)

It didn't matter that they couldn't get to Charlotte's island that first year, anyway. The builder wouldn't be finished with all the improvements before the following summer; Ketchum's clever winterizing would have to wait until then, too. The builder, Andy Grant, was what Ketchum affectionately called "a local fella." In fact, Charlotte had grown up with him—they'd been childhood friends. Andy had not only renovated the main cottage for Charlotte's parents a few years ago; he'd more recently restored the two sleeping cabins to Charlotte's specifications.

Andy Grant told Ketchum and Danny where the deer were in the Bayfield area, and Ketchum already knew a fella named LaBlanc, who called himself a hunting guide; LaBlanc showed Ketchum and Danny an area north of Pointe au Baril, in the vicinity of Byng Inlet and Still River. But, in Ketchum's case, it didn't matter where he hunted; the deer were all around.

At first, Danny was a little insulted by the weapon Ketchum had selected for him—a Winchester Ranger, which was manufactured in

New Haven, Connecticut, in the mid-eighties, and then discontinued. It was a 20-gauge, repeating shotgun with a slide action—what
Ketchum called "a pump." What initially insulted Danny was that the
shotgun was a *youth* model.

"Don't get your balls crossed about it," Ketchum told the writer.
"It's a fine gun for a beginner. You better keep things simple when you
start hunting. I've seen some fellas blow their toes off."

For the sake of his toes, Danny guessed, Ketchum instructed the
beginner to always have three rounds in the Winchester—one in the
chamber and two more in the tubular magazine. "Don't forget how
many shots you're carrying," Ketchum said.

Danny knew that the first two rounds were buckshot; the third was
a deer slug, what Ketchum called the "kill-shot." It made no sense to
load more than three rounds, no matter what the shotgun's capacity
was. "If you need a fourth or a fifth shot, you've already missed,"
Ketchum told Danny. "The deer's long gone."

At night, Danny had trouble keeping Ketchum out of the bar at
Larry's Tavern, which was also a motel—south of Pointe au Baril Station, on Route 69. The motel's walls were so thin, they could hear
whoever was humping in the room next door. "Some asshole trucker
and a hooker," Ketchum declared the first night.

"I don't think there are any hookers in Pointe au Baril," Danny
said.

"It's a one-night stand, then," Ketchum replied. "They sure don't
sound *married.*"

Another night, there was a prolonged caterwauling of a certain female kind. "This one sounds different from the night before, and the
night before that," Ketchum said.

Whoever the woman was, she went on and on. "I'm coming! I'm
coming!" she kept repeating.

"Are you timing this, Danny? It might be a record," Ketchum said,
but he walked naked into the hall and beat on the door of the longest
orgasm in the world. "Listen up, fella," the old river driver said. "She's
obviously *lying.*"

The young man who opened the door was menacing, and in a mood
to fight, but the fight—if you could call it that—was over in a hurry.
Ketchum put the guy in a choke hold before the fella had managed to

throw more than a punch or two. "I *wasn't* lying," the woman called from the dark room, but by then not even the young man believed her.

It was not how Danny had imagined he and Ketchum would be camping out, or otherwise roughing it, while they were hunting deer. As for the deer, the first buck Danny dropped in Bayfield required all three rounds—including the kill-shot. "Well, writers should know it's sometimes hard work to die, Danny," was all Ketchum told him.

Ketchum got his buck near Byng Inlet, with one shot from his 12-gauge. The next deer season in Ontario, they shot two more bucks—both of them at Still River—and by then the so-called improvements on Charlotte's island were complete, including the winterizing. Ketchum and Danny returned to Pointe au Baril Station in early February, when the ice on the bay nearest the mainland was two feet thick. They followed the snowmobile portage from Payne's Road, out of Pointe au Baril, and went across the ice and drifting snow to the back dock and Granddaddy's cabin.

Deer season was over, but Ketchum had brought his 12-gauge. "Just in case," he told Danny.

"In case *what*?" Danny asked him. "We're not poaching deer, Ketchum."

"In case there's some other *critter*," Ketchum replied.

Later, Danny saw Ketchum grilling a couple of venison steaks on the barbecue, which Andy had hooked up to the propane inside Charlotte's new screened-in verandah; the verandah was boarded up in winter to keep out the snow, because the outdoor summer furniture and two canoes were stored there. Unbeknownst to Danny, Ketchum had also brought his bow.

Danny forgot that Ketchum was a bow hunter, too, and that the archery season for deer in New Hampshire was three months long; Ketchum had had a lot of practice.

"That's poaching," Danny told the logger.

"The Mounties didn't hear any shots, did they?" Ketchum asked.

"It's still poaching, Ketchum."

"If you don't hear anything, it's more like nothing, Danny. I know Cookie's not a fan of venison, but I think it tastes pretty good this way."

Danny didn't really like deer hunting—not the killing part,

anyway—but he enjoyed spending time with Ketchum, and that February of '86, when they stayed for a few nights in the main cottage on Turner Island, Danny discovered that the winter on Georgian Bay was wonderful.

From his new writing shack, Danny could see a pine tree that had been shaped by the wind; it was bent at almost a right angle to itself. When new snow was falling, and there were near whiteout conditions—so that where the rocks on shore ended and the frozen bay began were all *one*—it struck Danny Angel that the little tree had a simultaneously tenacious and precarious grip on its own survival.

Danny sat transfixed in his writing shack, looking at that wind-bent pine; he was actually imagining what it might be like to *live* on the island in Lake Huron for a whole winter. (Of course he knew that Charlotte wouldn't have tolerated it for longer than one weekend.)

Ketchum had come into the writing shack; he'd been hauling water from the lake, and had brought some pasta pots to a near boil on the gas stove. He'd come to inquire if Danny wanted to take the first bath or the next one.

"Do you see that tree, Ketchum?" Danny asked him, pointing to the little pine.

"I suppose you mean the one the wind has fucked over," Ketchum said.

"Yes, that's the one," Danny answered. "What does it remind you of?"

"Your dad," Ketchum told him, without hesitation. "That tree's got Cookie written all over it, but it'll be fine, Danny—like your dad. Cookie's going to be fine."

KETCHUM AND DANNY went deer hunting around Pointe au Baril in November of '86—their third and last deer season together—and they went "camping," as they called it, on Turner Island in late January of '87, too. At Danny's insistence, and to Ketchum's considerable consternation, there was no more bow hunting out of season. Instead of his bow and the hunting arrows, Ketchum brought Hero along—together with the just-in-case 12-gauge, which was never fired.

Danny believed that the bear hound's reputation for farting was exaggerated; that January, Ketchum again used the dog as an excuse to sleep in Granddaddy's log cabin, which was unheated. With all the winterizing, the main cottage was a little too warm (and too comfortable) for the old woodsman, who said he liked to see his breath at night—when he could see at all. Danny couldn't imagine what Ketchum could see at night in Granddaddy's cabin, because there was no electricity or propane lamps there. The logger took a flashlight with him when he went off to bed, but he carried it like a club; Danny never saw him turn it on.

Ketchum had come to Charlotte's island only one time in summer, the same time when the cook had also come and gone. Charlotte never knew that Ketchum had the 12-gauge with him then, but Danny did. He'd heard Ketchum shooting a rattlesnake down at the back dock. Charlotte had taken the boat into Pointe au Baril Station; she didn't hear the shot.

"The rattlesnakes are protected—an endangered species, I think," Danny told the river driver. Ketchum had already skinned the snake and cut off its rattles.

In the summer, Charlotte had her boat serviced at Desmasdon's, the boat works where they dry-docked boats in the winter. Now, when Danny watched Ketchum skinning the snake, he was reminded of a poster on the ice cream freezer at Desmasdon's—it displayed the various snakes of Ontario, the Eastern Massasauga rattler among them. Those rattlesnakes really *were* protected, Danny was trying to make Ketchum understand, but the woodsman cut him off.

"Hero's smart enough not to get bitten by a fucking snake, Danny—I don't need to protect *him*," Ketchum started in. "But I'm not so sure about you and Charlotte. You walk all over this island— I've seen you!—just talking to each other and not looking where you're stepping. People in love aren't looking for rattlers; they're not listening for them, either. And you and Charlotte are going to have a *baby*, isn't that right? It's not the *rattlesnakes* that need protection, Danny." With that, Ketchum cut off the snake's head with his Browning knife. He drained the venom from the fangs on a rock; then he hurled the head off the back dock, into the bay. "Fish food," he said. "I'm a regular environmentalist, sometimes." He tossed the snakeskin up on the roof of

Granddaddy's cabin, where the sun would dry it out, he said—adding, "If the seagulls and the crows don't get it first."

The birds would get it, and they made such a ruckus over the snakeskin early the next morning that Ketchum was tempted to fire off his 12-gauge again, this time to drive the seagulls and the crows off the roof of the log cabin. But he restrained himself, knowing Charlotte would hear the shot; Ketchum went outside and threw rocks at the birds instead. He watched a gull fly off with the remains of the snakeskin. ("Nothing wasted," as the logger later described the event to Danny.)

That day, the Mounties came by in their boat to inquire about the gunshot the day before. Had anyone heard it? Someone on Barclay Island said that they thought they'd heard a shot on Turner Island. "I heard it, too," Ketchum spoke up, getting the two young Mounties' attention. Ketchum even recalled the time of day, with impressive accuracy, but he said that the shooting definitely came from the mainland. "Sounded like a twelve-gauge to me," the veteran woodsman said, "but gunfire can be both magnified and distorted over water." The two Mounties nodded at such a sage assessment; the beautiful but unsuspecting Charlotte nodded, too.

Then Joe had died, and Danny lost what little taste he had for killing things. And when Danny lost Charlotte, he and Ketchum gave up their dead-of-winter trips to Turner Island in Georgian Bay.

There was something about Pointe au Baril Station that stayed with Danny, though he didn't go there anymore. In fact, his parting from Charlotte had been so civilized—she'd even offered to share her summer island with him, when they were no longer together. Maybe he could go there in July, and she would go in August, she said. After all, he'd put his money into those improvements, too. (Charlotte's offer was sincere; it wasn't only about the money.)

Yet it wasn't Georgian Bay in the summer that Danny had adored. He'd loved being there with *her*—he would have loved being *anywhere* with Charlotte—but when she was gone, whenever he thought about Lake Huron, he thought mostly about that wind-bent pine in the wintertime. How could he ask Charlotte for permission to let him have a winter view of that little tree from his writing shack—the weather-beaten pine he saw now only in his imagination?

And how could Danny have had another child, after losing Joe? He'd known the day Joe died that he would lose Charlotte, too, because he sensed almost immediately that his heart couldn't bear losing another child; he couldn't stand the anxiety, or that terrible ending, ever again.

Charlotte knew it, too—even before he found the courage to tell her. "I won't hold you to your promise," she told him, "even if it means that I might have to move on."

"You *should* move on, Charlotte," he told her. "I just can't."

She'd married someone else soon after. A nice guy—Danny had met him, and liked him. He was someone in the movie business, a French director living in L.A. He was much closer to Charlotte's age, too. She already had one baby, a little girl, and now Charlotte was expecting a second child—one more than Danny had promised her.

Charlotte had kept her island in Georgian Bay, but she'd moved away from Toronto and was living in Los Angeles now. She came back to Toronto every September for the film festival, and that time of year—early fall—always seemed to Danny like a good time to leave town. They still talked on the phone—Charlotte was always the one who called; Danny never called her—but it was probably easier for both of them not to run into each other.

Charlotte Turner had been very pregnant—she was about to have her first child—when she won the Oscar for Best Adapted Screenplay for *East of Bangor,* at the Academy Awards in March 2000. Danny and his dad had watched Charlotte accept the statuette. (Patrice was always closed on Sunday nights.) Somehow, seeing her on television—from Toronto, when Charlotte was in L.A.—well, that wasn't the same as *actually* seeing her, was it? Both the cook and Danny wished her well.

It was just bad luck. "Bad timing, huh?" Ketchum had said. (If Joe had died three months later, it's likely Danny would have already gotten Charlotte pregnant. It had been bad timing, indeed.)

JOE AND THE GIRL HAD TAKEN some of the same courses in Boulder—she was a senior at the university, too—and their trip to Winter Park together might have been a belated birthday present that Joe decided to give himself. According to their mutual friends, Joe and the girl had been sleeping together for only a short time. It was the girl's first trip alone with Joe to the ski house in Winter Park, though both Danny and his dad remembered her staying at the house for a couple of nights over the last Christmas holiday, when a bunch of Joe's college friends—girls and boys, with no discernible relationship with one another (at least that the cook and his son could see)—were also camping out at that Winter Park house.

It was a big house, after all, and—as Charlotte had said, because she was closer in age to Joe and his pals than Danny and Dominic were—it was impossible to tell who was sleeping with whom. There were so many of them, and they seemed to be lifelong friends. That last Colorado Christmas, the kids had taken the mattresses from all the guest bedrooms, and they'd piled them in the living room, where both the boys and the girls had cuddled together and slept in front of the fire.

Yet, even with such a mob of them, and amid all the taking turns in the showers—it had surprised Danny and his dad that some of the girls took showers together—it was the cook and his son who'd noticed something special about that girl. Charlotte hadn't seen it. It was for just the briefest moment, and maybe it meant nothing, but after Joe *died* with the girl, the writer and the cook couldn't forget it.

She was pretty and petite, almost elfin, and naturally Joe had made a point of telling his father and grandfather that he'd first met Meg in a life-drawing class, where she'd been the model.

"One look at the girl doesn't suffice—it isn't nearly enough," the cook would tell Ketchum, shortly after that Christmas.

It wasn't just because she was an exhibitionist, though Meg clearly was that; as had been the case with Katie, Danny had seen for himself the first time, you simply had to look at Meg, and it was almost painful not to keep looking. (Once you saw her, it was hard to look away.)

"What a distraction that girl is," Danny said to his dad.

"She's trouble," the cook replied.

The two older men were making their way along the upstairs hall of that Winter Park house. The wing where the guest bedrooms were was a curious *L*-shaped addition off that hall—so architecturally strange that you couldn't pass the junction without at least glancing at the guest-wing hallway, and that was why Danny and Dominic noticed the slight commotion. Then again, their heads might have turned in that direction at the piercing shrieks of the young girls' laughter—not an everyday occurrence in the lives of the cook and his son.

Meg and another girl were emerging from one of the guest bedrooms, both of them wrapped in towels. Their hair was wet—they must have come directly from a shower—and they ran awkwardly in their tightly wrapped towels to the door of a different guest bedroom, the other girl disappearing into the room before Meg, who was left alone in the guest-wing hallway, just as Joe came around the corner of the L. It all happened so suddenly that Joe never saw his father or grandfather, and neither did Meg. She saw only Joe, and he clearly saw her, and before she slipped inside the guest room and closed the door—to more shrieks of laughter, from within the room—Meg had opened her towel to Joe.

"She shook her little titties at him!" as the cook would later describe the episode to Ketchum.

"A distraction, indeed," was all Danny had said at the time.

It was what Charlotte would have called "a throwaway line"—a reference to any extraneous dialogue in a screenplay—but after the accident that killed Joe and Meg, the *distraction* word lingered.

Why hadn't they been wearing their seat belts, for example? Had the girl been giving him a blow job? Probably she had; Joe's fly was open, and his penis was poking out of his pants when the body was discovered. He'd been thrown from the car and died immediately. Meg wasn't so lucky. The girl was found alive, but with her head and neck at an unnatural angle; she was wedged between the brake and the accelerator pedal. She'd died in the ambulance, before reaching the hospital.

What had led Joe and Meg to cut two days of classes in Boulder, and make the drive to Winter Park, at first seemed pretty obvious; yet two days of new, nonstop snow *wasn't* the prevailing reason. Besides, it had been a typical late-March snow, wet and heavy—the skiing must have been slow, the visibility on the mountain treacherous. And from the look of the ski house in Winter Park—that is, before the cleaning lady rushed in and made some attempt to restore order—Joe and the girl had spent most of their time indoors. It didn't appear that they'd done much skiing. Perhaps it had no more significance than most youthful experiments, but the young couple seemed to have made a game out of sleeping in every bed in the house.

Naturally, there would remain some unanswerable questions. If they weren't in Winter Park to ski, why had they waited until the evening of the second day to drive back to Boulder? Joe knew that after midnight and before dawn, the ski patrol was in the habit of closing U.S. 40 over Berthoud Pass, whenever there was any avalanche danger; with such a heavy, wet snow, and because it was the avalanche time of year, possibly Joe hadn't wanted to risk leaving before light the next morning, when they might still be blasting avalanches above Berthoud Pass. Of course the two lovers could have waited until daylight of the following morning, but maybe Joe and Meg had thought that missing two days of classes was enough.

It was snowing heavily in Winter Park when they left, but there was next to no ski traffic on U.S. 40 in the direction of I-70, and that highway was well traveled. (Well, it was a weekday night; for most schools and colleges that had a March break, the vacation was over.) Joe and Meg must have passed the snowplow at the top of Berthoud Pass; the plowman remembered Joe's car, though he'd noticed only the driver. Apparently, the plowman hadn't seen the passenger; perhaps the blow job was already in progress. But Joe had waved to the plowman, and the plowman recalled waving back.

Only seconds later, the plowman spotted the other car—it was coming in the other direction, from I-70, and the plowman presumed it was "a goddamn Denver driver." This was because the driver was going much too fast for the near-blizzard conditions. In the plowman's estimation, Joe had been driving safely—or at least slowly enough, given the storm and the slickness of the wet snow on the highway. Whereas the Denver car—if, indeed, the driver was from Denver—was fishtailing out of control as the car came over the pass. The plowman had flashed his lights, but the other car never slowed down.

"It was just a blue blur," the plowman said in his deposition to the police. (What kind of blue? he was asked.) "With all the snow, I'm not really sure about the color," the plowman admitted, but Danny would always imagine the other car as an unusual shade of blue—a *customized* job, as Max had called it.

Anyway, that mystery car just disappeared; the plowman never saw the driver.

The snowplow then made its way downhill, over the pass—in the direction of I-70—and that was when the plowman came upon the wreck on U.S. 40, Joe's upside-down car. There'd been no other traffic over the pass, or the plowman would have seen it, so the plowman's interpretation of the skid marks in the snow was probably correct. The other car—its tires spinning, its rear end drifting sideways—had skidded from the uphill lane into the downhill lane, where Joe was driving. From the tracks in the snow, the plowman could see that Joe had been forced to change lanes—to avoid the head-on collision. But the two cars had never made contact; they'd traded lanes without touching.

On a wet, snowy road, the plowman knew, a car coming uphill can recover from a skid—just take your foot off the gas, and the car slows down and stops skidding. In Joe's case, of course, his car just kept going; he hit the huge snowbank that had buried the guardrail on the steep side of U.S. 40, where the drivers coming up Berthoud Pass don't like to look down. It's a long way down at that section of the road, but the soft-looking snowbank was densely packed and frozen hard; the snowbank bounced Joe's car back into the uphill lane of U.S. 40, where the car tipped over. From *those* skid marks, the plowman could tell that Joe's car had slid on its roof down the steepest part of the highway. Both the driver's-side door and the door on the passenger side had sprung open.

How had one of Danny Angel's interviewers asked the question? "Wouldn't you say, Mr. Angel—regarding how *slowly* your son was driving, and the fact that he *didn't* hit the other car—that, in all likelihood, it was an accident your son and the girl would have survived if they'd been wearing their seat belts?"

"In all likelihood," Danny had repeated.

The police said it was impossible to imagine that the driver of the other car hadn't been aware of Joe and Meg's predicament; even with all the fishtailing, the so-called Denver driver must have seen what had happened to Joe's car. But he didn't stop, whoever he (or she) was.

If anything, according to the plowman, the other car had sped up—as if to get away from the accident.

Danny and his dad rarely talked about the accident itself, but of course the cook knew what his writer son thought. To anyone with an imagination, to lose a child is attended by a special curse. Dominic understood that his beloved Daniel lost his beloved Joe over and over again—maybe in a different way each time. Danny would also wonder if the other car ever had a driver, for surely it was the blue Mustang. That rogue car had been looking for Joe all these years. (At the time of the accident on Berthoud Pass, it had been almost fourteen years since that *near* accident in the alleyway in back of the Court Street house in Iowa City, when Max—who'd seen the blue Mustang more than once—and the eight-year-old Joe himself had sworn there was *no* driver.)

It was a *driverless* blue Mustang, and it had a mission. Just as Danny, in his mind's eye, had once imagined his slain two-year-old in diapers on Iowa Avenue, so had the plowman from Winter Park found Joe's actual body—dead in the road.

KISSES OF WOLVES

A T 7:30 ON A SATURDAY EVENING—IT WAS DECEMBER 23, the last night before the restaurant closed for the Christmas holiday—Patrice was chock-full. Arnaud was jubilant, greeting everyone at each table as if they were family. The owner's excitement was infectious. All the diners were informed of the upcoming changes ahead for the restaurant; a more casual atmosphere and menu awaited them in the New Year. "Lower prices, too!" Arnaud told them—shaking hands, bussing cheeks. When the restaurant reopened, even the *name* would be different.

"No more 'Patrice,' " Arnaud announced, gliding from table to table. "The new name is one you won't easily forget. It has, I think, a certain *edge!*"

"The new restaurant is called *Edge?*" Ketchum asked the Frenchman suspiciously. The old logger was increasingly hard of hearing—especially in his right ear, and Arnaud was speaking at the woodsman's right side. (There was a noisy crowd that night, and the place was crammed.)

Too much gunfire, Danny Angel was thinking. Ketchum had what he called "shooter's ear," but the writer knew that Ketchum was chainsaw-deaf in *both* ears. It probably wouldn't have mattered which ear Patrice was addressing.

"No, no—the name isn't Edge, it's *Kiss of the Wolf*!" Arnaud cried, loudly enough for the new name to register with Ketchum.

Danny and the logger had a window table for two, overlooking what they could see of Yonge Street—above the frosted glass. When the restaurateur had glided on to the next table, Ketchum gave Danny a penetrating stare. "I heard what the Frenchie said," the old river driver began. "Kiss of the fucking Wolf! Shit—that sounds like a name only a *writer* would have thought up!"

"It wasn't me," Danny told him. "It was Silvestro's idea, and Patrice liked it. Dad didn't have anything to do with it, either."

"Mountains of moose shit," Ketchum said matter-of-factly. "It's as if you fellas are *trying* to get caught!"

"We're not going to get caught because of the restaurant's name," Danny told the logger. "Don't be ridiculous, Ketchum. The cowboy can't find us that way."

"Carl is still looking for you—that's all I'm saying, Danny. I don't know why you want to help the cowboy find you."

Danny didn't say anything; he believed it was crazy to think that Carl could ever connect Kiss of the Wolf to the Baciagalupo name. The retired deputy sheriff didn't speak Italian!

"I've seen wolves. I've come upon their kill, too," the old woodsman said to Danny. "I'll tell you what a kiss of the wolf looks like. A wolf rips your throat out. If there's a pack going after you, or some other critter, they get you turning to face them, every which way, but there's always one who's getting ready to rip your throat out—that's what they're looking for, the throat-shot. Kisses of wolves aren't so pretty!"

"What do you feel like eating?" Danny asked, just to change the subject.

"I'm fairly torn about it," Ketchum said. He wore reading glasses— of all things!—but they failed to lend him a scholarly appearance. The scar from the eight-inch cast-iron skillet was too pronounced, his beard too bushy. The plaid shirt and fleece vest had too much of Twisted River about them to give Ketchum even a vestige of city life—not to mention fine dining. "I was considering the French-style grilled lamb chops, or the calf's liver with Yukon frites," the woodsman said. "What the fuck are Yukon frites?" he asked Danny.

"Big potatoes," Danny answered. "They're Yukon Gold potatoes, cut on the large side."

"The *côte de boeuf* kind of caught my attention, too," the logger said.

"The *côte de boeuf* is for two," Danny told him.

"That's why I noticed it," Ketchum said. He had been drinking Steam Whistle on tap, but he'd switched to Alexander Keith by the bottle; the ale had a little more to it. "Constipated Christ!" Ketchum suddenly exclaimed. "There's a wine that costs a hundred and sixty-eight dollars!"

Danny saw that it was a Barolo Massolino, from Piedmont. "Let's have it," the writer said.

"Just so long as you're paying," Ketchum told him.

OUT IN THE KITCHEN, it was bedlam as usual. The cook was helping Scott with the profiteroles, which were served with caramel ice cream and a bittersweet-chocolate sauce; Dominic was preparing the croutons and the rouille for Joyce and Kristine's fish soup as well. It had been the cook's task, earlier, to make the tagliatelle for the veal scallopini, and tonight the pasta would also be served with Silvestro's duck confit. But Dominic had made the tagliatelle long before the restaurant (and the kitchen) got busy; he'd started a red-wine reduction with rosemary, too.

It was noisier in the kitchen than usual that Saturday night, because Dorotea, the new dishwasher, had a cast on her right wrist and thumb, and she kept dropping the pans. Everyone was taking bets on what Ketchum was going to order. Silvestro had suggested the special cassoulet, but Dominic said that no sane woodsman would willingly eat beans—not if there was another choice. The cook predicted that Ketchum would have the *côte de boeuf* for two; Joyce and Kristine said that the old river driver would probably order both the lamb chops *and* the liver.

"Or he'll split the *côte de boeuf* with Daniel, and have either the lamb chops or the liver, too," Dominic speculated.

Something about the feel of the warm handle on the skillet with the red-wine reduction was distracting him, but the cook couldn't locate the true source of his distraction. Lately he'd noticed that his old memories were clearer—he meant more vivid—than his more recent memories, if that was actually possible. For instance, he'd found himself remembering that Rosie had said something to Ketchum just before, or just after, they'd all gone out on the ice together. But had Ketchum first said, "Give me your hand"? The cook thought so, but he wasn't sure.

Rosie had very distinctly said: "Not that hand—that's the wrong hand." She'd quickly created a little distance between herself and Ketchum, but was this before or somehow during the damn do-si-doing? Dominic did but didn't remember, and that was because he'd been drunker than Rosie *and* Ketchum.

Anyway, what was the wrong-hand business about? the cook was wondering; he didn't really want to ask Ketchum about it. Besides, Dominic was thinking, how much would the eighty-three-year-old logger remember about that long-ago night? After all, Ketchum was still drinking!

One of the younger waiters ventured a guess that the old riverman wouldn't order *anything* for dinner. He'd already had three Steam Whistles on tap and a couple of Keiths; the old logger couldn't possibly have room for dinner. But the young waiter didn't know Ketchum.

Patrice popped into the kitchen. "Ooh-la-la, Dominic," Arnaud said. "What is your son celebrating? Danny ordered the Barolo Massolino!"

"I'm not worried," the cook replied. "Daniel can afford it, and you can count on Ketchum drinking most of the wine."

It was their last night in the kitchen before the long vacation; everyone was working hard, but they were all in a good mood. For Dominic, however, the unknown source of his distraction lingered; he kept feeling the familiar handle of the warm skillet. What is it? he was wondering. What's wrong?

In the cook's bedroom in the house on Cluny Drive, the bulletin boards with those countless photographs all but eclipsed from view (or consideration) the eight-inch cast-iron skillet. Yet that skillet had crossed state boundaries and, more recently, an international border; that skillet surely belonged in the cook's bedroom, though its once-legendary powers of protection had probably passed (as Carmella once speculated) from the actual to the symbolic.

The eight-inch cast-iron skillet hung just inside the doorway to Dominic's bedroom, where it went almost unnoticed. Why had the cook been thinking about it so insistently—at least since Ketchum had arrived (in his usual unannounced fashion) for Christmas?

Dominic wasn't aware that Danny had lately been thinking about the old frying pan, too. There was a certain sameness about that skillet; it was unchanged. The damn pan just hung there in his father's bedroom. It was a constant reminder to the writer, but a reminder of *what*?

Okay, it was the same skillet he'd used to kill Injun Jane; as such, it had set Danny and Dominic's flight in motion. It was the same skillet Dominic had used to whack a bear—or so the myth began. In fact, it was the same eight-inch cast-iron skillet Danny's dad had used to clobber Ketchum—*not* a bear. But Ketchum had been too tough to kill. ("Only Ketchum can kill Ketchum," the cook had said.)

Danny and his dad had been thinking about that, too: Even at eighty-three, only Ketchum could kill Ketchum.

The young waiter now came back into the kitchen. "The big man wants the *côte de boeuf* for two!" he announced, in awe. Dominic managed a smile; he would smile again when Patrice popped into the kitchen a little later, just to tell him that his son had ordered a second bottle of the Barolo Massolino. Not even a *côte de boeuf* for two, and uncountable bottles of Barolo, could kill Ketchum, the cook knew. Only Ketchum, and Ketchum alone, could do it.

IT WAS SO HOT IN THE KITCHEN that they'd opened the back door to the alley—just a crack—though it was a very cold night, and an uncommonly strong wind repeatedly blew the door wide open. In the cold weather, Crown's Lane, the alleyway behind the restaurant, was a hangout for homeless people. The restaurant's exhaust fan blew into the alley, creating a warm spot—a good-smelling one, too. An occasional homeless person appeared at the door to the kitchen, hoping for a hot meal.

The cook could never remember whether Joyce or Kristine was the smoker, but one of the young women chefs was once startled by a hungry homeless person when she was smoking a cigarette in the alley. Since then, all of those working in the kitchen, and the waitstaff, were aware of the homeless people seeking warmth and a possible bite to eat in the near vicinity of the kitchen door. (This was also Patrice's delivery door, though there were never any deliveries at night.)

Now Dominic once more went to close the door, which the bitter wind had again blown wide open, and there was one-eyed Pedro—Patrice's most popular homeless person, because Pedro never failed to compliment the chef (or chefs) for whatever food he was given. His real name was Ramsay Farnham, but he'd been disowned by the Farnham family—a fine, old Toronto family, famous patrons of the arts. Now in his late forties or early fifties, Ramsay had repeatedly embarrassed the Farnhams. As a last straw, at an impromptu press conference at an otherwise forgettable cultural event, Ramsay had announced that he was giving away his inheritance to an AIDS hospice in Toronto. He also claimed to be finishing a memoir, explaining why he'd half-blinded himself. He said he had lusted after his mother his whole adult life, and while he'd never had sex with her—nor murdered his father—he had truly wanted to. Hence he'd blinded himself only in one eye, the left one, and had renamed himself Pedro—not Oedipus.

No one knew if Pedro's eye patch covered an empty eye socket or a perfectly healthy left eye, or why he'd picked Pedro for his new name. He was cleaner than most homeless people; while his parents would have nothing to do with him, perhaps there were other, more sympathetic members of the Farnham family who allowed Ramsay (now Pedro) to have an occasional bath and wash his clothes. Of course he was insane, but he'd received an excellent education and was preternaturally well-spoken. (As for the memoir, either it was forever a work-in-progress or he'd not written a word of it.)

"Good evening to you, Dominic," one-eyed Pedro greeted the cook, while Dominic was dealing with the windblown kitchen door.

"How are you, Pedro?" the cook asked. "A little hot food might do you some good on a cold night like this one."

"I've been entertaining similar thoughts, Dominic," Pedro replied, "and while I'm aware that the exhaust fan is most imprecise, I believe I detect something special tonight—something not on the menu—and unless my nose deceives me, Silvestro has outdone himself, yet again, with a cassoulet."

Dominic had never known Pedro's nose to deceive him. The cook gave the homeless gentleman a generous serving of the cassoulet, warning him not to burn himself on the baking dish for the beans. In return, Pedro volunteered to hold the kitchen door open—just a crack—with his foot.

"It is an honor to smell the aromas of Patrice's kitchen firsthand, unadulterated by the exhaust fan," Pedro told Dominic.

"Unadulterated," the cook repeated quietly, to himself, but to Pedro he said: "You know, we're changing our name—after Christmas."

" 'After Christmas' is a curious name for a restaurant, Dominic," the homeless man said thoughtfully. "Not everyone celebrates Christmas, you know. The duck is exquisite, by the way—and I love the sausage!" Pedro added.

"No, no—we're not *calling* the restaurant After Christmas!" the cook cried. "The new name is Kiss of the Wolf." The homeless man stopped eating and stared at the cook. "It wasn't my choice," Dominic told him quickly.

"You have to be kidding," Pedro said. "That is a *famous* porn film—it's one of the *worst* porn films I've ever seen, but it's famous. I'm certain that's the title."

"You must be mistaken, Pedro," Dominic said. "Maybe it sounds better in Italian," the cook added meaninglessly.

"It's not an *Italian* porn film!" the homeless man cried. He handed the unfinished cassoulet back to Dominic, the baking dish for the beans sliding across the plate of duck and sausage. (The baking dish briefly burned the cook's thumbs.)

"Kiss of the Wolf *can't* be a porn film," Dominic said, but Pedro was retreating into the alley, shaking his huge mane of hair, his grizzled beard wagging.

"I'm going to be sick," Pedro said. "I can never forget that film—it was *disgusting*! It's not about sex with wolves, you know, Dominic—"

"I don't want to know what it's about!" the cook cried. "I'm sure you're wrong about the title!" he called after the homeless man, who was disappearing down the dark alleyway.

"There are some things you can't forget, Dominic!" Pedro called, after the cook could no longer see him. "Dreams of incest, desiring your mother—bad oral sex!" the crazy man shouted, his words whipped by the wind but audible, even over the deep drone of the exhaust fan.

"Pedro didn't like the cassoulet?" Silvestro asked, when the cook brought the full plate and the baking dish back into the kitchen.

"He was bothered by a name," was all Dominic said, but the incident struck the cook as a bad omen for Kiss of the Wolf—even if Pedro had been wrong about the title of the terrible porn film.

As it would turn out, neither the cook nor his writer son could find a porn film called *Kiss of the Wolf*. Not even Ketchum had seen such a film, and Ketchum claimed to have seen everything—at least everything pornographic that was available for viewing in New Hampshire.

"I think I would have remembered that title, Cookie," the old logger said. "In fact, I'm sure I would have sent it to you. But what happens in it that's so special?" the woodsman asked.

"I don't know what happens in it—I don't *want* to know!" the cook cried. "I just want to know if it *exists*!"

"Well, don't get your balls crossed about it," Ketchum said.

"Apparently, it doesn't exist—at least not *yet*," Danny told his dad. "You know that Pedro is nuts, Pop—you know that, don't you?"

"Of course I know he's nuts, Daniel!" the cook cried. "Poor Pedro was just so convinced—he made it sound *plausible*."

That Saturday night before the Christmas break—the last night that Patrice would be Patrice—Danny and Ketchum had ordered three bottles of the Barolo Massolino. As the cook had told Arnaud, Ketchum drank most of the wine, but Ketchum had also been counting.

"You may *say* you have a couple of beers, and one or two glasses of red wine with your dinner, Danny, but you've had *four* glasses of wine tonight. Even three glasses of wine, on top of two beers, is kind of a lot for a little fella." There was nothing accusatory in Ketchum's tone—he was simply setting the record straight—but Danny was defensive about it.

"I didn't know you were counting for me, Ketchum."

"Don't be like that, Danny," the logger said. "It's just my job to look after you fellas."

Ketchum had complained about Danny's tendency not to lock the house on Cluny Drive after he came home from dinner. But most nights the cook came home later than his son, and Dominic didn't like fumbling around with the door key. The cook preferred to lock the front door after he'd come home, and before he went to bed.

"But wine makes you sleepy, doesn't it, Danny?" the woodsman had asked. "Most nights, I expect, you fall sound asleep in an unlocked house—before your dad is back home."

"Mountains of moose shit—as you would say, Ketchum," Danny had replied.

That was just the way they did things in Toronto, the cook and his son explained to the veteran river driver. Danny and his dad had locked each other out of the house before; it was a nuisance. Now, when they went out, they left the house on Cluny Drive unlocked; when they were both back in the house for the night, the last one to go to bed locked the damn door.

"It's the red wine that troubles me a bit, Danny," Ketchum had told the writer. "With red wine, you fall asleep like a rock—you don't hear anything."

"If I drink only beer, I'm awake all night," Danny told the logger.

"I like the sound of that a little better," was all the woodsman had said.

But the red wine wasn't really the problem. Yes, Danny would occasionally drink more than a glass or two—and it did make him sleepy. Still, the wine was no more than a contributing factor, and the restaurant's new name wasn't part of what went wrong at all. The problem was that after all their efforts to elude the cowboy—and the dubious name changes, which would prove to be pointless—Ketchum had simply been followed.

THE COWBOY HAD FOLLOWED Ketchum before, but Carl was none the wiser for it. The retired deputy had twice trailed the logger on his hunting trips to Quebec; Carl had even tracked Ketchum all the way to Pointe au Baril Station one winter, only to assume that the younger man the old woodsman was camping with was just some Ontario hick. The cowboy had no idea who Danny was, or what Danny did; Carl had wildly concluded that possibly Ketchum was "queer," and that the younger man was the old logger's lover! No little fella with a limp had materialized on these adventures, and Carl had essentially given up on following Ketchum.

One word would change everything—the word and the fact that both Ketchum and the cowboy did their *tire* business at the same establishment in Milan. Tires, especially winter tires, were important in northern New Hampshire. Twitchell's was the name of the tire place that Ketchum and the cowboy frequented, though the grease monkey who did the important talking was a young Canuck named Croteau.

"That looks like Ketchum's rig," Carl had said to the French Canadian—this was a week or more before Christmas, and the cowboy had noticed Ketchum's truck on the hoist in the garage at Twitchell's. Croteau was changing all four tires.

"Yup," Croteau said. The retired deputy observed that the Canuck was removing Ketchum's studded tires and replacing them with unstudded snow tires.

"Does Ketchum have an inside tip that it's gonna be a mild winter?" Carl asked Croteau.

"Nope," Croteau said. "He just don't like the sound of the studs on the interstate, and it's mostly interstates between here and Toronto."

"Toronto," the cowboy repeated, but that wasn't the word that would change everything.

"Ketchum puts the studded tires back on when he comes home after Christmas," Croteau explained to the deputy, "but you don't need studs for highway drivin'—out on the interstates, regular snow tires will do."

"Ketchum goes to Toronto for Christmas?" Carl asked the Canuck.

"For as long as I can remember," Croteau said, which wasn't very long—not in the cowboy's estimation. Croteau was in his early twenties; he'd been changing tires only since he got out of high school.

"Does Ketchum have some *lady* friend in Toronto?" Carl asked. "Or a boyfriend, maybe?"

"Nope," Croteau replied. "Ketchum said he's got family there."

It was the *family* word that would change everything. The deputy sheriff knew that Ketchum didn't have a family—not in Canada, anyway. And what family he'd had, the old logger had lost; everyone knew that Ketchum was estranged from his children. Ketchum's kids were still living in New Hampshire, Carl knew. Ketchum's children were grown up now, with kids of their own, but they had never moved away from Coos County; they'd just cut their ties to Ketchum.

"Ketchum can't have any *family* in Toronto," the cowboy told the dumb Canuck.

"Well, that's what Ketchum said—he's got family there, in Toronto," Croteau insisted stubbornly.

Later, Danny would be touched that the old logger thought of him and his dad as family; yet that was what gave them away to Carl. The cowboy couldn't think of anyone whom Ketchum had absolutely taken to—or had seemed at all close to, in the manner of family— except the cook. Nor had it been hard for the ex-cop to follow Ketchum's truck, unnoticed. That truck burned a lot of oil; a black cloud of exhaust enveloped following vehicles, and Carl had wisely rented an anonymous-looking SUV with snow tires. That December, on the interstate highways of the northeastern United States—they would cross into Canada from Buffalo, over the Peace Bridge—the cowboy's car was as nondescript as they come. After all, Carl had been a cop; he knew how to tail people.

The cowboy knew how to stake out the house on Cluny Drive, too. It wasn't long before he was familiar with all of their comings and go-ings, including Ketchum's. Of course the cowboy was aware that Ketchum was just visiting. While Carl must have been tempted to kill all three of them, the deputy probably didn't want to risk going up against the old logger; Carl knew that Ketchum was armed. The house on Cluny Drive was never locked during the day, or at night, either—not until after the last of them, usually the cook, had limped home to go to bed.

It had been easy for the cowboy to get inside and have a good look at the house; that way, Carl knew who was sleeping in each room. But there was more that he *didn't* know.

The only gun in the house was the one in the guest bedroom, where it was clear to Carl that Ketchum was staying. The cowboy thought it was an odd gun, or at least an unsophisticated weapon, for Ketchum to be carrying—a *youth*-model Winchester 20-gauge. (A friggin' *kid's* shotgun, Carl was thinking.)

How could the deputy have known that the Winchester Ranger was Ketchum's Christmas present for Danny? The old logger didn't believe in wrapping paper, and the 20-gauge, pump-action shotgun was loaded and stashed under Ketchum's bed—exactly where the cowboy would have hidden a weapon. It never occurred to Carl that the 20-gauge wouldn't be going back to New Hampshire with the veteran river driver, whenever it was that Ketchum eventually returned to Coos County. The cowboy would just wait and see when that would be—then make his move.

Carl thought he had several options. He'd unlocked the door to the fire escape in Danny's third-floor writing room; if the writer didn't notice that the door was unlocked, the cowboy could enter the house that way. But if Danny saw that the door was unlocked, and re-locked it, Carl could come into the house through the unlocked front door—at any time of the evening, when the cook and his son were out. The cowboy had observed that Danny didn't go back to his third-floor writing room after he'd had dinner. (This was because of the beer and the red wine; when the writer had been drinking, he didn't even want to be in the same room with his writing.)

Whether Carl entered the property via the third-floor fire escape or walked in the front door, he would be safe hiding out in that third-floor room; the cowboy only had to be careful not to move around too much, not until the cook and his son were asleep. The floor creaked, Carl had noticed; so did the stairs leading down to the second-floor hall. But the cowboy would be wearing just socks on his feet. He would kill the cook first, Carl was thinking—then the son. Carl had seen the eight-inch cast-iron skillet hanging in the cook's bedroom; of course the cowboy knew the Injun-killing history of that skillet, because Six-Pack had told him. Carl had amused himself by thinking how funny it would be to be standing in the cook's bedroom, after he'd shot the little fucker, just waiting for the kid to come to his dad's rescue with the stupid skillet! Well, if that was how it worked out, that would be okay with the cowboy. What was important to Carl was that he kill them both, and that he drive across the U.S. border before the bodies were discovered. (With any luck, the cowboy could be back in Coos County before then.)

The old sheriff was a little worried about encountering the Mexican cleaning woman, whose comings and goings weren't as predictable as the cook's—or the no-less-observable habits of his writer son. Compared to Lupita suddenly showing up to do a load or two of laundry, or compulsively attacking the kitchen, even Ketchum's routine was reasonably consistent. The logger went to a Tae Kwon Do gym on Yonge Street for a couple of hours every day. The gym was called Champion Centre, and Ketchum had found the place by accident a few years ago; the master instructor was a former Iranian wrestler, now a boxer and a kickboxer. Ketchum said he was working on his "kicking skills."

"Dear God," the cook had complained. "Why would an eighty-three-year-old man have an interest in learning a martial art?"

"It's more *mixed* martial arts, Cookie," Ketchum explained. "It's boxing and kickboxing—and grappling, too. I'm just interested in finding new ways to get a fella down to the ground. Once I get a guy on the ground, I know what to do with him."

"But *why*, Ketchum?" the cook cried. "How many more fights are you planning to be in?"

"That's just it, Cookie—no one can *plan* on being in a fight. You just have to be *ready*!"

"Dear God," Dominic said again.

To Danny it seemed that Ketchum had always been getting ready for a war. Ketchum's Christmas present to the writer, the Winchester Ranger, with which Danny had killed three deer, appeared to emphasize this point.

"What would I want with a shotgun, Ketchum?" Danny had asked the old logger.

"You're not much of a deer hunter, Danny—I'll grant you that—and you might never go back to hunting deer," Ketchum began, "but every household should have a twenty-gauge."

"Every household," Danny repeated.

"Okay, maybe *this* household especially," Ketchum said. "You need to have a quick-handling, fast-action gun around—something you can't miss with, in a close situation."

"A close situation," the cook repeated, throwing his hands in the air.

"I don't know, Ketchum," Danny said.

"Just take the gun, Danny," the logger told him. "See that it's loaded, at all times—slip it under your bed, for safekeeping."

The first two rounds were buckshot, Danny knew—the third was the deer slug. At the time, he'd handled the Winchester appreciatively—not only to please Ketchum, but because the writer knew that his acceptance of the shotgun would exasperate his father. Danny was adept at getting Ketchum and his dad riled up at each other.

"Dear God," the cook started up again. "I won't sleep at all, knowing there's a loaded gun in the house!"

"That's okay with me, Cookie," Ketchum said. "In fact, I would say it would be *ideal*—if you don't sleep at all, I mean."

The Winchester Ranger had a birch-wood forestock and butt-stock, with a rubber recoil pad that the writer now rested against his shoulder. Danny had to admit that he loved listening to his dad and Ketchum going at it.

"God damn you, Ketchum," the cook was saying. "One night I'll get up to pee, and my son will shoot me—thinking I'm the cowboy!"

Danny laughed. "Come on, you two—it's *Christmas*! Let's try to have a Merry Christmas," the writer said.

But Ketchum wasn't in a merry mood. "Danny's not going to shoot you, Cookie," the logger said. "I just want you fucking fellas to be *ready*!"

"IN-UK-SHUK," Danny sometimes said in his sleep. Charlotte had taught him how to pronounce the Indian word; or, in Canada, was one supposed to say the *Inuit* word? (An *Inuk* word, Danny had also heard; he had no idea what was correct.) Danny had heard Charlotte say the *inuksuk* word many times.

When he woke up the morning after Christmas, Danny wondered if he should move the photograph of Charlotte from above the head-board of his bed—or perhaps exchange it for a different picture. In the photo in question, Charlotte is standing, wet and dripping, in a bathing suit, with her arms wrapped around herself; she's smiling, but she looks cold. In the distance, one can see the island's main dock—Charlotte was just swimming there—but nearer to her tall figure, between her and the dock, stands the unreadable *inuksuk*. This particular stone cairn was somewhat man-shaped but not really a human like-ness. From the water, it might have been mistaken for a mark of navigation; some *inuksuit* (that was the plural form) were navigational markers, but not this one.

Two large rocks atop each other composed each manlike leg; a kind of shelf or tabletop possibly represented the figure's hips or waist. Four smaller rocks composed a potbellied upper body. The creature, if it was intended to have human features, had absurdly truncated arms; its arms were as disproportionately short as its legs were overlong. The head, if it was meant to be a head, suggested permanently windswept hair. The stone cairn was as stunted as the winter-beaten pines on the Georgian Bay islands. The cairn stood only as tall as Charlotte's hips, and given the perspective of the photograph above the headboard of Danny's bed—that is, with Charlotte in the foreground of the frame—the *inuksuk* looked even shorter than it was. Yet it also appeared to be indestructible; maybe that's why the word was on Danny's lips when he woke up.

There were countless *inuksuit* on those islands—and many more out on Route 69, between Parry Sound and Pointe au Baril, where Danny remembered a sign that said FIRST NATION, OJIBWAY TERRITORY. Not far from those summer cottages around Moonlight Bay, where Danny had driven in the boat with Charlotte one scorching day, there were some striking *inuksuit* near the Shawanaga Landing Indian Reserve.

But what *were* they, exactly? the writer now wondered, as he lay in bed the morning after Christmas. Not even Charlotte knew who had built the *inuksuk* on her island.

There'd been a carpenter from the Shawanaga Landing Indian Reserve on Andy Grant's crew, the summer the two sleeping cabins were under construction. Another summer, Danny remembered, one of the guys who brought the propane tanks to the island had a boat named *First Nation*. He'd told Danny he was a pure-blooded Ojibway, but Charlotte said it was "unlikely"; Danny hadn't asked her why she was skeptical.

"Maybe Granddaddy built your *inuksuk*," Danny had said to Charlotte. Perhaps, he'd thought, the various Indians who'd worked on Turner Island over the years had rebuilt the stone cairn whenever the rocks had fallen down.

"The rocks don't fall down," Charlotte said. "Granddaddy had nothing to do with our *inuksuk*. A native built it—it won't ever fall down."

"But what do they *mean*, exactly?" Danny asked her.

"They imply origins, respect, endurance," Charlotte answered, but this was too vague to satisfy the writer in Danny Angel; he remembered being surprised that Charlotte seemed satisfied with such a nonspecific description.

As for what an individual *inuksuk* meant—"Well, shit," as Ketchum had said, "it seems to matter which Injun you ask." (Ketchum believed that some *inuksuit* were nothing but meaningless heaps of rocks.)

Danny peered under his bed at the Winchester. Per Ketchum's instructions, the loaded shotgun lay in an open case; according to Ketchum, the case should remain unzipped, "because any fool intruder can hear a zipper."

It was obvious, of course, *which* fool intruder Ketchum meant—an eighty-three-year-old retired deputy sheriff, all the way from fucking New Hampshire! "And the safety?" Danny had asked Ketchum. "Do I leave the safety off, too?" It made a sound, a soft click, when you pushed the button for the safety, which was slightly forward of the trigger housing, but Ketchum had told Danny to leave the safety on.

The way the old logger put it was: "If the cowboy can hear the safety click off, he's already too close to you."

Danny looked first at the photograph of Charlotte with the *inuksuk* standing behind her, then at the 20-gauge shotgun under his bed. Perhaps the stone cairn and the Winchester Ranger both represented protection—the 20-gauge of a more specific kind. He was not unhappy to have the gun, Danny was thinking, though it seemed to him that every Christmas ushered in a morbid preoccupation—sometimes initiated by Ketchum (such as the Winchester) but at other times inspired by Danny or his dad. This Christmas Eve, for example, the cook could be blamed for beginning a downward spiral of gloominess.

"Just think of it," Dominic had said to his son and Ketchum. "If Joe were alive, he would be in his mid-thirties—probably with a couple of kids of his own."

"Joe would be older than Charlotte was when I first met her," Danny chimed in.

"Actually, Daniel," his father said, "Joe would be only a decade younger than *you* were—I mean, at the time Joe died."

"Whoa! Stop this shit!" Ketchum cried. "And if Injun Jane were still alive, she'd be eighty-fucking-eight! I doubt she'd even be speaking to any of us—not unless we somehow managed to elevate our conversation."

But the very next day, Ketchum had presented Danny with the 20-gauge shotgun—not exactly an *elevation* of their prevailing conversation, or their overriding fixation—and the cook had, seemingly out of the blue, begun to complain about "the sheer morbidity" of Daniel's book dedications.

True, *Baby in the Road* (as might be expected) was dedicated as follows: "My son, Joe—in memoriam." It was the second dedication to Joe—the third, overall, in memoriam. Dominic found this depressing.

"I can't help it if the people I know keep dying, Pop," Danny had said.

All the while, Ketchum had continued to demonstrate the sliding action of the Winchester, the ejected shotgun shells flying all around. One of the live shells (a deer slug) would be lost for a time in the discarded wrapping paper for other Christmas presents, but Ketchum kept loading and unloading the weapon as if he were mowing down a *horde* of attackers.

"If we live long enough, we become caricatures of ourselves," Danny said aloud to himself—as if he were writing this down, which he wasn't. The writer was still contorting himself in bed, where he was transfixed by the photo of Charlotte with the mysterious *inuksuk*—that is, when he *wasn't* drawn to the dangerous but thrilling sight of the loaded shotgun under his bed.

IT WAS BOXING DAY in Canada. A writer Danny knew always had a party. Every Christmas, the cook bought Ketchum some outdoor clothing—at either Eddie Bauer or Roots—and Ketchum wore his new gear to the Boxing Day party. Dominic never failed to help out in the kitchen; the kitchen, anybody's kitchen, was ever the cook's home away from home. Danny mingled with his friends at the party; he tried to remain unembarrassed by Ketchum's political outbursts. There was never any need for Danny to feel embarrassed—not in

Canada, where the old logger's anti-American ranting was very popular.

"Some fella from the CBC wanted me to go on a radio show," Ketchum told Danny and his dad, when the cook was driving them home from the Boxing Day party.

"Dear God," Dominic said again.

"Just because you're sober, don't think you're a good driver, Cookie—you best let Danny and me handle the conversation while you pay attention to the mayhem in the streets."

The cowboy could have killed them all that night, but Carl was a coward; he wouldn't risk it, not with Ketchum in the house. The deputy didn't know that the youth-model 20-gauge was under Danny's bed, not Ketchum's, nor could Carl have guessed how much the old logger had had to drink at the party. The cowboy could have *shot* his way into the house; it's doubtful that Ketchum would have woken up. Danny wouldn't have woken up, either. It had been one of those nights when the supposed one or two glasses of red wine with his dinner had, in reality, turned out to be four or five. Danny woke once in the night, thinking he should look under his bed to be sure that the shotgun was still there; he fell out of bed in the process, making a resounding *thump*, which neither his dad nor the snoring logger heard.

Ketchum never lingered long in Toronto once Christmas was over. A pity he hadn't brought Hero with him and then—for some reason—left the dog with the cook and his son *after* Ketchum went back across the border. Carl couldn't have entered the house on Cluny Drive, or hidden himself in the third-floor writing room, if Hero, that fine animal, had been there. But the dog was in Coos County, staying with Six-Pack Pam—terrorizing her dogs, as it would turn out—and Ketchum left early the next morning for New Hampshire.

When Danny got up (before his dad), he found the note Ketchum had left on the kitchen table. To Danny's surprise, it was neatly typed. Ketchum had gone up to the third-floor writing room and used the typewriter there, but Danny hadn't heard the creaking of the floor above his bedroom—he hadn't heard the stairs creak, either. Both he and the cook had slept through the sound of the typewriter, too—not a good sign, the old logger could have told them. But Ketchum's note said nothing about that.

> I'VE SEEN ENOUGH OF YOU FELLAS FOR A TIME!
> I MISS MY DOG, AND I'M GOING TO SEE HIM. BY THE
> TIME I'M BACK HOME, I'LL BE MISSING YOU, TOO!
> EASY ON THE RED WINE, DANNY. KETCHUM.

Carl was happy to see Ketchum's truck leave. The cowboy must have been growing impatient, but he waited for the Mexican cleaning woman to come and go; that way, the deputy had no doubt. With the guest bedroom empty—Lupita had made it up as good as new—Carl was convinced that Ketchum wasn't coming back. Yet the cowboy had to wait another night.

The cook and his son ate their dinner at home on the evening of December 27. Dominic had found a kielbasa sausage in the meat market and had browned it in olive oil, and then stewed it with chopped fennel and onions and cauliflower in a tomato sauce with crushed fennel seeds. The cook served the stew with a warm, fresh loaf of rosemary-and-olive bread, and a green salad.

"Ketchum would have liked this, Pop," Danny said.

"Ah, well—Ketchum is a good man," Dominic said, to his son's amazement.

Not knowing how to respond, Danny attempted to further compliment the kielbasa stew; he suggested it might make a suitable addition to the more bistro-like or low-key menu at Kiss of the Wolf.

"No, no," the cook said dismissively. "Kielbasa is too rustic—even for Kiss of the Wolf."

All Danny said was: "It's a good dish, Dad. You could serve it to royalty, I think."

"I should have made it for Ketchum—I never made it for him," was all Dominic said.

THE COOK'S LAST NIGHT ALIVE, he ate with his beloved Daniel at a Portuguese place near Little Italy. The restaurant was called Chiado; it was one of Dominic's favorites in Toronto. Arnaud had introduced him to it when they'd both been working downtown on Queen Street West. That Thursday night, December 28, both Danny and his dad had the rabbit.

During Ketchum's Christmas visit, it had snowed and it had rained—everything had frozen and thawed, and then it all froze again. By the time the cook and his son took a taxi home from Chiado, it had started to snow once more. (Dominic didn't like to drive downtown.) The imprints of the cowboy's footsteps in the crusty old snow on the outdoor fire escape were faint and hard to see in the daylight; now that it was dark, and snowing, Carl's tracks were completely covered. The ex-cop had taken off his parka and his boots. He'd stretched out on the couch in Danny's third-floor writing room with the Colt .45 revolver clasped to his chest—in the scenario he'd imagined, the old sheriff had no need of a holster.

The voices of the cook and his writer son reached Carl from the kitchen, though we'll never know if the cowboy understood their conversation.

"At fifty-eight, you should be married, Daniel. You should be living with your wife, not your father," the cook was saying.

"And what about you, Pop? Wouldn't a wife be good for you?" Danny asked.

"I've had my opportunities, Daniel. At seventy-six, I would embarrass myself with a wife—I would always be apologizing to her!" Dominic said.

"For *what*?" Danny asked his dad.

"Occasional incontinence, perhaps. Farting, certainly—not to mention talking in my sleep," the cook confided to his son.

"You should find a wife who's hard of hearing—like Ketchum," Danny suggested. They both laughed; the cowboy had to have heard their laughter.

"I was being serious, Daniel—you should at least have a regular girlfriend, a true companion," Dominic was saying, as they came up the stairs to the second-floor hall. Even from the third floor, Carl could have singled out the distinguishing sounds of the cook's limp on the stairs.

"I have women friends," Danny started to say.

"I'm not talking about *groupies*, Daniel."

"I don't have groupies, Pop—not anymore."

"Young fans, then. Remember, I've read your fan mail—"

"I don't answer those letters, Dad."

"Young—what are they called?—'editorial assistants,' maybe? Young booksellers, too, Daniel . . . I've seen you with one or two. All those *young* people in publishing!"

"Young women are more likely to be unattached," Danny pointed out to his dad. "Most women my age are married, or they're widows."

"What's wrong with widows?" his father asked. (At that, they'd both laughed again—a shorter laugh this time.)

"I'm not looking for a permanent relationship," Danny said.

"I can see that. *Why?*" Dominic wanted to know. They were at opposite ends of the second-floor hall, at the doorways to their respective bedrooms. Their voices were raised; surely the cowboy could hear every word.

"I've had my opportunities, too, Pop," Danny told his dad.

"I just want all the best for you, Daniel," the cook told him.

"You've been a good father—the *best,*" Danny said.

"You were a good father, too, Daniel—"

"I could have done a better job," Danny quickly interjected.

"I love you!" Dominic said.

"I love you, too, Dad. Good night," Danny said; he went into his bedroom and quietly closed the door.

"Good night!" the cook called from the hall. It was such a heartfelt blessing; it's almost conceivable that the cowboy was tempted to wish them both a good night, too. But Carl lay unmoving above them, not making a sound.

Did the deputy wait as long as an hour after he'd heard them brush their teeth? Probably not. Did Danny once more dream about the windswept pine on Charlotte's island in Georgian Bay—specifically, the view of that hardy little tree from what had been his writing shack there? Probably. Did the cook, in his prayers, ask for more time? Probably not. Under the circumstances, and knowing Dominic Baciagalupo, the cook couldn't have asked for much—that is, if he'd prayed at all. At best, Dominic might have expressed the hope that his lonely son "find someone"—only that.

Did the floorboards above them creak under the fat cowboy's

weight, once Carl decided to make his move? Not that they heard; or, if Danny heard anything at all, he might have happily imagined (in his sleep) that Joe was home from Colorado.

Not knowing how dark it might be in the house at night, the cowboy had tested those stairs from the third-floor writing room with his eyes closed; he'd counted the number of steps in the second-floor hall to the cook's bedroom door, too. And Carl knew where the light switch was—just inside the door, right next to the eight-inch cast-iron skillet.

As it turned out, Danny always left a light on—on the stairs from the kitchen to the second-floor hall, so there was plenty of light in the hall. The cowboy, slipping silently in his socks, padded down the hallway to the cook's bedroom and opened the door. "Surprise, Cookie!" Carl said, flicking on the light. "It's time for you to die."

Maybe Danny heard that; perhaps he didn't. But his dad sat up in bed—blinking his eyes in the sudden, white light—and the cook said, in a *very* loud voice, "What took you so long, you moron? You must be dumber than a dog turd, cowboy—just like Jane always said." (Without a doubt, Danny heard that.)

"You little shit, Cookie!" Carl cried. Danny heard that, too; he was already kneeling on the floor, pulling the Winchester out of the open case under his bed.

"Dumber than a dog turd, cowboy!" his dad was shouting.

"I'm not so dumb, Cookie! *You're* the one who's gonna die!" Carl was hollering; he never heard Danny click the safety off, or the sound of the writer running barefoot down the hall. The cowboy took aim with the Colt .45 and shot the cook in the heart. Dominic Baciagalupo was blown into the headboard of the bed; he died instantly, on the pillows. There was no time for the deputy to comprehend the cook's curious smile, which stretched the white scar on his lower lip, and only Danny understood what his dad had uttered just before he was shot.

"*She bu de,*" Dominic managed to say, as Ah Gou and Xiao Dee had taught him—the *she bu de* that means "I can't bear to let go."

The Chinese was, of course, meaningless to Carl, who, as he wheeled to face the naked man in the doorway, must have half understood why the cook had died smiling. Not only did Dominic know that all the yelling would save his son; the cook also knew that his friend Ketchum had provided Daniel with a better weapon than the eight-inch cast-iron skillet. And maybe there was a margin of last-minute recognition in the cowboy's eyes, when he saw that Danny had already taken aim with Ketchum's Winchester—the much-maligned youth model.

The long barrel of Carl's Colt .45 was still pointed at the floor when the first round of buckshot from the 20-gauge tore away half his throat; the cowboy was flung backward into the night table, where the lightbulb in the lamp exploded between his shoulder blades. Danny's second load of buckshot tore away what remained of the cowboy's throat. The deer slug, the so-called kill-shot, wasn't really necessary, but Danny—now at point-blank range—fired the shotgun's third and final round into Carl's mangled neck, as if the gaping wound itself were a magnet.

If Ketchum could be believed—that is, if he'd been speaking literally about the way wolves killed their prey—weren't these three shots from the 20-gauge Ranger exactly as kisses of wolves should be? Weren't they, indeed, not so pretty?

Still naked, Danny went downstairs. He called the police from the phone in the kitchen, telling them that he would unlock the front door for them, and that they could find him upstairs with his father. After he'd unlocked the door, he went back upstairs to his bedroom and put on some old sweatpants and a sweatshirt. Danny thought of calling Ketchum, but it was late and there was no reason to be in a hurry. When he reentered his dad's bedroom, there was no overlooking the kisses of wolves that had ripped the cowboy apart—leaving him like something sprayed from a hose—but Danny only briefly regretted the mess he'd made for Lupita. The blood-soaked rug, the blood-spattered walls, the bloodied photographs on the bulletin board above the shattered night table—well, Danny didn't doubt that Lupita could handle it. He knew that something worse had happened to her: She'd lost a child.

Ketchum had been right about the red wine, the writer was thinking, as he sat on the bed beside his father. If he'd been drinking only beer, Danny thought he might have heard the cowboy a few seconds sooner; Danny just might have been able to open fire with the shotgun before Carl could have pulled the trigger. "Don't beat up on yourself about it, Danny," Ketchum would tell him later. "I'm the one the cowboy followed. I should have seen that coming."

"Don't *you* beat up on yourself about it, Ketchum," Danny would tell the old logger, but of course Ketchum would.

When the police came, the lights in the neighboring houses were all ablaze, and lots of dogs were barking; normally, at that hour of the night, Rosedale is very quiet. Most of the residents who lived near the double shooting had never heard gunfire as loud and terrifying as that—some dogs would bark until dawn. But when the police came, they found Danny quietly cradling his dad's head in his lap, the two of them huddled together on the blood-soaked pillows at the head of the bed. In his report, the young homicide detective would say that the bestselling author was waiting for them in the upstairs of the house— exactly where he'd said he would be—and that the writer appeared to be singing, or perhaps reciting a poem, to his murdered father.

"She bu de," Danny kept repeating in his dad's ear. Neither the cook nor his son had ever known if Ah Gou and Xiao Dee's translation of the Mandarin was essentially correct—that is, if *she bu de* literally meant "I can't bear to let go"—but what did it matter, really? "I can't bear to let go" was what the writer *thought* he was saying to his father, who'd kept his beloved son safe from the cowboy for nearly forty-seven years; that had been how long ago it was when they'd both left Twisted River.

Now, at last—now that the police were there—Danny began to cry. He just started to let go. An ambulance and two police cars were parked outside the house on Cluny Drive, their lights flashing. The first policemen to enter the cook's bedroom were aware of the rudimentary story, as it had been reported over the phone: There'd been a break-in, and the armed intruder had shot and killed the famous writer's father; Danny had then shot and killed the intruder. But surely there was more to the story than that, the young homicide detective was thinking. The detective had the utmost respect for Mr. Angel, and, under the circumstances, he wanted to give the writer all the time he needed to compose himself. Yet the damage done by that shotgun—repeatedly, and at such close range—was so excessive that the detective must have sensed that this break-in and murder, and the famous writer's retaliation, had a substantial history.

"Mr. Angel?" the young homicide detective asked. "If you're ready, sir, I wonder if you could tell me how this happened."

What made Danny's tears different was that he was crying the way a twelve-year-old would cry—as if Carl had somehow shot his dad their last night in Twisted River. Danny couldn't speak, but he managed to point to something; it was in the vicinity of his father's bedroom doorway.

The young detective misunderstood. "Yes, I know, you were standing there in the doorway when you shot," the homicide policeman said. "At least, for the first shot. Then you came closer into the room, didn't you?"

Danny was violently shaking his head. Another young policeman had noticed the eight-inch cast-iron skillet hanging just inside the doorway of the bedroom—an unusual spot for a frying pan—and he tapped the bottom of the skillet with his index finger.

"Yes!" Danny managed to say, between sobs.

"Bring that skillet over here," the homicide detective said.

While he didn't relinquish his hold on his father—Danny continued to cradle the cook's head in his lap—he reached with his right hand for the eight-inch cast-iron skillet, and when his fingers closed around the handle, his crying calmed down. The young homicide detective waited; he could see there was no rushing this story.

Raising the skillet in his right hand, Danny then rested the heavy pan on the bed. "I'll start with the eight-inch cast-iron skillet," the writer finally began, as if he had a long story to tell—one he knew well.

V.

COOS COUNTY,
NEW HAMPSHIRE, 2001

—

CHAPTER 14

KETCHUM'S LEFT HAND

KETCHUM HAD BEEN HUNTING BEAR. HE'D DRIVEN HIS truck to Wilsons Mills, Maine, and he and Hero had taken the Suzuki ATV back into New Hampshire—crossing the border about parallel to Half Mile Falls on the Dead Diamond River, where Ketchum bagged a big male black bear. His weapon of choice for bear was the short-barreled, lightweight rifle Danny's friend Barrett had (years ago) preferred for deer: a Remington .30-06 Springfield, a carbine, what Ketchum called "my old-reliable, bolt-action sucker." (The model had been discontinued in 1940.)

Ketchum had some difficulty bringing the bear back across the border, the all-terrain vehicle notwithstanding. "Let's just say Hero had to walk a fair distance," Ketchum would tell Danny. When Ketchum said "walk," this probably meant that the dog had to *run* the whole way. But it was the first weekend of bear season when hounds were permitted; that fine animal was excited enough to not mind running after Ketchum's ATV. Anyway, counting Ketchum and the dead bear, there'd been no room for Hero on the Suzuki.

"It might be dark on Monday before Hero and I get home," Ketchum had warned Danny. There would be no locating the old logger over the long weekend; Danny didn't even try. Ketchum had gradually accepted the telephone and the fax machine, but—at eighty-four—the former river driver would never own a cell phone. (Not that there were a lot of cell phones in the Great North Woods in 'o1.)

Besides, Danny's flight from Toronto had been delayed; by the time he'd landed in Boston and had rented the car, the leisurely cup of coffee he'd planned with Paul Polcari and Tony Molinari turned into a quick lunch. It would be early afternoon before Danny and Carmella Del Popolo left the North End. Of course the roads were in better shape than they'd been in 1954, when the cook and his twelve-year-old son had made that trip in the other direction, but northern New Hampshire was still "a fair distance" (as Ketchum would say) from the North End of Boston, and it was late afternoon when Danny and Carmella passed the Pontook Reservoir and followed the upper Androscoggin along Route 16 to Errol.

When they drove by the reservoir, Danny recognized Dummer Pond Road—from when it had been a haul road—but all he said to Carmella was: "We'll be coming back here with Ketchum tomorrow."

Carmella nodded; she just looked out the passenger-side window at the Androscoggin. Maybe ten miles later, she said: "That's a powerful-looking river." Danny was glad she wasn't seeing the river in March or April; the Androscoggin was a torrent in mud season.

Ketchum had told Danny that September was the best time of year for them to come—for Carmella, especially. There was a good chance for fair weather, the nights were growing cooler, the bugs were gone, and it was too soon for snow. But as far north as Coos County, the leaves were turning color in late August. That second Monday in September, it already looked like fall, and there was a nip in the air by late afternoon.

Ketchum had been worried about Carmella's mobility in the woods. "I can drive us most of the way, but it will entail a little walking to get to the right place on the riverbank," Ketchum had said.

In his mind's eye, Danny could see the place Ketchum meant—an elevated site, overlooking the basin above the river bend. What he couldn't quite imagine was how different it would be—with the cookhouse entirely gone, and the town of Twisted River burned to the ground. But Dominic Baciagalupo hadn't wanted his ashes scattered where the cookhouse was, or anywhere near the town; the cook had requested that his ashes be sunk in the river, in the basin where his not-really-a-cousin Rosie had slipped under the breaking ice. It was almost exactly the same spot where Angelù Del Popolo had gone under the logs. That, of course, was really why Carmella had come; those many years ago (thirty-four, if Danny was doing the math correctly), Ketchum had invited Carmella to Twisted River.

"If, one day, you ever want to see the place where your boy perished, I would be honored to show you," was how Ketchum had put it to her. Carmella had *so wanted* to see the river basin where the accident happened, but not the logs; she knew the logs would be too much for her. Just the riverbank, where her dear Gamba and young Dan had stood and seen it happen—and maybe the exact spot in the water where her one-and-only Angelù hadn't surfaced. Yes, she might one day want to see that, Carmella had thought.

"Thank you, Mr. Ketchum," she'd said that day, when the logger and the cook were leaving Boston. "If you ever want to see me—" Carmella had started to say to Dominic.

"I know," the cook had said to her, but he wouldn't look at her.

Now, on the occasion of Danny bringing his father's ashes to Twisted River, Ketchum had insisted that the writer bring Carmella, too. When Danny had first met Angel's mom, the twelve-year-old had noted her big breasts, big hips, big smile—knowing that only Carmella's smile had been bigger than Injun Jane's. Now the writer knew that Carmella was at least as old as Ketchum, or a little older; she would have been in her mid-eighties, Danny guessed. Her hair had turned completely white—even her eyebrows were white, in striking contrast to her olive complexion and her apparently robust good health. Carmella was big all over, but she was still more feminine than Jane had ever been. And however happy she was with the new fella in her life—Paul Polcari and Tony Molinari continued to insist that she was—she'd held on to the Del Popolo name, perhaps out of respect for the fact that she had lost both the drowned fisherman *and* her precious only child.

Yet on the long drive north, there'd been no bewailing her beloved Angelù—and only one comment from Carmella on the cook's passing. "I lost my dear Gamba years ago, Secondo—now you've lost him,

too!" Carmella had said, with tears in her eyes. But she'd quickly recovered herself; for the rest of the trip, Carmella gave Danny no indication that she was even thinking about where they were going, and
why.

Carmella continued to refer to Dominic by his nickname,
Gamba—just as she called Danny Secondo, as if Danny were (in her
heart) still her surrogate son; it appeared she'd long ago forgiven him
for spying on her in the bathtub. He could not imagine doing so now,
but he didn't say so; instead, Danny rather formally apologized to
Carmella for his behavior all those years ago.

"Nonsense, Secondo—I suppose I was flattered," Carmella told
him in the car, with a dismissive wave of her plump hand. "I only worried that the sight of me would have a damaging effect on you—that
you might be permanently attracted to fat, older women."

Danny sensed that this might have been an invitation for him to
proclaim that he was *not* (and had never been) attracted to such
women, though in truth—after Katie, who was preternaturally
small—many of the women in his life had been large. By the stick-
figure standards of contemporary women's fashion, Danny thought
that even Charlotte—indisputably, the love of his life—might have
been considered overweight.

Like his dad, Danny was small, and while the writer didn't respond
to Carmella's comment, he found himself wondering if perhaps he
was more at ease with women who were bigger than he was. (Not that
spying on Carmella in a bathtub, *or* killing Injun Jane with a skillet,
had anything to do with it!)

"I wonder if you're seeing someone now—someone special, that
is," Carmella said, after a pause of a mile or more.

"No one special," Danny replied.

"If I can still count, you're almost sixty," Carmella told him.
(Danny was fifty-nine.) "Your dad always wanted you to be with
someone who was right for you."

"I was, but she moved on," Danny told her.

Carmella sighed. She had brought her melancholy with her in the
car; what was melancholic about Carmella, together with her undefined disapproval of Danny, had traveled with them all the way from
Boston. Danny had detected the latter's presence as strongly as

Carmella's engaging scent—either a mild, nonspecific perfume or a smell as naturally appealing as freshly baked bread.

"Besides," Danny went on, "my dad wasn't with anyone special—not after he was my age." After a pause, while Carmella waited, Danny added: "And Pop was never with anyone as right for him as you."

Carmella sighed again, as if to note (ambiguously) both her pleasure and displeasure—she was displeased by her failure to steer the conversation where she'd wanted it to go. The subject of what was *wrong* with Danny evidently weighed on her. Now Danny waited for what she would say next; it was only a matter of time, he knew, before Carmella would raise the more delicate matter of what was wrong with his *writing*.

ALL THE WAY FROM BOSTON, he'd found Carmella's conversation dull—the self-righteousness of her old age was depressing. She would lose her way in what she was saying, and then blame Danny for her bewilderment; she implied that he wasn't paying sufficient attention to her, or that he was deliberately confusing her. His dad, Danny realized, had remained sharp by comparison. While Ketchum grew deafer by the minute, and his ranting was more explosive—and though the old logger was close to Carmella's age—Danny instinctively forgave him. After all, Ketchum had always been crazy. Hadn't the veteran riverman been cranky and illogical when he was young? Danny was thinking to himself.

Just then, in the high-contrast, late-afternoon light, they drove past the small sign for ANDROSCOGGIN TAXIDERMY. "My goodness—'Moose Antlers for Sale,'" Carmella said aloud, attempting to read more minutiae from the sign. (She'd said, "My goodness," every minute of the drive north, Danny reflected with irritation.)

"Want to stop and buy a stuffed dead animal?" he asked her.

"Just so long as it's before dark!" Carmella answered, laughing; she patted his knee affectionately, and Danny felt ashamed for resenting her company. He'd loved her as a child and as a young man, and he had no doubt that she loved him—she'd positively *adored* his dad. Yet Danny found her tiresome now, and he hadn't wanted her along on this trip. It was Ketchum's idea to show her where Angel had died;

Danny realized that he'd wanted Ketchum for himself. Seeing his dad's ashes sunk in Twisted River, which was what the cook had wanted, mattered more to Danny than Ketchum making good on his promise to escort Carmella to the basin above the river bend, where her Angelù was lost. It made Danny feel ungenerous that he thought of Carmella as both a burden and a distraction; it made him feel un-kind, but he believed, for the first time, that Paul Polcari and Tony Molinari hadn't been kidding. Carmella truly must be happy—with her new fella *and* her life. (Nothing but happiness could explain why she was so boring!)

But hadn't Carmella lost three loved ones, counting the cook—her one and only child among them? How could Danny, who had lost an only child himself, *not* see Carmella as a sympathetic soul? He *did* see her as "sympathetic," of course! Danny just didn't want to be with Carmella—not at this moment, when the dual missions of sinking his father's ashes and being with Ketchum were entirely enough.

"Where are they?" Carmella asked, as they drove into Errol.

"Where are *what*?" Danny said. (They'd just been talking about *taxidermy*! Did she mean, Where are the dead stuffed animals?)

"Where are Gamba's remains—his ashes?" Carmella asked.

"In a nonbreakable container, a jar—it's a kind of plastic, not glass," Danny answered, somewhat evasively.

"In your luggage, in the trunk of the car?" Carmella asked him.

"Yes." Danny didn't want to tell her more about the container itself—what the contents of the jar used to be, and so forth. Besides, they were coming into the town—such as it was—and while it was still light, Danny wanted to get his bearings and have a look around. That way, it would be easier to find Ketchum in the morning.

"I'll see you bright and early Tuesday," the old logger had said.

"What's 'bright and early'?" Danny asked.

"Before seven, at the latest," Ketchum said.

"Before eight, if we're lucky," Danny told him. Danny had his con-cerns about how *bright and early* Carmella could get up and be fully functioning—not to mention that they were spending the night a few miles out of town. There was no proper place for them to stay in Errol, Ketchum had assured Danny. The logger had recommended a resort hotel in Dixville Notch.

From what Danny and Carmella could see of Errol, Ketchum had been right. They took the road toward Umbagog, past a general store, which was a liquor store, too; there was a bridge over the Androscoggin at the east end of town, and a fire station just west of the bridge, where Danny turned the car around. Driving back through town, they passed the Errol elementary school—they'd not noticed it the first time. There was also a restaurant called Northern Exposure, but the most prosperous-looking place in Errol was a sporting-goods store called L. L. Cote.

"Let's have a look inside," Danny suggested to Carmella.

"Just so long as it's before dark!" she said again. Carmella had been one of the earliest erotic stimulations of his life. How could she have become such a repetitious old woman? Danny was thinking.

They both regarded the sign on the door of the sporting-goods store with trepidation.

PLEASE NO LOADED FIREARMS INSIDE

"My goodness," Carmella said; they hesitated, albeit briefly, at the door.

L. L. Cote sold snowmobiles and all-terrain vehicles; inside there were dead stuffed animals, the regional species, enough to suggest that the local taxidermist was kept busy. (Bear, deer, lynx, fox, fisher cat, moose, porcupine, skunk—a host of "critters," Ketchum would have said—in addition to all the ducks and the birds of prey.) There were more guns than any other single item; Carmella recoiled from such a display of lethal weaponry. A large selection of Browning knives caused Danny to reflect that probably Ketchum's big Browning knife had been purchased here. There was also quite a collection of scent-elimination clothing, which Danny tried to explain to Carmella.

"So that the hunters don't smell like people," Danny told her.

"My goodness," Carmella said.

"Can I help you folks?" an old man asked them suspiciously.

He was an unlikely-looking salesman, with a Browning knife on his belt and a portly appearance. His belly hung over his belt buckle, and his red-and-black flannel shirt was reminiscent of what Ketchum usually wore—the salesman's camouflage fleece vest notwithstanding.

(Ketchum wouldn't have been caught dead in camouflage. "It's not like a war," the woodsman had said. "The critters can't shoot back.")

"I could use some directions, maybe," Danny said to the salesman. "We have to find Lost Nation Road, but not until tomorrow morning."

"It ain't called that no more—not for a long time," the salesman said, his suspicion deepening.

"I was told it's off the road to Akers Pond—" Danny started to say, but the salesman interrupted him.

"It is, but it ain't called Lost Nation—almost nobody calls it that, not nowadays."

"Does the road have a new name, then?" Danny asked.

The salesman was eyeing Carmella disagreeably. "It don't have a name—there's just a sign that says somethin' about small engine repairs. It's the first thing you come to, off Akers Pond Road—you can't miss it," the old man said, but not encouragingly.

"Well, I'm sure we'll find it," Danny told him. "Thank you."

"Who are you lookin' for?" the salesman asked, still staring at Carmella.

"Mr. Ketchum," Carmella answered.

"*Ketchum* would call it Lost Nation Road!" the salesman said emphatically, as if that settled everything that was wrong with the name. "Is Ketchum expectin' you?" the old man asked Danny.

"Yes, actually, he is, but not until tomorrow morning," Danny repeated.

"I wouldn't pay a visit to Ketchum if he *wasn't* expectin' me," the salesman said. "Not if I was you."

"Thank you again," Danny told the old man, taking Carmella's arm. They were trying to leave L. L. Cote's, but the salesman stopped them.

"Only an Injun would call it Lost Nation Road," he said. "That proves it!"

"Proves *what*?" Danny asked him. "Ketchum isn't an Indian."

"Ha!" the salesman scoffed. "Half-breeds are Injuns!"

Danny could sense Carmella's rising indignation—almost as physically as he could feel her weight against his arm. He had managed to steer her to the door of the sporting-goods store when the salesman called after them. "That fella Ketchum is a Lost Nation unto himself!" the salesman shouted. Then, as if he'd thought better of it—and with a certain measure of panic in the afterthought—he added: "Don't tell him I said so."

"I suppose Ketchum shops here, from time to time—doesn't he?" Danny asked; he was enjoying the fat old salesman's moment of fear.

"His money's as good as anybody's, isn't it?" the salesman said sourly.

"I'll tell him you said so," Danny said, guiding Carmella out the door.

"Is Mr. Ketchum an Indian?" she asked Danny, when they were back in the car.

"I don't know—maybe partly," Danny answered. "I never asked him."

"My goodness—I've never seen a *bearded* Indian," Carmella said. "Not in the movies, anyway."

THEY DROVE WEST OUT OF TOWN on Route 26. There was something called the Errol Cream Barrel & Chuck Wagon, and what appeared to be an immaculately well-kept campground and trailer park called Saw Dust Alley. They passed the Umbagog Snowmobile Association, too. That seemed to be about it for Errol. Danny didn't turn off the highway at Akers Pond Road; he simply noted where it was. He was sure Ketchum would be easy to find in the morning—Lost Nation or no Lost Nation.

A moment later, just as it was growing dark, they drove alongside a field encircled by a high fence. Naturally, Carmella read the sign on the fence out loud. " 'Please Do Not Harass the Buffalo'—well, my goodness, who would do such a thing?" she said, indignant as ever. But they saw no buffalo—only the fence and the sign.

The resort hotel in Dixville Notch was called The Balsams—for hikers and golfers in the warm-weather months, Danny supposed. (In the winter, for skiers certainly.) It was vast, and largely uninhabited on a Monday night. Danny and Carmella were practically alone in the dining room, where Carmella sighed deeply after they'd ordered their dinner. She had a glass of red wine. Danny had a beer. He'd stopped drinking red wine after his dad died, though Ketchum gave him endless shit about his decision to drink only beer. "You don't have to lay off the red wine *now!*" Ketchum had shouted at him.

"I don't care if I can't sleep anymore," Danny had told the old logger.

Now Carmella, after sighing, appeared to be holding her breath before beginning. "I guess it goes without saying that I've read all your books—more than once," she began.

"Really?" Danny asked her, feigning innocence of where this conversation was headed.

"Of *course* I have!" Carmella cried. For someone who's so happy, what is she angry with me for? Danny was wondering, when Carmella said, "Oh, Secondo—your dad was *so proud* of you, for being a famous writer and everything."

It was Danny's turn to sigh; he held his breath, for just a second or two. "And *you?*" he asked her, not so innocently this time.

"It's just that your stories, and sometimes the characters themselves, are so—what is the word I'm looking for?—*unsavory,*" Carmella started in, but she must have seen something in Danny's face that made her stop.

"I see," he said. Danny might have looked at her as if she were another interviewer, some journalist who hadn't done her homework, and whatever Carmella *really* thought about his writing, it suddenly wasn't worth it to her to say this to him—not to her darling Secondo, her surrogate son—for hadn't the world hurt him as much as it had hurt her?

"Tell me what you're writing now, Secondo," Carmella suddenly blurted out, smiling warmly at him. "You've been rather a long time between books again—haven't you? Tell me what you're up to. I'm just *dying* to know what's next!"

NOT MUCH LATER, after Carmella went to bed, some men were watching *Monday Night Football* at the bar, but Danny had already gone to his room, where he left the television dark. He also left the curtains open, confident in how lightly he slept—knowing that the early-morning light would wake him. He was only a little worried about getting Carmella up and going in the morning; Danny knew that Ketchum would wait for them if they were late. The lamp on the night table was on, as Danny lay in bed, and there on the table, too, was the jar containing his father's ashes. It would be Danny's last night with the cook's ashes, and he lay looking at them—as if they might suddenly speak, or give him some other indication of his dad's last wishes.

"Well, Pop, I know you *said* you wanted this, but I hope you haven't changed your mind," Danny spoke up in the hotel room. As for the ashes, they were in what was formerly a container of Amos' New York Steak Spice—the listed ingredients had once been sea salt, pepper, herbs, and spices—and the cook must have bought it at his favorite fancy meat market in their neighborhood of Toronto, because Olliffe was the name on the label.

Danny had gotten rid of most, but not all, of the contents; after he'd placed his father's ashes in, there'd been room to put some of the herbs and spices back in as well, and Danny had done so. If someone had questioned him about the container at U.S. Customs—if they'd opened the jar and had a whiff—it still would have smelled like steak spice. (Perhaps the pepper would have made the customs officer sneeze!)

But Danny had brought the cook's ashes through U.S. Customs without any questioning. Now he sat up in bed and opened the jar, cautiously sniffing the contents. Knowing what was in the container, Danny wouldn't have wanted to sprinkle it on a steak, but it still smelled like pepper and herbs and spices—it even *looked* like crushed herbs and a variety of spices, not human ashes. How fitting for a cook, that his remains had taken up residency in a jar of Amos' New York Steak Spice!

Dominic Baciagalupo, his writer son thought, might have gotten a kick out of that.

Danny turned out the lamp on the night table and lay in bed in the dark. "Last chance, Pop," he whispered in the quiet room. "If you don't have anything else to say, we're going back to Twisted River." But the cook's ashes, together with the herbs and spices, maintained their silence.

DANNY ANGEL ONCE WENT ELEVEN YEARS between novels—between *East of Bangor* and *Baby in the Road*. Again, a death in the family would delay him, though Carmella had been wrong to suggest that the writer was once more taking "rather a long time between books." It had been only six years since his most recent novel was published.

As had happened with Joe, after the cook was murdered, the novel Danny had been writing suddenly looked inconsequential to him. But this time there was no thought of revising the book—he'd simply thrown it away, all of it. And he had started a new and completely different novel, almost immediately. The new writing emerged from those months when what remained of his privacy had been taken from him; the writing itself was like a landscape suddenly and sharply liberated from a fog.

"The publicity was awful," Carmella bluntly said, at dinner. But this time, Danny had expected the publicity. After all, a famous writer's father had been murdered, and the writer himself had shot the killer—irrefutably, in self-defense. What's more, Danny Angel and his dad had been on the run for nearly forty-seven years. The internationally bestselling author had left the United States for Canada, but *not* for political reasons—just as Danny always claimed, without revealing the actual circumstances. He and his dad had been running away from a crazy ex-cop!

Naturally, there were those in the American media who would say that the cook and his son should have gone to the police in the first place. (Did they miss the fact that Carl *was* the police?) Of course the Canadian press was indignant that "American violence" had followed the famous author and his father across the border. In retrospect, this was really a reference to the guns themselves—both the cowboy's absurd Colt .45 and Ketchum's Christmas present to Danny, the Winchester 20-gauge that had blown away the deputy sheriff's throat. And in Canada, much was made of the fact that the writer's possession of the shotgun was illegal. In the end, Danny wasn't charged. Ketchum's 20-gauge Ranger had been confiscated—that was all.

"That shotgun saved your life!" Ketchum had bellowed to Danny. "And it was a *present*, for Christ's sake! *Who* confiscated it? I'll blow his balls off!"

"Let it go, Ketchum," Danny said. "I don't need a shotgun, not anymore."

"You have fans—and whatever their opposites are called—don't you?" the old logger pointed out. "Some *critters* among them, I'll bet."

As for the question Danny was asked the most, by both the American and the Canadian media, it was: "Are you going to write about this?"

He'd learned to be icy in answering the oft-repeated question. "Not immediately," Danny always said.

"But *are* you going to write about it?" Carmella had asked him again, over dinner.

He talked about the book he was writing instead. It was going well. In fact, he was writing like the wind—the words wouldn't stop. This one would be another long novel, but Danny didn't think it would take long to write. He didn't know why it was coming so easily; from the first sentence, the story had flowed. He quoted the first sentence to Carmella. (Later, Danny would realize what a fool he'd been—to have expected her to be impressed!) " 'In the closed restaurant, after hours, the late cook's son—the maestro's sole surviving family member—worked in the dark kitchen.' " And from that mysterious beginning, Danny had composed the novel's title: *In the After-Hours Restaurant*.

To the writer's thinking, Carmella's reaction was as predictable as her conversation. "It's about Gamba?" she asked.

No, he tried to explain; the story was about a man who's lived in the shadow of his famous father, a masterful cook who has recently died and left his only son (already in his sixties) a lost and furtive soul. In the rest of the world's judgment, the son seems somewhat retarded. He's lived his whole life with his father; he has worked as a sous chef to his dad in the restaurant the well-respected cook made famous. Now alone, the son has never paid his own bills before; he's not once bought his own clothes. While the restaurant continues to employ him, perhaps out of a lingering mourning for the deceased cook, the son is virtually worthless as a sous chef without his father's guidance. Soon the restaurant will be forced to fire him, or else demote him to being a dishwasher.

What the son discovers, however, is that he can "contact" the dead cook's spirit by cooking up a storm in the nighttime kitchen—but only after the restaurant is closed. There, long after hours, the son secretly slaves to teach himself his dad's recipes—everything the sous chef failed to learn from his father when the great cook was alive. And when the former sous chef masters a recipe to his dad's satisfaction, the spirit of the deceased cook advises his son on more practical matters—where to buy his clothes, what bills to pay first, how often and by whom the car should be serviced. (His father's ghost, the son soon realizes, has forgotten a few things—such as the fact that his somewhat retarded son never learned to drive a car.)

"Gamba is a *ghost*?" Carmella cried.

"I suppose I could have called the novel *The Retarded Sous Chef*," Danny said sarcastically, "but I thought *In the After-Hours Restaurant* was a better title."

"Secondo, someone might think it's a cookbook," Carmella cautioned him.

Well, what could he say? Surely no one would think a new novel by Danny Angel was a cookbook! Danny stopped talking about the story; to placate Carmella, he told her what the dedication was. "My father, Dominic Baciagalupo—in memoriam." This would be his second dedication to his dad, bringing the number of dedications "in memoriam" up to four. Predictably, Carmella burst into tears. There was a certain safety, a familiar kind of comfort, in her tears; Carmella seemed almost happy when she was crying, or at least her disapproval of Danny was somewhat abated by her sorrow.

As he lay awake in bed now, with little confidence that he would fall asleep, Danny wondered why he'd tried so hard to make Carmella understand what he was writing. Why had he bothered? Okay, so she'd *asked* what he was writing—she had even said she was *dying* to know what was next! But he'd been a storyteller forever; Danny had always known how to change the subject.

As he drifted—ever so lightly—to sleep, Danny imagined the son (the tentative sous chef) in the after-hours kitchen, where his father's ghost instructs him. Similar to Ketchum before the logger learned to read, the son makes lists of words he is struggling to recognize and remember; this night, the son is obsessed with pasta. "*Orecchiette*," he writes, "means 'little ears.' They are small and disk-shaped." Bit by bit, the sous chef is becoming a cook—if it isn't too late, if his dead father's restaurant will only give him more time to learn! "*Farfalle*," the somewhat retarded son writes, "means 'butterflies,' but my dad also called them bow ties."

In his half-sleep, Danny was up to the chapter where the cook's ghost speaks very personally to his son. "I had *so wanted* for you to be married, with children of your own. You would be a wonderful father! But you like the kind of woman who is—"

Is *what*? Danny was thinking. A new waitress has been added to the waitstaff in the haunted restaurant; she is precisely "the kind of woman" the cook's ghost is trying to warn his son about. But at last the writer fell asleep; only then did the story stop.

THE POLICE BUSINESS concerning the double shooting in Toronto was finished; even the most egregious morons in the media had finally backed off. After all, the bloodbath had happened almost nine months ago—not quite the duration of a pregnancy. Only Danny's mail had continued to discuss it—the *sympathy* letters, and whatever their opposite was.

That mail about the cook's murder and the subsequent shooting of his killer had persisted—condolences, for the most part, though not all the letters were kind. Danny read every word of them, but he'd not yet received the letter he was looking for—nor did he seriously expect that he would ever hear from Lady Sky again. This didn't stop Danny from dreaming about her—that vertical strip of the strawberry blonde's pubic hair, the bright white scar from her cesarean section, the imagined histories of her unexplained tattoos. Little Joe had given her a superhero's name, but was Lady Sky an actual warrior—or, in a previous life, had she been one? Danny could only imagine that Amy's life had been different once. Doesn't something have to happen to you *before* you jump naked out of an airplane? And *after* you've jumped, what more can happen to you? Danny would wonder.

That Amy had written him once, after Joe died, and that she'd also lost a child—well, that was one of life's missed connections, wasn't it? Since he'd not written her back, why would she write him again? But Danny read his mail, all of it—answering not a single letter—in the diminishing hope that he would hear from Amy. Danny didn't even know why he *wanted* to hear from her, but he couldn't forget her.

"If you're ever in trouble, I'll be back," Lady Sky had told little Joe, kissing the two-year-old's forehead. "Meanwhile, you take care of your daddy." So much for the promises of angels who drop naked out of the sky, though—to be fair—Amy had told them she was only an angel "sometimes." Indeed, most persistently in Danny's dreams, Lady Sky didn't always make herself available as an angel—obviously, *not* on that snowy night when Joe and the wild blow-job girl met the blue Mustang going over Berthoud Pass.

"I would like to see you again, Amy," Danny Angel said aloud, in the writer's fragile sleep, but there was no one to hear him in the dark—only his father's silent ashes. Evidently, in the drama enacted that night in that hotel room, the cook's ashes—at rest in the jar of Amos' New York Steak Spice—had been given a nonspeaking part.

DANNY AWOKE WITH A START; the early-morning light seemed too bright. He thought he was already late for his meeting with Ketchum, but he wasn't. Danny called Carmella in her hotel room. He was surprised at how wide awake she sounded, as if she'd been antici- pating his call. "The bathtub is much too small, Secondo, but I man- aged somehow," Carmella told him. She was waiting for him in the vast and almost empty dining hall when he went downstairs for break- fast.

Ketchum had been right about visiting in September; it was going to be quite a beautiful day in the northeastern United States. Even as Danny and Carmella drove away from The Balsams at that early- morning hour, the sun was bright, the sky a vivid and cloudless blue. A few fallen maple leaves dotted Akers Pond Road with reds and yel- lows. Danny and Carmella had told the resort hotel that they would be staying a second night in Dixville Notch. "Maybe Mr. Ketchum will join us for dinner tonight," Carmella said to Danny in the car.

"Maybe," Danny answered her; he doubted that The Balsams was Ketchum's kind of place. The hotel had an oversize appearance, an ambience that possibly catered to conventions; Ketchum wasn't the conventioneer type.

They quickly came upon the sign that said SMALL ENGINE RE- PAIRS, with an arrow pointing down an innocuous dirt road. "I'm at the end of the road," was all Ketchum had told Danny, though there was no sign saying this road was a dead end. Next came the sign that said (with the same neat lettering) BEWARE OF THE DOG. But there was no dog—no house or cars, either. Perhaps the sign was preparing them for an eventuality—namely, if they continued farther down the road, there would almost certainly be a dog, but by then it would be too late to warn them.

"I think I know the dog," Danny said, chiefly to reassure Carmella. "His name is Hero, and he's not really a bad dog—not that I've seen."

The road went on, growing narrower—till it was too narrow to turn around. Of course it could have been the wrong road, Danny was thinking. Maybe there still was a Lost Nation Road, and the crazy old salesman in the sporting-goods store had deliberately misled them; he'd definitely been hostile about Ketchum, but the old logger had always drawn hostility out of even the most normal-seeming people.

"Looks like a dead end ahead," Carmella said; she put her plump hands on the dashboard, as if to ward off a pending collision. But the road ended at a clearing, one that could have been mistaken for a dump—or perhaps it was a graveyard for abandoned trucks and trailers. Many of the trucks had been dissected for their parts. Several outbuildings were scattered throughout the premises; one weather-beaten shack had the appearance of a log-cabin smokehouse, from which so much smoke seeped through the cracks between the logs that the entire building looked as if it were about to burst into flames. A smaller, more focused column of smoke rose from a stovepipe atop a trailer—a former wanigan, Danny recognized. Probably, a woodstove was in the wanigan.

Danny shut off the car and listened for the dog. (He had forgotten that Hero didn't bark.) Carmella rolled down her window. "Mr. Ketchum must be cooking something," she said, sniffing the air. From the bearskin, stretched taut on a clothesline between two trailers, Danny assumed that the skinned bear was in the smokehouse—not exactly "cooking."

"A fella I know butchers my bears for me, if I give him some of the meat," Ketchum had told Danny, "but, especially in warm weather, I always smoke the bears first." From the aroma in the air, it was definitely a bear that was smoking, Danny thought. He opened the driver's-side door cautiously—on the lookout for Hero, assuming that the hound might see his designated role as that of guarding the smoking bear. But no dog emerged from one of the outbuildings, or from behind any of several sheltering piles of wreckage.

"Ketchum!" Danny called.

"Who wants to know?" they heard Ketchum shout, before the door opened to the wanigan with the smoking stovepipe. Ketchum quickly put the rifle away.

"Well, you aren't as late as you thought you would be!" he hailed them, in a friendly fashion. "It's nice to see you again, Carmella," he told her, almost flirtatiously.

"It's nice to see you, Mr. Ketchum," she said.

"Come on in and have some coffee," Ketchum told them. "Bring Cookie's ashes with you, Danny—I want to see what you've got them in."

Carmella was curious to see the container, too. They had to pass the strong-smelling bearskin on the clothesline before entering the wanigan, and Carmella looked away from the bear's severed head; it was still attached to the pelt, but the head hung nose-down, almost touching the ground, and a bright globe of blood had bubbled and congealed. Where the blood had once dripped from the bear's nostrils, it now resembled a Christmas ornament attached to the dead animal's nose.

" 'Amos' New York Steak Spice,' " Ketchum proudly read aloud, holding the jar in one hand. "Well, that's a fine choice. If you don't mind, Danny, I'm going to put the ashes in a glass jar—you'll see why when we get there."

"No, I don't mind," Danny said. He was relieved, in fact; he'd been thinking that he would like to keep the plastic steak-spice container.

Ketchum had made coffee the way old-timers did in the wanigans. He'd put eggshells, water, and ground coffee in a roasting pan, and had brought it to a boil on top of the woodstove. Supposedly, the eggshells drew the coffee grounds to them; you could pour the coffee from a corner of the pan, and most of the grounds stayed in the pan with the eggshells. The cook had debunked this method, but Ketchum still made his coffee this way. It was strong, and he served it with sugar, whether you wanted sugar or not—strong and sweet, and a little silty, "like Turkish coffee," Carmella commented.

She was trying hard not to look around in the wanigan, but the amazing (though well-organized) clutter was too tempting. Danny, ever the writer, preferred to imagine where the fax machine was, rather than actually see it. Yet he couldn't help but notice that the interior of the wanigan was basically a big kitchen, in which there was a bed, where Ketchum (presumably) slept—surrounded by guns, bows and arrows, and a slew of knives. Danny assumed that there must additionally be a cache of weapons he couldn't see, at least a handgun or two, for the wanigan had been outfitted as an arsenal—as if Ketchum lived in expectation that he would one day be attacked.

Almost lost among the rifles and the shotguns, where the Walker bluetick bear hound must have felt most at home, was a canvas dog bed stuffed with cedar chips. Carmella gasped when she saw Hero lying on the dog bed, though the bear hound's wounds were more striking than severe. His mottled white and bluish-gray flank had been raked by the bear's claws. The bleeding had stopped, and the cuts on Hero's hip were scabbed over, but the dog had bled in his bed overnight; he looked stiff with pain.

"I didn't realize that Hero had lost half an ear," Ketchum told them. "There was so much blood yesterday, I thought the whole ear was still there. It was only when the ear stopped bleeding a bit that I could see it was half gone!"

"My goodness—" Carmella started to say.

"Shouldn't you take him to a vet?" Danny asked.

"Hero isn't friendly to the vet," Ketchum said. "We'll take Hero to Six-Pack on our way to the river. Pam's got some gunk that works good for claw wounds, and I've got an antibiotic for the ear—while what's left of it is healing. Doesn't it serve you right, Hero?" Ketchum asked the dog. "I told you—you were too far ahead of me! The fool dog got to the bear while I was out of range!" Ketchum explained to Carmella.

"The poor creature," was all she could say.

"Oh, he'll be fine—I'll just feed him some of the bear meat!" Ketchum told her. "Let's get going," he said to Danny, taking the Remington .30-06 Springfield down from two pegs on the wall; he lowered the carbine across one forearm and headed for the wanigan's door. "Come on, Hero," he called to the hound, who rose stiffly from the dog bed and limped after him.

"What's the gun for? It looks like you got your bear," Danny said.

"You'll see," Ketchum told him.

"You're not going to shoot anything, are you, Mr. Ketchum?" Carmella asked him.

"Only if there's a critter in need of shooting," Ketchum answered her. Then, as if to change the subject, Ketchum said to Danny: "I don't imagine you've seen a skinned bear without its head. In that condition, a bear resembles a man. Not something for *you* to see, I think," the logger added quickly, to Carmella.

"Stay!" Ketchum said suddenly, to Hero, and the dog froze alongside Carmella, who had stopped in her tracks, too.

In the smokehouse, the skinned bear was suspended above the smoldering fire pit like a giant bat. Without a head, the bear indeed resembled a hulking man—not that the writer had ever seen a skinned man before. "Kind of takes your breath away, doesn't it?" Ketchum said to Danny, who was speechless.

They went out of the smokehouse and saw Carmella and the bear hound, standing transfixed exactly where they'd left them—as if only a violent change in the weather would have persuaded the woman and the dog to rethink their positions. "Come on, Hero," Ketchum said, and Carmella dutifully followed the hound to the truck—as if the old river driver had also spoken to her. Ketchum lifted Hero, putting the injured dog in the back of the pickup.

"You'll have to indulge Six-Pack, Danny," Ketchum was saying, as they got into the cab of his truck—Carmella taking up more than her share of room, in the middle. "Pam has something she wants to say to you both," Ketchum told them. "Six-Pack's not a *bad* person, and I suspect she just wants to say she's sorry. It was my fault that I couldn't read, remember. I never blamed Pam for telling Carl what really happened to Injun Jane. It was the only thing Six-Pack had over the cowboy, and he must have made her use it."

"I never blamed Six-Pack, either," Danny told him; he tried to read Carmella's expression, which seemed slightly offended, but she didn't say anything. There was a bad smell in the cab; maybe the smell had offended Carmella.

"It won't take too long, anyway—Six-Pack will have Hero to attend to," Ketchum said to them. "Hero barely tolerates Pam's dogs when he's *not* all clawed up. This morning could be interesting." They drove out the road advertising small engine repairs, though Danny somehow doubted that this was Ketchum's sign, or that Ketchum had ever been in the business of repairing other people's small engines; maybe the logger just fixed his own, but Danny didn't ask. The smell was overpowering; it had to be the bear, but why had the bear been in the cab?

"We met a guy who knows you—a salesman at L. L. Cote," Danny told Ketchum.

"Is that so?" the riverman said. "Was he a nice fella, or do I take it that you met the one asshole who works there?"

"I believe that's the one we met, Mr. Ketchum," Carmella said. The horrible smell traveled with them; definitely the bear had been in the cab.

"Fat fella, always wears camouflage—that asshole?" Ketchum asked.

"That's the one," Danny said; the bear smell almost made him gag. "He seems to think you're half-Indian."

"Well, I don't know what I am—or what the missing half of me is, anyway!" Ketchum thundered. "It's fine with me if I'm half-Injun—or three-quarters-Injun, for that matter! Injuns are all a lost nation, which suits me fine, too!"

"That fella seemed to think your road was no longer called Lost Nation Road," Danny told the old woodsman.

"I ought to skin that fella and smoke him with my bear!" Ketchum shouted. "But you know what?" he asked Carmella, more flirtatiously.

"What, Mr. Ketchum?" she asked him fearfully.

"That fella wouldn't taste as good as bear!" Ketchum hollered, laughing. They swerved onto Akers Pond Road and headed to the highway. Danny held the new glass jar with his dad's ashes tightly in his lap; the old container, now empty, was pinched between his feet on the floor of the cab. The glass jar was bigger; the cook's ashes, together with the herbs and spices, filled it only two-thirds full. It was once an apple-juice jar, Danny saw by the label.

Ketchum drove to that well-kept trailer park on Route 26, just outside Errol—the Saw Dust Alley campground, where Six-Pack Pam had a trailer. Six-Pack's home, which was no longer mobile—it was set on cinder blocks, and half surrounded by a vegetable garden—was actually two trailers that had been joined together. A kennel kept the dogs out of the garden, and a large, hinged door of the kind cats usually use allowed Pam's dogs free access between the kennel and the trailers. "I've tried to tell Six-Pack that a full-grown *fella* could come through that fucking dog door, though I suspect there's no fella around here who would dare to," Ketchum said. Hero had a hostile look about him as Ketchum lifted the dog from the back of the pickup. "Don't get your balls crossed," Ketchum told the hound.

Danny and Carmella had not seen Six-Pack, who was kneeling in her garden. On her knees, she was almost as tall as Carmella was standing. Pam got to her feet—unsteadily, and with the help of a rake. Danny only then remembered how big she was—not fat, but big-boned, and nearly as tall as Ketchum. "How's your hip?" Ketchum asked her. "Getting up off your knees isn't the best thing for it, I suppose."

"My hip is better than your poor dog," Six-Pack told him. "Come here, Hero," she said to the hound, who went over to her. "Did you kill the bear all by yourself, or did this asshole hunter finally get around to shootin' it?"

"This asshole bear hound got too far ahead of me. When Hero got to the bear, I wasn't in range!" Ketchum complained again.

"Old Ketchum ain't as fast as he used to be, is he, Hero?" Six-Pack said to the dog.

"I shot the damn bear," Ketchum told her peevishly.

"No shit—of course you did!" Pam said. "If you hadn't shot the damn bear, your poor dog would be dead!"

"I'm giving Hero an antibiotic for that ear," the logger said to Six-Pack. "I thought you might put some of that gunk you've got on his claw wounds."

"It ain't *gunk*—it's *sulfa*," Six-Pack told him.

The dogs in the kennel were an overeager-looking lot—mongrels, for the most part, though there was one that appeared to be close to a purebred German shepherd. Hero had his eye on that one, even with a fence between them.

"I'm sorry for your business here, Danny," Six-Pack Pam said. "I'm sorry for my part in it, however long ago it was," she added, this time looking directly at Carmella when she spoke.

"It's okay," Danny said to Six-Pack. "There was no preventing it, I guess."

"Everyone loses people," Carmella told her.

"I kinda fancied Cookie, once," Six-Pack said, now looking at Danny. "But he wouldn't have nothin' to do with me. I suppose that was part of what provoked me."

"You had the hots for *Cookie*?" Ketchum asked her. "High time I heard of it, I guess!"

"I ain't tellin' *you*—I'm tellin' *him*!" Six-Pack said, pointing at Danny. "I ain't sayin' I'm sorry to you, either," Pam told Ketchum.

Ketchum kicked the ground with his boot. "Well, shit, we'll be back for the dog later this morning—or maybe not till this afternoon," he said to Six-Pack.

"It don't matter when you come back," Pam told him. "Hero will be fine with me—I ain't plannin' on huntin' any bears with him!"

"I'll have some bear meat for you shortly," Ketchum said sullenly. "If you don't like it, you can always feed those mutts with it." Ketchum made a sudden gesture to the kennel when he uttered the *mutts* word, and Six-Pack's dogs commenced barking at him.

"Ain't it just like you, Ketchum, to get me in trouble with my neighbors?" Pam turned to Carmella and Danny when she said, "Would you believe he's the only asshole who can be counted upon to drive my dogs crazy?"

"I can believe it," Danny said, smiling.

"Shut up, all of you!" Six-Pack yelled at her dogs; they stopped barking and slunk away from the fence, all but the German shepherd, who kept his muzzle pressed against the fence and continued to stare at Hero, who stared back.

"I'd keep those two fellas separated, if I were you," Ketchum said to Pam, pointing to his bear hound and the shepherd.

"Like I need *you* to tell me that!" Six-Pack said.

"Shit," the logger said to her. "I'll be in the truck," Ketchum told Danny. "Stay!" he said to Hero, without looking in the hound's direction; thus again, Ketchum managed to make Carmella turn to stone.

—

OLD AGE HADN'T BEEN GENTLE to Six-Pack, who was Ketchum's age, though she was still a scary-looking bleached blonde. There was a scar on her upper lip—one Danny didn't remember. In all likelihood, the new scar was one the cowboy had given her, the writer thought. (What was wrong with her hip might have been something the deputy had done to her, too.)

When the woodsman had shut himself in the cab of his truck and turned the radio on, Six-Pack said to Danny and Carmella: "I still love Ketchum, you know, though he don't forgive me much—and he can be an awful asshole, when he's judgin' you for your faults, or for what you can't help about yourself."

Danny could only nod, and Carmella had been turned to stone; there was a momentary silence before Pam continued. "Talk to him, Danny. Tell him not to do somethin' stupid to himself—to his left hand, for starters."

"What about Ketchum's left hand?" Danny asked her.

"Ask Ketchum about it," Six-Pack said. "It ain't my favorite subject. That left hand ain't the one he ever touched *me* with!" she suddenly cried.

The old logger rolled down the window on the driver's side of his truck. "Just shut up, Six-Pack, and let them leave for Christ's sake!" he shouted; Pam's dogs started barking again. "You already got to say you were sorry, didn't you?" Ketchum called to her.

"Come on, Hero," Six-Pack said to the bear hound. Pam turned and went into the trailer, with Hero limping stiffly after her.

It was still only a little after seven in the morning, and once Danny and Carmella had joined Ketchum in the truck, Six-Pack's dogs stopped barking. There was half a cord of firewood in the bed of the pickup; the wood was covered by a durable-looking tarpaulin, and Ketchum had put his rifle under the tarp. Anyone following behind the pickup truck wouldn't have seen the old bolt-action Remington, which was hidden in the woodpile. There was no hiding the bear smell in the cab, however.

A Kris Kristofferson song from the seventies was playing on the radio. Danny had always liked the song, and the singer-songwriter, but not even Kris Kristofferson on a beautiful morning could distract the writer from the powerful stench in Ketchum's truck.

> *This could be our last good night together;*
> *We may never pass this way again.*

When Ketchum steered the truck south on Route 16, with the Androscoggin now running parallel to them on the driver's side of the vehicle, Danny reached across Carmella's lap and turned off the radio. "What's this I hear about your left hand?" the writer asked the old logger. "You're not still thinking about cutting it off, are you?"

"Shit, Danny," Ketchum said. "There's not a day that goes by when I don't think about it."

"My goodness, Mr. Ketchum—" Carmella started to say, but Danny wouldn't let her go on.

"Why the *left* hand, Ketchum?" Danny asked the woodsman. "You're right-handed, aren't you?"

"Shit, Danny—I promised your dad I would never tell you!" Ketchum said. "Even though, I suspect, Cookie probably forgot all about it."

Danny held the cook's ashes in both hands and shook them. "What do you say, Pop?" Danny asked the silent ashes. "I'm not hearing Dad raise an objection, Ketchum," Danny told the logger.

"Shit—I promised your *mom,* too!" Ketchum shouted.

Danny remembered what Injun Jane had told him. On the night his mother disappeared under the ice, Ketchum got hold of a cleaver in the cookhouse. He'd just stood in the kitchen with his left hand on a cutting board, holding the cleaver in his right hand. "Don't," Jane had told the river driver, but Ketchum kept staring at his left hand on the cutting board—imagining it gone, maybe. Jane had left Ketchum there; she'd needed to take care of Danny and his dad. Later, when Jane came back to the kitchen, Ketchum was gone. Jane had looked everywhere for the logger's left hand; she'd been sure she was going to find it somewhere. "I didn't want you or your father finding it," she'd told young Dan.

Sometimes, especially when Ketchum was drunk, Danny had seen the way the logger looked at his left hand; it was the way the riverman had stared at the cast on his right wrist, after Angel went under the logs.

Now they drove alongside the Androscoggin in silence, before Danny finally said: "I don't care what you promised my dad *or* my mom, Ketchum. What I'm wondering is, if you hated yourself—if you were *really* taking yourself to task, or holding yourself accountable—wouldn't you want to cut off your *good* hand?"

"My left hand *is* my good hand!" Ketchum cried.

Carmella cleared her throat; it might have been the awful bear smell. Without turning her head to look at either of them, but speaking instead to the dashboard of the truck—or perhaps to the silent radio—Carmella said: "Please tell us the story, Mr. Ketchum."

CHAPTER 15

MOOSE DANCING

IT WAS NO SURPRISE TO DANNY THAT THE STORY OF KETCHUM'S left hand was not immediately forthcoming. By the time the truck passed the Pontook Reservoir—and Danny noted the familiar drainage into the fields, as they drove down Dummer Pond Road—it was obvious that Ketchum had his own agenda. The story revealing whatever curious logic had persuaded the old logger to consider his left hand his "good" one would have to wait. Danny also noticed that Ketchum drove past the former haul road to Twisted River.

"Are we going to Paris, for some reason?" the writer asked.

"West Dummer," Ketchum corrected him, "or what's left of it."

"Does anyone call it West Dummer anymore?" Danny asked.

"I do," Ketchum answered.

Crossing the new bridge over Phillips Brook, they went the way young Dan had gone to school when Injun Jane was driving him. Long ago, it had seemed a never-ending trip from Twisted River to Paris; now the time and the road flew by, but not the bear smell.

"Don't get your balls crossed about it, Danny, but the Paris Manufacturing Company School—the actual schoolhouse—is still standing," Ketchum warned him. "Where the young writer-to-be spent a few of his formative years—getting the shit beat out of him, for the most part," the woodsman explained to Carmella, who seemed to be struggling with the concept of crossed balls.

It's probable that Carmella was simply fighting nausea; the combination of the rough surface of the dirt road with the rank smell in the truck's cab must have made her feel sick. Danny, who was definitely nauseated, tried to ignore the bear hair drifting at their feet, blown about by the air from the open driver's-side window of the lurching truck.

Even with a stick shift, Ketchum managed to drive right-handed. He stuck his left elbow out the driver's-side window, with the fingers of his left hand making only coincidental contact with the steering wheel; Ketchum clenched the wheel tightly in his right hand. When he needed to shift gears, his right hand sought the navel-high knob on the long, bent stick shift—in the area of Carmella's knees. Ketchum's left hand tentatively took hold of the steering wheel, but for no longer than the second or two that his right was on the gearshift.

Ketchum's driving was a fairly fluid process, as seemingly natural and unplanned as the way his beard blew in the wind from the open driver's-side window. (Had the window not been open, Danny was thinking, he and Carmella almost certainly would have thrown up.)

"Why didn't you put the bear in the back of the pickup?" Danny asked Ketchum. The writer wondered if some essential hunting ritual were the reason for the slain bear riding in the cab of the truck.

"I was in Maine, remember?" Ketchum said. "I shot the bear in New Hampshire, but I had to drive in and out of Maine. I have New Hampshire plates on my truck. If the bear had been in the back of my pickup, some game warden or a Maine state trooper would have stopped me. I have a New Hampshire hunting license," Ketchum explained.

"Where was Hero?" Danny asked.

"Hero was in the back of the pickup—he was bleeding all over," Ketchum said. "Live critters bleed more than dead ones, because their hearts are still pumping," the old logger told Carmella, who appeared to be suppressing a gag reflex. "I just buckled the bear in your seat belt, Danny, and pulled a hat over his ears. The beast's head looked like it was stuffed between his shoulders—bears don't have much in the way of necks—but I suppose we looked like two bearded fellas out driving around!"

Ketchum would have sat up taller in the cab than the dead bear, Danny realized. From a distance, the woodsman's beard and long hair were as black as a black bear's; you had to look closely at Ketchum to see the gray. Through the windshield of Ketchum's approaching truck, especially if you'd been passing with any speed, probably Ketchum and the bear had looked like two *young* men with heavy beards—younger than Ketchum really was, anyway.

"Hell, I wiped the bear blood off the seat," the river driver was saying, as the truck pulled into Paris. "I do wonder, though, how long the critter's *reek* will last. Bears do smell something awful, don't they?"

Ketchum dropped the truck down to first gear, his rough right hand briefly brushing one of Carmella's knees. "I'm not trying to feel you up, Carmella," the logger said to her. "I didn't plan on my stick shift ending up between your legs! We'll put Danny in the middle next time."

Danny was looking all around for the steam-powered sawmill, but he couldn't see it. Hardwood sawlogs had once been driven down Phillips Brook to Paris; the Paris Manufacturing Company of Paris, Maine, had made toboggans, the writer remembered. But where was the old sawmill? What had happened to the horse hovel and the tool shops? There'd been a mess hall and a hostelry—a seventy-five-man bunkhouse, as Danny recalled—and what had appeared to be (at the time) a rather fancy-looking house for the mill manager. Now, as Ketchum stopped the truck, Danny saw that only the schoolhouse remained. The logging camp was gone.

"What happened to Paris?" Danny asked, getting out of the truck. He could hear Phillips Brook; it sounded just the same.

"West Dummer!" Ketchum barked. He was striding toward the knoll where the mess hall had been. "Why they waited till ninety-six to take it down, I couldn't tell you—and they did a piss-poor job of it, when they finally got around to the bulldozing!" the logger yelled. He bent down and picked up a rusted pot and pan, clanging them together. Danny followed him, leaving Carmella behind.

"They *bulldozed* it?" the writer asked. He could now see sharp shards of metal, from the sawmill, poking out of the ground like severed bones. The horse hovel had collapsed and was left in a pile; the seventy-five-man bunkhouse or hostelry had been churned half-underground, with the childlike remains of bunk beds scattered in the low-lying juniper. An old washstand stood like a scooped-out skeleton; there was an empty, circular hole where the washbasin had been. There was even the rusted hulk of a steam-engine Lombard log hauler—rolled on its side, with its boiler dented, by the destructive but ineffectual force of the bulldozer. The Lombard rose out of a patch of raspberry bushes; it resembled the violated carcass of a dinosaur, or some other extinct species.

"You want to get rid of a place, you should *burn* it!" Ketchum railed. Carmella traipsed far behind them, pausing to pluck the burrs and the milkweed off her city slacks. "I wanted you to see this asswipe place first, Danny—it's a fucking disgrace that they couldn't even dispose of it properly! They were always dumber than dog shit in West Dummer!" the old logger hollered.

"Why is the schoolhouse still standing?" Danny asked. (Given how those West Dummer kids had abused him, Danny would have liked to burn the Paris Manufacturing Company School to the ground.)

"I don't know," Ketchum told him. "That schoolhouse has some frigging recreational use, I suppose. I see cross-country skiers here, now and again—and snowmobilers all the time, of course. I hear from those *energy* assholes that they're going to put these fucking windmills on the high ridges, all around. Three-hundred-and-fifty-foot-high turbines—they have one-hundred-and-fifty-foot blades! They'll build and service them with a thirty-two-foot-wide gravel-surfaced access road—which, as any fool knows, means they'll have to clear about a seventy-five-foot-wide path just to build the road! These towers will make a whorehouse of noise and throw a shitload of ice; they'll have to shut them down when there's too much snow or sleet, or freezing fog. And after the piss-poor weather has passed, and they start the stupid windmills up again, the ice that has frozen on the blades will get thrown eight hundred fucking feet! The ice comes off in sheets, several feet long but less than an inch thick. Those sheets could slice right through a fella, or a whole moose! And of course there's the flashing red lights to warn the airplanes away. It's wicked ironic that these *energy* assholes are the same sorry bunch of fuck-headed environmentalists who said that *river driving* wrecked the rivers and the forests, or they're the environmentalists' asshole *children!*"

Ketchum suddenly stopped shouting, because he could see that Carmella was crying. She had not progressed very far from the truck; either the raspberry bushes had blocked her way, or the debris from the bulldozed logging camp had impeded her. With the uproar Ketchum had been making, Carmella couldn't have heard Phillips Brook—nor could she see the water. The toppled Lombard log hauler, which was an utter unknown and, as such, forbiddingly foreign to her, appeared to have frightened her.

"Please, Mr. Ketchum," Carmella said, "could we see where my Angelù lost his life?"

"Sure we can, Carmella—I was just showing Danny a part of his *history,*" the old river driver said gruffly. "Writers have to know their history, don't they, Danny?" With a sudden wave of his hand, the woodsman exploded again: "The mess hall, the mill manager's house—all bulldozed! And there was a small graveyard around here somewhere. They even bulldozed the graveyard!"

"I see they left the apple orchard," Danny said, pointing to the scraggly trees—untended for years now.

"For no good reason," Ketchum said, not even looking at the orchard. "Only the deer eat those apples. I've killed my fair share of deer here." (Doubtless, even the deer were dumber than dog shit in West Dummer, Danny was thinking. Probably, the dumb deer just stood around eating apples, waiting to be shot.)

They got back in the truck, which Ketchum turned around; this time Danny took the middle seat in the cab, straddling the gearshift. Carmella rolled down the passenger-side window, gulping the incoming air. The truck had sat in the sun, unmoving, and the morning was warming up; the stench from the dead bear was as oppressive as a heavy, rank blanket. Danny held his dad's ashes in his lap. (The writer would have liked to *smell* his father's ashes, knowing that they smelled like steak spice—a possible antidote to the bear—but Danny restrained himself.)

On the road between Paris and Twisted River—at the height of land where Phillips Brook ran southwest to the Ammonoosuc and into the Connecticut, and where Twisted River ran southeast to the

Pontook and into the Androscoggin—Ketchum stopped his foul-smelling truck again. The woodsman pointed out the window, far off, to what looked like a long, level field. Perhaps it was a swamp in the spring of the year, but it was dry land in September—with tall grasses and a few scrub pine, and young maple suckers taking root in the flat ground.

"When they used to dam up Phillips Brook," the river driver began, "this was a pond, but they haven't dammed up the brook in years. There hasn't been a pond—not for a long time—though it's still called Moose-Watch Pond. When there was a pond, the moose would gather here; the woodsmen came to watch them. Now the moose come out at night, and they dance where the pond was. And those of us who are still alive—there aren't many—we come to watch the moose dance."

"They *dance*?" Danny said.

"They do. It's some kind of dance. I've seen them," the old logger said. "And these moose—the ones who are dancing—they're too young to remember when there was a pond! They just know it, some-how. The moose look like they're trying to make the pond come back," Ketchum told them. "I come out here some nights—just to watch them dance. Sometimes, I can talk Six-Pack into coming with me."

There were no moose now—not on a bright and sunny September morning—but there was no reason not to believe Ketchum, Danny was thinking. "Your mom was a good dancer, Danny—as I know you know. I suppose the Injun told you," Ketchum added.

When the old logger drove on, all Carmella said was: "My goodness—moose dancing!"

"If I had seen nothing else, in my whole life—only the moose dancing—I would have been happier," Ketchum told them. Danny looked at him; the logger's tears were soon lost in his beard, but Danny had seen them.

Here comes the left-hand story, the writer predicted. The mere mention of Danny's mother, or her dancing, had triggered something in Ketchum.

Up close, the old riverman's beard was more grizzled than it appeared from farther away; Danny couldn't take his eyes off him. He'd thought that Ketchum was reaching for the gearshift when the logger's strong right hand grabbed Danny's left knee and squeezed it painfully. "What are you looking at?" Ketchum asked him sharply. "I wouldn't break a promise I made to your mom *or* your dad, but for the fucking fact that some promises you make in your miserable life contradict some others—like I also promised Rosie that I would love you forever, and look after you if there came a day when your dad couldn't. Like *that* one!" Ketchum cried; his reluctant left hand gripped the steering wheel, both harder and for longer than he allowed his left hand to hold the wheel when he was merely shifting gears.

Finally, the big right hand released Danny's knee—Ketchum was once more driving right-handed. The logger's left elbow pointed out the driver's-side window, as if it were permanently affixed to the truck's cab; the now-relaxed fingers of Ketchum's left hand only indifferently grazed the steering wheel as he turned onto the old haul road to Twisted River.

Immediately, the road surface worsened. There was little traffic to a ghost town, and Twisted River wasn't on the way to anywhere else; the haul road hadn't been maintained. The first pothole the truck hit caused the glove-compartment door to spring open. The soothing smell of gun oil washed over them, momentarily relieving them from the unrelenting reek of the bear. When Danny reached to close the door of the glove compartment, he saw the contents: a big bottle of aspirin and a small handgun in a shoulder holster.

"Painkillers, both of them," Ketchum remarked casually, as Danny closed the glove compartment. "I wouldn't be caught dead without aspirin and some kind of weapon."

In the pickup's bed, nestled together on the woodpile under the tarp—along with the Remington .30-06 Springfield—Danny knew there was also a chainsaw and an ax. In a sheath above the sun visor of the truck, on the driver's side, was a foot-long Browning knife.

"Why are you always *armed*, Mr. Ketchum?" Carmella asked the river driver.

Maybe it was the *armed* word that caught Ketchum off-guard, because he *hadn't* been armed that long-ago night when the logger and the cook and the cook's cousin Rosie had started out on the ice—

do-si-doing their way on the frozen river. Right there—in the bear-stinking truck, in the woodsman's wild eyes—a vision of Rosie must have appeared to Ketchum. Danny noticed that Ketchum's fierce beard was once more wet with tears.

"I have made . . . *mistakes,*" the riverman began; his voice sounded choked, half strangled. "Not only errors of judgment, or simply saying something I couldn't live up to, but actual *lapses.*"

"You don't have to tell the story, Ketchum," Danny told him, but there was no stopping the logger now.

"A loving couple will say things to each other—you know, Danny—just to make each other feel good about a situation, even if the situation *isn't* good, or if they *shouldn't* feel good about it," Ketchum said. "A loving couple will make up their own rules, as if these made-up rules were as reliable or counted for as much as the rules everyone else tried to live by—if you know what I mean."

"Not really," Danny answered. The writer saw that the haul road to what had been the town of Twisted River was washed out—flooded, years past—and now the rocky road was overgrown with lichen and swamp moss. Only the fork in the road—a left turn, to the cookhouse—had endured, and Ketchum took it.

"My left hand was the one I touched your mom with, Danny. I wouldn't touch her with my right hand—the one I had touched, and would touch, other women with," Ketchum said.

"Stop!" Carmella cried. (At least she hadn't said, "My goodness," Danny thought; he knew Ketchum wouldn't stop, now that he had started.)

"That was our first rule—I was her left-handed lover," the logger explained. "In both our minds, my left hand was *hers*—it was Rosie's hand, hence my most important hand, my *good* hand. It was my more gentle hand—the hand least like myself," Ketchum said. It was the hand that had struck fewer blows, Danny was thinking, and Ketchum's left index finger had never squeezed a trigger.

"I see," Danny told him.

"Please stop," Carmella begged. (Was she gagging or crying? the writer wondered. It hadn't occurred to Danny that it wasn't the *story* Carmella wanted to stop; it was the *truck.*)

"You said there was a *lapse*. So what was the *mistake*?" Danny asked the old woodsman.

But they were cresting the hill where the cookhouse had been. Just then—in the bouncing, vomitous truck—there hove into view the deceptively calm river basin, and below the basin was the bend in the river, where both Rosie and Angel had been swept away. Carmella gasped to see the water. For Danny, the shock was to see nothing there—not a board of the cookhouse remained—and as for the view of the town from where the cookhouse had been, there was no town.

"The *mistake*?" Ketchum shouted. "I'll say there was a *lapse*! We were all drunk and hollering when we went out on the ice, Danny— you know that much, don't you?"

"Yes—Jane told me," Danny said.

"And I said, or I thought I said, to Rosie, 'Give me your hand.' I swear that's what I said to her," Ketchum declared. "But—being drunk, and being right-handed—I instinctively reached for her with my right hand. I had been carrying your father, but he wanted to slide around on the ice, too—so I put him down." Ketchum finally stopped the truck.

Carmella opened the passenger-side door and vomited in the grass; the poor woman kept retching while Danny surveyed the crumbled chimney of the cookhouse. Nothing taller than two or three feet of the bricks was left standing where once the cook's pizza oven had been.

"But your mother knew our rules," Ketchum continued. "Rosie said, 'Not that hand—that's the wrong hand.' And she danced away from me—she wouldn't take my hand. Then your father slipped and fell down, and I was pushing him across the ice—as if he were a human sled—but I couldn't close the distance between your mom and me. I didn't have hold of her hand, Danny, because I'd reached for her with my right one—the *bad* one. Do you see?"

"I see," Danny said, "but it seems like such a small thing." Yet the writer could see it, vividly—how the distance between his mom and Ketchum had been insurmountable, especially when the logs tore downstream from the Dummer ponds and onto the ice in the river basin, where they quickly picked up speed.

Carmella, on her knees, appeared to be praying; her view of where her beloved Angelù had been lost was truly the best in Twisted River, which was why the cook had wanted the cookhouse erected there.

"Don't cut off your left hand, Ketchum," Danny told him.

"Please don't, Mr. Ketchum," Carmella begged the old woodsman.

"We'll see," was all Ketchum would tell them. "We'll see."

IN THE LATE FALL of the same year he'd set fire to Twisted River, Ketchum came back to the site of the cookhouse with a hoe and some grass seed. He didn't bother to sow any of it in what had been the town of Twisted River, but in the area of the cookhouse—and everywhere on the hillside above the river basin, where the ashes from the fire had settled into the ground—Ketchum hoed the ashes and the earth together, and he scattered the grass seed. He'd picked a day when he knew it was going to rain; by the next morning, the rain had turned to sleet, and all winter long the grass seed lay under the snow. There was grass the next spring, and now there was a meadow where the cookhouse had been. No one had ever mowed the grass, which was tall and wavy.

Ketchum took Carmella by the arm, and they walked down the hill through the tall grass to where the town had been. Danny followed them, carrying his dad's ashes and—at Ketchum's insistence—the Remington carbine. There was nothing left standing in the town of Twisted River, save the onetime lone sentinel that had stood watch in the muddy lane alongside what had been the dance hall—namely, the old steam-engine Lombard log hauler. The fire must have burned so hot that the Lombard was permanently blackened—impervious to rust but not to bird shit, yet otherwise perfectly black. The strong sled runners were intact, but the bulldozer-type tracks were gone—taken as a souvenir, maybe, if not consumed in the fire. Where the helmsman had sat—at the front of the Lombard, perched over the sled runners—the long-untouched steering wheel looked ready to use (had there been a helmsman still alive who knew how to steer it). As the cook once predicted, the ancient log hauler had outlasted the town.

Ketchum guided Carmella closer to the riverbank, but even on a dry and sunny September morning, they couldn't get within six feet of the water's edge; the riverbank was treacherously slippery, the ground spongy underfoot. They didn't dam up the Dummer ponds anymore, but the water upstream of the river basin nonetheless ran fast—even in the fall—and Twisted River often overflowed its banks. Closer to the river, Danny felt the wind in his face; it came off the water in the basin, as if blown downstream from the Dummer ponds.

"As I suspected," Ketchum said. "If we try to scatter Cookie's ashes in the river, we can't get close enough to the water. The wind will blow the ashes back in our faces."

"Hence the rifle?" Danny asked.

The woodsman nodded. "Hence the glass jar, too," Ketchum said; he took Carmella's hand and pointed her index finger for her. "Not quite halfway to the far shore, but almost in the middle of the basin— that's where I saw your boy slip under the logs," the riverman told her. "I swear to you, Danny, it wasn't more than an arm's length from where your mom went through the ice."

The three of them looked out across the water. On the far shore of Twisted River, they could see a coyote watching them. "Give me the carbine, Danny," Ketchum said. The coyote took a long, delirious drink from the river; the animal still watched them, but not furtively. Something was the matter with it.

"Please don't shoot it, Mr. Ketchum," Carmella said.

"It must be sick, if it's out in the daytime and not running away from us," the woodsman told her. Danny handed him the Remington .30-06 Springfield. The coyote sat on the opposite riverbank, watching them with increasing indifference; it was almost as if the animal were talking to itself.

"Let's not kill anything today, Mr. Ketchum," Carmella said. Lowering the gun, Ketchum picked up a rock and threw it into the river in the coyote's direction, but the animal didn't flinch. It seemed dazed.

"That critter is definitely sick," Ketchum said. The coyote took another long drink from the river; now it didn't even watch them. "Look how thirsty it is—it's dying of something," Ketchum told them.

"Is it the season for shooting coyotes?" Danny asked the old logger.

"It's always open season for coyotes," Ketchum said. "They're worse than woodchucks—they're *varmints*. They're not good for anything at all. There's no bag limit on coyotes. You can even hunt them at night, from the first of January till the end of March. That's how much the state wants to get rid of the critters."

But Carmella wasn't persuaded. "I don't want to see anything die today," she said to Ketchum; he saw she was blowing kisses across the water, either to bless the spot where her Angelù had perished or to bestow long life on the coyote.

"Make your peace with those ashes, Danny," the woodsman said. "You know where to throw that jar in the river, don't you?"

"I've made my peace," the writer said. He kissed the cook's ashes and the apple-juice jar good-bye. "Ready?" Danny asked the shooter.

"Just throw it," Ketchum told him. Carmella covered her ears with her hands, and Danny threw the jar—to almost midstream in the river basin. Ketchum leveled the carbine and waited for the jar to bob back to the surface of the water; one shot from the Remington shattered the apple-juice jar, effectively scattering Dominic Baciagalupo's ashes in Twisted River.

On the far shore, at the sound of the shot, the coyote crouched lower to the riverbank but insanely held its ground. "You miserable fucker," Ketchum said to the animal. "If you don't know enough to run, you're definitely dying. Sorry," the old logger said—this was spoken as an aside, to Carmella. It was a smooth-working rifle—Ketchum's "old-reliable, bolt-action sucker." The woodsman shot the coyote on top of its skull, just as the sick animal was bending down to drink again.

"That's what I should have done to Carl," Ketchum told them, not looking at Carmella. "I could have done it anytime. I should have shot the cowboy down, like any varmint. I'm sorry I didn't do it, Danny."

"It's okay, Ketchum," Danny said. "I always understood why you couldn't just kill him."

"But I *should* have!" the logger shouted furiously. "There was nothing but bullshit morality preventing me!"

"Morality isn't bullshit, Mr. Ketchum," Carmella began to lecture him, but when she looked at the dead coyote, she stopped whatever else she was going to say; the coyote lay still on the riverbank with the tip of its nose touching the running water.

"Good-bye, Pop," Danny said to the flowing river. He turned away from the water and looked up at the grassy hill, where the cookhouse had been—where he'd disastrously mistaken Injun Jane for a bear, when all along she'd been his father's lover.

"Good-bye, Cookie!" Ketchum called out, over the water.

"Dormi pur," Carmella sang, crossing herself; then she abruptly turned her back on the river, where Angel had gone under the logs. "I need a head start on you two," she told Danny and Ketchum, and she started slowly up the hill through the tall grass—not once looking back.

"What was she singing?" the woodsman asked the writer.

It was from an old Caruso recording, Danny remembered. "Quartetto Notturno," it was called—a lullaby from an opera. Danny couldn't remember the opera, but the lullaby must have been what Carmella sang to her Angelù, when he'd been a little boy and she was putting him to bed. *"Dormi pur,"* Danny repeated for Ketchum. " 'Sleep clean.' "

"Clean?" Ketchum asked.

"Meaning, 'Sleep tight,' I guess," Danny told him.

"Shit," was all Ketchum said, kicking the ground. "Shit," the logger said again.

The two men watched Carmella's arduous ascent of the hill. The tall, waving grass was waist-high to her truncated, bearlike body, and the wind was behind her, off the river; the wind blew her hair to both sides of her lowered head. When Carmella reached the crown of the hill, where the cookhouse had been, she bowed her head and rested her hands on her knees. For just a second or two—for no longer than it took Carmella to catch her breath—Danny saw in her broad, bent-over body a ghostly likeness to Injun Jane. It was as if Jane had returned to the scene of her death to say good-bye to the cook's ashes.

Ketchum had lifted his face to the sun. He'd closed his eyes but was moving his feet—just the smallest steps, in no apparent direction, as if he were walking on floating logs. "Say it again, Danny," the old riverman said.

"Sleep tight," Danny said.

"No, no—in *Italian!*" Ketchum commanded him. The river driver's eyes were still closed, and he kept moving his feet; Danny knew that the veteran logger was just trying to stay afloat.

"*Dormi pur*," Danny said.

"*Shit*, Angel!" Ketchum cried. "I said, 'Move your feet, Angel. You have to keep moving your *feet*!' Oh, shit."

IT HAD BEEN a bitterly confusing morning for Six-Pack Pam, who liked to work in her garden early—even earlier than she fed the dogs or made coffee for herself, and while her hip lasted. First Ketchum had come and disrupted everything, in his inimitable fashion, and she'd put the sulfa powder on Hero's wounds—all this before she fed her own dear dogs and made the coffee. It was because of Ketchum's willful disruption of her day, and treating the wretched dog who'd been mauled by a bear, that Six-Pack had turned her television on a little later than usual, but she still turned the TV on soon enough.

Pam was thinking that it was partly her own fault: After all, she'd asked to see Danny and that Italian woman who'd been the cook's lover—the Injun Jane replacement, as Six-Pack thought of Carmella. Pam had wanted to make her peace with them, but now she felt conflicted. The shock of Danny being almost thirty years older than his father had been—that is, when Six-Pack had last seen the little cook—was upsetting. And, having made her apologies to Danny and Carmella, Pam was only now realizing that it was *Ketchum's* forgiveness she wanted; that was confusing, too. Moreover, treating Hero's wounds had made her cry, as if they were *Ketchum's* wounds she was impossibly trying to heal. It was exactly at this bewildering moment—at the height of her most bitter disappointment, or so Six-Pack imagined—when she turned on the TV.

The world was about to overwhelm her, too, but Six-Pack didn't know that when she saw the wreckage caused by the first of the hijacked passenger jets; American Airlines Flight 11, flying out of Boston, had crashed into the north tower of the World Trade Center, where the plane tore a gaping hole in the building and set it on fire. "It must have been a small plane," someone on television said, but Six-Pack Pam didn't think so.

"Does that look like a hole a *small* plane would leave, Hero?" Six-Pack asked the wounded Walker bluetick. The dog had his eye on Six-Pack's male German shepherd; both dogs were under the kitchen table. The stoic bear hound didn't respond to Pam's question. (Living with Ketchum had made Hero overfamiliar with being spoken to; with Ketchum, the dog knew that no response was expected.)

Pam just kept watching the news about the plane crash. On the TV, it looked like a bright, sunny day in New York City, too—not the kind of day a pilot has a visibility problem, Six-Pack was thinking.

Six-Pack was regretting that she'd ever said she once "kinda fancied Cookie"—hadn't that been how she'd put it? Pam could have kicked herself for saying that within Ketchum's diminished hearing. Every time she thought their relationship was improving, if not exactly back on track, it seemed to Six-Pack that she said the dead-wrong thing—or that Ketchum did.

She'd left a lot of men, and had been left by them, but busting up with Ketchum had hit her the hardest—even when Six-Pack considered that leaving Carl had caused the cowboy to very nearly kill her. The deputy sheriff had raped her on a dock at night—at the Success Pond boat launch. Afterward a couple who had witnessed it had taken Pam to the Androscoggin Valley Hospital in Berlin, where she'd spent a few days recuperating. This had led to Six-Pack getting a job in the hospital, which she liked; she had a cleaning job, most nights, while her dogs were sleeping. Talking to some of the patients made Pam feel less sorry for herself. Printed in small, neat letters on her hospital uniform was the word SANITIZATION. Six-Pack doubted that many of the patients ever mistook her for a nurse, or a nurse's aide, but she believed she was nevertheless a comfort to some of them—as they were to her.

Six-Pack Pam knew she would have to have her hip replaced, and every time the hip hurt her, she thought about the cowboy banging her on the dock—how he'd pushed her face against a boat cleat, which was what had given her the scar on her upper lip—but the worst of it was she'd told Ketchum that the woodsman really *should* kill Carl. This was the worst, because Six-Pack hadn't known how strongly Ketchum believed that he should have killed the cowboy *years* ago. (And when the deputy sheriff shot Cookie, Ketchum's self-recriminations never ceased.)

Pam was sorry, too, that she'd ever told Ketchum what Carl had done following that fatal collision on Route 110—this was out on the Berlin-Groveton road, where the highway ran alongside Dead River. Two teenagers who weren't wearing their seat belts had slammed head-on into a turkey truck. The turkeys were already dead; they'd been "processed," as they say in the turkey-farming business. The truck driver survived, but he'd suffered a neck injury and had briefly lost consciousness; when he came to, the driver was facing the two dead teenagers. The boy, who'd been driving, was run through by his steering column, and the girl, who was pinned in the passenger seat, had been decapitated. Carl was the first one from law enforcement on the scene, and—according to the turkey-truck driver—the cowboy had fondled the dead, decapitated girl.

Carl claimed that the truck driver was out of his head; after all, he'd snapped his neck and had blacked out, and when he came to, he was evidently hallucinating. But the cowboy had told Pam the truth. What did it matter that he'd played with the headless girl's tits—she was dead, wasn't she?

To which Ketchum had said—not for the first, or the last, time— "I should just kill that cowboy."

Six-Pack now said to Hero and her German shepherd: "You two should stop eyeballin' each other that way." It was a little after nine in the morning—exactly eighteen minutes after the first passenger jet had hit the north tower—when the second hijacked airliner, United Airlines Flight 175 (also flying out of Boston), crashed into the south tower of the World Trade Center and exploded. Both buildings were burning when Six-Pack said to the assembled dogs, "Tell me that was another *small* plane, and I'll ask you what you've been drinkin' with your dog food."

Hero tentatively licked some of the sulfa powder on his claw wounds, but the taste of it stopped the dog from licking further. "Don't that taste special?" Pam asked the bear hound. "You lick that off, Hero, I've got more."

In what appeared to be a calculated non sequitur, Hero lunged at the German shepherd; both dogs were going at it, under the kitchen table, before Six-Pack was able to separate them with the water pistol. She kept it loaded with dishwasher detergent and lemon juice, and she squirted both dogs in their eyes—they *hated* it. But it had hurt Pam's hip to drop down on all fours and crawl under the kitchen table with the fighting dogs, and she was in no mood to listen to President

Bush, who came on television at 9:30, speaking from Sarasota, Florida.

Six-Pack didn't despise George W. Bush to the degree that Ketchum did, but she thought the president was a smirking twerp and a dumbed-down daddy's boy, and she agreed with Ketchum's assessment that Bush would be as worthless as wet crap in even the smallest crisis. If a fight broke out between two small dogs, for example, Ketchum claimed that Bush would call the fire department and ask them to bring a hose; then the president would position himself at a safe distance from the dogfight, and wait for the firemen to show up. The part Pam liked best about this assessment was that Ketchum said the president would instantly look self-important, and would appear to be actively involved—that is, once the firefighters and their hose arrived, and provided there was anything remaining of the mess the two dogs might have made of each other in the interim.

True to this portrait, President Bush said on TV that the country had suffered an "apparent terrorist attack."

"Ya *think*?" Six-Pack asked the president on television. Characteristic of people who lived alone, discounting her dogs, Pam talked back to the people on TV—as if, like the dogs, the people on television could actually hear her.

By now, the Federal Aviation Administration had shut down the New York airports, and the Port Authority of New York and New Jersey had ordered all the bridges and tunnels in the New York area closed. "What are the dumb fuckers waitin' for?" Six-Pack asked the dogs. "They should close down *all* the airports!" Ten minutes later, the FAA halted all flight operations at U.S. airports; it was the first time in the history of the United States that air traffic had been halted nationwide. "Ya *see*?" Six-Pack asked the dogs. "Someone must be listenin' to me." (If not Ketchum, and definitely not the dogs.)

Six-Pack had soaked a clean sponge in cold water and was rinsing the dishwasher detergent and lemon juice out of the German shepherd's eyes. "You're next, Hero," Pam told the bear hound, who watched her and the shepherd impassively.

Three minutes later, American Airlines Flight 77 crashed into the Pentagon, sending up a towering plume of smoke; two minutes after that, they evacuated the White House. "Holy shit," Six-Pack said to the dogs. "It's lookin' more and more like an *apparent* terrorist attack, don'tcha think?"

She was holding Hero's head in her lap, rinsing the dishwasher detergent and lemon juice from the wounded bear hound's eyes, when, at 10:05, the south tower of the World Trade Center collapsed. After the tower plummeted into the streets, a billowing cloud of dust and debris drifted away from the building; people were running through the waves of dust.

Five minutes later, a portion of the Pentagon collapsed—at the same time that United Airlines Flight 93, which had also been hijacked, crashed to the ground in Somerset County, Pennsylvania, southeast of Pittsburgh. "I wonder where that one was headed, Hero," Six-Pack said to the dog.

The German shepherd had circled around behind Pam, and Hero was anxious that he couldn't see the shepherd; the bear hound's nervousness alerted Six-Pack to her devious shepherd's presence. She reached quickly behind her and grabbed a handful of fur and skin, squeezing as hard as she could until she heard the shepherd yelp and felt the dog twist free of her grip.

"Don't you try sneakin' up on me!" Six-Pack said, as the German shepherd slunk out the dog door into the outdoor kennel.

It was next announced on television that they'd evacuated the United Nations building—and the State and Justice departments, along with the World Bank. "I see all the important fellas are runnin' for cover," Six-Pack said to Hero. The dog eyed her warily, as if he were considering her contradictory behavior in the following manner: First she puts the bad-tasting yellow gunk on my cuts, then she squirts me in my eyes with the stinging-and-burning stuff, and lastly she tries to make me feel better; not to mention, where is that sneak-attack fuck of a German shepherd?

"Don't get your balls crossed, Hero—I ain't goin' to hurt you," Pam told the bear hound, but Hero regarded her mistrustfully; the dog might have preferred his chances with a bear.

At 10:24, the FAA reported that all inbound transatlantic aircraft entering the United States had been diverted to Canada. "Oh, that's brilliant!" Six-Pack said to the TV. "I might have begun with that idea a few fuckin' *months* ago! Like I suppose ya thought that the fellas fly-in' those first two planes were *from* Boston!" But the television ignored her.

Four minutes later, the north tower of the World Trade Center collapsed; someone said that the tower appeared to peel apart, from the top down, as if a hand had taken a knife to a tall vegetable. "If this ain't the end of the world, it's surely the start of somethin' close to it," Six-Pack said to the dogs. (Hero was still looking all around for that fuckheaded German shepherd.)

At 10:54, Israel evacuated all its diplomatic missions. Six-Pack thought she should be writing this down. Ketchum always said that the Israelis were the only ones who knew what was what; that the Israelis were closing down their diplomatic missions meant that the Muslim extremists, those militant Islamists who were determined to wipe out the Jews, were beginning their religious war by wiping out the United States—because without the United States, Israel would long ago have ceased to exist. Nobody else in the craven, so-called democratic world had the balls to stick up for the Israelis—or so Ketchum also said, and Six-Pack pretty much took what amounted to her politics from the old libertarian logger. (Ketchum admired the Israelis, and almost nobody else.)

Six-Pack had often wondered if Ketchum was half-Injun and half-*Jewish*, because the riverman periodically threatened to move to Israel. Pam had, more than once, heard Ketchum say: "I might make more beneficial use of myself killing those assholes from Hamas and Hezbollah, instead of picking on the poor deer and bear!"

SHORTLY AFTER ELEVEN THAT MORNING, the New York City mayor, Rudolph Giuliani, urged New Yorkers to stay at home; the mayor also ordered an evacuation of the area of the city south of Canal Street. By now, Pam was vexed at Ketchum and the two others for spending close to the whole morning scattering the little cook's ashes. But, knowing Ketchum, Six-Pack considered that the logger would have insisted on showing Danny what the woodsman called the "vandalism" that had been done to Paris—or West Dummer, as Ketchum obdurately called it—and either en route to Paris, or on the way back, Six-Pack knew that Ketchum would have paused to deliver a fucking *eulogy* to the confused, heartbreaking moose who danced their scrawny asses off in Moose-Watch Pond.

Pam felt a pang that she had not often accepted Ketchum's periodic invitations to join him in a middle-of-the-night visit to see the moose dancing. (Six-Pack believed that the moose were just aimlessly "millin' around.") It was also with a pang that Six-Pack regretted that she had not accompanied Ketchum on many of his proposed overnight "campin' trips," as she called them, to that grassy hill where the cookhouse had been; she knew this was hallowed ground to Ketchum, and that he liked nothing better than to spend the night there. Ketchum just pitched a tent and slept in a sleeping bag, but his snoring kept her awake half the night, and Pam's hip hurt her on the hard ground. Furthermore, Ketchum best liked camping at the cookhouse site when the weather had turned colder—especially, once there was snow. The cold weather made Six-Pack's hip throb.

"You're the one who keeps putting off the hip-replacement surgery," Ketchum routinely told her; Six-Pack regretted putting off the surgery, too. And how could she expect the old river driver to resume their long-ago relationship if she wouldn't go camping with him when he asked her?

When she'd suggested going to see a movie in Berlin instead, Ketchum had rolled his eyes at her. Six-Pack knew Ketchum's opinion of movies *and* Berlin. He liked to say, "I would rather stay home and watch Hero fart."

She wanted Ketchum to marry her, Six-Pack suddenly realized. But *how?*

Just after noon, with Ketchum and the other two having been gone the entire morning—and Pam feeling extremely pissed-off at them, and at the rest of the world—the Immigration and Naturalization Service said that the U.S. borders with Canada and Mexico were on the highest state of alert, but that no decision had been made concerning closing the borders.

"The fanatics aren't *Canadians!*" Six-Pack shouted meaninglessly at the dogs. "The terrorists aren't *Mexicans!*" she wailed. She'd held herself together all morning, but Six-Pack was losing it now. Hero went out the dog door into the outdoor kennel, no doubt thinking his odds were better with the German shepherd than with Pam.

It was no wonder that when Ketchum *finally* arrived, with Danny and Carmella, the logger saw his long-suffering Hero ("that fine animal") together with Pam's dogs in the outdoor kennel—Six-Pack's untrustworthy German shepherd among them—and took this to mean that Six-Pack had been neglecting his wounded bear hound. "Pam must be farting away her time, watching whatever abomination there is on daytime television," was how the ever-critical woodsman expressed himself to Danny and Carmella.

"Uh-oh," Danny said to Carmella. "You should be *nice* to Six-Pack, Ketchum," Danny told the old logger. "In fact, I think you should *marry* her—or try living with her again, anyway."

"Constipated Christ!" Ketchum shouted, slamming the door to his truck. Pam's dogs immediately commenced barking, but not the stoic Hero.

Six-Pack came out the trailer door from her kitchen. "The country is under attack!" Pam screamed. "Bush is flyin' around in *Air Force One*—the coward must be hidin'! The Israelis have all gone home to defend themselves! It's the beginnin' of the end of the world!" Six-Pack shouted at Ketchum. "And all *you* can do, you crotchety asshole, is rile up my dogs!"

"*Marry* her?" Ketchum said to Danny. "Why would I want to *live* with her? Can you imagine coming home every day to a deteriorated state of mind like *that*?"

"It's all *true*!" Six-Pack wailed. "Come see for yourself, Ketchum—it's on *television*!"

"On *television*!" Ketchum repeated, winking at Carmella—which doubtless drove Six-Pack around the bend. "Naturally, if it's on TV, it must be truer than most things."

But neither Six-Pack nor Ketchum had thought very much about where they *were*—in an orderly, fastidiously neat trailer park, in the Saw Dust Alley campground, where there were many stay-at-home women with young children, and some retired or unemployed older people (both men *and* women), and a few unattended teenagers who were skipping school while their working parents didn't have a clue.

It was Ketchum who clearly didn't have a clue about how many people had overheard him and Pam, and both Ketchum and Six-Pack were unprepared for the diversity of opinion among the trailer-park residents, who had been glued to their television sets all morning. Given that the walls of their trailers were paper-thin, and that many of them had been talking with one another in the course of the day's unfolding events, they'd expressed quite a variety of views—in regard to what some of them saw as the first installment of the Armageddon they were witnessing—and now this notoriously belligerent intruder had come into their small community *bellowing,* and the famously loudmouthed Ketchum (for the former river driver was indeed famous in Errol) seemed to be unaware of the developing news.

"Ain't you heard, Ketchum?" an old man asked. He was stooped, almost bent over—wearing red-and-black wool hunting pants on this warm September day—with his suspenders loosely cupping his bony shoulders, and his bare, scrawny arms dangling from a white sleeveless undershirt.

"Is that you, Henry?" the logger asked the old man. Ketchum had not seen the sawyer since they'd shut down the sawmill in Paris—years before they had bulldozed it half-underground.

Henry held up his left hand with the missing thumb and index finger. "Sure it's me, Ketchum," the sawyer said. "It's the war in the Middle East, the war between the Muslims and the Jews—it's started *here,* Ketchum," Henry said.

"It started long ago," Ketchum told the sawyer. "What's going on?" the logger asked Six-Pack.

"I've been *tryin'* to tell ya!" Six-Pack screamed.

There was a young woman with an infant in her arms. "It's a terrorist attack—no airport is safe. They've closed them all down," she said to Ketchum.

Two teenage boys, brothers who'd skipped school, were barefoot; they wore jeans and were shirtless in the midday sun. "Hundreds of people are dead—maybe thousands," one said.

"They were jumpin' from skyscrapers!" the other boy said.

"The president is missing!" a woman with two small children said.

"Well, *that's* good news!" Ketchum declared.

"Bush ain't missin'—he's just flyin' around, stayin' safe. I told ya," Six-Pack said to the logger.

"Maybe the Jews did it—to make us think it was the Arabs!" a young man on crutches said.

"If it's your brain that's addled, you don't need crutches," the old woodsman told him. "Constipated Christ—let me have a look at the TV," Ketchum said to Six-Pack. (The former river driver, now a reader, was possibly the only resident of Errol who didn't own a television.)

They traipsed into Pam's kitchen—not just Ketchum, with Danny holding Carmella's arm, but also Henry, the old sawyer with the stumps instead of a thumb and an index finger, and two of the women with young children.

The young man on crutches had hobbled away. Outside, the teenage boys could be heard by the kennel. After exchanging pleasantries with the dogs, one of the teenagers said, "Look at the tough bastard with one ear—he's been in a fight."

"Some fight," the second boy said. "It musta been with a cat."

"Some *cat*!" the first boy said appreciatively.

On Pam's kitchen TV, the media kept replaying that moment when Flight 175 crashed into the south tower of the World Trade Center—and of course those moments when first the south tower and then the north tower came down. "How many people were in those towers—how many cops and how many firemen were under those buildings when they fell?" Ketchum asked, but no one answered him; it was too early for those statistics.

At 1:04 P.M., speaking from Barksdale Air Force Base in Louisiana, President Bush said that all the appropriate security measures were being taken—including putting the U.S. military on high alert worldwide. "Well, that sure as shit makes us all feel safer!" Ketchum said.

"Make no mistake," Bush said on the TV. "The United States will hunt down and punish those responsible for these cowardly acts."

"Oh, boy," Ketchum said. "It sounds to me like *that's* what we should be afraid of next!"

"But they attacked us," the young woman holding the infant said. "Don't we have to attack them back?"

"They're suicide bombers," Ketchum said. "How do you attack them back?"

At 1:48, President Bush left Barksdale aboard *Air Force One* and flew to another base in Nebraska. "More flyin' around," Six-Pack commented.

"How many wars will that shit-for-brains start, do you imagine?" Ketchum asked them.

"Come on, Ketchum—he's the *president*," the sawyer said.

Ketchum reached out and took the old sawyer's hand—the one with the missing thumb and index finger. "Did you ever make a mistake, Henry?" the veteran river driver asked.

"A couple," Henry answered; everyone could see the two stumps.

"Well, you just wait and see, Henry," Ketchum said. "This ass-wipe in the White House is the wrong man for the job—you just wait and see how many mistakes this *penis-breath* is going to make! On this mouse turd's watch, there's going to be a fucking *myriad* of mistakes!"

"A fuckin' *what*?" Six-Pack said; she sounded frightened.

"A *myriad*!" Ketchum shouted.

"An indefinitely large number—countless," Danny explained to Six-Pack.

Six-Pack looked sick, as if the confidence had been kicked out of her. "Maybe you'd like to watch the moose dancin' tonight," she said to Ketchum. "Maybe you and me—and Danny and Carmella, too—could go campin'. It's gonna be a pretty night up by the cookhouse, and between you and me, Ketchum, we could come up with some extra sleepin' bags, couldn't we?"

"Shit," Ketchum said. "There's an undeclared war going on, and you want to watch the moose dancing! Not tonight, Six-Pack," Ketchum told her. "Besides, Danny and I have some serious issues to discuss. I suppose they have a bar and a TV at The Balsams out in Dixville Notch, don't they?" the logger asked Danny.

"I want to go home," Carmella said. "I want to go back to Boston."

"Not tonight," Ketchum said again. "The terrorists aren't going to bomb Boston, Carmella. Two of the planes flew out of Boston. If they were going to attack Boston, they would have done it."

"I'll drive you back to Boston tomorrow," Danny told Carmella; he couldn't look at Six-Pack, who seemed to be in despair.

"Leave me the dog—let me look after Hero," Pam said to Ketchum. "They don't take dogs at The Balsams—and you should stay the night there, Ketchum, 'cause you'll be drinkin'."

"Just so you're paying," Ketchum said to Danny.

"Of course I'm paying," Danny said.

All the dogs had come in the dog door and were huddled in the kitchen. There'd been no more hollering—not since Ketchum had shouted, "A *myriad*!"—and the dogs were anxious about so many humans standing around in Six-Pack's small kitchen without any yelling.

"Don't get your balls crossed, Hero—I'll be back tomorrow," Ketchum told the bear hound. "You don't have to work at the hospital tonight?" the former river driver asked Six-Pack.

"I can get out of it," she told him disinterestedly. "They like me at the hospital."

"Well, shit—I like you, too," Ketchum told her awkwardly, but Six-Pack didn't say anything; she'd seen her opportunity pass. All Pam could do was position her aching body between the two children (belonging to one of the young women) and that unreliable German shepherd; the dog was just plain bonkers. Six-Pack knew that her odds of preventing the shepherd from biting the kids were far better than the possibility that she could ever persuade Ketchum to live with her again. He'd even offered to pay for her hip replacement—at that fancy fucking hospital near Dartmouth—but Pam speculated that Ketchum's generosity toward her damaged hip had more to do with the logger's infinite regret that he'd not killed the cowboy than it served as a testimony to Ketchum's enduring affection for her.

"Everybody out. I want my kitchen back—everybody out, *now*," Six-Pack suddenly said; she didn't want to break down in front of a bunch of strangers. All but one of Pam's mutts, as Ketchum called them, sidled out the dog door before Six-Pack could say to them, "Not you." But the dogs were used to the everybody-out command, and they moved more quickly than the two women with young children or old Henry, the former sawyer and double-digit amputee.

Paying no heed to Pam's command, the lunatic German shepherd and Hero stood their ground; the dogs were engaged in a macho standoff, in opposite corners of the kitchen. "No more trouble from you two," Pam said to them, "or I'll beat the livin' shit out of you." But she'd already started to cry, and her voice lacked its customary firepower. The two dogs weren't afraid of Six-Pack anymore; the dogs could sense when a fellow creature was defeated.

—

THE THREE OF THEM WERE RIDING in the bear-fouled truck again—Danny once more in the middle, and Carmella as close to the open passenger-side window as she could get—when Ketchum turned on the radio in the stinking cab. It wasn't yet three o'clock in the afternoon, but Mayor Giuliani was having a press conference. Someone asked the mayor about the number of people killed, and Giuliani answered: "I don't think we want to speculate about that—more than any of us can bear."

"That sounds like a good guess," Danny said.

"And you're thinking about moving back here—isn't that right?" Ketchum asked Danny suddenly. "Didn't I hear you say that there was no real *reason* for you to stay in Canada—not anymore—and that you were inclined to come back to your own country? Weren't you recently complaining to me that you didn't really *feel* like a Canadian—and, after all, you were born here, you really *are* an American, aren't you?"

"I suppose so," Danny answered; the writer knew enough to be careful with Ketchum's line of questioning. "I *was* born here—I *am* an American. Becoming a Canadian citizen didn't make me a Canadian," Danny said more assertively.

"Well, that shows you how stupid I am—I'm just one of those slow fellas who believes what he reads," the old riverman said slyly. "You know, Danny, I may have been a long time learning to read, but I read pretty well—and quite a lot—nowadays."

"What are you driving at, Ketchum?" Danny asked him.

"I thought you were a *writer*," Ketchum told him. "I read somewhere that you thought nationalism was 'limiting.' I believe you said something about all writers being 'outsiders,' and that you saw yourself as someone standing on the outside, looking in."

"I *did* say that," Danny admitted. "Of course, it was an interview—there was a *context*—"

"*Fuck* the context!" Ketchum shouted. "Who cares if you don't *feel* like a Canadian? Who cares if you're an American? If you're a *writer*, you *should* be an outsider—you should *stay* on the outside, looking in."

"An exile, you mean," Danny said.

"Your country is going to the dogs—it has been, for some time,"

Ketchum told him. "You can see it better, and write about it better, if you stay in Canada—I know you can."

"We were attacked, Mr. Ketchum," Carmella said weakly; her heart wasn't in the argument. "Are we going to the dogs because we were *attacked*?"

"It's what we make out of the attack that counts," Ketchum told her. "How's Bush going to respond? Isn't that what matters?" the old logger asked Danny, but the writer was no match for Ketchum's pessimism. Danny had always underestimated the former river driver's capacity for following things through to their worst-possible conclusion.

"Stay in Canada," Ketchum told him. "If you're living in a foreign country, you'll see what's true, and what isn't true, back in the old U.S.A.—I mean, more clearly."

"I know that's what you think," Danny said.

"The poor people in those towers—" Carmella started to say, but she stopped. Carmella was no match for Ketchum's pessimism, either.

The three of them were in the bar at The Balsams, watching the TV at 4 P.M., when someone on CNN said there were "good indications" that the Saudi militant Osama bin Laden, who was suspected of coordinating the bombings of two U.S. embassies in 1998, was involved in the attacks on the World Trade Center and the Pentagon—this was based on "new and specific" information, meaning since the attacks.

An hour and a half later, after Ketchum had consumed four beers and three shots of bourbon, and when Danny was still drinking his third beer, CNN reported that U.S. officials said the plane that crashed in Pennsylvania could have been headed for one of three possible targets: Camp David, the White House, or the U.S. Capitol building.

Carmella, who was sipping only her second glass of red wine, said: "I'll bet on the White House."

"Do you really think I should *marry* Six-Pack?" Ketchum asked Danny.

"Just try living with her," Danny suggested.

"Well, I did that—once," the old riverman reminded him. "I can't believe Six-Pack wanted to fuck *Cookie!*" Ketchum cried. Then, out of consideration for Carmella, he added: "Sorry."

The three of them went into the dining room and ate an enormous meal. Danny kept drinking beer, to Ketchum's disgust, but Ketchum and Carmella went through two bottles of red wine, and Carmella retired early. "It's been a difficult day for me," she told them, "but I want to thank you, Mr. Ketchum, for showing me the river—and for everything else." Carmella was assuming that she wouldn't see Ketchum in the morning, and she wouldn't; even when he'd been drinking, Ketchum was an earlier and earlier riser. Both gentlemen offered to walk Carmella to her hotel room, but she wouldn't hear of it; she left them in the dining room, where Ketchum immediately ordered another bottle of red wine.

"I'm not going to help you drink it," Danny told him.

"I don't need your help, Danny," Ketchum said.

For a small person, which Danny was, the problem with drinking only beer was that he began to feel full before he felt drunk, but Danny was determined not to let Ketchum tempt him with the red wine. Danny still imagined that the red wine had played some role in the cowboy's murder of his father. On the very day the cook's ashes were scattered in Twisted River, Danny didn't want to belittle the memory of that terrible night when Carl killed Danny's dad, and Danny gave all three rounds of the 20-gauge to the cowboy.

"You've got to let yourself go, Danny," Ketchum was saying. "Be more daring."

"I'm a beer drinker, Ketchum—no red wine for me," Danny told him.

"For Christ's sake—I mean, as a *writer!*" Ketchum said.

"As a *writer?*" Danny asked.

"You keep skirting the darker subjects," Ketchum told him. "You have a way of writing around the *periphery* of things."

"I *do?*" Danny asked him.

"You do. You seem to be dodging the squeamish stuff," Ketchum told him. "You've got to stick your nose in the worst of it, and imagine *everything*, Danny."   •

At the time, this struck Danny as less in the spirit of literary criticism than it appeared to be a direct invitation to spend the night in the cab of Ketchum's truck—or in the smokehouse with the skinned, smoking bear.

"What about the bear?" Danny suddenly asked the woodsman. "Won't the fire in the smokehouse go out?"

"Oh, the bear will have smoked enough for now—I can start the fire up again tomorrow," Ketchum told him impatiently. "There's one more thing—well, okay, *two* things. First of all, you don't seem to be a city person—not to me. I think the country is the place for you— I mean, as a writer," Ketchum said more softly. "Secondly—though I would suggest this is more important—you have no need for the fucking nom de plume anymore. As I'm aware that the very idea of a pen name once affected you adversely, I think it's time for you to take your own name back. *Daniel* always was your dad's name for you, and I've heard you say, Danny, that Daniel Baciagalupo is a fine name for a writer. You'll still be Danny to me, of course, but—once again, *as a writer*—you should be Daniel Baciagalupo."

"I can guess what my publishers will say to that idea," Danny said to the logger. "They'll remind me that Danny Angel is a famous, best-selling author. They're going to tell me, Ketchum, that an unknown writer named Daniel Baciagalupo won't sell as many books."

"I'm just telling you what's good for you—as a writer," Ketchum told him almost offhandedly.

"Let me see if I understand you correctly," the writer said a little peevishly. "I should rename myself Daniel Baciagalupo; I should live in the country, in Canada; I should let myself go—that is, be more daring as a writer," Danny dutifully recited.

"I think you're catching on," the logger told him.

"Is there anything else you would recommend?" Danny asked him.

"We've been an empire in decline since I can remember," Ketchum said bluntly; he wasn't kidding. "We are a lost nation, Danny. Stop farting around."

The two men stared at each other, poised over what they were drinking—Danny forcing himself both to keep drinking and to continue looking at Ketchum. Danny loved the old logger so much, but Ketchum had hurt him; Ketchum was good at it. "Well, I look forward to seeing you for Christmas," Danny said. "It won't be that long now."

"Maybe not this year," Ketchum told him.

The writer knew he was risking a blow from Ketchum's powerful right hand, but Danny reached for the logger's *left* hand and held it against the table. "Don't—just *don't*," Danny said to him, but Ketchum easily pulled his hand away.

"Just do your job, Danny," the old river driver told him. "You do your job, and I'll do mine."

VI

POINTE AU BARIL STATION,
ONTARIO, 2005

—

CHAPTER 16

LOST NATION

FOR THREE WINTERS NOW, THE WRITER DANIEL BACIAGALUPO—who'd reclaimed the name that the cook and Cousin Rosie had given him—spent the months of January and February, and the first two weeks of March, on Turner Island in Georgian Bay. The island still belonged to Charlotte, the onetime love of Danny's life, but Charlotte and her family had no desire to set foot on the frozen lake or those frigid, snow-covered rocks in the heart of the winter, when they lived happily in Los Angeles.

Danny had actually improved the place—not only according to Ketchum's standards. Andy Grant had taped heated electrical cables to the waste lines that were used during the winter. These same pipes were also wrapped with a foil insulation and covered with an ice-and-water membrane. Danny could have had running hot water by applying similar heat-line and insulation methods to the water pipe running to the bay, but Andy would have had to do a lot more work—not to mention move the hot-water heater inside the main cabin to ensure that *those* pipes wouldn't freeze. It was simpler for Danny to chop a hole in the ice on the lake, and carry the water from the bay in a bucket. This amounted to a lot of chopping and carrying, but—as Ketchum would have said—so what?

There wasn't just the ice-chopping; there was a lot of wood to cut.

(Ketchum's chainsaw was a big help.) In the ten weeks Danny was there, he cut all the wood he would need the following winter—with enough left over for Charlotte and her family to use on those summer nights when it was cool enough to have a fire.

In addition to the woodstove in the main cabin, there was a propane fireplace in the bedroom and an electric heater in the bathroom—and Andy Grant had put fiberglass insulation between the floor joists. The main cabin was now sustainable for winter weather, and there was a second woodstove in Danny's writing shack, though there was no insulation there; the little building was small enough to not need it, and Danny banked the perimeter walls of the shack with snow, which kept the wind from blowing under the building and cooling off the floor.

Every night, Danny also banked the fire in the woodstove in the main cabin; when the writer awoke in the morning, it was only necessary for him to put more wood on the fire and fully open the flue. Then he tramped outside to his writing shack and started a fire in the woodstove there. Overnight, the only concession he made to his IBM typewriter was that he covered it with an electric blanket—otherwise, the grease would freeze. While the writing shack was warming up, Danny chopped a hole in the ice on the lake and brought a couple of buckets of water up to the main cabin. One bucket of water was usually sufficient to flush the toilet for the day; a second sufficed for what cooking Danny did, and for washing the dishes. Charlotte's oversize bathtub easily held four or five buckets, which included the two that had to be heated (near to boiling) on the stove, but Danny didn't take a bath until the end of the day.

He went to work every morning in his writing shack, inspired by the view of that wind-bent pine—the little tree that had once reminded both the writer and Ketchum of the cook. Danny wrote every day until early afternoon; he wanted to have a few remaining hours of daylight in which to do his chores. There was always more wood to cut, and almost every day Danny went to town. If there wasn't much garbage to haul off the island, and he needed only a few groceries, Danny would make the trip on cross-country skis. He kept the skis and poles, and a small haul sled, in Granddaddy's cabin near the back dock. (That was the unheated, possibly haunted cabin Ketchum and

Hero had preferred during their days and nights on the island—the cabin with the trapdoor in the floor, where Charlotte's grandfather, the wily poacher, had likely hidden his illegally slain deer.)

It was a short ski from the back dock of the island across Shawanaga Bay, and then Danny took the South Shore Road into Pointe au Baril Station. He wore a harness around his chest; there was a ring attached to the harness, between Danny's shoulder blades, where a carabiner held a tow cord to the haul sled. Of course, if there was a lot of garbage to take to town, or if he needed to do more extensive shopping in Pointe au Baril, Danny would take the snowmobile or the Polar airboat.

Andy Grant had warned the writer that he would need to have his own snowmobile as well as the airboat. There weren't many days in the winter months when boating conditions were unfavorable, except when the temperature climbed above freezing; then the snow sometimes stuck to the bottom of the hull, making it difficult for the airboat to slide across the snow-covered ice. That was when you had to have a snowmobile. But in early January, when Danny arrived at Charlotte's island, there was usually open water in the main channel out of Pointe au Baril Station—and often floating slabs of ice in the choppy water in the Brignall Banks Narrows. Early January was when the Polar airboat was essential—and, only occasionally, in mid-March. (In some years, albeit rarely, the ice in the bay began to break up that early.)

The airboat could cruise over ice and snow and open water—even over floating chunks of broken ice—with ease. It could go 100 MPH, though Danny never drove it that fast; the airboat had an airplane engine and a single, rear-mounted propeller. It had a heated cabin, too, and you wore guards to protect your ears from the sound. The airboat had been the most expensive element of making Turner Island habitable for Danny during those ten weeks in the coldest part of the winter, but Andy Grant had shared the cost with the writer. Andy used it as a work boat, not only in December, when the ice began to form in the bay, but from the middle of March till whenever the ice was entirely gone—usually, by the end of April.

Danny liked to be gone from Georgian Bay before the start of mud season; the ice breaking up in the bay held no attraction for him.

(There wasn't much of a mud season in Georgian Bay—it was all rocks there. But for Daniel Baciagalupo, mud season was as much a state of mind as it was a recognizable season in northern New England.)

Since Charlotte's family used the bedroom in the main cabin only sparingly, as a guest room, Danny kept some of his winter clothing in the closet year-round—just his boots, his warmest parka, his snow pants, and his ski hats. Naturally, Charlotte's and her family's summer paraphernalia was everywhere—with new photographs on the walls every winter—but Charlotte had left Danny's writing shack as it was. She'd found a couple of pictures of Ketchum with the cook, and two or three of Joe, which she had hung in the shack—perhaps to make Danny feel welcome there, not that she hadn't already done enough to make him feel warmly invited to use the place.

Charlotte's husband, the Frenchman, was evidently the cook in their family, because he left notes for Danny in the kitchen about any new equipment that was there. Danny left notes for the Frenchman, too, and they traded presents every year—gadgets for the kitchen and sundry cooking ware.

The more recently restored sleeping cabins—where Charlotte and her husband, and their children, slept every summer—were understood to be off-limits to Danny in the winter. The buildings remained locked; the electricity and propane had been turned off, and the plumbing drained. But, every winter, Danny would at least once peer in the windows—no curtains were necessary on a private family island in Shawanaga Bay. The writer merely wanted to see the new photographs on the walls, and to get a look at what new toys and books the kids might have; this wasn't really an invasion of Charlotte's privacy, was it? And, if only from such a wintry and far-removed perspective, Charlotte's family looked like a happy one to Daniel Baciagalupo. The notes back and forth with the Frenchman had all but replaced Charlotte's now-infrequent phone calls from the West Coast, and Danny still stayed out of Toronto at that September time of the year, when he knew Charlotte and her director husband were in town for the film festival.

Ketchum had advised the writer to live in the country. To the veteran river driver, Danny hadn't seemed like a city person.

Well, that the writer spent a mere ten weeks on Turner Island in Georgian Bay didn't exactly constitute *living* in the country; though he traveled a lot nowadays, Danny lived in Toronto the rest of the year. Yet—at least from early January till the middle of March—that lonely island in Shawanaga Bay and the town of Pointe au Baril Station were extremely isolated. (As Ketchum used to say, "You notice the birch trees more when there's snow.") There were not more than two hundred people in Pointe au Baril in the winter.

Kennedy's, which was good for groceries and home hardware, stayed open most of the week in the winter months. There was the Haven restaurant out on Route 69, where they served alcohol and had a pool table. The Haven had a fondness for Christmas wreaths, and they displayed an abundance of Santas—including a bass with a Santa Claus hat. While the most popular food with the snowmobilers were the chicken wings and the onion rings and the French fries, Danny stuck to the BLTs and the coleslaw—when he went there at all, which was rarely.

Larry's Tavern was out on 69, too—Danny had stayed there with Ketchum on their deer-hunting trips in the Bayfield and Pointe au Baril area—though there was already a rumor that Larry's would be sold to make room for the *new* highway. They were always widening 69, but for now the Shell station was still operating; supposedly, the Shell station was the only place in Pointe au Baril where you could buy porn magazines. (Not very good ones, if you could trust Ketchum's evaluation.)

It could be forlorn at that time of year, and there wasn't a lot to talk about, except for the repeated observation that the main channel didn't freeze over for all but a week or two. And all winter long, both the gossip and the local news provided various gruesome details of the accidents out on 69; there were a lot of accidents on that highway. This winter, there'd already been a five-vehicle pileup at the intersection with Go Home Lake Road, or near Little Go Home Bay— Danny could never keep the two of them straight. (To those year-round residents who didn't know he was a famous author, Daniel Baciagalupo was just another out-of-it American.)

Naturally, the liquor store—out on 69, across from the bait shop— was always busy, as was the Pointe au Baril nursing station, where an ambulance driver had recently stopped Danny, who was on his snow-mobile, and told him about the snowmobiler who'd gone through the ice in Shawanaga Bay.

"Did he drown?" Danny asked the driver.

"Haven't found him yet," the ambulance driver replied.

Danny thought that maybe they wouldn't find the snowmobiler until the ice broke up sometime in mid-April. According to this same ambulance driver at the nursing station, there'd also been "a doozy of a head-on" in Honey Harbour, and an alleged "first-rater of a rear-end job" in the vicinity of Port Severn. Rural life in the winter months was rugged: snow-blurred and alcohol-fueled, violent and fast.

Those ten weeks that Danny lived in the environs of Pointe au Baril Station were a strong dose of rural life; maybe it wasn't enough country living to have satisfied Ketchum, but it was enough for Danny. It counted as the writer's *requisite* country living—whether Ketchum would have counted it or not.

IN THE AFTER-HOURS RESTAURANT, the eighth and final novel by "Danny Angel," was published in 2002, seven years after *Baby in the Road*. What Danny had predicted to Ketchum was largely true—namely, his publishers complained that a book by an unknown writer named Daniel Baciagalupo couldn't possibly sell as many copies as a new novel by Danny Angel.

But Danny made his publishers understand that *In the After-Hours Restaurant* was absolutely the last book he would publish under the Angel name. And, in every interview, he repeatedly referred to himself as Daniel Baciagalupo; over and over again, he told the story of the circumstances that had forced the nom de plume upon him when he'd been a young and beginning writer. It had never been a secret that Danny Angel was a pen name, or that the writer's real name was Daniel Baciagalupo—the secret had been why.

The accidental death of the bestselling author's son—not to mention the violent murder of the writer's father, and the subsequent shooting of the cook's killer—had been big news. Danny could have insisted that *In the After-Hours Restaurant* be the debut novel by Daniel Baciagalupo; their complaining aside, and however reluctantly,

Danny's publishers would have agreed. But Danny was content to let his *next* novel (it would be his ninth) be Daniel Baciagalupo's debut.

In the After-Hours Restaurant got a warm reception and mostly good reviews—the author was often praised for a nowadays-atypical "restraint." Maybe the oft-repeated *restraint* word was what bothered the writer, though it was meant as praise. Danny would never know what Ketchum thought of *In the After-Hours Restaurant,* but *restraint* had never been a prominent part of the logger's vocabulary—not in the category of admired qualities, anyway. Would Danny Angel's last novel have satisfied the former river driver's demand that Danny let himself go—that is, be more daring as a writer? (Apparently, Danny didn't think so.)

"You keep skirting the darker subjects," Ketchum had told him. In the case of *In the After-Hours Restaurant,* would the nightly efforts of the gentle sous chef to teach himself his illustrious father's trade constitute more of the same "writing around the *periphery* of things"—as Ketchum had unkindly put it? (Danny must have thought so; otherwise, why wouldn't he have proudly put Daniel Baciagalupo's name on the new novel?)

"His most subtle work," one reviewer had written glowingly about *In the After-Hours Restaurant.* In Ketchum's unsubtle vocabulary, the *subtle* word had never been uttered in praise.

"His most symbolic undertaking," another critic had commented. There was no telling what Ketchum might have said about the *symbolic* word, Danny knew, but the writer didn't doubt what the fearless riverman would have *thought:* Symbolism and subtlety *and* restraint added up to "dodging the squeamish stuff," which Ketchum had already criticized Danny for.

And would the old logger have liked how Danny answered the repeated political questions he was asked during the promotional trips he took to publicize *In the After-Hours Restaurant*? (In 2005, the novelist was still answering political questions—and there were a few translation trips for *In the After-Hours Restaurant* yet to come.)

"Yes, it's true—I continue to live in Canada, and will continue to live here," Danny had said, "though the reason for my leaving the United States has been, as an old friend of my family once put it, *re-*

moved." (It had been Ketchum, of course, who'd used the *removed* word in reference to the deceased cowboy—more than once.)

"No, it's *not* true that I am 'politically opposed,' as you say, to living in the U.S.," Danny had said, many times, "and—just because I live in Canada, and I'm a Canadian citizen—I do *not* intend to stop writing about Americans, or about behavior I associate with being an American. It could even be argued that living in a foreign country—especially in Canada, which is right across the border—enables me to see America more clearly, or at least from a slightly less American perspective." (Ketchum would certainly have recognized the writer's sources for *that* answer, though the combative woodsman wouldn't necessarily have appreciated how tactful Danny usually was in answering those questions regarding the novelist's political opposition to his country of birth.)

"It's too soon to say," the writer was always saying—in response to how the attacks of September 11, and President Bush's retaliation to those attacks, had *affected* the United States; in response to where the wars in Afghanistan and Iraq were *headed;* in response to whether or not Canada would be *dragged into* a recession, or a depression. (Because the U.S. was fast approaching one, or both, wasn't it? From the Canadian journalists, that was generally the implication.)

It was going on four years since Ketchum had called the United States "an empire in decline"; what might the old logger have called the country now? In Canada, the questions Danny was asked were increasingly political. Most recently, it had been someone at the *Toronto Star* who'd asked Danny a battery of familiar questions.

Wasn't it true that the United States was "hopelessly overextended, militarily"? Wasn't the federal government "wallowing under massive debt"? And would the writer care to comment on America's "belligerent, warmongering nature"? Wasn't the bestselling author's "former country," as the Canadian journalist referred to the United States, "in decay"?

For how much longer, Danny wondered, would the answers to these and other insinuating questions fall into the too-soon-to-say category? The writer knew that he couldn't get away with that answer forever. "I am a slow processor—I mean, as a *writer,*" Danny liked to preface his remarks. "And I'm a *fiction* writer—meaning that I won't

ever write *about* the September Eleventh attacks, though I may use
those events, when they're not so current, and then only in the context
of a story of my own devising." (The combined evasiveness and vague-
ness of *that* cautious manifesto might have elicited from Ketchum
something along the lines of the embattled woodsman's mountains-
of-moose-shit expletive.)

After all, Danny was on record for saying that the 2000 U.S.
election—the one Bush "stole" from Gore—was, indeed, a "theft."
How could the writer *not* comment on the 2004 version, when Bush
had beaten John Kerry with questionable tactics and for the worst of
all reasons? In Danny's view, John Kerry had been a hero twice—first
in the war in Vietnam, later in his protests against it. Yet Kerry was
viewed with disfavor by America's bully patriots, who were either stupid or stubborn enough to *still* be defending that misbegotten war.

What Danny had said to the media was that his so-called former
country occasionally made him remember and appreciate Samuel
Johnson's oft-quoted "Patriotism is the last refuge of a scoundrel." Re-
grettably, that wasn't all Danny said. In some instances, sounding like
Ketchum, the writer had gone on to say that in the case of the 2004
U.S. election, the *scoundrel* was not only George W. Bush; it was every
dumber-than-dog-shit American voter who'd believed that John
Kerry wasn't *patriotic* enough to be the U.S. president.

Those remarks would be repeated—especially that bit about the
"bully patriots," not to mention singling out "every dumber-than-
dog-shit American voter." The novelist Daniel Baciagalupo had indeed written and published eight novels under the nom de plume of
Danny Angel, and Danny and his father had fled the United States
and come to Canada—an act of emigration to evade a madman who
wanted to kill them, a crazy ex-cop who eventually *did* kill Danny's
dad—but the way it appeared to most of the world was that Daniel
Baciagalupo had chosen to *stay* in Canada for political reasons.

As for Danny, he was getting tired of denying it; also, sounding
like Ketchum was easier. Danny, pretending to be Ketchum, had commented on a recent poll: Twice as many Americans had expressed
more unrestrained loathing at the prospect of gay marriage than
they'd registered even mild anxiety about the outcome of the war in
Iraq. "Bush's regressive gay-bashing is reprehensible," the writer had

said. (A comment like that further contributed to Danny's political reputation; sounding like Ketchum was very quotable.)

On the refrigerator in his Toronto kitchen, Danny had compiled a list of questions for Ketchum. But they didn't look like a list; they hadn't been assembled in an orderly way. There were many small scraps of paper taped to the fridge. Because Danny had dated each note, the recorded information on the door of the refrigerator resembled a kind of calendar of how the war in Iraq was proceeding. Soon the fridge would be covered.

Even the most anti-American of the writer's Canadian friends found his refrigerator politics a futile and juvenile exercise. (It was also a waste of Scotch tape.) And the same year *In the After-Hours Restaurant* was published, 2002, Danny had gotten in the habit of listening on the radio to a patriotic country-music station in the States. Danny could find the channel only late at night; he suspected that the signal was clearest when the wind was blowing north across Lake Ontario.

Did Danny do this to make himself angry at his *former* country? No, not at all; it was *Ketchum's* response to the crappy country music Danny wished he could hear. The writer longed to hear the old logger say, "I'll tell you what's wrong with dumb-shit patriotism—it's delusional! It signifies nothing but the American need to *win*." Might not Ketchum have said something like that?

And now, with the war in Iraq almost two years old, wouldn't Ketchum also have railed that the majority of Americans were so poorly informed that they failed to see that this war was a *distraction* from the so-called war against terror—not a furtherance of that avowed war?

Danny had no quarrel with seeking out and destroying al-Qaeda— "Seek out and destroy fucking Hamas and Hezbollah while you're at it!" Ketchum had thundered—but Saddam's Iraq had been a *secular* tyranny. Did most Americans understand the distinction? Until we went there, there'd been no al-Qaeda in Iraq, had there? (It didn't take much for Danny to be over his head, politically; he wasn't as sure of himself as Ketchum had been. Danny didn't read as much, either.)

What would the raging woodsman from Coos County have said about the United States declaring an end to "major combat operations" in Iraq in May 2003—less than two months after the war had begun? It was tempting to wonder.

The questions for Ketchum on Danny's refrigerator may have been a reminder of the war's folly, but the writer had to wonder why he'd bothered to keep such an overobvious account; it served Danny no purpose, other than to depress him.

To the separate but similar-sounding denials by U.S. secretary of state Colin Powell and British prime minister Tony Blair—who swore in May 2003 that intelligence about Iraq's weapons of mass destruction was neither distorted nor exaggerated in order to justify the attack on Iraq—Danny could imagine Ketchum saying, "Show me the weapons, fellas!"

At times, Danny recited the questions for Ketchum to the dog. ("Even the dog," Ketchum might have quipped, "is smart enough to know where this war is headed!")

Daniel Baciagalupo would be sixty-three this coming mud season. He was a man who'd lost his only child and his father, and he lived alone—not to mention that he was a *writer*. Naturally, Danny *would* talk and read aloud to the dog.

As for Hero, he seemed unsurprised by Danny's somewhat eccentric behavior. The former bear hound was used to being spoken to; it usually beat getting mauled by a bear.

THE DOG WAS OF INDETERMINATE AGE. Ketchum had been vague about how old this particular Hero was—meaning how many generations were descended from that *first* "fine animal," which the current Hero represented. There were more gray hairs on Hero's muzzle than Danny remembered, but the Walker bluetick's mottled-white and bluish-gray coat made the gray hairs of *age* harder to distinguish. And that Hero was lame was not only an indication that the dog was advanced in years; the claw wounds from the bear-mauling had healed long ago, though the scars were very visible, and that hip, where the bear had clawed Hero, suffered from some joint damage. The mangled, mostly missing ear had also healed, but the scar tissue was black and furless.

Most disconcerting to anyone encountering Hero for the first time

was that the veteran bear hound was missing an eyelid—on the opposite side of the dog's fierce face from his mangled ear. The eyelid was
lost in Hero's last confrontation with Six-Pack's German shepherd,
though—according to Pam—Hero had gained the upper hand in the
dogs' final, kennel-clearing fight. Six-Pack was forced to put the
shepherd down. She'd never held it against Hero, however; by Pam's
own account, the two dogs had always and sincerely hated each other.

To the writer, the battle-scarred bear hound was a living replica of
Coos County, where lethal hatreds were generally permitted to run
their course. (As elsewhere, Danny considered—whenever he happened to glance at the questions for Ketchum on his refrigerator
door.)

In January 2004, the number of U.S. soldiers killed in Iraq since
the start of the war had climbed to five hundred. "Hell, five hundred
is nothing—it's just getting started," Danny could imagine the old
logger saying. "We'll be up to five *thousand* in just a few more years,
and some asshole will be telling us that peace and stability are right
around the corner."

"What do you think about that, Hero?" Danny had asked the dog,
who'd pricked up his one ear at the question. "Wouldn't our mutual
friend have been entertaining on the subject of this war?"

Danny could tell when the dog was really listening, or when Hero
was actually asleep. The eye without the eyelid followed you when
Hero was only pretending to sleep, but when the dog was truly dead
to the world, the pupil and the iris of the constantly open eye traveled
somewhere unseen; the cloudy-white orb stared blankly.

The onetime bear hound slept on a zippered dog bed stuffed with
cedar chips in the Toronto kitchen. Contrary to Danny's earlier opinion, Ketchum's stories of Hero's farting *hadn't* been exaggerated. On
the dog bed, Hero's preferred chew toy was the old sheath for
Ketchum's biggest Browning knife—the one-footer that the riverman
used to stash over the sun visor on the driver's side of his truck. The
sheath, which had absorbed the sharpening oil from Ketchum's oil-
stone knife sharpener, was possibly still redolent of the slain bear that
had once ridden in the cab of the truck; from the way Hero seemed
neurotically attached to the lightly gnawed sheath, Danny understandably believed so.

The foot-long Browning knife itself proved to be less useful. Danny had taken the knife to a kitchen-supply store, where they'd tried unsuccessfully to resharpen it; Danny's repeated efforts to rid the knife of any residue of Ketchum's sharpening oil, by putting the knife in the dishwasher, had dulled the blade. Now the knife was dull *and* oily, and Danny had hung it in a most visible but unreachable part of his Toronto kitchen, where it resembled a ceremonial sword.

Ketchum's guns were another matter. Danny hadn't wanted them—not in Toronto. He'd given them to Andy Grant, with whom Danny went deer hunting every November. Killing Carl had made it easier for Danny to shoot deer, though he'd refused to fire a shotgun. ("Never again," he'd said to Andy.) Danny used Ketchum's Remington .30-06 Springfield instead. In a wooded area, even at reasonably close range, it was harder to hit a deer with that prized collectible, but the kick of the carbine—or the resonance of the short-barreled rifle's discharge, in his ear—was different from what Danny remembered of the 20-gauge.

Andy Grant knew the Bayfield area like the back of his hand; he'd hunted there as a boy. But, for the most part, Andy took Danny deer hunting on what was more familiar terrain for Danny—that area west of Lost Tower Lake, between Payne's Road and Shawanaga Bay. In the vicinity of the winter snowmobile portage, and sometimes within sight of the back dock on Charlotte's island, was a natural runway— a virtual game path for deer. That way, every November, Danny could look across the gray water at his winter destination. There were places on the mainland, overlooking Shawanaga Bay, where you could see the back dock on Turner Island—even the roof of Granddaddy's cabin, where Ketchum had once thrown the skin from that rattlesnake he'd shot.

For those November hunting trips, Danny always stayed at Larry's Tavern. In the bar was where he'd heard the rumor that Larry's would one day be sold, whenever the new highway advanced that far north. Who was Danny to say, as the old-timers in the bar often did, that Larry's should be spared? Neither the tavern nor the motel seemed worth saving to the writer, but he couldn't deny that both parts of the roadside establishment had long served a local (albeit largely self-destructive) purpose.

And every winter, when Danny arrived on Charlotte's island, Andy Grant loaned him Ketchum's Remington. ("In case of *critters*," Ketchum would have said.) Andy also left a couple of extra loaded cartridge clips with the writer. Hero invariably recognized the carbine. It was one of the few times the bear hound wagged his tail, for that bolt-action Remington .30-06 Springfield had been Ketchum's gun of choice for bear, and doubtless Hero was reminded of the thrill of the chase—or of his former master.

IT HAD TAKEN TWO YEARS for Danny to teach the dog to bark. The growling and farting, and the snoring in his sleep, came naturally to Hero—that is, if the bear hound *hadn't* learned these indelicate arts from Ketchum—but Hero had never barked before. In his earliest efforts to encourage Hero to bark, Danny would occasionally wonder if the old logger had disapproved of barking.

There was a little park and playground, probably as big as a football field, near Danny's Rosedale residence and adjacent to those two new condominiums on Scrivener Square, which—as luck would have it—did *not* block the writer's view of the clock tower on the Summerhill liquor store. Danny walked Hero in the park three or four times a day—more often than not on a leash, lest there might happen to be a German shepherd present in the park, or some other male dog who could have reminded Hero of Six-Pack's late shepherd.

In the park, Danny barked for Hero; the writer made every effort to bark authentically, but Hero was unimpressed. After a year of this, Danny wondered if Hero somehow didn't think that barking was a *weakness* in dogs.

Other dog-walkers in the little park were disconcerted by Hero's lean-and-mean appearance, and by the bear hound's preternatural aloofness from other dogs. There were also the scars, the stiff-hipped limp—not to mention the wonky-eyed, baleful stare. "It's only because Hero lost an eyelid—he's not really giving your dog the evil eye, or anything," Danny would try to reassure the anxious dog owners.

"What happened to that ear?" a young woman with a brainless breed of spaniel asked the writer.

"Oh, that was a bear," Danny admitted.

"A *bear*!"

"And the poor thing's hip—those terrible scars?" a nervous-looking man with a schnauzer had asked.

"The same bear," Danny said.

It was their second winter on Charlotte's island when the barking began. Danny had parked the Polar airboat on the ice off the front dock; he was unloading groceries from the boat, while Hero waited for him on the dock. Danny tried once more to bark at the dog—the writer had almost given up. To both Danny and the dog's surprise, Danny's bark was repeated; there was an echo of the bark from the direction of Barclay Island. When Hero heard the echo, he barked. Of course there was an echo attending Hero's bark, too; the bear hound heard a dog uncannily like himself bark back.

It had gone on for over an hour—Hero barking at himself on the dock. (If Ketchum had been there, Danny thought, the former river driver would probably have shot the bear hound.) What have I created? the writer wondered, but after a while, Hero had stopped.

After that, the dog barked normally; he barked at snowmobiles and at the once-in-a-while airplanelike sound of a distant airboat out in the main channel. He barked at the train whistles, which the dog could hear from the mainland—and, less frequently, at the whine of the tires on those big long-haul trucks out on 69. As for intruders—well, in those winter weeks, there were none—there was only a now-and-again visit from Andy Grant. (Hero barked at Andy, too.)

One could never say that Ketchum's bear hound was normal—or even *almost* normal—but the barking did much to alleviate the sheer creepiness of Hero's one-eared, gaping-eyed face. Certainly, Danny's fellow dog-walkers in that little park near Scrivener Square were less visibly anxious about the bear hound—and now that the dog barked, he growled less. It was a pity that there was nothing Danny could do about Hero's silent farting or his colossal snoring.

What the writer was realizing was that he hadn't known what owning a dog was like. The more Danny talked to Hero, the less the writer was inclined to think about what Ketchum would have said about Iraq. Did having a dog make you less political? (Not that Danny had ever been *truly* political; he'd never been like Katie, *or* like Ketchum.)

Danny did take sides, politically; he had political opinions. But

Danny wasn't an anti-American—the writer didn't even feel like an expatriate! The world that was captured in the barest outline form on his Toronto refrigerator began to seem less and less important to the author. That world was increasingly *not* what Daniel Baciagalupo wanted to think about—especially not, as Ketchum would have said, *as a writer.*

THERE'D BEEN AN ACCIDENT on 69 near Horseshoe Lake Road. A dipshit driving a Hummer had rear-ended a cattle-transport trailer, killing himself and a bunch of beef cattle. This happened the first winter Danny stayed on Charlotte's island, and he'd heard about the accident from his cleaning woman. She was a First Nation person— a young woman with black hair and eyes, a pretty face, and thick, strong-looking hands. Once a week, Danny drove the airboat to the Shawanaga Landing Indian Reserve; that was where he picked her up, and where he returned her at the end of the day, but she almost certainly didn't live there. Shawanaga Landing was mostly used in the summer months, both as a campsite and as a gateway to the bay. The residents of the reserve lived in the village of Shawanaga, though there were a few First Nation people who lived year-round in Skerryvore— or so Andy Grant had told Danny. (Both areas could be reached by road in the winter months, at least on snowmobiles.)

The young cleaning woman seemed to like riding in the Polar airboat. Danny always brought a second pair of ear guards for her, and after she'd met Hero, she asked why the bear hound couldn't come along for the ride. "The airboat is too loud for a dog's ears—well, for his one ear, anyway," Danny told her. "I don't know how well Hero can hear out of the mangled ear."

But the cleaning woman had a way with dogs. She told Danny to put her ear guards on Hero when he drove to Shawanaga Landing to pick her up, and when he drove back to Turner Island without her. (Surprisingly, the dog didn't object to wearing them.) And when the cleaning woman rode in the airboat with Hero, she held the bear hound in her lap and covered his ears—even the mostly missing one—with her big, strong hands. Danny had never seen Hero sit in anyone's lap before. The Walker bluetick weighed sixty or seventy pounds.

The dog devotedly followed the young woman throughout her cleaning chores, the same way Hero attached himself to Danny everywhere on the island when Danny was otherwise alone there. When Danny was using the chainsaw, the bear hound maintained a safe distance between them. (The writer was sure that Hero had learned this from Ketchum.)

There was an ongoing misunderstanding in regard to where the young First Nation person *lived*—Danny never saw anyone waiting for her at Shawanaga Landing, or any kind of vehicle she might have used to get herself to and from the boat landing. Danny had asked her only once, but the young cleaning woman's answer struck him as dreamy or facetious—or both—and he'd not asked her for clarification. "Ojibway Territory," she'd said.

Danny couldn't tell what the First Nation woman had meant—maybe nothing. He could have asked Andy Grant where she was actually from—Andy had put him in touch with her in the first place—but Danny had let it go. Ojibway Territory was a good enough answer for him.

And the writer had instantly forgotten the young woman's name, if he'd ever really heard it. Once, early in the first winter she worked for him, he'd said to her admiringly, "You are tireless." This was in reference to all the ice-chopping she did—and how many full buckets of water she hauled up from the lake, and left for him in the main cabin. The girl had smiled; she'd liked the *tireless* word.

"You may call me that—*please* call me that," she'd told him.

"Tireless?"

"That's my name," the First Nation woman had told him. "That's who I am, all right."

Again, Danny could have asked Andy Grant for her real name, but the woman liked to be called Tireless, and that was good enough for Danny, too.

Sometimes, from his writing shack, he saw Tireless paying obeisance to the *inuksuk*. She didn't formally bow to the stone cairn, but she respectfully brushed the snow off it—and, in her submissiveness, she demonstrated a kind of deference or homage. Even Hero, who stood eerily apart from Tireless on these solemn occasions, seemed to acknowledge the sacredness of the moment.

Danny worked as well in his writing shack on the one day a week when Tireless came to clean as he did when he was alone with Hero there; the cleaning woman didn't distract him. When she was done with her work in the main cabin—it didn't matter that, on other days, Danny was used to Hero sleeping (and farting and snoring) in the writing shack while he worked—the writer would look up from his writing and suddenly see Tireless standing by that wind-bent little pine. She never touched the crippled tree; she just stood beside it, like a sentinel, with Hero standing beside her. Neither the First Nation cleaning woman nor the bear hound ever stared at Danny through the window of his writing shack. Whenever the writer happened to look up and see them next to the weather-beaten pine, both the dog and the young woman had their backs to him; they appeared to be scouting the frozen bay.

Then Danny would tap the window, and both Tireless and Hero would come inside the writing shack. Danny would leave the shack (and his writing) while Tireless cleaned up in there, which never took her long—usually, less than the time it took Danny to make himself a cup of tea in the main cabin.

Except for Andy Grant—and those repeat old-timers Danny occasionally encountered in the bar at Larry's Tavern, or at the Haven restaurant, and in the grocery store—the First Nation cleaning woman was the only human being Danny had any social intercourse with in his winters on the island in Georgian Bay, and Danny and Hero saw Tireless just once a week for the ten weeks that the writer was there. One time, when Danny was in town and he ran into Andy Grant, the writer had told Andy how well the young First Nation woman was working out.

"Hero and I just love her," he'd said. "She's awfully easy and pleasant to have around."

"Sounds like you're getting ready to *marry* her," Andy told the writer. Andy was kidding, of course, but Danny—if only for a minute, or two—found himself seriously considering the idea.

Later, back in the airboat—but before he started the engine or put the ear guards on the bear hound—Danny asked the dog: "Do I look lonely to you, Hero? I must be a little lonely, huh?"

—

IN THE KITCHEN OF DANNY'S HOUSE on Cluny Drive—particularly as the year 2004 advanced—the politics on the writer's refrigerator had grown tedious. Conceivably, politics had *always* been boring and the writer only now had noticed; at least the questions for Ketchum seemed trivial and childish in comparison to the more personal and detailed story Danny was developing in his ninth novel.

As always, he began at the end of the story. He'd not only written what he believed was the last sentence, but Danny had a fairly evolved idea of the trajectory of the new novel—his first as Daniel Baciagalupo. Danny was slowly but gradually making his way *backward* through the narrative, to where he thought the book should begin. That was just the way he'd always worked: He plotted a story from back to front; hence he conceived of the first chapter *last*. By the time Danny got to the first sentence—meaning to that actual moment when he wrote the first sentence down—often a couple of years or more had passed, but by then he knew the whole story. From that first sentence, the book flowed forward—or, in Danny's case, back to where he'd begun.

As always, too, the more deeply Danny immersed himself in a novel, the more what passed for his politics fell away. While the writer's political opinions were genuine, Danny would have been the first to admit that he was mistrustful of *all* politics. Wasn't he a novelist, in part, because he saw the world in a most subjective way? And not only was writing fiction the best of what Daniel Baciagalupo could manage to do; writing a novel was truly all he did. He was a craftsman, not a theorist; he was a storyteller, not an intellectual.

Yet Danny was unavoidably remembering those last two U.S. helicopters that left Saigon—those poor people clinging to the helicopters' skids, and the hundreds of desperate South Vietnamese who were left behind in the courtyard of the U.S. Embassy. The writer had no doubt that we would see that (or something like that) in Iraq. Shades of Vietnam, Danny was thinking—typical of his age, because Iraq wasn't exactly another Vietnam. (Daniel Baciagalupo was such a sixties fella, as Ketchum had called him; there would be no reforming him.)

It was with little conviction that Danny spoke to the yawning, otherwise unresponsive dog. "I'll bet you a box of dog biscuits, Hero—everything is going to get a lot worse before anything gets a little better." The bear hound didn't even react to the *dog biscuits* part; Hero found all politics every bit as boring as Danny did. It was just the world as usual, wasn't it? Who among them would ever change anything about the way the world worked? Not a *writer*, certainly; Hero had as good a chance of changing the world as Danny did. (Fortunately, Danny *didn't* say this to Hero—not wanting to offend the noble dog.)

IT WAS A DECEMBER MORNING IN 2004, after the final (already forgotten) question for Ketchum had been taped to the door of Danny's refrigerator, when Lupita—that most loyal and long-suffering Mexican cleaning woman—found the writer in his kitchen, where Danny was actually writing. This disturbed Lupita, who—in her necessary departmentalizing of the household—took a totalitarian approach to what the various rooms in a working writer's house were *for*.

Lupita was used to, if disapproving of, the clipboards and the loose ream of typing paper in the gym, where there was no typewriter; the plethora of Post-it notes, which were everywhere in the house, was a further irritation to her, but one she had suppressed. As for the political questions for Mr. Ketchum, stuck to the fridge door, Lupita read these with ever-decreasing interest—if at all. The taped-up trivia chiefly bothered Lupita because it prevented her from wiping down the refrigerator door, as she would have liked to do.

Caring, as she did, for Danny's house on Cluny Drive had been nothing short of a series of heartbreaks for Lupita. That Mr. Ketchum didn't come to Toronto for Christmas anymore could make the Mexican cleaning woman cry, especially in that late-December time of year—not to mention that the effort she'd had to expend in restoring the late cook's bedroom, following that double shooting, had come close to killing her. Naturally, the blood-soaked bed had been taken away, and the wallpaper was replaced, but Lupita had individually wiped clean every blood-spattered snapshot on Dominic's bulletin boards, and she'd scrubbed the floor until she thought her knees and the heels of her hands were going to bleed. She'd persuaded Danny to replace the curtains, too; otherwise, the smell of gunpowder would have remained in the murderous bedroom.

It is worth noting that, in this period of Danny's life, the two women he maintained the most constant contact with were both cleaning women, though certainly Lupita exerted more influence on the writer than Tireless did. It was because of Lupita's prodding that Danny had gotten rid of the couch in his third-floor writing room, and this was entirely the result of Lupita claiming that the imprint of the loathsome deputy sheriff's body was visible (to *her*) on that couch. "I can still see him lying there, waiting for you and your dad to fall asleep," Lupita had said to Danny.

Naturally, Danny disposed of the couch—not that the imprint of the cowboy's fat body had ever been visible to Daniel Baciagalupo, but once the Mexican cleaning woman claimed to have sighted an imprint of Carl on that couch, the writer soon found himself imagining it.

Lupita hadn't stopped there. It was soon after Hero had come to live with him, Danny was remembering, when Lupita proposed a more monumental change. Those bulletin boards with their collected family history—the hundreds of overlapping snapshots the cook had saved, and there were hundreds more in Dominic's desk drawers— well, you can imagine what the Mexican cleaning woman thought. It made no sense, Lupita had said, for those special photos to be on display in a room where they were now unseen. "They should be in *your* bedroom, Mr. Writer," Lupita had told Danny. (She'd spontaneously taken to calling him that, or "Señor Writer." Danny couldn't recall exactly when this had started.)

And it followed, of course, that those photographs of Charlotte would have to be moved. "It's no longer appropriate," Lupita had told Danny; she meant that he shouldn't be sleeping with those nostalgic pictures of Charlotte Turner, who was a married woman with a family of her own. (Without a word of resistance from Mr. Writer, Lupita had simply taken charge.)

Now it made sense. The late cook's bedroom served as a second guest room; it was rarely used, but it was particularly useful if a couple with a child (or children) were visiting the writer. Dominic's double bed had been replaced with two twins. The homage to Charlotte in this far-removed guest room—at the opposite end of the hall from Danny's bedroom—seemed more suitable to what Danny's relationship with Charlotte had become.

It made more sense, too, that Danny now slept with those photographs of the cook's immediate and extended families—including some snapshots of the writer's dead son, Joe. Danny had Lupita to thank for this even being possible, and Lupita was the one who maintained the bulletin boards; she chose the new and recycled photographs that she wanted Danny to sleep with. Once or twice a week, Danny looked closely at the pictures on those bulletin boards, just to see what Lupita had rearranged.

Occasionally, there were small glimpses of Charlotte in the snapshots—for the most part, these pictures were of Charlotte with Joe. (They had somehow passed Lupita's unfathomable radar of approval.) And there were pictures of Ketchum galore, of course—even a few new ones of the woodsman, and of Danny's young mother with his even younger dad. These long-saved shots of Cousin Rosie had come into Danny's possession together with Hero, and Ketchum's guns—not to mention the chainsaw. The old photos had been spared any exposure to sunlight, pressed flat in the pages of Rosie's beloved books, which had also come into Danny's possession—now that the old logger could no longer read them. What a lot of books Ketchum had hoarded! How many more might he have read?

That December morning in 2004, when Lupita caught Danny writing in the kitchen, he was closing in on a couple of scenes he imagined might be near the beginning of his novel—even actual sentences, in some cases. He was definitely getting close to the start of the first chapter, but exactly where to begin—the very first sentence, for example—still eluded him. He was writing in a simple spiral notebook on white lined paper; Lupita knew that the writer had a stack of such notebooks in his third-floor writing room, where (she felt strongly) he should have been writing.

"You're writing in the kitchen," the cleaning woman said. It was a straightforward, declarative sentence, but Danny detected an edge to it; from the critical tone of Lupita's remark, it was as if she'd said,

"You're fornicating in the driveway." (In broad daylight.) Danny was somewhat taken aback by the Mexican cleaning woman's meaning.

"I'm not exactly writing, Lupita," he said defensively. "I'm making a few notes to myself about what I'm *going to* write."

"Whatever you're doing, you're doing it in the *kitchen*," Lupita insisted.

"Yes," Danny answered her cautiously.

"I suppose I could start upstairs—like on the third floor, in your writing room, where you're not writing," the cleaning woman said.

"That would be fine," Danny told her.

Lupita sighed, as if the world were an endless source of pain for her—it had been, Danny knew. He tolerated how difficult she could be, and for the most part Danny accepted Lupita's presumed authority; the writer knew that one had to be more accepting of the authority of someone who'd lost a child, as the cleaning woman had, and more tolerant of her, too. But before Lupita could leave the kitchen—to attend to what she clearly considered her out-of-order (if not altogether wrong) first task of the day—Danny said to her, "Would you please clean the fridge today, Lupita? Just throw everything away."

The Mexican was not easily surprised, but Lupita stood as if she were in shock. Recovering herself, she opened the door to the fridge, which she had cleaned just the other day; there was practically nothing in it. (Except when Danny was having a dinner party, there almost never was.)

"No, I mean the *door*," Danny told her. "Please clean it off entirely. Throw all those notes away."

At this point, Lupita's disapproval turned to worry. "*¿Enfermo?*" she suddenly asked Danny. Her plump brown hand felt the writer's forehead; to her practiced touch, Danny didn't feel as if he had a fever.

"No, I am *not* sick, Lupita," Danny told the cleaning woman. "I am merely sick of how I've been distracting myself."

It was a tough time of year for the writer, who was no spring chicken, Lupita knew. Christmas was the hardest time for people who'd lost family; of this, the cleaning woman had little doubt. She immediately did what Danny had asked her to do. (She actually welcomed the opportunity to interrupt his writing, since he was doing it in the wrong place.) Lupita gladly ripped the little scraps of paper off the fridge door; the damn Scotch tape would take longer, she knew, digging at the remaining strips with her fingernails. She would also scour the door with an antibacterial fluid, but she could do that later.

It's not likely that it ever occurred to the cleaning woman that she was throwing away what amounted to Danny's obsession with what Ketchum would have made of Bush's blundering in Iraq, but she was. Maybe in Danny's mind—way in the back, somewhere—the writer was aware that he was, at that moment, letting go of at least a little of the anger he felt at his *former* country.

Ketchum had called America a lost nation, but Danny didn't know if this was fair to say—or if the accusation was true *yet*. All that mattered to Daniel Baciagalupo, as a writer, was that his former country was a lost nation to *him*. Since Bush's reelection, Danny had accepted that America was lost to him, and that he was—from this minute, forward—an outsider living in Canada, till the end of his days.

While Lupita made a fuss over the refrigerator door, Danny went into the gym and called Kiss of the Wolf. He left a fairly detailed message on the answering machine; he said he wanted to make a reservation at the restaurant for every remaining night that Kiss of the Wolf was open—that is, until Patrice and Silvestro closed for the Christmas holiday. Lupita had been right: Christmas was always hard for Danny. First he'd lost Joe, and those Christmases in Colorado; then Danny's dad had been blown away. And every Christmas since that also-memorable Christmas of 2001, the writer was reminded of how he'd heard about Ketchum, who was lost to him, too.

Danny was not Ketchum; the writer was not even "like" Ketchum, though there'd been times when Danny had tried to be like the old logger. Oh, how he'd tried! But that wasn't Danny's job—to use the *job* word as Ketchum had meant it. Danny's job was to be a writer, and Ketchum had understood that long before Danny did.

"You've got to stick your nose in the worst of it, and imagine *everything*, Danny," the veteran river driver had told him. Daniel Baciagalupo was trying; if the writer couldn't *be* Ketchum, he could at least *heroize* the logger. Really, how hard was it, the writer was thinking, to make Ketchum a hero?

"Well, writers should know it's sometimes hard work to die,

Danny," Ketchum had told him when it had taken Danny three shots to drop his first deer.

Shit, I should have known *then* what Ketchum meant, the writer was thinking on that day when Lupita was madly cleaning all around him. (Yes, he should have.)

CHAPTER 17

KETCHUM EXCEPTED

DANNY DID HAVE SOME GLIMMER OF UNDERSTANDING IN regard to what Ketchum was up to—this had happened around the time of American Thanksgiving, in November 2001. The writer was having dinner one evening—naturally, at Kiss of the Wolf—and Danny's dinner date was his own doctor. Their relationship wasn't sexual, but they had a serious friendship; she'd been Danny's medical-expert reader for a number of his novels. She'd once written him a fan letter, and they'd begun a correspondence—long before he came to Canada. Now they were close friends.

The doctor's name was Erin Reilly. She was almost Danny's age—with two grown children, who had children of their own—and, not long ago, her husband had left her for her receptionist. "I should have seen it coming," Erin had told Danny philosophically. "They both kept asking me, repeatedly—I mean about a hundred times a day—if I was *all right.*"

Erin had become the friend in his Toronto life that Armando DeSimone had been to Danny in Vermont. Danny still corresponded with Armando, but Armando and Mary didn't come to Toronto any-more; the drive from Vermont was too long, and airplane travel had become too inconvenient for people their age, and of their disposition.

"The airport-security goons have taken every Swiss Army knife I ever owned," Armando had complained to Danny.

Erin Reilly was a real reader, and when Danny asked her a medical question—whether this was a concern he had for himself, or when he was doing research for a character in a novel—Danny appreciated that the doctor gave long, detailed answers. Erin liked to read long, detailed novels, too.

That night, in Kiss of the Wolf, Danny had said to his doctor: "I have a friend who has a recurrent desire to cut off his left hand; his left hand failed him somehow. Will he bleed to death, if he actually does it?"

Erin was a gangling, heron-like woman with closely cut gray hair and steely hazel eyes. She was intensely absorbed in her work, and in whatever novel or novels she was reading—to a flaw, Danny knew, and maybe the flaw was why he loved her. She could be blind to the world around her to an alarming degree—the way, with the passage of time, the cook had managed to convince himself that the cowboy wasn't really coming after him. Erin could joke that she should have "seen it coming"—meaning her husband's involvement with her receptionist—but the fact that they'd both kept asking Erin if she was *all right*, was not (in Danny's opinion) what his dear friend Erin *should* have noticed. Erin had written her husband's Viagra prescriptions; she had to have known how much of that stuff he was taking! But Danny loved this about Erin—her acute innocence, which reminded him of everything his father had been blind to, which Danny had also loved.

"This . . . *friend* who has a recurrent desire to cut off his left hand," Dr. Reilly slowly said. "Is it *you*, Danny, or is this a character you're writing about?"

"Neither. It's an old friend," Danny told her. "I would tell you the story, Erin, but it's too long, even for you."

Danny remembered what he and Erin had to eat that night. They'd ordered the prawns with coconut milk and green curry broth; they'd both had the Malpeque oysters, with Silvestro's Champagne-shallot mignonette, to start.

"Tell me *everything*, Erin," he'd told her. "Spare me no detail." (The writer was always saying this to her.) Erin smiled and took a tiny sip of her wine. She was in the habit of ordering an expensive bottle of white wine; she never drank more than a glass or two, donating the remainder of the bottle to Patrice, who then sold it by the glass. For his part, Patrice every so often paid for Erin's wine. Patrice Arnaud was Dr. Reilly's patient, too.

"Well, Danny, here goes," Erin had begun that night in November 2001. "Your friend probably would *not* bleed to death—not if he cut his hand off at the wrist, with a clean swipe and a sharp blade." Danny didn't doubt that whatever instrument Ketchum might use would be sharp—be it the Browning knife, an ax, or even the old logger's chainsaw. "But your friend would bleed a lot—a real spurting mess out of the radial and ulnar arteries, which are the two main vessels he would have severed. Yet this unfortunate friend of yours would have a few problems—that is, if he *wanted* to die." Here Erin paused; at first, Danny didn't know why. "Does your friend want to die, or does he just want to be rid of the hand?" the doctor asked him.

"I don't know," Danny answered her. "I always thought it was just about the hand."

"Well, then, he may get what he wants," Erin said. "You see, the arteries are very elastic. After they were cut, they would retract back into the arm, where the surrounding tissues would compress them, at least to a degree. The muscles in the arterial walls would immediately contract, narrowing the diameter of the arteries and slowing the blood loss. Our bodies are resourceful at trying to stay alive; your friend would have many mechanisms coming into play, all making an effort to save him from bleeding to death." Here Erin paused again. "What's wrong?" she asked Danny.

Daniel Baciagalupo was still thinking about whether or not Ketchum *wanted* to kill himself; over all those years with the incessant talk about the left hand, it hadn't occurred to the writer that Ketchum might have been harboring more serious intentions.

"Are you feeling sick, or something?" Dr. Reilly asked Danny.

"No, it's not that," Danny said. "So he *wouldn't* bleed to death—that's what you're saying?"

"The platelets would save him," Erin answered. "Platelets are tiny blood particles, which aren't even large enough to be real cells; they're actually flakes that fall off a cell and then circulate in the bloodstream.

Under normal circumstances, platelets are tiny, smooth-walled, non-adherent flecks. But when your friend cuts off his hand, he exposes the endothelium, or inner arterial wall, which would cause a spill of a protein called collagen—the same stuff plastic surgeons use. When the platelets encounter the exposed collagen, they undergo a drastic transformation—a metamorphosis. The platelets become sticky, spiculated particles. They aggregate and adhere to one another—they form a plug."

"Like a clot?" Danny asked; his voice sounded funny. He couldn't eat because he couldn't swallow. He was somehow certain that Ketchum intended to kill himself; cutting off his left hand was just the logger's way of doing it, and of course Ketchum held his left hand responsible for letting Rosie slip away. But Rosie had been gone for years. Danny realized that Ketchum must have been holding himself accountable for not killing Carl. For his friend Dominic's death, Ketchum faulted himself—meaning *all* of himself. Ketchum's left hand couldn't be blamed for the cowboy killing the cook.

"Too much detail while you're eating?" Erin asked. "I'll stop. The clotting comes a little later; there are a couple of other proteins involved. Suffice it to say, there *is* an artery-plugging clot; this would stem the tide of your friend's bleeding, and save his life. Cutting off your hand won't kill you."

But Danny felt that he was drowning; he was sinking fast. ("Well, writers should know it's sometimes hard work to die, Danny," the old logger had told him.)

"Okay, Erin," Danny said, but his voice wasn't his own; neither he nor Erin recognized it. "Let's say that my friend *wanted* to die. Let's assume that he wants to cut off his left hand in the process, but what he *really* wants is to die. What then?"

The doctor was eating ravenously; she had to chew and swallow for a few seconds while Danny waited. "Easy," Erin said, after another small sip of wine. "Does your friend know what aspirin is? He just takes some aspirin."

"Aspirin," Danny repeated numbly. He could see the contents of the glove compartment in Ketchum's truck, as if the door were still open and Danny had never reached out and closed it—the small handgun and the big bottle of aspirin.

"Painkillers, both of them," Ketchum had called them, casually. "I wouldn't be caught dead without aspirin and some kind of weapon," he'd said.

"Aspirin blocks certain parts of the process that activates the platelets," Dr. Reilly was saying. "If you wanted to get technical, you could say that aspirin prevents blood from clotting—only two aspirin tablets in your friend's system, and very possibly the clotting wouldn't kick in quickly enough to save him. And if he *really* wanted to die, he could wash the aspirin down with some booze; through a completely different mechanism, alcohol also prevents platelet activation and aggregation. There would be a real synergy between the alcohol and the aspirin, rendering the platelets impotent—they wouldn't stick to one another. No clot, in other words. Your hand-deprived friend would die."

Erin finally stopped talking when she saw that Danny was staring at his food, not eating. It's also worth noting that Daniel Baciaglupo had hardly touched his beer. "Danny?" his doctor said. "I didn't know he was a *real* friend. I thought that he was probably a character in a novel, and you were using the *friend* word loosely. I'm sorry."

DANNY HAD RUN HOME from Kiss of the Wolf that November night. He'd wanted to call Ketchum right away, but privately. It was a cold night in Toronto. That late in the fall, it would have already snowed a bunch of times in Coos County, New Hampshire.

Ketchum didn't fax much anymore. He didn't call Danny very frequently, either—not nearly as often as Danny called him. That night, the phone had rung and rung; there'd been no answer. Danny would have called Six-Pack, but he didn't have her phone number and he'd never known her last name—no more than he knew Ketchum's first name, if the old logger had ever had one.

He decided to fax Ketchum some evidently transparent bullshit—to the effect that Danny thought he should have Six-Pack's phone number, in case there was ever an emergency and Danny couldn't reach Ketchum.

I DON'T NEED ANYBODY CHECKING UP ON ME!

Ketchum had faxed back, before Danny was awake and downstairs in the morning. But, after a few more faxes and an awkward phone conversation, Ketchum provided Danny with Pam's number.

It was December of that same year, 2001, before Danny got up the nerve to call Six-Pack, and she wasn't much of a communicator on the phone. Yes, she and Ketchum had gone a couple of times that fall to Moose-Watch Pond and seen the moose dancing—or "millin' around," as Six-Pack said. Yes, she'd gone "campin' " with Ketchum, too—but only once, in a snowstorm, and if her hip hadn't kept her awake the whole night, Ketchum's snoring would have.

Nor did Danny have any luck in persuading Ketchum to come to Toronto for Christmas that year. "I may show up, I more likely won't," was how Ketchum had left it—as independent as ever.

All too soon, it was that time of year Daniel Baciagalupo had learned to dread—just a few days before Christmas 2001, coming up on what would be the first anniversary of his dad's murder—and the writer was eating dinner alone at Kiss of the Wolf. His thoughts were unfocused, wandering, when Patrice—that ever-suave and graceful presence—approached Danny's table. "Someone has come to see you, Daniel," Patrice said with unusual solemnity. "But, strangely, at the kitchen door."

"To see *me*? In the *kitchen*?" Danny asked.

"A tall, strong-looking person," Patrice intoned, with an air of foreboding. "Doesn't look like a big reader—might not be what you call a fan."

"But why the *kitchen* door?" Danny asked.

"She said she didn't think she was well-enough dressed to come in the front door," Patrice told the writer.

"*She?*" Danny said. How he hoped it was Lady Sky!

"I had to look twice to be sure," Patrice said, with a shrug. "But she's definitely a she."

In that Crown's Lane alleyway behind the restaurant, one-eyed Pedro had spotted the tall woman; he'd graciously shown her to the service entrance to the kitchen. The former Ramsay Farnham had said to Six-Pack Pam: "Even if it's not on the menu, they often have cassoulet at this time of year—I recommend it."

"I ain't lookin' for a handout," Six-Pack told him. "I'm lookin' for a fella, name of Danny—a famous writer."

"Danny doesn't work in the kitchen—his dad did," one-eyed Pedro told her.

"I know that—I'm just a back-door kinda person," Pam said. "It's a fuckin' fancy-lookin' place."

The former Ramsay Farnham appeared momentarily disdainful; he must have suffered a flashback to his previous life. "It's not *that* fancy," he said. In addition to whatever snobbishness was in his genes, Ramsay still resented his favorite restaurant's change of name; though no one had ever seen it, *Kiss of the Wolf* would always be a porn film to one-eyed Pedro.

There were other homeless people in the alleyway; Six-Pack could see them, but they kept their distance from her. It was perhaps fair to say that one-eyed Pedro was only a *half*-homeless person. The others in the alley were wary of Pam. Six-Pack's rough north-woods attire notwithstanding, she didn't look like a homeless person.

Even one-eyed Pedro could see the difference. He knocked at the service entrance to Kiss of the Wolf, and Joyce—one of the female sous chefs—opened the door. Before Joyce could greet him, Pedro pushed Six-Pack ahead of him into the kitchen.

"She's looking for Danny," one-eyed Pedro said. "Don't worry—she's not one of us."

"I know Danny, and he knows me," Six-Pack quickly said to Joyce. "I ain't some kinda groupie, or anythin' like that." (At the time, Pam was eighty-four. It's not likely that Joyce mistook her for a groupie—not even a *writer's* groupie.)

Kristine ran to get Patrice, while Joyce and Silvestro welcomed Six-Pack inside. By the time Patrice brought Danny back to the kitchen, Silvestro had already persuaded Pam to try the duo of foie gras and duck confit with a glass of Champagne. When Danny saw Six-Pack, his heart sank; Six-Pack Pam was no Lady Sky, and Danny guessed that something had to be wrong.

"Is Ketchum with you?" the writer asked her, but Danny already knew that Ketchum would have come in the front door—no matter how the old woodsman was dressed.

"Don't get me started, Danny—not here, and not till I've had somethin' to eat and drink," Six-Pack said. "Shit, I was drivin' all day with that fartin' dog—we only stopped to pee and gas up the truck. Ketchum said I should have the lamb chops."

That's what Six-Pack had. They ate together at Danny's usual table by the window. Pam ate the lamb chops, holding them in her fingers, with her napkin tucked into the open neck of one of Ketchum's flannel shirts; when she was done eating, she wiped her hands on her jeans. Six-Pack drank a couple of Steam Whistles on tap, and a bottle of red wine; she ordered the cheese plate in lieu of dessert.

Ketchum had given her very detailed directions to Danny's house, warning her that if she arrived near dinnertime, she would probably find Danny at Kiss of the Wolf. The logger had also provided Six-Pack with directions to the restaurant. But when she looked inside Kiss of the Wolf—Six-Pack was tall enough to peer over the frosted-glass part of the large window facing Yonge Street—some of those overdressed types among the restaurant's Rosedale clientele must have discouraged her from just walking in. She'd gone searching for a rear entrance instead. (That Rosedale crowd can be snooty-looking.)

"I put Hero's dog bed in the kitchen—he's used to sleepin' in kitchens," Pam said. "Ketchum told me to let myself in, 'cause you never lock the place. Nice house. I put my stuff in the bedroom farthest away from yours—the one with all them pictures of that pretty lady. That way, if I have one of my nightmares, I might not wake you up."

"Hero's here?" Danny asked her.

"Ketchum said you should have a dog, but I ain't givin' you one of mine," Six-Pack said. "Hero ain't the friendliest critter to other dogs—my dogs sure as shit won't miss him."

"You drove all this way to bring me Hero?" Danny asked. (Of course the writer understood that there was probably more purpose to Six-Pack's visit than bringing him the bear hound.)

"Ketchum said I was to see you in person. No phone call, not a letter or a fax—none of that chickenshit stuff," Six-Pack told him. "Ketchum musta meant it seriously, 'cause he put everythin' in *writin'*. Besides, there's other crap he wanted you to have—it was all in his truck."

"You brought Ketchum's truck?" Danny asked her.

"The truck ain't for you—I'm drivin' it back," Pam said. "You wouldn't want it for city drivin', Danny—you wouldn't want it anyway, 'cause it still smells like a bear took a shit in it."

"Where's Ketchum? What happened?" the writer asked her.

"We should go walk the dog, or somethin'," Six-Pack suggested.

"Someplace more private, you mean?" Danny asked.

"Christ, Danny, there's people here with their noses *born* outta joint!" Six-Pack said.

Kiss of the Wolf was crowded that night; since the name change, and Patrice's back-to-bistro renovation, the restaurant was packed most nights. Some nights, Danny thought the tables were too close together. As the writer and Six-Pack Pam were leaving, Pam appeared to be favoring her bad hip, but Danny soon realized that she'd meant to lean on the adjacent table, where a couple had been staring at them throughout their dinner. Because he was famous, Danny was used to—almost oblivious to—people staring at him, but Pam (apparently) hadn't taken kindly to it. She upset the wineglasses and water on the couple's table; suddenly seeming to catch her balance, Six-Pack struck the seated gentleman in his face with her forearm. To the surprised woman at the wrecked table, Six-Pack said: "That's 'cause he was gawkin' at me—as if my tits were showin', or somethin'."

Both a waiter and a busboy rushed to the ruined table to make amends, while Patrice smoothly glided up to Danny, embracing the writer at the door. "*Another* memorable evening—most memorable, Daniel!" Patrice whispered in Danny's ear.

"I'm just a back-door kinda person," Six-Pack said humbly to Kiss of the Wolf's owner and maître d'.

Once they were out on Yonge Street, and while they were waiting for the crossing light to change, Danny said to Six-Pack: "Just tell me, for Christ's sake! Tell me *everything*. Spare me no detail."

"Let's see how Hero's doin', Danny," Six-Pack said. "I'm still re-hearsin' what I gotta say. As you might imagine, Ketchum left me with a shitload of instructions." As it had turned out, Ketchum put several pages of "instructions" in an envelope in the glove compartment of his truck. The door to the glove compartment had been left open purposely, so that Pam couldn't miss seeing the envelope, which was pinned under Ketchum's handgun. ("A better paperweight bein' unavailable at that time," as Six-Pack said.)

Now Danny saw that Ketchum's truck was parked in the driveway of the Cluny Drive house, as if the former riverman had changed his mind about coming for Christmas. Appearing to guard his dog bed, Hero growled at them—a surly greeting. Pam had already put the sheath for Ketchum's foot-long Browning knife in the bear hound's bed; maybe it served as a pacifier, the writer considered. He'd spotted the long Browning knife on the kitchen countertop, and had quickly looked away from the big blade. The dog's farting had filled the kitchen—possibly, the entire downstairs of the house. "God, what's wrong with Hero's *eye*?" Danny asked Pam.

"No eyelid. I'll tell ya later. Just try not to make him feel self-conscious about it," Six-Pack said.

Danny saw that she'd put Ketchum's favorite chainsaw in the gym. "What am I going to do with a chainsaw?" the writer asked her.

"Ketchum said you should have it," Six-Pack told him. Perhaps to change the subject, she said: "If I had to guess, Hero has to take a crap."

They walked Hero in the park. Christmas lights twinkled in the neighborhood surrounding them. They brought the dog back to the kitchen, where Danny and Six-Pack sat at the kitchen table; the bear hound sat at what seemed a purposeful distance, just watching them. Pam had poured herself some whiskey in a shot glass.

"I know you know what I'm gonna tell ya, Danny—you just don't know the *how* of it," she began. "I see the story startin' with your mother—all because Ketchum was fuckin' your mom instead of learnin' ta read, ain't that right?" Six-Pack said. "So, anyway—here's the endin'."

LATER, WHEN THEY UNLOADED THE TRUCK TOGETHER, Danny was grateful that Six-Pack had postponed telling him the story. She'd given him time to prepare himself for it, and while he'd been waiting to hear what had happened to Ketchum, Danny had already imagined a few of the details—the way writers do.

Danny knew that Ketchum would have wanted to see the moose dancing one last time, and that this time the old woodsman *wouldn't* have invited Six-Pack to come with him. As it had snowed that day, and the snow had stopped—quite a cold night, well below freezing, was expected—Ketchum had said to Six-Pack that he knew her hip wasn't up to camping out at the cookhouse site, but that maybe she would like to join him there for an outdoor breakfast the next morning.

"Kind of a cold spot for breakfast, ain't it?" she'd asked him.

After all, it was past mid-December—coming up on the longest night of the year. Twisted River rarely froze over until January, but what was Ketchum thinking? Yet (as Pam explained to Danny) they'd had breakfast together at the cookhouse site before. Ketchum always enjoyed making a fire. He would set some coals aside, and brew the coffee the way he liked it—in the roasting pan, with the coffee grounds and eggshells in the snow he melted for the water. He would grill a couple of venison steaks and poach three or four eggs on the fire. Six-Pack had agreed to meet him there for breakfast.

But the plan didn't add up, and Pam knew it. Six-Pack had taken a look in Ketchum's pickup; there was no tent and no sleeping bag. If the veteran river driver was camping out, he must have been planning on freezing to death—or else he was intending to sleep in the cab of his truck with the motor running. Furthermore, Ketchum had left Hero with Pam. "I think the cold kind of gets to Hero's hip, too," he'd told her.

"First I heard of it," as Six-Pack said to Danny.

And when she'd shown up at the cookhouse site the next morning, Six-Pack knew right away that there was no outdoor breakfast in Ketchum's plan. The coffee wasn't brewing; nothing was cooking. There was no fire. She spotted Ketchum sitting with his back against the remains of the crumbled brick chimney, as if the logger might have imagined that the cookhouse was still standing—the burned-to-the-ground building somehow warm and cozy, all around him.

Hero had run to his master, but the dog stopped short of where Ketchum sat on the snow-covered ground; Pam saw that the bear hound's hackles were up, and the dog suddenly walked stiff-legged, circling the old logger. "Ketchum!" Six-Pack had called, but there'd been no response from the woodsman; only Hero had turned his head to look at her.

"I couldn't walk over to him—not for the longest time," Six-Pack told Danny. "I could tell he was a fuckin' goner."

Because it had snowed the previous day, and the snow had stopped before nightfall, it was easy for Pam to see how he'd done it. There was a trail of blood in the fresh snow. Six-Pack followed the blood down the hill to the riverbank; there were some big stumps above the bank, and she saw where Ketchum had wiped the snow off one of them. The warm blood had seeped into the stump, and Ketchum's ax was stuck so firmly in the stump that Pam couldn't pull it out. There was no left hand to be found; obviously, Ketchum had thrown it in the river.

Having seen the spot in the river basin where Ketchum shot the apple-juice jar containing the cook's ashes, Danny had no trouble imagining exactly where Ketchum had thrown his left hand. But it must have been hard work for the old woodsman to walk back up the hill to the site of the cookhouse; from all the blood Pam saw in the snow, she knew Ketchum must have been bleeding profusely.

"Once, when they was still drivin' hardwoods on Phillips Brook," Six-Pack told Danny, "I seen Ketchum stealin' some firewood for himself. You know, he was just pickin' some pulpwood outta the pile— them four-foot small-diameter logs didn't amount to much. But I seen Ketchum turn half a cord of pulpwood into kindlin' in less than half an hour! That way, no one would recognize the stuff—if they spotted the wood in his truck, sometime later. Ketchum just choked up on the handle of his ax—he held it in one hand, you know, like a hatchet—and he split them logs lengthwise, and then split 'em again, till they was skinny enough so he could chop them four-foot logs inta two-foot sticks of fuckin' *kindlin'*! I never seen him swing that ax. He was so strong, Danny, and so accurate—he just wielded that ax with one hand, like it was a fuckin' *hammer*! Those Paris Manufacturin' Company clowns never knew why their pulpwood was *disappearin'*! Ketchum said the assholes were too busy makin' toboggans in Maine—that's where they were truckin' most of their hardwoods. Them Paris peckerheads never noticed where their pulpwood was goin'."

Yes, Ketchum could split a four-foot hardwood log one-handed; Danny had seen how the woodsman could wield an ax, both as an ax and as a hatchet. And after Ketchum had cut off his hand, the old river driver was still strong enough to walk up the hill, where he'd sat down to rest his back against all that was left of the cookhouse chimney. There'd been a bottle of whiskey beside him, Six-Pack said; she told Danny that Ketchum had managed to drink most of it.

"Anything else?" Danny asked Six-Pack. "I mean—on the ground, beside him."

"Yeah—a big bottle of aspirin," Pam told the writer. "There were still plenty of aspirin left in the bottle," Six-Pack said. "Ketchum wasn't much of a painkiller person, but I suppose he took some aspirin for the pain—he musta just washed 'em down with the whiskey."

As Danny knew, the aspirin *hadn't* been "for the pain"; knowing Ketchum, Danny believed that the old riverman had probably *relished* the pain. The whiskey wasn't for the pain, either. Both the aspirin and the whiskey, the writer knew, were strictly to keep Ketchum bleeding; the logger had little forgiveness for anyone who had a job to do and did a piss-poor job of it. (Only Ketchum could kill Ketchum, right?)

"Ketchum couldn't forgive himself for failin' to keep Cookie alive," Six-Pack told the writer. "And before that—after your boy died, Danny—Ketchum felt he was powerless to protect *you*. All he could do was *obsess* about your writin'."

"Me, too," the writer said to Six-Pack. "Me, too."

SIX-PACK DIDN'T STAY for Christmas. After they'd carried Ketchum's guns up to Danny's bedroom on the second floor—Pam insisted that *all* the guns be stowed under Danny's bed, because this was what Ketchum had wanted—and once they'd lugged the boxes of Rosie's books up to Danny's third-floor writing room, Six-Pack warned the writer that she was an early riser.

"How early?" he asked her.

Ketchum's truck and Six-Pack Pam were gone when Danny woke up in the morning; she'd made coffee for him and had left him a letter, which she'd written by hand on several pages of the typing paper he kept in the gym. Six-Pack's handwriting was very familiar to Danny, from those years when she'd written Ketchum's letters for the then-illiterate logger. But Danny had forgotten how well Pam wrote—far better than she spoke. Even her spelling was correct. (The writer wondered if this was the result of all the reading-aloud she'd once done to Ketchum.)

Naturally, Six-Pack's letter included instructions for taking care of Hero, but most of her letter was more personal than Danny had expected. She was having the hip-replacement surgery at Dartmouth-Hitchcock hospital, as Ketchum had recommended. She'd made a few new friends at the Saw Dust Alley campground, that nice-looking trailer park on Route 26—the attacks of September 11 had served to introduce her to many of her neighbors. Henry, the old West Dummer sawyer with the missing thumb and index finger, would look after Pam's dogs while she was having the surgery. (Henry had volunteered to look after the dogs while Six-Pack was driving Ketchum's truck to Toronto and back, too.)

Six-Pack had also made some long-standing friendships at the Androscoggin Valley Hospital in Berlin, where she still worked nights as a cleaning person; she'd called her friends at the hospital when she found Ketchum's body at the cookhouse site. Six-Pack wanted Danny to know that she'd sat with Ketchum for the better part of that morning, just holding his one remaining hand, the right one—"the only one he ever touched me with," as Six-Pack put it in her letter.

Pam told Danny he would find some photographs pressed flat in the books that had once belonged to Danny's mother. It had been hard for Six-Pack not to burn the pictures of Rosie, though Pam did more than put her jealousy aside. Six-Pack admitted that she now believed Ketchum had loved the cook even more than the logger had once loved Rosie. Six-Pack could live with that—the left-hand business notwithstanding. Besides, Six-Pack said, Ketchum had wanted Danny to have those photos of the writer's mother.

"I know it's none of my business," Pam also wrote to Danny, "but if I were you, I would write *and* sleep in that third-floor room. It is peaceful up there, in my opinion—and it's the best room in the house. But—don't get your balls crossed about this, Danny—I suspect you are well acquainted with more than your fair share of ghosts. I suppose it's one thing to *work* in a room with a ghost, but quite another matter to *sleep* in the same room with one. I wouldn't know—I never had children, on purpose. My philosophy was always to do without those things I didn't dare to lose—Ketchum excepted."

Danny wrote the *Ketchum excepted* words on a scrap of typing paper and taped it to one of his outdated typewriters—another IBM Selectric II, the one he was currently using in that third-floor room he shared with Joe's ghost. The writer liked the phrase *Ketchum excepted;* maybe he could use it.

All that had happened three years ago, and counting. The only reason Danny hadn't thrown out his relic of a fax machine, which was still in the kitchen of that house on Cluny Drive, was that Six-Pack occasionally faxed him and he faxed her. Pam must have been eighty-eight or eighty-nine—the same age Ketchum would have been, if the old logger were still alive—and her messages via the fax machine had lost what literary pizazz she'd once demonstrated as a letter writer.

Six-Pack had grown more terse in her old age. When there was something she'd read, or had seen in the news on TV—and provided the item was in the dumber-than-dog-shit category of human stupidities—Six-Pack would fax Danny. Pam unflinchingly stated what Ketchum would have said about this or that, and Danny never hesitated to fax her back with the writer's version of the river driver's vernacular.

It was not necessarily what Ketchum might have said about the war in Iraq, or the never-ending mess in the Middle East, that particularly interested Danny or Six-Pack. It was what Ketchum would have said about *anything*. It was the old logger's *voice* that Danny and Six-Pack wanted to hear.

Thus we try to keep our heroes alive; hence we remember them.

THE MID-FEBRUARY STORM had blown across Lake Huron from western Canada, but when the wind and snow hit the Georgian Bay islands, the wind shifted and the snow just kept falling; the wind now blew from a southerly direction, from Parry Sound to Shawanaga Bay. From his writing shack, Danny could no longer see where the bay ended and the mainland began. Because of the whiteout from the storm, the fir trees on what Danny knew was the mainland appeared as a mirage of a floating forest—or the trees seemed to be growing out of the frozen bay. The wind whipped little spirals of snow skyward; these twisters looked like small tornadoes of snow. Sometimes, when the wind blew northward, along the length of Shawanaga Bay, there were *actual* tornadoes—not unlike the kind you see in the American Midwest or on the Canadian prairies, Danny knew. (Andy Grant had warned the writer to watch out for them.)

Tireless had called Danny on his cell phone. She didn't want to be an island cleaning woman today; it wasn't a good idea to be out in the Polar airboat, not when the visibility was this bad. In a similar storm, only a few years ago, Tireless told Danny, some butt-brained oaf from Ohio had run his airboat aground on the O'Connor Rocks—just a little northwest of Moonlight Bay. (Danny had to come that way in order to pick Tireless up at the Shawanaga Landing Indian Reserve.)

"What happened to him—the butt-brained oaf from Ohio?" Danny asked her.

"They found the poor fool frozen—stiff as a stick," Tireless told him.

"I'll come get you tomorrow, or the next day—whenever the storm's over," Danny said. "I'll call you, or you call me."

"Kiss Hero for me," she said.

"I don't kiss Hero a lot," Danny told Tireless. "At least I'm not inclined to."

"Well, you should kiss him more," the First Nation woman said. "I think Hero would be nicer to you if you kissed him a lot."

All morning, in the writing shack, Hero had been farting up a storm—the near equal of the snowstorm Danny was watching out his window. It was a morning when the writer wasn't tempted to make his relationship with the bear hound a *closer* one. "Jesus, Hero!" Danny had exclaimed several times in the course of the foul-smelling morning, but it was unfit weather for the Walker bluetick to be put outside. And despite the dog's unrelenting flatulence, the writing had been going well; Danny was definitely getting closer to the start of his first chapter.

Certain sentences now came to him whole, intact; even the punctuation seemed permanent. When two such sentences were born consecutively, one emerging immediately after the other, the writer felt especially riveted to his task. He'd written the first twosome of the morning on a piece of typing paper and had thumbtacked the page to the rough pine-board wall of his writing shack. Danny kept looking at the sentences, rereading them.

"As for the river, it just kept moving, as rivers do—as rivers do. Under the logs, the body of the young Canadian moved with the river, which jostled him to and fro—to and fro."

Danny liked the repetition. He knew this was first-chapter material, but the passage belonged at the end of the chapter—it definitely didn't sound like a beginning. Danny had circled the *under the logs* phrase, which the writer thought wouldn't be a bad chapter title. Yet much of the focus of the first chapter seemed to be on the cook; the focus really wasn't on the boy who'd slipped under the logs.

"You could not say 'the past' or 'the future' in the cook's presence without making him frown," Daniel Baciagalupo wrote. There were other, isolated sentences about this young cook; they were like landmarks or signposts for Danny, helping to orient the writer as he plotted his first chapter. Another sentence was: "In the cook's opinion, there were not enough bends in Twisted River to account for the river's name." There would be much more about the cook, of course; it kept coming. "The cook could see that the river driver with the broken wrist had come ashore, carrying his pike pole in his good hand," Danny wrote.

The cook would be a major point-of-view character in the first chapter, the writer imagined—as Danny also imagined the cook's twelve-year-old son would be. "The cook knew too well that indeed it was the young Canadian who had fallen under the logs," Daniel Baciagalupo wrote. And there was one sentence about the cook that the writer left unfinished—at least for the moment. "The cook had an aura of controlled apprehension about him, as if he routinely anticipated the most unforeseen disasters"—well, that was as far as Danny wanted to go with *that* sentence, which he knew he would have to complete another day. For now, it was enough to type all these thoughts about the cook on a single piece of paper and thumbtack the page to the wall of the writing shack.

"In a town like Twisted River, only the weather wouldn't change," Danny had also written; it could work as a first sentence to the chapter, but the writer knew he could do better. Still, the sentence about the weather was a keeper; Danny could use it somewhere. "Now it was that mud-season, swollen-river time of year again," Daniel Baciagalupo wrote—a better beginning sentence, but it wasn't really what the writer was looking for.

Everything about the Ketchum character was more fragmentary. Nothing about the Ketchum character came to Danny in a complete sentence—not yet. There was something to the effect that "Ketchum had done more damage to himself than breaking his wrist in a river drive"; Danny liked that line, but he couldn't see where the sentence was going. There was another fragment about Ketchum being "no neophyte to the treachery of a log drive." Danny knew he could and would use that, but he wasn't sure where—maybe in proximity to an as-yet-uncertain sentence about Ketchum lying on his back on the riverbank "like a beached bear." Yet these fragments also found their way to the writing-shack wall, where they were thumbtacked along-side the first chapter's other signposts or landmarks.

At this point, the writer could see the Angel character more clearly than he could see the Ketchum character—though it was obvious to Daniel Baciagalupo that the Ketchum character was more major. (Maybe *most* major, Danny was thinking.)

Just then—at what amounted to a wave of more noxious farting from the dog—Danny's cell phone rang again.

"*Buenos días,* Señor Writer," Lupita said.

"*Buenos días,* Lupita," Danny said.

The Mexican cleaning woman didn't call often. In those ten weeks of the winter when Danny lived on the island in Georgian Bay, Lupita looked after the house on Cluny Drive; she opened and read the author's mail, she replayed the messages on his answering machine, she kept an eye on the fax machine, too. Once a week, Lupita would com-pile a list of what she considered was important for Danny to know—in essence, what she believed couldn't wait until he returned to Toronto. She faxed the list of priority messages to Andy Grant's office in Pointe au Baril Station.

Danny always left a couple of checkbooks of signed blank checks for Lupita, who paid his bills while he was gone. Most of all, the Mex-ican cleaning woman demonstrably enjoyed reading the writer's mail and deciding what was important—and what wasn't. This doubtless appealed to Lupita's pride—her sense of herself as having an immeas-

urable authority, an almost managerial control over the bestselling author's domestic life.

Danny knew that Lupita would have seized any opportunity that
presented itself for her to take charge of the writer's wretched personal
life, too. If she'd had daughters, she would have introduced them to
Danny. Lupita *did* have nieces; she would shamelessly leave their photographs on the kitchen countertop, calling Danny (after she'd gone
home) to tell him that she'd "lost" some photos that were dear to her.
Perhaps he'd seen the pictures lying around somewhere?

"Lupita, the pictures are on my kitchen countertop—where you
evidently left them," he would tell her.

"The dark-haired beauty in the pink tank top—the one with the
wonderful smile and the gorgeous skin? My precious niece, actually,
Mr. Writer."

"Lupita, she looks like a teenager," Danny would point out.

"No, she's *older*—a little," Lupita would tell him.

Once Lupita had told him: "Just don't marry another *writer*. All
you'll do is depress each other."

"I'm not going to marry anybody—not ever," he told her.

"Why don't you stab yourself in the heart instead?" she asked him.
"Soon you'll be consorting with prostitutes! I know you talk to the
dog—I've heard you!" she told him.

If Lupita was calling him in Pointe au Baril, she was vexed about
something, Danny knew. "What's up, Lupita?" he asked her on the
cell phone. "Is it snowing in Toronto? We're having quite a snowstorm
up here—Hero and I are stranded."

"I don't know about that unfortunate dog, but I think you *like* to be
stranded, Mr. Writer," Lupita said. Clearly the weather wasn't on her
mind; that wasn't why she'd called.

Sometimes, Lupita became convinced that people were *watching*
the house on Cluny Drive; occasionally, they were. Shy fans, a few
every year—mildly obsessed readers, just hoping to get a look at the
author. Or lowlifes from the media, maybe—hoping to see what?
(Another double shooting, perhaps.)

Some sleazy Canadian magazine had published a map of where
Toronto's celebrities lived; Danny's house on Cluny Drive had been

included. Not often, but once a month or so, an autograph-seeker came to the door; Lupita shooed them away, as if they were beggars. "He gets paid to *write* books—not *sign* them!" the cleaning woman would say.

Some half-wit in the media had actually written about Lupita: "The reclusive writer's live-in girlfriend appears to be a stout, Hispanic-looking person—an older woman with an extremely protective disposition." Lupita hadn't been amused; both the *stout* and the *older* grievously troubled her. (As for Lupita's disposition, she was more protective than ever.)

"There's someone looking for you, Señor Writer," Lupita now told him on his cell phone. "I wouldn't go so far as to call her a stalker— not yet—but she is determined to find you, I can tell you that."

"How determined?" Danny asked.

"I wouldn't let her in!" Lupita exclaimed. "And I didn't tell her where you were, of course."

"Of course," Danny repeated. "What did she want?"

"She wouldn't say—she's very *haughty*. She looks right through you—if looks could kill, as they say!—and she boldly hinted that she knew where you were. She was fishing for more information, I think, but I wouldn't take the bait," Lupita said, proudly.

"Boldly hinted how?" Danny asked.

"She was *unnaturally* informed," Lupita said. "She asked if you were up on that island you'd once lived on with the screenwriter! I said, '*What* island?' Well, you should have seen how she looked at me *then*!"

"As if she knew you were lying?" Danny asked.

"Yes!" Lupita cried. "Maybe she's a witch!"

But every Danny Angel fan knew that he'd lived with Charlotte Turner, and that they'd gone to Georgian Bay in the summer; it had even been written somewhere that the allegedly reclusive writer was spending his winters on a remote island in Lake Huron. (Well, it was "remote" in the winter, anyway.) For a Danny Angel reader, this was basically an intelligent guess; it hardly meant that the woman looking for the writer had witchlike powers.

"What did this woman look like, Lupita?" Danny asked; he was tempted to ask the Mexican cleaning woman if she'd spotted a broom, or if the *unnaturally* informed woman had been attended by the smell of smoke or the crackling sound of a fire.

"She was really scary-looking!" Lupita declared. "Big shoulders—like a man! She was *hulking!*"

"Hulking," Danny repeated, reminding himself of his dad. (He was the cook's son, clearly—repetition was in his genes.)

"She looked like she lived in a gym," Lupita explained. "You wouldn't want to mess with her, believe me."

The word *bodybuilder* was on the writer's lips, but he didn't say it. Lupita's combined impressions suddenly caused Danny to conjure the spirit of Lady Sky, for hadn't Amy looked like she lived in a gym? Hadn't Lady Sky been capable of looking right through you? (If looks could kill, indeed!) And hadn't Amy been a *hulking* presence? Somehow the *haughty* word didn't suit Lady Sky, but the writer understood that this may have been Lupita's misinterpretation.

"Did she have any tattoos?" Danny asked.

"Mr. Writer, it's *February!*" Lupita cried. "I made her stay outside, in the cold. She looked like an Arctic explorer!"

"Could you see what color her hair was?" Danny asked. (Amy had been a strawberry blonde, he remembered; he'd never forgotten her.)

"She was wearing a parka—with a *hood!*" Lupita declared. "I couldn't even see what color her *eyebrows* were!"

"But she was *big,*" Danny insisted. "Not just broad-shouldered, but tall—right?"

"She would *tower* over you!" Lupita exclaimed. "She's a *giantess!*"

There was no point in asking if Lupita had noticed a parachute somewhere. Danny was trying to think of what else he could ask. Lady Sky had at first seemed older than the writer, but later he'd reconsidered; maybe she was closer to his own age than he'd thought. "How old a woman was she, Lupita?" Danny asked. "Would you guess that she was my age—or a little older, maybe?"

"Younger," Lupita answered, with conviction. "Not much younger, but definitely younger than you are."

"Oh," the writer said; he knew that his disappointment was audible. It made Danny feel desperate to have imagined that Amy might fall from the sky again. Miracles don't happen twice. Even Lady Sky had said that she was only an angel *sometimes*. Yet Lupita had used the *determined* word to describe the mysterious visitor; Lady Sky had certainly seemed determined. (And how little Joe had loved her!)

"Well, whoever she is," Danny said to Lupita on the phone, "she won't show up here today—not in this storm."

"She'll show up there one day, or she'll be back here—I just know it," Lupita warned him. "Do you believe in witches, Mr. Writer?"

"Do you believe in *angels*?" Danny asked her.

"This woman was too dangerous-looking to be an angel," Lupita told him.

"I'll keep an eye out for her," Danny said. "I'll tell Hero she's a *bear*."

"You would be safer meeting a bear, Señor Writer," Lupita told him.

As soon as their phone conversation ended, Danny found himself thinking that—fond of her as he was—Lupita was a superstitious old Mexican. Did Catholics believe in witches? the writer was wondering. (Danny didn't know what Catholics believed—not to mention what Lupita, in particular, believed.) He was exasperated to have been interrupted from his writing; furthermore, Lupita had neglected to say *when* she'd confronted the giantess in Toronto. This morning, maybe—or was it last week? Moments ago, he'd been on track, plotting the course of his first chapter. A pointless phone call had completely derailed him; now even the weather was a distraction.

The *inuksuk* was buried under the snow. ("Never a good sign," the writer could imagine Tireless saying.) And Danny couldn't bear to look at that wind-bent little pine. The crippled tree was too much his father's likeness today. The pine appeared near to perishing—cringing, snow-laden, in the storm.

If Danny looked southeast—in the direction of Pentecost Island, at the mouth of the Shawanaga River—there was a white void. There was absolutely nothing to see. There was no demarcation to indicate where the swirling white sky ended and the snow-covered bay began; there was no horizon. When he looked southwest, Burnt Island was invisible—gone, lost in the storm. Due east, Danny could make out only the tops of the tallest trees on the mainland, but not the mainland itself. Like the lost horizon, there was no trace of land in sight. In the narrowest part of the bay was an ice fisherman's shack; perhaps the snowstorm had swept the shack away, or the ice fisherman's shack had simply vanished from view (like everything else).

Danny thought that he'd better haul some extra pails of water to the main cabin from the lake while he could still *see* the lake. The new snow would have hidden the last hole he'd chopped in the ice; Danny and Hero would have to be careful not to fall through the thin ice covering that hole. There was no point in risking a trip to town today—Danny could thaw something from the freezer. He would take the day off from cutting wood, too.

Outside, the wind-borne snow stung Hero's wide-open, lidless eye; the dog kept pawing at his face. "Just four buckets, Hero—only two trips to the bay and back," Danny said to the bear hound. "We won't be outside for long." But the wind suddenly and totally dropped, just as Danny was hauling the second two buckets from the bay. Now the snow fell straight down in larger, softer flakes. The visibility was no better, but it was more comfortable to be out in the storm. "No wind, no pain, Hero—how about that?" Danny asked the Walker bluetick.

The dog's spirits had notably improved. Danny watched Hero run after a red squirrel, and the writer hauled two more (a total of six) pails of water from the bay. Now he had more than enough water in the main cabin to ride out the storm—no matter how heavily the snow kept falling. And what did it matter how long the storm lasted? There were no roads to plow.

There was a lot of venison in the freezer. Two steaks looked like too much food, but maybe one wasn't quite enough—Danny decided to thaw two. He had plenty of peppers and onions, and some mushrooms; he could stir-fry them together, and make a small green salad. He made a marinade for the venison—yogurt and fresh-squeezed lemon juice with cumin, turmeric, and chili. (This was a marinade he remembered from Mao's.) Danny built up the fire in the woodstove in the main cabin; if he put the marinated venison near the woodstove, the steaks would thaw by dinnertime. It was only noon.

Danny gave Hero some fresh water and fixed himself a little lunch. The snowstorm had freed him from his usual afternoon chores; with any luck, Danny might get back to work in the writing shack. He felt that his first chapter was waiting for him. There would only be the bear hound's farting to distract him.

"Under the logs," the writer said aloud to Hero, testing the phrase as a chapter title. It was a good title for an opening chapter, Danny thought. "Come on, Hero," he said to the dog, but they'd not left the main cabin when Danny's cell phone rang again—the third call of the day. Most days, in the writer's winter life on Charlotte's island, the phone didn't ring once.

"It's the *bear,* Hero!" Danny said to the dog. "What do you bet that the big she-bear is coming?" But the phone call was from Andy Grant.

"I thought I better check up on you," the builder said. "How are you and Hero surviving the storm?"

"Hero and I are surviving just fine—in fact, we're very cozy," Danny told him. "I'm thawing some of the deer you and I shot."

"Not planning on going shopping, are you?" Andy asked him.

"I'm not planning on going *anywhere,*" Danny answered.

"That's good," Andy said. "You've got whiteout conditions at your place, have you?"

"Total whiteout," Danny told him. "I can't see Burnt Island— I can't even see the mainland."

"Not even from the back dock?" Andy asked him.

"I wouldn't know," Danny answered. "Hero and I are having a pretty lazy day. We haven't ventured as far as the back dock." There was a long pause—long enough to make Danny look at his cell-phone screen, to be sure they were still connected.

"You and Hero might want to go see what you can see off the back dock, Danny," Andy Grant told the writer. "If I were you, I would wait about ten or fifteen minutes—then go take a look."

"What am I looking for, Andy?" the writer asked.

"A visitor," the builder told him. "There's someone looking for you, Danny, and she seems real determined to find you."

"Real determined," Danny repeated.

SHE'D SHOWN UP at the nursing station in Pointe au Baril, asking for directions to Turner Island. The nurse had sent her to Andy. Everyone in town knew that Andy Grant was protective of the famous novelist's privacy.

The big, strong-looking woman didn't have her own airboat; she didn't have a snowmobile, either. She didn't even come with skis—just ski poles. Her backpack was huge, and strapped to it was a pair of snowshoes. If she'd had a car, it must have been a rental and she'd already gotten rid of it. Maybe she'd spent the night at Larry's Tavern, or in some motel near Parry Sound. There was no way she could have driven the entire distance from Toronto to Pointe au Baril Station—not that morning, not in that snowstorm. The snow had blanketed Georgian Bay, from Manitoulin Island to Honey Harbour, and—according to Andy—it was supposed to snow all that night, too.

"She said she knows you," Andy told the writer. "But if it turns out that she's just a crazy fan, or some psycho autograph-seeker, there's enough room in that backpack for all eight of your books—both the hardcover and the paperback editions. Then again, that backpack's big enough to hold a shotgun."

"She knows me *how*—she knew me when, and where?" Danny asked.

"All she said was, 'We go back a ways.' You're not expecting a visit from an angry ex-girlfriend—are you, Danny?"

"I'm not expecting *anybody*, Andy," the writer said.

"She's one powerful-looking lady, Danny," the builder said.

"How big is she?" Daniel Baciagalupo asked.

"We're talking *giantess* category," Andy told him. "Hands like paws—boots bigger than mine. You and I together could fit in her parka; there would probably be room for Hero, too."

"I suppose she looks like an Arctic explorer," the writer guessed.

"She's sure got the right clothes for this weather," Andy said. "The snowpants, the snowmobiler's gloves—and her parka has a big old hood."

"I don't suppose you saw the color of her hair," the writer said.

"Nope—not under that hood. I couldn't even be sure of the color of her *eyes*," Andy said.

"And what would you guess her age was?" Danny asked. "About my age, maybe—or a little older?"

"Nope," the builder said again. "She's *way* younger than you are, Danny. At least what I could see of her. She's really *fit*-looking."

"With all the clothes she had on, how could you tell she was *fit*?" the writer asked.

"She came into my office—just to look at my map of the bay," the builder told Danny. "While she was locating Turner Island on the map, I lifted her backpack—I just picked it up off the floor and set it down again. It's about a seventy-pound pack, Danny; that pack weighs as much as Hero, and she left here carrying it like a pillow."

"She sounds like someone I met once," Danny said, "but her age is wrong. If she were the woman I'm thinking of, she couldn't be '*way* younger' than I am—as you say."

"I could be wrong about that," Andy told him. "People age differently, Danny. Some folks seem to stay the same; others, if it's been a while, you wouldn't recognize them."

"Oh, it's been a while—if she's the one I'm thinking of," Danny said. "It's been almost forty years! It *can't* be her," the writer said; he sounded impatient with himself. Danny didn't dare to hope that it was Lady Sky. He realized that it had also been a while since he'd *hoped* for anything. (He had once hoped that nothing terrible would ever happen to his beloved Joe. He'd also hoped that his dad would long outlive the cowboy, and that Ketchum would die peacefully—in his sleep, with both his hands intact. Daniel Baciagalupo didn't have a good record with hope.)

"Danny, it's dumb to think you can even *guess* what someone's going to look like after forty years," Andy said. "Some people change more than others—that's all I'm saying. Look," the builder said, "why don't I come out there? I could probably catch up to her on my snowmobile. I could bring her the rest of the way, and if you don't like her—or she's *not* the person you're thinking of—I could bring her back to Pointe au Baril."

"No, Hero and I will be all right," Danny said. "I can always call you if I need help getting her to leave, or something."

"You and Hero better be on your way to the back dock," Andy told him. "She left here a while ago, and she's got a real long stride."

"Okay, we'll get going. Thanks, Andy," Danny told him.

"You sure I can't come out there, or do anything for you?" the builder asked.

"I've been looking for a first sentence to my first chapter," the writer answered. "You wouldn't have a first sentence for me, would you?"

"I can't help you with that," Andy Grant said. "Just call me if you have any trouble with that woman."

"There won't be any trouble," Danny told him.

"Danny? Take that old Remington with you, when you go to the back dock. It's just a good idea to have the gun with you—and make sure she *sees* it, okay?"

"Okay," the writer answered.

Hero was excited, as always, to take a walk with Ketchum's .30-06 Springfield carbine. "Don't get your hopes up, Hero," Danny told the dog. "The odds are she's not a bear."

The snow was knee-deep on the wide-open path to the writing shack, and not quite as deep on the narrow path through the woods from Danny's workplace to the back dock.

When he passed his writing shack, the writer said aloud, "I'll be back, first chapter. I'll see you soon, first sentence."

Hero had run ahead. There was a grove of cedars, out of the wind, where a small herd of deer had bedded down for the night. Either Hero had spooked them, or the deer had moved on when the wind dropped. Hero was sniffing all around; there were probably deer turds under the snow. The snow in the cedar grove was flattened down where the deer had huddled together.

"They're gone, Hero—you missed them," Danny told the bear hound. "Those deer are on Barclay Island by now, or they're on the mainland." The dog was rolling in the snow where the herd had bedded down. "If you roll in any deer turds, Hero, I'll give you a bath—with shampoo and everything."

Hero hated baths; Danny didn't much like washing the uncooperative dog, either. In the Cluny Drive house, in Toronto, Lupita was the one who washed the dog. She seemed to enjoy scolding Hero while she did it. ("So, Señor Macho—how do you like having only one eyelid? But that's what you get for fighting, Mr. Macho—isn't it?")

There must have been three feet of snow on the roof of Grand-daddy's cabin, to which neither the writer nor the dog gave more than a passing glance. If that cabin had been haunted before, it was *more* haunted now; neither Danny nor Hero would have welcomed an encounter with Ketchum's ghost. If the old logger were a ghost, Danny knew that the poacher's cabin was just the spot for him.

The snow had drifted thigh-high onto the back dock. Across the frozen bay, parts of the mainland were visible in the whiteout, but the far shore didn't emerge distinctly; the mainland was blurred. The clarity of the shoreline was fleeting. In the distance, fragments of the landscape momentarily appeared, only to disappear the next instant. There were no identifying landmarks that allowed Danny to see exactly where the snowmobile portage from Payne's Road came into contact with the bay, but from the vantage of the dock, the writer could make out the shape of the ice fisherman's shack. It had not been blown away by the storm, yet the shack was so indistinct in the steadily falling snow that Danny knew the snowshoer would be halfway across the reach of the bay before he could see her.

What had little Joe said that day at the pig roast? "Plane. Not a bird." And then, because Danny had been watching Katie instead of the small airplane, he'd heard Joe say: "Not flying. *Falling!*" Only then did Danny see her: The skydiver was free-falling, hurtling through the sky, when the writer had first spotted her, only seconds before her parachute opened. And Amy herself had come *consecutively* more and more into view. First, it became clear she was a *woman* skydiver; then, all at once, she was *naked*. Only when Danny was beside her, in the pigpen—in all the mud and pig shit—did he realize how *big* Amy was. She'd been so *solid*!

Now the writer squinted across the bay, into the falling snow, as if he were waiting for another little airplane to appear on the vanished horizon—or for another red-white-and-blue parachute to pop open.

Whoever she was, she wouldn't be naked this time, the writer knew. Yet he also knew that, like the skydiver, she would suddenly just *be* there—the way an angel drops down to earth from the heavens. He was looking and looking for her, but Danny understood that in the whiteout of the snowstorm, the woman would just plain appear, as if by magic. One second, nothing would be there. The next second, she would be halfway across the bay and coming closer—one long stride after another.

What the writer had overlooked was the fact that Hero was a hunter; the bear hound had one good ear and a very good nose. The growl began in the dog's chest, and Hero's first bark was muffled— half swallowed in his throat. There was no one out there, on the frozen bay, but the bear hound knew she was coming; the dog's barking began in earnest only seconds before Danny saw her. "Shut up, Hero—don't scare her away," Danny said. (Of course the writer understood that, if she was Lady Sky, nothing could scare her.)

The snowshoer was in full stride, practically running, when Danny saw her. At such a pace, and carrying a backpack that heavy, she'd worked up quite a sweat. She had unzipped the parka to cool herself off; the hood, which she'd pushed off her head, lay on the back of her broad shoulders. Danny could see her strawberry-blond hair; it was a little longer than she used to cut it, when she'd been a skydiver. The writer could understand why both Lupita and Andy Grant thought she was younger than Danny; Amy looked younger than the writer, if not *way* younger. When she reached the dock, Hero finally stopped barking.

"You're not going to shoot me—are you, Danny?" Amy asked him. But the writer, who'd not had much luck with hope, couldn't answer her. Danny couldn't speak, and he couldn't stop staring at her.

Because it was snowing, the tears on Danny's face were mingled with the snow; he probably didn't know he was crying, but Amy saw his eyes. "Oh, hold on—just hang on—I'm coming," she said. "I got here as fast as I could, you know." She threw the backpack up on the dock, together with her ski poles, and she climbed over the rocks, taking her snowshoes off when she gained her footing on the dock.

"Lady Sky," Danny said; it was all he could say. He felt himself dissolving.

"Yeah, it's me," she said, hugging him; she pulled his face to her chest. He just shook against her. "Boy, you're even more of a mess than I thought you would be," Amy told him, "but I'm here now, and I've got you—you're going to be okay."

"Where have you been?" he managed to ask her.

"I had another project—*two*, actually," she told him. "They turned out to be a waste of my time. But I've been thinking about you—for years."

Danny didn't mind if he was Lady Sky's "project" now; he imagined that she'd had her share of projects, more than two. So what? the writer thought. He would soon be sixty-three; Danny knew he was no prize.

"I might have come sooner, you bastard, if you'd answered my letter," Amy said to him.

"I never saw your letter. My dad read it and threw it away. He thought you were a stripper," Danny told her.

"That was a long time ago—before the skydiving," Amy said. "Was your dad ever in Chicago? I haven't done any stripping since Chicago." Danny thought this was very funny, but before he could clear up the misunderstanding, Lady Sky took a closer look at Hero. The bear hound had been sniffing Amy's discarded snowshoes suspiciously—as if he were readying himself to piss on them. "Hey, *you*," Amy said to the dog. "You lift your leg on my snowshoes, you might just lose your other ear—or your pecker." Hero knew when he was being spoken to; he gave Amy an evil, crazed look with his lidless eye, but the dog backed away from the snowshoes. Something in Amy's tone must have reminded the bear hound of Six-Pack Pam. In fact, at that moment, Lady Sky had reminded Danny of Six-Pack— a *young* Six-Pack, a Six-Pack from those long-ago days when she'd lived with Ketchum.

"Jeez, you're shaking so much—that gun might go off," Amy told the writer.

"I've been waiting for you," Danny told her. "I've been *hoping*."

She kissed him; there was some mint-flavored gum in her mouth, but he didn't mind. She was warm, and still sweating, but not out of breath—not even from the snowshoeing. "Can we go indoors, somewhere?" Amy asked him. (At a glance, anyone could see that Granddaddy's cabin was uninhabitable—unless you were Ketchum, or a ghost. From the back dock of the island, it was impossible to see the other buildings—even when there wasn't a snowstorm.) Danny picked up her snowshoes and the ski poles, being careful to keep the carbine pointed at the dock, and Amy shouldered the big backpack. Hero ran ahead, as before.

They stopped at the writing shack, so that Danny could show her where he worked. The little room still smelled of the dog's lamentable farting, but the fire in the woodstove hadn't died out—it was like a sauna in that shack. Amy took off her parka, and a couple of layers of clothes that she wore under the parka—until she was wearing just her snowpants and a T-shirt. Danny told her that he'd once believed she was older than he was—or they were the same age, maybe—but how was it possible that she seemed *younger* now? Danny didn't mean younger than she was that day on the pig farm, in Iowa. He meant that she'd not aged as much as he had—and why was that, did she think?

Amy told him that she'd lost her little boy when she was *much* younger; she'd already lost him when Danny met her as a skydiver. Amy's only child had died when he was two—little Joe's age at the pig roast. That death had aged Amy when it happened, and for a number of years immediately following her boy's death. It wasn't that Amy was *over* her son's death—one never got over a loss like that, as she knew Danny would know. It was only that the loss didn't show as much, when so many years had passed. Maybe your child's death ceased being as visible to other people, after a really long time. (Joe had died more recently; to anyone who knew Danny, the writer had noticeably aged because of it.)

"We're the same age, more or less," Amy told the writer. "I've been sixty for the last couple of years, I think—at least that's what I tell the guys who ask."

"You look fifty," Danny told her.

"Are you trying to get in my pants, or something?" Amy asked him. She read those sentences, and the fragments of sentences, from the first chapter—the lines he'd thumbtacked to the pine-board wall of the writing shack. "What are these?" she asked.

"They're sentences, or parts of sentences, ahead of myself; they're waiting for me to catch up to them," he told her. "They're all lines from my first chapter—I just haven't found the first sentence yet."

"Maybe I'll help you find it," Amy said. "I'm not going anywhere for a while. I don't have any other projects." Danny could have cried again, but just then his cell phone rang—for the fourth fucking time that day! It was Andy Grant, of course, checking up on him.

"She there yet?" Andy asked. "Who *is* she?"

"She's the one I've been waiting for," Danny told him. "She's an angel."

"*Sometimes,*" Lady Sky reminded him, when he hung up. "*This* time, anyway."

What might the cook have said to his son, if he'd had time to utter some proper last words before the cowboy shot him in the heart? At best, Dominic might have expressed the hope that his lonely son "find someone"—only that. Well, Danny *had* found her; actually, she'd found him. Given Charlotte, and now given Amy—at least in that aspect of his life—the writer knew he'd been lucky. Some people don't ever find *one* person; Daniel Baciagalupo had found two.

SHE'D BEEN LIVING IN MINNESOTA for the last few years, Amy said. ("If you think Toronto's cold, try Minneapolis," she'd told him.) Amy had done a little grappling in a wrestling club called Minnesota Storm. She'd hung out with "a bunch of ex-Gopher wrestlers," she said—a concept that Danny found difficult to grasp.

Amy Martin—Martin had been her maiden name, and she'd taken it back "years ago"—was a Canadian. She'd lived a long time in the United States, and had become an American citizen, but she was "at heart" a Canadian, Amy said, and she'd always wanted to come back to Canada.

Why had she gone to the States in the first place? Danny asked her. "Because of a guy I met," Amy told him, shrugging. "Then my kid was born there, so I felt I should stay."

She described her politics as "largely indifferent now." She was sick of how little Americans knew about the rest of the world—or how little they cared to know. After two terms, the failed policies of the Bush presidency would probably leave the country (*and* the rest of the world) in a terrible mess. What Amy Martin meant by this was that it would then be high time for some hero on a horse to ride in, but what could one hero on one horse do?

Not much would change, Lady Sky said. She had fallen to earth in a country that didn't believe in angels; yet the Bible-huggers had hijacked one of the two major political parties there. (With the Bible-huggers, not much would *ever* change.) Moreover, there was what

Amy called "the cocksuckers' contingent of the country"—what Danny knew as the dumber-than-dog-shit element, those bully patriots—and they were too set in their ways or too poorly educated (or both) to see beyond the ceaseless flag-waving and nationalistic bluster. "Conservatives are an extinct species," Lady Sky said, "but they don't know it yet."

By the time Danny had shown Amy the main cabin—the big bathtub, the bedroom, and the venison steaks he was marinating for dinner—they'd established that they were bedfellows, at least politically. While Amy knew more about Danny than he knew about her, this was only because she'd read every word he'd written. She'd read almost all the "shit" that had been written about him, too. (The *shit* word was what they both instinctively used for the media, so that on the subject of the media they discovered they were bedfellows, too.)

Most of all, Amy knew when and how he'd lost his little Joe—and when his dad had died, and the how of that, too. He had to tell her about Ketchum, whom she knew nothing about, and while this was hard—except with Six-Pack, Danny didn't talk about Ketchum—the writer discovered, in the process of describing Ketchum, that the old logger was alive in the novel Danny was dreaming, and so Danny talked and talked about that novel, and his elusive first chapter, too.

They heated the pasta pots of lake water to a near boil on the gas stove, and with their two bodies in that big bathtub, the tub was full to the brim; Danny had not imagined it was possible to fill that giant bathtub, but not even the novelist had ever imagined that tub with a *giantess* in it.

Amy talked him through the history of her myriad tattoos. The when and the where and the why of the tattoos held Danny's attention for the better part of an hour, or more—both in the warm bathtub and in the bed in that bedroom with the propane fireplace. He'd not taken a close look at Amy's tattoos before—not when she was spattered with mud and pig shit, and not afterward, when she was wearing just a towel. Danny felt it would have been improper and unwelcome to have stared at her then.

He stared at her now; he took all of her in. Many of Amy's tattoos had a martial-arts theme. She'd tried kickboxing in Bangkok; for a couple of years, she had lived in Rio de Janeiro, where she'd competed in an unsuccessful start-up tour of Ultimate Fighting for women. (Some of those Brazilian broads were tougher than the Thai kickboxers, Lady Sky said.)

Tattoos have their own stories, and Danny heard them all. But the one that mattered most to Amy was the name Bradley; that had been her son's name, and her father's. She'd called the boy both Brad and Bradley, and (after he died) she'd had the two-year-old's given name tattooed on her right hip where it jutted out—precisely where Amy had once carried her child when he was a toddler.

In explaining how she'd borne the weight of her little boy's death, Amy pointed out to Danny that her hips were the strongest part of her strong body. (Danny didn't doubt it.)

Amy was happy to discover that Danny could cook, because she couldn't. The venison was good, though there wasn't quite enough of it. Danny had sliced some potatoes very thinly, and stir-fried them with the onions, peppers, and mushrooms, so they didn't go hungry. Danny served a green salad after the meal, because the cook had taught him that this was the "civilized" way to serve a salad—though it was almost never served this way in a restaurant.

It pleased the writer no end that Lady Sky was a beer drinker. "I found out long ago," she told him, "that I drink everything alcoholic as fast as I drink a beer—so I better stick with beer, if I don't want to kill myself. I'm pretty much over wanting to kill myself," Amy added.

He was pretty much over that part, too, Danny told her. He had learned to like Hero's company, the farting notwithstanding, and the writer had two cleaning ladies looking after him; they would all be disappointed in him if he killed himself.

Amy had met one of the cleaning ladies, of course, and—weather permitting—Lady Sky would probably meet Tireless tomorrow, or the next day. As for Lupita, Amy called the Mexican cleaning woman a better guard dog than Hero; Lady Sky was sure that she and Lupita would become great friends.

"I have no right to be happy," Danny told his angel, when they were falling asleep in each other's arms that first night.

"Everyone has a right to be a *little* happy, asshole," Amy told him.

Ketchum would have liked how Lady Sky used the *asshole* word, the writer was thinking. It was a word choice after the old logger's heart, Danny knew, which—in his sleep—led him back to the novel he was dreaming.

AMY MARTIN AND DANIEL BACIAGALUPO had a month to spend on Charlotte Turner's island in Georgian Bay; it was their wilderness way of getting to know each other before their life together in Toronto began. We don't always have a choice how we get to know one another. Sometimes, people fall into our lives cleanly—as if out of the sky, or as if there were a direct flight from Heaven to Earth—the same sudden way we lose people, who once seemed they would always be part of our lives.

Little Joe was gone, but not a day passed in Daniel Baciagalupo's life when Joe wasn't loved or remembered. The cook had been murdered in his bed, but Dominic Baciagalupo had had the last laugh on the cowboy. Ketchum's left hand would live forever in Twisted River, and Six-Pack had known what to do with the rest of her old friend.

One mid-February day, a snowstorm blew across Lake Huron from western Canada; all of Georgian Bay was blanketed by it. When the writer and Lady Sky woke up, the storm was gone. It was a dazzling morning.

Danny let the dog out and made the coffee; when the writer brought some coffee to Amy in the bedroom, he saw that she'd fallen back to sleep. Lady Sky had been traveling a long way, and the life she'd led would have tired anyone out; Danny let her sleep. He fed the dog and wrote Amy a note, not telling her he was falling in love with her. He simply told her that she knew where to find him—in his writing shack. Danny thought that he would have breakfast later, whenever Lady Sky woke up again. He would take some coffee with him to the writing shack, and start a fire in the woodstove there; he'd already built up the fire in the woodstove in the main cabin.

"Come on, Hero," the writer said, and together they went out in the fresh snow. Danny was relieved to see that his father's likeness, that wind-bent little pine, had survived the storm.

IT WASN'T THE KETCHUM character who should *begin* the first chapter, Daniel Baciagalupo believed. It was better to keep the Ketchum character hidden for a while—to make the reader wait to meet him. Sometimes, those most important characters need a little concealment. It would be better, Danny thought, if the first chapter—and the novel—began with the lost boy. The Angel character, who was not who he seemed, was a good decoy; in storytelling terms, Angel was a *hook*. The young Canadian (who was *not* a Canadian) was where the writer should start.

It won't take long now, Daniel Baciagalupo believed. And whenever he found that first sentence, there would be someone in his life the writer dearly desired to read it to!

"Legally or not, and with or without proper papers," Danny wrote, "Angel Pope had made his way across the Canadian border to New Hampshire."

It's okay, the writer thought, but it's not the beginning—the mistaken idea that Angel had crossed the border comes *later*.

"In Berlin, the Androscoggin dropped two hundred feet in three miles; two paper mills appeared to divide the river at the sorting gaps in Berlin," Danny wrote. "It was not inconceivable to imagine that young Angel Pope, from Toronto, was on his way there."

Yes, yes—the writer thought, more impatiently now. But these last two sentences were too technical for a beginning; he thumbtacked these sentences to the wall alongside the other lines, and then added this sentence to the mix: "The carpet of moving logs had completely closed over the young Canadian, who never surfaced; not even a hand or one of his boots broke out of the brown water."

Almost, Daniel Baciagalupo thought. Immediately, another sentence emerged—as if Twisted River itself were allowing these sentences to bob to the surface. "The repeated *thunk-thunk* of the pike poles, poking the logs, was briefly interrupted by the shouts of the rivermen who had spotted Angel's pike pole—more than fifty yards from where the boy had vanished."

Fine, fine, Danny thought, but it was too *busy* for a beginning sentence; there were too many distractions in that sentence.

Maybe the very idea of *distractions* distracted him. The writer's thoughts leapt ahead—too far ahead—to Ketchum. There was something decidedly parenthetical about the new sentence. "(Only Ketchum can kill Ketchum.)" Definitely a keeper, Danny thought, but most definitely *not* first-chapter material.

Danny was shivering in his writing shack. The fire in the wood-stove was taking its time to heat the little room. Normally, Danny was chopping a hole in the ice and hauling a couple of buckets of water out of the bay while the writing shack was warming up; this morning, he'd skipped the chopping and the hauling. (Later in this glorious day, he would have Lady Sky to help him with the chores.)

Just then, without even trying to think of it—in fact, at that moment, Daniel Baciagalupo had reached out to rub Hero behind the dog's good ear—the first sentence came to him. The writer felt it rising into view, as if from underwater; the sentence came into sight the way that apple-juice jar with his dad's ashes had bobbed to the surface, just before Ketchum shot it.

"The young Canadian, who could not have been more than fifteen, had hesitated too long."

Oh, God—here I go again—I'm *starting*! the writer thought.

He'd lost so much that was dear to him, but Danny knew how stories were marvels—how they simply couldn't be stopped. He felt that the great adventure of his life was just beginning—as his father must have felt, in the throes and dire circumstances of his last night in Twisted River.

A C K N O W L E D G M E N T S

SPECIAL THANKS TO THESE CHEFS AND RESTAURATEURS FOR their time and expertise: Bonnie Bruce at Up for Breakfast in Manchester, Vermont; Ray Chen and Christal Siewertsen at The Inn at West View Farm in Dorset, Vermont; Georges Gurnon and Steve Silvestro at Pastis Express in Toronto; Cheryl and Dana Markey at Mistral's in Winhall, Vermont.

My appreciation to these friends and relations, and various expert readers of earlier drafts of the manuscript; they also assisted me with my research: in New Hampshire, Bill Altenburg, Bayard Kennett, John Yount; in Vermont, David Calicchio, Rick Kelley; in Ontario, James Chatto, Dean Cooke, Don Scale, Marty Schwartz, Helga Stephenson.

In addition, to my wife, Janet, and my son Everett, to whom I read aloud the first draft of the manuscript; to two full-time assistants, Alyssa Barrett and Emily Copeland, who transcribed and proofread all the drafts; and to my editor and copy editor, Amy Edelman—*un abbràccio.*

S O U R C E S

Barry, James. *Georgian Bay: The Sixth Great Lake.* Toronto: Clarke, Irwin & Co., Ltd., 1968.

Chatto, James. "Host Story." *Toronto Life,* January 2006.

Gove, Bill. *Log Drives on the Connecticut River.* Littleton, N.H.: Bondcliff Books, 2003.

Gove, Bill. *Logging Railroads Along the Pemigewasset River.* Littleton, N.H.: Bondcliff Books, 2006.

Pinette, Richard E. *Northwoods Heritage: Authentic Short Accounts of the Northland in Another Era.* Colebrook, N.H.: Liebl Printing Company, 1992.

Riccio, Anthony V. *Boston's North End: Images and Recollections of an Italian-American Neighborhood.* Guilford, Conn.: Globe Pequot Press, 1998.

Stone, Robert. *Prime Green: Remembering the Sixties.* New York: Ecco/HarperCollins, 2007.

WAS AT A DINNER PARTY not long ago when the woman seated
next to me said, "Even your conversation has a *plot*." The *plot* word
was spoken disparagingly—with an almost involuntary disgust—as if
plot were a long-dead animal I had dragged to the dinner table, or
something I'd carelessly stepped in and had brought inside on one of
my shoes.

Evidently, the woman had very refined sensibilities as a reader—
her tastes were modern or postmodern, maybe, or perhaps she
was fashionably opposed to third-person omniscience (or other
nineteenth-century novelistic devices). She seemed offended by what
I represented: the long, plotted novel. I was a dinosaur—or worse, a
reactionary. She'd been seeking an intellectual conversation, too theo-
retical for me, and I'd done the unthinkable, or the unacceptable: I had
told her a story.

But that's what I do. And if you're telling a story—especially to il-
lustrate a point—you'd better know what happens in the story before
you start. Endings not only matter to me; endings are where I begin a
novel or a screenplay. If I don't know the ending, I can't begin—and I
don't mean that I need to know only what *happens*. I need to know the
tone of voice, and the last sentence (or sentences). I write not only to
a moment in time, but to a sound—a feeling. I have to know what that
feeling is, or I won't start.

From the last sentence, I work my way back to where the story be-
gins. This constitutes a kind of road map in reverse. That process—of
working my way backward through the plot, from the last sentence to

the first—usually takes a year or eighteen months, sometimes longer. But for twelve novels now, the last sentence has always come first. And those last sentences have never changed in the process—not even the punctuation.

Naturally, while writing my first four or five novels, I did not see my habit of beginning at the end as a "process," as I've called it; in fact, I would have been embarrassed to call it my *method*. I believed it was a curious habit; I thought it might change. But by the time I was writing my sixth novel, *The Cider House Rules*, I had accepted the pattern as inevitable. There was a refrain at the end of that novel, as there would be at the end of *A Widow for One Year*—something we recognize as dialogue we've heard before, perhaps in a different context. After *The Cider House Rules*, I didn't question my process.

Last Night in Twisted River has been in my mind longer than any other novel I've written—for more than twenty years. I began (and finished) other novels that had been in my mind for not nearly as long, because the last sentences of those novels were more quickly forthcoming. As much as I knew about the story of *Twisted River*, I couldn't grasp that last sentence; it eluded me for the longest time. But I always knew it was a fugitive novel; a father and son had to flee, and they would be on the run for fifty (or more) years. I also knew that the story began in a rough and rudimentary place, a kind of frontier town—a one-lawman town, and that lawman was an ornery fella. A logging camp was always a possibility, but I also considered a fishing village in Maine—maybe a lobstering town, near the Maritimes. That the story began in northern New England, somewhere near the Canadian border, was a must.

It was always a violence-begets-violence story. And I knew the approximate age of the son, twelve or thirteen, and that the father was a cook. I even knew that the son would grow up to be a writer—all this, for more than twenty years, but not the elusive last sentence! So I wrote other novels instead of this one.

I've written about writers before—in *The World According to Garp* and *A Widow for One Year*. But, in those novels, I never described my process as a writer; I did not make T. S. Garp or Ruth Cole the *kind* of novelist I am. In *Twisted River*, Daniel Baciagalupo *is* the kind of writer I am; I even gave Danny my educational biography. (We went to the same schools, graduated in the same years, and so forth.) What I did *not* give Danny was my life, which has been largely happy and very lucky. I gave Daniel Baciagalupo the *un*luckiest life I could imagine. I gave Danny the life I am afraid of having—the life I hope I never have. Maybe that's autobiographical, too—in a deeper, more meaningful, certainly more *psychological* way. (When you write about what you fear, about what you hope *never* happens to you—or to anyone you love—surely that's a little autobiographical.)

It DOESN'T SURPRISE ME that I begin with the plot. I was fifteen when I first read Charles Dickens's *Great Expectations*, the novel that made me want to become a writer. Consider the plot. A boy who grows up in a blacksmith's shop has a benefactor; someone has paid his way to the proper schools, and made a perfect snob of a London gentleman out of him. He believes he knows who his *benefactress* is— we believe it, too, though there's every reason to doubt that Miss Havisham has supported him. She is an awful woman, jilted at the altar, living with the rotting remains of her own wedding cake, hating all men and boys.

In truth, the boy from the blacksmith shop has a most mysterious benefactor, and we meet him in the first chapter of the novel. He is a convict escaped from a prison ship; he accosts the boy in the marshes, in a graveyard, and tells him he will eat his liver if the boy doesn't run home and get him something decent to eat and a file to saw off his leg-irons. That escaped convict is the boy's benefactor, and a far better representative of humane behavior—of redemption and forgiveness— than the cruel Miss Havisham. *Great Expectations* is a great story.

Before I was sophisticated enough to recognize other aspects of novel-writing, I noticed the plot. Look at Thomas Hardy's *The Mayor of Casterbridge*—the best first chapter in an English novel. A man gets so drunk that he sells his wife and infant daughter to a sailor. I thought, Whoa! How does Michael Henchard ever redeem himself? But I didn't know Hardy; the point is, there are actions you can never forgive yourself for. Michael Henchard won't recover from what he does in that first chapter; he is unforgivable. Henchard writes in his will that no man should remember him, but most readers will never forget him—I didn't.

The other writers who made me wish I could write like them were my fellow New Englanders Herman Melville and Nathaniel Hawthorne. Does *Moby-Dick* have a plot? Think about Queequeg's coffin; it has a purpose. Does *The Scarlet Letter* have a plot? Don't worry—I won't give it away. These novels, and the novels of Dickens and Hardy, were my teachers. I love plot, and other nineteenth-century novelistic devices; the nineteenth century is the model of the form for me.

But the last sentence of *Last Night in Twisted River* was a long time coming to me. Usually, I find the tone of voice before the actual last sentence. At the end of *The Cider House Rules*, I could hear that there was a refrain, and that it was a kind of benediction, before I wrote down the refrain itself: "Princes of Maine, Kings of New England." I knew that the last sentence of *A Prayer for Owen Meany* would be (what else?) a prayer. But what confused me about *Twisted River* was that the tone of that last sentence seemed elated; yet I knew what had happened to Daniel Baciagalupo. What did Daniel have to be happy about? I thought I must have been mistaken about the last sentence—I believed I was on the wrong track—so I kept waiting.

Then, in January 2005, I got it. What makes Danny happy is that he's *writing* again; it was that simple. What else would make Daniel Baciagalupo *elated*? After all, *Twisted River* is, in part, a novel about the writing process. And not only the *process*; in Danny's case, it's about the psychological motivation for becoming a writer. Everything that happens in his life—everything he's afraid of happening to the people he loves—makes him a writer. It hasn't happened to me like that, thank God.

Following that last sentence, I made my reverse road map very quickly. I got the first sentence in August of that same year; seven months from last sentence to first sentence is fast for me. And what I had then was a map of the *action* of the novel—the (to me) all-important plot. When I actually began writing, I knew everything that would happen; now I could concentrate on the language.

The actual writing of *Last Night in Twisted River* came quickly to me, like the road map in reverse. September 2005 to September 2008: Three years to write a novel is unheard-of for me—it usually takes longer. Having this one in my mind for more than twenty years must have helped.

DORSET, VERMONT
JANUARY 2010

PHOTO: © EVERETT IRVING

JOHN IRVING published his first novel, *Setting Free the Bears,* in 1968. He has been nominated for a National Book Award three times—winning once, in 1980, for the novel *The World According to Garp.* He also received an O. Henry Award, in 1981, for the short story "Interior Space."

In 1992, Mr. Irving was inducted into the National Wrestling Hall of Fame in Stillwater, Oklahoma. In 2000, he won the Oscar for Best Adapted Screenplay for *The Cider House Rules*—a film with seven Academy Award nominations. In 2001, he was elected to the American Academy of Arts and Letters.

Last Night in Twisted River is John Irving's twelfth novel.

www.John-Irving.com

A B O U T   T H E   T Y P E

This book was set in Caslon, a typeface first designed in 1722 by William Caslon. Its widespread use by most English printers in the early eighteenth century soon supplanted the Dutch typefaces that had formerly prevailed. The roman is considered a "workhorse" typeface due to its pleasant, open appearance, while the italic is exceedingly decorative.

Look for these

 Available as Vintage Canada paperbacks

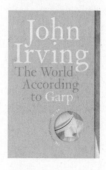